# West of Annapolis

## A Novel

### Ed Borger

Disclaimer

This is a work of fiction spanning the period from 1976 to 1984 and incorporates a blending of storytelling with factual historical background. Specific non-fictional events set at the U.S. Naval Academy in Part II during 1976-77 described in narration are provided to add a sense of depth and accuracy to the storytelling. Events described in Part III concerning the Vietnam War, Tonkin Gulf Incident and Operation Frequent Wind are based upon actual historical events, but actions taken by the fictional characters in the story did not actually occur. All characters within the story are fictional. Any resemblance to actual persons is purely coincidental. The exception is a cameo role by Heinz Lenz, a member of the Naval Academy physical education department and PEP instructor from 1968 to 1992. Other historical characters referenced in the story are Admiral Hyman Rickover, Vice Admiral James Stockdale and Fleet Admiral Chester Nimitz.

ISBN-13: 978-0-578-35624-2

# DEDICATION

To my wife, Sheila. Thank you for your love, support, and especially your patience during the many weekends I consumed chasing down this dream.

Also, to all the men and women of our armed forces. Thank you for your sacrifice, your service, for keeping us safe.

# CONTENTS

# PROLOGUE

My father's name was John Baumann. It's a German name. He was born in Meade, Kansas in 1919. He came from a large family of farmers clinging stubbornly to the desolate high plains of western Kansas in the wake of my great grandfather's immigration from Hamburg in the mid-1800s. I imagine life was challenging working the soil, plagued by season after season of either drought or flood. Once the Great Depression hit, my grandfather, eager to escape his farming roots, moved his young family east to Wichita in hopes of finding work. There was none. Instead, he spent many months on the road working as a laborer in the fields or in the salt mines. Then his wife died suddenly while giving birth, delivering their fourth child during one of his many extended work absences. My father, growing up unsupervised, ran wild in his teen years with his younger brother. He took to riding the rails with little money, no food, nearly freezing to death one night in a boxcar, making his way as far as California before returning to Kansas. Once safely ensconced back in the homestead, he committed himself to helping his family and reentered high school, graduating with honors in '39. He'd been smitten with California, I suppose, and returned to her warm breezes and blue ocean, settling in Pasadena, working part-time in a dairy, and studying to become an engineer at the local community college. Then Pearl Harbor hit in '41 and changed everything – for him and an entire generation. He enlisted in the Army Air Corps in '42, earning his wings as a B-17 pilot and marrying my mother, an 18-year-old war bride, shortly before shipping overseas to join the mighty Eighth Air Force. He flew 35 combat missions attached to the 486th Bomb Group based in Sudbury, England and was awarded the Air Medal and Purple Heart. When he returned, like many experienced flyers, he left the service and hired on with the airlines, beginning a 30-year career with United Airlines and raising a family. I was born in 1956 in San Francisco, California and grew up idolizing my war-hero, airline pilot father. As a young boy, I'd try on his oversized uniform jacket and hat, sleeves draping to the floor, his hat covering my eyes, and zoom around my parent's bedroom, arms extended, making the buzzing sound of a high-performance airplane. I watched every episode of the series, *Twelve O'Clock High* on TV. I built dozens of models of WWII bombers and fighters, imagining myself diving from the sky in my P-51 Mustang chasing Messerschmitts and Focke-Wulfs or making perilous bombing runs over Berlin in my B-17 dodging bursts of flak. All I wanted to do was follow in my father's footsteps, become a military pilot and do something heroic. But sometimes the path to hero is murky, laced with risk and uncertainty, something you can neither plan nor orchestrate. My father never cautioned me about fate or free will as I charted my course. He let me live the life he gave me, free to drift, free to succeed or fail, free to find my own way.

# West of Annapolis

# Part I

# 1

## SOUTHWEST OF SAN DIEGO

November 1982

WE WERE DESCENDING through a bumpy cloud layer at six thousand feet setting up for a long, tedious on-station patrol in the coastal waters off San Clemente Island in our P-3C Orion, a large four-engine turboprop aircraft named after the mythical hunter of the same name. I looked at my wristwatch. Midnight. Five bone-jarring hours of flying at low altitudes ahead as we commenced our mission – search, acquisition and tracking of a Soviet nuclear submarine – and with only sketchy locating data given to us by the nearby U. S. surface battle group. It would be a long night of flying for our twelve-man crew, requiring a focused coordinated effort with the ships below to find our target.

Once leveled off, I engaged the autopilot's altitude hold function, pushed back my seat and stood. "Just going to grab a quick stretch before the war starts, Colbs," I said, with a wink to my 2P, or copilot, Lieutenant (jg) Colby Reed, in the right seat. "Won't be gone but a minute."

Colby nodded and slid his left hand over the four power levers, acknowledging control of the big airplane. I patted our flight engineer, Chief Ralph Wilhelm, on the shoulder and squeezed through the tight fit behind his middle chair and the large center console in front of him. The prolonged sitting was the worst part of the job. As PPC, or Patrol Plane Commander, I spent practically the entire on-station period in either the right or left seat despite having a third pilot, or 3P, onboard. I'd make a quick walk through the cabin, offer some encouraging words to the crew, stretch my legs, then strap in for the duration.

The P-3C is built on the airframe of the Lockheed Electra, a 1950s civilian airliner. In place of the many rows of passenger seats are bays stuffed with mission electronics. The lengthy cabin has a galley with two bunks in the tail just aft of the main cabin door. Forward of the door on the port side are two acoustic sensor stations where the submarine acquisition and tracking take place. Further up the narrow aisle on the starboard side is the non-acoustic operator's station which handles the radar, the Magnetic Anomaly Detector

(MAD) and other aircraft sensors. Moving forward still are the mission computer equipment bays and immediately behind the cockpit are the Tactical Coordinator (TACCO) and Navigator (NAVCOM) stations, one on each side of the aisle. I had barely started my journey aft when I was waylaid by our crew's TACCO, Lieutenant Jamie Morgan.

"Hey, Mitch," he said, grabbing my flight suit as I passed his seat. "Just checked in with Alpha X-ray. They've given us updated tasking – a 16-buoy distro field they want in the water, ASAP." He pointed at his large, round scope with neat green symbols representing the placement of the buoys.

"Already?" This was unusual. Alpha X-ray was the anti-submarine warfare (ASW) coordinator on the battle group destroyer below and typically flailed a bit before deciding on how best to insert the newly checked-in P-3 into the ASW problem. "What's their rush?"

"Don't know, but something's up. Apparently CINCPAC needs to know what this guy's up to. Wants the sub reacquired and for us to send position, course and speed ASAP."

ASAP, I thought. The Navy loves that acronym. Everything ASAP. To me, *as soon as possible* meant whenever possible, or whenever I get around to it. To the Navy, I learned early on, it meant *immediately*. "Okay, guess I better get back up front."

"Yep. First fly-to point's already on your scope."

Whatever their rush, it was going to take about twenty minutes to deploy our 16-buoy search pattern. Then we'd need to replace any buoy failures. And there was always at least one. So, ASAP was just going to have to mean in due time to CINCPAC, not *inmediatamente*. The buoys our P-3 was designed to deploy were called search stores. We carried 84 of them, forty-eight externally launched and another thirty-six from inside. Our load tonight was all passive buoys designed for detecting and listening to the newer, ultra-quiet nuclear submarines. Just as the subs didn't want us to know of their presence, our passive buoys were designed for the same purpose. All part of the cat and mouse game of ASW.

"Flight, TACCO. Mitch, you up?" It was Jamie in my headset, the crewmate I'd just left behind.

"Roger, just strapping in. What's up?"

"Two minutes to first drop, it'll be DIFAR 1." DIFAR stood for Directional Frequency Analysis and Recording. DIFAR buoys made up most of our load tonight. Their hydrophones could provide valuable bearing information as well as general acoustic recording of the target.

"Yeah, inbound now. Got it on the scope, no problem. Hey, the sensor guys ready? I don't think they were expecting to go to work so soon."

"Of course, we're ready, Flight." It was Petty Officer Steve Hodges, our Sensor 1 operator, jumping in, pretending to sound offended.

"Sorry, thought you might still be enjoying your siesta," I said.

"No, sir. Gear's up, everything checks four-oh. Thought the flight station was still enjoying *their* siesta."

I let out a chuckle, appreciating the early banter. "Okay then, let's go to work."

"Roger that."

"DIFAR 1 away," cried Jamie.

The aircraft gave a slight shudder as the buoy ejected from the belly underneath. A minute later DIFAR 2 was away, and so on, until all sixteen buoys were up and operational in a neat 5 x 6 x 5 search pattern spaced at three nautical miles. Deploying a search pattern was performed with the assistance of our onboard mission computer, managing all the drop trajectories, pattern drift and other complexities, keeping everything routine – for now. Once the sensor operators called hot contact, mission computer or not, all hell would break loose. I was enjoying the peace and quiet as the airplane very smoothly flew its straight path, automatically deploying the first five buoys then banking gracefully in a one-eighty degree turn to line up for the next six.

Our mission technically started at 1900 yesterday evening with the standard three-hour preflight and two-hour transit from Moffett Field Naval Air Station in Mountain View to the rendezvous point with the battle group a hundred miles southwest of San Diego. We were initially scheduled to begin early yesterday, Wednesday, and be completed before Thanksgiving Day on Thursday. The crew had been eager to begin the four-day weekend, but their hopes were dashed by the last-minute change to the flight schedule calling for a 0600 landing on Thanksgiving morning. There were plenty of groans in the hangar when I told them our Wednesday "banker's hours" flight had been pushed to a late evening preflight and Thursday morning redeye impacting their Thanksgiving leave and quick departures from base. I pretended to be disappointed for the crew's sake but wasn't concerned about the delayed departure or erosion of valuable leave time. My leave plans would not be disrupted one iota, cemented the moment my mother called last week saying, "And you will be up for Thanksgiving, of course." My wife, Aimee, and I, and our two small children would once again dine at her insistence in her big, empty house along with whomever else she may've invited. Every year it was a different crowd.

"TACCO, Sensor 1. High probability we've got him on 8. Starting to paint the classic wandering 50-hertz line. Looking for secondaries now. Standby."

Our completed search pattern had been transmitting no more than ten minutes when Hodges thankfully broke my concentration and called subsurface contact on DIFAR 8. There was no mistaking it. A wandering 50-hertz frequency was not our battle group. U.S. vessels all had electrical systems that operated on 60-cycle electrical power. This was our guy, his warbling Russian-built generator a dead giveaway. "Inbound to 8," I cried, as I twisted the yoke, banking the aircraft in a 45-degree turn to get back to DIFAR 8. No sooner had I steadied on the new course than Jamie had four planned buoy drops he was sending to my scope centered around DIFAR 8. He wanted to convert to close aboard tracking in case this was our target. And it most certainly was. Hodges would be confirming it in a minute.

"Sensor 3, Flight, bring up the radar and give us several sweeps. Need to check for any surface traffic in the vicinity of our pattern." I wanted to narrow our search by confirming the signal on DIFAR 8 was not surface-related. Once Hodges picked up a second, corroborating subsurface frequency we'd have him nailed.

"Negative surface traffic in the area, Flight. I've got the battle group at 245 degrees, twenty-five nautical miles. Nothing near our pattern. Radar going back to standby."

"Roger, thanks, Three."

"TACCO, Sensor 1, okay, I'm calling positive contact on DIFAR 8." Hodges' voice was raised, sounding urgent. "High confidence, Type 1 Soviet nuke. Again, high confidence. Tracking him on both the 50 and 147-hertz lines. It's him, sir."

"Flight, TACCO, c'mon, Mitch. I need you on top of 8. We need more buoys in the water otherwise we're gonna lose him."

"Inbound now," I said. "Give me the new fly-to points for the drops. I don't see 'em."

"Mitch, they're up on your scope," Jamie shouted, in frustration. "Hit up-scale, for crying out loud!"

Colby reached across the center console from the right seat and mashed the scale button on our computer keyboard and, voila, four new fly-to points magically appeared on our scope. "Okay, got 'em now, Jamie. Sorry about that."

"No prob, just capture them. We need to be raining steel right now."

We also need to notify CINCPAC, I thought. "NAV, Flight, get an initial contact report to Alpha-X-ray, have 'em relay to CINCPAC with sub's position. Tell 'em to standby for course and speed."

"Already working on it, Flight."

"Copy, thanks."

The crew knew their jobs and were quickly embracing the challenging problem around them. I knew our NAVCOM, Lieutenant (jg) Alex Quigley, would have the report ready to go just as our Sensor 3 operator knew to sweep the area with his radar before I gave the order. Much of my commands were normal procedure but unnecessary. This is what we trained for, what we relished, the chance for a real-world hunt against a real-world target. The plan now was to circle DIFAR 8 with four more buoys in tight spacing in order to develop close tracking and generate an accurate position, course and speed that would get reported up the chain of command, all the way to the Commander, U.S. Pacific Fleet, if necessary.

"DIFAR 10 away," Jamie cried.

I put the aircraft in a hard-left bank to punch out two more buoys around the contact buoy, DIFAR 8. The mood in the flight station and cabin was electric, the unnecessary chatter on ICS ceased, becoming more clipped and succinct. The crew in back grabbed something to hold onto during our radical maneuvering to get more buoys around this guy. Years of experience and learned tactics had taught us to anticipate the sub's whereabouts and next move yet there was always an element of uncertainty, of guessing what might occur next in the mind of a Soviet submarine captain. Our prosecution of the target was moving to the next, more crucial stage.

"TACCO, Sensor 1, contact on DIFAR 10, still holding him on 8 as well. Sending you bearings now, 180 degrees on 10, 240 on 8. Should have course and speed soon."

"Okay, keep the bearings coming, Sensor 1. Mitch, another set of fly-to points on your scope. Get over and capture ASAP. I need at least two more buoys in front of this guy."

Sure, ASAP, I thought. "Roger, inbound now." The tactic was to follow the bearing lines and get buoys all around him and contain him until we knew where he was headed. I jerked the airplane hard right causing everyone in back to once again grab their seats as Jamie punched two more buoys from the belly in close succession.

"DIFAR 16 and 17 away."

"Flight, TACCO, hey Mitch, we're starting to develop a decent course and speed. I'd like to get lower in anticipation of generating attack criteria."

Things moved rapidly and with remarkable efficiency as we zeroed in on our prey. "What's his speed?" I asked.

"Erratic. He's slowed below four knots, maybe less. Computer's all over the map. He may even be dead in the water, who knows. Standby."

"Okay, let's get down to five hundred feet in the meantime." I punched the PA button on the interphone system and announced, "Okay, crew, this is Flight, we're going below 1,000 feet, LPAs required." This was another signal to the crew that we were in hot pursuit and things would become more hazardous at low altitude, hence the requirement to don life-preservers. The five-hundred-foot altitude also permitted faster deployment of buoys and the possibility to generate a MAD, an alert by our Magnetic Anomaly Detector, the stinger probe in the back of the aircraft, to a large manmade metallic object in the water below us.

"TACCO, Sensor 1, contact on DIFAR 17. I've got good Doppler inbound, am showing a relative speed of only two knots."

"Roger, computer fixing confirms. Two knots. Thanks, One."

Why's this guy dragging his ass, I wondered. Patrol speed was typically four to five knots. Nonetheless, things were proceeding nicely, right by the book. I was thinking of letting my 3P into the right seat to relieve Colby, to gain some close tracking experience.

Then, "Hold on, TACCO!" Suddenly the relative calm in the prosecution was interrupted by Hodges's frantic call, his voice up an octave. "I just got a loud whoosh on 17, sir."

"Loud whoosh?"

"Yes, sir. Sounds like we've got outer missile doors opening and pressurization of the launch tubes," he shouted.

"What!" Jamie yelled, matching Hodges's voice.

*Missile doors?* Did our lower altitude alert him? A submarine didn't routinely just open its missile doors. Was this some sort of cold war game he was playing? I ran through the rules of engagement in my head. Things had been heating up with our adversaries and there had been some recent stiff rhetoric from both the Soviet leader and our president. "NAV, advise Alpha-X-ray, he's opening his doors. And have 'em give us weapons status from CINCPAC just in case."

"Okay, TACCO." It was Hodges again. "We've got CPA of less than 500 yards on DIFAR 17," meaning the sub just made its closest point of approach to the buoy. "He's slowing. Two knots…one knot. He's practically DIW."

I swung the airplane to an inbound heading on buoy 17. "Sensor 3, Flight, bring up your gear. I want to MAD this son-of-a-bitch. Standby, three minutes to mark." A MAD would give us attack criteria. Theoretically, we'd drop our weapon on the MAD call by Sensor 3, but we were operating under "weapons tight," meaning punching out a Mark 46 torpedo or B-57 depth bomb would only be simulated.

"Flight, Sensor 1. Detecting air pressurization sounds on 17. Jesus, sir, he's at zero knots, confirm no blade signature!" I knew what Hodges was thinking and fearing. Opening the doors, pressurizing the missile tubes, stopping the boat were all steps in the ballistic missile launch sequence. When the sub captain pushed the button, air pressure would ultimately force the missiles up the tube and into the water where their rocket motors would light, taking them to some major U. S. city. A terrifying thought.

Al interrupted my concern, ratcheting the tension. "Flight, NAV, CINCPAC says weapons free, repeat, weapons free."

"You sure, NAV? You know what you're saying?" Al understood the concern in my voice. I was asking a life-or-death question – the lives of those on the sub or the lives of our citizens back home. It was really a no-brainer if the sub was ready to launch but I wanted verification. As I waited, we continued the run-in on buoy 17 with hopes of our MAD.

"Mitch," Al said, gravely, "The 'repeat weapons free' didn't come from me. I was echoing CINCPAC," he said. "Yeah, I'm sure. But I'll double-check. They're passing us the nuke weapon authorization codes over the secure teletype now."

*Are you fucking kidding me?* They want us to nuke this guy with a B-57 depth bomb? And start World War III? Instead, I answered very calmly. "Roger, NAV." I paused to take a breath. "Okay, Jamie, you hear? We need to activate the B-57 special weapon checklist.

"Roger, Flight, I've got the checklist open. This will be a special weapon manual drop from bomb bay station Charlie-4." He spoke it very mechanically, very professionally. "I will read with the normal challenge and the flight station will reply with the appropriate response. Copy?"

"Copy." I held the aircraft steady on a heading inbound to buoy 17 balancing the checklist in my lap. "Sensor 3, anticipate mark on target, two minutes. Be ready to call the MAD."

"Roger, Flight."

Jamie continued. "Circuit breakers?"

Wilhelm spun in his seat, looked at the panel and gave me a thumbs up. "All circuit breakers are in."

"Bomb bay station select and release mode?" Jamie replied to his own challenge as these switches were at his station. "Selecting station 4C. Release mode will be rack-release."

Back to me.

"Arming switch?"

"Arming switch to Special Weapon."

"AMAC monitor control panel?"

"Breaking seal wire. Moving from Safe to Arm."

"TA / TB switch to Weapon Monitor?"

"Weapon Monitor selected."

"Master Arm?"

"Master Arm is on."

"Bomb bay doors?"

"Bomb bay doors are coming open."

"Okay, Flight, last item on the checklist. Senior officer will release the special weapon. Mitch, you need to break the seal wire on secondary release panel Drop / Hold switch. Pilot will release the special weapon upon valid attack criteria."

"Seal wire broken, kill-ready light illuminated. Standing by to drop."

"Roger. This completes the special weapon checklist," Jamie replied. "It's all yours, Mitch. Punch it on the MAD."

"Sensor 3, Flight, one minute to mark on target. Holler if you get the MAD."

"Roger that, sir."

MAD or no MAD, I planned to punch the weapon out at our last known datum. This would be our only run to stop Ivan before his missiles started

7

flying. Our 20-kiloton nuclear depth bomb would obliterate every living thing in the ocean below in a one-mile radius.

"Flight, NAV, second message, this one from Third Fleet. *Weapons free. Repeat, weapons free.* There's our confirmation. Everyone's watching this one, Mitch."

"TACCO, Sensor 1, zero Doppler shift on 17, we're past CPA. The boat has stopped and is hovering. He's not hiding now. We've got all indications of a nuclear ballistic missile submarine prepared to launch its missiles, sir."

I selected the PA function on the ICS again. "Crew, this is Flight, we're staying at 500 feet to ensure we get the MAD. We'll climb at max power after the drop. I show thirty seconds to mark. I will call weapon away over the PA. Standby and brace for potential shockwave impact." I could hear rustling in the cabin as the crew moved to secure everything that wasn't nailed down. I prayed we weren't too late and no one on the crew would call a visual launch from the sea. Once their ballistic missile was away, there was no stopping it. If we were too late, another acronym for MAD, Mutually Assured Destruction, would be next, initiated by NORAD.

"Fifteen seconds to mark," I announced. Everything was quiet as a tomb on ICS, no one was speaking or moving. The aircraft was rock steady on its heading to the target. I looked down at the bright amber KILL READY light and gave a shiver, no turning back now. All aircraft systems were tight. "Ten seconds to target. Standby 3." I counted in my head, nine, eight, seven, six...

"MAD, MAD, MAD!" cried Sensor 3.

"Weapon away!" I replied, imagining a snap from the bomb bay rack below and a shudder from the aircraft as it quickly shed 500 pounds.

"Confirm, weapon in water," Hodges added. "Standby..."

The crew remained deadly silent, the drone of the aircraft engines the only sound.

"DETONATION!" Hodges screamed into his mic and tore off his headset.

We'd done it, our action decisive and devastating. We'd delivered a nuclear salvo atop a Soviet ballistic missile submarine as it was preparing to hurl its weapons of mass destruction upon every western city in the United States. The unthinkable had happened. World War III had begun.

# 2

## A SAFE HARBOR

EXCEPT THIS WAS ONLY A DRILL, a fleet exercise and training designed to sharpen our crew's skills and prepare us for the eventuality of the real deal. The target, our own USS *Guitarro*, played the role of the Soviet ballistic missile submarine tonight. The Soviet submarine sounds, augmented frequencies emanating from the *Guitarro*, the radio communication with CINCPAC fleet, and of course, the nuclear weapon drop, were all simulated for training purposes. World War III would have to wait for another day.

We were now on a descent path back to Moffett Field passing four thousand feet, setting up for the final approach. The long night of flying had tested the crew's proficiency and endurance, especially near the end of the on-station period as we struggled to generate many more attack solutions on the *Guitarro* as part of the fleet exercise and our crew training requirement. I'd be glad to be back on deck in about ten more minutes. As we broke out of a patchy cloud layer, I could see a magnificent mackerel sky developing through the aircraft's windscreen by dawn's arrival to the east. The tightly knotted overcast streaked with red-orange hues was growing more vibrant as sunrise approached. *Red sky in the morning, sailors take warning*, I thought. The simple rhyme was a throwback from my Boy Scout days and had been around for two millennia. It was pure folklore in the satellite age, but much needed rain was headed for the San Francisco Bay Area later today lending credence to the old proverb. And it was supposed to be a gusher said the forecasters, lasting throughout the long Thanksgiving weekend.

I needed to shed the sightseeing distractions and focus on the task at hand. The pace in the cockpit quickened during final as we glided softly above the winking lights of the Silicon Valley. We'd touch down well ahead of the rain that was due to start pounding the coast later this morning. Colby was flying from the left seat and I was backing him up from the right scanning the instruments and handling the radios. He disengaged the autopilot and gracefully banked our large ship to line up on the final approach course. Everything about the transit home had been uneventful, our successful training mission coming to a close, the crew eager to spread out and begin their well-deserved holiday break. My thoughts drifted back to my own preordained holiday plans and rendezvous with my mother and her potential guest list. I had no clue who she might've invited. She lived alone in the large house my father left behind after they'd separated five years ago and—

*Get out of your head for God's sake.*

We were still ten miles out on final and the unwelcome intrusion of our holiday plans plus my night flight hangover were distractions I needed to push aside. The lights surrounding the airfield loomed in the distance bringing my focus back to the present and serving as a reminder we were almost done. The runway and taxiway lights shimmered in the still darkness below, the sky radiating an even brighter shade of red. The high-intensity linear strobe lights, flashing in sequence, were guiding us to the tip of the runway at 120 knots. Almost home.

"Gear down, landing check," called Colby from the left seat. I was letting him make the landing and, as acting pilot, he initiated the checklist. We ran through the customary last-minute items calling for lowering of the landing gear, checking seat harnesses, confirming cabin landing condition and ending with me verifying, "Three down and locked," on the landing gear indicator. Then, acting as copilot, I made the radio call.

"Moffett Tower, good morning. Sierra Echo 310 with you, four miles, short final, runway three two right with the gear, full stop." Adding the full stop was perhaps unnecessary. There were no other P-3s in the pattern this morning doing touch and gos, so the tower had to know our intention to stop. Hell, there was no movement anywhere near the field on this dead Thanksgiving holiday. The full stop was simply force of habit.

*"Sierra Echo 310, Moffett Tower, good morning, sir,"* came the cheerful reply. *"Wind, three zero zero at five, cleared to land, runway three two right."*

"Cleared on the right," I confirmed.

Colby called for flaps forty, which was full extension for landing. The airplane slowly pitched over and decelerated to its final touchdown speed. A minute later, after a perfectly timed flare, our main landing gear tires greased the runway precisely on landing speed, precisely on runway centerline just beyond the painted numbers. I reached across the center console and gently punched my copilot's arm.

"And that, ladies, is how we do that," he replied, giving a relieved chuckle.

"Just don't let it go to your head, Colbs." It was a textbook landing, and he knew it. A landing that flawless, while requiring a repeatable skill honed by hours of training, was still rare and necessitated a bit of luck. All it took was a gust of wind or a slightly mistimed throttle excursion to turn a great landing into an average one.

I was fortunate to have drawn Colby as my copilot, or second pilot, as we referred to the position in the P-3 community. There were three pilots to a crew – the PPC, or Patrol Plane Commander; the 2P, or second pilot and then the 3P, the third pilot; the 3P being the most junior and still earning his qualification on the airplane. Colby was smart, meticulous and known as a "good stick," meaning a competent flyer. Soon he'd take over Crew 4 as the PPC when I received orders to my next duty station, which, at present, was somewhat of a controversy. My lifelong plan had been to leave active duty as soon as possible and join one of the major airlines and begin making the big bucks as fast as possible. United, American, Delta and others were hiring as fast as the World War II veterans were retiring, and the time to jump was now. However, if I took orders to my next duty station, a coveted shore assignment, I'd incur another three years of active service. Plus, there was the risk of not yet knowing what that assignment would be.

We were still rolling down the runway at a hundred knots. Chief Wilhelm, the flight engineer sitting between us, took over the throttles and slid them into beta, a reverse condition of the propeller blades that helped slow the big aircraft during the landing.

"Four thousand feet remaining," I called, as I read the passing runway markers. The aircraft was now down to eighty knots. More brake by Colby, more reverse prop by Wilhelm and we exited the active runway at a brisk thirty knots.

"Nice job, Willy," Colby said. "Have the nav give base a call and ask where they want us to park." Colby knew I would insist he take the first available taxiway to shorten our path to the ramp, so he gave the nose wheel steering a quick twist. The big plane pivoted leaving a trace of skid marks on the pavement. Behind us I could hear shouts from the crew as pens, cups, manuals, anything not secured, were tossed into the cabin aisle.

"Geez, Colbs, maybe a little more brake next time? This ain't the Daytona 500," I chided him although it was a maneuver I would've done myself, anything to shave a minute or two off the taxi time. I was proud of my copilot. "Hey, Nav," I called over the interphone, "Where're they parking us?"

Al had just talked to base. "Maintenance chief is reminding us to go to the birdbath first."

I rolled my eyes at Colby and cued the mic. "We're not going to the birdbath, Al, I can promise you that. Tell him to get our lineman out here pronto and get us a spot. We're in a hurry."

The birdbath was a carwash of sorts for airplanes and was located at the south end of the airfield. Returning P-3s from overwater missions were obligated to taxi through the big sprayers and rinse off any clinging salt air to lessen the effects of pesky airframe corrosion. The entire evolution took maybe twenty minutes and all P-3 squadron commanding officers made sure their crews rinsed off before they shut down for the day. Our crew had been put out enough by taking this last-minute Thanksgiving training flight and I wanted to give them a small reward by returning some of their holiday time.

From his middle seat in the cockpit, Wilhelm raised an eyebrow. "You

11

sure you want to skip the bath, sir? I mean—"

"Yes, I'm sure, Willy," I snapped. "I'm not wasting any more time taxiing around the field this morning than necessary," I said, thinking I was doing him a favor. "Don't you want to get home sometime before your wife pulls the bird out of the oven?"

"Roger that, sir."

We approached the squadron ramp with the two outboard engines already shut down and came to an abrupt halt. From the cockpit, both Colby and I searched the empty tarmac for our wayward lineman who was required to guide us to our assigned parking spot. "All right Al," I said in frustration over the interphone, "Ask the chief where the hell our lineman is."

"On his way," Al answered immediately, understanding my impatience. "He says he suspects you didn't go to the birdbath and wants to know why you're in such a hurry – if it's because of the message."

"Message? Nah. Tell him I'm in a hurry because his mother's back home in my bed."

Colby uttered a quick, nervous laugh then shut up. He knew I was taking a chance flaunting the birdbath directive and wasn't sure if he'd be implicated should the skipper find out. Wilhelm didn't make a sound. He would likely side with the maintenance chief despite my decision to save a little time from our crew day.

"Hang on, Al. I'm only kidding. What message? What was that second part?"

"Standby."

In a matter of seconds, Al was back on the interphone. "Okay, chief says you have a message in the duty office, says your wife called while we were flying, needs you to call her back."

"Aimee called? What time?"

"He didn't say."

"All right, thanks." This was odd. She would never call when I was in the air unless something important was up. I needed to get straight to a phone after shutting down.

As we pulled to a halt in our spot, I glanced at Wilhelm. He looked either tense or irritated, it was difficult to tell, that I'd elected to skip the birdbath. I felt it didn't need an explanation or that I owed him one. The reason for skipping wasn't that I knew about some message, and it wasn't to disrespect the skipper or the maintenance chief. It was simply a token gesture to Wilhelm and the crew in the wake of a disappointing last-minute schedule change by the squadron ops officer when COMSUBPAC moved the sub's availability. There were times, I felt, when bending a minor regulation as a trade for doing some good for the troops was permitted, and necessary. It was called leadership. But, as Wilhelm's expression reminded me, the Navy's long arm was always present, measuring the consequences of every action, ready to second guess any decision regardless of the greater good that might result. I was growing exhausted under the daily grind and looked forward to possible separation from active duty soon rather than accept orders to a new duty station. In my early years, I reveled in squadron life, especially after becoming a new patrol plane commander, a title similar to airline captain in civil aviation, and the ranking officer on the crew. The job was demanding, and I was grateful for the responsibility at such a young age. I led by example using the work-hard-play-hard maxim as my style. During our first deployment to Westpac, we thrived on the pressure from the many operational flights and basked in the exotic liberties in Thailand, Fiji, Reunion and Australia. Lately though, as my separation date approached, a subtle cynicism and quick temper were creeping around the edges of my personality and I knew the crew sensed the vibe. I chalked it up to the stress created from many months of disciplined Navy life. I was approaching my three-year anniversary with Patrol Squadron 25 and, like any short timer, was itching to punch out and pursue a new assignment, in my case, a career with the airlines. Still, there was something more behind my hair-trigger mood swings and compulsive behavior whenever authority intruded too deeply into my personal life. While my defiance may have appeared cool to my fellow junior officers in the squadron, it spelled trouble for anyone serious about making the Navy a career. Some well-intended senior officer would likely tell me it was a sign of immaturity, a sign I hadn't learned the lessons of a first-tour junior officer. And while this observation would be insightful and could steer me away from trouble, heeding it was another matter entirely.

Petty Officer Dave Buchanan, our crew's in-flight technician, had the main cabin door open and the aircraft ladder deployed as soon as we'd stopped at our assigned parking spot. I tossed my headset on the seat and headed back to talk to Jamie as the crew began their individual post-flight tasks of shutting down. Jamie was also a lieutenant but not as senior, so I held the dual position of crew Mission Commander and Patrol Plane Commander. Jamie's job was to coordinate and oversee the assigned mission as it pertained to the crew in the cabin, but I retained overall responsibility. Jamie and I were close friends based on our many travels together over the past three years and many flight hours we'd logged on the same crew. Jamie was powering down his station and gathering his flight gear as I passed.

"We got the qual, right?" I said. "I mean, how do you feel about it?"

Jamie stood up and took a long stretch. He hadn't been out of his seat for nearly seven hours. "More or less. At least that's what I'm putting in the purple. We'll know for sure at the debrief."

"I thought we nailed it. That's what you said when we left station." I was used to Jamie's conservative, cautious approach to his duties and, at times, viewed it as a weakness. To me, the debrief was a negotiation with the debriefing officer. You presented facts, used persuasion, told a harrowing

13

story of how you mixed skill and luck over the treacherous waters of Southern California that resulted in mission success for the crew, and for the squadron. The end goal was simply a qualification, another checkmark in the training log for all the hours, buoys and fuel spent by the sole crew. Despite the autonomy crews felt they were given to complete such a mission, there were plenty of eyes much further up the chain of command that closely monitored the success or failure of the crew's on-station time. I always had the confidence I could persuade any debriefing officer to award the necessary qualification after a mission if there were gray areas. This was my strength, what I brought to the table and why I would show up to the debrief in the first place. Tonight, though, there had been no gray areas. We'd nailed it starting with the simulated nuclear weapon drop.

"Well, I'm not so sure on that last attack criteria," Jamie said, already fretting, making room for disappointment. "Our heading might've been off a few degrees. I think we'll be okay though."

"Of course, we will," I said, observing Jamie repack his flight bag with his classified pubs, fitting them back like Chinese puzzle pieces. "Look, I need to cut out early, to check out this urgent message from Aimee."

"Was it urgent?"

"I'm sure it was. It's not like her to call. Not when she knows I'm flying."

"What about the debrief at the ASWOC?" ASWOC was the ASW Operations Center.

"It'll go fine. You'll soon be the senior officer on the crew and new mission commander. I'm delegating to you this morning. You and Al can cover it. You don't need me. That last attack was right down centerline. Just be confident. I may stop by Maintenance Control, make a peace offering to the chief about the birdbath but I need to get going."

"You're going to skip the debrief? You're kidding, right?" He knew it was customary for the plane commander to attend and, as a dual-hat mission commander, it was pretty much required, but Aimee's mysterious message was on my mind.

"C'mon, Jamie, this was just a training exercise, not a real-world Soviet. Besides, I really need to see what's happening on the home front."

"Okay, I've got it, I guess." Concern was written all over his face. "I hope everything's okay at home, Mitch. Let us know."

"Sure thing, buddy. I'm off." Jamie watched me walk to the rear of the airplane and step out the main cabin door. I could sense him tracking me from his station's large round window in silence, observing as I made a beeline across the tarmac to my waiting car in the squadron parking lot between the two large hangars. By walking away, I'd compounded his concern with the debrief by skipping it. Nonetheless, I opened the trunk to my 1977 MGB Roadster, the small, two-seat sports car I'd owned since my senior year at the Naval Academy, tossed my flight gear in the back and drove off.

It was a short journey around the runway to the main side of the base and our assigned living quarters, dwellings typical for stateside naval air stations in the 1980s. The quarters Aimee and I shared with our two children were part of a cluster of duplexes situated in a secluded part of base that featured vast common areas, expansive lawns, a playground of equipment and covered parking – simple but nice amenities for junior officer families. Being able to live on base was a huge perquisite given the booming economy and high cost of living beyond the gates in Silicon Valley. Moffett Field was a microcosm amidst the sprawl, a safe harbor supporting officer and enlisted housing, a commissary, a Navy Exchange along with many other services and conveniences that sustained family life in the military community.

There was no traffic as I cruised along the two-lane road bordering the southern edge of the airfield. The runway lights were still brightly illuminating the gloom of the heavy morning sky. A drop of rain met my windshield followed by intermittent spatters. Here it comes, I thought, the first of four days of stormy weather. I negotiated a quick series of turns past the base chapel, swung into one of two assigned parking spots outside our unit and glanced at my digital watch. 0710. I was curious how the debrief was going and felt a stab of guilt for skipping. I switched off the engine and looked towards the house trying to imagine what Aimee's call had been about. My stomach rumbled. I was really craving a hot breakfast and black coffee before heading north to the homestead. I was also in dire need of a nap after flying all night and facing the prospect of my mother and her Thanksgiving soiree later this afternoon.

I scanned the cluster of homes from the silence of my seat, impressed with the tidy appearance. Streetlamps flickered off, timed sprinklers came on mixing with the light rain. A child's Big Wheel sat atop the grass. An errant basketball rested in a neighbor's flowerbed. No sign of outdoor life had yet emerged. This was Aimee's and my home, the place we'd lived the longest in our four-year marriage. Base housing provided a pleasant, safe environment to raise a young family with every junior officer wife pitching in, covering for each other when husbands were absent on deployment. And the humble duplexes themselves held a certain level of charm. The clean lines of the two-story buildings were very efficient, very functional and pleasing to the eye. I had thought of ways to improve the design after we'd moved in but realized this was one military housing project that had gone right, leaving little room for creative ad-libbing. In high school, I'd shown a certain flair for the industrial arts, at one time pondering a career as an engineer-architect. I'd even toyed with the idea of returning to grad school. But that ship sailed long ago. I was following in my father's footsteps as a commercial airline pilot, an impressionable child's dream firmly ingrained in my DNA, entrenched long before I'd discovered Frank Lloyd Wright and his

15

concepts of organic design and sweeping horizontal lines.

I climbed from the MG and entered the warm house wondering where Aimee was. And where's the big emergency? No one was up, the familiar commotion in the kitchen absent. No Carlene fussing in her highchair, no Aimee prepping Sean for school, no hot breakfast. They were celebrating Thanksgiving morning by sleeping in, of course, yet a trace scent of freshly baked goods hovered in the air. I unzipped my flight suit in the surrounding silence and considered a run to the Navy Exchange to pick up some donuts when I spied the source of the lingering aroma, two freshly prepared pumpkin pies cooling on the kitchen counter. Presumably, Aimee had spent last night preparing dessert for the meal we'd share later today at my mother's, a task she'd cheerfully agreed to for the third year in a row. I was primed to slice into the pie with a large carving knife when Aimee appeared at the bottom of the stairs, her hair mussed and robe slightly undone. "Oh, no you don't, mister. Put that knife down right now," she said, in a raspy voice, still half asleep.

I recoiled in surprise. "God, Aimee, don't sneak up on me like that. I was only hoping for a little breakfast."

"There's some cereal in the pantry. Don't you dare touch those pies."

I watched as she cinched up her robe and stepped into some fuzzy house slippers. "So, what was that urgent message all about last night?" I said, poking in the fridge, downing some orange juice straight from the carton. "Things look pretty placid around here to me."

"Well, it *was* urgent, like nine hours ago. Your mother, of course – another crisis with Amber. She was positively inconsolable until I told her I'd try to reach you." She cocked her head. "Why didn't you call me back?"

I looked at my watch. "I was in the air. We took off at ten P.M. What time did she call?"

"Ten-oh-one." Aimee sat down at our small kitchen table. "Mitch, I'm sorry but this is getting old." She gave me a weary look. "I was there, covering for you when you were on deployment, covering every little thing when your mother was having one of her – how shall I say – meltdown moments? And believe me, there were plenty. Now that you're back, I need you to step in. I need a reprieve."

I opened the pantry door, moving aside tall boxes of cereal. "Tell you what," I said, smiling, still hopeful for a hot breakfast. "I'll call her back right now if you make me some of these pancakes." I held up a box of Bisquick. "And toast, and coffee. And some bacon too."

"Don't start, Mitch. Not now. Not in the face of our drive north today. I was up half the night making that dessert and the other half with Carlene. She's got the croup or something. Didn't sleep a wink." Aimee glanced up at the wall clock, "Of course, not until now. The Tylenol must've finally kicked in."

"Guess we both pulled the graveyard shift last night, huh?" I leaned down, kissed her forehead and grabbed the kitchen phone, punching in my old childhood number, one I had memorized since age five. It was early in the morning, but I knew Mother would be up moving about the kitchen, getting ready for her big day.

"Good morning," came her cheery, singsong voice.

"Good morning, Mother."

Her tone quickly changed. "Oh, good morning, Son. May I presume you're on your way?"

"On our way, Mother? It's seven-thirty. What's going on?"

"Well, as you can imagine, there's much to be done. I'm stuffing the turkey, polishing the silver, setting the table, then I've got to run over to—"

"Mother," I interrupted. "Why the urgent phone call last night at 10 P.M.?"

"Oh." Long pause. "Mitch, if you only knew."

I held my laugh. My mother's manipulation was so transparent, always beginning with some vague reference to suck you into her problem. "Is there something you want picked up on our drive to the house later today?" I said, hoping to get off easy.

Another long pause, a sigh. "I've got all I need, thank you very much. Everything's under control. It's Amber, dear. She's missing."

"Missing?" Amber was my sister. She hadn't lived at home since graduating from high school five years ago heading for parts unknown, to either Washington or Oregon. I hadn't seen her in two years. "What do you mean, missing? I thought you said she was coming home for Thanksgiving dinner this year."

"She's been invited but who knows. I couldn't reach her last night, and believe me, I tried. Her phone must've been off the hook. I thought it got turned off again, like last time. I gave her money to pay the bill but—"

"Mother," I said, halting her again in mid-sentence. "What's going on, is she missing or not?"

"Well, not exactly. No, thank God. You just need to come. Come as quickly as you can. We can talk about it later."

"We'll be there at two." I took a deep breath, fighting off my night-flight fatigue. "Are you sure everything's all right? There's nothing I can pick up on the way?"

"Don't be absurd. I've got it covered. Everything's been planned for weeks."

"Okay then, see you at two."

"Yes, at two. And thank you, Son. I love you."

"Love you too, Mother."

"Oh, yes, and I love Aimee and everyone in your darling little family. Just get here soon."

"We—"

Click.

"—surely will." I turned to Aimee. "Amber's missing, huh?"

"*Was* missing. For about an hour while your mother frantically dialed her apartment every ten minutes. Then she called me. She just *knew* there'd been some horrible accident. I told her to call the police, which I knew she wouldn't do. Then I told her I would try to reach you."

"And she said—"

Aimee put on her best Mother expression. "Oh, thank you, dear. Thank you, thank you, thank you. Mitch will know what to do."

I laughed. "You do that pretty good you know."

"Years of practice."

We were both exhausted. We needed to be brave and get on with the excruciating day ahead, anticipation of another drama-filled Thanksgiving Day with Mother, Amber, and whoever else might show up unannounced. I trudged up the stairs and stepped into a hot shower, turning the water up as high as I could stand it. It felt good, letting the flesh on my back turn a bright shade of pink melting away the muscle tension from sitting upright all night.

Within a minute, Aimee was calling me. I wasn't sure it was her voice over the rush of water or my imagination. "Mitch, telephone," she cried again. She was in the bathroom and I could hear her plainly now.

"Who is it?" I yelled, perhaps a bit too loud, given that Aimee was standing just outside the curtain. "Mommy Dearest?" A second phone call from Mother could not be good. "She wanting us to pick up some strangers from the homeless shelter and invite them along to dinner?" Every year, my mother wistfully nurtured the impulse to invite the homeless to her Thanksgiving meal but never acted on it.

"Ha, ha, very funny. They're asking for Lieutenant Baumann. Sounds like the squadron," she said, bringing me back to reality.

I shut off the water and toweled off. For a moment, I couldn't imagine why they'd be calling me at home on Thanksgiving, especially after landing from an all-night exercise. Then it dawned on me, something had gone wrong at the debrief. I walked into the bedroom and picked up the extension on the nightstand.

"This is Lieutenant Baumann," I said, confidently, into the receiver.

"Mitch?" It was Duncan Kinder, a lieutenant (jg), the VP-25 squadron duty officer. The man with two last names, Duncan had the misfortune of being one of the least senior officers in the squadron thus drawing an SDO duty slot over the long holiday weekend. "Skipper's looking for you. And I need to tell you, man, is he pissed."

Oh, sure, the debrief, I knew it. My stomach knotted. "Is he at the hangar?" I quickly summoned a vision of him pacing around the duty office repeating, where the hell is that goddamn Baumann?

"No. He wants you to call him at home. Said it's about your flight."

"Right now?"

"At 1500 this afternoon, said he'll be unavailable until then."

Unbelievable. I wondered how the CO found out so quickly that I'd skipped the debrief.

"Did he say what it was about?"

"Yeah. And, man, was he pissed."

"You already said that, Dunk. What was he so pissed about?"

"You blew off the debrief for crying out loud. The debriefing officer called the ops officer, the ops officer called the XO, the XO called the skipper and the skipper called me. Chewed me out like I personally skipped the debrief. Ordered me to call you."

Silence.

"Mitch, you still there? Did you hear me? You've got to call the skipper."

"Yeah, Dunk. I heard you. I'm standing naked here in the shower. I'll call him this afternoon after I get to my parent's house. Tell him that if he calls back."

"Precisely at 1500."

"Yeah, yeah, 1500. Got it."

"You need his number?"

I stood letting water drip onto the bedroom carpet. I didn't have the skipper's home number and didn't have anything to write with in my naked condition. I opened the nightstand drawer rifling through the junk, aimlessly searching for a pen.

"Mitch, you still there?"

More silence.

"Look, man, I don't want to see you go down. The skipper will find you. Please, you need to call him back."

I had to reply. It wasn't fair to Duncan, letting him dangle. I assured him I'd find the number and call Skipper Wilson precisely on time. This seemed to satisfy him. I ended the call wishing him a happy Thanksgiving. He laughed. "Yeah, right."

# 3

## THE HOMESTEAD

"C'MON, AIMEE, LET'S GO. We're burning daylight." I was behind the wheel of our Chevy Suburban, the antithesis of my tiny MG parked in the adjacent spot in front of our duplex. The engine was idling, the truck loaded and ready for our excursion north – almost ready, that is. Aimee was still dressing Carlene, our two-and-a-half-year-old daughter, stuffing her into her jacket. They were somewhere inside the house with the front door standing wide open. I felt the usual irony in this situation, the last person in our foursome wanting to face my mother but the first one ready to get underway. Sean, our six-year-old son, was buckled in the backseat playing with one of his Masters of the Universe superheroes. I marveled at his fascination with these toys and the company that manufactured them. Sean had a budding collection of about a dozen of these characters while their creator had visions of marketing at least a hundred. They were adding a new hero or villain every week and at ten bucks a pop it was like a license to print money. I spun around from the front seat to face Sean. "Which one you got there, buddy? Is that He-Man?"

Sean responded without looking up. "No, Daddy, I already told you, it's Man-at-Arms."

I smiled. Sean looked adorable sitting there completely serious about making sure I didn't mix up one superhero with another. "They're both good guys though, right? He-Man and Man-at-Arms?"

"Yes." Sean gave an exasperated look as if I should know simply because I was an adult.

Adults were supposed to know everything, and it seemed to embarrass Sean if he discovered a gap in Daddy's knowledge. It was a very burdensome responsibility when parenting a six-year-old with a highly active imagination.

Aimee stepped out on the porch, hands on her hips, and called in an elevated voice. "Mitch, can you come in here for a minute? We forgot something."

What more could we possibly need? I didn't relish getting out of the truck. The rain had started in earnest and I wasn't wearing a jacket or carrying an umbrella. I made a quick dash to the front door and hopped inside.

20

"What's up?"

Aimee had Carlene in her rain boots and was zipping her tiny down jacket with the hood up guiding her to the car. "Go into the kitchen and grab the gift bag sitting on the counter. I forgot to put it in the car."

"Gift bag?"

"Just get it for me, please. I've got my hands full." Her expression said don't start asking a bunch of questions right now.

I scooped up the bag and moved toward the front door prepared to lock the deadbolt when the phone began to ring from the kitchen. I glanced at the Suburban. Aimee and the kids were settled in and ready to depart awaiting their driver. I turned back toward the kitchen, annoyed at my dilemma, and guessed at a range of possible callers – my mother, one of the neighbors, Duncan at the duty office or the skipper himself. As concerned as I was with the ringing, I ignored it, inserting the key into the front door and locking the deadbolt into place. Within two minutes we were underway, exiting Moffett Field's main gate in a steady rain, pointed north to my childhood home in Millbrae. The drive would only take thirty minutes, but I decided to extend it by traveling on I-280, the more circuitous route up the Peninsula. A few more miles but less traffic, I reasoned. I had no intention of getting to the house any sooner than my mother expected us. She had said "two-ish" but the translation was, be here exactly at two or you're late.

I loved this remote section of the I-280 corridor filled with its rolling pastures, horse farms and verdant hillsides as far as the eye could see. And yet, in as little as five miles in any direction, there were neighborhoods as dense as the streets of Calcutta. Or Los Angeles, where Aimee grew up. Aimee and her two older brothers moved to Tarzana, an upscale community in the southern belt of the San Fernando Valley, in the early 1960s after her mother remarried. This was approximately the same time we moved to Millbrae. Aimee said she loved the Bay Area but would occasionally wax nostalgic about the Valley, the nearby scenic Topanga Canyon and the warm beaches of Malibu. When she entered her LA-is-great mode I would let her ramble until she got to the part about her family's beloved Dodgers. I'd always been an avid Giants fan, following in the footsteps of my father, and I grew up despising the LA Dodgers. The rivalry was mostly fun for me, part of the game itself, and Aimee and I would good-naturedly rib each other when the two teams met. It was a different story with Aimee's stepfather, Bill. Bill always presented an acerbic edge when the debate between Northern and Southern California surfaced and, despite him liking me, used the rivalry and my alliance to the Giants as if to prove some sort of character flaw. Out of self-preservation, I found myself avoiding a variety of social and political topics, which, early in our relationship, broke Aimee's heart. Aimee and her stepdad had weathered a complex family history. She mostly hated him, and would rail against all his shortcomings but, for whatever reason, once she introduced me to him, she felt it imperative we get along. I grew comfortable with the defined barriers, accepting them as a natural rule in coping with in-laws. I knew, as did Bill, that our hostility extended beyond any baseball competition. Whenever we discovered we were at opposite ends of an issue we were experts at pushing each other's buttons, always ragging each other, first good-naturedly as old buddies might do but then he or I'd get in a low blow causing Aimee to intervene. Although when we were talking, sometimes jabbing, sometimes kidding, I felt I understood Bill in ways better than my own father. My father had taken me to the Giants games at Candlestick Park at age six, thus beginning my loyalty to the team. It was one of the few bonding experiences we shared until I started high school. Then things changed. My father became distant, almost reclusive. He and my mother separated. By the time I graduated from the Naval Academy in 1977, Dad was completely out of the picture, gone, separated from my mother, his new life unfolding like scenes in a foreign film. I had been contemplating these events a good deal lately. My father's silent treatment had mystified and confused me.

"You've been awfully quiet since we left," Aimee said, breaking the silence. Sean was holding his toy and looking out the window. Carlene had fallen back asleep. "Why didn't you answer the phone back at the house?"

She caught me by surprise, ending my daze from the road. "You heard it ringing? All the way from the car?"

"Of course, I heard it." She turned to watch the passing scenery. "It was your mother, wasn't it?"

I didn't feel like getting into the range of possibilities of who or why, so I remained quiet.

"You really shouldn't ignore her, you know. I'm sure she just needed a quick favor, maybe to pick up something along the way."

"Oh, sure. I can hear her now. *Oh, Mitch, darling, on your way up here could you please swing by the convent and pick up Mother Teresa? I've invited her to Thanksgiving dinner along with many of our community's homeless to help ensure my special place in heaven.*"

Aimee surprised me with a quick laugh. She was usually not keen on my running sarcasm.

"Actually, Aims, I'm pretty sure it wasn't Mother."

"Who then? The squadron?" She remembered the call during my shower. "What do they want?"

"Probably something routine." I wanted to provide more detail, but the possibilities were many and still simmering like ingredients in an unpleasant stew. "I need to call the skipper when we get to the house," I said, and left it at that. The thought of calling the squadron CO from my mother's house on Thanksgiving to get berated on a trivial matter was maddening and incomprehensible. I'd skirted some regulations, minor ones, but obviously enough to irritate him. And the transgression, although trivial, would likely move me one step closer to my career decision. I was nearing a point all junior officers face as they approach the completion of their service obligation. For pilots, it was five years from the day you earned your wings. I had less than a year remaining until that decision point and would need to submit my resignation request soon. Hell, there was really no decision. I would pull the plug and beat a path to the airlines so fast there'd barely be time for the ink to dry on my discharge papers. It was what John Baumann, my father, had done after his military service during World War II and what I would do next year. I knew this day would arrive even before I received my appointment to the Naval Academy. But as we drove northward to my mother's house, the airline option no longer seemed like the obvious path. Sure, it made sense given my ripening frustration with Navy life, but I no longer felt I was leaning toward the knee-jerk airline reaction most pilots find when their time is up. The decision would require some level of critical analysis before abandoning such a stable and honorable career as a naval officer.

The drizzle from the storm ended and I reached to shut off the truck's wipers. The blades were making an annoying screeching sound as they dragged across the dry windshield. Carlene was awake in her car seat and chatting to no one in particular. Aimee turned around to face both the children when I spotted a familiar landmark. "Sean, Carlene, what do I see? Look. Look over there."

I pointed ahead, out the windshield. I was eager for them to see.

Little Carlene was first to reply. "Bah-boo house! Bah-boo house!"

Aimee joined Carlene with encouragement. "Yay, Bubble House! There it is."

Perched atop the lofty canyon wall at eye level with the bridge we were now traversing was an unusual residential structure very much out of place with the surrounding conventional homes of the wealthy Hillsborough neighborhood. The house was a series of cement pods, or bubbles, painted white resembling something almost prehistoric.

"It's really called the Flintstone House, Daddy. That's what Evan's family calls it," Sean asserted. Evan was Sean's best friend and lived next door on base. He was a year older than Sean and, lately, an authority on most everything.

"Yes, Sean," I said. "I suppose that's a good name too."

But I always liked Bubble House. I coined the term, watching it come together back in the early '70s. But the finished product did appear straight from the town of Bedrock. The construction project was highly experimental at the time and I remember driving to the site many times, only a few miles from home, for closer inspection while on leave from the Naval Academy. There was something inexplicable about the shape and design that stirred my soul, offering maybe a pang of regret. And it always commanded my attention from the bridge, especially when driving alone, reminding me of the career choices I'd firmly made.

Aimee drew a deep breath and exhaled audibly. We were exiting the freeway, only minutes from home and my mother's hovering presence. Her sigh was a barometer reporting the impending change in the weather. Our big Suburban approached the long, windy street to my childhood home on Latera Way. Latera meandered through the neighborhood and ended in a cul-de-sac with our house, a large, low-profile 1960's rancher, at the center of the dead-end where the blacktop spread into a wide circle, which as a kid, had been perfect for bike riding and games of tag. I shut off the engine and the truck's interior became a tomb, the only sound the ticking dashboard clock. There was no excitement from Sean in the backseat. Carlene appeared to have dozed off again and her peaceful breathing amplified the hushed silence.

I eyed the front porch catching a glimpse of the living room drapes quiver back into place, a set of eyes suddenly disappearing. It was Mother, preparing for her usual spring from the double doors feigning surprise, rejoicing that her only son had returned home to his poor, lonely mother on this important holiday. My stomach tightened in anticipation. There was a time when I welcomed coming home despite how bad things were with my parents or Amber. This house had remained a refuge during my time at the Academy and I would either forgive or overlook the domestic problems that persisted while home on leave. As a child, I was either not aware or simply too naïve to understand the grownup world and its complexities that existed in our home. Our house always presented a neat facade. We had a swimming pool, a big yard, situated in an upscale neighborhood of large homes. Yet there had been a transition from normalcy over the last ten years and I couldn't put all the blame on my mother. My father's growing absences near the end puzzled us all. But my mother's spiral downward, aided by alcohol and an over-willingness to play the victim, made her too easy a target for my disappointment with the entire family. Mother was now living alone, legally separated from my father in what should have been their golden years, two retired empty-nesters with plenty of time, a fat airline pension and free flight benefits to travel the globe. To live through the turmoil, witnessing this alternate ending, had taken a toll on us all. "Well, Aims, looks like we're the only ones here, praise God." I gestured at the empty driveway and lack of strange cars in front of the house.

"I don't think so," she said.

"What are you talking about? We're late, the last to arrive. Where's the bus full of shut-ins? Where's the Pope and his entourage?"

"Stop. Please, just stop," Aimee interjected, unable to be coaxed into a second laugh so near the house. "Amber's coming and she's invited a friend.

Your mom also mentioned someone else, a neighbor perhaps. I don't know who."

I raised an eyebrow. "Amber?" Amber had been absent the last two Thanksgivings living up in the northwest but had moved back to the Bay Area sometime when I was on deployment. "According to Mother, she's missing."

"She'll be here. And a friend."

"Boyfriend or girlfriend?"

"Mitch, let's not get into this now. I'm fully aware of the stress your family causes but if you keep this up, I'll get out of this car and walk the thirty miles back to base."

"Okay, okay." I leaned across the console and kissed her cheek. "I'm sorry. Please stay."

Abruptly, Sean broke in. "Daddy, are we going inside or what? I need to go tinkle."

I had to smile. How could you not love Sean and his perfect timing? "In a minute, buddy. Hang on." I turned to Aimee, lowering my voice. "I know how you feel but every year it's the same and every year I look forward to leaving the moment I walk through that door. And you know all the reasons. It's not fair to bring you down with me. It's the whole Amber thing. I haven't seen her in two years, and I don't know how I'll react."

"You'll hug her and tell her it's great to see her, that you've missed her." She offered a simple smile. "That's how you'll react."

"That easy, huh?"

"That easy."

"Do we really know what Amber's been up to the last two years? Unemployed, living on a commune up north with some guy that looks like Frank Zappa, doing drugs and taking checks from my mother on a regular basis. And believe me, I know about the checks. Mother lets me know every time she sends one and Amber cashes it."

"And this is your problem, how?"

"Okay," I admitted. "Maybe it isn't my problem."

"Bingo."

"No. It is my problem. She's everyone's problem. Do you realize how much I've tried to help her since junior high? How I've tried to steer her away from all the bad decisions she's made until her life got so…" I lowered my voice in deference to the kids, "so messed up that she practically lives like a bag lady. And she's absolutely oblivious to it – takes zero responsibility, whatsoever. It's like, *Oh, dear me, why does shit keep falling from the sky wherever I go?* Believe me, I've tried to help her."

"And how's that working out?" Aimee said, smugly, keeping her voice soft.

"It's not. You know that." I drew a deep breath and returned my voice

25

to a normal level. "Okay everybody, let's go inside and see Grandma and have a happy Thanksgiving."

I said it loudly enough to finally wake up little Carlene, who replied, "Yay, happy 'Sgiving!'"

Aimee guided Sean to the porch as they walked hand in hand. I followed, carrying Carlene and her diaper bag in my arms. Mother showed little restraint at the front door offering her usual shrieks and overplayed enthusiasm. She'd observed us sitting in the car and spied our approach on the walkway suddenly jerking open the door and popping out before Aimee had the chance to ring the chime. "My, my! You finally made it!" she cried. "I was *so* worried. I thought maybe there'd been an accident." She leaned down embracing both Sean and Aimee in unison as they held hands. "How are you doing, my dears?" She stood and gave Aimee a quick peck on the cheek.

Aimee smiled warmly. "We're fine, Cynthia. How are you?"

"Well, everything's perfect now that my family is here." She looked down at Sean. "My, you're getting tall, young man." She brushed his hair with her hand. "But so very thin," clearly registering disappointment, implying Aimee might not be feeding him enough.

Aimee remained silent, unwilling to acknowledge the dig.

"Can we go swimming later? Huh, Grandma?"

"No, Sean," Aimee cut in. "It's much too cold and rainy. Brr."

Sean maintained his look to Grandma as if Aimee hadn't spoken.

"Of course, you can go swimming, dear."

Aimee gave her a look.

"Oh. Well," she said, backtracking. "Better check with Mommy first, sweetheart."

"No, Sean. We're not going swimming today. End of discussion." Her words registered loud and clear, even to my mother, who quickly fell silent.

I stepped forward and handed Carlene to Mother's extended hands. Carlene threw her arms around grandma's neck, resting her head on her shoulder and placing her thumb in mouth. Both were enjoying this tender reunion as I peered into the living room from the threshold. Carlene was handed back to Aimee. My mother and I were face to face, hands at our side. I reached out first. I hugged her with one arm and kissed her cheek. "How are you, Mother. Happy Thanksgiving."

She appeared disappointed, expecting a much bigger show of affection but unwilling to make the first move herself. "Oh. Yes. And happy Thanksgiving to you, Son." She leaned in and whispered sharply, "You're late. Why do you do always do this? I was so worried."

I peeked at my watch on my free arm. "Mother, it's only 2:15." I drew her close again. "You don't look so worried."

"And you don't know your own mother," she said pulling away to reenter the house.

I wasn't going to engage. I'd made a promise. Instead, I took note of the other guests deeper inside the living room presenting only silhouettes from my view on the porch. No additional cars were parked in the motor court or sitting on the street. Aimee brushed by me to greet one of the two young women standing in the dining room. I did a double-take. Was that Amber? I couldn't believe I didn't recognize my own sister. She looked different, refined, better than I'd expected, but still bearing the worn countenance from the hard life she'd chosen. Her shaggy auburn hair was cut to a neat shoulder-length, much shorter and tidier than when I'd seen her two years ago. Aimee hugged Amber like a lost friend, much more tender and familiar than I'd seen in the past. I was marveling at their renewed connection when my mother reached for my arm and led me to an older woman, at least eighty years old, seated on the sofa. Okay, here we go, I thought. Time to meet one of her mystery guests.

"Mitch, Son, this is Mrs. Hagl," she said proudly. "You remember her." If my mother was frustrated from our late arrival at the front door, she'd quickly forgotten it.

Mrs. Hagl remained seated, offering a warm smile and extending her hand. I was relieved I didn't have to hug her, pretending to recognize this person I'd clearly never met. "Pleased to meet you, Mrs. Hagl." I took her delicate hand and shook it politely.

"It is Klara, darling. I am always Klara," she spoke, in a very thick, discernable German accent.

"Oh, of course, Klara, forgive us," my mother quickly interjected. "Mitch remembers you. It's just been a very long time." She turned to me with a frozen smile as if to say, don't you dare embarrass me, not the moment you walk into my house. I looked at Aimee, who was being introduced to Amber's guest, a slovenly dressed woman that appeared the same age as Amber. Aimee was smiling, playing the gracious in-law role she did so well with my family.

"Mitch, you remember." Mother leaned in, pinching my arm, providing the clue I wished she had in the first place. "Harold's grandmother."

"Oh, Miss Klara, of course, now I remember. I'm very sorry. It's been more than ten years. So how is Harold and the rest of your family?" Harold and I had been friends in grade school, and I presumed his parents still lived in the neighborhood.

"Oh, they leave me today. Harold is a Porsche mechanic, like his father, and lives in San Jose. Krystal is married and living in..." Klara paused, looking to my mother for help remembering the city name.

"Chico, dear, up in the central valley," my mother offered, then turned to me and whispered, "And what a hell hole."

"Ah, yes, Chico. Thank you, my dear," Klara replied. "I've never been there." She winked in my direction. "They tell me it's a hell hole."

I smiled. Two could play this game.

My mother didn't miss a beat. Instead of turning three shades of red she instantly replied, "Well, it *is* very hot in the summer. Oh, but it's a marvelous place to start a new family. Things are *so* cheap there. Ha, ha."

This was vintage Mother – take a misspoken slur and turn it into a compliment as if her ill-timed statement was planned from the outset. Despite her gaff, Klara's news brought me back into the picture. So, Harold was working as an auto mechanic now, probably for his father, August. However, August was no longer a mere Porsche mechanic, as Klara had described, and hadn't been for many years. When he and his new wife, Cornelia, came to the United States from Germany in 1951, he may have started as a mechanic but by the time they'd moved into our neighborhood in 1964 he was co-owner of a very posh Porsche Audi dealership in San Carlos, always driving one of their newest cars off the lot. I'd also lost track of Krystal unaware she'd gotten married and moved to Chico. She was a year older than me and was strikingly beautiful at an early age with long legs and a thick mane of blond hair. We'd ended up in the same sixth-grade class when I got skipped ahead a year in school and I'd kept an eye on her from afar throughout our years in high school.

Aimee had her back to me and continued her chat with Amber and her friend in the far corner of the living room. Mother disappeared to the kitchen, Carlene leading her by the hand after being promised a cookie. I figured this was the best time to break the ice with Amber after not seeing or speaking to her for so long. I made a straight line for the threesome feeling self-conscious and out of place. I resolved to keep my vow, made only minutes ago, to curb my sarcasm and drop any trace of judgment from my voice. My best move would be to make introductions to Amber's girlfriend first.

I extended a hand. "Hi, I'm Mitch, Amber's brother."

The girl snickered and looked at Amber. Her wavy black hair fell in uneven chunks down her lower back. It was choppy as if she'd cut it herself with a pair of dull scissors. She was wearing a simple black t-shirt with elastic waistband pants and exuded a strong scent of patchouli oil

Amber spoke. "Mitch, you guys have met. This is Dez. We went to Mercy together."

"Dez? Oh, sure," I said, after a beat. "Dez." Again, here was another soul I'd presumably met and should remember. Amber's look told me I'd fare much better simply by faking it.

"Don't worry," Dez said. "If it helps, I don't remember you either."

I nodded politely and turned to my sister. "So, how are you doing, Amber? Long time, huh?" I was trying my best to maintain good behavior, if for no one's sake but Aimee's, who stood next to me bracing for World War III. Amber was dressed casually in a beige cardigan and designer jeans. Her hair looked professionally cut. Her clean appearance and smart clothing stood in stark contrast to her friend, Dez, who seemed intentionally underdressed for a guest at Thanksgiving.

"Two years. Same place, same holiday, huh?" she said, matter-of-factly.

"Where are you living now? Where have you been?"

Amber and Dez exchanged looks and laughed. "Oh, here and there."

"Here and there?" I tried to keep derision out of my tone, but it was difficult. "Have you been back to see Mother in the last two years?"

"What do you care? It's not like I've seen you putting in regular appearances at Chez Baumann."

"Hey, I've been on deployment."

"Oh, that's right. So, while you were saving the world from communism, yeah, I came home. Spent part of my summer right here living with Mother, in fact. Any more questions?"

"C'mon, Amber. I'm only trying to catch up." I couldn't believe how fast things were deteriorating. And I was being nice.

"Catch us up? Bullshit. This is an interrogation. You know what I've been up to and where I've been. You get the news, I'm sure."

Aimee, who had been watching our blunt exchange, decided best to intervene. "Hey, guys, time out. We can talk about this later over dinner. I bring peace offerings." She held up a festive gift bag with colorful tissue and two wrapped presents inside. This was the bag I'd fetched from our kitchen earlier and assumed it was a hostess gift for my mother.

"Amber, this is just a little something from Mitch and I – for your, uh, going away."

Again, I was playing catch-up. "Going away? Amber's going away, where?"

"I'll tell you later, Mitch," Aimee said.

"No, seriously, going away, where?" I continued.

Aimee clenched her teeth and lowered her voice, speaking as she faced Amber. "Not now. Just drop it, please."

Amber laughed. "You mean he doesn't know?"

Me: "Apparently not."

Aimee: "I thought I'd let him find out at dinner tonight."

Amber: "Oh, perfect."

Dez: "Why not just tell him now?"

Amber: "Nah, let him dangle."

All three girls laughed.

I wasn't about to continue with their guessing game and their laughter provided the opportune moment to slip from the room. Their girly secret could wait. I needed some air, and we'd only just arrived. I entered the family room, passing the kitchen where Klara and my mother were busy with Thanksgiving meal preparations. Carlene had pulled up a stool to the counter and was pretending to help the grownups. Sean was standing at the large sliding glass door, cookie in hand, surveying the swimming pool in the backyard. "C'mon, Sean-boy, let's go outside," I said.

"But it's raining out there, I hope you know." *I hope you know* was the latest phrase he'd picked up from his best friend, Evan. Lately, Sean and Evan added it to all their statements as if to claim the final authority on any topic. He would tell Aimee, we're out of milk, *I hope you know*, or, the school bus is late again, *I hope you know*. It was a cute way for a six-year-old to assert himself but was also something we hoped he'd soon outgrow.

"It's letting up," I said. "Let's take a walk."

"Can we go swimming?" he asked, dead serious.

"No, c'mon." I noticed two coolers full of beer and soft drinks on the patio and thought we could have some fun skipping ice chips across the water. I slid the glass door open, and we stepped into a light spit of rain. I suspected we were between storm bands and the heavy stuff wouldn't start coming down again for another hour. I needed some time to grab a bit of air and step away from the stuffy atmosphere I'd left behind. Sean began tossing ice cubes one by one into the water while droplets of rain danced on the pool's surface. I walked past the pool deck into my mother's small garden containing willow and elm shade trees among rows of her prized roses, geraniums and baskets of hanging fuchsias. An empty hummingbird feeder hung from the lattice just above my head. Beyond the garden was a short flight of stairs, just three steps, leading down to a narrow deck at the end of the property where the terrain dropped off sharply. This was our "million-dollar view" to the east, one that would hypnotize my father for hours when he needed to be alone. The rear deck was long and slender, only six feet wide, and contained a wicker couch with two matching chairs where he'd sit peering up and down the expansive San Francisco Bay for hours. Mount Diablo was the prominent peak on the horizon with Oakland, Alameda and Contra Costa County fanning out in all directions. From our perch on this side of the bay, San Francisco airport's runways, three miles out, seemed almost close enough to touch.

"What do you think, Sean? Nice view, huh?" It really was spectacular, one I never tired of.

"I'm cold."

"Oh, so I take it you don't want to go swimming." I laughed and tousled his hair.

"Uh-uh."

"That's fine," I said. "I'll walk you back to the house, but I think I'll stay outside a bit longer, okay?"

I guided Sean toward the edge of the pool deck and watched him run the remaining distance to the house, tug on the heavy sliding door and reenter the family room. I walked back to the deck and resituated myself on the big wicker chair my father used to sit. Heavy layers of swollen clouds hung to the east. The rain had temporarily ceased, and visibility was decreasing under the low, gray ceiling. I needed to brush aside the skirmish in the living room. I had made a conscious effort to be affable, to go along, especially after not seeing Amber in two years yet I felt I'd let Aimee down again, that she'd see me as the antagonist. As much as I wanted to deny it, a pattern had formed. My behavior had noticeably changed, especially over the last year and I blamed it on my upcoming career decision. I was impatient, defiant, angry. Those were Aimee's words, and if I completely agreed with her, which I didn't, she'd say the problem had been going on longer than a year. I wasn't the person Aimee described and I didn't see that I had a problem.

And yet...

From my vantage point on the deck, I could look down and see both my old elementary and high schools, easily recognizable landmarks with their large playgrounds and athletic fields. The elementary school, Portola Valley, was huge, thirty classrooms at least, and had recently been closed due to sagging enrollment. Mills High School, however, was still open and in full operation. I spotted the football field with its recently upgraded rubberized track, its tall light stanchions and prominent grid lines etched into the grass. My eyes wandered to the adjoining baseball diamond, an inescapable memory flooding back like the tide.

I frowned.

The memory was familiar, one I'd replayed many times, always fantasizing about a more desirable outcome, one that made me the hero. It provided an insight to my personality that would likely validate some of Aimee's observations, traits she'd bring up in our disagreements I felt were unjust and only uttered to provoke me. I'd never told her this specific story from my senior year in high school, never in its complete, unvarnished truth. Aimee knew I played baseball, she'd seen the pictures in the yearbook, she knew I played first base, occasionally filling in as pitcher, and was competent at both positions. She even knew, again from my yearbook, that we came painfully close to winning the Central Coast Sectional Division I playoffs in 1973 and a trip to the state finals. That was all she knew. She didn't know how I'd let the team down, myself down, and cost us the game by getting ejected in the top of the third inning.

We were playing on our home field against our rival high school down the peninsula. The playoff would decide who would represent the central coast in the state championship series. Mills had never gone this far in the post-season in our fifteen-year history and practically everyone in Millbrae, including the mayor, had turned out to watch us play on this beautiful spring afternoon. The school added extra bleachers to accommodate all the parents and local fans wanting a seat. Missing from the crowd, however, was my father, who was on another of his extended trips with the airline. As a captain, his workweeks usually lasted four days on followed by five days off, or sometimes vice versa. When I was in grade school, I noticed my father was home more than the other fathers in the neighborhood. Somewhere during junior high, however, he began to stay away longer, extending his time by more than a week at a stretch. In high school, he was gone all the time making only brief, irregular appearances at home. When it became evident he'd miss this important playoff game like many other regular season games, I was very angry with him and my mother. This was a difficult time for me, trying to adjust to an absentee father and a mother who didn't acknowledge his absence or seem to care.

I'd started the game as pitcher, and we were in a seesaw battle with the score tied 2-2 after two full innings. As we hustled onto the field to start the top of the third my teammates ran by the mound offering pats of encouragement. I felt distracted and was running out of gas too early. During the between-inning warmup, my throws were not hitting the spot Jake Wallace, our catcher, had set as a target. He kept repositioning his glove until finally walking to the mound. "Settle down," he said. "You've got their pitcher in the nine-spot and he can't hit. Easy out. Their number one and two hitters are due next, and they hate the curveball, remember? Keep 'em high and breaking and we'll get through this. You and me." He handed me the ball and jogged back to the plate in his heavy gear, repeating, "You and me, you and me."

Their first batter, the pitcher, did go down as predicted but only after clobbering the ball into deep center. The crowd sent out a collective gasp fearing a homerun, but our centerfielder ran it down at the warning track snagging the ball in midair at the last second. Not the easy out Jake had promised, I thought. Next came the top of their lineup. I'd faced their leadoff hitter in the first inning and had him chasing the curve, always behind, just as Jake had said. This time my first pitch, a real roundhouse beauty, leapt off his bat for a single into right field. "No problem, no problem," I could hear Jake saying. He signaled for another curve to the next batter. Ball one. I followed with a series of fastballs, but nothing worked. The guy ended up fouling off ten consecutive pitches before walking, wearing me down in the process and putting runners at first and second.

I was losing control and felt enraged. I picked up the rosin bag and threw it down in frustration as their number three hitter approached the batter's box. He was a beefy kid known for his power and thunderous swings and my goal was to keep the pitches high, get him to chop the ball at one of our infielders. Jake gave me the target I needed with his glove but had to adjust quickly. My first pitch hit the dirt in front of the plate, the exact opposite of where it needed to go. Our coach was staring daggers at me from the dugout.

My next two pitches were the opposite, too high, and Jake had to stand to catch them. Suddenly I was facing a 3 and 0 count with two runners on. Not good. I began to silently chant, looking at Jake. *You and me, you and me…* My next pitch was perfect, a change-up down the middle for a strike. He just stood limply, expecting the walk. Instead, he got call strike one.

Now comes the finale, which I always recall in slow motion – my last pitch, in my last game, of my last season. And the pitch will go down as a dark footnote in our school's history. I am exhausted after losing the last batter after fourteen pitches and angry at getting behind in the count on this next guy. The game still has six innings to go and I'm just not visualizing its ending. In fact, I wonder if I'll even finish the inning.

I will not.

As I let my final pitch fly, I only think about getting the ball over the plate, letting the chips fall where they will. Most of my pitches this inning have not gone where I wanted them to go, where they needed to go. This last pitch is no exception, the ball beginning a trajectory of high and inside heading straight for the batter. There isn't time for him to properly react, to spring from the ball's path, so he instinctively turns his back and braces for impact. The ball ricochets off his shoulder, spins into the air and lands near his foot. For a moment, time stands still, there isn't a sound in the park as the ball twirls to a rest. My gut reaction is to appear defensive, resolute, show no remorse. The batter is fine, in fact jovial, as he kicks the ball back to me soccer-style, like, hey, no hard feelings. Oh, but there are plenty of hard feelings. I'm seeing red, I'm furious. "Just take your base, douchebag," I yell, pointing at first. Surprisingly, he doesn't take my polite suggestion, deciding instead to throw down his bat and rush the mound. Jake tackles him from behind. Benches clear, players from both sides spill onto the field. "It was an accident," I want to say. But it's too late, and no one cares. The melee has begun. My teammates quickly form a barricade around me as it appears everyone wants a piece of the pitcher. Punches get thrown, a few players on both sides get knocked down, some are thrown to the ground but remarkably no one gets bloodied or injured. In fact, I never was touched. The barrier my teammates created kept me at a clean distance until the fray was halted by the coaches and umpires. As the dust settles, I marvel at this miracle, but not for long. The home plate umpire threads his way through the crowd and grabs my arm. He walks me to the edge of the playing field directly in front of my coach and fans and gestures wildly, just like they do in the Bigs, "You're OUTTA here!"

The rain resumed after an hour lull. Drops began dotting my forehead forming rivulets of water down my face onto my shirt, hastening my return from memory lane. The sky had closed in and the vast San Francisco Bay, so much a part of the deck's panorama, was socked in, no longer visible.

33

How long had I drifted off? I needed to get out of the rain and take care of the unpleasant duty I'd promised myself before we'd arrived. I needed to call the skipper.

I moved quickly past the swimming pool to the sliding door and removed my shoes before entering the kitchen. My mother spied me creeping by. "Oh, Mitch, there you are. Where on earth did you disappear to? And you're soaking wet. We're going to be sitting down in a few minutes. I want you to play host. Please pick out some wine for us, perhaps a white and a—"

"In a minute, Mother. I need to make a phone call. Can I use the extension in the den?"

"A phone call? Who possibly needs calling on Thanksgiving?"

"I'll tell you afterward. Just excuse me for a moment." I turned to walk away.

"Oh, please, do as you wish." She tossed a fresh dishtowel at me. "And dry off your hair, maybe run a comb through it. You look like you a drowned rat."

The towel landed squarely on my shoulder. "Yes, Mother."

I made my way through the family room toward the den near the back of the house. The Dallas Cowboys were playing on the TV console with the sound muted. No one was paying attention to the game. Amber and Dez were playing with Sean and his Masters of the Universe collection on the floor. Aimee was sitting on the sofa reading a book to Carlene who was in her lap, thumb in mouth. Everyone went silent and looked up as I passed. "Quick call to the squadron," I said, mainly to Aimee, who offered no hint of understanding even though I'd told her earlier.

The room we all referred to as the den was set up as my father's office, a room he hadn't used in years. My mother had decorated it for him shortly after we'd moved in filling it with many of my father's Army Air Corps memorabilia from his World War II pilot days flying B-17s – pictures of his crew, his Air Medal and Purple Heart, a listing of his 35 combat missions. It was an impressive wall, one that had remained static since my third grade, one that I regarded as décor rather than artifacts of my father's history. Despite him no longer living at home, my mother kept the room completely unchanged, down to a framed desktop picture of the two of them on Miami Beach after my father returned from the war. I studied the black and white photo, circa early 1945, barely recognizing either of them. They were so young, my mother about to turn nineteen, my father, twenty-four. I was puzzled yet pleased she'd preserved this room, not dumping the pictures or placing them face-down as would typically be her nature.

I took a deep breath. Time to face the music, I thought. Although my perception of the transgression was trivial, calling the CO was never trivial. I only hoped phoning him at his home during the holiday weekend would find him in a festive mood. But first I needed to call Duncan, the squadron duty officer, for the skipper's home number.

Duncan picked up on the first ring. "VP 25 Duty Office, Lieutenant Duncan Kinder, this is a non-secure line, may I help you, sir?"

"Dunk, it's me, Mitch."

"Mitch! Holy cow. Where are you? I've been calling your home number every half-hour."

"I told you, I was headed out. What's the crisis now?"

"The debrief thing. No one's leaving it alone. My phone's been ringing off the hook since this morning. Apparently, it didn't go well. Jamie called, feels awful and was trying to reach you. All I had was your home number. He's afraid he's going to take a lot of heat. Ops officer also wanted to talk to you until I told him the skipper's involved. Everyone's waiting. Jeez, Mitch, I hope you're not in trouble because—"

"Okay, okay, calm down, Dunk." I massaged my temples. "Skipper's really upset, huh?"

"Yeah, Mitch, he's pretty steamed."

"All right, let me have his home number. I'll call him right now."

"Right now."

"Yes, Dunk, right now."

"Okay, cool. You should be okay. He was doing a lot of screaming but you know what that usually means, right?"

"Yep, I know. And thanks. I didn't mean to put you on the spot. He wasn't yelling at you, you know." But he'll soon be yelling at me, I thought. That was a given.

We bid goodbye and Duncan wished me luck. I reminded myself to remain calm once the storm started, that when the skipper, Commander Sam Wilson, started yelling the hard part was over, and he just needed to provide a bit of theatrics to drive his point home. This was known throughout the squadron as his "Yosemite Sam" mode from the feisty Warner Brothers cartoon character. The fitting nickname was applied behind his back shortly after he took over as CO when he brought this comical yet intimidating Texas cowboy bully to real life. The skipper was short, barely five-foot-nine, and had a bit of a handlebar mustache and swagger just like Yosemite Sam. At happy hours, after everyone was sufficiently liquored up, we'd trot out our best Yosemite Sam Wilson imitations and funniest stories. One story in particular was fairly insightful. Skipper Wilson insisted all his candidate patrol plane commanders fly their final check ride with him before he signed their approval paperwork. He was a tough but fair instructor and very meticulous on the rudimentary skills of airmanship, especially during the approach and landing phases. Anticipation of these check flights would keep a pilot awake the entire night before, reviewing every possible contingency and the entire NATOPS flight manual emergency procedures section. So, on this particular check ride, the student PPC made a sloppy approach to the runway, coming in too high and sinking too fast. He managed to salvage the landing by shoving on some power at the last second to grease it in – a big no-no. The skipper, in the right seat, immediately jumped all over him. He ranted and raved, ending in true Texan form with an animal metaphor. "That approach was like flying up an elephant's ass," he screamed. "It was high, and it stunk." Soon after the story made its rounds, a big poster of Dumbo the Flying Elephant was hung in our squadron wardroom by an anonymous officer. It showed poor Dumbo turning around and frowning, surveying his hindquarters with a big red circle and slash over his ass, the international symbol implying, "No Elephant's Asses". We began calling each other's bad approaches EAs, or Echo Alphas. The skipper loved it and adopted the term himself. He roared approval at the Dumbo poster and commended the junior officers who created it. It was all about generating camaraderie in his wardroom and keeping morale high. He wanted his aircrews loose and aggressive, especially when we were on deployment. Blustering was his way of correcting a minor mistake or bending the rules using his command presence as the final say. And a humorous story always followed, one even the skipper himself might retell in the bar with the victim at his side. Skipper Wilson had many admirable traits and we all lived to please him, to carry out his orders, to gain his respect. It was when he looked you calmly in the eye with grave concern, without going ballistic, you knew you were in genuine trouble.

I slowly pressed each button on my father's desk phone, carefully inputting the numbers Duncan had provided. I was shaking, but just mildly.

The phone rang in my ear. Once, twice, three times. Maybe no one's home, I thought. Hallelujah.

Suddenly, "Hello?" It was a woman's voice.

"Uh, hello, Mrs. Wilson? I'm sorry to interrupt your Thanksgiving. This is Mitch Baumann. Is Commander Wilson in? He asked that I call."

"Oh, Mitch," came her sunny reply. "Happy Thanksgiving to you. And please don't apologize. He's right here, dear. Hang on."

Skipper Wilson was on the phone in two seconds. "Mitch?"

"Yes, sir."

"Goddamn it, Mitch. Where the hell have you been?"

"Traveling, sir. I've been—"

"I don't give a shit where you've been."

But you just asked, I thought, before realizing these were questions he didn't want answered. This was not a two-way conversation, not yet.

He continued. "What happened this morning? What makes you think you've got the right to just blow off the debrief? You think you're special? Those coordinated ops flights are the most expensive training exercises we fly to meet squadron readiness. We pay for the sub's time, burn up more fuel and shit more sonobuoys than most operational flights on real world Soviets.

They're rare and valuable on-top time, not something I want fucked up, especially by a smart-ass lieutenant who thinks he's too good to finish the job and attend the debrief with his crew."

I remained silent.

"You're the Mission Commander, are you not? You have overall responsibility for the success of the mission, do you not? You're my representative in the air *and* at the goddamn debrief on the ground. Are you soft, or what? Did you forget everything you were ever taught? Because the alternative is much worse. It means you willfully disrespected the debriefing officer, your crew, the squadron and *me*. Which is it, Mitch? Stupidity or insubordination? There's no third option."

I remained still, holding the receiver a good twelve inches from my ear.

"I don't want to ever hear of you skipping out of a debrief again. *Ever.* You got that?"

"Yes, sir." I was hoping we were though, that he'd said his piece. But he switched gears.

"And what gives you the goddamn right to skip the birdbath, for Christ's sake?"

Oh, of course, the maintenance chief, I thought. He couldn't stay quiet, he owed me no favors.

"Yeah, I heard about that one too. I take it as a deliberate *fuck you* to my directive, a direct affront to my authority. What the hell's wrong with you, Mitch? Everyone washes off after going feet wet, even the Commodore, you got that? What's your excuse?"

He finally took a breath and waited for a response. After a dressing-down like that, there was only one response, one I'd learned as a plebe at the Naval Academy. "No excuse, sir," I said. "I was wrong, and it won't happen again. In the future, I will wash the airplane and I will attend the debrief. I'm sorry." By accepting full responsibility, as my training had taught, and by apologizing, I was signaling uncle. I had taken my medicine and wanted to end the unpleasant call. I was hoping this was it, that he was letting me off with a warning, albeit a colorful, profane-laced Yosemite Sam warning.

"Stow the apology," he said, calmly. "We still need to talk. I want to see you in my office first thing Monday morning at 0700. You got that?"

"Yes, sir."

Click. He was gone.

My face was numb. It was not Skipper Wilson's practice to continue a rant days later. Once he got it off his chest, he was done, turn the page, a new start. Whatever he wanted to say Monday morning was purposely held back in the phone call. I sat in my father's office, spun in his big desk chair and pondered my fate. Was this the confrontation I was pursuing, a subconscious exit strategy, one that would force a decision with my career path of either remaining in the Navy or going airline? I certainly would not have planned this telephone encounter or the face-to-face Monday meeting with a very angry commanding officer. But what was my excuse for playing it loose with simple regulations? Crew leadership? Not likely. This was not me. I knew better.

I stood up and walked from the den. It would do little good to continue dwelling on my future meeting with Skipper Wilson and the root cause of running afoul with squadron regulations, be it short-timer apathy or subliminal career sabotage. Best just to get through the upcoming meal, head home and try to enjoy the remainder of the long weekend before facing the early Monday encounter, regardless of consequences.

I appeared to be late when I entered the formal dining room. Everyone was already standing behind an assigned seat at the table while Aimee fastened Carlene into her highchair, one that had been mine when I was her age. I walked up to the only empty spot, a chair next to Aimee, and everyone's eyes locked on me.

"Everything okay?" Aimee asked, in a hushed voice directly in my ear.

"Sure, everything's great. Why wouldn't it be?" I said, a bit too loudly, casting an eye at everyone.

"I just thought," Aimee glanced at my mother and then the other guests, "maybe the squadron was looking for you. That you might have to leave or something. Forget it," she said, reaching to refill the wine glass she'd carried into the dining room.

"It's forgotten," I said, for the room's benefit. I whispered toward her, "I'll tell you later." I deeply wanted to confess, and Aimee always played the role of my sympathetic sounding board. I loved her for that but now was not the time.

My mother, feeling the tension, said, "Son, why don't you make yourself useful and fetch the turkey from the kitchen. I'd like you to do the honors this year of carving and serving."

"This year, Mother? I've done it every year since Dad left."

She ignored my remark and continued, "And Amber will lead us in grace, won't you, dear?"

I immediately looked at Amber. She hadn't led grace at our table since she was ten years old, and it was the obligatory children's prayer, *God is great, God is good, let us thank Him for our food.* Amber didn't return my look and simply nodded at my mother. Dez, standing next to Amber, stared down at the carpet, appearing aloof and disconnected.

"So, Dez," I said, wanting to draw her back in, "Did I hear Amber correctly, that you went to Mercy together?" Mercy was a ridiculously expensive all-girl Catholic high school located in the wooded hills above Burlingame and served mainly as a prep school for high achievers bound for major universities such as Stanford or USC. It also served, in Amber's case, and presumably Dez's, as a rigid institution with a set of inflexible rules designed to course-correct troubled girls that got off to a bad beginning in the public junior high schools. Amber had started experimenting with drugs and alcohol at thirteen and my mother's response was to throw money at the problem by sending her to an exclusive private school that would isolate her. What she hadn't counted on were the Dez's of the world and other druggie girls with wealthy parents that had the same idea.

Dez looked up to respond but not directly at me. "Yeah. Me, Amber, MJ, Omi, the rest of the crew, we all went to Mercy."

"The crew?" I said, slightly mocking her choice of noun.

Amber quickly jumped in. "What's your point, Mitch? And why your sudden interest in the Mercy alumni?"

"I'm not interested in the Mercy alumni, Amber." We were ending our sentences with names, reminiscent of our fights as children. "I'm only curious if Dez, MJ and Omi were nicknames, that's all."

"Dez is right here, Mitch. Why don't you ask her?"

"Now, children." It was Klara, in her soft German accent. "It's Tanksgiving and you haven't seen each other in two years. You shouldn't fight. You should rejoice and be tankful for your blessings." She displayed an odd giddiness, unfazed by the bickering.

I looked kindly at Klara, acknowledging her attempt at diplomacy. "Thank you, Miss Klara. I was only trying to bring Dez into the conversation." I looked over at Dez and winked, like, no hard feelings then walked into the kitchen to fetch the turkey, a golden brown 25-pound giant fresh from the oven and sitting on my mother's finest silver serving tray. Before I could grab the carving utensils, my mother appeared, facing me across the center island. "Just what do you think you are doing?" she spoke, phrasing it more as a challenge than a question.

"What do you mean? Fetching the turkey, like you asked."

"No, what you said earlier. Reminding everyone at the table you've been filling in since Dad left."

"I mean, I've been carving, filling in every year since Dad left. What's the big deal?"

"Filling in for him?" It was just the two of us, alone in the kitchen, and she was circling like a prizefighter ready to pounce. "As if—"

"Mother, please, leave it alone." She understandably contained some bitterness in the wake of my father's departure, and it had embarrassed her at some level, I'm sure, making her feel vulnerable, yet also fueling feelings of anger, especially at odd, unpredictable times.

"Filling in for him…" she whispered again, busying herself at the stove.

"Yes, okay, have it your way. I'm filling in for him," I shot back, no longer confident we were discussing the same subject.

"Oh, you pretend you're so important. You disappear in the backyard for hours. You dodge your family to make important calls showing the world the Navy can't function without you, not even on Thanksgiving."

I was stunned by her sudden accusatory tone and fierce loyalty to a husband that had disappeared, leaving us all in the lurch. "Who are we talking about here, Mother? Me or my father?"

"You figure it out," she said dismissively, pivoting from the stove. As she whirled around, she appeared woozy and stumbled, dropping a bowl of homemade stuffing onto the tile countertop. The ceramic bowl hit hard and shattered into several large pieces.

I ran to her. "Mother! Are you all right?" She reached out and leaned into my arms. I thought she was about to faint, and I held her close. "Mother...?"

She was gently sobbing but there were no tears. "I'm sorry," she said. "It's just that sometimes—"

"Don't worry about it," I said, pulling her closer. "I know, this has to be hard. Every year, it's the same, time passes... It's been hard on all of us."

"No, no, I'll be fine." She spoke as though nothing had occurred. "I'm fine now."

She straightened her shoulders and righted herself. I let go and stepped back. "Are you sure you're feeling all right? Maybe you should lie down for a few minutes."

"Don't be absurd. Everything's fine. The bowl was wet and slipped, that's all." She smoothed her apron and went back to the stove to fill another container with the remaining stuffing. "Run along. I'll be there in a moment." There was that familiar lilt in her tone and a spring in her step, suggesting we weren't to talk of this any further and forget it ever happened.

I hoisted the huge turkey from the counter, carried it into the dining room and began carving, saying nothing.

"...Dez is a nickname," Dez spoke, breaking the silence at the table as I sawed a turkey leg. "It's short for Desdemona."

Her delayed response combined with the kitchen incident caught me off-guard. Amber stared at her, possibly hearing this fact for the first time herself. I continued slicing and spoke, "Desdemona? As in Shakespeare's Desdemona?" I vaguely recalled the character from Othello but that was where my knowledge ended.

"Both my parents are Anglophiles – Shakespeare freaks, actually. Of course, they think nothing of naming their daughter after a tragic character from Othello."

"I take it she dies?"

"Of course, she dies. But not before disgracing her family and deeply disappointing her father."

"I guess we always end up disappointing the ones we love," Amber spoke, looking directly at me.

I ignored the remark. Amber *was* a disappointment, and she knew it, but by jabbing me with her comment she could shift some of the burden like it was my fault for setting the bar too high. "So, Miss Klara, where is your family today?" I was curious where her son, August, and his wife, Cornelia were today and why she was left alone.

I could see my mother dying to intercede before Klara cut her off. "They fly up to Vancouver yesterday to be with Cornelia's mother and her family. I couldn't go since I'm here from Germany on a visa."

My mother burst in from her silence. "August is working on getting her a green card so she can live here until she dies, I mean, live here indefinitely." She turned to Klara, "And it must be so hard traveling back and forth to Germany at your age, my dear. I know I certainly couldn't do it. Those long flights are just *horrific*. Imagine, not letting an elderly mother stay with her son when she needs him most. They should have let her in immediately."

I caught the obvious dig about a son not going the extra mile for his mother. "Mother, why don't you write a letter? Address it personally to the Secretary of State, George Shultz, and complain about such treatment?"

My mother considered the question seriously, not as intended sarcasm. "Oh, I would. But I'm afraid I'm not a relative and I'd carry no weight in the case. In fact, I've given Cornelia many such suggestions, to write our congressman, the senators and yes, even the State Department." Of course, she ignores all my advice and my good intentions. I guess she never did much care for me."

"Oh, my dear, no," Klara spoke, playing right into my mother's hand, "Cornelia and my son think you are wonderful. They say all the time, 'Cynthia is so caring and thoughtful, she is always checking on us.' You are especially thoughtful on this Tanksgiving to invite me and help while they are gone."

My mother basked in the compliment but felt compelled to add, "Well, I'm sure she thinks I'm being a busybody."

I wanted to say, no, you *are* being a busybody. Instead, I turned to Klara and asked, "Miss Klara, you may have mentioned, but where in Germany do you live now?"

"I live in Koblenz. It's a small city near Frankfurt, a nice, clean city. I still walk to the market. I have a tiny apartment, but I must climb the stairs every day, there is no Aufzug, uh, no lift."

"And she's on the third floor, for God's sake," my mother interjected, proud of knowing this small fact and galled at the same time. "Can you imagine? Eighty-two years old and still climbing three flights of stairs."

Klara nodded at my mother. "Yes, my dear, but it is good exercise for me." She laughed.

"Are you from Koblenz? Do you have other family there?" I was curious as I knew Krystal, her granddaughter, was born in Germany and her mother,

41

Cornelia, flew back from the United States to give birth so Krystal could eventually obtain dual citizenship – another fact that galled my mother.

Klara paused. "No, my August is all I've got, living here in America. We move from Hamburg right after the war. August was still a boy, maybe fifteen, just starting the Oberschule."

"Oberschule?"

"It's like your high school, dear. Of course, Germany's schools were such, problems, back then."

"You mean during World War II?"

"Ja. He begin Gymnasium in Hamburg but the war made it – made it, how do you say, um-possible?"

"*Impossible*," my mother corrected. "I can just imagine."

"Thank you. Ja, impossible." Klara spoke in a soft, wistful voice but had a look of resolve on her face, not inviting pity. "School was not a priority back then. It was all about the factory work."

"So, Hamburg was affected by the war, that's why you left?" I knew from studying history and our den wall that my father had bombed Hamburg and which cities around Germany had suffered the most but felt the need to be respectful, maybe end the line of conversation entirely.

"Yes, dear, the bombings lasted many days. We could no longer live in Hamburg, we – there was no wasser or electric, no food. I took August, we move south. But the *Hungersnot*, the famine was everywhere and—"

My mother jumped in holding up her hand like a traffic cop. "—and that concludes our history lesson for today," she said. "Let's all join hands as Amber prepares to lead us in grace."

"Wait," I said. "Let her finish."

She made direct eye contact with me, a look that said we are not probing the grisly details of famine at my Thanksgiving table, thank you very much. "Now, Amber…"

Klara, aware of the silent communication passing between my mother and me, smiled down at her plate and said, "Well, perhaps ve finish another time."

"Yes, that would be lovely, dear," my mother fired back. "Amber, are you ready?"

All eight of us, including Carlene, buckled in her highchair, sat at our places around the table and joined hands. My mother, sitting at the head of the table and to my left, looked up from her prayerful posture as if to warn me of something. It reminded me of when I was a kid. She was giving me that look, a familiar expression that said, behave, young man, and do not make a scene.

I looked back at her, in true innocence, and mouthed, "What?"

*"We give thanks for all the blessings and goodness for which we have before us at this table and in this house,"* Amber began. *"And we give thanks for all the love and*

*support that surrounds us in this room…"*

With my head bowed, I opened my eyes to slits and stared at the thick beige carpet under my feet. My mother's right hand trembled mildly in my left. As Amber prayed, I quickly noticed she had not used the word *Lord* or *God* or made reference to any particular saint in her preamble despite her Catholic school background. So, what was "love and support" really supposed to be referencing? Support for cooking a turkey?

*"…for my parents, especially Mother…"*

My mother's hand tightened around mine.

*"…for being there for me, when I needed them most, especially now. We give thanks to Dez, to Aimee, for the love they've shown me and the guidance to…to come to grips with who I am…"*

Oh, this is going deep, I thought. Much deeper than anything I've been privy to, that's for sure.

*"…and the responsibility I must now face."*

And the responsibility *I* must face come Monday morning, I thought, with a shiver.

*"Give me strength as I prepare for my…for my ordeal, and help me through the many difficult weeks ahead…"*

Okay, she's going someplace, I thought, someplace bad. Then it hit me. Oh, for Christ's sake, she's going to jail. She's going to *jail.* She's done another stupid thing, ripped off a 7-Eleven for beer or hit someone in a DUI, and this time she's going to…

*"…that I will spend in rehab."*

Rehab? Again? I lifted my head slightly and peered at Aimee. Her head was reverently bowed, her eyes closed. How come she never told me? I wanted to ask her right here, straight away. I remembered my mother's look, the one that reminded me to not make a scene. I looked over at my mother, her head also bowed, eyes shut. Okay, no scene, Aims but we're going to have a little talk on the drive home.

*"Make me a stronger person, someone that my family, even little Sean and Carlene, can once again look up to…"*

Once again?

*"…and someone to be proud of when I return. We now ask for forgiveness for our sins and transgressions in our great Savior's name, Jesus Christ. In the name of the Father, Son and Holy Ghost, amen."*

All right, now there're four years of Catholic school talking, I thought. I watched as Amber, Aimee, Dez, my mother, even Klara, gave the sign of the cross reflexively like a group of cloistered nuns, or perhaps by some pre-spoken agreement. Sean looked at me after their religious gesticulation unsure of its meaning or if we should follow suit. He giggled nervously so I reached across the table and high-fived him, appeasing his need for a brief ritual of his own.

The dinner itself proceeded peacefully considering the 800-pound gorilla Amber had let loose during grace. We made idle chitchat about the weather, the changes in the neighborhood, who'd moved, who'd died. My mother, always to be counted on to toss a grenade into the conversation was conspicuously hushed as we ate our turkey, sweet potatoes and cranberry dressing. Upon finishing her meal and without announcement she decided it was time to start clearing the table. She picked up her plate and silverware and strode into the kitchen expecting others to follow. "We'll take dessert back here in ten minutes, I just have some things to prepare," she said. Her prim hostess manners were certainly a contrast to prior year's Thanksgivings where we'd sit at the table for hours after finishing our first and second helpings to ponder life, chat, or scream passionately about whatever political topic of conversation my mother deemed worthy or controversial. Tonight, things were clearly amiss. The news that tumbled out during Amber's prayer was something my mother didn't want dissected, putting a lid on all forms of her usually lively confrontational banter. Actually, the change was refreshing but I still found myself curious about the prayer as we stood alone in the kitchen.

"Well, that was some news," I said. "About Amber, I mean. I take it that's why you were, how shall I say, showing some decorum during dinner and acting a bit more reserved than usual?"

"I always show decorum at my dinner table, not just tonight. And don't start with me, Mitch, not now. Show some respect. You have *no* idea what Amber's been through this past last year, what we've all been through," she said, obviously annoyed at my ignorance of Amber's woes yet unwilling to have shared them with me in the first place. I'd been back from deployment from Japan since June and she'd said nothing about a second trip to rehab for Amber.

I wondered about Aimee and what she knew – obviously more than me if she was hugging Amber in sympathy and buying her going away presents. I turned from the kitchen to find her. I wanted to ask why I was always kept in the dark about these significant developments in my sister's plight but always taking the hit for not knowing of them or being appropriately involved. This was a game all women in my life seemed to play lately, reserving the right to not tell me something yet becoming totally exasperated like talking to a three-year-old when I ultimately had to inquire about it. I walked into the family room and spotted Amber and Dez through the sliding glass door, outside on the patio. They were standing on the far side of the swimming pool, under the eaves of the garden shed, smoking their cigarettes. My mother would never let anyone smoke in the house since she quit years ago and would banish anyone to the patio to partake in what she now called, "that disgusting habit". This was not a new development with Amber, smoking, yet it looked foreign and out of place to me, especially when she was cleaned up and dressed nicely, looking the part of wanting to rejoin mainstream society.

Aimee helped my mother bring the coffee and her pumpkin pies to the table. We reassembled in the dining room for the last course of the meal. The evening would thankfully be over soon. Still, I felt shortchanged in getting caught up on all the real news during the conversation dearth at dinner. We hadn't yet discussed Amber's rehab plans or what had prompted her reentry. Nor had we broached the topic of my father or his whereabouts, something I'd counted on my mother bringing up so dutifully at the mere mention of his name. My guess was she hadn't heard from him lately and didn't want to admit being clueless like the rest of us. That's when I opened my mouth, just as she was slicing up the pie for everyone. "So, Mother," I announced, formally, wanting my question to convey a sense of gravity. "What's our father been up to lately? Still up in Mendocino living at the Art Colony?" I'd only seen my father twice since his early retirement from United Airlines in 1977, and not since he pulled up stakes from his San Bruno condominium in 1980, moving north to a remote coastal hippie commune near Ukiah. Art Colony were her words, a euphemism intended to soften the blow that her estranged husband had willfully moved to a decaying art community full of homeless bums, long past its revitalization of the 1950s.

"Oh, no, Mitch, darling," she said, her voice rising in her patented saccharine trill. "You need to stay abreast of your father's life. He left that place long ago." My mother looked pleased with herself, either because he'd finally left *that place* or because she knew something I didn't.

As I was about to reply, Aimee gave me a look of caution, as if to say, please, don't go there.

"Long ago, Mother? You told me he just moved up there. How are we supposed to stay abreast if you don't tell us?"

"Tell him, Amber," she said, smugly.

"He left that place. Long ago," she said, winking at me. "He's living in Coeur d'Alene."

"Coeur d'Alene?" I was stunned. "As in France?"

"It's in Idaho, Mitch," Aimee chimed in rather flatly.

"Idaho. Hmm. Okay, living in Idaho." So even Aimee knows, I thought. Sure, why not?

"With some woman named Ramona," my mother added, in need of ratcheting the tension, seizing even higher ground with her knowledge. Here came all her classic bombshells that were missing at dinner. My mind was now reeling, which, of course, was her sole intention. And, yes, I'd asked for it. But still.

"Ramona, huh?" I looked around the table. "Anything else I might have missed in the last year?" Klara was looking across the table at me as if she too wanted to communicate something, or maybe just offer a little sympathy.

45

It was difficult to tell. "Speak now. Please."

Silence.

We finished our pie without so much as a word between us. Amber finally got up to pour more coffee for everyone and carried the gift bag, the one Aimee had given her, back into the dining room. "So, Aimee, thank you," she said, as she removed the tissue paper and reached inside the bag. "What have we here? Feels like a book."

"Books," Aimee said. "There are two, actually."

I was surprised. Amber was allowing discussion to begin on her upcoming rehab experience while throwing me a lifeline, offering us to pivot from the awkward moment I'd started regarding our father. She unwrapped a hardback book with a blue and gold jacket. I vaguely recognized the female author and the book as one of her latest trashy romance novels she regularly cranked out. "Her newest, right?" Amber said. "You know me, one of my guilty pleasures. Thank you, Aimee."

Aimee offered a crooked, embarrassed smile. "Yeah, sort of a beach book, something you can veg out with. It's really the other book I wanted to get for you."

Amber reached in again and unwrapped a second book – some eloquent title on personal and spiritual growth. "Oh, what's this?" She hesitated, as if recognizing this self-help book, written by a pretentious shrink with an initial for a first name, might contain some dark truth about her.

"Have you heard of it?" Aimee said, hopefully. "It's really a wonderful book. I've known so many people who have read it."

I wanted to ask Aimee if she'd read it. Probably, I wasn't sure. Since Carlene had been born, she'd picked up her reading at a voracious pace, mostly consuming Eastern philosophy and navel-gazing self-improvement stuff with an occasional trashy romance of her own thrown in the mix. To me, this book represented another publisher's venture into preying on weepy, self-loathing chicks searching to blame their problems on either an overbearing mother, a misogynistic father or the entire dysfunctional family.

"No, I haven't read it, but I've heard about it," Amber said. "It's supposed to be really, uh, insightful?"

"Oh, yes, and much more," Aimee said, speaking passionately. "He not only demonstrates a lucid understanding of human behavior but also gives you the practical tools to change your life."

"So, you've read it?" I said.

"Of course, I've read it," Aimee said, passing me a look that said, and so should you. "It came highly recommended at one of our Officer's Wives Club meetings."

Bingo, my suspicion was confirmed. This writer's audience was probably ninety percent white, educated females just dying to toss a lead weight belt to all the drowning loser men that had wronged them along the way.

"Well," Amber ventured, "I recognize I do need a change. To change my life, that is. I'm sure these books will help me endure another rehab." She appeared on the verge of tears, not necessarily from Aimee's kindness but from her fear of confronting a life full of bad choices. I'd seen this performance before when, as a teenager, Amber would get all sorrowful and bawl like a baby after being caught sneaking out the window in one of her many drug-addled escapades.

"So, when do you leave for rehab, Amber?" I said, wanting to derail any potential pity party that was developing.

"Next week, Mitch. Why? You planning on seeing me off?"

"Depends. I don't even know where you're going." In high school, she spent six weeks one summer at an addiction rehabilitation center for teens cleverly disguised as a fashionable resort up in the San Bernardino Mountains on Lake Arrowhead. The program, which kept her off drugs for a year, was paid for courtesy of my father as I was certain this upcoming stay would be.

"I'm going to Colorado. The clinic's in Aspen."

"Aspen? Wow. You planning on bringing your skis?" I knew she didn't ski.

"Gee, I don't know, Mitch," she smirked. "You planning on wearing those gay Murjani jeans when you come for a visit?"

Aimee turned to hide a smile.

"Hey, these are Jordache," I replied, trying to sound offended but suppressing a tiny smile of my own.

"And it's going to be for three long months," Mother said, ignoring the prattle. "She's even going to be gone for Christmas if you can imagine. But I've heard marvelous things about the Columbine Care Center, that in ninety days they can cure anybody, for life."

"I'm sure they'll cure me just fine, Mother," Amber muttered.

"Oh, yes, dear. Maybe you'll even be able to quit smoking," she said, hopefully, like it would be thrown in as a freebie, a side benefit to living a monk's life of abstinence for thirteen weeks.

"Actually, Mrs. Baumann," Dez said, "they let you smoke whenever you want. They practically encourage it, to use, you know, as sort of a crutch."

"Oh. Well. I wasn't aware of that," said my mother, clearly disappointed. "That's a different approach."

Wonderful, I thought. Take away their drugs and alcohol but let them deal with lung cancer and emphysema long after leaving the loving arms of Columbine. I was pondering what a racket these luxury rehab centers were when the front doorbell rang. The deep bass chime halted the conversation, and we turned our heads in the general direction of the foyer. Despite the late hour and dinner's completion, I couldn't help imagining this was some set of indigent stragglers from the homeless shelter that had crossed their wires with my mother's invitation time. "Mitch, daring, will you see who's at our front door, please?" asked my mother.

"You mean you don't know?"

"I most certainly do not," she said, indignantly, sensing what I was thinking, that some invited guests might in fact be showing up to claim their free turkey dinner.

I rose from my chair. "All right," I said, on the way to the door, "Better start throwing some of that stuffing and gravy back in the microwave." I switched on the porch light and opened the front door. The sight that greeted me gave me a start – two grave-faced policemen in uniform. Unless my mother had included the Millbrae Police Department on her guest list, this was not a social call. My first thought was of Amber that as in high school, something had happened to her and the police had arrived as bearers of the bad news. But that was impossible. She was sitting at our dining room table. I'd just seen her. The cop's presence couldn't be attributed to her. Still, my protective instinct caused me to step onto the porch and shut the door behind me before anyone, especially my mother, could detect the cops or the nature of their visit. "Yes, officers? Is something wrong?"

"Good evening, sir. There's been a small accident down the hill involving a blue 1969 Volkswagen and a few of the neighbors believe the car might belong to someone at this address." The officer looked down at his notebook. "An Amber Baumann?"

I was perplexed. "Amber? I don't believe she owns a Volkswagen. A Beetle, you say?"

"I didn't say, but yes, sir."

"Well, if she owns it, I don't see how it could've been involved in an accident. Amber is sitting inside the house and has been for most of the day."

The second officer spoke up. "No, sir. The car was unoccupied. It appears to have rolled down the hill on its own accord, sideswiping a parked vehicle then coming to rest after crashing through the living room window of…" He looked at his notepad. "Of, the residence at 1175 San Lupo Drive. White house, yellow trim." He pointed in the general direction.

"My God. Was anyone hurt?"

"No, but the family on San Lupo was pretty upset, as you can imagine," the first cop said.

"Yes, I can imagine."

"Car came right through the window in the middle of their dinner," said the second cop.

"You don't say." I wanted to act as matter-of-a-fact as the cops but was shaken by their abrupt news and instinctively knew Amber was linked. This would be exactly the type of trouble, the same shit-from-the-sky that had plagued her since turning fourteen. I knew the stricken house they referred to but not the family. Oh, but my mother would know them. This little calamity, assuming the VW was Amber's, was going to embarrass her plenty. She'd be baking them cookies and bringing them food and flowers for the next six months.

"Sir, we need to verify the vehicle belongs to, uh, Ms. Baumann. If she's inside, can you ask her to come down to the accident site? It should only take about thirty minutes to clear up. The tow truck and fire department are on their way now."

"Fire department?"

"Yes. They have to seal up the living room window, cover it with some plywood, maybe add some waterproofing, a tarp, perhaps." The temperature had turned cooler since sunset and the rain was still coming down, light but steadily.

"My God," I uttered a second time. The damage was substantial. I needed to get down the street to the house myself but so did Amber. "Officers, if you will excuse me, I'll go get Ms. Baumann and we'll meet you down at the site. Will that work?"

They said it would and turned to leave. I opened the front door and stepped back inside the cozy house, recapturing the pleasant aroma of turkey and warm apple pie lingering in the air. From the foyer, I drew a deep breath and called out, "*Amber!*"

Officers Warren and Demarco, the names printed on their business cards, were cordial enough, not friendly, not menacing, simply professionals pulling the late shift on a dreary Thanksgiving evening. Amber, Dez, my mother and I set out on foot to meet them at the accident site in the rain, an easy walk past our cul-de-sac and down the hill on San Lupo Drive. The three women huddled under a large umbrella and I walked out front, letting the rain once again soak my hair and run down my face. We spotted the two cops standing between their cruiser and a fire engine that had just pulled up. The engine's red lights were still flashing, and some floodlights had been trained on the house revealing a surreal scene of a Volkswagen Beetle wedged in a shattered picture window, its forward trunk buried inside the house with its ass-end tilted three feet in the air suspended precariously above some juniper bushes. The tow truck arrived ten minutes later, the driver and firemen arguing about how best to extract the derelict vehicle. Amber spoke to the officers and claimed that, yes, she had driven the car and parked it at the corner of Latera and San Lupo earlier in the day but no, she did not own the vehicle. She had borrowed it from her roommate. There were tears, of course, laced with apologies and excuses, explained to the officers in sobs as the one named Demarco took notes. My mother immediately ran to the owners of the stricken home and talked in her animated form hugging them and pointing up towards her house on the cul-de-sac. I kept my distance, observing her gesticulations but not hearing her speak, holding Amber's hand as she talked to the police. When she finished her statement, her sobbing continued. I took her shoulder and pulled her close, consoling her, stroking her hair. "It's all right," I kept repeating. "It'll be okay."

"Oh, Mitch, I don't know what happened. I locked the car. Why'd it have to roll down the hill like that?"

"It'll be okay," I reassured her. "It was an accident."

She seemed puzzled, either from my unexpected comforting or the car's sudden independent streak. "Thank you," she finally said, whispering in my ear and kissing my cheek before slipping from my arms. I'm sure it was a tender scene, Amber and I acting as one huddled close, appearing very supportive of one another in this minor crisis while Mother ran open loop with the neighbors.

I turned to Officer Demarco, "Are we finished here?"

He nodded, shutting his pad.

The entire interview was completed in thirty minutes and Amber, along with Dez and my mother, were soon safely back inside the house. I remained at the site to watch them drag the car from the front window, talk to the neighbors about what they'd witnessed and help tidy up. I walked back to the house and stepped inside the foyer. Aimee had Sean and Carlene bundled up and was ready to leave. The kids were tired. We should've been on the road an hour ago. That exact statement was plainly written on Aimee's face. We hastily said our thank-yous and goodbyes, loaded the kids in the Suburban and were pointed south to base in five minutes.

By remaining at the accident site I learned Amber's errant VW did in fact begin its roll down the hill spontaneously after her parking brake gave way. Either the brake's cable or the friction pad itself failed. They'd decide all that at the wrecker's yard in a post-accident investigation. The tow truck driver, a burly fellow with a Scottish accent, had told me the car was left in neutral. "How could anyone park a stick-shift on a hill and leave it in neutral?" he lamented to me as if I'd done it myself. I wanted to respond, welcome to my sister's life, but didn't. I also learned the name and location of the junkyard where the car would be towed. It was a total loss, no doubt. If the initial crash through the window didn't do the trick, the extraction certainly did. When they hooked up the rear bumper to the winch and pulled, the poor car teetered on the window ledge then fell hard onto the garden below, snapping the trans-axial and causing the small engine to drop from its mounts onto the front lawn. The entire evolution was ugly and I was glad my mother and Amber weren't present to witness it.

The Suburban was quiet as we entered the freeway heading south. I was still grappling with news of my father taking up with some woman named Ramona and moving to the boonies of Idaho. Whatever was going through his head these days, I couldn't imagine. I would likely get to meet this Ramona, assuming one day she could be my stepmother, and ask her some very hard questions. I looked forward to a potential meeting but also dreaded its outcome, fearful of gaining knowledge that my father may no longer be playing with a full deck. She could provide some insightful clues perhaps, becoming the link that could clear up this man-of-mystery persona my father had developed since his retirement from United Airlines. Still, the idea that he had found another woman in his life at sixty-two and formed a deeper than platonic relationship confounded me. And, as far as I knew, he was only legally separated from my mother, not yet divorced.

I glanced over at Aimee in the passenger seat sitting quietly, her head turned away staring out the window. Both the kids were fast asleep. "I've reached a decision," I said, cutting through the silence, "I'm getting out of the Navy at the end of next year." She held her response longer than I'd anticipated. An uneasiness had existed between us since dinner and I wanted to ease the tension, to halt her obvious message of intentional silence.

"So, that's it, huh? No discussion, no what's best for the family? Just what's best for Mitch?"

"C'mon, Aimee. We've covered this a hundred times. We've talked about our options if I resign. Either I extend in the squadron and get out next year or take orders to shore duty somewhere and get out in three years. I've decided I want out sooner rather than later."

"And did that mystery phone call this afternoon bring you to this conclusion?"

I was surprised she brought up the phone call with the skipper. "I don't know, maybe. Do you even know who I was talking to?"

"You never said anything. You told me to just forget it."

"No, you told *me* to forget it," I said. "I told you everything was fine."

Aimee's face grew dark and she turned away, back to her window.

"Okay, I'm sorry. I know what you meant. I wasn't very forthcoming because I didn't want to get into it in front of my mother."

Silence.

"Aimee?"

"What? The frustration was clear in her voice. "What do you want, Mitch? How do you want me to respond?"

"I spoke to the skipper. That's what the call was earlier, before we left home. It was the duty officer telling me I needed to call him, which I finally did, from Mother's house."

"And?"

"And, there was some trouble with our flight last night. I forgot to do some things and he was pissed, needed to yell a little bit. I wasn't too worried though, that's his usual MO, to yell." I took a deep breath. "But—"

"But, what?"

"But he said he wants to see me in his office, first thing Monday morning. He was calm about it like there's more to the problem, which worries me."

"So, you think submitting your resignation letter will be a preemptive strike?"

"Maybe that's what's on my mind. I guess I'll see on Monday." I needed to continue, more for my sake. Aimee had intuited more about the situation than I realized. "I know I've been a bit cynical about Navy life lately and letting it leak out in subtle, and not-so-subtle ways. The reason the skipper was pissed was he found out I didn't wash off the airplane, a small thing, right? Then I decided to skip the debrief to get an earlier start on our weekend. Maybe not so small. So, yeah, he was mad about the whole mess and probably justified. I wouldn't have behaved this way last year or on deployment and, to be honest, I'm not sure what's driving my behavior now. Maybe I'm trying to force a change, to let people help make the change for me. Hell, I don't know. All I do know is I'm sick of the Navy, sick of flying."

"Sick of flying? I thought the whole point of leaving the Navy was to start flying for the airlines." She looked me in the eye. "That's your plan, right?"

"Right. Something like that. God, I don't know. I was even thinking about grad school again this morning, becoming an architect. What do you think about that?"

"*Architect?*"

"Oh, relax. It's just a notion. I need to see what the skipper wants on Monday morning. You know, take it one day at a time."

"Mitch, you know I'm supportive of whatever path you choose – stay in, get out, airlines, no airlines, grad school, anything. Just stop being so passive about it. We're in this together, you know." She gestured toward the backseat at Sean and Carlene.

"Yeah, I know. Probably should just drop it until I get home from the meeting on Monday. Too many unknowns right now."

We resumed our silence, but the atmosphere had improved. We'd talked at the root of the problem, my growing dissatisfaction with the Navy, not solving anything, maybe even widening our options, but reopening a positive line of communication, nonetheless. And my mind was still racing in the wake of our Thanksgiving visit and Amber's accident. "Can we change subjects for a minute?" We'd had very little chance to talk at Mother's.

"Okay."

"What are we going to do about Amber?"

She sighed. "What do you mean, *we?*"

"All right, not we. I get it, she's not your sister. What am *I* going to do?"

"Mitch, I don't think you do get it. Amber's a big girl, she's made her choices. It's her life, her consequences, not yours. You don't need to do a thing other than offer support, maybe some encouragement."

"I do offer encouragement, you know, when I'm around, when I see her."

"Oh, you mean like, hey, Amber, you bringing your skis to rehab? That kind of encouragement?" Aimee smiled to indicate she was going easy on me, knowing I'd truly been helpful in Amber's latest crisis, barely an hour old.

"I know. I just get frustrated with her. I don't get her. I never did. But God knows, I've tried to help her as far back as junior high school. I could see the problems coming like a freight train, way ahead of my parents."

"And you tried to advise her, guide her, perhaps even caution her, right? "Right. So?"

"So, sometimes when you offer advice, even when you honestly believe you're helping, you come off sounding a little judgmental."

"Judgmental?"

"Yeah, judgmental. And that's the quickest way to get someone like Amber to head for the hills. My God, you come off sounding like one of those TV evangelists."

"Oh, so you think I'm actually responsible for her running to drugs, is that it?"

"Of course, not, Mitch. I'm just saying you may not be filling the big-brother mentor role like you think. Amber needs someone she can trust, someone she can identify with and eventually look up to as a role model."

"And that's not me, I'm not a proper role model?"

"No, you're not. You haven't been a junkie, you haven't stolen from people, you haven't run from the law or rolled your roommate's car down a hill into a house. She needs someone that has lived through those experiences and gotten their life together, turned things around for themselves. A role model that has shared her struggles. That's what will turn her around."

"And where do you find someone like that? In the drug booby-hatch, living in the room next door?"

"Maybe. Or a counselor there, perhaps. I'm hoping the book I gave her will help."

"The book? The one you gave her at dinner tonight?"

"Yes."

"You want my opinion on that?"

"I don't know. Do I?"

"That book is totally wrong for her, Aims. First, you're assuming she'll read it, then, that she'll understand it. That thing isn't written for druggies hoping to kick their habit. It's for college-educated women chock-full of insecurities, designed to talk them out of their depression and assuage their guilt because they hate themselves."

Aimee started laughing, "That's what it's about, huh?"

"Yeah. And I'll bet the good doctor summarizes at the end by saying it's okay to hate your family, not yourself. That it's practically your duty to blame your current misery on Mommy and Daddy and all your sibs if you ever expect to crawl out of your pathetic hole."

She was shaking her head. "Mitch, you are so wrong about that book. I'd ask you to read it but you're in no shape to receive the grace it truly offers. It'd be a waste."

"You're right, it would be a waste. I'm not interested in reading it. And I know Amber certainly won't be reading it."

"Stop! You don't know that," she said, clearly hurt.

I'd gone too far.

"You know nothing of that book, and you know even less about your sister. She's been through a life-changing experience, Mitch. She's screaming for help to turn her life around once and for all. She begged your parents for this rehab. She wasn't ordered to go like the last time."

I'd heard this line before. "So, what changed?"

"Amber had a – let's call it an accident – while you were gone on deployment, around April. I promised I wasn't going to tell you but—"

"But, you changed your mind. Now I get to hear another exciting chapter from, *Welcome to My Sister's Life*."

"Okay, forget it."

"C'mon, Aims, I'm kidding. Tell me what happened, please."

"No chance. Just stay on your side of the car and don't talk to me, not for the rest of the evening."

It was after 10 P.M. when we rolled into our covered parking spot at the duplex on base. We worked together in silence unbuckling the kids from the car and carrying them to the house, dodging rainwater spilling from the parking canopy's metal roof. I had Sean over my shoulder while Aimee, carrying Carlene, struggled to get the front door unlocked with her one free hand. Like two parental automatons, we took our charges up the stairs to their respective rooms, laid them in bed, asked if they needed water, Aimee changed Carlene's diaper, we switched on their nightlights and bid them goodnight. All this was performed silently, in unison, no questions or comments necessary from either of us. It wasn't until we were settled in our bedroom, undressing for bed, when I brought up Amber again. "Aimee, I'm sorry," I said. "I'll put the attitude aside. Please tell me what happened to Amber while I was on deployment?"

"I don't know, Mitch, sometimes you're absolutely exhausting. I know your family stresses you out, but I bear the brunt of your sarcasm whenever we go up there, not them."

"I wasn't sarcastic."

"Oh, don't even say that. You were hanging your mother out to dry with that whole homeless shelter, do-gooder crap before we even left the house this morning. Then, when you found out Amber was coming you cut her into little bits in the car out front. And that Dez girl, what'd she ever do to you?

"What do you mean?"

"I mean flipping her shit at dinner over her name? And don't think she didn't pick up on it. You thought you were being cute, but everyone saw through it."

"Did you see how she was dressed?"

"So *what*? Does that give you permission to attack her over her name?"

I certainly didn't expect this stinging recap of our evening. I wanted to hear about Amber, but not at the price of listening to how I'd screwed up. "No, I didn't attack her because of her name. When I'm in a tense situation I tend to bleed stress by using humor. That stuff about Mother? Yeah, I believe she puts on airs and is a bit of a drama queen. I don't like it, it's revolting, so I joke about it. I even made you laugh on the drive up. And Amber? What a complete waste of a life. I can't help it, I know she's not my problem, but I somehow feel responsible. I can't control her so I use humor, or yes, sarcasm, to rid the stress she causes me every time I see her or hear about her antics. She's never going to change, Aims. This second rehab, and the thousands of dollars it's costing – someone – my father, don't hold your breath, she's been in this situation before. She'll screw it up. Her track record precedes her."

"She's going to change this time, Mitch. She already has. And you'd have seen it tonight if you'd opened your eyes."

"My eyes were open, and I didn't see a thing." My words were without conviction, they were a knee-jerk reaction to Aimee's challenge. Amber did look different tonight and I'd noticed. Gone were the ratty clothes, the foul mouth, the defensive posturing. We'd still snipped this evening, but she surprised me with how contrite she was during her prayer, something she'd have never done in the old days. And her words after dinner revealed, perhaps, a dawning of accountability, a sense of *mea culpa*? "Okay, maybe I did notice a change. So, what's different this time?"

Aimee drew a deep breath and exhaled slowly through pursed lips. "Okay," she began, "Amber got arrested in April. She did thirty days in the county jail, adult jail, not juvenile detention like before and—"

"Wait, wait. So you believe – I'm supposed to believe – thirty days in jail changed her? What was the charge?"

"DUI."

"DUI? For God's sake, Aims, this is the same old racket. Amber probably has more DUI arrests than Foster Brooks. A DUI conviction and a short stint in jail isn't going to turn her life around."

"You're right. Please stop interrupting and let me finish." Her tone said this is your last chance, mister, you had better not screw it up.

"I'm sorry. Please go on."

"Okay, so, back in April, Amber is out driving with some guy, maybe her boyfriend at the time, I don't know, but they're out in his car, and Amber is at the wheel. They're both high on coke, that's what the police report said, and he's doing lines in the car so he's letting her drive."

"Was it the guy who looks like Frank Zappa?"

"What? I don't know. Does it matter?" She paused to consider the question. "Okay, no, actually. This guy was relatively clean-cut with the exception of a goatee and some gold chains. Looked like a real shithead."

I smiled. "Okay, I'm listening. Please continue."

"So, they're driving down El Camino doing about fifty and come to this intersection where an old lady in a Cadillac has stopped beyond the crosswalk and the front half of her car is sticking out into traffic. Amber isn't paying attention, or the drugs have skewed her reaction time, and she grazes the left front end of the stationary Cadillac, tearing off the bumper and raking the side of her car from front to back, scraping off paint and gouging the passenger door. All in all, more significant than a fender-bender but not a horrible accident."

"So, no one was hurt?"

"No." Aimee let out a hiss. "Not yet. So, Mr. Shithead jumps out of the passenger seat and runs back to the lady in her Cadillac screaming and yelling, you wrecked my Firebird, you wrecked my car, you stupid bitch, not realizing Amber had caused it. When he sees the lady isn't moving, he demands she get out of her car to face the consequences. The lady remains calm. She sees this madman rushing at her and she locks her doors tight, to wait until the police arrive. Mr. Shithead is having none of this. He runs circles around her car, so hopped up on coke, yelling and ripping at all the door handles. In the meantime, the lady's dog, a yellow toy poodle, is sitting in her lap yapping its head off at the crazed stranger. And then, for whatever reason, the lady makes a mistake. Somehow Mr. Shithead talks her into powering down her window, or maybe she did it voluntarily to tell him to please go away."

"Oh, no."

"Yeah. Either way, he sees he's made progress. He gets right in her face and demands she step from the car to view the damage she's caused and to provide her insurance information. She says no, she's staying put until the police arrive. He says, get out or I'll pull you out. She says no, get away. The little poodle is so frightened it's turning circles in her lap and continuing to bark. He says get out, I'm not asking you again. When the lady refuses for the fourth time, Mr. Shithead reaches into the car, plucks the tiny dog from her lap and flings it into high-speed traffic on El Camino Boulevard. The cars have no time to react and the dog is killed instantly, run over by multiple vehicles before traffic can clear a space around it."

"My God, Aimee." I was nauseated. "Why'd you tell me that?"

"Hang on."

"And where was Amber in all this?"

"I'll get to it, let me finish. Next, our hero, this vile douchebag, realizes he's gone too far, even by his warped standards, and decides to flee on foot before the cops arrive, leaving Amber behind to deal with the dead dog, the car damage, the drugs stashed in their car, everything. But Amber is so devastated after witnessing this heinous act by her boyfriend she disregards her own predicament and runs directly to the grief-stricken woman, now hysterical, kneeling over her mashed dog in on-coming traffic. One of two cops, having just arrived on the scene, stops the cars and escorts Amber and the lady to the curb. Meanwhile, the other cop notices the drugs on the Firebird's front seat and begins a thorough search of their vehicle. Amber is arrested and placed in the back of the squad car. By the time they start their hunt for Mr. Shithead, he's long gone."

I was still reeling from Aimee's graphic image of the tiny dog being hurled into oncoming traffic. I had no idea who this fucker was or why Amber was constantly drawn to these degenerates, but I did know if he was standing in front of me at this moment I'd make him pay for what he did to that innocent little animal. I would torture him first, then kill him, no doubt. "Did they ever find the guy?"

"He got farther than you'd imagine. It took them two days and two hundred miles to track him down in Reno. He had several warrants out for his arrest, the biggest right there in Nevada, so Amber was charged and arraigned alone in San Mateo."

"So, please tell me, Aimee, please tell me this guy is not out walking the streets today, that he's been locked up in San Quentin, serving time as some bad boy's girlfriend."

"Yeah, so, he was a pretty big fish and Amber was able to offer testimony against him in return for a plea bargain of just thirty days in jail. Otherwise, she was facing three to five mandatory, just like him. Since they found ten ounces of cocaine and other drugs in the car they charged him as a dealer, not with just simple possession. Amber was lucky, it could've easily gone the other way had they not found the guy."

"That's quite a story, Aims. I had no idea." Many questions, many emotions were spinning through my head. "I can see how this would change a person, I mean that whole dog thing, that's really what helped turn her around, right?"

"Of course, it was. She'd hit bottom with that accident. It shocked her back to reality, made her realize how badly she'd strayed. I know this sounds awful but having her witness what she did was probably the best thing that could've happened. She's like you, she's got a soft side for animals, especially dogs. That's what I find so endearing about you both. Her system needed that kind of jolt."

I had to agree. While Aimee was telling the story, as soon as she got to the dog part, I knew I would've reacted the same under similar circumstances.

I'd have dropped everything and run directly into traffic to rescue the animal and help the poor woman – exactly as Amber did. The hell with the car damage, the drugs and the police. We were both dog lovers who couldn't resist reaching down to nuzzle someone's dog at the park, to love on any animal straining at its leash begging for a pet. Aimee knew this about Amber, she knew it about me, and she knew the effect her story would have.

I finally eased under the cool covers of our bed and massaged my temples. God, it felt good to finally lie down in a real bed. The nightstand clock registered 11:15, its large LED numerals glowing in my face. Aimee and I kissed goodnight and switched off the light. In the quiet darkness of the room, just before dozing, I mumbled, "How come no one ever told me about this?"

"You were gone, on deployment."

"I mean after, when I got back? This was a huge, Aimee."

"It kept us all pretty busy, that's for sure. But we worked it out."

*We. We* worked it out, as in the ones left behind. There was simply so much that I didn't know, so much that had happened at home behind the scenes with my family while I was overseas for six months. And it was up to them to deal with every contingency, every possible domestic problem in my absence, from routine car maintenance to the extraordinary arrest of my sister, using whatever resources available. I tried to imagine the phone calls, the crying, the counseling, the appointments with lawyers, court appearances, the myriad of decisions needing to be made, all without me. Aimee and my mother must've formed a pretty tight bond as they struggled through the ordeal. And what role did my father play, where might he have fit in all this? There were just too many questions, too many variables. My head hurt, my ears were ringing. I was beyond ordinary exhaustion from the long visit and my all-night flight. We'd both endured a very long day.

"Aimee?" I whispered, mustering the last of my strength.

"Hmm?"

"I love you. Thank you. For everything."

There was no response. Her gentle breathing filled the dimly lit room. She was sound asleep.

# 4

## ON THE CARPET

MONDAY MORNING, 0545, came much too quickly. I lay in bed repeatedly mashing the snooze button on the alarm, then shoving myself in the direction of the shower at the last possible moment. I dressed in a freshly laundered khaki uniform, attached my wings and collar devices, checked my shoeshine, downed a Carnation Instant Breakfast and headed out the door. The weekend had slipped away, wasted by my alternate fretting about the upcoming meeting with the skipper and the righteous indignation I felt at being called on such a trivial matter. I drove my MG from the main side of base around the runway toward the flight line avoiding some flooded areas from the Thanksgiving storm that had thankfully passed. I imagined a pristine blanket of snow covering the Sierras and perfect ski conditions now awaiting those souls lucky enough to have a weekday off. I approached the last stop sign before entering the squadron parking lot, flanked by the two large hangars. The road actually crossed the flight line and I had to wait as a fully loaded P-3 taxied across my path bound for take-off. I was envious of the crew onboard. Despite their having to come in at zero dark thirty this morning for the preflight, they were going somewhere, getting the hell out of Dodge. No one on that plane had a 0700 rendezvous with an irate skipper.

Plenty of parking spaces were available between the towering walls of Hangar 2 and 3 at this early hour. These cavernous structures were built during World War II, initially designed for Navy blimps but now home to seven P-3C squadrons, swallowing up the large planes like children's toys. As I pulled into a random spot, I noted the reserved CO and XO spots were occupied, taken by Yosemite Sam's late-model Audi Quattro and the XO's vintage Corvette. Great, they're both here, already hard at work, I thought, and it's only 0630. I sat in the car and let the radio drone, having no intention of showing my face before the appointed time. Dr. Don Rose, KFRC's morning DJ, was conducting his typically hilarious show, trying his best to make me laugh to no avail. I'd been humorless and pensive the entire weekend. Aimee had tried to distract me on Sunday by offering to take a drive down the coast to Monterey with the kids, maybe dinner and a movie later, even a day hike in the Santa Cruz mountains now that the storm had passed. I appreciated her gestures, but no one could've dragged me off the sofa or pried the TV remote from my hand.

I checked my watch, time to leave the warm protection of the car. I had fifteen minutes to get upstairs to the CO's office. I entered the squadron through the duty office lobby and walked onto the hangar floor, passing two P-3s – one going through a major engine inspection with its cowlings and engine covers spread out all over the floor, the other sitting silently with its electrical umbilical attached, all parts intact, appearing ready for flight. I made my way to the coffee mess, a small space next to Maintenance Control serving as a break area for the maintenance troops and other squadron personnel.

"Good morning, Mr. Baumann," came the chipper greeting from the enlisted gal working behind the counter.

"Ah, Ms. Ansley, how are we this fine Navy morning?" Heather Ansley was an airman, a non-rated E-3, striking for Intelligence Specialist Third Class with a goal of eventually working for the squadron's air intelligence officer. She was chatty and pretty and one of the first five women assigned to a Moffett Field P-3 squadron. Heretofore, women could not serve in a seagoing operational squadron, but patrol aviation was considered soft sea duty since we didn't deploy on aircraft carriers. To date, though, women could not serve as members of the aircrew, they were restricted to support roles in maintenance, personnel or operations, known affectionately, or derogatorily, as ground-pounders.

"Been a long night, sir. Had the mid-watch again." She watched as I fished a quarter from my pocket. "Coffee's over there," she said, pointing to the silver urn.

"It's fresh, right? Not like that sludge sitting up in the wardroom?" I winked at her.

"Yes, sir. I just made it twenty minutes ago, should still be some left."

She knew what I was thinking, that the maintenance chiefs around here drank up coffee like camels at an oasis stop. There were just enough remnants in the big urn to fill my Styrofoam cup. "So, I hear you'll be joining us up in Adak for the detachment come January," I said.

"Yep. I leave with the first two airplanes. I can't wait."

I smiled. "You know we're talking about Adak, Alaska, right? Land of perpetual gray and gloom?" Adak was a naval outpost flung far out in the Aleutian archipelago, basically a tundra-covered rock in the middle of nowhere.

"Sir, I stand the mid-watch in the VP-25 coffee mess. To me, Adak is Shangri-La, and I've never seen the place."

"Exactly. Be careful what you wish for, honey."

Her eyes narrowed. "Okay, I will. *Honey.*"

I chuckled. "Touché, Ms. Ansley." She was quick, indirectly calling me on my unintended harassment breech all the while flashing a flirtatious grin.

And she had a point. You could spend night after night in a damp hangar selling gedunk, the Navy term for candy, to sailors or start your real naval career working in an air-intelligence office 750 miles from the Soviet border on the Kamchatka Peninsula. It was a no-brainer. "When are you scheduled to leave?"

"Forty days and a wake-up. And only twenty more working in this dump. I'll be packed and waiting at the bottom of the aircraft ladder a week before we go."

"I'll bet you will." I moved for the door, absorbing her obvious joy of anticipation.

"Have a nice day, sir."

"You too, Ms. Ansley." I waited until I was outside to whisper, "Just be careful up there," before making my way up the ladder to the second floor. I was happy for her. She was starting a new adventure and was thrilled. Who could blame her for being a little giddy and naïve about the realities of a forward deployment site? And the men up there were going to love her, that was a given. She'd be a big fish in a little pond, with more offers for sex than a hooker in Olongapo. I held that thought, sorry I'd made the comparison. Heather was not a prostitute and I was saddened to already know her fate when she had no idea, at least of the magnitude of what was to come. All she wanted to do was serve, do something exciting, blaze a trail, not have to endure blatant come-ons and lewd innuendo from the sex-starved sailors in the barracks. And yet, I'm sure she sensed the excitement, the social interaction. At times, she might even encourage it, just not at the level it would be returned. I'd seen the problem of inserting females into a traditionally male domain firsthand when women were first admitted to the Naval Academy in July of 1976. I was a first-class midshipman when they were integrated into the Class of 1980 as plebes, breaking the 131-year all-male tradition. The women at the Academy experiment was a disaster slowly righting itself after nearly seven years of missteps characterized by gross harassment and sex scandals, all well-publicized in the *Washington Post* and other newspapers around the country. Part of me wanted to warn her, to protect her, as the Navy continued to place willing, almost gullible women in harm's way, in the name of gender equality.

Patrol Squadron 25's CO and XO offices were part of a suite of rooms connected to the squadron admin department, a row of six worn desks in a cramped space, now unoccupied until the official start of the workday at 0730. Over the desks hung a large banner of a red fox, our squadron's namesake, which was also painted on the tails of our nine aircraft. I stepped quickly past the XO's open door without looking in, not wanting to invite his attention if he was in. I approached the CO's office, his door also open, lights on, and cautiously peered inside. He was sitting behind his desk, red pen in hand, perusing the message boards, a task he performed every morning before any of his department heads could get a chance at them. I glanced at my watch. Exactly 0700. I entered, assumed a loose form of attention and said, "Good morning, Skipper. Lieutenant Baumann reporting as ordered."

He looked up behind a pair of reading glasses I'd never seen, suddenly aging him, making him look almost tame. "Ah, Mitch, sit down. Just another minute here."

I took one of the two imitation leather chairs across from him. He appeared neither pissed nor glad to see me, just distracted, which I took as a good sign. Behind him, covering the entire wall, was an oversized red, white and blue flag of Texas, his beloved Lone Star state, adding even more to the legend of Yosemite Sam, which he happily nurtured. He continued to read and initial message after message, letting the silence build. I understood his intention and had no choice but to let the game play out. Loud, boisterous people, such as Skipper Wilson, would be uncomfortable with dead air and would start to fidget, the effect he was hoping to create in me. I held still, staring straight at the white star of his pretentious flag without a twitch as he pretended to ignore me.

"Mitch." he finally said, making eye contact.

I waited for him to finish the sentence, maybe with an indignant, *What the fuck?* He remained quiet so I followed his cue. "Skipper, ah, good morning, sir."

"Enjoy your nice, long weekend, did you?"

"Yes, sir. It was a welcome break." My reply was sincere and hopeful, overlooking his emphasis on the word *long* like we were exchanging pleasantries over coffee after the Thanksgiving holiday.

"You get a chance to read the Purple from your event?" He was referring to the Navy's color-coded operational message system – in this case, the mission summary from our flight.

How could I have possibly read it? I thought. It's sitting in that stack on your desk. "No, sir, I haven't read it."

"Says here you flew six passes over the TOI and conducted six simulated attacks. That sound right?"

"Yes, sir."

"And how many attacks were graded as valid?"

He knew I couldn't answer since I didn't attend the debrief. He had me, which was the whole point. I felt all the attacks were valid. "Six," I said, with confidence.

"Six, huh?"

"Yes, sir."

"EHEHEHEH!" He made a loud buzzer sound, the kind a game show contestant receives in the face of a bad answer. "Guess again."

"I don't know, Skipper. I'm sure we got at least three good ones," which was the minimum required.

"Nope. I only see two." He looked up from behind his reading glasses again, pointing at a line on the page.

My stomach dropped. "That can't be. There should have been at least three good ones in the mix. Did they do a full mission replay on the computer?"

He glared at me. "Gee, Mitch, I don't know," he said, his voice full of sarcasm. "I wasn't at the debrief. Did *you* ask them to do one?"

Again, he knew the answer. I remained silent.

"Mitch?"

"No, sir. I didn't ask them to do one."

"Oh, that's right. Thank you for refreshing my memory. My mission commander, the one I expect to attend all debriefs with his crew, decided he was too busy that day and couldn't be bothered, that he couldn't spend the extra hour to complete his duty. Well, congratulations, deadbeat, you blew the qual. Your crew is no longer in alpha status and I can't send you to Adak in the normal rotation. You're no good to me, Mitch, you and your entire band of trained idiots, idle and useless." He paused and narrowed his eyes. "You know, you were one of my go-to crews in Westpac this summer. You met my every expectation which makes this gaffe very hard for me to fathom. Very hard, indeed."

He surprised me with the compliment. Up until now, I had no idea where the crew and I stood with him. Commander Wilson was not one to lay on the praise in private. There was an ulterior motive in play. "Skipper, I'm sure if I was to go back and talk to the debriefing officer, he'd—"

"He'd what? Award you the qual four days after the fact? That flight's history, Mitch. It's in the archives. Christ, the Purple's been released, and I just signed the squadron readiness report to the Wing – one less alpha crew, one less available to send to Adak in January."

I couldn't believe he was giving up this easily. "Let me go back to the ASWOC and find the DBO. We can do a reconstruct. They rarely run the replay tapes unless we ask them or there's a protest by the crew." Then it dawned on me. "Do you know if Lieutenant Morgan asked for a replay? Did he try to dispute the DBO's decision not to award the qual?"

The skipper pounded his fist on the desk. "Goddamn it, Baumann, those are questions I ask you, not the other way around." He quickly steadied his coffee mug after sloshing half its contents onto the blotter. "So, here's the deal. There'll be no tracking down the DBO, no appeal, no begging from anyone in this command to get the qualification reinstated after it was denied. You'll either fly another training mission or go into the simulator for a redo. And it won't be until February because I'm told the subs aren't available and WSTs are booked solid for two months."

I let his words fade. "Skipper, may I speak freely?"

63

Despite holding all the cards, he eyed me suspiciously, like he figured I'd have the balls to try to change his mind. "Speak."

"It seems we could save a lot of time and money if you'd let me talk to the DBO. They're all reasonable over there. They were aircrew once too. Wouldn't you and the ops officer rather have Crew 4 back in alpha status, not have to pull us from the planned Adak rotation, not send us back to SoCal for a re-fly, and not burn all those extra flight hours?" I sat up straight in my chair to deliver what I felt would be my final appeal. "You've decided to single me out, make an example of me. Yes, I get that. I screwed up. I should have attended the debrief. We should have gotten the qual. I'm sorry. Still, this seems like a pretty high price to pay, for both my crew and the squadron, just to teach me a lesson."

The skipper pondered my statement, giving it thorough consideration. "Mitch, I hear you're planning to drop your resignation letter soon," he said, abruptly changing tack. "Punch out early and skip orders to shore duty? That true?"

I was stunned. First, how could he have possibly heard this fact? Sure, I'd mentioned it casually to some fellow officers but presumed it'd been in confidence. Second, why was he using this on me now, to what relevance? I'd not seriously discussed resigning with anyone except Aimee and I was certainly not prepared to spar with the CO about my undecided career options, especially in light of my recent foul-up.

He raised both hands. "Don't worry, I don't expect an answer, not now. But I do wonder where you've picked up this petulant, childish attitude since returning from deployment. You were one of my best crews out there, one of a handful I could launch with assurance of getting the job done, from locating a Soviet nuke to those complex coordinated ops exercises we fly with the carrier battle group. Twelve years from now, you're sitting in this chair. It could be you, you know that? Your performance, your leadership, your airmanship, have been that good since joining VP-25, well above average. You made PPC early, you're one of only three junior officer mission commanders in the squadron. I even recommended you for early promotion on your last fitness report. And now what? You come off deployment like you want to break every reg in the book. Your attitude sucks. I can't even count on you to return with a simple qual on a training flight. You haven't lost your skill or your edge, Mitch, you've lost your respect – for the Navy, for this command and for me. Am I right?"

"Skipper, I haven't lost my respect for you or the command. I just skipped—"

"No? What about the birdbath directive? What about going lost com on Thanksgiving when I had the duty office calling you every half-hour? And what about taking that pilot trainer up to Klamath for lunch when I specifically told all my PPCs, no more lunches up in Klamath, period?"

I winced.

"Yeah, I heard about that one. You think that shit stays hidden? I let it slide because your crew was a huge part of our success in Westpac this summer. Thought maybe you had amnesia or missed the last all-officers meeting where I warned everyone."

Klamath Falls was a small airport just over the California border in Oregon. Pilots had the freedom to choose multiple airports up and down the West Coast to practice instrument and visual approach procedures in the landing pattern. Klamath was a popular destination because it was an underutilized airport in a low-density air traffic environment perfect for touch and gos. And it had a greasy spoon café on the ramp where you could taxi up to its door. Lately though, some of the local tree-huggers had taken exception to seeing military aircraft parked on the transient line with the crew inside enjoying a quick lunch on government time. Rather than inform these bozos that the field was designated as joint-use, that it was government subsidized, and that the meal wasn't costing taxpayers a dime, the wing commander at Moffett simply put out a directive to the squadrons - no more lunch stops at Klamath until further notice. I wasn't at the AOM but heard about the new policy later. "I missed the announcement that day, Skipper," I said.

"Yeah, well, no more. Hear this announcement. As punishment for disobeying my directives and your careless conduct following your training flight, I'm restricting you to base starting next Monday extending through the Christmas and New Year holidays. And you will stand permanent SDO watch from December 15 through January 1. Your holiday leave request is denied, and you won't be going to Adak in January on the four-week cycle with Crew 2. Without alpha status, I can't send you even if I wanted to. When you get your qual, you'll be put in the rotation in March for the six-week cycle with Crew 3."

Six weeks instead of four, I thought. Great.

"We'll consider this an unofficial reprimand. Nothing formal, no letters in anyone's jacket. Do your time, your slate's clear. Any questions?"

I started to reply but no words came out.

"Good. Go. You're dismissed."

I don't recall departing the CO's office and descending the steep metal ladder onto the hangar floor. My head was still spinning. I understood the skipper's disappointment, his theatrical ire, even his punishment, but I felt he was being vindictive to intentionally let our qual slide, to punish the crew by taking us out of the Adak rotation. He had an axe to grind, it was personal. But why the crew? I thought. The more I considered our flight and unjust verdict, the more I wanted to fix it, despite the skipper's caution not to. The DBO was either lazy or incompetent and I knew if I could find him and expose him, he would give our mission a second look. I first needed to find Jamie and ask what really happened at the debrief and why the hell he didn't officially protest the decision by not signing the log.

I made my way toward the squadron duty office. Lieutenant Jake Burgess, the on-duty SDO, was at his desk when I walked in. He was the PPC on Crew 2, a year behind me at Annapolis and had played fullback on the football team. Jake was dressed in his service dress blues, the proper uniform for the watch. He looked tired, his double-breasted jacket rumpled, and he needed a shave – Fred Flintstone in a uniform. The harsh glow of the florescent bulbs highlighted his fatigue, but he was happy to see me when I stepped in. His assistant SDO, a young petty officer on his crew, was seated at an adjacent desk. The duty driver, an even younger kid, was parked on a chair in the corner immersed in an issue of *Hot Rod* magazine. The air in the confined space was warm and foul, a pungent mix of body odor, burnt coffee and stale cigarette smoke. "Jake, you look like hell," I said. "Don't tell me you didn't get any sleep in the bunk room last night."

"Are you kidding? We're the host squadron this month, remember? Goddamn Brits arrived unannounced this morning at 0100 in their Nimrod. Needed fuel, a parking spot and rides to the BOQ before their final leg back to Kinloss. Then, just as I'm about to hit the rack, our boys from Crew 5 show up. Wait, let me rephrase that, our helpless idiots from Crew 5 show up at 0330 to preflight their torpedo exercise to Barbers Point. Had to unlock the Comm Office, order box lunches, practically point them to their airplane." He turned to his petty officer assistant, "By the way, did you get an off-time for SE-02?"

"No, sir. Not yet."

"I saw 'em taxi by me on the ramp around 0630," I volunteered. "Probably off by now."

"Huh?" Jake glanced at his watch. "Gee, Mitch, you think? That was like an hour ago."

Again, he turned to his assistant, "Call the tower, get an off-time and remind them it's their job to call us, the lazy pricks."

"I see you're in a fine mood this morning. Must've been a hell of a watch," I said.

"It was. No sleep whatsoever. I've got one more hour, and so help me, if my relief is even a minute late, I'll—" Jake looked down at the clipboard on his desk. "Say, what had you in here at 0630 anyway? I don't see you on the flight schedule."

"Meeting with the skipper."

"The skipper?" He was genuinely curious. "About what?"

I glanced at Jake's enlisted assistant, his ears perked in our direction, then back at Jake. "Not much, other than my crew won't be joining you in Adak in January. We're going in a different slot, probably in March. Not sure yet."

"March? You're giving up a four-week slot for a six? What happened?"

"I don't know," I lied. "Skipper just wants to mix things up a bit, I guess. Look I'll tell you later, when we're alone. It's complicated."

"Sure, Mitch," he said, correctly intuiting something was amiss. "No sweat. I thought the plan was to have the two most senior crews up there in January to ensure the detachment got off on the right foot."

"It was. It is. I don't know." I wanted off the topic. "Hey, speaking of senior, what are you doing pulling the SDO watch at the end of the Thanksgiving weekend? Shouldn't one of the nuggets have it?"

"Oh, yeah. Last-minute change. Seems our Ensign Willkie, who was on the watch bill for Sunday, forgot about his Monday class in San Diego. He didn't forget about the class, mind you, just the day of transit time he'd need to get down there. So, he calls the ops officer on Thanksgiving Thursday, who tells Duncan Kinder, the SDO, to start calling any officer he can find to fill the watch. He said, and I quote, *Grab the first person that picks up the phone.*"

"So, you picked up?" I said, grinning.

"Yep. Broke the biggest unwritten rule in the Navy. Never answer the goddamn telephone on leave, especially at home on a long weekend. Can you believe that shit? What a rookie move."

I thought about my current predicament with the skipper exacerbated by *not* answering the telephone on Thursday. "Sometimes I think you stand to lose either way. It's a Catch-22."

"You're right," he said, not understanding my full meaning. "Pick up the phone, don't pick up the phone, who cares? The big Navy banana will always find you. Sure, it messed up my weekend a little but so what? We've got to help each other out, man. It wasn't like I was headed out of town or had big plans, you know?"

"Yeah, I know." I instantly felt a knife planted in my side. Jake had retained a healthy spirit throughout his young career, not yet crushed under the inevitable strain of regimented Navy life. I'd carried the notion since the Academy that, right or wrong, the Navy was this ancient, monolithic authority that needed testing, not a full-blown palace revolt mind you, just subtle resistance from within to make it stronger. I didn't want to admit this resistance was perhaps counterproductive to the mission, whether saving someone's life in a firefight or simply covering a watch for a buddy when there was a schedule glitch. It was just that sometimes Navy life posed an unwelcome paradox so vast it could drive a Buddhist monk to commit self-immolation.

"Hey, Mitch, you still with us?" It was Jake, bursting through my bubble. "Huh?"

"You sort of drifted off there, Major Tom."

"Yeah, sorry," I said, coming back to reality. "I just remembered why I came in here in the first place. I was looking for my TACCO. Have you seen Jamie around this morning?"

"I saw him go by earlier. He should be at his desk up in Admin. Didn't you notice him when you came out of the skipper's office?"

I did not. The truth was, I was in such a funk after my meeting with the skipper, Farrah Faucet could've been splayed across Jamie's desk in her scant one-piece and I wouldn't have noticed. "I'll go check again," I said. "Thanks."

"Don't mention it. Hey, it's a bummer you won't be going up to Adak with us. I was looking forward to our crews working together. You know, flying, hanging out in the club, backing each other up, all that shit. It's rough country up there."

"Yeah, it is. On both counts." I turned to leave, eager for some fresh air. "Go get some sleep, Jake."

Jamie was at his desk when I walked back into the admin spaces on the second deck of the hangar. He looked fresh in his khaki uniform and was aggressively attacking a pile of paperwork spread out before him. I stood directly in front of his desk and cleared my throat. He made no sign he was aware of my presence. I kicked the metal desk hard, forcing him to steady his coffee cup and look up. He was stunned, the precise effect I was after. "Good morning, shipmate."

"Mitch, man, you scared the piss outta me. What are you kicking my desk for? I saw you standing there."

"I don't think so," I said, smiling.

"Yeah, I did. I saw you come out of the skipper's office earlier too. What's going on?"

"That's what I came to talk about. You have a minute?" I again made note of the huge stack of paperwork on Jamie's desk and the stressed look on his face.

"Well, I'm way behind but—" He waved an arm over his work. "Sure. For you, always."

Jamie was the squadron legal officer, his ground job when we weren't flying, and he hated being bothered when hard at work. Jamie reported to a lieutenant commander department head but on most days worked directly for the skipper preparing charges for CO's Mast, a non-judicial punishment hearing for disposal of small offenses committed by the sailors in the command such as UA or drunk and disorderly. Jamie was not a lawyer and did not belong to the Navy's Judge Advocate General Corps. He was a line officer like the rest of us and was sent to two weeks of legal training, armed with just enough information to be dangerous. The Navy's theory was they'd train line officers to function with low-level authority to handle routine legal matters under the UCMJ and escalate higher-level problems, such as summary and general court-martials, to the JAG office across the field. What it came down to mostly was babysitting all the juvenile misbehavior caused by drunken enlisted kids straight from boot camp and away from home for the first time or dealing with someone who failed their drug urinalysis test. The case would generate layers of paperwork, all prepared by Legal, include a statement and signature from the accused, then go to mast in front of the skipper. He'd dole out some restriction, occasionally take some stripes or pay and be done with it, next case. Typically, there'd be two or three cases a week. It was a never-ending cycle for Jamie and he always claimed to be behind. "What happened at debrief on Thursday?" I asked, wasting no time getting to the point. "You hear we didn't get the qual?"

"I kind of figured it was headed that way." Jamie looked up from his stack. "Man, why didn't you come with us? We could've really used you."

"I know. The skipper helped drive that point home just now. I'm sorry, I truly am. I should have never left you hanging like that. Still. What went wrong? What happened at the debrief?"

"Nothing really happened. The DBO looked at Al's navigation log printout, compared the aircraft headings to the sub's course and only counted two of our six attacks as valid. The rest were outside attack criteria."

"How far outside? Did he say? I'm guessing less than five degrees."

"Yeah, something like that," Jamie admitted, sorrowfully.

"I knew it. Five measly degrees! That's borderline tolerance of our acoustic tracking gear, Jamie. You've told me that a hundred times. Why didn't you challenge the DBO's decision? Whatever possessed you to sign the log?" I couldn't believe he'd caved so easily.

"Well, the guy that normally signs for our crew didn't show up that day," Jamie said, directly confronting me for the first time. "The DBO kept asking, 'Where's your mission commander, why isn't he here?' He probably took it as a sign of disrespect and intentionally hammered us on the five-degree technicality."

"Of course, he did. What an asshole."

"Well, you should've been there," Jamie said, standing firm.

"Well, you should've challenged the decision."

Jamie didn't respond. He was upset and felt betrayed.

Our longstanding friendship was in the balance. It dawned on me that all three of them, the skipper, the DBO, Jamie himself, were aligned against me in their opinion. "You're right," I said, calmly, after the moment of silence. "I should have been there." I went on to describe my earlier meeting with the skipper, the yelling, the disappointment, the restriction, and the fact our crew would not be going to Adak in January on the shorter rotation cycle. I watched as Jamie absorbed the news without a trace of emotion, even when he discovered he was stuck going to Adak for six weeks instead of four. I apologized a second time then asked in an official capacity, "Can the skipper really restrict me like that? Is it even legal, I mean, without a proper CO's

Mast?"

"Mitch, believe me, you don't want this to go to mast. He'd win. There'd be documentation, he'd be forced to enter it into your service record. It would follow you for your career. You say he told you, 'Serve your time and your slate's clear,' right?"

"Something like that."

"Then consider it a gift, an unofficial reprimand. You're in hack, Mitch. That's the old Navy term for it. It shouldn't even affect your fitrep."

"Still, restriction at Christmas?"

"Yeah, I know. That does suck."

We sat in silence as the admin office came to life with the morning arrival of the yeomen. I thought about my mother and the excuses I'd have to make about missing Christmas at the homestead. She'd already started planning the whole affair with Aimee over the telephone two days after Thanksgiving. There'd be her usual outcry and hurt feelings. After our little Thanksgiving together, I imagined restriction to base not being such a bad thing when Jamie interrupted, changing the subject. "So, you hear Stevie Nicks is getting married?"

"Huh?"

"Yeah, I know you're crushed. Everyone knows you have a thing for her." Jamie was now grinning ear to ear, eager to spring the news.

"What are you talking about, a thing for her?"

"Oh, don't even try to pretend you don't. I heard it on the radio this morning driving in, she's getting married in January."

"To who? Lindsey, I suppose?"

"No. Some dude that was married to her best friend, apparently a widower now. Come on, admit it, you're bummed. We all know about the poster and the letters."

I laughed. "Yeah, we all got a little crazy on deployment." Jamie's accusation was true. About halfway into our six-month Westpac tour, I became obsessed with all things Stevie Nicks. I listened to nothing but her solo album, *Bella Donna*, over and over on my Walkman and anything that featured her sultry voice by Fleetwood Mac. I sent away for her renowned "gypsy" poster, the adorable candid shot taken backstage during their *Rumors* tour capturing the glimmer of innocence in those soulful brown eyes. I hung it at the foot of the bed in my BOQ room while writing ridiculous amounts of letters to her fan club, fantasizing she'd send a personal reply. All this came out when I drunkenly confessed it one night to Colby and Jamie at the O-club in Kadena. They never let me live it down.

"As a concerned friend, I just thought you'd want to know."

"Certainly. And, as a concerned friend, just let me say I haven't forgotten about Colby's obsession with Cheryl Ladd and his surfing the AFRTS channels endlessly at night in his Q-room for reruns of Charlie's Angels when he should've been crew resting. And then your obsession with trying to build a Star Trek transporter beam that was actually going to move water through the ether from one end of the hangar to the other."

"Hey, don't mock me," Jamie said, trying to keep from laughing. "Gene Roddenberry got it right. The hardware just doesn't exist in the twentieth century."

"Oh, and that Isaac Asimov thing, what was it called, a Disinto? You were going to design and build one of those. To prove what?"

"Again, another sad limitation of twentieth-century technology. That's what I proved."

"You're such a nerd, Jamie."

"And proud of it."

The stress and separation caused by months of deployment intensified odd quirks in both the officers and enlisted men and it arrived with remarkable precision at the three-month period. My obsession with Stevie Nicks had been real but we all knew that hanging posters, listening only to her music, writing endless letters, and expecting a personal reply, was a manifestation of the acute stress mostly confined to overseas duty. Colby never made mention of Cheryl Ladd or watched another Charlie's Angels episode once we returned to the States. And Jamie secretly burned all his transporter and Disinto blueprints.

"You guys got a lot of mileage out of my Stevie thing," I said.

"Yeah, everyone got a little wacky out there, not just you. Kept us all sane in the long run, gave us something to laugh about later."

"I guess."

"So, what's going on, Mitch?" Jamie said, turning serious. "You were a blast on deployment. What's gotten into you now that we're back?"

"I don't know." It seemed pointless to deny what everyone now perceived as a problem. "I guess I'm having trouble with all the bullshit."

"But you used to let the bullshit roll off your back. Why the change?"

"No clue, Jame. I'm just not dealing well with authority right now. Don't you ever feel that way about the Navy sometimes?"

"Yeah, but I don't disobey the CO or his directives to satisfy my urge. Do you know how self-destructive that is? You should let that stuff go before you act. Count to ten or something."

"Count to ten, huh?" I smiled at his feeble attempt at anger management instruction. "Look, I know you mean well. And I know you're concerned you have to fly with me. You're probably asking, 'Is this guy even safe?'"

"Mitch, I wasn't—"

"Of course, I'm safe. You have nothing to worry about. We'll get the qual we missed on Thursday. We'll go to Adak in the new rotation, and we'll perform heroically. You can count on it."

"Mitch—"

"No, please. You should get back to your paperwork. Get all those sailors who failed their whiz-quiz to mast on time." Suddenly, I had to get out of the office, away from Jamie, the CO, the squadron, the hangar, the entire base. I ran down the stairs to the parking lot, jumped in my MG and sped for the back gate.

# 5

## RESTRICTION

I JUST DROVE. I headed up the busy 101 freeway to Woodside Road, then west, into the small town of Woodside itself. There was something that drew me to this unique part of the Peninsula. I loved the quaint village aura, the vast equestrian estates and streets with names like Whiskey Hill Road and Turkey Farm Lane. I continued west, motoring through the township toward the steep forested climb to Skyline Boulevard. This is where my little sports car shinned, up the narrow switchbacks, taking hairpin turns at 40-miles-per-hour, shifting alternately between second and third. I was free, if only briefly, from Navy life and the dense crush of humanity – it was all in my rearview mirror. The road was empty as I made my way up the mountain. I pulled into a small dirt parking lot at the summit with a magnificent view of the Pacific Ocean and killed the ignition, rejoicing in the sudden silence around me, spoiled only by random cooling ticks from the engine. Despite being pleased with my decision to escape the hangar, I knew there might be consequences for cutting out so early on a workday. I closed my eyes, bleeding all Navy stress from memory. Still dogging me, however, was the bomb my mother had intentionally dropped during Thanksgiving about my father disappearing to Coeur d'Alene with this Ramona woman. She was forcing me to relive bits of our family history, effortlessly, playing us all like a master puppeteer.

I felt the need to assess the situation, to assure myself of the facts, to admit this much I know was true: John Baumann, my father, separated from my mother, Cynthia, in November 1976, after 32 years of marriage during my senior year at the Academy. In early 1977, he retired suddenly from United Airlines, three years before his sixtieth birthday, the normal retirement age for commercial pilots. He moved into a small condominium in San Bruno during the same period. His new residence was less than six miles from home, but it may well have been the moon given the limited number of times I saw him before moving north to Mendocino in 1980. Mendocino was a shock to us all, a wake-up call informing us that Dad may not be the stable, predictable machine he'd been for years. My initial conclusion, and hope, regarding his radical move was to label it a stunt, a calculated plan to divert our attention, mainly at my mother for her years of excessive family theatrics. But when he failed to establish any type of reasonable contact with Amber or me, and only ended up sending my mother her monthly support checks, all hope evaporated. He was seemingly lost, adrift, searching for something, God knows what, in an isolated art colony west of Ukiah. And just as I come to terms with having a father living a hippie lifestyle in Mendocino, my mother announces he's moved to Idaho and is shacked up with some gal named Ramona. Come on. Ramona? Coeur d'Alene? We had no family or geographic connection to that part of the country. It was just too bizarre.

I didn't feel like driving home, not yet. I started the car and continued down the mountain toward La Honda, a small, eclectic community wedged deep in the Santa Cruz Mountains. I pulled up to the parking lot at La Honda Center, a rustic inn and grocery well past its prime. An aged gentleman, looking much like the town drunk, trudged up the steps into the store. La Honda was much like I imagined Mendocino – a dope-driven haven of loose, arty drifters. My father might've been well-served coming here instead, La Honda being much closer and sporting its own checkered history in the 1960's hippie movement, hosting the unsavory likes of the Merry Pranksters and the Hells Angels.

The MG's small interior suddenly felt too small for my cramped body. I needed to stretch and find a restroom inside the bodega. I also needed to grab a soft drink for the road. I followed the path of the wino up the stairs and entered the store, desperate to find a can of anything cold behind the refrigerator's glass door. The fluorescent lights of the store hummed. The air reeked of a dampness of the past, a sweet rotting perfume of mildew and stale tobacco. As I inspected the meager soft drink selection, a weak voice called from an aisle over. I caught only part of it, "…goin' my way?"

I turned to face this disheveled, wild-eyed old man – the wino up close.

"Excuse me?" I responded in a tone to discourage any potential panhandling.

"…you're goin' my way," he said, this time phrasing it more as a statement than a question.

"No, I don't believe so," I replied.

He stood motionless, staring at me. Beyond the weary expression, there was a twinkle of intelligence, almost a clairvoyance about him, not the wild man I'd initially perceived. It occurred to me I was wearing my Navy khaki uniform and flight jacket, apparel they don't typically see in these parts. "Do you need a lift somewhere, sir?"

"Nah. What I need is two dollars. You got two bucks on you, Skippy?"

Money would certainly be easier than a ride, I thought. I opened my wallet, figuring I was getting off cheap. "Here you go," I said, thrusting two ones at him.

He held off taking them. "I know where you're headed, young fella," he said. "And I appreciate the offer to ride along but I been down that road once or twice already."

"I'm only going back over the mountain."

"Sure you are," he said, snatching the bills from my hand. "Much obliged." He departed the store's entrance, carefully negotiating the rickety wooden steps, pausing at the bottom before turning around to gather himself one final time. "Lose that anger, son." The old man's clear brown eyes pierced my soul like a laser. "Life's short and we're here but for a flicker." He kept his lock on me. "You drive safe now."

I remained frozen, struck by the fact he didn't buy anything with his newfound cash, no booze, nothing. He pocketed the money and left. I had a fleeting desire to chase after him, to question his odd behavior and unclear message. Was it a test, a riddle? I mean, two dollars worth of advice saying life is short and then you die? Instead, I paid for my Coke and watched from the cash register as he labored down the road, a stooped, frail image fading to black under a canopy of cypress trees.

*Lose that anger, son.* It came as a whisper in my head, but it wasn't the old man's. *Dad?* Suddenly I was gripped by a wave of nausea and tunnel vision forcing me to brace against the counter to steady my wobbly knees. In the distance, a different voice broke through the haze. *...hey, you okay...you all right?* It took several minutes to regain my senses as the storekeeper behind the counter, obviously relieved I wasn't going to take a dive, fed me ice cubes to munch on. Standing there in the old man's wake, dabbing ice across my forehead, an idea crystallized, a vision of why I'd come here in the first place. I would pay a visit on my father and ask him the hard questions. I would drive solo if necessary, all the way to Idaho, after returning from Adak in the spring. Nothing seemed clearer or more settling.

I arrived on base, remembering little of the drive back from La Honda, my MG parked neatly under the awning in front of our duplex as if by magic. I'd been in a deep trance, still rattled from my encounter with the old man, my eureka moment to visit my father eclipsed by a recurring truth pounding in my head. Who was I kidding? A visit wasn't going to erase family history. Despite our differences, my over-achievement and Amber's drug use, we'd both strived for the same result growing up – attention from inattentive parents as their marriage slowly dissolved around us. My wristwatch said 1 o'clock. I wasn't going back to work at the hangar across the field. I had nothing pressing today with my ground job as pilot training officer and my direct boss, the squadron training officer and department head, Lieutenant Commander Bill Van Arkel, was on the crew that launched to Hawaii at 0630 this morning. Essentially, I was free to play hooky. I made a note to check in with the duty office later as I walked from my car into a quiet house. Aimee was sitting at the kitchen table sipping coffee and scanning the newspaper. "Mitch," she said, clearly surprised to see me. "You didn't tell me you'd be home for lunch."

"This isn't lunch. I'm home for the day." I leaned down and kissed her, a quick brush on the lips.

"Flying tonight?"

"No. I probably won't be flying until after the New Year," I said. "Where is everyone?"

"I just put Carlene down for her nap. Sean's still in school. You caught me enjoying a little me-time." Aimee stood and put her arms around me, gently kissing my neck, nipping my ear lobe with her teeth. She met my eyes in an alluring fashion. "You come home for a little action, sailor boy?"

Two minutes ago, I was probably the farthest thing from her mind and now here she was, suggesting sex. I loved that about her but after my morning meeting with the skipper and indelible imprint left from my drive, I doubted I'd be much good in the bedroom. "Say, Aimee," I said, delicately changing the subject. "What if we skipped Mother's for Christmas this year?"

She pushed away to better assimilate what I'd just said. She looked confused, perhaps hurt. "Sure, let's skip," she said. "You have a better plan. Maybe take us to Hawaii?" Her eyes still conveyed hope of a liaison upstairs or the trip to Hawaii. It was hard to tell.

"No, sorry. No Hawaii. I just thought we could spend Christmas here, show Carlene Santa visited our house rather than carting everything up to Mother's."

"Mitch, it'll break her heart, not having us there at Christmas, especially with Amber gone."

"I know, I know. And we'll get her usual, poor-dear-me, pity party. Leave me stranded on the biggest holiday of the year crap."

"Stop it, now. You told her yourself we'd be up for Christmas. She's been calling every day and planning it all. She's invited other guests. What's changed?"

"What's changed with you?" Her defense of my mother surprised me.

"C'mon, Mitch, we've been driving up to your mother's every Christmas and Thanksgiving since we've been stationed here and I've done every one of them – cheerfully, I might add."

I turned to the sink for a glass of water.

Aimee's eyes narrowed on me. New thoughts were forming. "So, how'd your meeting with the skipper go?"

Her abruptness caught me off balance. "That's why I'm home talking about Christmas."

"I guess it didn't go so well, huh?"

"How'd you manage that conclusion?"

"It was all over your face when you walked in," she said. "You come home four hours early and look like you've been to a funeral."

I remained silent.

"Well, have you?"

"A funeral? Of course, not. I was driving around. My meeting was at seven. When it was over, I just went out, out for a drive off base, that's all."

"A drive?" she said, skeptically. "Like, where?"

"Like, does it matter? Just out."

Again, she studied me for deeper clues, a detective hunting for a confession.

"All right, I drove over the hill to La Honda, okay? I needed to get away for a few hours. I think I'm supposed to drive up to Idaho to see my father." I had no intention of letting this half-baked notion spill out, at least not initially, but I wasn't ready to go into the details of my morning meeting and restriction over the holidays.

"Oh? And when might this be?"

"I don't know yet."

"Well, as long as you've thought it through."

"I haven't. Obviously."

"Are you going to give him a heads-up or just show up out of the blue?"

"Geez, Aims, I don't know, probably just show up. The idea just occurred to me this morning."

"Don't get me wrong, Mitch. I think it's an important step to take, seeing your father, given all you've told me about your relationship with him, or lack thereof. I think it's a wonderful idea. You need to start communicating with him again. But I don't think driving up there and surprising him will work."

"You don't, huh?"

"No. You'd be getting in his face just to challenge him. Like saying, 'Explain your behavior for the past five years.' And you don't want that. You want to show him you're there out of love and concern."

"No, I want him to explain his behavior for the past five years. And for a hell of a lot more than that. I have no idea who the man is, Aimee. I mean, I thought I did, at one time. I was going to be like him. You know, follow in his footsteps."

"Talk it out with him then. Just don't go up there angry, with that chip on your shoulder."

"But I am angry."

"Boy, don't I know it," she said, mainly to herself.

"What's that supposed to mean?"

"Mitch, this shouldn't come as news to you. You've been carrying that anger, that poison, around since you got back from deployment, probably longer."

"I have not," I replied but the denial didn't ring true.

"And I suspect someone's finally called you on it. So, I'll ask again, how'd your meeting with the skipper go?"

"Not so great." She wasn't going to let me off the hook.

77

"Then talk to me. Tell me about it. Tell me again about the plan to see your father. I think you're on the right track there."

"I don't know. I told you, the idea to drive up there just popped into my head this morning. That's it, that's the plan, the whole thing. There are some questions I'd like to ask him, that's all. But it'll have to wait until I get back from Adak." I watched her face as I talked. There was something different in her eyes, a more attentive, compassionate expression genuinely interested in listening. Normally she'd retreat when she observed a mood swing and we'd stew in silences, sometimes lasting days. But this time I let it all spill out, telling Aimee everything, my intentional disobedience of the skipper's directives, blowing off the debrief after our training mission, letting the crew down, not getting the qualification and getting stuck with a less preferable rotation to Adak. And I saved my punishment, my restriction to base over the holidays, for last. I studied her expression as I concluded, wary of any disappointment. I felt better though, at peace, recounting my deeds aloud, complete with cause and effect. Confession doth the soul good, I thought.

"My, that's quite a story, Mitch. Quite an admission. But what caused it, what on earth would've set you off to do all those things?"

"I don't know. I think it stemmed from getting stuck flying on Thanksgiving. When we landed, I just wanted off the airplane, away from base. I wanted to start the weekend. We had plans, right?"

"Oh, yeah. And I know you were just dying to get up to your mother's." She smiled.

"I know." I grinned back. "It makes no sense, does it?" I started laughing, a little at first, then, almost uncontrollably. We both stood. I drew her close and we hugged, kissing each other with purpose, with passion like we hadn't in weeks. She took my hand and led me upstairs.

It was almost 3 o'clock when Sean came through the front door from school, right on time, according to Aimee, lying next to me in bed. We'd enjoyed a welcome respite in the middle of the day, a little afternoon delight, providing a chance to rekindle the intimacy in our relationship that had disappeared since my getting back from Westpac in June. Aimee was great, our afternoon lovemaking a wonderful diversion from the stress that had encircled us in the wake of the Thanksgiving weekend. Aimee lay next to me, a single sheet pulled over her bare chest, breathing in a soft rhythm. We both wanted to linger in bed, to keep the mood alive, but Aimee sighed and dutifully arose. She pulled her mussed hair back into a ponytail, slipped into her silk robe and headed downstairs to meet Sean in the kitchen. I remained in bed admiring a portrait of us on the dresser, a magnificent picture of Aimee pinning my wings on my summer white uniform after graduation from flight school in Corpus Christi, Texas. We were tanned, newly married and happy to be done with flight school, brimming with optimism about our upcoming navy life in California. The low autumn sun, approaching its solstice, streamed through the window warming the room and casting long shadows across the floor. I suddenly felt very sluggish, as if I couldn't rise from the bed if I had to. I closed my eyes for just a few minutes, to rest, maybe take a quick nap before dinner. When I awoke, the room was dark, Aimee was back beside me, softly snoring, sound asleep. The digital alarm clock at bedside read 5:00 A.M. I had blacked out for more than thirteen hours.

My first day of restriction to base, and punitive SDO watch, fell on a Wednesday. It was December 15th and I was surprised by the level of activity around the hangar despite a very light flight schedule leading into the holidays. By order of the skipper, I was to stand fifteen 24-hour watches consecutively. I was allowed to sleep in the bunk room adjacent to the duty office at night or, when there were no scheduled flights, I could go home to sleep but had to carry a beeper and return within ten minutes of my Assistant SDO's page. The ASDO was a twelve-hour watch and typically rotated with enlisted members of my crew. I felt bad because, without me, my crew was being temporarily ripped apart to fill holes in the flight schedule with other crews or to stand watch with me leading into the holiday season. In a sense, they were being punished too, which I'm sure was part of the skipper's plan, to spread the pain and allow me to feel the guilt. When I'd held a short, impromptu meeting to inform the crew about the changes, they'd been more shocked about our new Adak rotation dates than the fact they'd have to divide up some extra watches over the holiday leave period.

Nearing the end of the workday, my 2P, Colby Reed, strolled into the duty office. I hadn't eaten since coming on watch at 0800 and he must've known it. "Hey, let's go grab some chow at the Prop Stop," he said. "I'm buying."

"The Prop Stop? Are you kidding?" The Prop Stop was a greasy spoon café located in the hangar next to the engine overhaul shop and run by a retired Filipino petty officer and his family. The food was marginal, the aroma a blend of fried Lumpia and jet engine solvents. "Besides, why're you hanging around here this late? Don't you need to go Christmas shopping or something?"

"Nah. Just thought we could talk, that you could use some company."

"Well, that's mighty decent of you, Colbs. Now don't go feeling sorry for me," I reminded him. "I'm eating this shit for breakfast."

"And that's why you're dying for one of Chief Santos's monkey burgers. C'mon."

We walked across the hangar floor and sat down in the dimly lit dining area of Le Prop Stop. Not surprisingly, we had the place to ourselves. I sensed Colby had an agenda and felt obligated to lead me away from the duty office to discuss it. He wasted no time. "So, Larsen wants to pull me off the crew permanently, send me to Adak in January with Crew 5."

"What?" I was taken aback. "When did he tell you this?" Lieutenant

Commander Bob Larsen was the squadron operations officer, a decent guy, who oversaw the flight schedule and aircrew readiness. I knew if he was making a change it had to have come from the CO or XO. He'd never just randomly shift crews around this close to our Adak detachment.

"He didn't tell me. He asked if I wanted it, asked me to consider it."

"Consider it? Why on earth would you do that? I'm leaving in less than a year, you'll get my slot and stay with Crew 4. Why would you jump now?"

Colby stared down at his coffee cup. "I don't know. I think they want me ready to take over Crew 5 in June."

"Did Larsen promise you that? Is that what this is all about?" The move didn't make any sense. "Or, are they just trying to get you away from me, like I'm a bad influence or something?"

"Now, Mitch, he didn't say that. I'm going to be ready for my PPC board in a few months and Crew 5 will have an opening in June. I think that's where he's going."

"What about Abbott? He's the 2P on Crew 5. What happens to him?" The answer was already forming. I was the pilot training officer and knew him well. Jim Abbott was an underachiever and weak stick. He was neither on track to have his PPC board by June nor likely to ever be trusted by the skipper. I could see the writing on the wall – take a hot, up-and-coming pilot like Colby away from a conduct case like me, reward him with his own crew and saddle me with a dullard like Abbott. This was payback. This was the skipper.

"Look, Mitch. They aren't forcing this. I can tell them I'd rather stay with you and eventually take over Crew 4. In fact, that's what I want to do. We kicked ass on deployment. I've never been with a crew as tight as you made us, both flying and on the beach. I want to carry on the tradition but—"

"But?" I picked up on Colby's hesitation. "Come on, finish. But—"

"Yeah," he continued. "But things changed after deployment."

I sighed. "Okay, here we go again. I'm no fun, I'm self-destructive, I'm angry, I'm not safe to fly with. Pick one, or all of the above. Right?"

"No. Well, yes. I mean to say, well, something's changed. We've always been a bit of a renegade crew, all junior officers, a little cocky, playing outside the lines but always delivering. I think the skipper even encourages that behavior – work hard, play hard, cuts us slack where he can, you know. And we reeled in every bit of that slack on deployment. But you're still expecting it now. And when you don't get it, you blame others, you blame the system, and, yeah, you get self-destructive."

I couldn't look at Colby. He was harping on a familiar theme and I had to stop him in his tracks. "Anything else, Doctor?"

"Come on, man. I mean well. I'm your friend. Always will be. I know you've got a lot of shit on your plate, a lot you came home to. Want to punch out early, fly for the airlines, follow your old man. Lost touch with him because he's living off the grid, somewhere up in – Mendocino?"

"Coeur d'Alene."

"Huh?"

"Forget it," I said. "Continue."

"And your sister thing, what a wreck. I don't know, Mitch. Maybe some time off and delaying Adak is what you need, to take a break, refocus."

"Is that what I need? In your professional opinion?"

Colby grunted, his eyes darting back to his coffee.

I was surprised by his accurate recounting of my personal life. I remember on deployment, a rant in the O-Club after a lot of Japanese sake. I'd told him some stories, mainly complaining about my wayward sister, but the memory was hazy. I never intended to spill my guts about the machinations inside the House of Baumann. "Look," I said. "I'm sorry. I'm your friend too. I'll get through this punishment. Let's get together after the holidays – you, Linda, Aimee and me."

"Sure, Mitch, that'd be great. We'd like that." Colby stood to leave. "Just the same though, I think I'm going to tell Larsen I'm taking the move to Crew 5."

I grunted back. This was his intention from the start. Still, the words stung. He'd make the move, of course he would. It was the smart play for Colby and his career. But I felt betrayed, as if he were carelessly tossing aside years of friendship and mentoring I'd provided him as 2P on our crew.

When the Friday before Christmas rolled around, things were thankfully quieting down around the squadron spaces and duty office. There would be no more flights until December 27, and those were scheduled as "banker's hours" in the 0900 to 1600 block – a pilot trainer and a post-maintenance check flight, both with minimum crew. I would still have to come in each day but I'd be sleeping in my own bed for the next ten nights. Just after 1600 the final parade of officers and enlisted entered the duty office with leave papers to sign. They'd be scattering far and wide until January 1st. Petty Officer Rod Kennedy, the Sensor 2 operator on my crew, and acting ASDO, signed them all out, wishing them a Merry Christmas and Happy New Year. I tried to do the same but it was tough. I got looks of sympathy from some of the officers from other crews, one even volunteering to come in and substitute for me the day after Christmas. I thanked him but said that wouldn't be allowed, wouldn't even be worth asking the skipper, but thanked him again for the thought.

The stampede finally ended at 1700. It was down to just me, Petty Officer Kennedy and the duty driver, a young airman apprentice from the maintenance department. I figured we were the last three souls in our side of the hangar, which had turned into a ghost town this late Friday afternoon. I jokingly turned to Kennedy and asked what he was fixing us for chow tonight.  Before he could answer, my boss, Lieutenant Commander Bill Van Arkle, the VP-25 Training Officer, popped inside the door, surprising us all. Kennedy wasted no time jumping to his feet to greet him.  "Commander V, good afternoon, sir.  What brings you down here this late in the day?"

Bill Van Arkle was a laidback department head.  He was a Naval Flight Officer and the TACCO on Crew 5.  He'd recently been passed over for full commander, a victim of the Navy's competitive system to screen officers for command of a VP squadron, apparently failing to break out of the pack.  Van Arkle was never in the hunt for command and would be lucky to make commander in the next selection board and retire as an O-5 with his twenty-year pension intact.  I finally stood up too, feeling self-conscious, knowing he didn't expect it.  "Yes, good afternoon, sir.  How was Hawaii?"  He'd been on the crew that went to Barbers Point a few weeks back for the torpedo exercise.

"Gimmie a break, Baumann.  Stay seated, both of you."  He gave me a weary smile.  "Hawaii?  What a Charlie Foxtrot.  I don't know why they say those torp-exes are such a great deal.  Yeah, sure.  Go out there, drop your bombs, spend the rest of the time sitting on the beach sucking down Mai Tai's under the proverbial palm tree in paradise, right?  Bullshit."

"Didn't go well, huh?"

Van Arkle laughed.  "Well, the good news was we got the qual, even after missing our range time by three hours at Barking Sands.  Before and after, though everything went to hell.  They screwed up our reservations at the Q, had us scheduled on the wrong dates.  Everything was full, had to spend the night thirty miles away in the barracks with the jarheads on Kaneohe Bay – only thing available, they said.  Of course, I'm the senior officer, so it all fell on me.  Took three tries to load the torps properly, three hours late for takeoff, had a chips light on landing, went through a full engine change after that.  Yep, I think it's safe to say, things didn't go well.  If I ever see another "good deal" torp-ex to Barbers Point, I think I'll pass.  But, you know me, I can't complain."

We all laughed.  His story was funny and so full of typical Navy fuckups, but that was Van Arkle.  Shit seemed to follow him around, not real bad shit, just the irritating kind, like rain at a picnic or a flat tire on the way to the supermarket.  And when it happened, he just shrugged his shoulders and accepted his ugly fate as it came, as if he had no control.  He was an amiable sad sack that probably was never competitive from the day he entered the Navy.  When the laughter subsided, he turned a serious gaze to me and said, "Mitch, I need a word in private.  Let's take a walk."

This sounded ominous, and strange coming from Van Arkle.  We stepped outside the duty office and walked side by side onto the hangar floor past the row of parked P-3s.

"So, how're you doing with the SDO gig?" he said.  "Tough punishment if you ask me."

My predicament was between the skipper and me and I didn't feel like getting into details. Van Arkle had been on his way to Hawaii that morning and, even though in my chain of command, was never officially involved. Instead, I told him I was fine, I'd survive, and my punishment was considered an "unofficial" reprimand.

"Whew. Unofficial," he said, sounding relieved. "Something like that could really freeze a career in its tracks." He added a resigned chuckle. "Believe me, I know."

I didn't want to ask him how he knew. I really didn't care. "Look, Commander, what'd we step outside for? You wanted to tell me something?"

"Yeah. I guess you know my crew is taking your place in Adak in January, right?"

"Yes, and I'm sorry about that. We really wanted to go. Missed getting the qual, but you heard about all that, I'm sure."

"No, don't apologize. We're thrilled to go, believe me. Four weeks of gray and rain beats the shit out of six weeks any day. That's not what I came to talk about." We stopped walking and faced each other. "Mitch, what's the story with this Jim Abbott fellow? He's on my crew but you're the Pilot Training Officer. Is he on track to finish his PQS for 2P anytime soon? Is he even safe?"

I was reminded of my conversation with Colby about Abbott. "He's behind, and, no, he's not the brightest bulb in the strand. Why do you ask?"

"Not the brightest bulb? Why this idiot almost killed us all when we were departing the range after the exercise in Hawaii. We're in the clag, picking up our clearance back to Barbers and ATC tells him to make a left turn, but he makes it wide and to the right and nearly plants us into the mountainside."

"I hadn't heard," I said, but a picture was forming in my mind. The Barking Sands Missile Range on Kauai sits at the base of some very rugged, mountainous terrain, often shrouded in tropical cumulus rain clouds that form quickly and move across the island. Jim Abbott wouldn't be the first pilot to encounter a near-miss with the lush, green mountains of Kauai but he'd had prior issues. After this incident, I knew he was moving perilously close to a special pilot evaluation board, one that could strip him of his wings.

"It's been kept under wraps since it's not clear yet how close we actually came to impact. Skipper's been dragging his feet releasing the hazard report."

"Uh-huh," I said, filing away the information. The whole Colby-for-Abbott swap was becoming obvious now. The skipper wanted to keep Abbott home until the incident could be resolved, and who better to send in his place than my hot, up-and-coming copilot, Colby Reed. I didn't want to interpret the potential move as more revenge by the skipper, but it certainly seemed he was cherry-picking our crew and saddling me with a group of misfits. I'd been given an odd duck on deployment, Wayne Horseman, our new 3P. Wayne, or "The Horse" as he liked to be called, would become a competent pilot but alienated the crew on his first flight with us, telling us in all seriousness the Navy wasn't his true calling, that he could've become a rock star back in college when he had the chance. We'd hear him sing and play guitar from behind the door in his BOQ room in Kadena after a few beers, blasting away on his tiny Fender amp. He sounded patently awful and was blind to the fact he couldn't carry a tune in a bucket. But his lack of talent wasn't what worried me. It was his misdirected passion and immunity to criticism. He truly thought he was great, absorbing his squadron-mate's laughter as a sign of jealousy. Socially, the guy was off-center and living in a dream world. Many in the squadron had picked up the same vibe. It would be just like the skipper to assign me another eccentric, someone potentially dangerous and oblivious to his shortcomings. "You'll be happy with Colby as your 2P up there, sir," I finally said, trying to sound supportive to Van Arkle but also pissed that Colby had been taken without my consultation or endorsement.

"I'm sure we will," he said, smiling, confirming the switch was a done deal. He turned to leave. I offered a quick salute, almost as an afterthought, which he didn't seem to notice. Van Arkle walked toward the hangar exit, his tiny figure dwarfed by the monstrous hangar doors, now retracted, providing a gaping hole nearly 200 feet across and 150 feet high. He delicately danced over the door's intricate rail system and headed for his parked car in the lot beyond. Van Arkle was unmoored, a man of little worry, projecting this constant state of ignorant bliss. I didn't get him. How could you commit yourself to a twenty-year career in the Navy and then not find the motivation to fuel it, to seek promotion and command?

A damp wind picked up and blew through the hangar giving me a chill. I looked around the empty structure as if it no longer offered protection, as if I were the last man on a sinking ship. What am I doing here? I thought. In trouble, on restriction, struggling in a once-promising career I should end soon before it certainly ends me. My talk with Van Arkle left me feeling despondent. There was a churn in my stomach, a helplessness brought on by the vague notion I was sabotaging my life for some unknown reason and couldn't stop it.

December 24, Christmas Eve Day, 0700. I was late getting up for my watch and sat at the kitchen table alone in my underwear and robe staring at my coffee. Aimee and the kids were still upstairs asleep. I was contemplating blowing off the drive across the field on this rainy holiday to report in. The flight schedule was a blank page. Only those with the duty would be at the hangar today. I could simply call my ASDO, who'd been on since 0600, check in and ask if anything was going on or if he needed me. This would be bending the rules but also very low risk. The skipper was five hundred miles south in San Diego for the holidays, I'd checked his leave papers for his contact information, and all the department heads were similarly scattered. I picked up the phone to make the call. *Don't do it*, a voice said. I dialed and listened to it ring. *Hang up.* Then, on the other end, "Patrol Squadron 25 Duty Office, Petty Officer Dubois, this is a non-secure line, may I help you, sir?" Hearing Dubois' dull, detached monotone, my ASDO for the day, I came to my senses. I slammed down the phone, ran upstairs and quickly changed into my service dress blues. Petty Officer Dubois was not a member of my crew. He was a conduct case that had been ordered on the watch bill today, at Christmas, for some minor infraction at mast, allowing his enlisted brethren, the ones in good standing, to enjoy their time off. It'd be too risky to assume this dimwit would call me the instant something went wrong or cover for me if a VIP turned up looking for the squadron duty officer.

I raced across the field in my MG and breezed into the duty office before 0730, well before anyone could ask where I'd been on this Christmas Eve Day. "Morning, Dubois," I said. "All quiet on the Western Front?"

"Yes, sir, all quiet." He was sitting at his desk reading the sports section of the *San Francisco Chronicle*. He didn't even look up, let alone rise to greet me. "XO's upstairs in his office," he added like it was common knowledge the executive officer would come in the day before Christmas as any other day.

"Say that again?" I was flabbergasted, hoping I'd heard wrong. "And look at me this time! The XO's upstairs?"

"Yes, sir," he said, setting down the newspaper. "Did I do something wrong?"

"Un-fucking-believable." I raced outside to the parking lot and, sure enough, the XO's piece of shit Corvette was sitting in its spot. *Damn, how'd I miss that?* I stuck my head back into the duty office. "Just sit tight," I told Dubois. "I'm going upstairs. And for God's sake, ditch that newspaper. Now."

Scurrying up the ladder to the second deck catwalk I wished I'd had time to shave, to put on a fresh uniform. I was in slovenly form but needed to greet the XO, to show him I was present and ready to offer any assistance for what I regarded as an unusual appearance. I could only guess what he was after. His door was open and the lights on as I approached. I walked purposely forward, directly into his office and up to his desk in my service dress blues. "Good morning, XO. Lieutenant Baumann. May I be of assistance, sir?" I wanted a shock reaction, to appear proactive in the wake of my absence downstairs.

"Ah, Mitch. Merry Christmas," he said, with a false grin, putting his green pen down to meet my eye. "Missed you downstairs. Guess you were out, making the rounds, eh?"

"Merry Christmas, XO. Yes, sir, something like that." We stared at each other, him in his freshly starched khakis and me in my rumpled service dress blues. "Do you require any assistance, sir? May I bring you anything?" I gestured with my arm indicating the bare hangar and lack of regular office support. I was hoping he'd tell me, no thank you, that he'd be departing soon.

"Cut the crap, Mitch. You were miles from here when I walked in. Probably sound asleep at home when Petty Officer *Doofus* downstairs called to alert you. And from the looks of it, you rolled right out of your rack wearing that uniform. Am I right?"

"No, sir. I never spoke to Petty Officer *Dubois* before arriving this morning," I said, correcting his slur. I couldn't believe he was mocking an enlisted man's name. He probably barely knew the guy. "I was in by 0730."

"But not after having a pleasant evening at home and relaxing snooze in your own bed."

"Sir, part of my restriction to base is being allowed to sleep in my quarters at night if there are no scheduled flights or host activities during the period." I was indignant despite his rank and my sloppy appearance.

"Yeah, sure, whatever. Just get your ass over to the communication center and bring me the message boards. That's what I came for in the first place. They should've been here on my desk waiting for me. Comprende?"

"Yes, sir." Our eyes locked. "I comprende just fine." Without waiting to be dismissed, I turned on my heel and walked out.

Commander Richard Fowler arrived at VP-25 in May to assume his duties as executive officer. Per Naval Aviation custom and regulation, he would relieve the commanding officer after one year and become the new commanding officer. Commander Fowler was a sub-par aviator with no inherent leadership skill whatsoever. His flair for administration and intuitive sense for Navy politics had offset other crucial deficiencies the Bureau of Naval Personnel used to screen officers for command. He was living proof the screening process itself was flawed, that someone with strong administrative acumen alone had slipped through the net this late in the process. Since arriving at VP-25, Fowler's style had been bullying and mercurial, lacking any trace of humor. He was addressed by his title, *XO*, by everyone in the squadron. He was known as Dick by his friends and Dickless by the junior officers. Soon after we'd returned from deployment a couple of "anonymous" JOs played a sophomoric prank on him, one well within the boundaries of officer discretion but one that had him so enraged he was threatening a summary court-martial. One morning after he'd arrived at work and parked his coveted Corvette in its spot, three politically charged bumper stickers suddenly appeared on the back of his car, the first: ☮ *No Nukes* ☮. Another: *Greenpeace Now.* And finally: *I Support the ACLU, Shouldn't You?* By nature, naval officers and their families generally ran along politically conservative lines, especially during the Reagan era. We either detested or laughed at the civilian liberals. So, there were many snickers around base when the XO's easily recognized '63 Corvette showed up at the Navy Exchange, the Credit Union and even Wing Headquarters sporting these leftwing slogans. It took more than a week of driving around base and out in town before he discovered them. Even the skipper noticed the stickers and gave a nod to JO initiative and ingenuity, laughing all the way to his office one morning. But when the XO spotted them, he blew a gasket. The pair of peace signs anchored to each end of the *No Nukes* sticker were especially inflammatory. To him, they may as well have been swastikas or a hammer and sickle. He told the skipper and department heads he'd conduct a board of inquiry, he'd interrogate the officers, he'd convene a court-martial, that this was calculated disrespect to a senior officer. Finally, after a particularly long rant on the subject at a department head meeting, the skipper turned on him and said, "For Christ's sake, give it a rest, Commander Queeg." That remark should've been the final word. It wasn't. His war against the JO's had just begun.

I was out on the catwalk heading for the hangar deck when I spotted a female figure near the bottom of the ladder. I recognized her. It was Heather Ansley, the airman from the coffee mess. She was dressed in dungarees, the working uniform for sailors, which, on most women, looked horribly unattractive. But on Heather, it made her look rebellious and stylish like she could appear in a designer jeans ad. Her long blond hair was pinned in a bun and she was wearing a touch of mascara and eyeliner. Upon closer inspection, I could see she'd been crying. I prepared to greet her, but she spoke up. "Oh, Mr. Baumann, sir, they said I needed to find you, that you could help me."

"At your service, ma'am." I leaned in, taking note of her red eyes. "Everything okay?"

"Yes, sir. I have to drive up to Oak Knoll today for an appointment and I need my medical record. They told me over at the clinic my record was here, you know, as part of the batch that needs to go to Adak next week with us."

"You have a medical appointment at Oak Knoll? On Christmas Eve day?" Oak Knoll was the Navy's regional medical center thirty miles away in Oakland.

"Yes, sir. And they told me I had to bring my record. It's up in Personnel, isn't it? Can you unlock the filing cabinet and get it?"

I thought about it for a moment, realizing I was going to disappoint her. "I doubt it. They don't give us the keys to all that stuff." I could see she was on the verge of tears again. "But let's go upstairs and take a look, maybe the cabinets are unlocked."

Heather nodded and we climbed the stairs. She had that deer-in-the-headlights look, completely detached as if operating on autopilot. When we got to the main office space, I gestured for her to sit down before I began yanking on filing cabinet drawers. Nothing opened, everything was locked tight, per regulation. I looked up at her feeling worthless, like if ever there was a time she needed a man's help, and I couldn't deliver. "Sorry, all secure," I said. "Maybe I could call one of the yeomen. She looked up from her chair, detecting the hollowness in my voice. I'd heard it myself, knowing full well Yeoman First Class Vijray and his key ring were 7,000 miles away in the Philippines for two weeks of holiday leave with his extended family.

"It's okay, sir. At least you tried."

I was puzzled by her quick resignation and put on a fatherly expression, the best I could muster. "Heather, what's the matter? Are you sick?" It was just the two of us in the darkened office space. I purposely used her first name, a breach of etiquette between officer and enlisted. But she needed a human connection, not a sterile, professional one.

"I'm pregnant," she blurted out. Her large eyes glared back at me. "I just found out this morning."

"Wow. I, uh—"

Tears started rolling down her cheeks. "You're the first I've told. No one knows but the Navy nurse and that stupid corpsman at Sick Bay."

"And they're not going to let you go to Adak?" I felt awful. Her world was crashing in around her the day before Christmas. And yet, avoiding Adak sounded wonderful to me.

"No. I'm going. I want to go. That's why they're sending me to Oak Knoll. Today. I need to get checked by a doctor and get the okay. The clinic in Adak will monitor my progress, you know, all the prenatal stuff. The corpsman and nurse, they made it all sound routine." She sniffled and managed a weak smile."

This was so goddamn typical. The Navy recruits a willing, innocent girl of nineteen, allows her to break the glass ceiling by joining an operational fleet squadron then throws her in the barracks with a bunch of horny sailors and when she turns up pregnant, they treat it as just part of the routine, like it goes with the territory. Except in nine months, she'll be useless to the squadron, she'll be a single mother and non-deployable, so they'll rotate her back to shore duty, sending some male sailor in her place. The great social experiment I'd witnessed at the Naval Academy was now being played out in the fleet with similar, predictable results. I glanced down at her left hand and saw no ring, of course. "Heather, who did this to you? Can you tell me?" It was a blunt question, well outside my boundaries, but I was pissed. Not pissed at her but at the Navy and all the liberal do-gooders, especially in Congress, that voted their collective conscious for women's rights but never considered the obvious consequences.

"You don't know him, sir," she said, looking down at her shoes. "He's not in our squadron."

"But he's a sailor, right? From here on base?"

She hesitated, still not making eye contact. "Umm, yeah. Look, I don't want to make this your problem. I probably shouldn't have—"

"No, no. It's not your fault." I cut in, halting what must've felt like an interrogation, an officer intruding on an enlisted person's sex life. I sat down across from her to deflect that impression. "Heather, I'm sorry for all the questions. I'm just concerned for your sake, that's all. Don't worry, I'm not going to go find this guy." *Oh, but I'd love to; I'd love to find him and kick his ass.* "That's between you and him." Her eyes finally met mine, showing relief. "What I'd like to do is get the filing cabinet open for you." I gave one final, useless tug.

Heather offered an appreciative smile and started to cry again. "That's okay, sir. I'm not going to the appointment. I don't want them saying, 'Oh, here's another stupid, knocked-up sailor chick. Shows up for her exam. Forgets her record. Claims they lost it,' et cetera, et cetera."

"They won't say that," I said, handing her a tissue.

"Yes, they will. You should've seen that corpsman. I'm reminded every day I don't belong here, that I don't fit. Like the only reason I joined the Navy is for sex, that I couldn't possibly want a job or a career or anything." She paused and took a breath. "Well, I just made it easy for them. I helped prove their point."

She was in a tough spot and needed a friend. I understood her view. It wasn't necessarily true but very easy to draw her conclusion, to grasp her perception built on months of repeated propositions for sex or sneers of you-don't-belong. "Do you have someone that can go to the appointment with you?"

"No. I already told you, I'm not going."

"Yes, you are. Look, you don't need your medical record. Just go and they'll give you a chit to insert later on." I glanced at my watch and stood up. I was late and needed to get over to the communication center to retrieve the XO's precious message boards. Heather stood up with me, realizing our talk was over. I could tell she was alone, not just for Christmas but since she'd arrived at Moffett; her expressions and body language made it abundantly clear. Staring into her trusting eyes, I felt an invitation to reach out and offer comfort, a hug perhaps, some intimate gesture of support. As male and female, we both sensed the moment but as officer and enlisted we couldn't tear deeper into the time-honored etiquette between the ranks. I needed to step back before anyone, mainly the XO in his nearby office, got the wrong impression. "You need to go," I said. "Get up to Oak Knoll, today."

"I'll try, sir." She hurried from the office, head down, making her way to the stairs.

I stood alone wondering if I'd just helped or hurt her, if I'd done the right thing and what her future held. In the aftermath, I felt invested in her situation – emotional, protective, responsible for whatever path lie ahead.

"You still here?" came a voice from behind, shocking me back to reality. "You're supposed to be over at the comm center. What's the problem?"

It was the XO, who'd just sprung from his office. I was uncertain if he'd seen the exchange with Heather. "On my way, sir. Just got sidetracked for a moment."

"Sidetracked? Your whole career is about to be sidetracked, Baumann. What were you doing with that girl just now?"

"Helping her, sir. I was trying to find her medical record."

"Medical record?" he scoffed. "Never mind that. I want you to find me the message boards, ASAP. What's the matter? You have a learning disability?"

My face flushed. I remained silent. *Control, control.*

"Hey, don't answer that. I wouldn't want you to incriminate yourself," he said, chuckling at his own lame remark. He then gave me the once-over, as if sizing me up for the first time. "Look, Baumann, I know your type. You think the Navy's some sort of dodge allowing you mark time until you can go fly for the airlines. You live under the protection of the junior officer's creed – no career commitment, no accountability, not a care in the world. Life's just one big frat party freeing you to lob smack from the cheap seats." The XO got right up in my face and continued. "I'm putting you on notice, son. This little mutiny you're staging is coming to an end. You pull any of your shenanigans or challenge my authority while I'm O-in-C in Adak, you'll be doing a lot more than standing an SDO watch over Christmas."

"O-in-C in Adak?" I said. This was not good news. I think he enjoyed springing it on me to see my reaction.

"Yep, I'm the man for the second half of the detachment. Since you were so monumentally incompetent and missed getting your crew qual, we've ended up together. Shipmates, in fact." He flashed a phony grin. "So, take heed, Mr. Baumann. I'll be watching you, real close, under the microscope, you might say. None of your bullshit or bending of the rules this time, or else it'll cost you more than a finger-wagging and restriction if you catch my drift." He finally dropped the smile. "Now run along. Go fetch those message boards."

O-in-C stood for Officer-In-Charge. In this case, the XO would be the senior officer in charge of the detachment in Adak, something usually reserved for a lieutenant commander department head being groomed for command, not an incumbent executive officer. Why the skipper wanted Commander Dickless at the helm up there was beyond me. Life on the rock had just doubled in shittyness if that was even possible. *And the hits just keep on coming.*

# 6

## PREPARATION FOR ADAK

OVER THE HOLIDAY BREAK, I was bothered by a recurring idyllic memory that accentuated my dour mood – the kind in the movies where the young, romantic couple is daydreaming in bed with soft sunlight streaming in. Aimee and I had just wed in Corpus a week prior and were nestled under the covers on a lazy Sunday morning whispering wishful things to one another, things that began with the word *Someday*. Mitch: *Someday we'll own a big yellow Lab and go camping in the mountains on a pristine lake, we'll cook trout for breakfast over an open fire and hike to the top of a nearby peak.* Aimee: *Someday we'll fix up one of those old bungalows in Sacramento, we'll rake leaves on a crisp fall day, sip hot cocoa on the porch and help the kids carve pumpkins for Halloween.* I shook my head in amazement. Camping out, carving pumpkins, sipping hot cocoa… How indulgent our distant fantasy-tripping seemed in the wake of my run-in with the XO. I'd been numbed to the fact that concepts of such simple joy were still possible. By the time the New Year holiday rolled in, my mood was so low, melancholy would've been an improvement. My restriction, which kept me chained to base for most of the month was bad enough. Then on December 31st, I received the marvelous news BUPERS was freezing all VP squadron officer's orders for three months to save money. This would extend the period I had left in VP-25 to June, delaying my rotation to shore duty and separation from the squadron on time. My restriction officially ended on January 1st when I was relieved by a new squadron duty officer, the first in fifteen days.

On January 2nd, Aimee suggested we head south for a four-day vacation and drive down to Disneyland with the kids, so we loaded up the Suburban and fled town. The sensation of passing through the Moffett Field main gate, blending back into the civilian horde of the Silicon Valley after nearly a month was liberating, providing me the giddy sensation of a prisoner freshly sprung from the gates of San Quentin. We ate at family restaurants along the way, stayed at the Disneyland Hotel and rode the monorail into the park. The kids were totally jazzed by the Disney experience. Even Sean, our precocious little six-year-old, forgot himself and joked with Mickey Mouse on Main Street and screamed joyfully on Space Mountain and Pirates of the Caribbean. Sean's delight was a metaphor for us all. It was a time to heal, a time of simple laughter. We were suspended in that blissful moment of togetherness, recapturing our unity and letting the tension that had dogged us since Thanksgiving melt away like spring snow. We were near the end of our second day, watching the kids spinning wildly on Alice's Mad Tea Party ride when Aimee came up from behind, put an arm around my waist and gave a squeeze. The sun was low in the west, the shadows long and leisurely, creating one of those Kodak moments. "This has been a wonderful break, Mitch," she said. "Life should always be this good." I smiled and nodded yet a part of me was already distracted, already fretting about our final push to Adak, of flight schedules and training commitments.

We arrived home late on Wednesday night after an eight-hour car ride. I had to report to work early Thursday for our crew's scheduled simulator event, a second run at our sub qualification, this time in the Weapons System Trainer known as the WST. The spontaneous Disney trip and four-day basket leave was a blessing, a gift by the skipper that wouldn't be charged as official leave time. Even though he ran a tight ship, screamed a lot and missed nothing, you had to admire the guy. He must've taken pity on me after the harsh punishment and wanted to show I was still in good standing, that there'd be no permanent repercussions. I wanted to thank him and inquire about the status of my orders but that would have to wait. I'd first need to earn the elusive crew qual we'd missed on Thanksgiving.

The WST is located inside Moffett Field's Hangar One, one of the largest enclosed structures in the world and, built in 1933 to house the colossal airship USS *Macon*, is listed in the National Register of Historic Places. It dominates the skyline from almost any point in the northern Silicon Valley and can create its own weather inside when the doors are closed. The WST is housed under its huge dome in a series of low-silhouette modular buildings. I walked up to the main entrance of the simulator complex and slid my green military ID card to the sailor behind the glass. He glanced at it, said nothing, and handed me a badge labeled "Aircrew" on a lanyard and buzzed me through the door. Once inside I instantly noticed the familiar change in climate which was much cooler and dryer and maintained the perpetual odor of overcooked coffee, stale air and hot, humming electronics. I stepped onto the raised floor, a loose set of plates under which ran miles of computer cable. My flight boots thudded down the hollow corridor with each step. Jamie, our TACCO, and both acoustic sensor operators from our crew, AW1 Hodges and AWSN Kennedy, were seated in the small briefing room when I arrived. They were eager to get started and understood, as did I, this second shot at our qual was not to be squandered with more eyes watching than usual. The stress inside Jamie was pushing him to try harder, to be perfect today. I was impressed with his energy and professionalism, refreshed myself, and ready to get underway.

"Gentlemen," I said, as I grabbed a seat at the table. "Seems we're light. Where's our intrepid navigator?"

"Galley. Coffee," Jamie said, without looking up from the mission briefing packet he'd been given, quickly absorbing every detail. Our instructor, a lieutenant from VP-31, was presumably readying the WST in the control center and had handed Jamie one of the many simulated mission packets that would be our "exam".

Our crew, Crew 4, was twelve strong but the simulator missions only required the tactical nucleus, or "Tac Nuc," which was five. A single pilot, the TACCO, the NAVCOM and the two acoustic sensor operators. The rest of the crew was not needed. The two flight engineers, the inflight technician, the ordnanceman and the non-acoustic operator would be simulated by the instructor at his console as the mission dictated.

The P-3C Weapons System Trainer represented the latest computer technology the Navy could buy. The vast systems housed in these modular buildings cost more than the airplanes they were designed to simulate but were operated at a fraction of the cost. A four-hour submarine detection and tracking mission could be simulated using identical avionics in an exact replica of the P-3's entire cabin, or more commonly referred to as "the tube." The acoustic gear, the NAVCOM and TACCO stations, the onboard computer, the radar, even the aircraft seats were hardware pulled from the Lockheed production line to make the mission experience as real as possible. The best part of the simulator missions was the two-hour transit time to and from the search area was eliminated. Crews would sit down at their stations, plug in and the instructor would activate a series of switches, press a few buttons, magically transporting the "aircraft" to the Bering Sea, the Tsugaru Straits or G-I-UK Gap. Even the actual oceanic environmental conditions could be simulated in the search area. In an adjoining room was the P-3's cockpit, or flight station. Again, this was an impressive array of simulation and actual hardware designed to give pilots the look and feel of the real airplane. The simulator would supply its software-based control laws to the cockpit avionics, the yoke, the column, the throttle quadrant, and pilots would suddenly be flying the mission along with their cabin crew next door which was known as the coupled mode. Today, since I was the only pilot, I would not be flying the mission in the cockpit simulator fully coupled. Instead, I'd be sitting out front next to the instructor at his console with a headset turning a simple knob designed to steer the airplane while on station. A keyboard would accept my altitude changes along with throttle movements for airspeed. I was completely happy with this arrangement. To break up the monotony I could grab coffee or snacks from the galley, use the restroom, gab with the instructor or walk back into the tube and mess with Jamie or Al at their stations. Our mission would be a piece of cake.

The five of us walked into simulator #1 and let our eyes adjust to the dim lighting. Jamie and Al sat down in adjacent seats on each side of the aisle and immediately began to power up their stations, checking the simulated sonobuoy and weapons loads along with the navigation system and initial position of the aircraft. Today's mission would start us at 16,000 feet, 250 miles southwest of Adak, searching for a Soviet Delta II ballistic missile nuclear submarine in the cold waters off the Aleutians. We'd have the full 48 externally launched sonobuoys plus 36 more inside, capable of being launched by our "simulated" ordnanceman upon Jamie's request. All 84 of our buoys, called "search stores," were passive, designed to maintain a stealthy presence lest we alert the sub before we could kill it. We'd also have four 500-pound Mark 46 torpedoes loaded in the bomb bay, known as "kill stores," to launch when the appropriate attack criteria was achieved. To attain our qualification, we needed at least three valid attacks.

Seated ten feet aft of Jamie and Al, facing sideways, Hodges and Kennedy were doing similar preflight checks, running their sophisticated acoustic gear through its built-in test, or BITE. To me, their AQA-7(V) DIFAR (Directional Frequency Analysis and Recording) avionics and all the associated subsystems were pure magic. I didn't understand its intricate operation, the constant tuning, adjusting, listening and button-pushing required to detect a sub signature from the surrounding oceanic chaff. Suffice to say their gear represented the pinnacle of acoustic submarine detection technology for 1983 and cost the taxpayers plenty. It was designed for simplicity but was highly complex and required years of experience to master. Antisubmarine warfare, or ASW, despite all the recent tech advancements, was still an art. And Jamie, who wouldn't drop the f-bomb but maybe once a year, liked to say Hodges could play the AQA-7 like fucking Mozart. We were all that confident in his abilities and had formed a tightknit band around him and his assistant, Kennedy, giving them anything needed once we were on station in hot tracking mode.

I was standing behind Jamie sipping coffee, looking at his TACCO screen when the instructor unfroze us. "And away we go," I said, slapping Jamie on the shoulder. He turned around, headset on, eyes bugged out, his expression saying, what the hell are you standing here for? I made my way out front, threw on a headset and took a seat in the plastic chair next to our instructor-evaluator. I stuck out a hand and introduced myself. His name was Bill Pearson, a lieutenant like me, but a few years ahead in his career path. He was assigned to VP-31 as an NFO instructor, having already completed his operational squadron tour across the field. Bill pointed at the screen in front of me, indicating Jamie had set up a sixteen-buoy search pattern I needed to start flying. I twiddled with the heading knob and aligned the aircraft for the first row of buoy drops. Jamie had set up the standard search pattern for our target as prescribed by the ASW Tactical Manual, a sixteen-buoy distributive field spaced at four nautical miles arranged in three rows.

Our simulated P-3 approached the first buoy drop at 200 knots. As I captured the computer release point, Jamie called, "DIFAR 1 away," over the interphone system. This would cue Hodges to tune channel 1 on his sono-receiver system and begin the process of listening and recording. After another minute of flying, Jamie would call DIFAR 2 away, and so on until all sixteen buoys were deployed in a symmetrical pattern and sending back valid RF signals. Sometimes the instructor would simulate a failure of one of the buoys and we'd have to go back to replace it, which was a pain but totally realistic. Today he decided not to give us any search pattern failures, which I took as a bad sign. It meant he'd likely kill one when we were in the more vulnerable close aboard tracking phase.

"TACCO, Sensor 1, all buoys up and operational," Hodges informed the crew over the ICS.

"Thanks, One," Jamie responded. You could hear disappointment in his tone as he was thinking the same thing I was, that we'd likely lose a crucial one later when things got hot and heavy. "Let me know as soon as you think you have something."

"Roger, TACCO."

Our mission was off to a slow start. After nearly two hours of droning around at low altitude and burning up valuable sim time with nothing but useless ICS chatter, we were at a dead end with nothing to show, zero subsurface contact. It was like our instructor was purposely jerking the sub around giving us his version of the Kobayashi Maru and setting us up for certain failure. Jamie finally made a proclamation on ICS. "Mitch, I'm moving our search eastward and tightening up the spacing. I'll have another sixteen-buoy pattern on your scope in a minute."

"Roger."

After our second pattern had hit the water, Al and I huddled around Jamie at his station for a brief conference. We were off headset and stood in the aisle, Jamie fussing about the dwindling clock and our narrowing options. Al estimated the chances of successfully completing our crew qualification in the remaining two hours had shrunk from something like eighty percent to thirty percent. He stated the numbers with a detached ease, like a Vegas oddsmaker.

"And how did you compute that, Einstein?" Jamie said. "Using your fingers and toes?" He was in no mood Al's negativity or unfounded speculation.

"Simple math probability," Al responded, coldly.

I'd never taken a course in probability, but thirty percent sounded about right. We all sensed we were about to miss our second shot at the qual. "Come on, ladies," I said. "Let's get back to our stations." I turned to leave. "Something good will come up."

"Hey!" came a scream from behind. "Why aren't any of you answering?" It was Hodges, yelling at us from his station ten feet away. "Get on headset, now. We've acquired!"

The three of us instantly broke our huddle and scrambled back to our chairs to don headsets. Jamie's voice was up a full octave on ICS, "Where is he, One, where is he? What buoy?"

"DIFAR 5. And it looks like direct path!" said Hodges.

If this truly was direct path contact, we'd soon be tracking the sub close aboard setting up for our first kill. Very welcome news, indeed. Direct path meant just what the term implied. Sound from the sub was emanating in a straight path to the buoy's hydrophone. Direct path in standard ocean water would only extend two to four miles – that's how close the sub was to our buoy. Remarkable luck.

The ICS chatter came alive as we converted to developing a rough course and speed that was refined by dropping more buoys at closer intervals. The goal now was to establish a very accurate sub track, one that would enable a CPA, or Closest Point of Approach, of 500 yards or less to any single sonobuoy. A 500-yard CPA by the sub would yield attack criteria and allow us to bomb the buoy with one of our Mark 46 torpedoes. Jamie was calling for multiple buoy drops in front of the sub as fast as I could get the airplane into position. We were employing what was humorously referred to as the "Sherman-Williams" tactic, a mad effort to "cover the earth" with buoys like paint advertisement said, to hang onto the contact and quickly convert to attack criteria. Jamie set up an attack barrier two miles in front of the sub, a line of four buoys spaced at 1,000 yards. When the sub penetrated the barrier, attack criteria would be automatically generated. My challenge would be to get the buoys in the water per Jamie's pattern now on my scope, then position the aircraft over the attack buoy the instant the sub made its CPA. "Descending to five hundred feet," I said. We were heading for low altitude and banked over at 45-degrees. In a real-world mission, this was where the pilots earned their pay.

The four-buoy barrier went into the water easily enough, both Hodges and Jamie refining the sub's course and speed to determine exactly when CPA would occur and which buoy. "Okay, TACCO," Hodges said, "I got him directly inbound DIFAR 7, estimate CPA in one minute."

"Concur," was Jamie's terse response. A double-click of his mic also sufficed as acknowledgment when he was busy. I knew he was balancing several crucial tasks at once and I was doing my damnedest to get us into position for the attack. It was a delicate dance, one that required the airplane, the sub and the weapon to converge on a single point in a 30-second window.

"Okay, Flight, time to kill this commie bastard," Jamie said. "Here comes the weapon fly-to-point on your scope. We need to run through the on-line Mark 46 checklist pronto, one minute to drop." The screen at my console automatically decluttered nonessential information and boldly displayed the weapons FTP in dead center. The flight director command bars came alive giving me precise steering guidance to the drop point. The torpedo would release automatically upon capture if all went well.

"Standing by, Mark 46 check," I said. I flipped open my pocket checklist and quickly ran through the setup with Jamie in the customary challenge and response.

"Roger, Mark 46 checklist" Jamie answered. "Release selection switch?"

"Release selection is auto."

"Master arm?"

"Master arm is on."

"Bomb bay doors?"

"Bomb bay doors coming open." I pushed a switch on my console. As soon as the simulated doors finished opening, my computer weapons release button went from green to bright amber, as it did at Jamie's station.

"Okay, we're armed. Checklist complete, clear to drop," Jamie said. "Just hit that FTP, Mitch."

"I'll do my best. Be ready to punch it manually if I don't capture."

Double-click of his mic.

We were flying at just under 200 knots to the release point. Our wings were level, and I was on proper heading and altitude to capture the tiny symbol. I knew Jamie had his finger on the trigger if I missed.

We were – just – about –

"Weapon away!" Jamie cried.

"Confirm, weapon in the water, TACCO," Hodges said after ten seconds had passed. He would continue to monitor the attack buoy to verify the sound of a kill. I'd never heard the sound or tone the WST would give the acoustic operator to signal we'd killed the target. I imagined a recorded sound bite from an old movie like the *Bedford Incident* where the nuclear ASROC blows the Russian sub to smithereens. I made a mental note to ask Hodges about it at debrief.

"Score that as a successful kill." It was Bill, our instructor, on ICS. "One down, two to go," he said in his monotone voice.

After all the work and sweat getting us to this point, the atmosphere in the tube and the control room was downright anticlimactic. There was no explosion, no whooping it up by the crew, no slapping each other on the back like in the movies. We knew this was simply an exercise, a simulation, a test. And our test was only one-third complete. Jamie quickly set up another attack barrier which the sub penetrated, and we generated a second successful attack. Afterward, Bill slightly altered the course of the sub and we had to drop some extra buoys before laying our final attack barrier and getting off attack #3 to end the exercise. Bill looked at me and I nodded. "Okay, gentlemen, that's a wrap," he said over ICS, punching the freeze button on the simulator.

We'd completed the entire problem in just two hours and thirty minutes, well under the allotted four hours. Probably a squadron record. Now we could whoop it up. I threw off my headset and ran back to the tube. Jamie and Al had already walked aft to Hodges' and Kennedy's sensor station and were congratulating them. We were all smiles, high-fiving each other like high school kids after winning the big game when Jamie looked at his watch. "Wow, is it really only 10:30? It feels like late afternoon. I've been up since five worrying about this stupid event."

"Well, no worries now," Al said. "You nailed it."

Jamie exhaled a sigh of relief. "Yeah, we did, didn't we?"

Bill stuck his head into our little mix. "Debrief in five minutes, gentleman. Conference room out front."

We gathered our gear and walked to the same room we'd met in earlier. Jamie, Al and I grabbed a seat around the table. Hodges set down his acoustic grams, basically a thermal paper printout of the sub traces from our mission, on top of Jamie's official notes and Al's navigation log. "Anything else, sir?" he said, mainly to me.

"Nah, we won't need you," I said. "Dismissed. And super job today, both you and Kennedy."

"Thank you, sir. I'll pass that along."

Hodges was a pro, not only a whiz at ASW but a class act, a leader. He was dependable in a pinch, supportive of his crewmates or any person in need, the type of guy you'd want around in any circumstance. He was scheduled to take the Chief Petty Officer exam next month and would easily pass, making him the youngest E-7 in the squadron. I waved him on his way and began tossing a green apple up in the air, one I had grabbed from a basket in the galley. "You know, we're going to lose him when he makes chief," I said after he closed the door.

"Don't say that. I don't want to lose another crew member to a trade, not before we go to Adak," Jamie said.

"We're not going to lose him before we go to Adak."

"We lost Colby. And that was the worst trade since the Sox let Babe Ruth go."

"Forget Colby," I said, not wanting to get into the whole Jim Abbott for Colby Reed swap. "Look, we'll be fine up there. And the next time I see Colby, I'll tell him you compared his value to the Babe. I'm sure he'll be flattered."

Despite our success, something, perhaps the trade, was bugging Jamie. In the silence that followed, I continued lobbing my apple toward the ceiling, seeing how close I could get to the acoustic tiles without actually touching them.

"This guy likes to keep the suspense going, doesn't he?" Al said, referring to our instructor, who was past his five-minute promise.

"What suspense?" I said. "We nailed it. You said so yourself."

The door opened as I lunged across the conference table to snag an errant apple toss. Bill entered the room. If he was surprised by my strange action, he didn't show it. He sat down across from us, slid our mission artifacts in front of him and casually flipped through the stack, barely looking at any of the information. He looked nervous and his quick perusal was simply a way to heighten whatever drama he was trying to create with his late entry. Finally, he looked up at Jamie and spoke. "Well, gentlemen, I've got good news and bad news. Which first?"

We responded in unison. Jamie: "Good news." Me: "Bad news."

For whatever reason, Bill indulged Jamie first. "The good news is the TACCO and sensor operators did everything correctly throughout the mission. A textbook performance."

"Thank you, sir," Jamie replied.

I shot him a hard look unable to tell if he was being sarcastic or overly servile. I mean, *thank you, sir?* This wasn't the training command. We weren't still ensigns in flight school.

Bill continued. "The bad news is—" He looked at me then back to the artifacts, afraid to speak. "And this is a tough call, the reason I was late. The bad news is, I can't award the qual."

Jamie gasped. Al quickly stood as though he might grab Bill by the throat.

"What do you mean you can't award the qual?" I said, also standing to confront him. "You saw our three attacks. You saw everything from your console in the control room. What's the problem?"

"The second and third were questionable, not flown down the sub's track."

"What! Al roared. "Look at my log, our aircraft heading was right on." Al looked at me for corroboration, especially since I was doing the flying. "Mitch?"

"The torp acquired," I said, looking at Bill. "Doesn't that make it a valid attack?"

"Hardly."

"Hardly? Oh, so the weapon acquired the sub, blew it the fuck out of the water, and you say, no, sorry, not a valid attack?"

Bill's eyes narrowed. "I don't care if the weapon acquired and blew up Flipper," he said. "You're required to meet the Mark 46 torpedo drop parameters on all your attacks by flying the proper altitude, airspeed and heading. And watch your language."

"Okay, okay, calm down," I said. "Let's take our seats. Al, slide over your nav log. I want to take a look." I glanced at Jamie. His color was pale, his eyes closed. I paged through Al's computer printout to locate the nav parameters at the attack times.

"You're making this harder, not easier," Bill said.

"Oh, come now," I said, smiling. "We're all friends here. Let's just have a look. I know we were at least close." I slowly flipped through the log. It revealed at best a five-degree heading deviation and maybe a few knots of airspeed over max delivery velocity on the second attack. The third attack was a bit sloppier but, in my opinion, well within the scope of a charitable DBO. Jamie had already resigned himself to our predicament. He appeared to be having a flash-forward moment of career doom thinking the same as me, that this was a repeat of our Thanksgiving debacle in SoCal where we'd failed to receive the qual by a very non-charitable DBO. I needed a way for Bill to save face, to give him an out by taking him away from our group. I had a couple of cards to play. "Bill, may we have a word out in the hall, just you and me?"

"What now?" We both stood. He looked nervous as we stepped into the narrow corridor. "I suppose this is the part where you kick my ass?"

I put my arm around him. "Bill. Buddy. Come on, those attacks were certainly within tolerance of our tracking gear. We easily made those kills. Come on."

"They were marginal at best," he said in his nasal voice.

"You mean after all we did, in record time, and by the book as you so eloquently put it, you're not going to award the qual?"

"Your nav log leaves me little choice. People higher up than me are going to see it."

I dropped my arm, "Did you know our attacks were outside the box? As you watched from your console?"

"I suspected they were but—"

"All right then. You suspected they were." Here came my last card. "Yet you halted the sim after our third attack. We certainly could've achieved several more attacks in the time remaining, you know, for insurance. But you cut us off an hour before our time expired." I winked and smiled again to remind him we were still friends. "You know, you were in our shoes once. A successful TACCO on the other side. You know how hard we worked today. We gave you a textbook performance, right? Your own words. We earned that qual." Even as I applied the grease, I knew I'd put Bill in a tough spot. I'd given him the signal we were done after attack #3 and he'd made the decision to freeze the problem. I knew what he was thinking, the event was over, the sensor operators dismissed, records pulled, systems powered down. I was casting blame, but also providing him wiggle-room.

"Well," Bill said. "We can't just restart the sim, now can we?

"No, we can't."

"And we can't track everyone down and bring them back to their seats?"

"I know," I said, smiling, happy to play along. "Damn the bad luck."

There was a silence as Bill pondered our fate and the box he'd put us in by hitting the freeze button. "All right, let me see that log again." He heaved a sigh. "This is truly is a gift, Baumann. You know that, right?" He grabbed the doorknob and reentered the conference room. I followed him back inside trying to suppress my grin, not wanting to spike the football and celebrate too early. He calmly picked up Al's navigation log from the mission and slid out his black felt-tipped marker from his breast pocket, uncapped it and, in a big flourish, signed his name, rank and title across the front page. He capped the pen and stood to leave. "Enjoy Adak, boys," he said, slipping from the room.

We remained quiet in his wake until Jamie and Al let out an exuberant cheer, proclaiming victory over both the sub and potential controversy that could've ended badly. I was as relieved as they were, probably more so, happy to have atoned for my reckless behavior by skipping the debrief on Thanksgiving. By signing the log, Bill was attesting to the fact he'd reviewed our documents, given us a thorough debrief and was satisfied we'd met the requirements for the ASW crew qualification. Case closed. We were headed to Adak.

"Mitch, what the hell did you say to him out there in the hall?" Jamie asked.

"Yeah, you got pictures on him or what?" Al said.

"I simply thanked him for his time, his expertise and reminded him he was once aircrew too."

Jamie raised an eyebrow.

"Well, you must've charmed the pants off him," Al said. "That's for sure."

"Putty in my hands."

After our WST experience and delicate negotiation with Bill, I was feeling a greater need for control, to foresee potential problems and avoid the pitfalls before they occurred as I prepared for Adak and subsequent visit with my father. I'd been edgy all week pondering my fate and how much control I truly had as I packed for my six-week stint up north. Aimee came into our bedroom where I was sorting socks and underwear, tossing them into a suitcase. "Well, Aims, two more days and I'm gone. I can't believe how fast time has flown."

Aimee sat down on the bed in front of me. It was almost 6 P.M. and she was dressed nicely, like she was headed out, maybe to some officer's wives club function. It didn't really register what she might be doing since I had been preoccupied with packing and other deployment preparations over the last couple of days. "Yeah, it always seems that way when I know you are leaving." She looked up. "Are you ready for this, Mitch?"

"Of course. It'll go fine. I'll be home before you know it." I was trying to keep things light, ignoring the obvious stress we knew the six-week separation would cause. I was leaving at a time when Amber had just returned, fresh from rehab, and would potentially be in that fragile state adjusting to real life again. She'd be living with Mother, the two forced to cope with each other's idiosyncrasies and independent personalities. Part of me was relieved to be getting away from the ensuing drama but if needed I could offer little help or support while isolated in Adak. It would all be on Aimee, again. Then there was the issue of my father and the promise I'd made myself. On impulse, I said, "When I get back, I'm driving up to Coeur d'Alene." The announcement again just fell out, unplanned and unrehearsed.

"Good. I think you should go," Aimee said, without giving it a moment's thought. "You haven't seen your father in a very long time."

"That makes it harder to go, not easier."

"Yes."

"The fact that I haven't seen him in three years. And only twice in the last five."

"I know."

"God, Aimee. I don't even know the man. I haven't the slightest idea what I'd say to him if I faced him, right here, right now."

"I know."

"Please. Say something more than, 'I know.'" It was obvious she wasn't eager to discuss the topic so close to my departure. Still, I pressed on. "I'm not sure if it's the right decision to go up to Idaho or not. Part of me wants to just ignore him, ignore the whole mess he's left us. You know, he's making it very easy to do just that, let him fade like a distant memory.

"What do you want me to say, Mitch? I already told you to go. It's a good decision."

"But why should I be the one to reach out to him? Doesn't he owe it to me, to Amber, to reconnect? To want to reconnect with his grown children?"

"You're the one searching for answers, not him."

"Okay, fine." I stopped sorting my clothes and looked up. "I read you loud and clear. Let's drop it." I was tense, but there were things I felt needed saying on the verge of my departure. We'd kept things light over the last two months, tiptoeing around issues that had been brewing since Thanksgiving and creating a false sense of domestic peace. We'd taken family drives to the beach, we'd socialized more with our neighbors on base, we'd made love more often, I'd been to Sean's school many times to pick him up and to attend his open house. I'd also kept a lower profile at the squadron, flying only two pilot trainer flights – one with my new 2P, Jim Abbott, who was truly a rock but someone that could be managed, and one with the skipper for my annual check, which had gone well. All in all, life seemed back on track but there was an underlying stress that Aimee and I couldn't deny. I was simply looking for validation, some moral support of my decision to drive up to Idaho. Apparently, Aimee thought it best to ignore confronting my family's dysfunction until I got back, limiting my distractions in the face of a six-week absence. There was also the issue of my orders, orders that should've arrived in January but were delayed. As it stood, I'd receive them later this month while in Adak and likely be allowed to detach from the squadron in May or June. I'd already been given the unofficial word I was headed to VT-3 in Pensacola, Florida as an instructor pilot. This was no surprise as orders such as these were common for many pilots after completing their first operational tour. I just wasn't sure if I should accept them. I gave a deep sigh and resumed parsing the clothes into my bag.

Aimee stood up from the bed. "You know, Mitch, life is hard. That's one of the greatest truths. But once you understand this truth, and truly accept it, you transcend it and life ceases to be hard."

"Huh?" This bit of armchair psychology had likely come from one of her self-help chick books. "Aimee, please don't lecture me with stuff you read off the pop-psych book rack. Is that why you came in here? To cast pearls of wisdom before I leave that have no basis in reality?"

Aimee narrowed her eyes. "It has *plenty* of basis in reality. And I didn't come in here to *lecture* you. I came in to tell you we're going out to dinner with Mark and Lisa. I've got a sitter coming. We leave in thirty minutes." With that, she strolled from the room.

I followed her out. "What? Out to dinner? When did that get decided?" I maneuvered in front of her in the narrow hallway. "I leave for Adak day after tomorrow. I've still got things to do. Why'd you set this up for tonight? Did it ever occur to ask me?"

"I told you last week I wanted to go to our little Italian place one last time before you left. Tonight's the night. I suppose you're going to tell me you're not going?" We stood frozen, eye to eye, her sharp look demanding an answer.

"Aimee, c'mon. You could've asked first. I've got to finish packing and then I've got a full day tomorrow." I knew as I finished, I was sealing my fate. There was a way to fit dinner in, but the idea was sprung too quickly, too much of a surprise. My gut reaction was to say no.

"Okay, so there's nothing more to discuss." She tried to step around me in the confined space. "Get out of my way, please," she said. I moved aside as she squeezed past and headed down the stairs clacking her heels in loud succession.

Mark and Lisa were Evan's parents and had moved in next door only a few months after us. Mark was an instructor pilot at VP-31, the thought crossing my mind that he was perhaps friends with my new buddy, Bill Pearson. Mark and Lisa were nice enough and their son Evan was fast friends with Sean, both in the first grade. Aimee and Lisa had become close when I was in Westpac last year. I liked Mark well enough but both he and Lisa were strong evangelical Christians and were members of some mega-church out in town. Conversations with Mark would begin innocuously, discussing Navy life, squadron politics and our mutual plans to leave the military when our time was up but he'd invariably steer the discussion back to the Lord. *The Lord has plans for Lisa and I to do mission work in the Congo. The Lord warns us of Satan's presence in the workplace. The Lord has encouraged me to invite you and Aimee to church with us.* I enjoyed discussion on Christianity and religious philosophy; Aimee and I were Christians and supported the biblical teachings. What I found I didn't enjoy were Mark's judgmental attitudes and inflexible viewpoints on the subject. I could take the guy in small doses and by forgetting our dinner date, which truly was an honest mistake, the side benefit was no lengthy debate on the sins of the world and Jesus's vengeful second coming. Lisa was not as in your face as Mark with her faith and I'm certain that's why she and Aimee got along. Lisa was more of a follower but had a rebellious streak. She'd sometimes come over to our patio to sip wine or sneak an occasional cigarette with Aimee while I was on deployment forging that special bond of sisterhood extending beyond religious beliefs or political convictions. Shortly after I'd made my decision not to attend tonight's dinner, Aimee headed next door gabbing with Lisa most of the evening.

I went to bed early after a shower and never heard Aimee come home but when I awoke after midnight, she lay next to me sleeping soundly, her chest rising and falling in peaceful rhythm. I was pleased that she chose to find her way to our bed. Sometimes she'd be so furious, and tonight clearly could've been one of those nights, she'd sleep downstairs on the living room sofa using only a throw pillow and the TV comforter, a message saying she'd rather rough it on the couch than stay in the same room as me. A million thoughts raced through my head as I lay awake staring at the ceiling – mainly how I was going to patch things up with Aimee but also the numerous personal and squadron prep items that needed tending, the flight up to Adak, the weather, which airplane they'd give us, additional passengers, et cetera. The digital numerals on the nightstand clock ticked off, 12:30, 12:45, 1:00. I listened to the nocturnal beat of the house, the heater switching on, the low-pitch warble of the refrigerator downstairs. I desperately needed to get back to sleep. This would be my last chance for sustained rest before preflight the following morning at 0600.

I must've finally dozed off because I was jolted out of a dream to the sound of a telephone, the extension on the nightstand ringing next to my ear. At first, I thought I'd overslept but the big green numerals on the clock read 2:35. Only one legitimate caller would ring at this hour of the night – the VP-25 duty office. It was the SDO, I knew it. I just didn't know why. I answered in an intentionally groggy voice, "This is Lieutenant Baumann."

"Mitch?" A woman's voice.

"Yes?"

"Oh, Mitch." A pause. "Oh, Mitch, thank God, you haven't left."

"Amber?"

She was crying, talking fast and slurring her words. I couldn't understand any of it.

"Amber, slow down, honey. *Please*, slow down." My heart raced. I was thinking of all possibilities of trouble, and she'd only been home a week. "What's wrong? What's happened?"

At some point, Aimee stirred from her side of the bed and sat up. "Mitch, what's the matter? Is it the squadron?"

I held up a hand and shook my head. Again, to Amber: "Go slowly, you're not making any sense."

"Oh, Mitch, you need to come home, you need to come home. It's Dad."

"Dad? Where is he?" I couldn't imagine him returning home, especially at two in the morning. Still, I had to ask, "Is he there?"

"No, he's not here. Dad is— He's gone, Mitch."

"Gone?"

"He's dead." More sobs, more crying.

I dropped the receiver to my lap in stunned disbelief as Amber continued crying. She was inconsolable and unable to offer any details so I ended with, "Okay, sit tight, tell Mother I'm on my way up."

I slid my feet from the bed onto the floor and faced the window. The messenger of death and tragedy always comes in the middle of the night, and it seems so goddamn cliché. I have early memories of my maternal grandmother passing, waking to my mother crying after receiving the news from her sister after we'd gone to bed. I was five. I recall learning of my cousin finally succumbing to childhood leukemia – my father's brother, Hank, making the call to our house at 3 A.M. I was seven. Then there were the countless times of either the police calling or visiting our door long after midnight when Amber was in trouble back in high school.

Now this.

# 7

## A CHANGE IN PLANS

I SURVEYED THE SMALL CROWD attending the burial service from behind my father's casket. I faced them, waiting my turn to speak, and watched as the pastor recited the old, familiar scriptures from the Committal, ones you always hear in movies but rarely, if ever, experience firsthand, at least before you're thirty.

*"...for as much as it has pleased Almighty God to take out of this world the soul of John Baumann, we therefore commit his body to the ground, earth to earth, ashes to ashes, dust to dust..."*

How can it please Almighty God when He sends us down here in the first place? I thought. And then to take us before our time? This made no sense to me. I again looked at the crowd, heads bowed reverently displaying no emotion, no reaction, just passive submittal to whatever this guy needed to say to appropriately end the obligatory ritual. A drizzle from the heavy overcast began to seep into my black jacket, flecking it with tiny dark spots. No one carried an umbrella as this was not rain, merely a heavy dose of San Francisco fog hovering about our heads delivering a visible coat of moisture to everyone's clothes, our hair, the grass, the folding chairs, the casket before me. I waited patiently for our rent-a-pastor, who wanted to be known simply as Don, to finish his sermon. I would close the service, as my mother had informed Don, "With a few well-chosen memories and fitting remarks", meaning ones that would make her look good, "from John's eldest son." I was still in somewhat of a funk given all that had transpired in the last five days to bring our family to this point.

We were standing in the middle of Golden Gate National Cemetery in San Bruno, a grassy, 160-acre expanse amid some of the Peninsula's most prime real estate. The cemetery had row upon row of identical white headstones, spreading as far as the eye could see, each depicting a deceased U.S. veteran, many of whom served and died in actual battle, including twelve Medal of Honor recipients. I was told this last fact proudly by the local Department of Veteran Affairs rep two days prior as my mother and I signed paperwork confirming my father's eligibility and the plot he'd receive. My father's wish, one he'd made known in a will that surfaced only four days ago, was that he be buried here, among thousands like him who had served in World War II. This was a simple request, one the government granted despite the short notice and dwindling space on the grounds. What was not simple was validating the will, making arrangements to ship his body, planning the funeral, notifying family and friends and then extricating myself from my Adak deployment all in the course of five days. It took my mother and me the entire first day after his death, working with the officials in Kootenai County, Idaho over the phone to understand exactly what had happened. I say exactly but that's a misnomer as many details remained sketchy. Without traveling to Idaho, I would likely never gain full knowledge or understanding of the events. What we did know went like this: my father, John Baumann, age sixty-three, was involved in a small plane crash at 6:30 P.M., around dusk, in a Beech Baron he'd been piloting back from Missoula, Montana to the Coeur d'Alene airport. He was the sole pilot carrying no passengers after dropping his student pilot in Missoula. The twin-engine Baron lost altitude approximately four miles east of the airport over Lake Hayden and crashed in twenty feet of water, just yards from shore. The accident was witnessed by several residents on the lake but took more than an hour to get rescuers to the aircraft. Witnesses told the county sheriff it looked like the plane was trying to land. It came in at a shallow approach angle, skipped on the water once, flipped over and sank. By the time divers got to the inverted aircraft and pulled the cockpit door open, my father had drowned, still strapped to his seat, likely rendered unconscious at impact. Most of these details were provided over the phone by the local sheriff but the part regarding my father's recent will and the transporting of his body back to the Bay Area was aided by Ramona Trapani, my father's girlfriend, mistress, partner or whatever. I still wasn't clear on which.

Today's mourners at graveside numbered an even twenty, all appropriately clad in a dark suit or black dress. That is all except Amber, standing next to our mother, and another woman hanging noticeably back from the main cluster wearing some sort of medical smock. I made the count while awaiting my turn to speak as the good reverend droned on. He was now quoting from the Martin Luther King speech with the line, *"...free at last, free at last, thank God almighty, free at last."* I thought that'll be everyone's sentiments exactly after I finish my piece. When Don said his final "free at last" he abruptly slapped his Bible shut, gave a nod to the crowd and stepped aside. His ending caught everyone by surprise, including me. Nonetheless, I straightened my shoulders, took a step forward and reached inside my breast pocket for some notes I'd made. The paper was nothing more than doodles I'd made on the ride over. I needed a prop, something to make it look like I'd done my homework and was prepared to pay homage to my beloved father. I'd prepared virtually nothing. Before speaking, I glanced up at Aimee and the kids. Aimee was holding Carlene in one arm while little Sean held my mother's hand, fidgeting nervously and appearing somewhat lost. Amber was on my mother's other side dressed in an all-black Gothic Victorian maxi dress and matching derby hat. Amber owned scads of black clothing items, none of which were appropriate for a funeral, but she must've decided the Gothic maxi would do fine. What surprised me was my mother, the Queen of Appropriateness and Decorum, must've agreed or chose to ignore the ridiculous outfit when they left the house, which looked more like a Halloween costume than funeral attire.

I cleared my throat. "Thank you all for coming. Mother and I, my wife, Aimee, our two children, and my sister Amber, deeply appreciate your support and attendance today in our time of mourning." I glanced over at my mother, her head bowed respectfully, very much playing out the part of the newly bereaved widow. Continuing, "I realize some of you, many of you, knew my mother and father before I was born." I was paying tribute to the United Airlines faces I recognized, both retired and active pilots. Some of these men and their wives attended parties at our house when I was no older than five and dated back to the early '50s, spanning my father's glory years as a young captain flying DC-6s and -7s. The men, deep lines etched into their faces, looked old and tired, some well beyond sixty. Their wives, once young beauties drawn from the stewardess ranks, looked aged and worn, much like old thoroughbreds whose racing days were long past. My mother, a war bride and certainly never a stewardess, was always charming and warm to these women but maintained an air of superiority about her, especially after the parties broke up. I had to admit, my mother was much better maintained, and better looking than these wilting ladies with bad complexions who'd probably been smoking and drinking since they were eighteen.

"Spread out before us are the markers of many heroes." I paused, allowing the mourners to take in the view. "My father was my hero, and a true war hero. My earliest memory of him was driving to the airport, down the Old Bayshore Highway, to see him off, my mother driving and my father in the right seat dressed in his airline uniform ready for his trip. His appearance, his confidence and quiet demeanor made a deep impression on me, traits directly influencing my life, guiding me to make choices that have brought me to this point in my life, one that will allow me to follow in his footsteps..." I paused again and scanned the crowd. I'd run out of whatever prepared words I'd composed beforehand. I was flying blind, and they sensed it. "One that *may* allow me to follow in his footsteps, as you never know what the future holds." I looked at Aimee, who remained passive, eyes fixed on the distant horizon, holding Carlene against her shoulder. I launched into some history, noting mainly from my mother, that it would not be appropriate to end my eulogy here.

"My father loved California. After many winters growing up in Kansas, he embraced the warm climate, the shimmering ocean, the palm trees and orange groves spread as far as the eye could see. Those tall palms, he said, row upon row swaying in the gentle breeze reminded him of paradise, so foreign to his midwestern roots, yet so peaceful. He rented a room in Pasadena, enrolled in college, found a part-time job and was making a life after a troublesome beginning. Then, suddenly on December 7, his world changed. His generation, and millions like him, joined the service without hesitation and were whisked away to a world at war. But before shipping out to Europe as part of the Mighty Eighth Air Force, he met my mother at a dance. They married, spending precious days together before his six months of combat duty in the deadly skies over Germany. He fought without question, never wavering, defending our nation's freedom, an honorable cause that forged his beliefs and values in the years to come. He returned from war, raised a family and embarked on a career as an airline pilot. He was my role model, a rock of stability." I surveyed the crowd, their attention now focused, hanging on my every word. I continued.

"When I was on deployment in Japan recently, I noticed a road sign at the entrance to a small town written in both Kanji and English, the English having been translated literally, I'm sure. It simply stated, *Do Always the Right Thing*. This was advice, I'm sure, to drivers on the proper attitude to display when operating a motor vehicle within the city limit. What the sign did was remind me of John Baumann, my father, thousands of miles away and a generation apart. Always do the right thing. If he had a motto, if he had any words to impart, these would have been it, words he taught me without ever having to speak them."

I noticed for the first time my Uncle Hank, Dad's younger brother by three years, had suddenly materialized in the small crowd before me. If he'd been there from the start of the service, I'd missed him. He appeared focused, intent on hearing my eulogy, yet bewildered at the setting before him. Uncle Hank was the baby of the family, the youngest of the three Baumann children, and had endured a bumpy road pockmarked with the loss of a child, divorce, and most recently, bankruptcy. He was rash, spontaneous and loved to talk big, always creating the illusion he was atop the world which drove my father crazy. Normally a calm, rational man, my father would become unhinged after he and his brother had too much to drink and Hank's bragging started. I'd always feared a fistfight would break out. We began to see less and less of Uncle Hank after they'd lost their daughter. He later divorced my Aunt Carol and dropped off the radar completely. Seeing his face return amidst the mourners today was a shock to the system.

I needed to refocus and wrap up the eulogy. I'd led everyone this far and I didn't want to mess it up. I had an obligation to my mother to keep up appearances, to conjure up a happy image of family life and create damage control around the mysterious circumstances surrounding my father's death. "My father loved our mother," I said, turning back to Amber. "He provided us a wonderful home to grow up in and he was very attentive, very supportive." I was on shaky ground as he was gone so much of the time, yet I continued. "He came to our school events, my baseball games, Amber's choral music concerts, as much as he could despite his busy schedule." I took a deep breath. "And, so let me just say—" Gradually, without warning there was an abrupt shift my equilibrium, a sense the crowd was seeing through my grand illusion.

"And so let me wrap up," I hesitated, "with the truth. The truth is that – that I never knew the man. I never knew him. I wish he were here to explain everything." I turned to his coffin, intentionally lowering my voice and avoiding my mother, who I knew would be going into mock cardiac arrest. "I wish I knew today so many of the things I wanted to ask you. To end the mystery of your silences, your long absence from my life, a life I think you'd be proud of." I stepped up to his coffin, placed a hand on its metal lid and said, "Goodbye, Father. You've left me a lifetime of questions. Maybe one day we'll meet again and sort it all out…" A wave of nausea rushed in, my knees buckled, and my voice began to falter. I couldn't go on. There was a weight pressing on my soul, a physical force overpowering me, pushing me to my knees.

I was quickly helped to my feet and led away from the casket by one of the younger United pilots I didn't recognize. I wasn't crying but visibly shaken, completely operating outside myself. He threw an arm around me and escorted me past the assembled group. Instinct told me to pull away, to run like hell, but I maintained my composure, clinging loosely to whatever decorum my mother had instilled at an early age. I also felt her laser eyes bore-sighted on my back. "It's okay, it's okay," he kept saying, his arm still draped around my shoulder.

I looked up. He was taller than me, at least six-foot-three. "I'm sorry, I guess that wasn't very proper, now was it?" Now my tears came, large ones that ran off my cheeks onto my jacket. "I should have prepared more, I should have—"

"Hey, you did fine," he said. "That's one of the toughest things a son has to do. Don't be so hard on yourself."

"I didn't do fine. I'm going to pay for this later. You saw my mother," I said, quickly dabbing an eye with my sleeve.

He looked in her direction. "Nope, she's cool, steady as a rock," he said. "You're clear."

Steady as a rock. I knew that look. The calm before the storm, the frozen stance and her patent, pasted-on smile.

"The name's Jeff Bailey," he said, thrusting out his right hand, his left arm still around my shoulder. "I flew with your father in his final two years before he retired. I was his first officer. That's my wife over there, two down from your mom." He lifted his chin and nodded. "Really sorry for your loss."

"I'm Mitch. I'm sorry too. Have we met?" I said, hating to always ask that question but figuring, under the circumstances, I'd get a pass.

"No, we haven't met. And to be honest, I didn't know John had a son until today."

My emotions were raw, and I felt my anger rise. "Oh, thank you. Thank you for that," I said.

"Don't take it the wrong way," he said, his voice just above a whisper. "We didn't talk much about our personal lives when we flew. Your father was the quiet type, not saying much of anything, really."

"No argument from me there," I said, sarcastically.

"Well, we talked some," he said. "Look, you probably should get back over there." We both noticed Reverend Don and others supervising the lowering of my father's casket into the grave. "Give me a call sometime. We should talk."

My father's last copilot at United, this Jeff Bailey fellow, pressed a business card into my palm and walked ahead to rejoin his wife. I glanced at the card. It appeared he was now in the private aircraft charter business. I blended back in with the mourners and we stood in silence, watching the mechanical device slowly lower the suspended coffin into the grave. I remembered Don telling us before the service that my mother, Amber and I would each take a symbolic shovelful of dirt and toss it into the hole before the backhoe, parked off to the side, would complete the task after we'd departed. Amber, closest to the grave, picked up the shovel and threw in a generous scoop of dark earth into the hole and stared down inside as if to confirm it'd made it. My mother followed, daintily sprinkling her dirt like water from a watering can. I snatched the shovel from her hand, not making eye contact, feeling virtually nothing at this point, mechanically going through the motions. I was about to lay the shovel down, wanting nothing more than to depart the cemetery, to end this agonizing scene when the solo woman I'd noticed earlier, the one wearing nurse's scrubs, appeared and took the shovel from my hand. She nearly had to wrest it away as I stood, shocked by her intrusion into our family nucleus, staring in frozen awe as she tossed in some earth of her own. She had tears in her eyes, the only one of us showing visible emotion. When she finished, she handed back the shovel, looked me straight in the eye with unflinching confidence and spoke softly, respectfully, "I'm Ramona."

We hung back as the crowd began to thin, everyone eager to escape to the warmth of their nearby automobiles. The drizzle had stopped, our footfalls wafting scents of freshly mown grass and pungent eucalyptus from the surrounding trees. My mother, not waiting to be escorted by her lingering son, walked ahead with Amber and slid into the backseat of her awaiting black Mercedes. I would drive them back to the homestead, Aimee and the kids following closely behind in our Suburban. My mother had planned a small reception afterward, a wake of sorts, for the neighbors and attendees.

I myself wanted nothing more than to be pointed south, back to base, after this excruciating farce. "I'm Mitch. John's son," I said to Ramona as we made our way through the wet grass. "We spoke on the phone."

"Yes."

"Did you fly in this morning from Coeur d'Alene?"

"I drove. I arrived early this morning."

"You drove? Unbelievable." Nearly a thousand miles, probably an all-day, all-night trek. This explained the scrubs and her hungover appearance. "You must be exhausted," I said. When I went in for a closer look, I realized she was actually quite beautiful under her dark circles and bloodshot eyes. She looked to be forty-something with an olive complexion and a thick mane of black hair. Her pretty, oval face was simply stunning, marked with only light traces of advancing age. But to me, she may as well have been an alien from another planet, adding even more mystery to my father's shrouded lifestyle rather than bringing clarity. Who was this woman? I thought. And where'd he dig her up?

"I'm fine," she said, staring at her shoes. "It was important for me to be here, to say goodbye." She lifted her head, her dark eyes meeting mine. "Really, though, the other reason I came was to meet you and ask you to return with me. Come back to Coeur d'Alene."

I stopped walking. "Come back? To Coeur d'Alene?" I was astounded she'd make such a suggestion.

"Yes."

"Look, Ramona, whoever you are, I can't just – I'm in the Navy. I'm supposed to be in Alaska in two days. Why would I drive up to Idaho – I mean, what's up there? Do I need to sign for something, or pay for something on my father's behalf?" Now I was beginning to think the worst, that she was wanting compensation or some other favor in return for her assistance in the aftermath of my father's death.

"You really should come up, sooner than later."

"Is that all you want? For me to come up there? Isn't there some other reason you're here now, that you drove all this way?" My suspicions were evident, and she noticed.

"There's nothing I want from you," she said. "Or your family." She wasn't projecting anger. It was more a rebuke, a tone you take when someone's totally stepped out of line. "You say you never knew the man, that you didn't know your own father? That's just sad, Mitch Baumann. Well, I did know him, certainly better than his *perfect* son." Perfect rolled off her tongue like a dirty word. "Certainly better than his alcoholic wife or his wayward daughter."

"Hey, wait a minute." I was stunned. "You can't say those things, not about me or my family. Who the hell do you think you are?"

"Grow up, Mitch." She spoke in a motherly fashion, ignoring the question. "There are no secrets in this world. There's really no sense to them. I offer help, that's all. If you want help, come see me when you get back from – wherever. If you don't want help, fine, don't come. I really don't care."

"Obviously, you do, otherwise you wouldn't be here."

Ramona paused as if to consider a clever comeback. Instead, a smile emerged, and she reached out and hugged me. She held me tight as I stood there confused, rigid in her arms. "John told me about you," she whispered in my ear. "I loved him, loved him dearly. And we were getting close, so close."

Close to what? I wondered. Close to him finally divorcing my mother and marrying her? Again, I was thinking the worst and feared blurting out another insensitive comment or question. I politely returned her hug, staring off in the distance. There was my mother's silhouette shaped in the backseat of her car, door open, waiting impatiently, tapping her foot on the pavement, tap, tap, tap. Ramona and I separated. She was crying and clutching a tissue, one she'd pulled from her scrubs pocket.

"Take care of yourself, Mitch. Let your anger go. And remember, I come in peace." She began a brisk walk to her own car, dabbing her eyes until she reached the driver's door. Before getting inside she turned around, smiled bravely and flashed me the peace sign. Her quickly formed V was a likely gesture for an oddball, aging hippie like Ramona but her body language conveyed a sense of sweetness and spontaneity, not the gold digger I had pegged her for. She slipped into the driver's seat as swiftly as she'd appeared, spun the car towards the gate and was gone. I stood alone among the thousands of white headstones spread out in all directions and breathed in the thick, verdant air. What was that all about? It didn't make any sense. Poof, she's here, poof, she's gone. Behind me, the backhoe started its engine breaking the graveyard silence. I turned toward my mother's black Mercedes idle at the curb and sighed, slowly making my way in her direction.

My Uncle Hank was the first to arrive in Latera Court in a very tired red 1973 Cadillac. He'd always had a thing for Caddys, fitting his image of having plenty of money and living large, although this automobile had seen better days. The rear power window had failed in a half-open position, and when he stepped from the driver's seat, the door gave a loud torque POP, echoing in the quiet cul-de-sac. I had just escorted my mother inside the house in anticipation of her guest's arrival from the funeral when Uncle Hank motioned me over to his car. I hadn't seen him in nearly fifteen years, shortly after his divorce from my Aunt Carol, and he'd aged considerably in the interim. His regularly close-cut beard was grizzled and flecked with gray, his complexion ruddy, reminding me of Papa Hemingway or a drunk Santa Claus. He'd taken off his tie and·unbuttoned his shirt. The first thing he said was, "How'd he die?" No pleasantries, no hello Mitch, how are you doing Mitch, no what have you been up to in the last fifteen years Mitch? Just, *how'd he die?*

I told him what little I knew – small plane crash, ditched in a lake, flipped over, drowned pinned to his seat.

Uncle Hank leaned against his beater car and stroked his scruffy beard. "Drowned, you say?"

"Yes. Drowned."

He shook his head, muttering something I didn't catch.

"Uncle Hank, let's go inside," I said. "We can finish our talk in the house."

He scanned the cul-de-sac as if someone were watching. He looked jittery and distracted, a wildness about him. Rather than walk inside he explained he couldn't stay long, he had to be somewhere but seemed eager to get some things off his chest. He recounted some facts about him and my father, ones I'd heard only bits and pieces. We revisited his version of memory lane saying he'd joined the Army immediately after my father had signed up for the Army Air Corps, a mere two weeks after Pearl Harbor. My father, age twenty-one, had some college experience and was taken into the Air Corps cadet program, entering pilot training. Uncle Hank, barely eighteen, became an infantry soldier, first fighting in Italy as a private, then in Patton's Third Army as a sergeant near the end of the war. My father was commissioned a second lieutenant and subsequently flew thirty-five harrowing missions over Germany in B-17s, first as a copilot before getting his own crew. Uncle Hank said he spent years agonizing over the disparity, always bitter in the shadow of his older brother. I asked him if my father ever made him feel inferior or was it just something he imagined. Both, he said. Then, out of respect, he corrected himself, admitting it was probably his imagination. There was a huge rivalry here, something I never fully understood. They'd grown up without a mother along with their older sister, Meta, having been raised by a tyrannical grandmother and an absentee father who drifted job to job in the work-scarce Depression. This much I knew. What I didn't know, as Uncle Hank filled in the details, was their mother had died in childbirth while delivering a baby boy who died three days later. His name was Russell. Hank looked at me wide-eyed, astonished I'd never heard this family detail. "We were a pair," he said. "We ran wild," always dodging both their older sister's and grandmother's efforts to corral them. They got picked up for shoplifting, for vandalism. They were threatened with reform school. In his teen years, my father took to riding the rails with some of his buddies leaving my uncle behind which, even now, clearly bothered him. "When he got back, he'd changed. Something happened out there. I never knew what. John came home a new man, a model citizen, alien to us all. He reentered high school, graduated a year later and left for California, never saying boo to me or anyone. We were a pair," repeated Uncle Hank, sadly. "I never understood what happened to him." Uncle Hank was grappling with his own issues. If we shared anything in our odd moment of grief, it was closure on two generations of family issues. I could tell Uncle Hank had carried some notion he'd eventually confront their fifteen-year estrangement and patch things up. I knew how he felt. I was on the cusp of driving all night to Coeur d'Alene myself. The sudden loss had thrown us both.

Inside the house, my mother held court regaling her guests with stories about how much of a saint, John, her husband had been despite their breakup. I wasn't about to stop her, but it rankled me to hear praise about a man who'd left her in the lurch five years ago. Some guests were neighbors that moved in after my father's departure having never met him. You could see troubled looks on their faces as she waxed nostalgic on their glorious marriage and the strong man that he was. It was classic Mother. I drifted slowly toward the kitchen to avoid having to corroborate her biased memories of John. Aimee was replenishing a cold-cut platter and chatting with another woman, someone I recognized but hadn't seen in many years. It was Cornelia Hagl, Klara's daughter-in-law, our longtime neighbor from one street over. We politely hugged and I asked about her children, Harold and Krystal. She confirmed what Klara had told us at Thanksgiving. Harold was working with his father at the Porsche Audi dealership and Krystal had moved north to Chico to start a family. This information was glossed over as I could tell she had something more to deliver. She asked about Klara's visit. "And I heard she told you about the war, about the bombings, my dear?" I nodded my head. I recalled Klara briefly recounting the horrid conditions near Hamburg before my mother had cut her off. "Well, I'm sure you've heard all about it, from your father, yes?" I told her I hadn't. She looked surprised as if I were being intentionally vague on the subject. "Oh, my. Someday you come visit us, you come talk to August." She added that August was working today otherwise he'd be here, and it was a shame he couldn't attend the funeral. The conversation lapsed, ending with another invitation to visit. Cornelia didn't wish to continue, nor did I, and I didn't feel like prying beyond her open invitation of offering information I'd likely heard before. I told Aimee to grab the kids and let's go. I was ready to head south to base.

During the drive down the 101, Aimee and I conversed very little. The events of the last five days had drained us and now Adak was staring me in the face. I was to depart in two days for what would only be a five-week detachment, the first week a casualty of my bereavement leave. The mood in the Suburban was somber – a combination of fatigue, sadness and lingering anger from our argument the night I got the call about my father's sudden death. Aimee was like that. She could forget about a fight or crossly spoken words in the face of a larger intrusion, such as a death in the family, and function as if things were peachy between us, then days later, she could reclaim her injured feelings as if no time had passed. She had been wonderful at the funeral and very supportive throughout the week, but I knew things could return to pre-funeral levels in an instant and even a heartfelt apology may not bring her back into my arms.

# 8

## ADAK, ALASKA

THE DRIVE FROM OUR QUARTERS to Base Operations the next morning took a brief three minutes and we rode in uncomfortable silence, the kind that precedes a long separation. Aimee had loaded up the kids like the good Navy wife at 0600 to take the short ride in our Suburban to see me off. Moffett Field Base Ops was located on the main side of the base near Hangar One, not the far side where crews normally departed. Our trip to Adak today came with a twist. The squadron P-3C we were scheduled to fly didn't make it home from Adak the day before with Crew 7 as it required an unplanned engine change. Since the squadron had no aircraft to spare, our ops officer, Lieutenant Commander Larsen, decided we'd ride up in the Air Force cargo plane with the replacement engine then Crew 7 would hitch a ride back on the same cargo plane. No one was happy with this arrangement except, of course, Crew 7. They were scheduled to rotate out and would've taken their chances on the *Hindenburg* if it meant departing Adak on time. I had hoped to get some added stick time along with my two pilots before beginning operations in Adak. Plus, no self-respecting naval aviator wanted to depend on the Air Force for a ride. We felt Air Force pilots were a bunch of weenies that couldn't find the latrine without a checklist. I was already imagining what rigid set of rules would be in force once airborne.

As we rounded the final curve toward Base Ops, the tiny two-story structure was dwarfed in the foreground by the huge C-5A Galaxy chocked behind it. The long, bulbous fuselage poked out well beyond the building and the insanely high T-tail rose nearly seven stories in the air, well above the roofline of its host. I was amazed the Air Force had sent a C-5 for this cargo errand given its astronomical cost of operation simply to transport a lone P-3 engine with a crew of twelve, and our bags. It was like sending the *Titanic* across Lake Tahoe with a single bag of mail. Even Sean was impressed and shrieked when he spotted the mammoth aircraft from the car. I had promised him a quick tour inside "the world's biggest airplane" to bribe him out of bed this morning and he was going to ensure I delivered.

We pulled into the parking lot and crossed the ramp toward our awaiting air taxi. I carried my two bags, one in hand, one on a strap, while little Sean walked beside me holding my free hand. Aimee carried Carlene in her arms. She'd finally awakened, thumb in mouth, and was also staring at this big machine filling the landscape in front of her. We approached members of my crew assembled under the wing as they gawked inside the massive intake of one of the four jet engines. The first to greet us was our assistant flight engineer, or second-mech as we called them, AD2 Roy Chavez. Both Aimee and Sean had met Chavez after we'd returned from deployment at an informal squadron welcome home party. Chavez wasted no time grabbing Sean's tiny hand and saying, "Let's take a look inside, buddy. You want to do that?" Sean said he did. The two of them eagerly ran toward the door two levels below the cockpit. You couldn't have kept Sean off that plane with an armed Marine guard blocking the entrance. More crew members arrived with their gear as Aimee and I made our way to greet Jamie and my two pilots – newly added 2P, Jim Abbott and my regular 3P, Wayne Horseman, aka, the Horse. Jamie was sitting on the tarmac with his duffle bag open, his foot shoved deep inside apparently trying to cram some extra reading material inside, magazines, paperbacks and the like. "There's a weight restriction on this flight, you know," I said, breaking the ice, giving him a startle.

"What? They never said—"

I grinned down at him.

"Oh. You're just kidding, right?"

"No. Look at that beast." I gestured with my arm. "It'll never get off the ground with all those extra Hustlers and Penthouses stuffed in your bag."

Jamie looked at me seriously, then at Aimee. "Those are *not* Penthouse magazines, Mitch. They're—" He stopped abruptly and stood up, withdrawing his flight boot from the bag. "Aimee, I don't know how you put up with this royal pain in the ass." He leaned forward and gave her a quick peck on the cheek. Jamie could be quite the charmer when he wanted to. He was single and adored Aimee, probably had a crush on her. I think Aimee sensed it too and felt it her duty to always be setting him up, to find him a future wife among the slim pool of female officers or attractive civilian employees on base.

"They're called training publications, big guy," Horse interjected. "Your porn, that is."

"For the last time, it's not porn," Jamie insisted. "They're part of my Scientific American collect— Oh, forget it. You guys are assholes. Excuse my language, Aimee."

"They are assholes," Aimee agreed, smiling before realizing her slip. She'd never met the two men standing next to me and had just implicated all three of us. "I'm sorry," she said. "Just this guy." She pointed her thumb in my direction and offered an embarrassed laugh.

"Aimee, this is Jim Abbott and Wayne Horseman, our two other pilots,"

I said, making quick introductions.

Aimee offered her hand. Each shook it before she turned to me and whispered, "What happened to Colby? Wasn't he your copilot?"

I motioned for her to walk with me. We strolled back toward Base Ops and I took Carlene from Aimee's arms to give her a break. Sean rejoined our side after his quick tour. "They moved Colby to Crew 5," I said.

"When did they do that? You never told me."

"It's no big deal, Aims. Really." I could tell she was agitated, either because they moved him or because I didn't tell her, maybe both.

"I thought he was taking over your crew. You said you and he would fly together until you left the squadron, that Colby was your guy and you trusted him."

"Yeah, well, he's got a chance at getting his own crew earlier with this move," I said. "It's good for him and better for his career." I was not so much toeing the Navy's party line as I was trying to convince Aimee everything would be okay with the change. She knew crew members weren't typically swapped so close to deployment.

"What's this new guy like? Jim? Do you trust him?"

"Of course," I lied. "He'll be fine. Don't worry."

"Well, I get worried, Mitch. It's my job. I've heard your stories about Adak before – mountain peaks everywhere, icy waters, crappy weather, crews always close to *buying the farm*, as you put it. Or were those just entertaining sea stories?"

"Just sea stories," I assured her. "Relax."

Aimee quieted and stared past the runway. I wished I'd steered her away from Jim and Wayne. Aimee was perceptive and could tell, like many in the squadron, that Jim was a rock, a zero, just by looking at him. There was just something drifty, non-engaging, in his eyes.

Her silence persisted.

"Aimee? I'm fine with the crew change, really."

"It's not so much that, Mitch."

What then? I thought. Is she still pissed about last week? I had yet to openly apologize. "So, what is it?"

"Look, I don't want to get into this now," she said. "You're leaving."

"No, tell me." I was trying my best to keep a level tone. "What's the problem?"

"Mitch, just leave it alone, please. This can wait."

"Aimee, c'mon."

She sighed. "Okay, just so you know, you wanted to hear this." Aimee took a moment. "You're just so distant and sullen. I know your father just died and I know you may think you're being cute with the guys back there, but I bear the brunt of your stress and hostility. I'm just not feeling real close to you right now. There's too much tension in the air."

119

"Of course, there's tension," I retorted. "I'm tense. I'm leaving on a five-week detachment that should've been four. Five weeks in a place that ain't exactly Club Med."

Aimee smiled at the Club Med remark and stared at her shoes. "Look, just take care of yourself up there, Mitch, and come home safe. Then you can jump to the airlines, maybe get a more normal life."

I gazed at the horizon and thought of my father and his "normal" life.

"That's what this is all about, right?" She was back-peddling. "Getting to the airlines. That's what you want?"

"How the hell should I know?" My tone was stiff. "All I want is to get through this deployment. You're always bugging me about the airlines. Is that because *you* want the airlines?"

Aimee took a step back. She was livid after my accusation and needed to withdraw. "I wasn't *bugging* you," she hissed. "I don't always *bug* you about the airlines. I won't bring it up again, I can promise you that." She jerked Carlene back from me in one quick move.

"Look, I'm sorry. Let's just get through this separation. Things will be fine when I get back. They'll be fine. I'm sorry."

Nothing from Aimee.

"C'mon, Aims, don't be that way."

Again, nothing.

"Okay, fine. Be that way." I gave her and Carlene a group hug as she stood rigid in my arms. I tried. I tried my best, I thought. I turned to leave and walked across the expansive ramp toward the jumbo cargo plane, picked up my bags and slung them through the door. When I turned around to look in Aimee's direction she and the kids had disappeared. Gone.

We had just gone feet wet somewhere north of Point Reyes on the California coast and were climbing through 30,000 feet on our way to Adak in my first flight on the legendary C-5. Since being released from our seats in the cargo bay shortly after takeoff, I found a secluded spot upstairs in the passenger deck and strapped on my Walkman with Tom Petty blasting at full volume in the tiny headphones. I wanted to be left alone and rid my mind of that awful sendoff. I was hurt. Distant and sullen? What the hell did she know about distant and sullen?

My crew of twelve was onboard, spread out over the aircraft. I figured both flight engineers, Wilhelm and Chavez, were up in the flight deck grilling our Air Force hosts on all the technical details about their machine. Horse might've been up there with them or searching for an AC outlet to plug in his electric amp and guitar. I knew Abbott wasn't up in the flight deck. The guy had about as much curiosity as a patient in the coma ward and was probably sleeping in the crew rest area. Hodges and Kennedy were holed up in the galley studying classic Soviet sub recognition signatures along with our

Sensor 3 operator, AW2 Gilbert Moss. I was impressed and proud of all three of them. Al Quigley, our NAVCOM, was several rows behind me spread out over five seats with pillow and blanket, reading one of Jamie's sci-fi novels. Jamie himself was writing in a journal, something he did every day like clockwork when we were on deployment. The guy was destined to make admiral, that was for certain, his journal notes someday enabling one hell of a memoir. I had no clue where our ordnanceman, AO2 Kevin Cox, or our in-flight tech, AT2 Dave Buchanan disappeared to but they were aboard somewhere. Our Air Force flight crew, derisively referred to as *Zoomies* by us Navy folk, didn't turn out to be the nerds I'd expected despite the aircraft commander, a lieutenant colonel named Dean Martin – no joke – delaying our departure for an hour while we waited for a full complement of box lunches. What is it with the Air Force and box lunches? I thought. To them, the aircraft is not mission capable unless the 402nd Box Lunch Recharge Squadron shows up in their catering truck with lights flashing to deliver the aircrew their meals. This morning they were parked on the Naval Air Station and Mr. Martin was so incensed that the Navy blew off his lunch request that he was going to hold up the whole show until they delivered as ordered. I mean, for a box lunch? Are you kidding me?

I was getting into the music. Petty was singing *Listen to Her Heart* in his stoner drawl, the swagger and jangling guitar helping to dissolve my dismal mood and lift the enveloping funk since takeoff. A vision of Aimee had intruded my thoughts, of her standing on the ramp with Carlene in her arms, her morose expression and downcast eyes. Petty's lyrics reminded me of how she'd been before I met her, somewhat untamed, an independent streak a mile wide, out with her girlfriends drinking margaritas and smoking cigarettes in the bars around Pensacola. Our separation was widening both physically and metaphorically as I lay paralyzed in the airline seat. I regretted leaving her standing on the tarmac, offering nothing more than, *Okay, be that way.* As I replayed the scene, I resolved I'd call her later, get to a payphone as soon as we landed. It was a spontaneous promise and would challenge me to avoid getting defensive if she picked up, a caution to choose my words wisely and apologize. That's when I felt something bounce off my forehead. My eyes shot open and there was Horse, standing over me gripping a football, an impish grin on his face. He reached down and lifted an earphone from my head. "Hey, get up," he said. "Let's go toss this thing around the cargo bay." He spun the football in his left palm.

I looked at him skeptically. "Don't you have something to do, something you need study?" Horse had a mountain of PQS to complete, his Personnel Qualification Standard, as he was our junior pilot still working on his qualification in the airplane. "Maybe curl up with your NATOPS manual?"

"Fuck NATOPS," he said. "We're talking football in an airplane at 30,000 feet. We'll never get a chance like this again. Let's go."

We descended the ladder into the cavernous cargo bay. The space was empty, completely unused except for our Allison T56 turboprop engine anchored down on its pallet near the front. There was plenty of room to toss a football. Before Horse threw me the first pass I marveled at the cleanliness and order of the big ship. Everything was exposed in the airframe around me – flight control wires, hydraulic lines, wire bundles – but it looked so precise and well-maintained. The cargo floor was shiny, and the aircraft had a new-car smell. This was not the case with the Navy-owned P-3s. Our squadron airplanes rolled off the Lockheed production line in 1968. They had fifteen years of hard use in both the cockpit and cabin. While the mechanical and electrical systems were in perfect working order, the seats, curtains, lav, galley and bunk areas were very tired, like pictures I'd seen of the Soviet-run Aeroflot Airlines interiors. VP-25 was scheduled to transition to the new P-3C Update III but that was a year in the future.

Horse started off with a short lateral pass but soon we were hurling the football in deep overhanded arcs. Horse was running post patterns and I'd hit him with the ball just before he crashed into a bulkhead. This was great fun and a welcome diversion from the stress that had been building over the last week. As the ball flew back and forth, I kept looking around for some Air Force crew member, the loadmaster perhaps, to enter the space and tell us something absurd akin to Doctor Strangelove. *Gentlemen, you can't play football in here, this is a cargo hold.*

Again, I marveled at the expense this engine delivery must be costing the taxpayers. The C-5 took off from Travis Air Force Base yesterday with minimum crew and took the 400-mile flight down to the Lockheed assembly plant in Burbank, California. They loaded up the shiny new engine and flew the short distance back to Moffett Field, parked on the transient line in front of Base Ops before shutting down for the night. And this morning, as we showed up, LTC Dean Martin – no joke – and his crew added the required fuel (and box lunches) and we took off for the five-plus hour flight to Adak. I had learned after talking to Martin the Air Force needed to burn some leftover training hours in the fiscal quarter thus providing additional justification for using the overkill delivery system. We'd arrive over Adak with just enough fuel and minimum cargo to make our alternate, Shemya Air Base, an even smaller outpost farther west in the Aleutian chain, in case of bad weather. These lighter-than-normal conditions would be necessary to make the landing in Adak on its 7,700-foot runway. It would also be necessary for the C-5 to have no cargo and minimum fuel to get airborne on the same medium-length runway tomorrow. Their aircraft would pop up like a cork in high seas but need nearly every foot to do it. C-5 pilots were used to having at least 10,000 feet of runway in front of them and the austere field landing and takeoff in Adak would be part of their agrarian training and indoctrination. Welcome to our world, Zoomies.

Horse and I were getting bolder, firing the football as high as possible, brushing the overhead and completing 20-yard passes to each other. Finally, and we should have seen this coming, an errant throw from Horse hit a large overhead light fixture knocking it from its mount. There was a momentary bright electrical arc followed by darkness in the front half of the bay, presumably when the circuit breaker popped in the cockpit. I quickly scooped up the football and looked around to see if anyone noticed. All quiet – just the two of us alone in the big space. I hid the football under my flight jacket, and we slinked upstairs to the passenger cabin laughing the entire way. Three hours later we touched down on Runway 23 at 1130 local time in undoubtedly the best weather I'd ever seen on the rock. Clear blue skies, no wind and a temperature hovering near 50 degrees. The weather hadn't been decent for long because I spotted patches of snow and ice near the taxiways with streaks of water bleeding into the median melting quickly under the mid-day sun.

We taxied to a stop on the ramp and our ever-efficient Air Force C-5 crew wasted no time getting the mammoth nose of the plane tilted in the air to begin offloading the humble cargo. Senior Chief Rich McKenna, our detachment's acting Maintenance Officer was there to greet us and sign for his precious engine, one he'd have his troops installing before the night was over on SE-05, the P-3 that we should have flown from Moffett in the first place. "Welcome to Adak, Mr. Baumann," he said. "Let my guys grab your crew's bags and throw 'em in the duty van. They'll take you up the hill to the BOQ." He lowered his voice and added, "And by the way, sir, I heard. Sorry for your loss."

"Thanks, Senior." I appreciated his condolences. "You think you could've ordered any nicer weather?" I said, gesturing at the sun and cobalt sky.

"A gift for you, sir. It's supposed to get nasty again tomorrow though, back to cold and fog. You know the drill." He grinned, wanting to spoil whatever hope I might've held that the balmy weather would continue.

Yeah, I knew the drill. NAS Adak's weather sucked. This was my fifth visit since coming to VP-25 and would likely be the longest at nearly six weeks. Counting this trip, I'd amassed over a hundred days in the Navy's version of Siberia. I looked northeast twenty miles across the sound at Great Sitkin Island, its snow-capped peak rising 6,000 feet straight from the sea. This majestic now-extinct volcano was a rare sight given today's brilliant weather conditions and I marveled at its distant beauty. The other great peaks of Adak stood out in sharp contrast against the clear sky, serving reminder of how close they were to the airfield and what was not visible during an actual instrument approach. While the white mountains surrounding the base were a breathtaking sight, the stark terrain underfoot remained an ugly moonscape virtually free of vegetation. Halfway across the island lay what they call the "Adak National Forest." On my first visit to the rock, I'd lost a twenty-dollar bet to a senior crew member who said there was a legitimate forest on the opposite side of the airfield. Bullshit, I'd said, and agreed to the wager. After a short ride on a dirt road leading through several muddy bogs, we came to a 400 square-foot patch of windblown Sitka spruce no higher than ten feet obviously trucked in and planted by some local Aleuts or long-gone U.S. servicemen. A sign was stuck in the ground that proclaimed, "You are now entering (and leaving) Adak National Forest." I'd been suckered and had no choice but to pay the bet. As far as I know, they are the *only* clump of trees clinging to life on this barren wasteland.

"Mandatory in-chop briefing at the ASWOC at 1500," said the Squadron Duty Officer, sticking his head into the van as we awaited transport up the hill to our quarters. The SDO was the 2P on Crew 6 and had arrived a week ahead of us. The briefing was expected, part one of a two-part re-indoctrination to NAS Adak, Third Fleet's most western frontier. The second part was an area familiarization flight for the pilots – multiple practice missed approaches, touch and gos and full-stop landings to all the runways on the field. Technically speaking, our squadron detachment was an asset under Third Fleet, but we'd also be working closely and occasionally serving under Commander Task Group 72, part of the Navy's Seventh Fleet based in Yokosuka, Japan. Due to the overlap, both commanders were adamant that their aircrews get fully briefed and refamiliarized with the strategically important mission and hazards of operating in this potentially lethal environment. No one was excused from the in-chop briefing or allowed to blow off the fam flight regardless of how many prior visits made to the rock. You either completed the evolutions or your crew was grounded until you did.

Horse and Abbott looked across at me in the van, Horse rolling his eyes. "Yes, it's mandatory for everyone on the crew, including 2Ps and 3Ps," I reminded them. Jamie was already at the ASWOC along with Al. We had their bags and flight gear in the van and would ensure they got their single room with twin beds at check-in. Junior officers were always two-to-a-room in the cramped VP wing of the Adak BOQ.

"Just make sure we don't get stuck in dumpster alley like last time," Horse said. "I couldn't study or sleep with those goddamn garbage trucks banging away all night. No privacy whatsoever."

I looked around and lowered my voice. "What he means is he had no privacy whatsoever to jerk off or blast that stupid guitar of his all hours of the night." I smiled and winked at Abbott getting nothing in return but his blank stare. Horse laughed and cursed at me, recognizing this was all part of the virile deployment banter and I was starting it early. The good-natured razzing was intended to keep us loose, but there was something about Abbott, something that unsettled us as our laughter subsided.

"Hey, you up for this?" I said, turning to Abbott in all seriousness, staring directly into his stoned expression.

"Up for what?"

"Are you kidding? *This*. Adak." I waved my arm around the van. "You ready to go fly?"

"Not really. But here I am."

I kept my eyes locked on Abbott and noticed Horse, behind him, grinning like an idiot and giving me the loco sign. I wasn't amused. Horse could appear resigned or laugh at Abbott's behavior, but I couldn't. I'd need to set aside some personal one-on-one time with this space cadet either later today or tomorrow.

After checking in and dropping off our gear I walked alone back down the hill to the flight line to meet Jamie. In my eagerness to celebrate the unseasonable weather I'd left my flight jacket back in the room and began to regret it. Low hanging clouds were scudding in from the west and a breeze had picked up, carrying a marked chill that wasn't present when we landed. The weather was deteriorating right before my eyes. Jamie met me at the entrance to the ASWOC, a set of ugly modular buildings lashed together next to the VP hangar. "Have you lost your mind, Mitch?" he said. "Walking down here in short-sleeve khakis like that? They're predicting snow flurries by 2100." He looked at his watch. "In about five hours."

"So? Is the briefing going to last five hours? I don't think so."

"Just don't expect to borrow my parka."

"Never crossed my mind," I said. "By the way, I got you and Al all checked in at the Q. You guys are together, I'm rooming with Horse."

"Horse?" Jamie said. It was typical for the PPC and 2P to room together leaving the junior 3P to fend for himself and find a roomie from another crew.

"Yeah. Abbott's new and he's so – you know, there's just something kinda fucked up about him."

"No kidding, Mitch. Why you ever let Colby get away is beyond me."

"I didn't *let* him get away," I said. "He was moved by Larsen."

"Yeah, whatever." Jamie lowered his voice and looked around. "I don't think our boy Mr. Abbott will be around too much longer, anyway. He's stepped in some deep do-do and his time is running out rather quickly."

"Yeah, I figure everyone in the squadron knows about him nearly flying into the side of Kauai."

Jamie shook his head. "No, that's not it," he said, still speaking softly. "Well, it's a part of it but—"

"But, what?" It wasn't like Jamie to backbite or to spread idle rumors. "You know something?"

"Look, Mitch, I'm sorry, I probably spoke too soon but my advice is to keep him out of the seat unless you absolutely need him. And when you do need him, make sure you're in the seat next to him, not Horse, okay?"

"Hey, don't give me that crap. If you know something, especially if it concerns safety of flight, I expect you to tell me."

"I'd love to, but I can't. He's safe, at least officially, according to the XO. I can't go into any details. Maybe later."

Jamie, in his role as legal officer, was privy to much of the bad-boy behavior within the squadron, both officer and enlisted. I understood there were things he couldn't tell me but now I was on edge. Abbott was my responsibility along with the rest of the crew and if he had a personal issue I should have been told. Nonetheless, I remained quiet and held the door open for Jamie as we entered the ASWOC for the briefing.

The bright sunlight made it difficult for my eyes to adjust as we passed security making our way into the dreary conference room. Even in my blinded condition I knew this place well, the pervasive odors of stale air and burnt coffee guiding me through the narrow corridors. The conference room itself was already packed with officers and enlisted ready to begin as Jamie and I grabbed the last couple of chairs against the wall. Ensign Chris Cook, our squadron Air Intelligence Officer, was standing in front of the group awaiting his petty officer assistant to bring up the situation map on the screen, a green stroke-character computer projection of the surrounding Aleutian chain with various targets of interest plotted and marked with ID tags. I scanned the room noting others in attendance. Lieutenant Commander Bill Olivares, the ASWOC Operations Officer was seated in the front row. A grave-looking female lieutenant who I didn't recognize from the Naval Facility (her ID badge declaring NAVFAC in bold letters on the lanyard around her neck and LT MOORE on the blue nametag over her right breast pocket) sat with her two male Operations Specialist Petty Officers, or OSs. My entire crew, less the flight engineers and ordnanceman, were present as well as the on-duty SDO and our intrepid detachment Officer-in-Charge and XO, Commander Fowler. I'd forgotten he'd taken over as OINC and his presence startled me as he walked in and took a seat next to LCDR Olivares. His eyes darted around the room before settling on me, giving me a shudder and causing me to look away.

Chris began. "Good afternoon, gentlemen. And ladies," he added, nodding politely at Miss NAVFAC. She returned his acknowledgment with a thin, fake smile. I knew Chris; he was not patronizing her. I also knew how she must've felt – one of only a handful of female officers on an island crawling with men. "ASW operations remain relatively quiet throughout the Pacific theater as of 0600 Zulu although we have five targets of interest I'd like to discuss, two having just been upgraded to high priority by CINCPAC. The first is Papa-63, a Soviet Echo-class transiting the La Perouse Strait north of Hokkaido. We've had good locating data from VP sorties flown out of Misawa. We believe he's transiting into the Sea of Japan, back to his homeport in Vladivostok." The second and third, Papa-20 and Papa-71 are Soviet Yankee SSBNs, located here in Eastpac, approximately 300 miles off the coast of California." Chris pointed at two green symbols in the middle of the black screen representing the vast Pacific Ocean. "It appears Papa-71 is -20's relief as we already see -20 heading off station." Sadly, this was all routine stuff, transiting Echos in Westpac with nuclear-tipped cruise missiles and Yankees relieving one another off the California coast, their ballistic missiles pointed at every major city in the western US. It was all part of the Cold War churn, Moscow and Washington holding each other in check. I'd been up since 0500 Moffett time and the warm conference room combined with Chris's droning voice made closing my eyes and dozing off very tempting.

"Excuse me, Chris." It was the NAVFAC lieutenant, "Are we tracking Papa-20 and -71 with VP assets or just SOSUS?" SOSUS was a highly classified network of hydrophone arrays spread throughout the ocean floor in strategic locations. The term stood for Sound Surveillance System and was first deployed by the Navy in the 1950s. It consisted of miles of sonar arrays attached to land-based listening posts run by the Naval Facility Command in both the Pacific and Atlantic theaters, including the station here in Adak.

"Just SOSUS right now, ma'am," said Chris, apparently not on a first-name basis with his counterpart up the hill. "We've had strong SOSUS AOPs throughout Papa-20's on-station period and Third Fleet didn't feel it necessary to burn flight hours just to confirm." AOP stood for Area of Probability, an ellipse generated from multiple intersecting SOSUS bearings.

"Where's the data coming from. Which stations?" she persisted.

"Mainly the Point Sur NAVFAC," said Chris. "But there's been confirmation from Coos Bay and spurious contact reported by Centerville Beach up near Eureka."

"So, no need to launch the P-3s?" It was more a statement than a question. Both the XO and LCDR Olivares's eyes had been bouncing back and forth during the two officers' exchange.

I knew where this was headed. The NAVFAC lieutenant was taking a moment to grandstand, to show everyone in the room how unnecessary P-3s were. A waste of money, gas and risked lives flying low and slow over the ocean when all you needed was a guy on dry land with a headset stuck over his ears to do basically the same thing. She'd just as soon see the arrogant P-3 aircrews and their boy-toy airplanes the hell off Adak and leave the serious submarine hunting to the NAVFAC.

"What's your point, Lieutenant?" It was our XO, Commander Fowler, taking her to task. I recognized that tone. He needed to grandstand a bit himself, more for his sake than ours.

"Sir?"

"What are you suggesting? No need to launch VP?"

127

"I'm sorry, sir," she said. "I was merely observing SOSUS monitoring alone seems to do the trick keeping tabs on the Yankee SSBNs on patrol."

"And what happens when your Yankee SSBN decides to launch its missiles, to start World War III? What then? The SOSUS arrays going to take him out?"

"No, sir. I was only saying—"

"You were only saying nothing. Tell me, who's going to launch a Mark 46 torpedo or drop a nuclear depth bomb when ordered by Third Fleet to stop them? The NAVFACs? And where the hell do you think all those acoustic sub signatures come from that enable you to locate and track these boats in the first place?"

Lieutenant Moore remained silent.

"I suggest in the future when you attend these briefings you sit attentively, take notes and keep your mouth shut. You only embarrass yourself and your command. You got that, honey?"

The room became deadly silent, the only sound from the projector fan whirring softly in the background. Moore was aghast. She stood up, grabbed the satchel next to her chair and strutted from the room without another word. Her two enlisted assistants weren't sure if they were to follow. As they watched their boss scurry out the door, they looked at each other quizzically, then stood and politely excused themselves. Part of me wanted to say, yay, score one for patrol aviation but it felt wrong. The silence in the room confirmed what we all knew. Fowler was way out of line pretending to protect our reputation as if it needed protecting, and he used his rank to intimidate the junior lieutenant. His gut reaction to bully someone, especially a woman, spoke volumes about his character.

"Go ahead, continue your briefing, Chris," said the XO, in a much gentler tone as if he'd just disposed of a pesky fly buzzing about the room.

"Aye, aye, sir," he responded, unable to look Fowler in the eye. "The two remaining targets of interest, and these are the ones upgraded to high priority by CINCPAC, are a Victor III SSN, designated Papa-72 and a Delta III SSBN, designated Papa-50. Last known contact with the Victor III was here," Chris pointed, "Two hundred miles south of the Komandorski Islands heading into open waters of the Pacific Ocean." He paused, apparently without sufficient information to continue. My intuition told me he was hoping this was where Lieutenant Moore would have spoken up offering a NAVFAC perspective, her main reason for being asked to attend today's briefing in the first place. Without her input, Chris simply continued to the other target. "The Delta III, just reacquired by SOSUS yesterday, departed Petropavlovsk on 12 March confirmed by satellite imagery and is headed into the Bering Sea 150 miles northwest of Shemya. We believe this is the same sub that participated in the ballistic missile test launch in the Sea of Okhotsk last month and is being shadowed by a Soviet trawler, a *Moma*-class AGI, the

*Aleksey Chirkov*, located here." Again, Chris pointed at the contact near the green computer polygons representing the Aleutian chain around Shemya.

This was noteworthy intelligence, and I suspected some relevant NAVFAC data were missing due to Dickless's needless chest-thumping. Operations in Adak would likely get hot again after weeks of quiet. Chris concluded his briefing by noting the aircraft carrier, the USS *Carl Vinson*, was south of Pearl Harbor transiting to Westpac with two *Spruance*-class destroyers, the *Ingersoll* and the *Paul F Foster*, to commence a six-month deployment. She was scheduled to enter the Seventh Fleet AOR in a few days and would pick up the rest of her escorts at that time, including the USS *Phoenix*, a *Los Angeles*-class nuclear attack submarine. I stood up to leave, eager to get out of the cramped space and into fresh air when the XO jumped out of his chair and got in my face. "Zero-five will be finished with its engine change during the mid-watch," he said. "They'll be doing the high-power run-ups at 0400. I want you rested and ready to fly the PMCF first thing in the morning. Check the flight schedule for your preflight time."

PMCF stood for Post Maintenance Check Flight and was performed with minimum crew – two pilots, one flight engineer and an observer in back. I was surprised he wanted me to conduct the flight as it would violate the standing order for all freshly arrived aircrews to first complete the required island familiarization. "What about the fam flight?" I said. "Aren't we supposed to do that first?"

He studied my face as if I were intentionally trying to undermine his decision, his order. "Always looking for an out aren't you, Baumann?"

"No, sir."

*"No, sir,"* he repeated, mocking me. "You let me worry about who flies the fam flights and who doesn't. I want your ass ready to launch in SE-05 tomorrow morning and land with a fully mission capable aircraft. Then we'll talk about fam flights. Copy?"

"Yes, sir."

Jamie and Al followed me out of the ASWOC having overheard my entire exchange with XO. "Man, what an A-hole," Al said, on our walk back to the BOQ.

"*A-hole?*" Jamie said, smiling like, what, are we still in the third grade?

"Yeah. As in A-Number-One Flaming Asshole."

"Oh, well, now that you clarify it."

Al wanted agreement, not sarcasm. He turned to me. "Mitch, don't you think?"

"Par for the course for ol' Dickless," I said, and let it go at that.

It was after 7 P.M. and dark when we met in the lobby of the BOQ to take the short walk up the hill to the Husky Club. Horse had talked us into having a little fun, of drowning our sorrows in beer to help forget our first night in purgatory. There was nothing going on at the BOQ, the restaurant and bar having closed at six per their usual "winter hours." And since the XO had penciled in his own name for the PMCF tomorrow fearing the wrath of Third Fleet, I was free to have a beer and agreed to Horse's plan. The Husky Club was officially for the enlisted ranks but was the only decent bar in Adak, so the brass looked the other way when crews of officers and enlisted mingled socially to blow off a little steam. The four of us, Horse, Jamie, Al and I, left Abbott back at the Q at his request. He said thanks but no thanks, he wasn't interested. "What a strange ranger that guy is," Al observed, as we departed. "What the hell's he doing in the Navy anyway?"

"Good question," said Horse. "The bigger question is how the hell did that nimrod end up on our crew?"

We were clustered in a tight pack in the middle of the road walking against a stiff, cold wind. From my hooded Navy-issue parka I could see snowflakes swirling in my tunnel vision illuminated by the low-hanging streetlamps. The late afternoon rain had turned to a mix of snow and sleet at sunset as the temperature plummeted below freezing creating an icy glaze on our path. Jamie glanced at me, a signal asking not to betray his trust regarding his earlier remarks about Abbott. "Great night for a walk," I said. "Whose idea was this, Horse?"

"Hey, you'll be thanking me after your first beer."

"Only if you're buying," I replied, shortly before plunging my foot into a slush-filled pothole, instantly soaking my shoe and sock. "Goddamn it." I was furious. "Fucking Adak weather."

Al laughed at my dripping leg. "Just another day in paradise," he said, chuckling.

Horse stopped dead in his tracks as though experiencing his first lucid thought in a fortnight. "You know," he began, "just the mere existence of Adak, this hell on Earth, allows paradise to exist elsewhere. Think about it. While we're here doing penance for man's sins on this godforsaken rock, others are sitting on warm beaches in Bali, enjoying unimaginable pleasures and communion with nature. It's God's cruel joke, the paradox within our universe, the yin and the yang, you know?

"Oh, yeah, Mr. Sunshine?" I said, shaking off my boot. "When did you get so fuckin' philosophical?"

"Hey, I'm just sayin'."

"Yeah, and so am I."

"Now, boys," Jamie said, intervening. "We're supposed to be having fun, right?"

We continued our trudge up the hill in silence and entered the hot, smoky atmosphere of the infamous Husky Club. The place was alive with music and packed with clusters of inebriated sailors wearing a typical variety of faded t-shirts and grubby jeans. We were lucky and spotted an unoccupied table on the officer side of this seedy, come-as-you-are dive. Jamie, Al and I seated ourselves on one of the benches while Horse made his way to the bar and ordered two large pitchers of Budweiser, presumably taking my earlier cue to buy. Decent of him, I thought, and wondered if he could also grab me a towel. I peeled my sock down and inspected my numb, frozen foot.

"Tsk, tsk," Al said. "I think you'll live."

"Appreciate your concern, dork."

"No charge."

As we waited for Horse to return, I noticed a familiar face sitting alone two tables over. It was Heather, Airman Ansley, from the coffee mess, now part of our Adak squadron detachment. I wondered how her new job in the Air Intelligence Office was working out. "Excuse me, guys, I need to go talk to someone," I said. "I'll be right back." I watched them exchange puzzled looks as I sat down across from Heather at her table.

Heather looked up, surprised, almost embarrassed, as if I'd caught her doing something wrong, which I had. There was a mixed drink in front of her and she was smoking a cigarette. "Mr. Baumann, uh, hello, sir. I heard your crew arrived today." She offered a weak smile. "Welcome to Adak."

It was none of my business, but something was clearly amiss, and I decided to call her on it. "Heather, what the hell?" I said, in a low, fatherly voice. "Last time we talked you'd just found out you were pregnant. Now, this?" I waved my arm in displeasure at her cigarette and alcohol. "You think this is a wise move in, what, your second trimester?"

"I lost it, sir."

The music was loud, but I was certain I'd heard her correctly. I just needed a moment to absorb the news. "Huh?"

"The baby, sir. I lost it." She brushed away an invisible tear. "About two weeks ago."

"Oh. Heather. I'm sorry." I knew I shouldn't have pried. This was certainly none of my business and I'd ventured too far. "Why are you even here? Wouldn't they want to send you home, maybe take some leave?"

"I'm scheduled to rotate out in a few days. Back to Moffett. Back to the coffee mess."

"The coffee mess?" I figured something must've gone wrong with her AIO job. "Can't you take emergency leave, go home? Get away from Moffett and the Navy? You really should."

"I appreciate your concern, sir, but I really can't go home. My parents never knew I was pregnant in the first place. And I don't feel the need to explain any of this to them now. Besides—" She stopped, intentionally.

"Besides, what?" It was a natural response. Still, I was concerned with what might follow. "Besides, what?" I repeated, over the loud music.

"Besides, it doesn't matter, sir. You really want me to go on?"

I nodded.

"Okay, I left home right after high school. My parents were awful. Couldn't get far enough away from them and their stupid rules. They never trusted me and said I had to start paying rent if I planned to stay. Well, they never expected me *not* to stay so I decided to give them a shock. Joined the Navy and blew town two days after graduation." She paused to wipe another tear. "And see how that turned out? Guess I showed them, huh?"

"You need to talk to them, Heather." A vision of Amber flashed in my mind. "You can't let this pass without letting them know about your situation. Think of it as an opportunity."

"Nope. I'm not going home. And I'm not telling them. No offense, sir, but do you know what it's like to be a woman? A woman trying to succeed in a male world while carrying all the burdens of a female?"

I smiled and stood. "Afraid you got me there." It was time to leave. "Take some time off, Heather. Go home. Talk to them." I thought of my father. "Before it's too late."

"Maybe..."

"I'm serious. Do it."

"I'll think about it, sir."

"Okay then." I turned and walked back to our table. Horse had just set down two huge pitchers of beer. I knew Heather wouldn't think about it. She was being nice. Another sailor girl, presumably waiting for me to leave, reseated herself in the chair across from Heather and they resumed their chat.

"Who's the chick?" Al said, who'd been leering at me the entire time from two tables over.

"Who's what chick?" Horse asked, innocently.

"The one over there. The one Mitch was hitting on." Al pointed his thumb in Heather's direction.

"I wasn't hitting on her, you jerk. I was talking to her."

Jamie, who'd been silent since sitting down, looked in the direction of Al's thumb. "Why that's our Airman Heather Ansley," he said. "Worked for Chris Cook in AIO office, coffee mess before that. Nice girl."

"So, you know her too?" I said to Jamie.

"Obviously not as well as you." This drew some sniggers from Al and Horse.

"Cut the crap," I said. "She just needed some – advice. Let's leave it at that."

"Sure, Mitch."

It wasn't long before the two pitchers were gone and the Horse, God bless him, was at the bar ordering, and paying for two more. When he returned to the table, he was carrying a pitcher in each hand and had two women with him. "What the hell has he done now?" I yelled into Jamie's ear over Derek and the Dominos' *Layla,* which was blasting from the sound system at a hundred decibels. People were beginning to dance.

"Gentlemen," Horse said, grinning broadly, "I present to you OS3 Robin MacHold and OS2 Kerry Sullivan. They work at the NAVFAC and you may call them Robin and Kerry."

"Bullshit we're calling them Robin and Kerry," I said to Horse, reminding him of certain officer-enlisted protocols despite the Husky Club's informal atmosphere. "No offense, ladies. We just need to keep it professional. But please, sit down and join us."

Horse's look said, yeah, keep it professional, like you and Heather over there. The girls sat down, and he filled their glasses with the first two pours from the pitcher. "So, Petty Officer Third Class MacHold, Petty Officer Second Class Sullivan," Horse said, mocking me. "We just arrived on the rock today. Dropped in to pay homage to the infamous Husky Club." He lifted his beer mug in the general direction of the bar.

"All right, Horse, I get it," I said. "Just keep the first names here at the table, not after we leave."

"Roger that, Cap'n. So, we just landed today and—"

"Ooh, did you guys come in on that big C-5 this morning?" Robin cut in.

"We did in fact, ma'am," Horse said, proudly. "Had us a little football game on the way up too."

"A football game?" Kerry said. "In an airplane?"

"It wasn't a football game," I said. "C'mon, Horse, get real. We were just playing a little catch." Hearing my lighter, more honest version still sounded amazing for an airplane in flight.

"I'd love to fly on one sometime," Robin said, continuing to eye Horse. "Maybe play a little catch myself."

I studied Robin and Kerry in their casual civilian attire. Both were attractive twenty-somethings, Robin in her early twenties, Kerry maybe pushing closer to thirty. Neither appeared engaged or married, no sign of rings. Kerry was clearly the dominant of the two personalities, but Robin had a youthful curiosity and did more of the talking – gushing, really. She gushed at Horse's boastful narratives, especially when he told of his expensive Rickenbacker electric guitar and how he sang and played lead at dozens of gigs back at Georgia Tech, his alma mater. According to his version, he was on his way to becoming a rock star before the Navy shanghaied him and took that option off the table.

"The Navy took nothing off the table, *Mister Axeman*," Jamie said, after hearing enough on the subject. "You joined up after completing two years of volunteer ROTC. You had no service obligation after graduation like Mitch and Al and me."

"Hey, I had to go out and earn a living too," Horse said, feigning hurt feelings.

"Oh, that's right, I keep forgetting. It's tough making ends meet on a rock star's salary."

The entire table broke up in laughter removing whatever tension may have been incurred by Jamie's challenge. Even Horse showed he was a good sport by laughing. I had to admire the guy. He had a sizable ego, as did all of us, and needed continual stroking, especially in social situations. And tonight, Robin and Kerry were brought in to fulfill that purpose, to listen to his sea stories with amusement and awe. Horse was fun to hang out with, a laugh a minute, but you had to take him in small doses and Jamie's recommended daily allowance of Horse ran lower than most. Jamie was correct in that Uncle Sam had paid for all four years of his education at Rensselaer Polytechnic Institute under a full ROTC scholarship. Al and I were given the same deal at the Naval Academy, thus upon graduation, all three of us owed the government a five-year minimum payback of active-duty service. Horse had taken the ROTC courses voluntarily and active duty was optional, a technicality that probably didn't need mentioning but Jamie cut no one slack once he grew bored or impatient with them.

At some point, Horse left our group, presumably to get more beer. The talk turned professional, of the upcoming ASW operations that would soon unfold out of Adak. Kerry lowered her voice, an indication that what she was about to say may be classified. "The tempo has been slow lately but that's going to change soon."

"Yeah, we got the in-chop briefing at the ASWOC this afternoon," I said. "That Victor III is headed back this way, right? Is that what you're tracking on SOSUS?"

"No. We never really had the Victor. It's the Delta that seems to have everyone's attention."

"A simple Delta III starting its patrol?" Jamie said. "What makes that so attention-grabbing?"

Kerry looked around and lowered her voice another notch. "It's not a simple Delta III. At least we don't believe it is." She turned to me, "Didn't you say you got the briefing today? Didn't Lieutenant Moore talk to you guys?"

Al spoke. "Umm, yeah. That didn't go so well."

"Huh?" Again, Kerry looked at me. "What'd you all do? Sleep through it?"

I remained silent, returning her gaze.

Robin nudged her under the table, reminding her she was addressing a group of officers. "Okay, strike that last remark. I'm sorry. Look, we really can't go into it here, but we suspect, and we need satellite to confirm, that Papa-50 is a new prototype Delta IV. They just test-launched a ballistic missile in the Sea of O a few weeks ago and we think it's armed with the new SS-N-23 Skiffs."

Al let out a respectful whistle.

"Yeah," Kerry said. "Improved 7,000 nautical mile range, four 100-

kiloton warheads—"

"Yeah, yeah," Jamie cut in. "Five-hundred-meter accuracy, hit any target in the US while parked in its own backyard," he said, finishing her sentence. "Still, it doesn't do anything our Trident boats don't do." Jamie was referring to the Trident intercontinental ballistic missiles our new Ohio-class submarines were beginning to deploy. It wasn't a case the Soviets would achieve a technological breakthrough with the Delta IV and its missiles, but they were certainly spending money at an alarming rate to gain parity. Maybe their classic "strength through numbers" strategy of more ships, more airplanes, more troops, was no longer cutting it.

I was starting to get a headache. It wasn't long before Horse reappeared at the table, this time with a cute Navy nurse on his arm. I recognized her from the dispensary, a perky anorexic blond always spouting the virtues of veganism when you came in with a sore throat or the flu. She assisted the flight surgeons, wrote prescriptions for minor ailments and was a bit of a flirt with the senior officers when they arrived for their appointments. She was now with Horse and showed no indication of being put off by his lower rank of junior grade lieutenant. I always marveled at Horse's ability to sniff out and lure what little talent existed in these forward deployment sites to rally around him. I was certain, as in Kadena, he was running his Creedence Clearwater bullshit again – one where he tells practically every woman in the bar he's John Fogerty, doing USO tours for the Navy. Horse's resemblance to Fogerty was eerie though. He had the split front teeth, wore flannel shirts, had his hair fashioned into a mop (pushing Navy grooming regs) and talked a good guitar story like he played Woodstock alongside the Grateful Dead and Janis Joplin. "Robin, Kerry, gentlemen," Horse said, gracing us with yet another female introduction, "This is, uh, Lieutenant Aubrey..." He careened his neck to read her nametag, "Mosko, Mosk-o-witz. Now that's gonna be a hard one to say by the shank of the evening."

Nurse Aubrey laughed at Horse's joke like it was the funniest thing she'd ever heard. "Hello, boys," she grinned, waving with one hand while sipping a mixed drink from a tiny straw with the other. Unlike most in the club, she was wearing her khaki uniform and an oversized flight jacket covered in squadron patches. Al and I nodded politely in her general direction. Kerry looked away and mumbled, "We've met," her stuck-up attitude conveying she didn't appreciate Aubrey's presence and perhaps felt a tug of competition.

There were now two pitchers of beer and a pitcher of margaritas on the table. I had no idea who was paying but the pitchers kept coming, apparently faster than we could finish them. Jamie hadn't been drinking much. He seemed distracted and was quick to spring from the table when he spotted LCDR Olivares walk through the door bundled up in his parka, the fur-lined hood still surrounding his face. Jamie threaded his way through the crowd to greet him at the door. They were friends, kindred spirits – both NFOs,

135

nerdy science freaks and closet Trekkies. Olivares remained at the entrance and I watched from a distance as they spoke, unable to hear a word. It was business, that was obvious, Olivares doing most of the talking, Jamie replying in swift, respectful nods. Suddenly my attention was broken when the margarita pitcher, half full, was knocked over, spilling its sticky contents all over the table, mostly in Al's direction.

"Goddamn it, Horse, you fuckin' derelict," Al roared.

"Hey, sorry about that, let me help clean it up," Horse said. He was laughing, carelessly tossing paper napkins around the table as ice chunks slid off the edge into Robin's lap.

"Why's he keep callin' you Horse?" Aubrey said, with a slur in her speech.

I shot Al a knowing glance. Al rolled his eyes. Horse really was running his Creedence bullshit. Jamie made his way back through the crowd and reseated himself next to me. He looked grim. "Drink up, boys. We gotta wrap up this party. They're launching the Ready 1 at 0400 tomorrow and we've got a preflight at 1200, launch at 16."

"The Delta?" I said.

"Looks like it. I've got to run. Gonna walk back down the hill with Lieutenant Commander O."

"You're leaving us now? Why?"

"Because we've only got another..." Jamie paused to look at his wristwatch, "Twenty minutes. It's almost midnight."

"Hey, I haven't seen any flight schedule with our names on it," I said, holding up my glass of beer. "I'm going to at least finish this."

"C'mon, Mitch, I just informed you." Jamie was referring to the Navy's twelve-hour "bottle to throttle" rule which prohibits consumption of alcohol twelve hours before a scheduled preflight. If we had a 1200 preflight, we'd need to knockoff the drinking, like he said, in twenty minutes.

"Yeah, yeah, we'll head down in a bit." I lowered my voice. "By the way, what else were you guys talking about over there?"

"Huh?"

"That was more than Olivares telling us we've got a preflight at noon. What gives?"

Jamie smiled. "Pretty perceptive for being half in the bag, Mitch. I'll grant you that." He turned for the door, aching to speak but unable. "Look, I still can't talk. I'll tell you tomorrow morning for sure."

I watched as he ran to catch up with LCDR O. I was being left out of something big and felt a knot of anger form in Jamie's wake. We elected to hang out until our midnight prohibition. Horse and Nurse Aubrey were speaking in hushed tones to one another and starting to make out. Kerry and Robin slid closer to Al and I, Kerry rolling her eyes at the lively couple at the other end of the table. I topped off everyone's glass with the last of the beer. "I knew it," Kerry said, looking very serious. "Third Fleet wants this guy bad. We don't have the best locating data, be a needle in a haystack, but I think they want the P-3s on him before he disappears into open ocean."

"Typical," I said. "Go out, drop a thousand buoys, zero contact. Show the flag to CINCPAC, make it look like we at least tried."

"Hey!" Al said, coming out of his alcoholic haze. "Fly with us. Tomorrow. You can help us find Ivan." He spoke it loud enough for Horse and Aubrey to stop their cozy activity two seats down.

"Brilliant idea, Al," Horse shouted back, pointing at Kerry and Robin. "Both of you. Fly out with us on station. Have a look at those sono-thingies in the back."

Robin looked hopeful. "I'm in," she said. "We're not on duty tomorrow. C'mon, Kerry, let's go fly."

Everyone turned to me. My thoughts raced to AW1 Hodges, our prima donna sensor 1 operator, and how his ego would take two girls from the NAVFAC staring over his shoulder for four hours in the cramped space. "Sure, why not?" I said, thinking of the XO's lack of diplomacy earlier. "An olive branch in the spirit of better NAVFAC – VP relations."

"Yeah, for ol' Dickless," Horse said, practically for the whole bar to hear. He and Aubrey rose, Horse helping her into her parka. After she'd slid her arm into the bulky jacket, he leaned down close to my ear. "Won't make it too late tonight, boss, I promise."

"Don't," I said. "We fly tomorrow."

"But on the other hand, I'm not going to blow this either. Got my mojo working. She thinks I'm Fogerty, you know?"

"Sure, Horse."

He turned to Aubrey and draped an arm around her narrow waist and steered her toward the door. Horse was so damned cocky, so obviously full of himself and so naïve to his own bullshit. Still, this was a guy you wanted on your crew. Given time, he would wise up and grow into a competent pilot and crew leader. You just needed to knock him off his pedestal from time to time, give him a reality check.

"Hey, Horse," I yelled, raising my glass as he departed with Nurse Aubrey.

He spun around, a drunken grin plastered on his face, the gap in his front teeth even more apparent.

"Keep on Chooglin'."

He nodded big, understanding the reference but not the obvious sarcasm.

Al and I said our goodbyes to Kerry and Robin a little past midnight, promising to meet at the ASWOC at noon, and headed back down the hill. A mixture of sleet and rain pelted us as we steadied ourselves on the slick roads. I entered our empty BOQ room and made sure to leave the door unlocked so Horse wouldn't wake me when he stumbled in. It had been a long day and I was certain tomorrow would be even longer. I fell face down on my rack dead tired, the room spinning, my last thought of Aimee and my unfulfilled promise to call her.

I awoke at 0700 to Horse snoring peacefully in his rack. He hadn't made a ruckus returning from his liaison with the senior officer and, thankfully, I'd heard nothing. Conversely, I wouldn't be able to razz him later about his probable post-dawn arrival. I slipped into my flight suit and parka, tiptoed from the room, and headed to the hangar to meet Jamie. Last night's sleet had ended, and the roads were relatively dry but a low, gray overcast hung over the island restricting visibility to the hangar building and surrounding apron. The flight line was busy with activity, the XO's crew pre-flighting SE-05 for its PMCF and a VP-46 airplane turning its engines, readying for its operational flight. When did they get in? I wondered. VP-46 was another squadron based at Moffett Field and had apparently launched one of their aircraft to Adak to lend support in the upcoming ops on the Delta.

"Morning, Mitch," Jamie greeted me, as I stepped into the duty office. "Let's take a walk upstairs to the conference room." We were dressed in identical flight gear except for his blue VP-25 ballcap partly concealing a bird's nest of blond hair. He appeared to have had less sleep than me, holding his Styrofoam cup of steaming coffee in his hand. "Care to grab some joe first?"

I swung my nose in the direction of the urn which contained coffee made sometime last week. "Think I'll pass."

Jamie took a sip from his cup and promptly dumped it in the trashcan. "Blech, I hear you." He pointed at the door leading to the stairs. "Follow me."

The squadron conference room was cold and damp. It was set up like a 1950s classroom with a dozen rickety desk-chair combos and a large portable blackboard that had been rolled off to the side. Despite the passageway being empty, Jamie closed the door behind us and we each settled into a desk. I spun mine to face him. "So," I began, "What's been so worth hiding, secret agent man?"

Jamie tightened his lips.

"What the hell's going on, Jamie?" I was nervous. The suspense he'd created was killing me.

"Yeah, I understand your reaction, Mitch, and I feel awful for not being able to say anything sooner but until now this has been super confidential, between me and the skipper. I just briefed the XO last night."

"Briefed him about what?"

"Abbott's gone. Busted. He's headed back to Moffett this morning with VP-91."

"Busted?"

"Yeah, he's a doper, Mitch. Popped positive twice on his whiz quiz for THC."

"What?" I paused to absorb the news. "I'll be a— I *knew* there was something screwed up about the guy. Marijuana, huh?" This was bad. Unlike the enlisted ranks where first-time drug offenders were usually dealt a reduction in rank, restriction, or both, officers were immediately separated from the Navy and given a less-than-honorable discharge. Poor Abbott would never fly again or get a decent job in the civilian world. "What do you mean, twice?"

"Yeah, it's part of the complicated chain of custody with officers. When the DAPA office provided the weekly results and Abbott's name came up positive, we had to wait two weeks to get another urine sample. The second specimen is handled with more eyes, more scrutiny and if also comes back positive, legal action is taken. That's what I've been doing in my spare time these last two weeks, preparing Abbott's court-martial while we waited for the second test to come back. What a friggin' nightmare of paperwork."

"So, you say he's going home today, on the VP-91 bird?"

"Yep. Read him his rights myself in front of the base master-at-arms around 0100 this morning, moved to his own room in the Q until he can pack his bags."

I felt bad for Abbott, but I was also overjoyed. He was gone before he could become my problem, before he could fly us into any mountains. But there was a new problem. "If he's packing his bags, who's unpacking their bags?"

"Huh?"

"Jamie, Abbott's gone. You just said so. Who's flying as 2P on our mission today?"

"Ah, Mitch," Jamie said, grinning. "I'm glad you asked. Open the door and check the passageway."

"Suspense right till the end, eh, partner?" My first thought was the XO. He'd be filling in as the PPC on our flight, relegating me to 2P. *2P on my own crew.* Jamie's grin disarmed me. The XO would not be the surprise waiting in the hall if there *was* someone in the hall. I stood up and yanked the conference room door open, wanting to be the one to give the surprise. "Colby?" I was stunned. "Holy shit! When did you get in?"

"Yeah, some prick must've pulled some strings," he said, smiling back at me in full flight gear. "Been up here once already, served my time. But here we go again. Crew 4, back for more. Isn't that our motto?"

I reached out and embraced him in a bear hug. "Welcome to Adak, buddy. Again."

Twenty minutes later we were enjoying a hearty bacon and eggs breakfast in the officer's mess of the BOQ. It was fantastic seeing Colby again, and a huge surprise, him popping in virtually out of nowhere. I was still getting used to his presence at the table as we spent the morning catching up on squadron gossip and our upcoming flight. At 1130, we walked down the hill, entered the ASWOC's security door and were met by Jamie in the briefing area, the same room as yesterday. Standing behind Jamie in the shadows were Kerry and Robin, both dressed in ill-fitting flight suits presumably borrowed at the last minute from the VP-25 pararigger shop. Jamie stepped forward shooing us back into the passageway away from Kerry and Robin. He didn't look happy. "Mitch, what the hell?" he whispered. "What were you thinking?"

"I don't know, Jamie. Thinking about what?" I was growing tired of his drama.

"About inviting two women on an operational flight. You can't do that. Especially in the PARPRO system on a high-pri Soviet Delta."

I knew he was partially right but inviting the girls seemed like such a good idea last night. "Hey, women fly on our airplanes all the time," I said.

"Yeah, on training missions and reposition flights, not on real-world Soviet targets. You at least need a letter from the Wing giving them special permission."

I looked at my watch. "Well, no time for that now is there?"

"No, there sure isn't."

"C'mon, Jamie, they're qualified ASW experts. They can help us."

He gave a resigned shrug and turned away to take his seat in the briefing room. "Okay, Mitch, whatever. You're the boss."

Robin stepped forward after watching our exchange. She looked oddly attractive in her baggy flight suit and pinned-up hair. "Is there a problem?" she said, genuinely concerned for her and Kerry. "Are we not allowed to come?"

"Nah, you're good," I said. "However, as a precaution why don't you and Petty Officer Sullivan wait in the squadron duty office. We'll come get you when we get closer to our planeside briefing time."

The two women made their way to the door clearly sensing something amiss.

"Who're the girls?" Colby said, innocently, as they departed.

"Two NAVFAC OSs. Met them last night at the Husky Club and invited them along. It was Horse's idea."

"And you said yes."

"Sure, why not? I believe they can truly help. What's wrong with that?"

"Oh, nothing. Jamie's just watching out for you. Probably hanging on a technicality.

Colby and I took our seats behind Jamie. We were joined by Al and Horse and our three sensor operators at two minutes past 1200, Horse looking like he'd just dragged himself from his rack.

Chris Cook entered the room and took center stage. "Gentlemen, let's begin," he said, addressing our small group without his usual small talk. He was bleary-eyed, having been up since midnight, giving his fourth aircrew briefing in a row. "This briefing is classified secret. Your event is Alpha Kilo 44-83, call sign Lima Echo 440. You're the fourth of four scheduled sorties on Papa-50, a Soviet Type III nuclear submarine, suspected Delta IV prototype, now commencing its patrol in the Bering Sea 300 miles northwest of Shemya. Our best locating data is…" Chris's format was rote. He was making it sound like every other brief, very canned, very routine. But when he got to the phrase "Delta IV prototype" everyone sat up in their chairs. Jamie was scribbling away on his pad. So, Kerry was right, I thought. Now I felt better allowing the women to tag along, better able to justify their presence if pressed. Chris continued deeper into his briefing. "You will enter the PARPRO boundary using rough-cut Juliet as your airspace at time 0400 Zulu…" I took a deep breath to absorb the gravity of his last sentence. This was going to be a tough mission, one of the most challenging a VP crew is tasked with. Not only were we being asked to locate and track a very high-priority Soviet sub with sketchy locating data and no previous acoustic intel, but we were going to have to do it in the tricky PARPRO system right in the Soviet's backyard. PARPRO stood for Peacetime Aerial Reconnaissance Program and was designed to provide positive radar surveillance in a large block of oceanic airspace in close proximity to the Soviet Union, in this case within twenty miles east of the Kamchatka Peninsula. We'd be monitored and controlled by a branch of the Fifth Air Force known as Sky King. Sky King coded messages would be transmitted over HF radio warning us if we strayed too close to the Soviet landmass or if we were about to be intercepted by a pair of MIGs out of Petropavlovsk. It would be Al's responsibility to maintain very precise navigation and listen closely for any Sky King messages transmitted in the blind over the noisy HF radios and my responsibility as PPC and mission commander to comply with all the PARPRO contingency procedures. And there were plenty. The entire evolution from takeoff to landing would be tricky, leaving very little room for error by any crew member. Chris concluded his briefing reminding us of our wheels-up time of no later than 1600 local. At this point, LCDR Olivares got up to the front of the room to speak. "Sensor operators, you're excused for your separate acoustic intelligence brief on the TOI. Officers, please remain seated." This was an unusual twist. Normally, when Chris finished, we pilots were dismissed to begin the aircraft preflight.

LCDR O walked over and locked the door, his dramatic gesture giving him our full attention. "Gentlemen, this part of the briefing is classified top-secret," he said. "As you know, you are the final VP event on Papa-50. You should be given hot contact by VP-91 at your on-station time and are to track and record as many CPAs as possible, gaining the best possible acoustic intel on the target. At off-station time of 0800 Zulu, or thereabout, it is anticipated you will pass contact to—" He paused to make eye contact, reaffirming he had everyone's attention. "This is the top-secret part. You will pass contact to the USS *Phoenix*, the fast attack submarine that broke off from the *Vinson* battlegroup two days ago specifically for this target. You are to transmit contact reports via secure teletype on Papa-50's position, course and speed every fifteen minutes during your last hour on station to guide the *Phoenix* and aid in the handoff. Third Fleet's goal is to put her in trail of Papa-50 for the duration of what we believe is a post-shakedown patrol. I want to make it very clear, you are neither permitted to discuss the *Phoenix's* mission with your sensor operators nor acknowledge her presence should they observe the sub's signature on their grams during your on-station period. Is that clear?"

Nods from everyone.

"Okay, that concludes the top-secret portion of the briefing. Are there any questions?"

Colby leaned over to whisper in my ear. "How come we can't tell Hodges and Kennedy?" he said. "Seems wise to warn them they might see a second subsurface contact, don't you think?"

"They don't have a TS clearance," I whispered back. "Or the need to know. US sub positions while operational are classified top-secret."

"Yeah, but Hodges is gonna be the first person on the airplane *to* know."

"Look, I'll give him a heads-up when we get out of here. Officially we can't say anything. O is just doing his job."

"Oh." Colby smiled, catching my drift that this was just another onerous Navy reg designed to protect the overall success of a mission rather than enable it and that we'd work around it.

# 9

## FINAL FLIGHT

THREE HOURS LATER COLBY AND I were seated in the cockpit of SE 05 reviewing last-minute on-station weather reports and preparing for the pre-start engine checklist. But before we could start engines, we had to gather as a crew for the final planeside briefing at the rear of the aircraft near the galley.

Horse stuck his head in the cockpit. "Just finished fueling, buoys loaded. Jamie said to tell you the Arm-Ord test looked good. External preflight complete, Mitch. Buttoned up, ready to go."

"Good, good." I eyeballed my 3P closely. "How you feeling, Horse?"

"What do you mean?" he said with a smile. "I feel great. Four-point-fucking-oh, as a matter of fact."

"Mighty glad to hear it because you look like shit," I said. "Spread the word, planeside in fifteen minutes, at 1530. And tell Willy to come up here when he gets a chance."

"Roger that, boss." He turned and was gone.

"You want Willy to cue up his tape for planeside, right?" Colby said.

Colby was referring to Chief Wilhelm's cassette recorder he had wired into the interphone system from his flight engineer station. He used it to pipe music over the ICS during the on-station period and would conclude our preflight by playing John Lennon's *Nobody Told Me*, our crew theme song, over the PA system to announce it was time to gather for planeside. "No music yet," I said. "I want to ask him what he made of the maintenance write-ups after the number four engine change."

"Oh, I can tell you that," Colby responded. "Seems they had a little difficulty last night."

"I'll say."

"Willy says everything checks out though, that Maintenance was able to get it signed off."

"Colby, there were five friggin' pages of footnotes on the MAF. I couldn't even read some of the scribbling."

"Yeah, the replacement engine Lockheed shipped up here was brand-new and required all the latest mods to the propeller gearbox before they could mate it."

"And let me guess, the prop didn't have them?"

"Nope. Senior Chief McKenna and the Lockheed tech rep spent half the night on the phone with Ham Standard in Connecticut reviewing the description of every mod letter on the prop and gearbox to ensure they were either compliant or needed a waiver."

"Waiver?"

"Some of the mods weren't applicable. They just needed to hear it from Ham Standard after careful review over the phone."

This news concerned me, but I trusted Chief McKenna. He would not sign off on anything that wasn't kosher. "How'd the PMCF go?" I asked.

"Well, as you know, the XO flew it. Took her up for ten minutes, turned around and declared fully mission capable on the post-flight."

"Ten minutes?" I was pissed. "He was up for only ten minutes? I take it he did no inflight shutdown or restart to test number four?"

"Not sure. Don't know how he could have though given the flight time. You want me to call Maintenance and have them ask?"

I could just envision that scenario. *Hello, XO, sir? Lieutenant Baumann wants to know if you did your job and conducted a proper and thorough post-maintenance check flight on SE 05.* I didn't feel like another confrontation with Dickless, either before or after our flight. I just wanted to avoid him altogether. "No, forget it," I said, tossing my checklist onto the glare shield. "Let's get back for the planeside." I gave Colby a final appraisal in his copilot seat. He looked tired, distracted. "You okay? You get enough rest on the plane ride up?"

"Oh, yeah, sure," he said, after a beat. "I'm fine."

"Well, I'm glad you're up here. But if you ask me, man, I'd say you got screwed having to come back to Adak a second time. You served your sentence in January."

"I volunteered to come back," he said.

"Volunteered? Have you lost your mind?"

"I had to get out of Moffett. Things were too tense at home. Linda and me."

"Linda?" I was afraid to continue but Colby was too close a friend to let it drop. "You guys doing all right?"

"Not really," he said, which was an understatement. "We agreed to a separation, probably a divorce. At this point, volunteering to get out of Dodge was the best thing for both of us."

His news stung and once again a flash of Aimee greeted me from yesterday's goodbye. This was Navy life for you, always providing the most perfect subterfuge to wreck a marriage. "The separation been hard for her?" I wanted to tread lightly, fearing more bad news.

"She cheated on me, Mitch." He turned to face me in his seat. "Not once, but twice," he deadpanned. "The first time was in May when we were in Westpac. She actually confessed when we got back."

"She admitted to an affair? Out of the blue?"

"Yeah, very matter of fact, like it was my fault for being gone. Like she couldn't help herself, could no longer cope, or some such bullshit. I wanted to take the news in stride, you know, for the sake of the kids and the marriage. Her open confession implied she was willing to share the blame, but she wanted me to admit my faults too, that no one is perfect. Rather than get into it, I recommended counseling."

"What'd she say?"

"Oh, she agreed, wholeheartedly. Wanted us to go as a group, in fact."

"A group?"

Colby hesitated. He wanted to continue but was choking up, or perhaps starting to get angry. "This guy she cheated with – it wasn't their first time. They'd been seeing each other before I left for Japan. So, she agrees to counseling and says, 'Only if Beau can come. If you want to do this, I need Beau there too.'"

"Beau?"

"Yeah. Can you believe that shit? Like, oh, sure, let's do a three-way – me, my husband and the guy I cheated with." Colby paused, quickly touching his eye with an index finger. "Needless to say, it didn't happen, but my mistake was to sweep it under the rug, forgive her and pretend the affair never happened since I was back from deployment."

"But when you were in Adak—"

"Yeah, she and Beau. Again," he said, completing my sentence. "Caught 'em red-handed this time."

"Colbs, man," I said in a soft, consoling voice. "I'm sorry. Is there anything I can do?" The offer for help sounded lame but was the best I could do sitting alone with him in the noisy cockpit five minutes before our planeside and grueling eight-hour mission.

"Yeah," he replied, looking me dead in the eye. "Do yourself a favor, Mitch. Always call your wife before you decide to just show up a day early from Adak and surprise her."

At 1525, the crew, along with Kerry and Robin, began assembling in the aft section of the aircraft next to the main cabin door. This is the area where the ordnanceman and IFT sit during flight and is the most spacious zone on the P-3 with ample room to gather twelve crewmen and additional passengers. Since the P-3's introduction, crews have preferred this inside venue for the planeside brief, out of the elements, the last evolution before taxi and takeoff. As I made my way down the aisle from the flight station, Wilhelm's cassette tape of *Nobody Told Me* started blasting from the PA speakers throughout the cabin signaling us to start gathering. We adopted the tune as our crew theme song on deployment when Al heard it in a bar one night in Kadena. The lyrics were perfect, a fitting testimony to the bizarre ironies of Navy life. Lennon was singing from the overhead speaker, *Nobody told me*, repeating over and over, issuing a warning there'd be days like these.

Robin and Kerry were enjoying the song, singing along, its relevance obviously not lost on them. Lennon soon wrapped up and Wilhelm appeared, sliding the cassette tape into the breast pocket of his flight suit. "And there will be more music available on ICS Conference 2 throughout our flight," he said, to the entire group.

"You mean you guys listen to music on headset during the mission?" Kerry said.

"Only if you want to," Al replied. "It's on a separate ICS channel."

"That's so cool, just like United Airlines," Robin added.

"Yeah, except United Airlines doesn't play Johnny Cash and Marty Robbins over and over ad nauseam," Al said before turning to Chief Wilhelm. "Willy, if I hear *El Paso* one more time, I swear I'm gonna shove that goddamn tape down the freefall chute."

"Okay, okay, knock it off," I said. "Leave poor Willy's tapes out of this." I cleared my throat and scanned the crew huddled closely in our flight suits, heavy boots, all strapped into our LPAs, eyes locked on me, ready to go. Horse and Colby were standing close to one another. Despite Horse's marginal rest and Colby's marital distraction, they looked alert and eager to begin the flight. I also appreciated Al's earlier razzing of Wilhelm. It was solely intended for the crew's benefit, to keep the camaraderie alive, no malice toward Willy whatsoever. "Good afternoon, all," I began. "I will take a few minutes to provide the safety overview for today's flight then Lieutenant Morgan will review the tactical situation on station. First, a warm Red Fox welcome to Petty Officers Sullivan and MacHold." I quickly eyeballed Hodges, our Sensor 1, for a reaction and observed nothing but a blank stare so I continued. "They join us from the NAVFAC and are here to observe, however, if you girls care to lend a hand with any of your knowledge on the target of interest, I'm sure Petty Officer Hodges will be glad to oblige." Again, no reaction from Hodges. "Just a reminder, we'll be flying in the PARPRO system this evening. I'll let the TACCO, Lieutenant Morgan, provide more information when I finish. Our call sign for this flight is Lima Echo 440. Weather on-station will be bumpy at certain altitudes but not too bad. We're behind a stationary front stalled over Shemya and temperatures will be cooler than seasonal with icing possible down to the deck. Weather back in Adak for landing is not so great, forecasting 500 feet overcast, 5,000 broken, visibility one-half mile with possible fog and ice from 0400 Zulu, so we could be in for possible divert." I paused to ensure everyone was still paying attention. "Okay, emergency procedures are per NATOPS." I quickly ran through the litany of crew actions in case of fire, ditching or bailout, which was a mandatory part of the brief. "Are there any questions?" There were none. Everyone had heard it a thousand times.

It was Jamie's turn. "Okay, as Lieutenant Baumann said, we'll be flying in the PARPRO system for this mission in a block of airspace just east of the Kamchatka peninsula. We are required to monitor the HF HICOM frequencies in both the cockpit and cabin. Al will monitor at the Nav station and I expect whoever is in the right seat up front to also monitor. Please stay coordinated and alert for any Sky King messages transmitted in the blind, be prepared to copy any coded messages that begin with, 'Sky King, Sky King, do not answer.' These messages will alert us to the status of the airspace and any special instructions or actions we'll need to take in the event of straying off course or of an interception by a Soviet MIG. Copy them down verbatim in both the cockpit and nav station. Is that clear?" Jamie looked around the group, all serious faces, a few nods. "Okay, if all goes to plan, our mission today is to take hot contact on Papa-50, a Soviet Delta IV SSBN, from a VP-91 crew that arrived on-station…" Jamie looked at his wristwatch. "About two hours ago. Hopefully, they'll hang onto him, turn over hot and give us smooth sailing for the four hours to follow."

"Did you get an update from the ASWOC on the VP-46 event?" I asked. VP-46 was our sister squadron in Moffett, the Gray Knights. They were the second event now inbound back to Adak.

"Yes, the -46 crew reported hot contact when they departed an hour ago, which is really amazing given the time-lateness of the locating data. Hopefully, -91 will hold on to him."

"Yay. Score one for the *Gay* Knights," Horse chimed in. Muffled laughter rippled through the crew.

"Okay, that completes the tactical situation. Mitch, do you want Cox or Buchanan to instruct the ladies on their ditching stations and how to use one of the parachutes?"

"Hmm, oh yeah, forgot about that. Buck, show our guests how to don their chutes and where they'll sit for take-off and landing."

"Roger, boss."

Robin gave Kerry a wide-eyed look. "Parachutes? Nobody said anything about parachutes."

It was time to prepare for departure. We all came together for a final group high-five, bouncing off each other's chests like we'd won the Super Bowl, another silly but morale-building ritual formed during deployment. After the little dance, we split up and headed to our respective stations, everyone energized to pull together and overcome all the usual setbacks that would no doubt challenge us on-station. I was more concerned with the forecast weather slated for our arrival back in Adak.

The engine start and taxi from our parking spot on the ramp to takeoff position proceeded normally. I glanced at my watch from the right seat as

147

we pulled to a stop facing the active runway. Five minutes to four, right on time. As the mission commander, it was my responsibility to meet our PARPRO wheels-up time of 1600 local plus or minus ten minutes. Anything later would have to be reported up the chain to the Fifth Air Force, bringing shame upon the crew, the squadron, the Wing and the CO. Colby was in the left seat, making the takeoff. It was my intention to be in the left seat for the landing upon our return given the possibility of a divert to Anchorage if Adak was below minimums. Shooting the approach at night in bad weather would be hazardous. The landing would be mine even though it was Horse's turn.

*"Lima Echo 440, taxi, position and hold, runway five,"* came the call from the tower.

"Position and hold, runway five, 440," I replied. "Colby," I said, facing him across the center console, "When Willy sets takeoff power, I want you to remain on the brakes until I tell you to release. I want to watch number four as it spools up."

Colby nodded.

The second call from the tower came a minute later. *"Lima Echo 440, Adak Tower, wind calm, clear for takeoff, runway five."*

"Flight Engineer, set takeoff power," Colby said, looking straight ahead, keeping his eyes out the windscreen.

Chief Wilhelm advanced all four power levers in a smooth, rapid push forward. Our P-3C, loaded to max gross take-off weight of nearly 135,000 pounds, squatted forward as the nose strut compressed from the straining of the four spinning turboprops, aching to begin its roll down the runway and take flight. All our eyes focused on the number four engine instrument column. Colby stood on the brakes as directed, holding the big aircraft stationary on the runway numbers.

"Number four shaft horsepower, turbine inlet temperature coming up nicely. RPM holding steady at a hundred percent," reported Wilhelm over the din in the cockpit. "Looks good, sir."

"Just a tad longer, Colby," I said, waiting until everything felt right, until all four engines were spooled and instruments synced. One final scan. "Okay, release the brakes. Let's go."

Colby tapped the top of the rudder pedals and we were immediately pushed back into our seats feeling the surge of four engines at max power and the thrust from the four big propellers. "Eighty knots," I said, monitoring the airspeed during our take-off roll. All four engines remained normal as we approached our decision speed. "Refusal," I called out at 120 knots, meaning we were now committed to flight regardless of engine anomaly or failure. We continued accelerating down the runway, with approximately 2,000 feet remaining. At 130 knots, I called, "Rotate." With both hands, Colby pulled back on the yoke, gently raising the nose, lifting us from the runway at a fifteen-degree angle toward our assigned altitude.

"Gear up," called Colby. "Set Condition Four." We were underway and climbing.

Condition Four was an after-takeoff aircraft check conducted by the TACCO while the rest of the crew remained strapped in. Jamie would make a quick walk through the cabin inspecting the avionics racks, hydraulics bay and main electrical load center for any sign of trouble that might necessitate a quick return to base. Afterward, Condition Three would be set, allowing removal of our LPAs and free movement around the cabin. It was shortly after Condition Three was set that I pushed back from the right seat and allowed Horse to take my place. I wanted to be fresh when we arrived on station in two hours and headed to the bunk near the galley. Sleep was probably out of the question, but I could at least shed some of the fatigue that had dogged me since our preflight briefing at the ASWOC. Making my way back past the acoustic sensor station I bumped into Kerry and Robin as they emerged from their takeoff positions, two windowless floor seats wedged between the memory units of aircraft's mission computer.

"Excuse us, sir," Robin spoke, in a frustrated tone seeming to say she was sorry she'd come. "Oh, and thanks again for bringing us on the flight. We'll try to stay out of the way,"

"Nonsense," I said. "You're along to help. I expect you to pitch in once we've got contact and are tracking."

Kerry spoke up. "Are we even supposed to be here?" she asked, rather pointedly. "I mean, didn't Lieutenant Morgan say this was a tactical flight and passengers weren't allowed?"

"Who said you're passengers? Consider yourself aircrew for this flight, here as observers in an official capacity." This was stretching things a bit, I knew, and I'd certainly be on thin ice if questioned from above about designating them aircrew. But they truly could help our cause, especially if we ended up tracking both a Soviet and U.S. sub later in the mission. However, I knew if we hadn't been in the Husky Club drinking heavily last night, no chance they'd be aboard with us tonight.

"What are we supposed to do? I can tell your Sensor 1 operator doesn't want us anywhere near his gear once we're on station," Kerry said.

"That's not true," I replied. "Did he tell you that?" I knew Hodges. He didn't have to say a word. His projected arrogance and cold stare at planeside spoke volumes. These gals weren't blind.

"Not in so many words, sir."

"Well, there you have it. If he doesn't let you near the acoustic recordings on his grams you find me and I'll have a talk with him. In the meantime, cheer up. We're going to make history tonight." I winked at them and continued back to my bunk, climbed up and shut my eyes trying to ignore the card game already in progress between Kennedy, Buchanan and Cox at the galley table below me. They were killing time, like me, knowing we were in a lull, the calm before the storm, until we arrived on station.

It wasn't difficult finding a comfortable position lying on my back despite wearing my bulky flight jacket and thick boots. The cabin air being sucked aft was cold and dry and I fought the urge to shiver. I had a headset on playing Wilhelm's music on ICS to drown out the heavy ambient noise. Thankfully, he'd chosen a Creedence tape from Horse's collection and Fogerty was belting out *Run Through the Jungle*, a rather haunting tune, in his raspy tenor voice. I found my mind wandering back to the conversation with Colby during preflight when we sat alone in the cockpit. His news about separating from his wife and her infidelity disturbed me more than I realized. Oh, I knew all about the deployment infidelities, on both sides, but it hadn't hit so close to home until now. Aimee and I knew Linda. She seemed stable and normal, not someone to cheat then threaten to drag both husband and boyfriend into the same counseling session, for crying out loud. What a train wreck. Colby's predicament sickened me, but I felt strangely buoyed by his confession, his confidence to relate such personal heartbreak. This is where men struggled, I thought, in these unguarded human moments, blinking only for an instant to succumb to vulnerability and check the ego. We, too, could have weepy chick moments. I was pained by Colby's struggle and impressed with his ability to push through it. There was really no other choice.

Time passed slowly. At some point, I must've dozed off because a new song transitioned in my headset and I had no recollection of the previous one. As I lay pondering how far we might be from on-station, there was a noticeable surge of power added to all four engines without an associated sense of climbing, which would have been normal. We should be pulling back power and starting our descent, I thought, not the other way around. I jumped from the rack and quickly threaded my way forward. In the cockpit, Chief Wilhelm had his NATOPS manual opened to Part 5, the cross-hatched Emergency Procedures section, using his flashlight to illuminate the page in the semi-darkness of fading twilight.

"This can't be good," I said, announcing my presence. "What've we got, Willy?"

Chavez, our second mech, was sitting on the radar console directly behind Colby. "We had an intermittent prop pump light on number four, sir," he said. "Willy's checking it out."

Colby turned his head around from the left seat. Horse was at the controls from the right. "Ah, Mitch. Glad you're here. I was just about to call you," he said. "Yeah, one of the prop pump lights on four came on a few minutes ago."

I looked directly at the warning lights atop the number four engine column, all black, no prop pump light. "And—"

"And, first thing NATOPS says is to increase true airspeed so Willy pushed all four engines up to 10-10 and it cleared."

"It cleared? You do an indicator light check?"

Chief Wilhelm turned around in his middle seat to face me. "Yes, sir. I even replaced the bulb just to be sure. Checks four-oh." He continued reading aloud from the propeller section in NATOPS. "If RPM is stabilized at less than 100 percent and advancement of the power levers causes—"

"Yeah, yeah, I know what it says. Did anyone check out the window for visible prop fluid leaking around the spinner?"

Horse was sitting on the right side closest to the number four engine. "We hit it with the spotlight. Hard to tell, but I didn't see anything."

"Willy, you think we're pitch-locked?" Pitch-lock was a built-in safety mechanism to the prop that, upon prop fluid loss, would lock the variable-pitch blades to prevent an overspeed and a potential runaway propeller.

"No, sir. We've had zero RPM flux. Rock steady at 100 percent the entire flight. And no noticeable vibration. Haven't had to touch the Sync Servo or Sync Master switches either."

"Okay, so, steady RPM, no vibration, no visible prop fluid leak around the engine and the prop pump light is now out, bulb checks good," I recounted. "That about cover it?"

Horse and Colby nodded in unison.

"Willy?"

"I think we're good, sir. NATOPS says to continue operation."

"Okay, I concur," I said, making the decision as the PPC. "We continue."

A minute later the computer display in the cockpit showed us capturing the top-of-descent waypoint indicating we'd reached our on-station ingress point. Colby spoke into his headset mic and turned back in his seat. "Mitch, Nav says we're here. You want to switch now before we start the descent?"

"Yeah, let's swap," I said, eager to get back in the seat.

Horse decoupled the autopilot and put us into a manual 3,000-foot-per-minute descent to 8,000 feet, our assigned relief altitude with the off-going VP-91 aircraft. Chavez also took the opportunity to spell Wilhelm in the flight engineer seat. I'd barely finished strapping in when Jamie was squawking in my headset. "Flight, TACCO," he said.

"Go ahead."

"Bad news, Mitch. We're talking to the -91 crew on Nestor right now." Nestor was a secure-voice UHF radio link. "They lost contact on the Delta about two hours ago. They're turning over cold to us."

"You're kidding me, cold contact?" I was outraged. "Fucking reservists." VP-91 was a Navy Reserve squadron out of Moffett Field staffed purely with "weekend warrior" aircrews, men that flew maybe once or twice a month, and rarely, if ever, on such a high-priority target as our Delta IV. Olivares must've been in a bind placing them in the rotation. "The Gay Knights should've had a second bird up here instead of these guys."

"Now, Mitch, take it easy on them. They're claiming the water went to dog shit down there, median detection ranges from nearly four miles down to half a mile. Sub went through a vicious current anomaly and began changing course. Anyway, if it's true, no one would've hung on to him."

I drew a deep breath. "So, what's the plan, Stan?"

"We start from scratch. I'm setting up a 16-buoy distro field right now around their last contact buoy. Standby, I'll have a fly-to-point to the first drop on your screen in a minute."

"Roger that." Now that we were leveled at 10,000 feet, I told Horse and Chavez to standby to loiter the number one engine. Loitering meant to shut down one of our four engines on-station to conserve fuel. It was a common practice used by all aircrews on long missions except in cases of icing or bad weather. We ran through the engine shut down checklist which included pulling the e-handle and feathering the propeller, leaving the blades at a 90-degree angle to create the least drag while idle.

"Feather button light out, prop correctly positioned, sir," Chavez called, ending the checklist. We were now a three-engine airplane with considerably increased range. Under certain circumstances, crews would loiter a second engine, the number four, to conserve even more fuel. I was considering that option once our gross weight decreased should we be given direction by the ASWOC to "PLE." PLE meant to remain on-station to our "Prudent Limit of Endurance" rather than depart at the scheduled off-time. PLE was a likely scenario this evening given our mission setback with the VP-91 crew losing contact. "Prudent" was a weasel word though. It provided an escape for the watch officer back on dry land who gave the order to remain on-station to the max limit. It exonerated him in the event the crew ended up not having enough fuel to divert, or worse, ended up going swimming because they messed up their fuel management in a valiant attempt to salvage the mission. Our 16-buoy search pattern had been in the water no more than twenty minutes when Petty Officer Sullivan came up to the cockpit and tapped me on the shoulder. "Hey, Sully, how's it going so far? Pretty good, I hope."

"Sir, nobody calls me Sully," she said, rather curtly. "Sully was my father's nickname."

"Okay, I take it back. Sorry." She was clearly displeased about something more than my name slip. "How're things back there?"

"Well, that's what I came to talk about." She lowered her voice and moved closer to my ear. "Once our search pattern was fully deployed, I offered some helpful advice to Hodges."

"Good, good. And—"

"I told him to set up one of his search bands around the 247-hertz line. It's not one of the TOI's briefed frequencies but a weak secondary I'd noticed when we had him on our SOSUS grams a few days ago."

"And let me guess, he wasn't very enthusiastic?"

"He told me he didn't need help from some skirt about how to run his gear."

"He said that?" I had to keep from smiling. That was exactly something Hodges would say.

"Yes, sir, he did." She appeared on the verge of tears. "Look, I don't want to seem like a schoolgirl tattling on the class bully but—"

"No, no. It's fine. When I get out of the seat, I'll have a talk with him." I turned to Chavez, "In the meantime, I want to put number four in the bag. Are we light enough to loiter four yet?"

Chavez looked at our fuel totalizer, pulled out a laminated graph and did a quick calculation with his finger. "Yes, sir. We're about 10K under. Should be good."

"Okay, standby engine shutdown checklist on number four." I made a PA announcement over the interphone to Cox in the back of the plane. "Petty Officer Cox, I need you in your aft observer seat. We're loitering four."

Instantly Jamie was blabbing in my headset. "You really want to do that, Flight?"

"Of course, I do. What do you mean?"

"Well, Third Fleet policy doesn't permit us to loiter two engines."

"C'mon, Jamie, we loitered two all the time in Kadena."

"That was when we were under Seventh Fleet. CTG 72 policy permits two-engine operation above 2,000 feet. Third Fleet and Wing 10 do not."

"When did you get so picky on this stuff?" I said. "You need us to depart station on time, got a hot date back home?" I was kidding him.

There was a noticeable pause before Jamie's cool response. "Mitch, I'm just quoting the Wing 10 Op Order, providing you guidance, that's all. Obviously, it's your decision."

"I thought you'd be pleased. I'm buying us more time to find this guy, put the *Phoenix* in trail, make us all heroes."

No response. Either Jamie was interrupted by something on his scope or using silence to show disagreement with my plan. No matter, it was my call. I turned to Chavez and read the first item on the shutdown checklist. With that, the loiter proceeded normally and within a minute we were flying on just the two inboard engines, increasing our ability to remain on-station by at least an hour past scheduled off-time.

Another minute went by when Wilhelm, resting in the aft bunk, reentered the cockpit and touched my shoulder from behind. "Did we just loiter number four, sir?"

As if he couldn't see all the warning lights lit up atop the number four engine column. I turned my head. "Yes, we did, Einstein." He was second-guessing me too. "Something wrong?"

"Well, we did have that prop pump light earlier."

"And you and Lieutenant Reed cleared it." I was annoyed, anticipating

153

this was his point. "I thought we agreed, NATOPS said to continue operation."

"Yeah, but not to shut it down later. *Sir.*"

"Goddamn it, Willy, you weren't here," I snapped. "It was my decision and I made it. We'll just have to deal with any consequences later." His observation regarding the prop pump light was valid but came too little, too late. Jamie's badgering earlier was also on my mind. I wanted to dissuade further discussion and was thankful when Petty Officer Moss, our non-acoustic sensor operator, interrupted on ICS.

"Flight, Sensor 3, I believe I've got an ESM fix on that Soviet AGI, sir. That surface ship we were briefed on earlier?"

"You mean the *Alex Jerkoff*?" Horse chimed in, laughing, directing his comment at Al.

"That would be the *Aleksey Chirkov*," Jamie corrected. "Where is he, Three? Can you send me the fix?"

"Coming up now," Moss said. "Do we want to do a run-in, get a look at him? IRDS is operational." IRDS was our Inferred Detection System, basically a camera mounted in the nose of the aircraft with a video monitor at the Sensor 3 station allowing visual identification of a surface contact under the blanket of night.

"How far?" I asked.

"About seventy miles, Flight," Jamie replied. "Might as well ID him. Nothing going on here, pattern's cold."

I thought about our fuel situation and the need to go below 2,000 feet to RIG the ship. We'd need to restart number four and do a lot of unnecessary maneuvering just to get a single pass on him. "Forget it," I said. "He's well beyond our buoy RF horizon. Not a requirement to run in on him, right, TACCO?"

"Not yet. Be good to get a course and speed on him though."

Jamie was thinking the same as me. It would be valuable to know where he was headed since we were not permitted to sweep him with our radar to develop a track. The main concern with these Soviet AGIs loitering in the area was their ability to receive and record our buoy pattern, same as we do from the aircraft. We didn't want the Russians to know we'd located their precious submarine. And we certainly didn't want them recording *our* sub, the *Phoenix*, as it also passed near one of the hydrophones in trail. The operation order required a mission abort if an AGI was within twenty nautical miles of the contact buoy. "Let's bag it, Jamie. I want the crew focused on getting the Delta back."

Double-click of his mic. I was happy he decided not to second-guess me this time. I needed to get out of the seat and talk to Hodges. I'd promised Sullivan. And I needed to do it in private, off ICS. Part of me was pissed for his treating our NAVFAC guests like a macho shithead but part of me also understood the verve and confidence he possessed when running his station. He was a superstar amongst his peers and I felt the need to let him behave like one. Whatever I said to him would need to be handled very diplomatically lest we lose any opportunity for the girls to help us reacquire the target. I climbed out of the left seat, letting Colby slide back in and stopped at the TACCO station directly aft of the cockpit. "Anything yet?" I asked Jamie.

He pushed his headset off his right ear. "Nope. We're thirty minutes in, all buoys in the pattern cold. I'm open to suggestions, even from the bus drivers up front," he grinned.

"Actually, I do have a suggestion," I said. "And don't look so surprised. Did Petty Officer Sullivan talk to you earlier?"

"No."

"She said she asked Hodges to set up one of his searches around the 247-hertz line and he told her to buzz off."

"The 247-hertz line isn't a briefed freq, Mitch. He knows that."

"Yeah, but she said the NAVFAC noticed it as a weak secondary, that it is definitely the TOI. Wouldn't it make sense to take a peek at that part of the spectrum every now and then?"

"Certainly, it would." Jamie stroked his chin twice as an idea formed. "Go back there and tell Kennedy to set up around the 247-hertz line on his waterfall. Don't make a big deal of it though. Just walk around to his side of the station and quietly tell him your plan. Let Hodges keep doing what he's doing. If he notices, tough shit, you'll be forced to pull rank on him, but hopefully it won't come to that."

I knew Hodges would notice any instructions to Kennedy, as soon as I gave them. He was no fool and I was surprised Jamie thought it might work. Instead, I approached Hodges directly and motioned for him to lift one side of his headset. He obliged, dividing his attention between me and the thermal grams in front of him. I knelt low and spoke in whispers. "I need to tell you what happened at our briefing this afternoon at the ASWOC after you were dismissed. It's regarding the top-secret portion of our mission."

I had his full attention now.

"This is to remain solely between us. No one else. Do you understand?"

"Yes, sir."

I went on to explain about the *Phoenix*, that we were to hand over contact of the Delta IV to her and emphasized the position and presence of the *Phoenix* were top-secret.

Hodges smiled, apparently pleased to be privy to such highly classified information. "This is all great, sir, but we're presently cold. Sixteen buoys in the water with nothing. I suggest we punch out a BT buoy, update the environmentals and move our search eastward." East was the last known course. "Until we find Ivan, we can't help the *Phoenix*."

"I'll discuss it with Lieutenant Morgan. In the meantime, you know how imperative it is we find this guy, right?"

"Yes, sir."

"That we exhaust every possible option?"

"Yes, sir."

"That you're open to every possible suggestion?"

"Yes, sir."

I was leading the horse to water and he knew it. "All right then, I want you to set up your gear to also look for that 247-Hertz line. Let's find this guy." I patted both sensor operators on the shoulders before making my way aft toward the galley where Kerry and Robin were seated, talking in whispers, an uninviting expression on Kerry's face.

"Well?" Kerry said, eying me skeptically.

"Well. Hodges says he's very sorry. He feels badly things got off to such a rough start."

Robin let out a quick laugh.

"Cut the crap, sir," Kerry said. "I mean, I'm a pretty good judge of character. You're going to have to do better than that."

"Better than what? Look, all I know is Hodges has been reenergized. Says he's made some poor decisions lately, but his work is back to normal. He now has the utmost enthusiasm for the mission." I said this with a smile, paraphrasing the computer HAL from *2001, A Space Odyssey*. "He'd rather face shut down than fail to achieve the mission objectives."

Robin began singing, *"Daisy. Daisy,"* in a deep-voiced, sagging tempo. *"Give me your answer, do."* I joined in, matching her pace, *"I'm half-crazy, all for the love of you."*

"Good one, MacHold," I said, giving her a high-five. The moment of levity provided a good chance for escape. I spun around and moved up the aisle to Jamie's station, laughing to myself. The more I thought about these girls, the more intrigued I became, stirring my sense of imagination. Robin seemed simple, uncomplicated, yet surprisingly quick with her well-timed humor. Kerry was more mysterious and serious-minded, a tougher read. I tried to envision where she went, what she did in her off-duty hours on such a desolate naval outpost as Adak.

"What's so funny?" Jamie said, tossing his headset onto the console and massaging his neck. "I could use a laugh about now."

"One of our girls wants to pull the plug on Hodges. Thinks he's jeopardizing the mission."

"What?"

"Don't worry," I said. "I talked to both he and Kennedy."

"Oh, that. Turns out that was completely unnecessary. I should have known better."

"What are you talking about?"

"Hodges took her suggestion, Mitch. Long before you walked back there. Been centered around the 247-hertz line since our pattern hit the water."

"Then why'd he insult her?"

He ignored the question, rolling his trackball, distracted by a pop-up on his screen. "Did you tell Hodges about the *Phoenix*?"

"What?" Either Jamie was a mind reader or Hodges flat out betrayed our confidence only minutes after I'd warned him not to. "Yeah, I told him what's going on." I maintained eye contact. "It's a stupid requirement, Jamie. How are we going to know if we complete our mission unless he detects the sub on his gear and tells us? For Christ's sake, you or I won't see it on those grams."

"We're not supposed to see it. We're just supposed to record it. Then pretend it never happened. I wish you hadn't said anything to him about this. It could make things difficult later on."

"Later on? What do you mean, later on?" I sensed Jamie's concern if Hodges blabbed but was surprised he called me on it.

"Nothing, nothing. Look, let's just reacquire the Delta. We can bury a lot of missteps if we find this guy and hand him to the bubbleheads, let them chase him all over creation."

I left Jamie alone and headed to the cockpit. Bury a lot of missteps? I thought, shaking my head at his ominous reference. So, I made some command decisions tonight, maybe not exactly as others might do, but always in the best interest of the mission, right? I tapped Horse on the back, indicating for him to get out of the seat and get some rest. I no sooner strapped in and adjusted my headset when I overheard Hodges on ICS. "TACCO, Sensor 1, I think we've got him, sir."

The bored interphone chatter ceased immediately as we began the difficult dance confirming we had the target, which we did, and then localizing him to develop an accurate track, culminating in the kill, or in this case, the handover to the USS *Phoenix*. I took the aircraft down to 2,000 feet, a better altitude to accurately deploy our tracking buoys while Jamie began setting up five-buoy wedge-shaped attack barriers, one after another. The sub maintained a steady easterly course at four knots for most of the on-station period, allowing the tracking exercise to settle down and become almost routine. I stress *almost*. The initial urgency and panic on ICS slowed but the problem was becoming buoy management. Jamie had deployed the wedges very close together, gaining fantastic acoustic intelligence on the target but using the DIFARs at an alarming rate, running us into a shortage before the scheduled handover time with the *Phoenix*. Still, it was textbook ASW, just like flying in the WST – the sim back at Moffett. The crew was being taxed, working feverishly to hang on to him while further refining position, course and speed but everything was under control. We were a team again firing on all cylinders.

Al spoke up. "Flight, Nav. You were right. We just got a PLE message over the VP broadcast. It says to remain on station at least until 0700 Zulu, sending contact information on the Delta every fifteen minutes commencing immediately."

"Can we make it to 0700 Z, Flight?" Jamie asked, "and still have enough fuel for our alternate?"

"Of course, we can. We've got two engines in the bag. We can stay out here all night if we have to." The PLE message meant the *Phoenix* was farther from the Delta's position than Third Fleet anticipated based on our initial contact report, requiring us to push our scheduled departure until a handover could be verified. "You have enough buoys to last until 0700Z?"

"It'll be tight. I need to go back to dropping one at a time in a loose track until we put the Phoe-, uh, until later, praying he doesn't change course or speed." Jamie's stutter was involuntary and I'm sure Hodges recognized it. And, I'm sure Jamie was cursing me under his breath *knowing* Hodges recognized it. Quit worrying about it, I thought. Focus ahead, not in the rearview.

Two hours and seventy-five buoys later we achieved what we'd set out to do – we were at PLE and had hung onto the Delta with barely enough buoys and fuel remaining to continue. However, according to Jamie, off ICS, we still had no sign of the *Phoenix*. The proper and secure method of performing a VP to SSN handover of a Soviet sub is to keep track of the target at 500-yard intervals, sending contact positions in the blind until scheduled off-station time. If no updated tasking comes from Third Fleet via the VP broadcast, it is assumed the US sub has positioned itself in trail and you depart station on time, trusting your acoustic recordings will yield both US and Soviet subs during post-mission analysis at the ASWOC. Since we were ordered to PLE, I wanted some evidence we had the *Phoenix* on our grams and she was in trail before we pulled up stakes and left. Jamie did too but wouldn't admit it. I needed to have a little caucus in the back of the cabin with him and Hodges. "Colby," I said, leaning across the center console, "I'm going to jump out of the seat, just for a minute. Don't worry about getting Horse up here."

"Sure, Mitch. We're at 2,000 feet though. Don't be gone too long, otherwise—"

"Yeah, yeah. Hang on." I hopped around Wilhelm, who'd relieved Chavez minutes ago, and met Jamie, seated at his station. "Call Hodges up here, now," I said. He understood my urgency and made the call to Hodges on ICS. Within seconds Hodges appeared and we were in conference at the TACCO station, speaking quietly. "Okay, between the three of us, we know about the *Phoenix* and her mission," I began. "No need to sidestep that any longer. And here's the situation: we've got about ten more minutes of fuel before we hit PLE, we're out of DIFAR buoys and we have no indication of a second sub on the grams. That about summarize it?" I was ready to continue, expecting no replies when Hodges spoke up.

"Sir, we're recording the *Phoenix* right now," he said, very calmly.

"*What?*" Jamie and I yelled, in unison.

"Why didn't you say something?" I continued.

"I didn't think I was supposed to." His pained look said, isn't that right, sir?

Jamie jumped out of his seat and ran back to the sensor station with Hodges and me closely on his heels. "Show me, where is she?" Jamie demanded, pointing at the thermal paper scrolling slowly along on Hodges' gear.

"Right here."

"Right *where?*" Jamie said. "I don't know what I'm looking at."

"Right next to my annotation. Right here," he said as if talking to two school children on a field trip. "And here's Ivan, over here." Hodges closely traced the paper with his index finger, following two narrow fuzzy-gray lines centered around the primary tracking frequency of each sub. "Coming in for a nice CPA on buoy 12, right now. Notice the subtle frequency shift from the Doppler effect?"

"Nice," Jamie said, finally smiling. "Okay, I see it now. That's the CPA, the line shift, correct?"

Both looked at me, hoping to see a similar display of awe. "I don't see a thing," I said, staring at a gibberish of lines of varying length and intensity and scribbles of annotation in Hodges's handwriting. "But if you say so." Despite not understanding the data before me, I wasn't going to dull the moment by not savoring the fragile success we'd just achieved. We'd done it. We'd taken cold contact on a high-priority Soviet target and converted it to a 300-yard CPA and put a US nuclear attack sub in trail. We were heroes. Yet, by the same token, there was a sense of uneasiness among us, a projected concern from Jamie that we'd sidestepped a security directive and shouldn't be entitled to celebrate in front of the crew. A silence hung in the air. The hell with it, I thought. I high-fived Jamie then turned to Hodges, repeated the gesture while patting Kennedy's shoulder as he turned in his seat. Both Robin and Kerry, who'd been hanging back since witnessing the significant event on the grams saw our joy and tenuously moved in for a closer look. I eagerly pointed at Hodges's scribbling, pretending I understood it, and thanked them profusely for their help before running back up to the cockpit remembering I'd promised Colby I'd only be gone for a minute. I shooed Horse out of the left seat, who'd stepped in at Colby's insistence not knowing how long I'd be gone. After I'd buckled in, Colby asked, "Everything okay back there? We get her done?"

It occurred to me that Colby and Horse, and the remaining crew, were likely in the dark about the recent event occurring at the sensor station, bringing our mission to a close. I pressed the PA button on the ICS panel and cued my mic. "Attention, all. Just a word as we prepare to head off-station and begin the two-hour transit. First off, congratulations and thank you to everyone, including our guests, Petty Officers Sullivan and MacHold." I knew both Robin and Kerry would appreciate being acknowledged, having worked diligently alongside Hodges and Kennedy since we'd reacquired the Delta. "We've completed everything we were tasked by Third Fleet to accomplish tonight and I appreciate everyone's contribution. It was a total crew effort. As we head back, please ensure all your tapes, logs and transcripts are completed and ready for debrief upon landing. You can bet this one's going to get some heavy scrutiny." I paused to emphasize my sincerity. "Thanks again to all. And, one final item, aft observer, please standby on the starboard side for restart of the number four engine. Two minutes."

"Flight, Nav." It was Al. "I just copied the latest VP broadcast. They must know we're off-station. Says the weather for landing in Adak has gone to shit. Ceiling below 200 feet, quarter-mile vis in fog and freezing rain. Says to make contingency for Elmendorf in event of a missed approach. Oh, and reminding us that Shemya is closed due to runway repair, do not consider as an alternate."

"Roger. Thanks, Al. We'll get a weather update from ATC when we pick up our clearance in a bit." I leaned over to Colby. "We'll take one good shot at Adak but a night in Anchorage looks to be in our future." Elmendorf Air Force Base, with its 10,000-foot runway, sat on the outskirts of Anchorage and was an additional three hours from our primary destination. "By the way, did you see anything in the NOTAMs about Shemya being down for repairs?"

"No."

"Did you *check* the NOTAMs?" It was the 2P's duty to review the NOTAMs during preflight.

"Of course, I checked, Mitch," he said rather defensively. "And I didn't see anything about Shemya."

I knew Colby wouldn't lie but I also knew something as significant as a runway closure would be a glaring entry on any NOTAMs printout. He'd clearly missed it. Colby had a long transit flight with VP-91 from Moffett to Adak this morning and was battling personal issues at home. I knew he was not functioning at a hundred percent and would have to count on his experience in the right seat as we set up for the black-hole approach going into Adak. My mind was also on how much icing we'd sustained on-station. The weather had been mostly clear at our search altitude of 16,000 feet but we were in and out of the clouds at 2,000 feet while the outside air temperature hovered at zero degrees Celsius during tracking. I was eager to restart number four. I'd get number one relit once we put some more miles behind us. We'd need every drop of fuel for one approach attempt into Adak before flying the thousand-mile diversion to Anchorage. I turned to Wilhelm in the middle seat. "Standby engine restart checklist, number four."

I made sure our airspeed was adequate, maintaining 210 knots indicated. Wilhelm began the restart, first restoring the e-handle to its in position and ensuring the Sync Servo switch was turned off. After completing these preliminary items things happened very quickly, compressing time and warping my sense of passage. Per the checklist, Wilhelm restored fuel and ignition and we watched the gauges on number four return to life. Within seconds the engine achieved fuel flow, oil pressure and RPM, stabilizing at 100 percent. Wilhelm called normal light off and I released the aft observer from his station over ICS. I needed to wait several minutes before fully restoring power to the engine while the oil temperature rose to operating limits. It was during this waiting period that things went awry. We first experienced an abnormal vibration, an undeniable shudder throughout the cockpit as the prop governor struggled to maintain RPM control before releasing the engine to spin wildly beyond 110 percent. The noise in the cockpit doubled in intensity and both number four prop pump lights illuminated steadily. Without performing a full NATOPS check, Wilhelm and I knew we were pitch-locked. I instinctively retarded all three engines, which was the correct procedure, and we watched the RPM on four drop accordingly below 100 percent. Colby and I remained alert as Wilhelm reached for his NATOPS manual once again reviewing the emergency procedures for a pitch-locked propeller, reading aloud. I knew the section cold but was reassured hearing his voice as if the engineer who designed the system was with us in the cockpit. I pushed the power levers back up hoping to stabilize number four near the 100 percent mark. I knew we'd have our hands full nursing the engine back to Adak, struggling to maintain optimum RPM. But at least we were flying, and the emergency was under control. I asked Al to give us a single waypoint on our scope for Adak. We'd fuel chop the engine just before starting the approach, again per NATOPS.

Petty Officer Chavez was sitting atop the radar cabinet directly behind me and leaned into my ear. "Sir, we probably should restart number one now, don't you think?" He made his observation calmly and respectfully. His words no sooner sprang from his lips than it hit me how foolish we'd been. We allowed ourselves to become so distracted by the propeller malfunction we completely forgot number one was still loitered.

"Hold up, guys," I said, interrupting Wilhelm's reading. "What's say we restart number one?" Colby and Wilhelm exchanged puzzled looks as if I were speaking in tongues.

Then, suddenly, WHAM!

A horrible high-pitched screeching of tearing metal, both loud and intense, ripped through the cockpit. There was a simultaneous flash of bright

161

light from the right window followed by a Christmas tree of colorful warning lights around the cockpit. Then, for only a millisecond, shocking silence, an eerie relief from the previously loud warbling of the pitch-locked propeller. The silence was quickly shattered by a blaring fire warning horn on number four. A shrill of rushing air moved through the cabin behind me as if a big gash had been carved into the fuselage.

I've read about the fight-or-flight reaction that kicks in during an emergency or encounter with high stress. It's a part of the primitive brain function that provokes a kneejerk response in a dire situation. My instant reaction to the deafening noise, the warning lights, the engine fire, surprisingly, was denial. *This is impossible. This can't be happening. Not to me.* I didn't fully understand the nature of our emergency, but denial kept me in the seat, kept me fighting, kept me from panicking. I unconsciously recognized fighting would be in my better interest of survival. Only later would I assimilate we'd thrown a propeller blade from the number four engine and it had torn through the fuselage somewhere aft of the cockpit. Right now, the order of the day was to stay in the seat, stay calm and stay alive.

"Feathering number four," Wilhelm yelled, his adrenaline pushing his voice to a higher level. He pulled out the number four e-handle and released the fire extinguishing agent into the engine. His instinctive response and quick actions brought me back into the picture.

"My airplane," I yelled, taking control.

"Your airplane," Colby replied after Wilhelm locked out the screaming warning horn. "We're losing number three, Mitch," he quickly added. "Everything's rolling back."

My eyes locked on number three's instruments. It had just flamed out. I watched helplessly as shaft horsepower, turbine inlet temperature, RPM and fuel flow bled off like air from a punctured tire, realizing, as we all did, number three had probably suffered damage from the explosion of number four. We were now a single-engine airplane at a mere 2,000 feet above sea level. Number two was our only power source and we were sinking slowly, unable to maintain altitude on one engine. We'd need to get number one going pronto to arrest our inevitable descent into a very cold, churning sea below. The airplane was shedding electrical loads automatically due to single generator operation and Wilhelm wasted no time with the APU start checklist. Unfortunately, after several tries, it wouldn't light. The APU, mounted in the lower right side of the forward fuselage, had likely been damaged by the same event that caused number four to explode and number three to flame out.

"Starting number one," Wilhelm now called out, his voice calmer as he worked through our dwindling set of options. If we were to stay out of the drink, number one was our only hope. Wilhelm ran through the procedures quickly, without a checklist. He'd started engines hundreds of times in his career, always as trained, always with a checklist but speed was of the essence and he needed to work fast. He made sure to depress the pressure cutout override switch before pulling on the feather button, praying for swift rotation and ignition. "Come on you son-of-a-bitch, light off. Light off!"

"One thousand feet," Colby called, reading from the altimeter. Our altitude had been cut in half in the last two minutes. Two more minutes and we'd be jumping into life rafts.

I depressed the PA button. "CREW, PREPARE TO DITCH! Prepare to ditch! Don QD1 exposure suits if you have time. Nav, TACCO, get out a mayday report to Anchorage Radio on HF. NOW! Ditching likely in two minutes. Two minutes. Take ditching stations and standby, I will give a final brace-for-impact." I could hear an organized madhouse break loose from the cabin above the din of rushing air as they scrambled to get on their exposure suits.

Jamie stuck his head into the cockpit. "Mitch, Al's hurt. Chavez is taking him back to the galley. Looks like the prop or whatever tore into the skin came through just aft of his station, cut his shoulder and leg pretty bad. I'll get the mayday out, assuming the HFs still work." He looked out the left window into the black void. "Can't you get number one going?"

"Working on it," I yelled over my shoulder, "Just get the mayday out!" Turning to Wilhelm, I said, "Willy, what's going on? Why won't it light?"

He didn't respond. He was laser-focused on our last option. Wilhelm reached down to the fuel management panel in the center console and recycled the number one fuel boost pump switch after verifying the circuit breakers behind him were in. He then pulled down on the feather button again. We felt the familiar airframe shutter as number one began rotation, all eyes fixed on the engine instruments.

I said a short prayer. Colby called out, "Passing five hundred feet!"

Wilhelm remained silent, not wanting to jinx things or perhaps uttering a prayer of his own.

"Mayday, mayday!" I heard Jamie transmit on the HF radio. "This is Lima Echo 440, a Navy P-3, declaring an emergency." He repeated the call two more times, pleading for a response. I punched off the HF radio button to my headset, needing to shed the distraction.

Mercifully, number one came to life after rotating for what seemed like an eternity, RPM moving to 100 percent and turbine inlet temperature spinning up rapidly in a clockwise direction, but we were still sinking. "Passing two hundred feet," Colby called out. "For God's sake, Mitch, pull up!"

"Too slow, we'll stall." I wasted no time putting full power to both left engines desperately trying to arrest our sink rate and gain some airspeed. Time seemed suspended as we floated on the ragged edge of the flight envelope.

"One hundred feet!" Colby called, his scan solely fixed on the radio altimeter.

I delicately applied some back pressure to the control column, thinking stall or no stall, our flight will end right here in a watery crash if I don't level us off. I was greeted immediately with the sickening feeling of stall buffet, a natural airframe tendency warning of impending loss of controlled flight. I eased the yoke forward.

"Fifty feet! Mitch, we're going the wrong direction!" he said, with more alarm, convinced we were headed into the drink.

I was caught in a delicate balance of pushing and pulling on the yoke until finally, luckily, after what seemed like hours but was only seconds, our airspeed slowly inched back up the dial and our rate of descent nulled. I pulled back aggressively after stealing a glance at the radio altimeter, the needle bouncing spuriously between twenty and thirty feet off the raging sea below. This time the aircraft cooperated showing no signs of buffet and began a shallow climb. We were turning things around, ever so gradually, our paper-thin gap with the sea widening as the altimeter crept in a clockwise direction. I was thankful for the solid blackness out the windscreen but keenly aware of the permeating scent of salt air into the cockpit.

As airspeed slowly increased, I had to apply more left rudder and fiddle with the trim to compensate for the asymmetrical thrust before beginning a delicate climb to 10,000 feet. We'd be limited to this altitude due to the obvious pressure vessel breach by the prop blade. Safe and climbing, I needed the crew to begin assessing the full damage and understand any additional limitations we'd have during the cruise, approach and landing phase. Wilhelm immediately began working on a two-engine max range cruise calculation at 10,000 feet to see if we had enough fuel for Anchorage in the event of a missed approach. I first wanted him to confirm we had enough fuel to make Adak.

Jamie finally flagged down a Japan Airlines 747 monitoring the frequency who relayed our mayday call to Anchorage Radio. *"Navy Lima Echo 440, this is Anchorage,"* the controller replied. *"Read you loud and clear now, sir. State your position and nature of emergency, over."*

"I've got it, TACCO," Colby said, taking over the communication from his seat. "Anchorage, we've had a prop malfunction, dual engine failure, loss of pressurization and structural damage. We have at least one injured. Requesting 10,000 feet direct Adak for an emergency landing, over."

"Ask him about Shemya," I shouted across the cockpit. "What about Shemya?"

"And Anchorage, requesting priority direct Shemya, if able."

The controller, obviously briefed before his watch, replied instantly stating Shemya was closed for maintenance but to standby, he would request their ability to support an emergency landing. He also asked Colby to restate our current position, fuel state and souls on board.

"Willy," Colby said, "They want our fuel state in pounds and endurance."

Wilhelm looked down at the totalizer. "Twenty-four thousand pounds. Hang on, I'm working on range. Something's really fucked up here."

I smiled, imagining Colby relaying Wilhelm's words verbatim. My mirth was short-lived as I realized we had another problem besides fuel. I was experiencing less and less lateral control of the aircraft. Since the emergency, I'd been hand-flying, daring not to engage the autopilot. The aircraft had responded in a predictable manner with two engines out on the same side – tricky but manageable with proper trim. Now I was having difficulty maintaining heading. Correction to the right or left with the yoke felt very stiff, very uncharacteristic, like the power steering had been cut. I looked down at the hydraulic control panel and noticed we were dangerously low in pressure on both the number one and two systems. The warning light on the master caution panel was on, but so were many others. Keeping our asses out of the water had been our priority. We were just beginning to sort out the other problems. "Willy," I said calmly. "Check the hydraulic pressures. Are we really losing both systems?"

He glanced at the gauge and threw up his hands in resignation. "Oh, for Christ sake, one emergency at a time you miserable whore," he said, imploring at the overhead, making it clear he was talking to the airplane, not me. "It's entirely possible we're losing hydraulic fluid, sir. We're losing fuel, that's for certain. Our fuel flow indicators say we're burning at 3,500 pounds an hour yet every time I recheck the performance graphs it looks like we're burning at 10,000."

"That is fucked up."

"Obviously. We've got a fuel leak, a bad one. I just shut off the auto-transfer system. Take a look at tanks three and four."

"Dropping pretty fast?" It was hard to discern any change. I hadn't been hawking them minute by minute like he had but there was noticeably less fuel in tanks three and four than one and two.

"We lost a lot when number four came apart. The blades tore up number three and ripped into our skin like a can opener. Fuel's bleeding from a ruptured tank or broken fuel line. Either way, we're not going to see Anchorage by a long shot. And, yeah, the hydraulic lines run under the starboard side of the fuselage. One of the blades could've clipped 'em along with the APU fuel line. I'm going to start transferring fuel out of tanks three and four, but we've already lost about 10,000 pounds."

"What about the hydraulic system?" I said.

"Well, if we lose them both, we'll go boost-out." Wilhelm flashed an odd, crooked smile. "Ever fly boost-out before, sir?" He knew I hadn't. Boost-out is not something you practice or ever want to practice on a P-3. It's an emergency backup allowing manual movement of the control surfaces. You are flying without hydraulic assistance, or, without boost, as the term implies. The pilot at the controls does all the work. Pure seat of the pants flying, just like an old DC-3. Our conversation was interrupted when Anchorage Radio cut in. *"Navy Lima Echo 440, Anchorage."*

"Go ahead," Colby replied.

*"Shemya reports they can reopen runway 28 in two plus three zero hours after clearing equipment. Airport currently below weather minimums, forecast for 1000 Zulu is 500 overcast, visibility one-quarter mile in fog. Say position and intentions and they will attempt to clear, over."*

Colby looked to me. We were 100 miles from Shemya on a course to Adak which lay 300 miles beyond. If we wanted Shemya, we'd have to enter a holding fix while we waited for them to clear, burning precious fuel, destroying any option to proceed to an alternate in the event of a missed approach. "No, tell 'em we'll press on to Adak. Cold Bay and King Salmon will be our alternates, in that order." I let my own words sink in. God, this was a tough call. Too many variables, I thought. It was on that razor's edge of damned if you do, damned if you don't. Still, I told Colby to pass our intentions to Anchorage. Colby complied. Neither he nor Wilhelm batted an eye, wanting no part of the decision.

The next two and a half hours in transit were spent preparing for the approach and landing in Adak. Our aircraft, SE-05, was in stable condition. Cabin pressurization was gone, making it impossible to keep the inside air temperature above 45 degrees but, nonetheless, had stabilized. The crew wore parkas. Wilhelm had stopped the hemorrhaging of fuel, giving us enough to reach Adak at our miserably low and slow altitude of 10,000 feet. Engines one and two were performing well at the higher power settings. We were running them at the maximum continuous TIT operating limit of 1010° C to get all the airspeed possible. I took the opportunity to get out of the seat and stretch, letting Colby fly and Horse monitor. The approach and landing would be a very difficult evolution given our challenged aircraft and anticipated weather. I needed to be fresh, or at least fresher than I currently felt walking back into the cabin. My first concern was Al lying in the bunk aft of the galley. I was worried the hit he took, and severity of his injuries, required immediate medical attention. I approached his side. He was flat on his back, his right leg elevated and wrapped heavily in towels and a tourniquet. Kerry was applying pressure to his calf. Robin was adjusting his head to keep pressure off the shoulder. She had a wet rag folded over his forehead, shielding his eyes. There were half a dozen towels on the floor smeared in fresh blood. Al was conscious but just barely. One look at his face told you the pain was excruciating. "His lower leg was punctured by whatever tore through the floor," Kerry said. "Very sharp and jagged, ripped the flesh up and down his calf. The towels have slowed the bleeding but certainly not stopped it."

"How's his shoulder?"

"Dislocated, I think," Robin said. "Something heavy fell on him just as the floor collapsed."

Both first-aid kits were open, their contents strewn on the galley table. "I'm guessing we have nothing to give him for the pain," I said.

"Aspirin," Robin replied. "I just gave him four."

"Aspirin?" I repeated, shaking my head.

"Hey, Mitch," Al spoke, in a weak voice. "How's it going up there?" He remained still, the wet rag blocking his sight.

"Fantastic. We're about an hour out of Adak. Have you down soon, brother, and on some better drugs."

"So, we're going to make it? We're not going swimming?"

I was surprised by his desire to make chitchat. This was not easy for him and I wanted to appear positive, engaging. "Hell, no, we're not going swimming. Not unless you want to."

"Not especially. I do have a request though."

"Anything."

"Ask Willy to come back here and serenade me with *El Paso*. I was a bit rough on him earlier."

I took Al's left hand and gripped it tightly, admiring his spirit. "Will do, buddy. As soon as he's free." I turned to Robin, "If something changes, come up and let me know ASAP, okay?"

"Aye, aye, sir."

My tour of the cabin wasn't complete. I met with Petty Officer Buchanan, our in-flight technician, and got his damage assessment of the avionics, primarily the navigation and communication systems. He showed me we'd lost some things, but not much. The main damage was to the C-racks, directly behind Al, which held the number one HF and some crypto gear. I carefully inspected Al's navigation station. Everything facing forward was fine but the seat and the bulkhead behind him were mangled, twisted metal like the floor below. This was where one of the propeller blades cut through the fuselage, in line with the prop arc, directly aft of C1. It was a miracle Al escaped with only moderate injury. Buchanan went on to report the wire bundles to the VOR and LOC receivers took a hit, making them questionable. The inertial navigation system appeared stable and intact. He said we lost the mission computer when the main electrical bus was shed but the main load center along with UHF 1 and the VHF were fine. My main concern was the questionable VOR and LOC receivers. With the weather at minimums, these were two key systems we'd need to fly the Instrument Landing System, or ILS, into Adak to have even a small chance of getting into the airfield.

After the tour, I briefly sat with Kerry in the galley. I was fighting off fatigue that threatened to consume me in the wake of the excitement and knew if I lingered, I wouldn't be able to get back up. "Thanks for helping out with Al," I said. "You and Robin are doing a terrific job."

"He's in bad shape, sir. I don't know where that joking around was coming from."

"Yeah, that's just Al. Trying to keep things light."

"Joking in the face of danger? That makes no sense. You think I was laughing when we were two minutes from hitting the water back there?"

"Of course, not. The humor comes later."

"This is later, and I'm still petrified," she said, wiping the corner of her eye. "I'm not finding humor in any of this. Regret is more the emotion."

"Regret you came?"

She looked up afraid she'd hurt my feelings. "Oh, no, it's been great. Well, I could have done without all *this*." She waved her arm at Al and the bloody mess of towels. "Don't you feel regret in certain moments?"

"You mean, did my life pass before my eyes right before we hit the water?" I said, staring at the galley table. "Not really, there wasn't time. We were too busy, thank God. But now that you mention it..." I looked up into her moist eyes and continued, my words forming without thought. "I regret not getting to know my father before he died."

"Oh?" she said, surprised at this random bit of information. "I'm sorry. Were you not close?"

I ignored the question. "I regret not calling my wife yesterday. We had a fight before I left. I intended to call her but didn't, for whatever reason. I didn't make time. So, regrets? I guess it's true what they say – never go to bed angry. Or on deployment," I added hastily. I had no idea my emotions were running raw, this close to the surface. "You?"

"I regret signing up for another year in Adak," she responded, without hesitation. "The tour's a year. I agreed to a second and now I'm regretting it. I did it for the wrong reasons."

"Regretting signing up for another year on the rock? C'mon, Sully, that's a no-brainer." I hoped she didn't mind me calling her Sully, recognizing the bond I was trying to create.

"I guess I did it for the attention. People pay attention to me up here. It's like I'm someone. I matter."

I didn't respond.

"'Another year in Adak?' they said. 'Why not?' I replied. I figured I'd rather have people appreciate me here than go back home and be ignored, told I'm plain and worthless."

Her low self-esteem surprised me, but I understood we were no longer discussing her work. "Sully, you're not plain and—"

She lifted her index finger, placing it over my lips, hushing me. "I am what I am, sir. But after tonight, I see my self-serving behavior for what it is. Even agreeing to come on this flight, like, oh, sure, another chance to get laid. Robin even joked, maybe we'll join the mile-high club. It sounds so, I don't know, cheap and misguided." She tightened her lips and made a brave smile. "Anyway, I'm leaving. I'm going to request a change of duty, transfer off Adak when we get back." Kerry reached for my hand and held it in hers, tightening the grip. "We will make it back, won't we, sir?"

I stood from the table. I wanted to tell her the truth, that the approach and landing would be the most difficult and challenging flying I'd ever attempted but realized hearing the words would rip at my own confidence. "Of course, we'll make it," I said, tossing a pen from my flight jacket at her. "Here. Start filling out those transfer papers, right now."

Halfway up the aisle, I had to stop to calm my rapid pulse rate and concentrate on slow, deep breaths. It was reminiscent of my high school baseball experience, coming off the bench in a desperate situation as a relief pitcher, pumping pure adrenalin, with all eyes pinned on me. I swallowed the last sip of water from a paper cup Sully had given me and entered the darkened cockpit. "Okay, guys, let's do the Teaberry Shuffle," I said, tapping Colby on the shoulder. I climbed into the left seat as Colby vacated. Colby moved into Horse's spot on the right and Wilhelm relieved Chavez in the middle. The entire evolution took no more than a minute as we neared our top of descent point approximately forty nautical miles from Adak. Once settled in the seat, I noticed the aircraft was completely unresponsive to yoke and column movements. No matter how hard I pushed and pulled or tugged on the yoke, nothing happened. We had finally lost both hydraulic systems during my break. "Colby, how the hell have you been flying for the last half hour? I've got nothing here."

"Yeah, been doing it all with trim, which seems to work fine for maintaining heading and altitude, just can't maneuver."

Which would be peachy, I thought, if we didn't have to *fucking land*. "Well, that won't cut it any longer," I said, turning to Wilhelm. "Okay, Willy, guess it's time to go boost-out and see how she flies."

"Roger that, sir." We let out a collective gasp as he pulled the boost-out levers at the foot of the center console placing us in uncharted waters. Initially, there was no change as I gently coaxed the big airplane to turn. Nothing. The controls remained frozen, our flight path still trimmed in straight and level. In a surge of panic, I pushed with all my might on the column and twisted the yoke. This action freed the controls but seemed to have no effect on heading or altitude. Gradually though, our left wing dipped, and we began a turn. I twisted the yoke back to the right and again, as if in slow motion, the left wing rose and we resumed level flight. If the risk of flying an approach on two engines was considered a five on a scale of ten, doing it full boost-out would be a ten. I was no longer flying a slick-handling Chevy van. We were now a Mack truck with two flat tires.

Colby had taken over the comms from the right seat. We had just switched from Anchorage Radio and were in range talking to Adak Approach Control. "Tell 'em we want the GCA to runway 23," I said. "We can't fly the ILS." I didn't want to take a chance with our navigation receivers, which were either out of commission or unreliable. Flying a GCA, or Ground Controlled Approach, where the controller provides guidance commands to the runway threshold using a precision approach radar requires only a working VHF radio, one we verified after initial contact with Adak. Colby made the request while I experimented with the new handling characteristics independent of hydraulics. I found I had to lead any pitch or roll command several seconds more than normal, using twice the muscle. Otherwise, the aircraft appeared controllable. I would just have to learn to anticipate, be well out in front of any situation. We were getting very close to the island and I was eager to set up for the approach.

*"Lima Echo 440, Adak Approach, standby your request for the GCA, runway two-three. Say current position, souls on board and fuel state."*

Say current position? I thought. This was ridiculous. We were less than forty miles from the airfield and they still weren't painting us on radar.

Colby responded. "We're on the Adak 090 radial, 35 DME, fourteen souls on board, one critically injured. Fuel state— Standby." He paused and looked at Wilhelm, who held up three fingers. "Fuel state minimal, three-thousand pounds, approximately four-five minutes."

Forty-five minutes of flight time remaining was a generous estimate. I calculated we had enough gas for one approach and maybe one go-around at best. In our severely wounded state, I was not planning on any go-around. We would land on the first try. I was getting impatient and jumped on the radio. "Adak, request instructions and clearance for the approach immediately. It is urgent, repeat, urgent we get the GCA to two-three. We can't fly the ILS and we're low on gas." My request was anything but courteous. I was yelling.

*"Lima Echo 440,"* came a different voice, likely the tower chief stepping in for his younger controller. *"Roger, sir, understand you're declaring minimum fuel. We're setting up for the GCA now. Still need to locate your position on radar. Please recycle your transponder, squawk 2500 and ident."*

Colby complied, dialing in the new squawk code and pressing the ident button.

*"There we go. Hallelujah,"* said the chief, relief flooding his voice. *"Lima Echo 440, radar contact. You are fourteen miles east of the outer marker, turn left heading 270, descend and maintain 4,000, Adak altimeter 29.10. This will be a precision radar approach to runway 23."*

Colby read back the instructions. "And say current weather at the field."

Here it comes, I thought. More bad news.

*"Current Adak weather reporting 500 overcast, 2,000 broken, visibility one-quarter mile in fog and freezing rain. Wind calm, surface temperature three zero."*

We'd been flying an easterly heading for the last two hours and I needed to make a full one-eighty to follow the new heading assignment. I dialed in some additional elevator trim and wrestled the airplane into a wide left turn. We'd overflown the island by more than thirty miles and the course correction by the controller represented a significant navigation error. Not horrible but not trivial either given the likely trauma the inertial navigation system suffered during the accident. And there was some good news in the weather report despite the atrocious ceiling and visibility. The calm wind would make the approach less challenging to fly, requiring fewer corrections on final.

*"Lima Echo 440, approaching runway 23 final approach course. Turn left heading 240 to intercept, descend and maintain 2,000."*

Colby again echoed the controller's instructions. We were approximately twenty miles from the airfield and being set up on a long straight-in, one that would allow plenty of time to establish the proper airspeed, heading and vertical guidance from the GCA controller. We discussed the flaps and landing gear situation, agreeing that without hydraulics we'd be stuck making a no-flap landing. Wilhelm and Chavez would pull the nose and main gear handles to drop the gear manually as we got closer. Our final concern was the landing rollout. Again, without hydraulics, we'd have to rely on backup air braking – something I'd never done or tested. Events were now piling up in accordion fashion, squeezing me, giving me fewer and fewer options.

Adak Approach interrupted. *"Lima Echo 440, switching to GCA control. You are eighteen miles from the airfield. Remain this frequency and we'll pick you up on the other scope."*

It was the tower chief again, the senior man on the ground, reminding us he would be directing us and that he needed to move to the GCA radar console – two small scopes that painted the aircraft in both a lateral and vertical profile to provide proper three-dimensional guidance.

*"Lima Echo 440, GCA radar contact. You are sixteen miles from touchdown, slightly left of course. Turn right heading 235, maintain current altitude to intercept glide path."*

He was very calm, very professional, his relaxed monotone assuring everyone on headset, especially me, that things were under control. His voice was our sole lifeline to the runway, and he needed to make it seem routine. I tugged at the yoke to steady up on heading 235.

"Okay, Willy, time to drop the gear," I said. "Get Chavez to freefall the main now. Once we have indication they're down, go ahead and release the nose." Chavez would have to go back to the hydraulic service center to release the main landing gear, after which Wilhelm would pull the nose gear release handle from his station up front. In less than a minute, I felt the vibration and added buffet on the airframe from the lowered main gear, thank God. Chavez came running into the cockpit to report he'd let the gear go.

Wilhelm lowered the nose gear. By all indication, including reports from the aft observers, Buchanan and Cox, the gear was locked into place.

*"Lima Echo 440, ten miles from touchdown, on course, drifting slightly below glide path, ease your rate of descent. No need to acknowledge further transmissions. If no transmissions are received for thirty seconds, abandon the radar approach and execute the published missed approach."*

The controller no longer required us to respond and read back his instructions. This would reduce the workload in the cockpit allowing focus solely on the runway in front of us. He would instantly know if we copied his guidance by tracking our blip's movements on the sensitive scopes. I called for the landing checklist and told the crew to set Condition Five, requiring them to strap in and don their helmets.

*"Lima Echo 440, eight miles from touchdown. On course, slightly above glide path, increase rate of descent."* After a beat, *"Now on glide path, drifting slightly right of course. Turn left heading 225."*

"Flight, TACCO." It was Jamie. "Condition Five set. Al's still in the bunk, Sullivan's holding onto to him."

"That's no good, Jamie. She needs to be strapped in. Get a belt across Al and get her to a ditching station. Al will be fine. We're going to be on the deck in two minutes."

"Roger."

*"Lima Echo 440, six miles from touchdown, now left of course, turn right to 240, going slightly below glide path, ease it up a bit."*

I was all over the map, behind the aircraft, pushing, pulling, adjusting trim, anything to follow the chief's endless stream of guidance corrections.

*"Five miles from touchdown, now on course, returning to glide path. Wind 200 at 5, check wheels down and locked, cleared to land."*

We were picking up a bit of ground effect from Cape Cod, the nickname for the spit of land near the end of the runway, giving us momentary lift.

*"Four miles from touchdown. Course good. Glide path good. Looks okay."*

About time, I thought. I caressed the yoke. "Come on, baby, hang on, almost home." We now had the glow from the approach lights in the windscreen illuminating nothing but a thick soup of swirling fog. "Colby, tell him to dim the lights. Too much glare." The lights came down instantly before Colby could finish the request. Everyone was on it, doing their job.

*"Two miles from touchdown. On course, on glide path, advise when runway in sight."*

Nothing. Nothing but flapping wiper blades and blinding white fog in front of me. Nothing but the harsh reflection of our landing lights in my peripheral view.

*"One mile from touchdown. Approaching decision height."*

Still nothing.

Seconds passed in silence.

*"Lima Echo 440, overlanding threshold. You are below decision height. Execute the*

*missed approach and go around. Repeat, go around."*

We never visually acquired the runway at the mandatory two-hundred-foot decision height or informed the controller. Procedure said to go around.

"Mitch, you hear? They're telling us to go around," Colby said, his voice echoing the controller's urgency. "Go around!"

"We're continuing," I yelled back, glancing at the radio altimeter, which had now sprung to life.

Fifty feet, forty feet, thirty feet, twenty, ten...BAM.

We slammed the ground at 130 knots, hitting solid pavement, presumably the runway, but I had no idea where or how much pavement remained. At present speed, we'd bust through the other end in less than thirty seconds. "Brakes, brakes, brakes!" I called to Colby. Wilhelm took over the power levers easing number one and two into beta, fighting the asymmetrical yaw induced by the loss of three and four. The air brakes appeared to be working but we were still a missile at 100 knots, screaming to the end of a 7,700-foot runway we still couldn't see. The combination of a higher speed no-flap landing and Wilhelm's inability to apply full reverse thrust worked against as we struggled to bring our 80,000-pound ship to a halt. We crossed the runway 18 intersection at a clip of 80 knots, passing a dozen emergency vehicles in a blur, their red lights twirling in an eerie glow ready to give chase. Only 2,500 feet of asphalt remained. Colby and I were standing on the brakes, Wilhelm applying as much reverse thrust as possible to keep us from skidding off the edge of the runway. "More thrust, Willy. More." I yelled. I was willing to trade a little yaw for shorter stopping distance.

"One thousand feet remaining," Colby called, noting the final runway marker.

Below 80 knots, I had little sense of our actual speed without a visual reference. I started preparing my mind for runway departure and an emergency evacuation. I thought about Al. "Stop you miserable piece of shit," I implored. "Stop!" The lights signaling runway end were now in view, a menacing hazy bloom of red coming into focus, morphing into dozens of tiny lights on six-inch stands. We were mercifully coming to a halt. The lights disappeared, passing beneath our belly in slow motion.

Slowing, slowing, slowing...stopped.

Our flight came to rest twenty feet beyond the runway's threshold in a soft bed of gravel. I peeled off my headset and could hear cheering from the back. My first thought was of Aimee. I've got to call Aimee.

Events blurred. I was surrendering my grip on reality, my mind completely willing to disassociate from the events of the past eight hours. A madhouse of activity ensued after Cox got the main cabin door opened and stairs deployed. Firefighters surrounded the aircraft and rushed to the wounded right wing. Rescuers entered the galley and had Al on a stretcher and into an ambulance in no time, our entire crew evacuated onto the tarmac in less than two minutes. I pushed my way through a horde of officials, vaguely remembering my name being called, hopping into the ambulance to ride to the hospital with Al. Jamie appeared, his eyes scanning the back of the ambulance until spying me sitting with Al. His look was one of surprise, as if I shouldn't be abandoning him with the crew, that there would be a shitload of officers asking a shitload of questions. It could wait, the investigation would take months. I wanted to be with Al and the hell away from the melee developing at the end of the runway. The short ride in the ambulance was my escape, my deliverance.

Activity at the Adak base hospital was no less hectic. They'd been expecting a multitude of severely injured aircrew and were prepared for the worst. All base doctors, nurses and corpsmen had been called in and mobbed the ambulance as we pulled up. Once I assured them I was fine and only there to assist Al, I was shunted aside and allowed to stand in the emergency room corner as they took scissors to Al's flight suit and dove into his mangled leg. I never thought of myself as squeamish when it came to blood and ripped flesh but when the flight surgeon began extracting small bits of metal fragments from Al's leg, dropping them into a stainless-steel bucket, I had to turn and leave the room. Al was unconscious, on some sort of IV drip, presumably morphine. He didn't need me any longer.

"Don't worry, he'll make out all right," came a male voice from behind me as I entered the hospital corridor. "He'll be fine."

His voice caught me off-guard. I didn't notice anyone follow me out. He was a doctor, early thirties, wearing a khaki uniform under a green lab coat, the medical insignia clearly visible on his collar. "Will he?" I said. "His leg doesn't look to be fine." I was desperate for some good news.

"Well, he may need a medevac to Elmendorf for further surgery when he's stable, some therapy after that, but, yeah, he'll live." The doctor smiled as if the last part was meant as humor. He held out his hand to shake. "Jim Parks. Are you the pilot? On the plane that just landed?"

"Yeah."

"Wow, congratulations," he said, continuing to pump my hand. "We were all listening to the tower frequency. Outstanding. Simply outstanding." He paused to assess my condition, giving me a quick, professional once-over. "So, how are you holding up? Anything I can do?"

"I need to get to a phone," I said, not considering my physical state or the feat we'd just pulled off. "Is there one around?"

"Oh, sure, you bet. You can use the one in my office. Follow me." We walked down a dimly lit corridor to the other end of the small hospital. Doctor Jim stopped at his door, pushed it open and flicked on the lights. "Sit down, sit down," he said, pointing to his desk. "Dial 8 to get an Autovon line. And take your time, please."

Jim quickly disappeared, eager to give me privacy. The quiet isolation in his wake was intoxicating and surreal given the pandemonium in the flight deck less than an hour ago. I swiveled in his chair and stared at the framed photographs neatly arranged at the top of his desk. I felt like a snoop, an intruder in someone's home but these happy strangers were all staring at me, beckoning a closer look. One photo was taken at Jim's college graduation. Or was it med school? A younger Jim in cap and gown, a huge grin on his face, was flanked by proud parents and a few family members in the background. The other shots were more intimate, taken later in life, of Jim and an adorable five-year-old girl in pigtails. His daughter? A single parent? In a second shot, a large Buddha statue taken somewhere in Asia was in the background, the two of them facing each other with silly, mock-surprised expressions on their faces, so obviously enamored with each other, so wrapped up in their little moment. I scanned other photos around the desk for the wife, the mother – some indication to say this was a complete family. But, alas, I found no such evidence, nothing. A sadness crept in and I had to suppress a sudden urge for tears. I was heartsick, I was broken, I was exhausted. I needed to quit stalling and make my call. I carefully dialed the number to our house on base, not bothering to check what time it might be in California or wonder if Aimee had heard anything about the accident. She picked up on the second ring.

I was nervous and waited a moment before speaking. "Aimee?"

"Mitch?" She was surprised to hear my voice, not bone-weary from a restless night of worry waiting for me to call. Obviously, she'd heard nothing.

"Yeah, hi. How's it going?"

"What's wrong, Mitch?" she said, detecting the flatness in my voice, divining trouble in an instant.

"That's why I called, to tell you I'm fine. We had a little problem on our flight tonight but it's over. I'm safe and everything's fine."

"Oh, my God! Mitch. What happened? Where are you?"

I explained the nature of our flight, giving her the short version, the propeller and engine failure and our emergency landing back in Adak, omitting certain details and downplaying the overall seriousness. I purposely skipped Al's injury, especially since I knew his wife, Anne, had likely not been notified of either the accident or his condition.

"How horrible," she responded. "Are you sure you're okay?"

"Yes. I'm fine." I studied the photos on Jim's desk again. The graduation picture disturbed me the most. It was his parents. The whole thing seemed rigged. Yet, I knew in my heart that nothing in the photo was rigged, that it was me. *Not everyone's parents skip their son's graduation, you know.* I felt my gut tighten and again fought back the rush of tears, moving my eyes to the photos of Jim and his sweet little girl. "How are the kids?" I said, fumbling for their photos in my wallet, desperate to replace Jim's desktop images with something tangible of my own. Before Aimee could answer, my wallet fell from my hands and dropped to the floor. I began sobbing, no longer able to contain my emotions. Aimee could hear me. She was talking, offering solace, but I couldn't understand a word she was saying. I just kept repeating, "I'm sorry. I'm sorry we fought before I left." I was weeping openly, letting everything fall out over our scratchy 3,000-mile phone connection. I was drained. I'd been up for twenty-four hours and was emotionally spent and inconsolable. "I'm sorry, Aimee, I'm sorry. I'm so—" I was incoherent, rambling, incapable of further conversation. Time to end it, I thought.

"Mitch, slow down. Please. I'm right here."

"I'm sorry, I can't talk anymore." Less sobbing. "I've got to—"

"Mitch, I'm right here, honey, slow down. Please, keep talking to me. The kids are fine. We're all fine. We're right here at home waiting for you. Please, don't hang up."

"No, Aimee, I've got to go," I said, finally gathering myself. I could hear voices in the hall. "I'm sorry. They need me."

"Mitch? Please, don't—"

"I love you," I said, and hung up.

I stepped out of Jim's office and switched off the light. I realized the shock I'd given Aimee in sharing my post-accident trauma and needed to end the call for both our sake. A commotion had developed at the other end of the long hallway. I moved toward it, fighting every instinct to run the other way, knowing my temporary absence had created a stir. I wiped my puffy face with a towel I'd snagged from Jim's office, took a deep breath and stepped toward the group. The XO, Dickless himself, was among them. I easily spotted his towering figure, a half-head taller than the others, moving toward me.

"Ah, Baumann, there you are. Glad you could join us," he said, in his usual sarcasm, scanning me head to toe as if I'd lost my marbles. "What the hell happened out there tonight?"

"You want the whole story right here?" I was in no mood. Instead, "Well, sir, we had a problem."

"You bet your ass you had a problem. Where'd you go just now? Where've you been?"

"I didn't go anywhere, sir. I've been at the hospital the whole time. I came to be with Al Quigley, my NAVCOM."

He looked me over again suspiciously before turning his eyes to the ER doors where Al lay. "Don't worry about Al. Who told you to come to the hospital? I want you over at the ASWOC with your crew, where you should've been in the first place. You need to provide a preliminary written statement about the accident, get debriefed on the mission and submit to a drug test. Don't give me this be-with-Al crap. You can't hide out here."

"I'm not hiding out anywhere."

"Whatever. Just get over to the ASWOC and complete your duty." His eyes narrowed their gaze. "By the way, if the investigation shows you did anything improper with that engine on station—" He moved closer, lowering his voice. "And if you think the skipper's going to cover for you on this one, you've got another thing coming. Not with the visibility this thing will shine. I think maybe a certain someone's really stepped in it this time, wouldn't you say?"

"Gee, I don't know, XO," I said, cutting him off. I was hot. "I heard the engine wasn't properly PMCF'd. That maybe a certain *someone* didn't conduct the required inflight shutdown and restart check like they were supposed to. Maybe we should shine a little visibility on that!" I was fatigued beyond reason, my accusation spilling out with little regard for consequence. I needed to disengage, to get away before things got out of hand. I stepped around Fowler, who made no effort to stop me, and bolted for the hospital exit. At least one thing he said earlier was correct. I needed to be with my crew.

# 10

## NEW ORDERS

WE WERE HOME WITHIN A WEEK. The Patrol Wings Pacific safety officer and staff decided to continue the accident investigation back at Moffett Field where they'd have access to deeper resources and, of course, wouldn't have to travel to Adak themselves. Al had already been flown back from Elmendorf to Oak Knoll Naval Hospital. He'd be able to keep his lower leg but likely wouldn't pass a flight physical and always carry a limp. After being removed from flight status and without a full crew, it was an easy decision for the Wing to fly us back home and send a new airplane and crew in our place.

I'd anxiously been pacing about the house all morning, keeping Aimee on edge, in anticipation of my 0900 meeting with the skipper. I hadn't talked with him since getting back and knew he was interested in hearing my version firsthand. After my encounter with the XO, I'd felt uneasy about the hero status everyone in Adak had lavished on us after hearing our tale. I knew in my gut it was more a hero-goat thing, and all depended on the result of the accident board. They could either side with my decisions, make me the future poster child for how to properly handle a catastrophic propeller failure, or they could find fault with any number of things and fashion a hangman's noose that would strip me of my wings, or worse, discharge me from the Navy. "Relax," Aimee said. "They're not going to kick you out of the Navy. That propeller decided to come loose on its own and rip through the airplane. You saved it from crashing. How are they going to blame you when you saved the crew's life?"

I loved her selectiveness, her blatant naivety to a problem that wasn't hers. Aimee was smart and able to quickly grasp many sides of a complex issue. But when it suited her, she'd make a simple argument as if a blind man could see her side, not expecting a pointed retort with perhaps a more enlightened view. Still, I couldn't step on her good intentions. "Regardless of how the meeting goes," I said, "I think I'm going to tell the skipper I'm initiating paperwork today for my resignation. It's time to get off active duty, regardless."

"Oh? So, we're back to that option?"

"What do you mean back? I said, with some frustration. "We've been discussing it for the past two years."

"Yeah, but it's always a minefield with you," Aimee said. "As long as you're not running from something."

"I'm not."

"That you're doing it for the right reasons."

"I am."

"That it's not about your father."

"My father? What the hell's that got to do with anything?" I was thrown by how easily she'd changed subjects, not quite understanding the reference.

"Are you still mourning him?"

"I don't know."

"Did you ever mourn him?"

"Christ, Aimee, I don't know. Why are you asking me this now?"

"Because it's relevant," she said, raising her voice. "Because if you don't—"

"Okay, okay, time-out," I said, matching her volume. "You want to know the truth?" I took a breath, gathering my thoughts. "I can't mourn him. How can I mourn the man when I feel nothing, not now, not for a long time." I waited for a reaction. "Even at the funeral, it was like I'd flatlined, no spikes, no valleys, no sense of emotion. I kept asking myself, shouldn't I be crying? Shouldn't I be showing more empathy out of respect? I felt nothing, just hollowness, no perception of loss, no sadness."

"Mitch, you've got to mourn him, you must, or it will come back years later, I can assure you, and then it will be much harder to deal with. You have to let it go."

"Let *what* go? How do you let go of nothing?" I wanted off the topic. "Look, Aims, I let him go a long time ago, long before he died. Probably as far back as high school."

"That's impossible."

"How can you say that? You don't know me, at least not back then." I was certain we'd never discussed life at Baumann Haus, not in those years, not in the detail she'd need to piece together the complex puzzle I still hadn't solved myself.

"Of course, I know you, Mitch. I live with you, remember? We share a life together, a bed together, we have two wonderful children together. And I see a good man, a confused man that's been trying to impress his father his entire life. You loved and respected him more than you realize."

"Bullshit," I said, overreacting to her steering the conversation and implied clairvoyance. "You're way off base."

"Am I?" We were standing near the front door. Aimee moved closer, inches from my face. "Mitch, I want to help. I love you. I'm not the enemy here."

179

"I know, Aims, I know." I looked at my watch. "Look, I'm late. I've got to get to the squadron. I have my meeting at nine." I pecked her on the cheek as she stared back incredulously, not wanting to end the discussion. "I love you too."

The drive around base to the hangar took no more than five minutes and I couldn't rid myself of Aimee's perceptive, unwelcome advice. I didn't intend to abruptly cut her off, but she had us headed down a rabbit hole neither of us were prepared for. I needed to focus on my meeting with Skipper Wilson. There wouldn't be trouble like last time, but Wilson was sharp, always anticipating, bobbing and weaving, one step ahead of his prey. I needed to be sharp too, especially when bringing up my resignation and not accepting orders. When I arrived at the squadron, I didn't waste time with the usual watercooler chitchat. I made a beeline from my car to the outer admin office on the second deck. Petty Officer Vijray, the skipper's overworked yeoman, greeted me and directed me to the skipper's inner sanctum to wait, saying he'd just stepped down the hall to use the head. His big Texas flag welcomed me, reminding me of our last encounter, where he ended up recounting his displeasure in no uncertain terms and restricting me to base. I turned away from the flag and oversized desk to admire a set of framed black and white photos on the opposite wall. They showed a young Lieutenant Wilson in his glory days, back when he flew P-5M Marlins out of Sangley Point in the Philippines. He had a baby face not yet lined with age and that easily recognized cocky grin and non-reg handlebar mustache, standing with his crew gathered around the big seaplane. A more recent color shot showed him in full dress whites with his wife in a flowery sundress at his recent VP-25 change-of-command ceremony. I studied the photo and thought if I stayed in, would that be Aimee next to me in a pretty sundress? Would I even want command? A whiff of Aimee's perfume suddenly filled my senses. I pressed my hands to my face and breathed in, momentarily intoxicated by the pleasant intrusion. Her fragrance clung to my skin, trace evidence of our early morning sex. *I can't seem to forget you your Wind Song stays on my mind.* I laughed aloud recalling that cheesy yet provocative television ad. Aimee was like that. She could be unshakeable and thoughts of her would linger in my mind for hours after making love, at all the inappropriate times. Still, as I stood in the skipper's empty office, I remained off-balance and disturbed by her earlier observation and opinions about my father. She'd had a tough childhood herself and oft times felt entitled to spread around her hard-earned knowledge on the legacy of dysfunctional domestic behavior.

Aimee's biological father walked out on her when she was four, leaving behind a wife and three kids, never to be heard from again. The family struggled until Aimee's mother met Bill and married him a few years later, mostly out of desperation. Growing up, Aimee never got along with her stepfather. They disagreed, they fought, they mostly ignored each other.

Then, in 1968, when she was thirteen, the unthinkable happened. Aimee's mother died suddenly from a rare form of cancer. Her two older brothers scattered after the funeral, the older one, eighteen, to Canada to avoid the draft and the younger one, fourteen, to live with a cousin until joining the Navy at seventeen. Aimee was left to fend for herself in those years while her stepfather worked long hours as an executive at an aerospace firm near the LA airport. She resented him for his indifference to her teenage needs and grew to truly despise him for his dalliances in the wake of her mother's death, never appearing to mourn her, perpetually bringing home secretaries and other female companions to spend the night. Aimee left home in 1975 after completing her associate's degree in communications from a local community college and moved across the country to live with her Navy brother, stationed in Pensacola, Florida. She was working as a nightshift disk jockey at a local radio station, building a life after a tough start, when we met in a bar on Seville Quarter during my second-class summer at the Naval Academy. Our budding romance, never hearts and flowers, was sustained solely by sporadic letters we both found difficult to write. Initially, we stumbled then things abruptly fell apart. I was a midshipman at Annapolis. She was a DJ in Pensacola. I was heartbroken and soothed my grief by admitting to everyone at school that we mutually agreed to end it, that we'd botched the intricacies of managing a long-distance relationship, nothing more. It was a credible story, a valid excuse for sure, but also a lie. Aimee broke up with me, plain and simple.

Outside I heard footsteps. I breathed deeply, savoring the last of her fading scent, overhearing Vijray inform the skipper I was in his office. He entered in fresh khakis, all smiles, immediately pumping my hand in his very firm grip. "Mitch, good morning. Thanks for stopping by," he said, as if I'd shown up unannounced, honoring him with my presence. He waved me to a chair and sat down behind his big metal desk. "So, what the hell happened out there?" he said, still grinning. "What'd you do to one of my airplanes?"

"Well, sir—" I was prepared to give him the entire story, an expanded version of my written statement to the accident board. "We took off from NAS Adak at precisely 1600 with a full load of fuel, weighing approximately—" I stopped. I could tell from his expression this wasn't what he wanted to hear. "Uh, how much detail would you like, Skipper?"

He jumped in immediately. "What I want to know is how the hell you landed boost-out with two engines in the bag?" he said, moving to the end of my carefully planned narrative.

I proceeded to tell him how we used heavy trim to fly the leg back to Adak and how I relied on it during final approach to make smaller adjustments to keep us on course and glide path.

"And the gear came down without a hitch? No hydraulics?"

"Free-fall worked no problem, sir." We went on to discuss what it felt like when one of the prop blades tore into the fuselage, how close we got to the ocean on a single engine and how long it took to get number one restarted. This wasn't an interrogation. I was Chuck Yeager telling my heroic tale in a bar to some uninitiated junior aviator, not the CO of a squadron with nearly three times my flight hours. Wilson listened mostly in awe, shaking his head at the harrowing parts and giving a respectful whistle when I told him we came to rest just beyond the runway's end using only backup airbrakes.

"Shit hot, Baumann. Just shit hot." He reached across the desk to again shake my hand. "Damned lucky too, I'd say." He was truly impressed and utterly captivated by my no-shit sea story. I felt the urge to rise, hoping we might be finished but the skipper remained seated, so I followed his lead. I was not dismissed yet. The room grew quiet. His expression changed, suggesting there was unfinished business. "So, what's your plan, Mitch? You getting out or what?"

Good, I thought. I wanted to discuss this too, and best do it while he's in a good mood. "Yes, sir. I've been planning to submit my resignation letter soon, leave active duty in December when my obligation's up."

He looked down at some paperwork on his desk. "You have orders now, to VT-3 in Pensacola? That right?"

"Yes, sir. They came in while I was in Adak. I haven't accepted them though." Officers receiving permanent change-of-station orders had to acknowledge them with BUPERS before being allowed to detach from their current command. It was mainly a formality unless you were planning to separate from active duty. If I accepted the orders, I'd be obligated to complete them, picking up an additional three-year commitment.

"So, you plan to ride out your time and remain in the squadron until the end of the year?"

"Yes, sir. Of course, I'll need your endorsement."

"Yes, of course," he said, eyeing me carefully. "Mitch, you really want to do this? You know what happens next month, right?"

I understood the event he was referring to but not its relevance to my situation. His one-year term as VP-25 commanding officer was ending in May. "Your change of command, sir?"

"Bingo. And you're sure you *really* want to do this?"

Do what? I thought. Maybe he's trying to talk me into staying in the Navy. Maybe he's trying to explain that this office and all its infinite power will one day be mine. "Skipper, I'm flattered. I'm glad that you, that the Navy, wants to retain me." I struggled for words, feeling I was missing something in his message. "I'm just not sure I'm cut out for it, for the long haul that is."

"What'll it take to get you to accept orders and forget this early resignation BS? Something better? Life on the Redneck Riviera and Evelyn's Grunge Bar not appealing enough to you and Aimee?"

He threw me by bringing Aimee into it, that he even remembered her name. "No, Skipper, it's not that—"

"Well, what then, goddamn it? I'm not kidding. I'll get you something better, but you need to play ball. You'll need to accept. I won't have the Bureau cut new orders just so you can turn them down."

"Can I think about it, Skipper?" I said, realizing I needed to end the meeting. I wasn't going to come to a decision sitting in his office. "Maybe talk it over with Aimee?"

"No, Mitch. And here's why. In less than six weeks, Dick Fowler takes over as CO. You catching my drift? You really want to stay?"

I understood completely or thought I did. Commander Fowler, the XO, aka Dickless, was expected to get command in May and take over the squadron as part of the normal rotation. This was no surprise. I was confident I could weather the storm. "I'll take my chances, sir."

The skipper rose, gesturing for me to keep my chair. He walked over and shut the door to the outer office, careful to ensure it was locked. Now I knew I'd missed something and braced for impact. "He plans to court-martial you," he said, in a hushed voice. "You know that? If you stick around, your new CO is going to have you court-martialed, as sure as the Texas day is long."

The shock was so immediate all I could do was laugh. It seemed so ludicrous, after what I'd just accomplished, after all the praise the skipper had just bestowed. "No way," I said. "I can't believe he'd do that."

"Believe it," he shot back. "He's tossing around claims of violating the twelve-hour rule, taking non-authorized personnel – two women, mind you – on a tactical mission, sharing top-secret information with an enlisted man, not to mention willful disobedience of a standing order and destruction of government property." He paused for effect, looking up from behind his reading glasses. "Any of that stuff true, Mitch?"

I remained quiet.

"Because it has shades of someone I know written all over it."

This was preposterous. Here I'd "Yeagered in" a severely damaged aircraft to a miraculous landing after we'd located a high-priority Russian submarine and guided a US nuclear sub into position to trail it all over the Pacific. *And the XO was going to fucking court-martial me?* I sat in silence, hoping there was more to the skipper's accusation, that he'd soon burst out laughing, ha, ha, just kidding, had you going there for a moment, didn't I?

He remained serious. "Mitch, leave now. Detach," he said, in a reassuring, fatherly voice. "Take orders and get out while you can. I will help."

"I get the feeling you have someplace other than Pensacola in mind, sir?"

"I'm prepared to offer you a deal I've worked out with your detailer. A different tour, two years, max. A company officer billet at the Naval

Academy." He carefully studied my reaction. "What do you say?"

"Naval Academy?" I was floored. Company officer jobs were highly sought after and rarely came available due to the large number of applicants and few slots. He really was going out on a limb to save my ass from the big, bad XO. Still, I was conflicted. "When would I report?"

"June 10. Day after the change of command."

He had all the answers and was making it too easy. "Sir, thank you for your interest, your concern but—" I let the thought finish in my head, stemming a sudden rush of despair.

"But?" he said. "There is no but. Don't tell me you need to think about this one. Look, I can get you some leeway on the reporting date. Take some leave, let the accident investigation run its course, talk it over with your wife, but I advise in the strongest possible terms you take me up on this offer. Do you follow?"

I followed. It was no secret he and the XO disagreed on many fronts, their personalities and leadership styles clashing like badly meshed gears. The CO did not pick his XO, a Navy selection board picked him, and a flawed one at that. Many heard Wilson admit he was pleased to receive orders back to NAVAIR in Washington, DC. Away from Moffett Field, to the opposite coast, he'd add in private, making it clear *opposite coast* was a euphemism for his misgivings about Fowler taking the reins of command. And here he was, offering me a lifeline, orders back to the Naval Academy, which I had my own misgivings about. What had made me stay away since graduation and voluntarily skip my five-year reunion lay buried in a pile of grief and haunted memories, unfinished business from my first-class year. I simply could not accept his generous offer, no way, but finally ended the discussion by thanking him and saying, "I'll talk it over with Aimee, sir."

# West of Annapolis

# Part II

# 11

## JUST VISITING

TECUMSEH COURT at the U.S. Naval Academy serves as a gateway to Bancroft Hall, the world's largest college dormitory. A massive expanse of beige tile-brick spread in all directions, T-Court, as it is more commonly known, provides the perfect foreground for tourists to take in the spectacular French Renaissance architecture of the Yard around them and to observe the midshipmen as they gather outside for daily noon meal formations. At the far end, opposite Bancroft's grand entrance, is the bronze statue of Tecumseh himself, once figurehead of the USS *Delaware* and now proudly on display in this prominent part of the Yard. Tecumseh has also been named the "God of 2.0" by the midshipmen, reminding them of the minimum grade point standard as they pass to and from class. They honor Tecumseh by tossing pennies at his base and dressing him in colorful war paint when expecting good fortune, like a football victory over Army, success during final exams, or, as the case today, culmination of the academic calendar, the celebration of Commissioning Week and graduation itself.

Tecumseh was in full regalia as I stood beneath his presence on this warm May afternoon under a bright blue sky. I was awaiting an appointment with my detailer, Hal Wilkinson, a lieutenant commander from BUPERS in Washington, class of '74, and company-mate when I was a plebe. I looked at my wristwatch and realized I was early. I'd been jittery since agreeing to come on this exploratory trip back east, my first to the Naval Academy since graduation. The agreement I'd made with the skipper was to pay a visit, talk to some people, Hal included, get a feel for the place and then decide if duty here was what I wanted. The problem was I'd already made up my mind on the flight out. I'd turned it over and over, replaying practically my entire career in VP-25, and all logic pointed to skipping orders and punching out at the earliest opportunity. I just needed a way to explain this to Hal in a very concise, courteous manner. I wasn't even sure I'd recognize him after nearly nine years and, chances were, our little meeting wouldn't last more than ten minutes once I sprung my intentions. I could even change my airline reservation and be on the non-stop home tonight out of Baltimore if I wanted.

"Hey, they let anyone through the gate these days, don't they?" a voice boomed from behind.

I turned, surprised to see Hal, virtually the same as the day he'd graduated except for a thick but neatly trimmed mustache, his taut lacrosse-honed body still intact under freshly pressed summer whites. His uniform was lined with an impressive row of ribbons under gold naval aviator wings. Last time I'd seen Hal he'd just slid on fresh ensign shoulder boards at his graduation. "Hal Wilkinson," I said, his wings, ribbons and lieutenant commander boards practically compelling me to add "sir" as I did when he was my squad leader back in '74. I reached out and shook his hand with a firm grip. "How the hell are you? I'm surprised you even recognized me." I was wearing civies and my aviator sunglasses.

"Are you kidding, Baumann? You think you can hide under those geeky civilian clothes? Blend in like a bloody tourist? Once a mid, always a mid."

"Takes one to know one, Hal," I said, grinning. "Why the uniform?"

"In case you haven't noticed, it's Friday, a workday over at Disneyland East. Drove out here right after lunch."

"Uh-oh, did I miss the memo? Should I be in whites too?"

"No, no, of course not. You're on leave for God's sake. I understand this is an unofficial trip for you, paid your own airfare out, lodging and such. Don't worry, your skipper explained everything."

"He did, huh?" I wondered how much detail he and Hal had shared behind my back. Was Hal's mission to convince me to take orders, save me from throwing a promising naval career down the drain? "He explained everything?"

"Sure did. Said you were a bit conflicted about your future and orders back to dear Old Ivy would be just the ticket to refresh your senses."

I had to laugh. Hal had definitely talked to Wilson, a University of Texas grad and Longhorn, who loved using the term *Old Ivy* when referring to the Naval Academy in the presence of its JO alumni. It was simply his good-natured way of poking fun, conjuring up an image of the snobbery and cliquishness associated with an Academy officer. I didn't take offense, names like that went with the territory.

The sun was intense standing in the open air of T-Court. Hal suggested we follow a path to shade under the canopy of trees along Stribling Walk. In the distance, we could hear cheering and shouting as a large crowd of midshipmen gathered around the Herndon Monument. Ah, yes, the Friday before graduation, the plebe recognition ceremony, known simply as *Herndon*, had just gotten underway. The plebes were starting to form a human scaffolding around the twenty-foot obelisk in an effort to hoist a man to the top. At the apex sat a Dixie cup, a version of the sailor's hat, worn by plebes during their summer indoctrination. To complete the ritual, one of their classmates had to make it to the top, replace the Dixie cup with a regular combination cover, thus officially ending their plebe year and allowing recognition as fourth-class midshipmen. We walked closer to the monument and stood at the outer perimeter of the huge crowd gathered to watch as the plebes worked feverishly in the mud trench surrounding its base. "So, I heard the story of your flight up in Adak. Impressive stuff, Mitch, especially for a P-3 puke." Hal was an F-14 pilot that had completed his first tour with a fighter squadron on the West Coast before becoming a detailer. This much I knew. "You get any official recognition out of it?"

I pondered my recent conversation with the skipper. "Yeah, they put me in for an air medal, but it was subsequently downgraded to a letter of caution," I laughed.

"You're kidding, a letter of caution? In your jacket?"

"Of course, I'm kidding, Hal. It was a joke. You don't get out much, do you?"

"Hey, watch it, Baumann. I've crossed more oceans, flown off more carriers and sailed over more blue water than you'll ever see stuck on those desert islands sucking up all that per diem." He winked at me, indicating no hard feelings but enjoying his jab at the P-3 community's landlubber mentality.

We paused to look in the direction of the mob. The plebes were getting closer to the top of the monument, now three tiers high, bare feet resting on strong shoulders below, all hands clasped firmly together. Shouts and cheers were coming from their classmates from the outer ring on the ground as a female plebe appeared to be making her way closer to the top. "So, Mitch, we're glad you came out. I think it'll help with your decision, but I must say in my two years as a detailer, this one has certainly gone outside the lines."

"What do you mean?"

"It means we had you headed to VP-31, but when orders got pushed three months, we suddenly needed more primary instructors in Pensacola, so then it was VT-3. Not bad orders, but something we'd give a five-percenter, not a one-percenter. You look great on paper, hit all your quals early, recommended for early promotion on your last fitrep, top one-percent, glowing write-ups by both your skippers with—"

"Then why outside the lines?"

"We had you classified as likely to separate, not someone planning to stay beyond rotation from shore duty. And of course, we don't give primo orders to someone planning to punch out, leave active duty early."

I was stunned. "How'd you know I was planning to punch? I never communicated that in my dream sheet."

"Oh, we have ways, Baumann," Hal smiled, using his best Gestapo accent. "People talk, we listen. Department heads, peers, classmates. As much as you'd like to think, we're not braindead at the Bureau stamping out orders like some random number generator. So, VT-3 keeps you alive should you decide to stay in but it's not prime."

"But Naval Academy is?"

"Oh, yeah. Ninety percent of the company officers we select get picked up for lieutenant commander either ahead or in their zone, stay in for at least the full twenty. Your skipper's betting the ranch on you, that you won't punch."

"But I haven't officially decided yet. That's why I'm here, right?"

"Your orders are cut, they're on my desk. We just need the Commandant to give the nod, my boss will sign off and they'll be on the message boards by Monday." Hal looked me in the eye. "You do know about the interview with the Commandant, right? It's set for tomorrow."

"Yes, I know about the interview." I reminded myself of my decision on the plane and my plan to flea tonight if necessary.

"It'll be quick, I promise." An interview with the Commandant of Midshipmen wasn't typically part of the selection process but since I was out here, everyone thought it'd be a good idea for me to drop in, pay my respects. "You know, somewhat informal, sort of a meet and greet," Hal continued. "You did bring your whites though, right?"

"Yes, Hal." I was beginning to feel squeezed, like my option to fly home tonight was slipping away, that I was committed to fulfilling everyone else's expectations and promises. "So, all I have to do is meet the 'dant and the job is mine, the orders on their way?"

"Yeah, more or less," Hal said. "Look, think it over, talk to your wife tonight, but as they say, this is a limited offer, call now, operators are standing by, ha, ha."

The plebes were getting very close to the top. The female we'd seen earlier was no longer in the high position, having fallen or been given a subtle nudge by one of her male classmates. I shook my head amazed that after seven years, women at the Academy were still not fully accepted into the Brigade. The first women in the class of '80 had a rough Herndon ceremony in 1977 when they, as plebes, attempted the climb along with a thousand of their male counterparts. Back then, it was feared that since women were lighter, they would be the obvious choice to try to boost to the top and complete the event in record time. There was a huge move afoot by all classes to prevent such a scenario. Word was put out days before the ceremony, *NOGOH* – No Girls On Herndon. T-shirts had been printed by the hundreds with that exact slogan and later confiscated in advance when discovered by the Commandant. I was there as a first-class, having endured the first year ever with women, witnessing, and dare I say participating in, the blatant sexual harassment they bore along with a much harsher plebe indoctrination than most of the men. This was purely a bold attempt to run them off before they could gain a foothold in the previously all-male institution and quickly erase the huge mistake Congress had made in the first place. Needless to say, it didn't work, not then, not now, but it appeared some residual resentment remained as I viewed the current climb underway. Suddenly, I was reminded of Maddy and my heart sank. Why'd I come back here today? I thought. What the hell was I thinking?

"Hal, let me ask you a question," I snapped. "When you say, more or less, does that mean the decision is mine? Because if you guys haven't made up your mind, then I'd just as soon get the hell out of here, tonight."

"Cutting right to the chase, eh, Mitch?" Hal studied me carefully before continuing. "Okay, let me ask you, what's the story with this Commander Dick Fowler, your XO?"

I was surprised to hear his name and laughed. "What's the story? I'm not sure I follow."

"Well, he calls my boss last week, the director for all 1300-designator officer assignments, a four-stripper coming off a CO tour himself, A-6 driver, great guy. Anyway, they don't know each other, your XO and my boss, but they end up having a long chat and Fowler recommends we take a pass on you. Said some other things too."

Why that SOB, I thought. It'd be just like Dickless to poison the well. "He said that? In the face of my skipper's "glowing" recommendation?"

"He did. That's why this one's gone outside the lines, needs to be handled carefully, like I said earlier."

"That's the reason for the interview tomorrow?"

"Partly. Honestly though, Mitch, we're taking your CO's recommendation, your exceptional fitness reports, your long list of accomplishments in VP-25 and what will be, I'm sure, a positive endorsement by the Commandant, but my boss wanted me to settle this thing, this unusual phone call from your XO."

"Wait a minute. Hold on. I thought it was my decision, that I come out here, take a look around, talk to you, see the place, decide for myself. In truth, I thought you were here to sell *me* on the concept, not the other way around. Now I'm looking at an interview, having to answer for this "unusual" phone call. So, tell me Hal, is it my decision or has it come down to this?"

Hal's eyes wandered around the Yard before settling on me. "This," he said.

"I thought so. In that case—"

"Now hold on yourself, Mitch. Look at it from our view. My boss gets a call from a full commander, the next commanding officer of VP-25 mind you, and this commander doesn't have some very nice things to say. He paints a picture of a reckless pilot that is a bit of a hotdog, someone that doesn't like playing by the rules, who may not be as stellar as he looks on paper. He just wants me to get to the bottom of it, give him my recommendation. I'm voting for Mitch, so, yes, you do control your own destiny. Just get through the interview with the Commandant tomorrow and you'll be out here lickety-split."

"Lickety-split, eh? That tech jargon for a fighter jock?"

"Of course, not," Hal said, without skipping a beat. "It's how fast a P-3 puke's sister swims out to meet troop ships."

We shared a laugh, releasing some of the mounting tension. "Did you know he was a battalion officer back here in '77?" I said. "Fowler, that is – when I was a firstie."

"He mentioned it to my boss he was stationed here. Did he know you back then?"

"Nah, we never crossed paths, opposite sides of the world," meaning opposite sides of Bancroft Hall. "Is any of this relevant?"

"Everything's relevant, Mitch. We just count some stuff more than others. Is there anything else we should know? About you and Fowler?"

Fowler served as 1st Battalion Officer from 1976 to 1979, an odd assignment for someone having just been promoted to commander coming off a department head tour supposedly in the hunt for command of a VP squadron. Typically, if you screened for command at the end of your DH tour, you were quickly stashed somewhere to await orders to a squadron as executive officer. In Fowler's case, he'd come to the Academy and stayed for nearly three years, then served on the Deputy CNO's staff for another three, then began his XO tour. I say odd because there's never a gap of six years between a DH and XO tour. But there were a lot of things odd about Fowler, and I'm certain Hal's boss had sensed it during the call. "Did he say anything about a court-martial? Fowler?"

"A court-martial? Good God, no. Should he have?"

"Probably not. I think he was threatening one though. He was the OINC up in Adak during my flight and didn't particularly agree with the way I handled things. I'm pretty certain the skipper told him to stick it. He was always threatening some level of discipline with either the junior officer or enlisted ranks." I told Hal about the bumper sticker incident and the XO's completely off-the-rails response during a department head meeting. I recounted some other stories as well. Hal was starting to get the picture and laughed tremendously at the bumper sticker prank.

"Sounds like you've had an amazing first tour, Mitch. You'll do fine tomorrow. Call home tonight, talk things over with your wife. You really should get away from that prick."

"Don't I know it," I replied. Still, I was conflicted, uncertain duty at USNA was what I wanted, if I could tolerate being here again, if I really wanted to remain in the Navy afterward. Our little meeting had drawn to a close, Herndon conquered by the class of '86. It was time to wrap things up and say goodbye to Hal, at least until tomorrow morning when, and if, I showed for my appointment with the Commandant. "Have a good evening,

Hal. Great seeing you again."

"Thanks, man. See you in the morning, right?"

Maybe you will and maybe you won't, I thought. We reached out and shook hands briefly, possibly for the last time.

Almost like he was reading my mind, Hal continued, "It'll be a great tour for you, Mitch. A great experience for you and Aimee. Don't make any rash decisions. Think it over."

"I know, Hal. I will. And thanks for taking the time today."

"No, thank *you*," he replied, glancing away then back at me. "Hey, one last question."

"Yeah?"

"Did they ever resolve the, you know, the case?"

I remained silent, a shudder rippling through my body, unprepared for his change of subject.

"You remember, the female plebe, class of '80?"

"Yes, yes, I remember," I said, wishing he hadn't brought it up. "No news, from what I hear, although the investigation is still officially open. After six years though, who knows?"

"Yeah, it's been a long time, he said, sensing my reticence and limited knowledge dissuading further conversation. "Take care of yourself, Mitch," he said, turning to leave, a note of sadness in his voice.

"You too, Hal."

I lingered in his wake, enjoying the warmth of the late afternoon sun, meandering further down Stribling Walk toward Mahan Hall, its filigreed clock tower rising boldly above a leafy canopy of oaks and maples. The Academy Yard was alive in all its magnificent springtime glory – the rich beds of tulips, forsythia and azalea in full bloom, the fountained-terrace of Michelson and Chauvenet Halls framing the blue estuary of the Severn River as spinnaker-adorned sailboats pressed toward the bay. It's stunning how beautiful the place is, how you fail to recognize its grandeur when, after four long years, you seem to remember it only from behind a book, or a watch belt, or a parade uniform.

The huge crowd had moved on from Herndon and the groundskeepers were already cleaning up, replacing the muddy row of trenches with fresh sod and preparing to power wash the greasy goo from the monument's facade. I rejoiced with the fourth-classmen and shared the thrill of having shed the burdensome title as plebes, who were likely out in town at this moment grabbing a beer, exercising their newly awarded drinking privileges. And even with three challenging years ahead, Herndon was truly a liberating experience for anyone who stood in those trenches. The ritual created a lasting camaraderie that would sustain you during your remaining time at the Academy, providing one of the happiest and most memorable days in your four-year toil toward graduation. I was reexperiencing the elation myself standing in its simmering aftermath.

It was time to leave the Yard and head back into town toward my sponsor's house in the small village of Eastport. I swung an immediate left at Gate 3 and strolled through picturesque Annapolis harbor packed with families and tourists on my way to crossing the Eastport bridge. I was halted on the sidewalk's entrance as the drawbridge was raised for a slow-moving sailboat to pass underway on motor power, its naked mast poking through the gap in the road above as it returned from sea. Waiting, I surveyed the murky water below and was reminded of an incident on this bridge in 1976 during my first-class year the Saturday before Army Week as we prepared for the annual Army-Navy football game. I was on duty that weekend as the Battalion Officer of the Watch, more commonly referred to as the Bow Wow, when I got a call from the OOW, a full lieutenant commander, who was at the base hospital demanding I come over ASAP to write up four third-class midshipmen and escort them back to Bancroft Hall. They were all intoxicated, having kicked off Army Week in style by consuming too many pitchers of beer in town before heading back to Mother B with just minutes to spare before taps at 2300. Needless to say, they didn't make taps when one of these brilliant youngsters, the term for a third-class midshipman, and presumably the drunkest in the bunch, decided to take a leap off the Eastport bridge into Spa Creek thirty feet below in full service dress blues, combination cover, white scarf, gloves and overcoat. In my interview with the group at the hospital, I was informed by the jumper himself that he must've slipped, or leaned on a defective railing, or both. He couldn't recall. He was still quite drunk sitting in his hospital gown, shivering under a tightly wrapped wool blanket. His frightened classmates had sobered up and were more forthcoming in their statements. They admitted our would-be jumper had climbed onto the narrow guardrail to prove his sobriety and affirm his ability to walk any straight line, goddamn it, be it on the sidewalk or the bridge's protective railing. But once atop the railing, he was egged on by his classmates to intentionally jump, to do it in the spirit of the upcoming big game. "Show some balls," they taunted. On his way down, with arms flailing and cap flying, his loud cry to the world that night, or at least to the citizens of Annapolis, was, "BEAT ARMY!"

The Annapolis Harbor Patrol fished him out of the icy water minutes later as he frantically dog-paddled in circles with the weight of ten pounds of soggy clothing threatening to pull him under. Now dried out and somewhat embarrassed, I escorted him in a van from the hospital back to Bancroft Hall, one of his classmates carrying the waterlogged uniform stuffed into a plastic bag. I was directed by the OOW to fry them all for drunk and disorderly and conduct unbecoming, punishment considered "Class A" offenses, carrying a full 75 demerits each. Our jumper was the only one to eventually receive back-to-back Class A's and ended up restricting for six months, all the way to June Week. It was harsh punishment for an Army Week infraction and surprised everyone when the news leaked out. Beat Army fever runs high during Army Week and over-enthusiastic conduct is often overlooked or forgiven. Back in the day, you could practically get away with torching the Superintendent's residence as long as you yelled "Beat Army" while you did it. But no more. It was the first year of women at the Academy and the administration was determined to winnow out the drunken, Neanderthal behavior that had crept in since allowing upper-class midshipmen to consume beer out in town. Someone was to be made an example of – in this case, the jumper and his beered-up friends in my battalion.

I continued over Spa Creek to my sponsor's home, a modest but beautifully maintained Cape Cod less than a mile from Annapolis harbor across the bridge. My sponsors themselves, the Reardon's, Jack and Irene, were a wonderful couple assigned to me when I was a plebe back in 1973 and I'd maintained contact, a friendship with them both, ever since. Midshipman sponsors are a godsend for a plebe adjusting to the rigors of Academy life, offering refuge during weekend liberty, perhaps a nice meal on Sunday or just a place to kick back, watch TV and destress for an afternoon. Today, Jack and Irene came to the rescue, offering me a place to stay for the night as it would have been impossible to get a room at any hotel within a thirty-mile radius of the Chapel dome during Commissioning Week. Jack was a retired Navy captain, class of 1940, serving twenty-six years as a submariner beginning with the USS *Sawfish* in the South Pacific during WWII and retiring from active duty, settling in Annapolis in 1968. Their basement walls, where I was staying, were lined with plaques and pictures of World War II subs, of crewmen, combat action, exotic ports, and Jack's framed commissioning pennant from the USS *Tang* from 1960. Jack drove diesel boats his entire career, never making the transition to nuclear power even after applying and being accepted into Admiral Rickover's nuclear program in the late 1950s. According to Jack, he later told Rickover to take his program and shove it, a risk that would typically spell disaster for anyone, but Jack eventually got command of the *Tang* and later, a full sub squadron. Touché, Admiral, sir. Still, Rickover's connections and broad influence, finally serving as the Director of Naval Reactors, held sway over the entire Navy during his sixty years of active service. His presence was huge. He'd served in both World War I and II and was the indisputable father of the nuclear navy. Careers hung in the balance over his whims and dictatorial nature. In the mid-1960s, his heavy hand had helped revamp the entire academic curriculum at the Naval Academy forcing a change that eventually brought a halt to USNA's "trade school" mentality and more in line with a major university's accredited engineering program. In 1975, the Academy named their new engineering complex after him, creating what was later derided as "the Rickover curriculum" by many line officers. They believed these academic changes came at a price, a softening of the more rigorous military instruction that had prevailed for over a century, tried and proven methods that had given us Admirals Dewey, Nimitz, Halsey, Spruance and thousands of officers whose mettle had been successfully tested in battle throughout history.

Significant changes to the plebe indoctrination system followed in the late 1960s which many of the alumni faithful argued was a watering down of the entire academy experience – training designed not to separate the weak from the strong but an ordeal simply to be endured by all. Women at the Academy, again, these voices argued, was the next step in the de-evolution, another chink in the armor, less Sparta, more Athens, weakening the military for the sake of social experimentation. During my time as a midshipman, especially my first-class year, I felt I was at the vortex of these changes. I lived with them in the day-to-day grind of Bancroft Hall. The introduction of women *had* complicated things, not by lowering the bar of demanding physical standards and bucking tradition that everyone had feared but creating the complex issue of female integration into the rowdy, testosterone-laden military environment of Bancroft Hall. I would be remiss if I claimed the integration had gone smoothly but it wasn't the doomsday scenario everyone had predicted. Yes, there were problems – fraternization, harassment, sexual misconduct and the early misstep of the administration trying to cope solely by using the admin conduct system and passing out demerits. But we tried to meet the problems head-on, we did our best to anticipate – the Academy leadership, the company officers and the entire first-class regiment assigned to the plebe detail during that first summer, which allowed the Academy to emerge mostly unscathed during the inaugural year of the women. It wasn't until after I'd graduated the inevitable sex scandals arrived, creating nationwide public awareness, embarrassment for the Academy, court-martials, separations – a PR nightmare for any institution. The ship eventually did right itself after many changes as evidenced by the growing number of women in the ranks seven years later but there was a stain, a tarnishing of the image, a questioning of the mission. And I had sensed a lingering resentment of the women's presence today on Herndon, not nearly as strong as Induction Day when women first walked through the gates in 1976, but present nonetheless.

Irene prepared a marvelous homecooked meal I shared in the Reardon dining room that evening with just her and Jack. It was great reconnecting and hearing the latest on their three grown sons, the oldest a 1968 graduate who had completed two tours in Vietnam as a Marine infantry platoon leader and company commander. Irene reported he was now safely stationed back at the Marine Barracks in Washington DC as a freshly minted lieutenant colonel on the Commandant's staff. Their other two boys were out west, the youngest having recently graduated from medical school. All three were thriving, which was obviously reflected in Irene's enthusiastic chatter. Jack was quiet during dinner as was his nature, letting Irene do most of the talking. He did offer encouragement about my returning to Annapolis and made it abundantly clear that orders as a company officer should be something I should jump at and not waste a moment of thought on the subject. I figured he'd have trouble understanding any reticence on my part, so I kept quiet about my meeting with Hal earlier. I did tell them about my father's recent passing and offered a quick explanation of the circumstances. Both offered heartfelt condolences, but Jack seemed clearly disturbed by the news. He raised some pointed questions regarding my father's behavior and any change in his routine leading up to the accident – was he jittery? Was he upset? Did he have trouble sleeping the night before, or at any time? Was there a recent change in his health? On and on. How the hell would I know any of that, I thought. These were questions I couldn't answer and, sensing a gap of knowledge and discomfort on the subject, Jack begged off and apologized. How could he have known my father had moved to Coeur d'Alene and isolated himself from our family unless I told him, which was never my intention.

When I descended the stairs to their basement at 10 P.M., I was bushed. I flopped onto a pull-out sofa bed craving sleep but there was one last item on my to-do list before switching out the light. I had promised to call Aimee to let her know how things wrapped up today with Hal and my thoughts about our moving east. I crawled to the opposite corner of the room to locate the extension phone and was again sidetracked by Jack's career memorabilia surrounding me on the walls of their snug basement. My admiration of Jack and his military service ran deep, and I couldn't avoid the obvious comparison of him and my father, especially in the wake of our brief conversation at dinner. Jack Reardon and my father, John, were cast from the same mold – both Midwesterners, only two years apart, their youth forged in the Depression, fought in World War II, Dad experiencing combat in Europe, Jack in the Pacific, and each raising a family of baby-boomer children in the wake of prosperity that followed. Except I perceived huge differences. It was my mother I wanted sitting at that table upstairs at dinner tonight next to her loving husband John, still happily married, enthusiastically bragging about their son, Mitchell and daughter, Amber and how wonderful they'd turned out. I wanted resolution, I wanted peace but most of all I craved the life the Reardon boys must've had under Jack and Irene. Amber and I were still struggling, each in our own way, trying to cope in the aftermath of a tumultuous upbringing and the recent, sudden death of our mysterious father. I needed to halt this morose train of thought. Summoning feelings of regret and anger in my sponsor's basement 3,000 miles from home wasn't going to undo a single thing. It wasn't time for regrets. It was time to call Aimee.

I dialed O and placed the collect call, giving my name as Mitchell to the operator. It was only 7 P.M. in California. I listened as Aimee accepted the charges. She came on the line laughing, "Mitchell, huh? So, you're going formal now that you're on the east coast?"

"I just felt like using it. Don't worry, you can still call me Mitch," I tossed back. "How you doing, Aims? You sound happy."

"I am. I had a good day. You sound tired. Did the flight out go okay?"

I'd taken a redeye, flying all night from San Francisco, landing in Baltimore this morning and awake ever since. "Yeah, right on time. I had the meeting with my detailer at two, just finished dinner with Jack and Irene. I'm sitting in their basement now. So, tell me about your good day."

She hesitated. "Well, I got a job offer this morning. At a radio station in San Jose."

"A job offer? At a radio station?" My mind was reeling. "I didn't even know you were looking. When did this come about?"

"Mitch, I told you I wanted to go back to work when Sean got a little older. Don't sound so surprised. We discussed this."

"I know, but so close to my taking orders? What if we end up moving? Then what?"

"You told me there was no way you'd accept orders back to the Naval Academy, that you were only going to look around, to appease everyone."

"I know. I know I said that. It's just that – well, it's complicated. Things are still up in the air, it could go either way. I should know more tomorrow." I glanced up at a picture of Jack and Irene staring back at me, one from their younger days in the Navy. "I really wish you hadn't started looking for a job, at least not right now."

Aimee sighed. "And I really wish you had offered me congratulations."

"Okay, yes, I'm sorry. Congratulations, Aimee."

"Gee, Mitch, that sounded so heartfelt."

There was a brief lull, both of us afraid to talk for fear of starting a long-distance argument over the phone. I didn't want that to happen. There was still a ton I needed to tell her based on my meeting with Hal. "I'm sorry. I think it's wonderful you finally were offered a job back in radio. Congratulations." I truly meant it.

"Thank you." She sounded satisfied. "And if it means anything, I haven't accepted yet. I know things can change with us. I figured you didn't travel all the way out there just to tell them to shove it. When will you know?"

"Like I said, probably tomorrow. I have an interview with the Commandant."

"Then you'll decide?"

"Something like that. Again, it's up in the air. Apparently, they still need to offer *me* the job, not the other way around."

"And you're going to accept, right?" she said, her voice falling.

"Don't sound so disappointed, Aims. I'm not sure. I need to think about it. I get the feeling your job offer has changed things with you, yes?"

"Nothing's changed," she snapped. "I told you, I didn't accept, for the very reason we're talking here. I support you either way, you know that. But I think it's important you're either all in or all out with this, no halfway. And I'm just not hearing that in your voice. If things come to a head tomorrow, I'm betting you won't decide. You're still waffling."

She was perceptive as usual, drilling right to the heart of the matter. "I'm not waffling," I said, sounding defiant.

"Okay, Mitch, what is it then? Do we pack our stuff and move to Annapolis or not?"

"I don't know! I just told you, I have this interview tomorrow. It's out of my hands."

"All right, so I'm offering you the job, right here, right now, on the phone. Do you accept or not?"

"Aimee, c'mon. What's gotten into you? Why the urgency everything gets settled tonight?"

"Why do you think, Mitch? A decision is going to be made affecting our future, probably in the next twenty-four hours. I think you'll be happier if you do the choosing. And you'll be much easier to live with afterward. Don't you want to be a part of the solution? Don't you want a say in the matter?"

"Of course, I want a say," I said. "But there are things. There are issues."

"Then talk to me. Tell me."

"I can't! I truly don't know what I'm supposed to do. I'm being ripped in half. I have a past with this place, okay? There are issues, open issues." I paused, steadying my voice. "And yet I'm flattered. To have the skipper, my detailer and others rooting for me, willing to go to bat and offer me this, this opportunity, to be stationed here. Why it's such a beautiful place, Aimee. You should have seen it with me this afternoon. Anyone would jump at the chance to do a two-year tour here."

"Then take it. If they offer it, take it," she said, without conviction. "If that's what's in your heart."

"*My* heart? You sound disappointed. What's in *your* heart? And spare me the *I support you either way, Mitch*. You must have your own desires."

"I do. I love California, you know that, but I can move anywhere for two years if that's what you want. I'll always want to return though, and yes, resume my own career at some point. But this is about you now. You need to focus, bear down. Quit acting like an old lady and just decide."

"I am focused, I am coming to a decision," I said, meekly.

"Oh, please. One week it's, 'I'm resigning, getting out early to fly for the airlines.' The next it's, 'I'm sick of flying, I want to go back to grad school.' Then it's, 'What do you think about extending and moving to Annapolis?' Well, which is it? We can't just sit around waiting for you to make up your mind because it's not happening. This round and round has been dragging on for at least a year."

She was right, of course, but as I'd felt earlier, it was like everyone had their own desires and expectations, forcing a narrowing of my options simply because I wasn't as fast on my feet about making a decision. And I had reasons. I drew a deep breath. "Aimee, I need to tell you a story, a couple of them, actually. Why this place has left such a mark. Maybe it'll help, I don't know."

"Okay. I'm listening, Mitch. I've got all night."

There was a tenderness to her voice, but she didn't sound enthusiastic. And who could blame her? I'd dragged her down a path with so many forks we were both lost, and she doubted I still held the compass. I was apprehensive but plodded ahead. "It was when the girls came," I said. "That's when the problems began."

"Huh?"

"My problems. Really, they were my problems. My first three years at the Academy were no picnic but I thrived, even during plebe year. It wasn't until first-class year rolled around that my life went to hell on a sled. My parents split up, Amber got into deeper trouble, you *Dear John'd* me—"

Aimee leapt in, "Now wait a minute, if that's where this is going—"

"No, no, it's not. I'm sorry." I was certainly not trying to imply Aimee had wrecked my final year, only that her letter and my family woes may have contributed in some manner. I was sorry I'd led with that. "Okay, let me start over," I said, choosing my words carefully. "It began when I volunteered for plebe detail my first-class year, before the other personal stuff hit. I never realized what a challenge it was going to be integrating women into the Brigade, and what a personal struggle it would become for me."

"Go on," she said, returning to her less-than-eager tone.

"Okay, so the first story still haunts me with regret over something I could have controlled but didn't." I paused, giving her a moment to assimilate what I'd said and the potential magnitude of what was to follow. "Her name was Sara Sedgley."

"Sara? We're talking about a person?"

"Yes. She was one of three girls assigned to Oscar Company, two platoons of plebes formed for the summer. The other two girls were Amanda White and Madison O'Connor. Amanda was from Spokane. She was rather plain looking, shaggy brown mop of hair and had one desire – to blend in, to be average and not make waves or be singled out as one of the first women attending a service academy. Maddy was from nearby Annandale, Virginia and was anything but plain. She was highly competitive and came with an impressive resume – top of her class, champion swimmer, certified scuba instructor, played guitar and sang lead in an all-girl rock band – all before landing at USNA."

"Hmm, impressive," Aimee, said, unsure where I was headed.

Her guarded monotone kept me from adding that Maddy was very noticeable, cute but not beautiful, tomboyish but able to be feminine, with light auburn hair, large brown eyes and a warm, engaging smile – a definite standout in a crowd. "The three girls were roommates," I continued, aloud. "Part of 27th Platoon, Oscar Company and I was their company commander for the first set. Sara was from Olathe, Kansas. She was not cute or pretty or any of those things. She was slightly overweight and moved slowly, always the last to formation. She had a timid demeanor but a strong Christian faith, witnessing to her classmates in their rooms when she should have been studying. She'd chosen a difficult path and didn't seem to understand her classmate's mostly negative reaction to her helpful, spiritual nature.

"But Academy life was hard on all the women, not just Sara. They really took it in the shorts starting on Induction Day, the moment after taking the oath of office in T-Court. They soon acquired a wide array of derogatory nicknames – midshipwomen, midship-chicks, plebettes, ploobs – plebes with boobs – on and on. They were picked on and harassed in ways the administration never dreamed of. Maddy was sharp, the most outgoing of the three and had the most self-confidence. She dodged more of the extreme name-calling or just rolled with it. Amanda was quieter but assertive when she needed to be. She just wanted to fly under the radar, not make waves and survive the summer, which she did. Sara was different. She was shy and lacked self-confidence, especially when being addressed by the first-class running the plebe detail. She was not pretty like Maddy, she was not thin like either of them. She was short and pudgy and not pleasant to look at, especially in her baggy white-works uniform, Dixie cup and sweaty upper lip. She stumbled on her plebe rates – required knowledge – and was on excuse squad many times during first set for "throbbing blisters" and given a chit excusing her from marching and other rigorous physical activity. She became an instant shit-screen for her classmates, picked on by both them and my first-class squad leaders on the detail. Sara Sedgley quickly morphed into Sara Sludge-ley. It was later shortened to Sara Sludge, Miss Sara Lee and Miss Sara Lee Poundcake used by her plebe classmates behind her back, referring strictly to her weight. She was simply known as Miss Sludge to the first-class on the detail. That's what bothered me the most, that my classmates were using this cruel nickname to address her in ranks, making it stick like glue for everyone to hear and use freely. And I, as company commander, ashamedly admit, initially let it slide.

"She was weak and got weaker as plebe summer dragged on. She was consistently derided by many for being fat, for being lazy but mostly for being unattractive, dumpy and downright ugly. I decided to call a halt to it a week before first set ended, before we'd be replaced by our classmates on second set. I told the firsties under me, no more "Miss Sludge," no more excessive piling on, that she will be treated equally and fairly. My emphasis was on Sara as a human being, not as a woman, not as a female plebe here to ruin our hallowed institution, but as a person, and that this excessive harassment stops now. I was in a delicate situation. I was temporarily their company commander. I wrote their grease for the summer, but I was also their classmate and would return as their equal in the fall once the academic year started. As expected, I received mixed messages and a mixed level of support. Nonetheless, I carried on with my next step to round up the plebes, all seventy of them, in Oscar Company. I did it when Sara wasn't present, at sickbay perhaps or somewhere out of the company area. I wanted to do it informally, placing them at ease and not under duress. I assembled them by calling a "plebe ho," rousting them from their rooms after evening meal. I sat them down on the floor at the end of one of the passageways in the company area, dragged a chair over in one hand, a can of Pepsi in the other, sat down to face them – just a nice, informal fireside chat. All seventy sat relaxed on the deck, their eyes locked on me wondering what was about to happen. I started by talking about teamwork, about camaraderie, about esprit de corps. While I agreed that first there must be a tearing down of the individual, a reforming of a common base, which was the whole point of Plebe Summer, the company must rally around to help each other, to help the weaker, the slower and provide encouragement, that there must be ground for mutual respect and care for each and every classmate. I looked at the plebes, still wearing blank expressions but appearing respectful, attentive. I was getting through, some of them got it, I knew, but most remained expressionless. I decided they needed a shock to the system, something not in my planned script. I paused, making direct eye contact and said, 'Okay, just to drive home the point, let it be known from here on, no more Sara Lee Poundcake, and no more Miss Sludge to her face. No more derogatory, demeaning names, period, or someone's going down for 50 for direct disobedience of an order.' I stood from my chair, dismissed them back to their rooms and walked away. This may have been a mistake, my downfall, to specifically bring up Sara and demand they stop picking on her under threat of being fried for DDO since I would be departing in a week for my first-class summer cruise. I had unknowingly set the stage for the opposite to occur, increasing scrutiny on her in the weeks to come. And the long-term fallout, especially with my classmates, would come in September with the return of the Brigade."

There was a brief silence, an awkward pause on the other end. "That's a truly awful story, Mitch," Aimee said, returning to life. "It's just sickening to hear of the cruelty you describe but you did the right thing. There was no mistake in that. Why do you say, your downfall?"

"I waited too long to blow the whistle, first with my speech and then placing several on report. In the end, I lost some of my classmate's support for calling them on something that ran rampant throughout the plebe regiment that summer. It cost me some friendships too."

"Yes, but you protected a weaker person against some horrible bullying."

"I protected no one."

"That's not true. Why do you say that?"

"Because, Aims, she didn't make it. The taunts and catcalls continued behind my back before I left for cruise then came back with a vengeance during second set. Sara was broken, humiliated and physically exhausted. By the end of Parents Weekend, she was processed out of Oscar Company, volunteering to resign, to quit and end the torture she'd endured over the past eight weeks."

"I'm sorry, Mitch. I'm sorry you were put in that situation but there's no shame in what you did."

"The story's not over. Before she left Bancroft Hall for the last time, she came back to the company area, presumably after taps, and pinned her picture on the bulletin board, an unflattering but sweet 3 x 5 Polaroid taken in her new tropical white uniform, along with a typed Bible verse. Underneath, it read:

> *For God sees not as man sees, for man looks at the outward appearance, but*
> *God looks on the heart.* 1 Samuel 16:7

I was treated to the sight when I got back from my cruise the morning after she'd posted it. Sara had sent a message to us all in her meek Christian way, driving a stake to the heart of anyone with a conscience. Of course, the cowards without had already defaced it, scribbling a hateful epitaph below: *Another bitch bites the dust.*"

We agreed to end our call after Aimee reassured me I had done all that I could. She was being nice and recognized the injustice that had occurred and its relevance to the role I played. By standing in the Yard today, I had allowed Sara and many other memories to come crashing back into my life much like a marauding bear ransacking a campsite. I set the phone down on its cradle and massaged my temples knowing I simply couldn't close my eyes and shut everything off from that summer. The sofa bed's flimsy mattress offered little comfort as I stared at the ceiling, doubtful a merciful sleep would arrive and end the noise in my head. But it wasn't the mattress or story of Sara's demise holding sleep at bay. Sara was merely a prelude, an unwelcome introduction to my first-class year. Most everything that followed revolved around Maddy. Maddy was my last thought as sleep finally came – a fitful, restless sleep.

# 12

## A RETURN TO MOTHER B

Tuesday, July 6, 1976
Induction Day, Tecumseh Court, 1700
1,300-plus voices in unison:

*"...bear true faith and allegiance to the same,*

*"that I will obey the orders of the officers appointed over me,*

*"that I take this obligation freely without any mental reservation or purpose of evasion,*

*"and that I will faithfully discharge the duties of the office on which I am about to enter, so help me God."*

The shadows were growing longer, the trees in the Yard beginning to cast a welcome shade over the throng of family onlookers, their sons, and now daughters, taking the oath of office in Tecumseh Court after an arduous first day of processing – a blur of filling out forms, of immunization shots, mug shots, initial uniform and gear issue, room and roommate assignments, all culminating in the swearing-in as midshipmen in the United States Navy on this hot, sticky Maryland summer afternoon. The sights and sounds of people around me gradually faded in, taking full shape, the familiar oath resonating in my head. I had been returned to 1976, standing at attention on one of the curved ramps leading to Bancroft Hall in my tropical white long uniform, three fresh stripes on my shoulder boards, facing the Class of 1980, watching these new plebes, now ex-civilians, affirm their oath to the Superintendent, the Commandant, and the entire first-class regiment before them. They already looked wide-eyed and exhausted, and their adventure was just beginning. In less than an hour these fresh-faced, shell-shocked individuals, 1,280 men, and for the first time, 81 women, standing in their shapeless white-works uniforms, tennis shoes and Dixie cups would be our charges for the next eight weeks, to train, to run ragged, to break if necessary, in order to transform them into functioning military servicemen, beginning their four-year toil to commissioned line officers in the U.S. Navy or Marine Corps.

I looked to my left, one of my Oscar Company squad leaders and classmates for three years, Caleb Wise, was standing at loose attention, his eyes locked on the plebes like lasers, likely thinking the same as me; *For the next eight weeks, we own your asses.* His comment surprised me.

"I think I'm gonna be sick," he whispered, without turning his head.

"Huh?"

"Look. Just look at 'em. Makes me sick to my stomach."

"Look at who?" I said, thinking he was referring to the entire class of plebes, the sea of white, before us.

"All the bitches," Caleb said, keeping his voice low. "I swear, they'll be gone before this set is out. It'll be my personal mission."

I didn't respond. His clear reference was to all the female inductees but specifically to the three girls of Oscar Company. God have mercy, I thought. Caleb wasn't the first to brag like this. Plans of running the women off had been brewing ever since it was announced they were coming. I wasn't planning on making it my personal mission, but I did intend to be firm, to make sure they carried their share of the load, performing to standards – both physically and mentally. I made a note to keep an eye on Caleb, for his own sake.

The oath of office was now complete. The Superintendent made a few closing remarks, congratulating the plebes on the huge challenge they'd accepted and wishing them the best of luck in the weeks to come. He appeared as a benevolent father figure, playing to the huge crowd of parents standing behind them, delivering assurance and implying that their sons, and daughters, would be in good hands. If they only knew, I thought. After being dismissed, the newly formed Class of '80 was permitted to say goodbye to their families in Tecumseh Court, to mill about as a group in the fading light one last time before heading back to their respective company areas for evening meal formation and the march down to the Wardroom. I decided to linger after dismissal, to walk on the periphery of the large group of kids tearfully hugging Mommy and Daddy, siblings and girlfriends, many of whom they would not see until Christmas. I thought of my own Induction Day three years before. No Mommy or Daddy, no girlfriend, just me – a 17-year-old kid 3,000 miles from home ready to take on the world. If I were to reflect on any one point in my life where I became an adult, that was the day. I wasn't just beginning a summer adventure; I was beginning a life. For the first time ever, I was independent. I had a roof over my head, clothes on my back, pay in my pocket and three squares a day. It was a liberating jolt of adrenaline. Yet, like all my new classmates, I was petrified. I watched the Class of '80 mingle with their loved ones in their final minutes of freedom. It was a tender moment to observe as a member from the other side, to see these kids break the tie that binds, bidding a final farewell and taking the amazing leap of faith just as I had done three summers before.

There are approximately 360 identical tables in the Academy's colossal T-shaped dining hall, also known as the Wardroom. Each table seats twelve midshipmen, an entire squad, with two seats at each end and eight facing each other. The food, compared to most colleges, is excellent and served family-style on large trays by mess stewards. I was sitting with Caleb's squad tonight as we dined on a delicacy of steak and lobster, aka surf and turf, served only on special occasions. A large tub of vanilla ice cream and strawberries was waiting for dessert. The first-class knew there'd be leftover lobster tails and ice cream as most of the plebes, now suffering the effects of shock and sheer exhaustion, did not have much of an appetite.

"Mr. Brownfield!" Caleb bellowed from the seat next to me. "The name and hometown of the person on your left. Go!"

Mr. Brownfield, one of our plebes, cocked his head slightly to read his neighbor's nametag.

"What the hell are you doing! Get your eyes in the boat. I'll ask again, who is the girl on your left and where is she from?" Caleb glared impatiently.

Plebes were required to learn and memorize many facts, many figures, called rates, during the course of their summer training but at this first meal, one of the few requirements was to know the names and hometowns of their twelve fellow squad-mates. Mr. Brownfield hesitated, then spoke softly, with no confidence, "Uh, her name is Sara Sludge and she's from uh, Kansas, sir."

"Kansas, huh? Where in Kansas?"

"Kansas City, sir?"

"Are you guessing, Mr. Brownfield?"

"No, sir."

"*What?*" Caleb stormed. "You better not be guessing." He turned to Sara. "Tell me, Miss Sludge, is that your last name or did they misprint your nametag?"

"Sludge is not my last name, sir."

A few male plebes at the table sniggered. Caleb ignored them.

"Turn, Mr. Brownfield. Read it. Carefully." Caleb said as if talking to a child, pointing at Sara. "What does it say?"

"Sedgley, sir. Sorry."

"*Sorry?*" Don't ever say you're sorry to me, plebe!" He turned back to Sara. "Miss Sedgley, is your classmate correct? Are you from Kansas City?"

"No, sir. I'm from Olathe, Kansas, sir," she said, rather smugly.

"No-sir-I'm-from-Olathe-Kansas-sir," Caleb mocked, throwing his arms up in despair. "Mitch, I don't believe it. I'm not sure what's worse, Brownfield dicking up Miss Sedgley's name and hometown or Miss Sedgley bilging the hell out of her classmate just now." Turning back to Sara, "Do you realize what you just did, Miss Sedgley? he said, as if it were blatantly obvious to everyone at the table.

Sara looked confused so I jumped in to save her, ending Caleb's fun. "Miss Sedgley, what Mr. Wise means when he says, 'You just bilged your classmate,' is you made him look bad in order to save yourself," I said.

"Never do that, to him or anyone. In the future, in a similar situation, the proper response to an upperclassman is, 'Request permission not to bilge my classmate, sir.' He may order you to bilge him but at least you showed some balls, uh, some backbone letting him be the bad guy." I pointed at Caleb. "Letting him make your classmate look bad. Sometimes he might feel charitable and say, 'Don't bilge him,' and let you both off the hook. You never know. Understand?"

"Yes, sir."

A lull developed after my little speech allowing some of the hungrier plebes to shovel down some chow before Caleb sprang to life again. "Okay, people, listen up. It's getting way too quiet at this end of the table. We need a little conversation. And don't make me pick on someone. I want a volunteer. Who wants to tell me about *A Message to Garcia*?"

*A Message to Garcia* was a pamphlet handed out earlier this morning to the arriving plebe class that told a story of dubious origin about an American first lieutenant, Rowan, who was given a message from President McKinley to carry to the leader of the insurgents, Garcia, holed-up somewhere in the vast mountainous region of Cuba just before the outbreak of the Spanish American War. After arriving in Cuba, Rowan disappeared into the jungle on foot, and, after a month of traversing the country, delivered his message to Garcia as instructed. The pamphlet had been handed to every new class as far back as anyone could remember and provided an example of the urgency, and in this case, tenacity, required when carrying out an order. Plebes were told to be conversant with its theme at their first evening meal. Caleb flashed a look of mock indignance when no one spoke up at his invitation. "No volunteers, eh? My God, what's this place coming to?" He glanced at the nametag of the female plebe to his right, the second of the three in his squad. "Okay, Miss, uh, White, enlighten us about *Garcia*."

Amanda paused before looking up. "Sir, I think it's about—"

"Hang on, hang on. You *think*, Miss White? Don't think, just tell me!"

"Sir, it's about, uh, the importance of getting a message to whom it's addressed for fear of the dire consequences. Something like, for the want of a nail, the shoe was lost, then the battle and the entire kingdom?"

"*What?*" Caleb roared. "No, no, no. That's way too vague. Where'd you get that crap? From the back of a cereal box?"

Caleb was screaming recklessly, flaming was the term, but it was obvious, even to the plebes, he was enjoying his theatrical display of temperament, his witty putdown. Still, I thought if he was trying to inspire participation and critical discussion on the topic, he'd pretty much blown it. I turned to Maddy O'Connor, one of the few plebes yet to be called on during the meal. "Miss O'Connor, what do you think the theme is? What was Rowan telling us in his zeal to deliver the message?"

Maddy had been sitting quietly, attentively, throughout dinner. She was doing her best to keep a low profile but was too stunning in her appearance. Most of her classmates and firsties on the detail recognized her by the minor celebrity status she'd achieved modeling the new women's uniforms, pictures added to the MHP, the midshipman regulation book, after accepting her appointment. A few of the pictures even made their way into newspapers around the country and a national women's magazine – all before her reporting today. I'd been one of many to see the pictures, figuring this girl, whoever she was, would be doomed the moment she walked through the gate and was shocked when she turned up in Oscar Company. Now, here she sat with her modest haircut and white-works uniform, silently spooning in her strawberries, hoping to blend in.

Maddy gave my question considerable thought. She knew Amanda's answer wasn't necessarily wrong, it was possibly one of the themes, but, intuiting what Caleb was after, responded boldly, succinctly, "Sir, it's about not questioning an order or the mission. You don't piss and moan and make a thousand excuses. You just salute and report back when you're done – sir."

Caleb and I exchanged surprised looks. "Well. I guess that about covers it," I said, turning to Maddy, "Nice job, O'Connor. I doubt Rowan himself had even thought of that one."

If Caleb was impressed, he didn't show it. He just moved on, instructing the plebes how to properly dismiss themselves from the table by requesting permission to shove off. And most did, almost instantly, leaving Caleb and I with more leftover lobster tails and ice cream than we could possibly eat.

Wednesday, July 14, 1976

Eight days into Plebe Summer, I was at my desk after plebe taps reviewing the schedule of events of upcoming training evolutions for our company. Neil King, one of my two platoon commanders, walked into the room and grabbed a chair across from me. "Whatcha working on?"

"Weekly's," I said, waving my hand over a stack of binders in front of me, not making eye contact. I was amazed at the complex level of detail and behind-the-scenes planning necessary to synchronize thirty-six platoons, 1,300 individual's summer training matrices, to ensure everything ran like clockwork and everyone got to each event on time, each day, filling the calendar from reveille to taps. Every plebe had their own schedule to manage, which mostly matched the entire platoon of 38, each platoon conducting the training evolutions as a unit. And it was the first-class detail's responsibility to get the plebes, by marching them in formation, to their next evolution. Today we marched them to PEP, to drill practice, tailor shop detail, a signals class and an honor code lecture. There were also permanent slots in the schedule for the three daily meal formations, the meals themselves and special instruction periods afterward in the company area, known as "come-arounds," where we basically drilled them on their rates, lining them up in formation, putting them in a brace, screaming and yelling in their faces until they were completely terrorized and humiliated. Sometimes we'd spice things up and use the periods for a little fun and games – things known as carrier quals, greyhound races, snowflake drills and a host of other antics all designed to ensure they receive the proper plebe experience. Just another day in the life of the poor plebe, and ours still had 300 to go.

"Yeah, friggin' schedules," Neil said, shaking his head. "Twenty pounds of shit in a ten-pound bag. Hey, did you hear what happened over in Delta company yesterday?"

I looked up. "No, what?"

"They actually fried the Delta company commander for failing to get his two platoons to a human relations lecture on time. Apparently, it caused quite a stir, rippling through the day and the instructor, a crybaby female lieutenant, was pretty steamed. She couldn't fry the entire lot of plebes who were dropped on her doorstep, so she took it upon herself to call the Commandant, who called the batt officer, who called the Delta company officer and directed him to fry the poor bastard in charge, in this case, his company commander."

"Now there's some real Navy justice," I said. "Thanks for the warning."

"Yeah, no slop whatsoever between evolutions anymore. And blame it on us when it hiccups." Neil paused, changing subjects. "Hey, Mitch, I need a quick favor tomorrow."

"Anything, roomie." Neil was my long-time roommate during academic year and had been since we were plebes. We were fast friends, having endured three long years of this place, of our own plebe summer, triumphing on Herndon, shipping out on youngster cruise and drinking like fish all over the Med, double dating at homecoming and hanging tough through many all-nighters when the rigors of second-class year academics hit. Neil had heard all the ups and downs of Aimee and me and our long-distance relationship since meeting her in Pensacola during our second-class summer. I knew many similar personal details of Neil. I'd met his family, spent time at his home in San Diego. We were as close as any two friends could be.

"I've got Batt Office watch in the morning with three of our plebes and need to post at 0600. Can you march my platoon to PEP tomorrow?" PEP stood for Physical Education Program and was basically one hour of early morning calisthenics performed en masse with the entire plebe regiment on the artificial turf on Farragut Field. It was led by a no-nonsense staff PE instructor and a cadre of buff midshipman aides.

"Be glad to. I need the workout myself," I said, having skipped the initial two sessions due to paperwork.

"Great. After Flores completes reveille check, we form-up on the Red Beach at 0615 in PE gear and double-time over. Try to arrive on the turf no later than 0630. You know Lenz, he's a stickler for punctuality. Plenty of time to get them there though."

"No problem."

"Thanks, man, getting late. Got a hot date with my rack." He turned and was gone.

"Sweet dreams," I called out.

Reveille, a series of ear-splitting bells, came much too early at 0600. I'd stayed up late trying to compose a long letter to Aimee, struggling for words, grappling with the status of our relationship, which was currently on life-support for some unknown reason. I'd ended up hitting my own rack at two A.M. feeling beat-up and clueless regarding the care and feeding of a long-distance romance. At 0601, I shook away the cobwebs and threw on my sneakers, shorts and red PEP t-shirt while Dan Flores, my current roommate and company sub-commander, went door to door making sure all the plebes were turned out. Twenty minutes later, 27th platoon was assembled in formation on the Red Beach, a tiled terrace behind Bancroft Hall, in full PE gear, ready to roll. But three were missing. "All right, where're the girls?" I asked. No sooner did I open my mouth than Maddy and Amanda slipped into ranks, Maddy clearly distraught over something. "Miss O'Connor, where's your classmate, Miss Sedgley?"

"Sir, she's in our room," she said, out of breath. "She can barely walk. She's got blisters on both feet, sir."

"Blisters? She needs to be out here. Now." I looked at the plebes, standing at attention, all eyes locked on me. "Oh, for the love of— Platoon, at ease!" I dashed back into the Hall, down a passageway, passing Oscar company's 28th platoon departing for the PEP field on time. I entered the girl's room and found Sara sitting on the edge of the shower stall applying a damp washcloth to her bare feet. She attempted to rise, to sound off, but I made a gesture to remain seated. "What's the problem, Sedgley?" Why are you late?" She'd been crying and slid the washcloth away revealing some nasty sores on her heel and toes.

"I'm sorry, sir. I just can't."

I winced at the raw wounds and oozing puce. "Yeah, that looks pretty horrible," I said. "Okay, stay put. You can straggle down to Medical at sick call. Are you able to do that?"

She nodded and struggled to her feet.

After helping her to a desk chair, I jogged from the room realizing we were late for PEP, wondering if I should have left her stranded to find Medical by herself. Nothing I could do now. I quickly called the platoon back to attention and we made the brisk run in formation to Farragut Field.

Approaching the seaward entrance, I could see the turf lights were on blending with the hazy summer sunrise. Coach Heinz Lenz, the PEP leader, was already upon his platform bellowing over the PA system. "Let's go, let's go, line up, line up. It's a beautiful morning, NAVY!" he sang out in his distinctive German accent. "Today we do ze strength workout starting with—" Lenz halted his monologue, spying our approach from the rear. "Who is this entering my field?" he said. "You're late, you're late." He turned to a midshipman assistant on the platform for a quick word then turned back. "*Oscar Company!* Is that you, *Oscar Company?*" he yelled rhetorically for the entire regiment to hear. "C'mon, get moving, *Oscar Company!* You are holding up ze whole Navy!" I felt my face redden. Geez, could you scream Oscar Company a little louder? I thought. I don't think they heard you the first time.

During the remainder of PEP, I received sympathy nods from classmates in the other companies, knowing it could have easily been one them singled out and publicly shamed by Lenz. He pulled no punches when it came to order and punctuality. My plebes, however, looked terrified during the entire exercise period fearing the worst would come later. They didn't know much in their brief Navy careers but understood perfectly well the cardinal rule that shit flows downhill.

"We need to teach those little pricks a lesson," Caleb said, when we got back. "That we are never late to PEP again. Ever." Both he and Dan suggested we run some uniform races after evening meal.

"Yeah, but it was my fault," I said. "I gave us the late start."

"And Lenz coulda had one of his henchmen fry your ass if he wanted," Caleb said, lowering his voice. "You didn't get a deuce in yard-mail today, did you?" A deuce was a Form 2, a conduct report.

"Of course not. Lenz wouldn't put me on report. That's not his style."

"Still, we should run 'em around a bit tonight. Teach 'em all a lesson, that the girls should've been dressed out, in formation sooner and not caused the ruckus in the first place."

Uniform races were an exercise designed to teach speed and efficiency, the ability to change from one uniform to another in only a few minutes, to stand ready for inspection and repeat many times with some level of variation. I agreed with Caleb, we hadn't put them through this drill and it was time to send a message, to have a little fun.

At 1900, Dan Flores strode up and down the company area screaming, "Oscar Company! Plebe ho!" at the top of his lungs until both platoons were flushed from their rooms, assembled in formation and standing at rigid attention. They were frightened, correctly surmising there'd be consequences for today's embarrassment on the PEP field. All six of my squad leaders and both platoon commanders dressed in their grease tropical whites tightly ringed the formation hovering like jackals. "Okay, plebes, listen up," Dan said, waving a fresh stack of Form 2s in their faces. "Before the night is over, these deuces will be consumed. Used up. Gone. And they will be filled out on the spot by each offender himself, I might add, then signed by yours truly." Dan paused to enjoy their glum, puzzled looks. "And for what, you might ask? Well, there's a rumor going around that a certain company had difficulty making it to their first evolution on time this morning. You were *late*, gentlemen. All of you."

He should've said *we*. *We* were late.

"And late doesn't cut it. Not here, people. And it certainly doesn't cut it in the fleet." Dan got right in a plebe's face. "Does it, Mr. Buell?"

"No, sir!".

"Does it, people?!"

"NO, SIR!" all screamed in unison.

"Mr. Catton, what happens when people show up late?" Dan said, zeroing in on another plebe.

"Uh, they get fried, sir?"

"NO, YOU IDIOT! They miss ship's movement, they miss the battle, they lose the war! Do you want to lose the war, Mr. Catton?"

"No, sir!"

"Okay, good answer." Dan stepped back. "So, here's the deal. We're going to run some uniform races. You're going to be sent to your rooms to change into the uniform of our choice then get your asses back here in formation in five minutes. And if you don't bust out of those rooms like Clark Kent doing Superman, mark my words gentlemen, these deuces are going to start flying."

Caleb stepped up, taking over in tag-team style. "Okay, folks, here we go. White-Works Echo, wear raingear! MOVE, MOVE, LET'S GO!" He clicked a stopwatch. "Back here in five minutes – clock's running!"

Both platoons scattered like a herd of stampeding buffalo thundering down the passageway, each plebe screaming, "Go Navy," or "Beat Army," after squaring their corners back to their rooms. In the wake of their flash departure, one plebe remained, standing off to the side. Sara had been excused from the races and now leaned on her crutches alone in timid silence. I figured Caleb would use the time to start drilling her on her rates, asking her things like what's the menu for morning meal, who are the officers of the watch, etc., etc. He didn't. None of us did. Sara presented a sad picture, a downtrodden woman appearing lost and out of place. Under more traditional circumstances, chivalry called for her protection, for one of us to rush in and offer aid or comfort. Instead, we pretended to ignore her, adding to the awkward silence.

With thirty seconds remaining, the first of the plebes returned and began filling up the ranks, many others right on their heels. "...Seven! Six! Five! Four..." Caleb counted down, reading from his watch. More plebes scrambled in until all seventy were back in formation, standing at rigid attention, breathing heavily, covered with black raingear ponchos, Dixie cups and, presumably, White-works Echo underneath. "All right people, good, very good. All of you made it in the nick of time." Without a break came his next command, "This one's going to be a little tougher, get the ol' sweat pumps running. And I'm betting some of you *won't* make it. Here we go. I want to see sweatshirt, sweatpants and jockstraps all under White-Works Alpha, raingear again on top. GO!"

Again, all seventy fanned out in a mad dash knowing five minutes wouldn't cover the time needed to don all parts of this bastardized uniform. During their absence, one of my other squad leaders, Lonnie McCann, decided to take some Pledge and a rag to a silver tile in the center of the passageway where the plebes would be returning and squaring the corner. He sprayed and polished the tile to a slick, glossy shine. "Heh, heh. One last hurdle for 'em," he said, flashing a sadistic grin.

Lonnie was a joy to have on the detail, always one step ahead of the plebes. He was a promising African American football recruit, a tailback from Baltimore, and had suffered a catastrophic knee injury in practice our plebe year before playing a down. When his football aspirations were cut short, his attitude plummeted as did his grades, and he pondered quitting. Instead, he stuck it out, turning things around his third-class year, bringing his QPR back above 2.0 and making the Commandant's List both semesters. He was slated to be our 27th Company Commander in the fall.

As the first plebes hit Lonnie's waxed tile and pivoted ninety degrees, they were sent flying, arms flailing like Keystone Cops, all struggling to get back up and rejoin formation. Caleb, Dan, Lonnie and I couldn't contain our laughter, Dan shouting, "Square that corner, mister!" as each plebe took a tumble, their followers side-stepping the growing human pile on the floor. By some fluke, three of the seventy plebes returned to ranks under the five-minute deadline, the rest straggling in, some as late as two minutes. All were sweating profusely under their raingear. True to his word, Dan started passing out blank Form 2s to all the latecomers as Caleb roared, "Unsat, people! Grossly unsat!" Then he turned to the three early arrivers. "Oh, but congratulations to Brownfield, Harrington and Poole. I don't know how you did it, gentlemen, but you did. The rest of you, you're all down for 15 apiece – Late less than five, reporting self. Let's go, start filling out those forms."

I called to Lonnie for all to hear, "I think we should have a look under that raingear."

"You're right, Mitch," Lonnie called back, stepping in front of the two platoons. "Appearances can be deceiving. Hold up, everyone. Time for a little inspection. We're going to check out what's under those ponchos. Especially you three right here, Brownfield, Harrington and Poole." Lonnie pointed an accusatory finger at them. "Everyone take off your raingear, now. Drop it to the deck."

The plebes slowly unbuttoned their outer garment, dropping it as ordered. What came next surprised no one. We knew about the temptation to cut corners and shave time – we'd been in their shoes once ourselves and had set them up intentionally. Many of the plebes, the late ones, were dressed smartly in full White-works Alpha bulging slightly from the sweats underneath. However, the early arrivers, including Brownfield, Harrington and Poole, had nothing on but t-shirts and gym shorts and, in some cases, nothing but their jockstraps.

"I don't even *believe* what I'm seeing!" screamed Lonnie, as though he'd just uncovered a major smuggling ring. He stood in front of Brownfield, who was naked except for his jock, Corfam shoes and combination cover. "Mr. Brownfield," he said, his voice dripping with indignation, trying to hold back laughter. "Just what the hell uniform is this? Jockstrap Alpha?"

"I'll find out, sir."

"You bet your ass, you'll find out," he said, getting in his face. "Are you nice and cool under there, Mr. Brownfield, while your classmates are sweating their balls off? I hope you're nice and cool because it's about to get real hot. Caleb, hand this man his deuce."

Caleb handed Brownfield a blank Form 2 and said, "Let's see, what shall we fry him for? Out of uniform? Late less than five? Indecent exposure? Nudity? Bad taste?" Caleb and Lonnie were enjoying their charade, even some of the plebes were smiling listening to them go at it.

"I say we gig him on everything," Lonnie said. "Should add up to enough demerits to keep him marching until Parent's Weekend."

"How about *during* Parent's Weekend," Caleb added. "You like that, Brownfield? March the entire Parent's Weekend? Miss seeing Mommy and Daddy?"

"No, sir."

"Getting hot enough for you now, Mr. Brownfield?" Lonnie said.

Before Brownfield could reply he was ordered by Caleb to step out of ranks in his near-naked condition, front and center.

"Miss White?" Caleb called, as Brownfield stood at attention in front of the platoon.

"Yes, sir."

"Does Mr. Brownfield look hot to you?"

"Uh, no, sir. I mean, uh, yes, he does look like he's been sweating – sir." Amanda was completely flummoxed, recognizing the implied sexual nature of the question. Laughter rippled through the ranks. It was a light moment, a humorous exchange, but I was getting uncomfortable with where it was headed.

"Miss Sludge, what about you? Is Brownfield hot?"

Sara leaned forward on her crutches, embarrassed to look up. "Yes, sir, I think he's hot, sir."

Everyone in ranks hooted wildly, a mix of laughter and jeers. Sara blushed. Brownfield basked in the attention ignoring the jeers, puffing up his chest, flexing his muscles, gaining confidence as if he were a Chippendale dancer on display. Before I could call a halt to it, Caleb turned to Maddy.

"Miss O'Connor, is Brownfield hot?"

Maddy took her time, eying him carefully, like sizing up a contestant on the Dating Game. She sensed the moment called for a witty reply, something other than simple agreement that yes, Brownfield was indeed hot.

"C'mon, O'Connor. It's a simple question. Is Brownfield hot?"

Maddy smiled, winked at Brownfield and said, "Request permission not to bilge my classmate, sir."

The entire company broke up in raucous laughter, plebes and firsties alike. It was a clever way to knock Brownfield off his pedestal and allowed me the opportunity to seize the moment, to close the evening on a high note before things got completely out of hand. I stepped forward. "Oscar Company, atten-hut!" Everyone quieted down. "Okay, good job tonight, people," I said. "I think we learned a thing or two about how to be prompt and why. And why we don't cut corners with our uniforms." I turned to Brownfield next to me, standing bare in just shoes, cover and jockstrap. "Isn't that right, Mr. Brownfield?"

"Yes, sir."

"And just to show good faith, to all those with Form 2s in hand – you too, Brownfield – go ahead and toss them when you get back to your rooms. You've been granted amnesty, so to speak. You'll live to fight another day. So, tomorrow morning, we're going to form up on time and we're going to get to PEP on time. Is that clear?"

"YES, SIR!" in unison.

"Okay, dismissed. Get out of here."

"You shouldn't have let them off the hook, Mitch," Caleb said, back in my room after taps. "We should've fried every last one of them. Wasn't that the point of tonight?"

I had asked Lonnie and Caleb to stop by Dan's and my room before turning in. "I saw where it was headed," I said. "We just needed to cool it a bit, for your sake."

"Cool what? We were just having a little fun. We used to do locks-socks-jocks-and-boondocks all the time back in our day. Remember? Entire platoons in jockstraps."

"That was before the girls," I said.

"The girls have seen jockstraps before," Lonnie chimed in.

"C'mon. This wasn't about jocks. You guys know what I'm talking about. Is that your strategy? You think all the sexual innuendo is going to make them uncomfortable? Run them off? Not likely. What it will do is get us all in trouble. Like it or not, guys, the girls are here to stay."

"Says who?" Caleb challenged.

215

"Says Congress, for crying out loud. You're not going to change it by—"

"By what? Embarrassing them a little?

"Try sexual harassment," I said, letting that sink in.

"Well, Congress is wrong, man," Lonnie said. "What's the point of letting women into a service academy if they can't serve at sea?"

"I think the philosophy is you have to start somewhere."

"I think Congress should've started with understanding the impact of women serving in naval combatants, Marine infantry units, submarines and fighter aircraft," Caleb responded. "What good is it to say, 'Here's your appointment to the Naval Academy, Miss Gish, and, oh, by the way, since you can't serve in a combat role after graduation you get to go straight to PG school, or become a public affairs officer, or join the Civil Engineer Corps. We'll even send you to law school so you can become a JAG. No, ma'am, no sea duty for you.'"

"The Navy needs to fill shore billets too," Dan said, playing devil's advocate.

"Yeah, so fill 'em. Fill 'em with every sailor chick you can find so the men can stay at sea forever," Caleb retorted, raising his voice, "I repeat, until they let women serve in combat, they have no business being here. None whatsoever. What's the mission of this place? To prepare men to become line officers, right? To fill leadership positions in combat roles, to fight. Not to prepare us for grad school or to become lawyers in the JAG Corps."

"Caleb's right," Dan said. "I can't see women ever serving in combat. I mean, what if they were captured? What if they became POWs?"

"Yeah, I can just picture one of 'em checking into the Hanoi Hilton," Lonnie imagined.

"Or slogging through the jungles of Vietnam carrying an M-16, or crammed into an attack sub, hot-racking it with some other poor slob," Caleb replied. "It's pathetic just considering the possibilities."

"Yet here it is, a reality in 1976," Lonnie said. "I'm with Caleb. They're deadwood, Mitch. They're just taking up space."

"Hey, I wouldn't mind if Miss O'Connor took up some of my space," Dan said. "You know, right here, in my rack to—"

"All right, all right, enough," I said, cutting Dan off. "We're better off trying to solve world hunger than women at service academies tonight. Let's turn in, get some rest." I looked at my watch. "Reveille in six hours."

Caleb and Lonnie said goodnight and made a quick exit. We'd all been classmates and friends for three years, bonding together in ways many other college students would never experience. And despite our closeness, our camaraderie, I felt something slip away tonight, perhaps battle lines being drawn over this contentious, hot debate. And the debate was rife with anti-women sentiment, having been fueled by propaganda from many sources including the media. Lonnie's last comment before bed was not an original thought. He'd been quoting. Early in the spring when the Brigade knew women would be admitted but hadn't yet arrived, *The Log*, a satirical magazine for the midshipmen, ran a cartoon showing a perspective female plebe having freshly arrived at the Naval Academy main gate dressed in astronaut garb, holding a helmet by her side. Asked by an upperclassman why the suit and helmet, her reply: "Sir, my uncle says all of us girls will be taking up space."

# 13

## A VISITOR

Sunday, August 1, 1976

IT WAS A RAINY SUNDAY, exactly a week before the first set ended, and I'd just finished inspecting the on-coming plebe watch section in the Rotunda before evening meal. I was the designated Midshipman Officer of the Watch, known as the MOOW, and one of the duties was to inspect the watch team of plebes alongside the OOW in Bancroft's main rotunda before they posted. The MOOW is the senior midshipman watch stander, a duty that rotates daily. He wears the uniform of the day, in this case, tropical white long, a blue and gold MOOW armband and carries a sword sheathed along his side. He rates a salute from all midshipmen – even his first-class classmates. It's a fairly high position of authority and comes with a seat at the OOW table in the Wardroom at the base of the Anchor, the same table that is used to honor visiting dignitaries and where the Commandant or Superintendent might sit should they decide to dine with the Brigade.

I had just popped back to my room to retrieve my raingear when the Company Mate of the Deck, the CMOD, a plebe on watch in our company area, came in to tell me I had a visitor at Bancroft's main office. "A visitor? In Main O?" I asked.

"Yes, sir."

"Who? Did they say?"

"The message only says a visitor. Sorry, sir."

"Okay, never mind. I'm headed back that direction anyway. Tell them I'll be right down."

"Aye-aye, sir."

This was odd. I wasn't expecting visitors this evening, or any evening for that matter. For a moment I wondered if it could be Aimee but doubted she would travel the nearly thousand miles from Pensacola and show up unannounced. She'd had her chance to visit me numerous times over the last year, for the Valentine's formal, Easter break, my second-class Ring Dance, June Week – invitations all turned down for various reasons with vague excuses. Still, butterflies danced in my stomach with anticipation she might just surprise me.

When I arrived at Main Office and saw the figure waiting in the Rotunda near the reception desk, his back to me, I nearly collapsed. This was a bigger surprise, with bigger odds against turning up than Aimee herself. It was my father standing alone looking anxious like a patient awaiting a cancer diagnosis. My first thought was panic. Was it Amber? Mother? Their marriage? His job? It could be any number of things, none of them good, given the discord at home in the last few years. Still, I felt a pang of joy inside, hope perhaps, as I walked up from behind and called out, "Dad?"

My father spun around, surprised. I moved briskly the last few yards with open arms and embraced him. He hesitated for a moment, but I drew him closely as an old friend reunited after many years. I fought the urge for tears, very self-aware of being in full uniform, sword at my side, standing in this very public area of Bancroft Hall. He stepped back to admire me as if his young son had suddenly grown up sprouting an adult body and military uniform while he wasn't looking. It didn't quite convey the look of a proud parent thrilled with the success of his grown child, a midshipman about to graduate from the Naval Academy but held a glint of admiration, nonetheless. Upon closer inspection, I sensed something else in his deep-set eyes, perhaps a lack of focus. There was an agedness in his step, a frailness in his posture – things I'd not seen before. His hair was thinner, grayer, but he still carried that strong jaw, the dark complexion and confident demeanor, one that had dominated my childhood and earliest memories. "Hey, Speed, how are you?" he said, his attention wandering to a battleship mural behind me.

Speed was short for *speed demon*, a childhood nickname he coined when I was maybe three. It felt odd hearing this echo from my past, simultaneously heartwarming and unsettling. I realized I hadn't seen him since Christmas seven months earlier and speaking only by phone once since. "Dad, what brings you back here? Everything all right at home?"

"They had me flying into Boston this week. Thought I'd drop down but wasn't sure if you were still here or not."

"You almost missed me. I finish first set next week, then I'll be gone until September for summer cruise in the Med."

"First set?"

"Plebe detail. I'm on the summer training detail, helping to, you know, indoctrinate the new plebe class." I was certain I'd told him this. A shudder passed through me afraid he was asking if I was still a midshipman at the Naval Academy, like he wasn't sure. "Dad, again, is everything all right at home? You okay?"

"Yes, yes, we're fine," he replied, his eyes once more wondering over my shoulder. "Amber will be home soon from her summer on Lake Arrowhead looking forward to her senior year at Mercy. Mother's well. And I'm looking forward to retiring soon. Right around the corner, you know."

219

"Retiring?" He'd be sixty in four years, the mandatory retirement age for airline pilots. To me, 1980 was a dot on the horizon, not right around the corner. And why the positive spin on everything? Amber, spending her summer on Arrowhead? What a joke. She was spending her summer in rehab. And Mother well? Only if she's given up her jumbo wine glass and joined AA.

"Last time we spoke, you mentioned a girlfriend. Are you still seeing her?"

"Aimee?" I'd mentioned her to both my parents in a moment of lovesick optimism at Christmas and was surprised he remembered. "She's still down in Florida and no, we're on the outs for some unknown reason. Troubles with a long-distance relationship, who knows." I didn't feel a positive spin with Aimee was within me.

"Sorry to hear."

"Yeah, me too."

Despite its suddenness, I was warming to the appearance of my father. His presence and conversation suggested a renewed interest in my life which had been absent throughout high school and college. We were struggling to reconnect, meandering the Rotunda with no destination in mind. Dad seemed tired and we took a seat on a small marble bench near the broad staircase leading up to Memorial Hall. My mind raced with why he was here, what I should say, how to fill the void. "So, how about those Giants?" I blurted out. "Been to any games lately?" I hadn't followed the team closely since they'd traded Willie Mays in '72. Dad had always been a faithful San Francisco fan, win or lose and I felt guilty abandoning the team now that they were on the skids in a four-year slump.

"They're turning things around," he said. "Won their fourth in a row last night. This could be the year."

"That's great, Dad." This was my father, the team optimist even in their darkest hour. "The *Post* gives 'em practically no coverage out here." To him, the Giants were always one draft choice shy or one key trade away from winning it all. I admired that in him. Bringing them up though was a stall tactic, a diversion to buffer the more serious level of conversation I sensed was coming. My father had been a muted presence so much of my teen years, showing little interest. Yet here he was on a surprise visit, acting humble, contrite, obviously carrying something weighty on his mind. I longed for a return to this closeness, the rare individual attention I'd get when he'd take me golfing on long summer evenings, just the two of us, where he'd teach me the game's joys and frustrations. Or when I'd caddy for him and his United golf buddies and hang out in the clubhouse afterward. Other times, playing catch on the lawn after dinner, him helping me with my model airplanes, taking me flying in a rented Cessna... Those dulcet memories still clung to my heart but were colored with a profound sense of sadness. *God, he was so different back then.* I needed to break the spell. He was here on a mission and his retirement comment earlier had me worried. "Dad, really, is everything all right?"

He remained quiet, choosing not to make eye contact instead staring up at the battleship mural that'd caught his attention earlier, the USS *South Dakota* slicing through the water at flank speed, straddled by enemy fire, high above the Rotunda floor. I turned to view it with him. Her guns were ablaze, she was alive and in the fight. After a moment, he said, barely above a whisper, "It's not too late for you to quit, is it?"

*Quit?* Had I heard him correctly? "Of course, it's too late to quit, Dad," I responded instantly. "I've already incurred an obligation. Besides, why would I quit now? Why would you even suggest such a thing?"

He shrugged, not expecting a challenge. "No reason. Just wanted to know if you've considered your future after graduation."

"My future?" I'd just been punched in the gut. Hard. His question seemed so out of the blue, so random and hurtful. What kind of thing was that to ask a son, anyway? Not: *Aren't you excited to graduate, Son? What are your plans after graduation? You want to fly? You want to follow in my footsteps, you say? That's great, Son. I'm so proud of you, Son.* No, instead I get: *You can still quit, can't you?* Deep down, though, this was not a surprise. No matter what I set my sights on, no matter what I accomplished in my teen years, all I got was indifference and inattention, a lack of presence in both flesh and spirit. "I'm going to finish, Dad," I said, flatly. "I'm going to graduate in June."

"Of course, you will," he said, mainly to himself.

I felt like screaming out. Our conversation was driving me to the brink of causing a scene with his callous, insensitive remarks. I stood from the bench thinking it was time for him to leave, for us to part ways, when I spotted a familiar face coming toward us from the fourth wing exit. It was Trey McDavid, a classmate and fellow aero engineering major. Trey was the current plebe regimental commander with five stripes on his shoulder boards, the top post for the summer. He recognized me with my father and made a beeline approach, smiling broadly and snapping off a smart salute for dual reason – one, I was the MOOW, and two, he was acknowledging my guest. When in uniform, it's tradition to salute a fellow mid that's "dragging." Trey, gracious and always mindful of protocol, would never forget to honor a classmate and friend with a salute. I introduced Trey to my father and without hesitation, he replied, "World War II, right? The B-17 pilot?"

I was amazed at his memory. My father also showed surprise until I explained Trey was in my room last year prepping for one of our lab courses and noticed pictures under my desk blotter of him with his B-17 aircraft and aircrew. Trey's interest in my father's war experience was more than just polite inquiry. He'd truly been fascinated. My father kept quiet, not reacting to my explanation. It was certainly not the reaction I'd hoped for when you learn your proud son has shared his old man's story under the blotter on his desk, bragging in pictures to anyone caring to take notice. Trey sensed the awkward silence and stepped in, shaking my father's hand, obviously pleased to meet him. "Hey, evening meal formation goes outside in fifteen minutes," he said, dressed and ready, his own sword dangling from his belt. "You guys dining in tonight?"

I had no plans. My father's pop-in visit hadn't given me the chance. As the MOOW, I needed to observe formation in T-Court since the rain had lifted and the regiment would be back outside. I was free for dinner but would need to remain in the Yard.

"Why don't you bring your father to dinner in the Wardroom with us? The MOOW sits at the OD's table anyway, there'll be some extra seats." He turned to my father, "Join us, sir. It'd be an honor." Trey took most of his meals at this table as the regimental commander.

I was pleased with Trey's timely suggestion. I didn't want the visit with my father to end but we were headed down the wrong path earlier. "What do you say, Dad? Care to eat chow in the dining hall with us and a thousand screaming plebes?"

He agreed it'd be fine. Trey reminded me to fill out a special request chit that I quickly took care of at Main O as my father made his way up the steps and loitered in Memorial Hall. Mem Hall, as it's known, is an enduring tribute to the Naval Academy alumni who gave their lives while serving operationally or in actual combat throughout the wars and conflicts in our history. As of 1976, there were 2,447 names, of which 952 were listed as KIA along with 73 Medal of Honor recipients. Names, some with accompanying group photos, are enshrined serving as a reminder of the profession we're in, the ultimate price these men paid in defense of our nation.

"Dad?" I called out, jogging up the steps. He was browsing the artifacts. "I haven't been up here since I was a plebe. Pretty solemn place, don't you think?"

He simply nodded.

I was puzzled by his cool attitude, his lack of response. To me, Mem Hall was a humbling experience, a reminder to every visitor the cost of our freedom. And it spoke directly to the midshipmen by posing the question: are you prepared to serve your country, to follow in these men's footsteps if necessary? Dad seemed to be picking up an entirely different vibe as we browsed past name after name listed by graduation year on the granite tablets. The lists grew especially long with the alumni that served in World War II. We continued our stroll in silence until I couldn't take it any longer. His comment about quitting had formed an acid in my stomach. I stopped to confront him. "Dad, isn't this something I'm supposed to want? To graduate from here? Doesn't Mem Hall fill you with a sense of, I don't know – honor? Pride? You fought and served with many of these men."

"It's a fitting place to pay homage to those that perished," he said.

"Victims of man's inhumanity to man."

"I'm sorry?"

"War, Son. It shouldn't be glorified."

We walked on, my face growing numb. I didn't understand. I fumbled for words. "But shouldn't it be remembered?"

No response.

"Dad, please. Talk to me. I know you went to war, willingly, and I'm sure you saw some things, horrible things. But you never spoke about them." *Until now.* "Shouldn't we memorialize these brave men that fought and died for a just cause, defending our freedom?"

He breathed a deep sigh. "We should but—" He halted at the top of the steps staring down the long descent, his previous thought slipping away. "You know, I never really expected you to do this."

"Do what?"

"To join the service, become a pilot, follow in my footsteps. You had other options. Berkeley, Stanford—"

"But I wanted this option," I shot back. He was causing me to question everything, my whole future in the blink of an eye. "I'm doing this for me too."

"That was the whole point, the reason I went to war," he continued, ignoring my comment. "A mandate for future generations. To fight, so someday you wouldn't have to." He shook his head. "Pretty naïve notion, I suspect, given the rise of communism and the Cold War, Korea, Vietnam… But ending World War II should've been a turning point for us, a reason for hope."

"Dad—"

"So, yes, remember these honorable men—" He gestured at the walls. "But look around and ask yourself, what's all this blank space on the granite tablets for?"

"I—"

"And now women are here? Wanting to join the fight?" He shook his head again at the notion of women, women of his generation, heeding the call to arms and forsaking their traditional role in society to voluntarily dive into the horrors of war.

I remained silent. What more could I say? He'd found a way to halt the conversation simply because he knew. *The Horrors of War.* He'd been there.

We slowly descended the stairs to the Rotunda. "I had some problems on my flight into Boston last night," he said, staring ahead.

"Problems?" We halted at the bottom of the stairs. "As in mechanical problems? Aircraft problems?"

"No. There was an incident in the cockpit. I'm flying back to San Francisco in the morning as a non-rev temporarily off flight status. I need a rest, Son."

*An incident?* This was worse than any mechanical. "My God, what happened? Can you tell me?"

"I don't remember everything and I'm not sure what's going to happen when I return home."

"But are you all right?" I asked again. "Did you have some sort of breakdown?"

"I'm not sure what happened up there. I wanted to let you know, though. In case—" He stopped.

"In case what?" I needed to ask more questions. *Does Mother know? Have you spoken to her? Anyone else? Why me?* He seemed done talking. We stepped outside the main entrance to Bancroft Hall into the low-hanging sun. The plebes and first-class were beginning to arrive in T-Court in preparation for evening meal formation. I needed to break off. "Dad, I'm sorry, I'm going to have to step away for a minute to view the formation with the Officer of the Watch."

After the entire Regiment finished marching into Bancroft Hall, my father and I proceeded to the Anchor, a raised circular podium next to our VIP table in the Wardroom. I wanted to feel pride in myself and the Academy in his presence – his witnessing the impressive formation, my uniform, my sword, the three stripes on my boards, an important member of the plebe regimental staff. But my mood, my delight, was crushed, neutralized by what, I couldn't fathom. This was not the man I knew as a child. Something inside him was foreign, changed, almost haunting in its demeanor.

The plebes finished filing into the Wardroom and stood at attention behind their seats at their respective company tables. My father and I stood next to the OOW as they shook hands making brief introductions. Trey was poised at the Anchor waiting to call the plebe regiment to attention and make the routine announcements. He clanged the big ship's bell four times, quieting the hall. "Regiment, atten-hut!" he commanded, with the help of the microphone in his hand. The hall became silent. "Attention to announcements." He went on to read about ticket pickup for Parents Weekend, cancellation of tomorrow's sailing training due to inclement weather, on and on, finally ending his monologue with, "Regiment, seats."

Trey made his way down from the Anchor prepared to take the seat next to me when he glanced at my father, froze in his tracks and muttered something to himself. He quickly stepped back up and grabbed the mic. "Regiment, attention to one final announcement," he called. The chatter in the Wardroom again died. "I just want to draw attention to a special guest we have dining with us tonight. United Airlines pilot, Captain John Baumann, the father of Midshipman Lieutenant Mitch Baumann, joins us at the OD's table for evening meal. Captain Baumann served in World War II as a B-17 Flying Fortress pilot and flew 35 combat missions over Germany. We're honored to have him as our guest tonight, and we thank him for his service."

Spontaneous applause spread through the Wardroom, slowly at first, gaining momentum until the plebes and first-class alike were back on their feet giving a standing ovation. The group at our table rose as everyone, all 1,500 were up and clapping. Everyone, that is, except my father. He remained seated, looking uneasy, like a spooked animal aiming to take flight. The attention seemed incomprehensible to him, that maybe if he ignored it, it would go away. Finally, embarrassed for both of us, I leaned in and whispered, "Dad, for God's sake, stand up. Please. Give a wave, a nod, something. They want to see you." My father stood slowly, appearing disoriented, then gathered himself for a modest, anticlimactic wave to the crowd.

To say dinner was strained would be an understatement. You could see the look on Trey's face that he felt bad, like he did something wrong, perhaps disrespectful, to dishonor my father with his brief introduction. I passed a look back that said thank you, and no, in fact, you did nothing wrong. I was the one that felt bad.

My father and I bid a hasty goodbye after dinner leaving both of us rattled. I reached out to hug him a final time, to tell him everything would be okay, but he didn't seem to hear. The hug felt awkward, lacking any personal connection and I felt a sting in its aftermath. He was in a different place, his world slipping away. What lay ahead for my mother and our family was unclear. He got into his cab outside Gate 1 and disappeared.

I wouldn't see him again until after graduation. Things began to unravel shortly after his arrival home, bringing changes that would ripple through our lives in the years to come, changes I would learn about via one-sided rants from my mother during long-distance phone calls. I got a better picture when I went home at Christmas but not one in sharp focus with all the details. Who was this man I called my father? Certainly not the same one that piloted a B-17 in the war, not the same one I remembered as a young boy donning his airline uniform, strong, reliable, unshakable, his garment bag slung over his shoulder, chart bag in hand, heading out the door for another cross-country trip.

Monday, August 2, 1976

Another part of the job as MOOW is to randomly inspect rooms throughout the Brigade, or in this case, the plebe regiment, when the occupants are otherwise busy, at lectures, drill, sports, etc. It was Monday morning and time to start my rounds. My company was gone, their rooms and entire company area deserted. Typically, the MOOW would impose his presence on other company areas, not his own, letting his pen fly when he spied a room with an unmade rack, a gross shower or sink area or articles left adrift. I wasn't keen on inspecting my own company as putting them on report would reflect badly on me. Still, here I was, needing to begin somewhere.

I entered a random room, our girl's room, the three white nameplates on the door reading, *M. C. O'Connor '80, S. A. Sedgley '80, A. R. White '80*. The color scheme was inverse to the men's black nameplates, invented by the administration to quickly distinguish male rooms from female, to warn all entering of the strict rules applying to the opposite sex. Of course, my choice wasn't random as the white nameplates were scarce among the sea of black and designed to set off alarm bells making it impossible to mistake one room for another. I was curious and eager to inspect, not having been in the girl's room since the set began and their empty space presented little risk. The room itself was immaculate, of course, standard for plebe summer, and there was nothing to write them up for. The racks were taut, the shower and sink area sparkled and their desks were tidy. I lingered, my attention drawn to a cluster of photos under Maddy's desk blotter forming a mini collage. I moved in for a closer look fascinated by the variety of shots and the cute girl posing candidly for the camera. There was just something warm and inviting about Maddy that drew you in – her easy smile, emotions on the sleeve, a subtle sexuality running beneath the surface intertwining the physical and inspiring fantasy. Oh, this girl has broken hearts, I was certain. It was clear in every picture. And yet the pictures were nothing but homespun innocence – Maddy with Mom and Dad at high school graduation, Maddy on stage with her girl-band playing lead guitar, Maddy with her swim team, Maddy in scuba gear, Maddy frolicking with a golden retriever, Maddy entering the room behind me without a sound. POOF. "Sir! Midshipman Fourth Class O'Connor, 8-0-4-4-5-1! Oscar Company Mate of the Deck, sir!" she proclaimed, sounding off as required.

I nearly jumped out of my skin at her sudden presence. "JEEE-zus, O'Connor, don't do that!" I replied, yelling my oath to the ceiling before whirling around to face her. "You surprised the hell out of me just now."

Maddy suppressed a tiny smile, enjoying the fleeting moment of shock given to her company commander. "I'm sorry, sir. You surprised me too."

"What are you doing here?"

Her expression seemed to say: What are *you* doing here, sir?

"Aren't you supposed to be at small arms training on the range today with the rest of the company?"

Maddy pointed down at her watch belt and silver buckle, "CMOD duty, sir."

"Yeah? Me too. MOOW duty." I pointed down at my sword and smiled, legitimizing my presence in the room but looking guilty for the obvious snooping.

"May I be of service, sir?" Again, this was the proper response for a CMOD when spotting an officer, or in this case the MOOW, in the company area.

"Yes, Miss O'Connor, you may be of service." She was standing at rigid attention. "Why don't you stand at ease. Please."

She relaxed her shoulders, but only slightly. As she did, a dainty bracelet with small, ornate pieces of silver slid below the sleeve of her white-works and became visible on her wrist. It made a soft tinkling sound.

My eyes were immediately drawn to it. "Oh, and what's this?"

"Just a charm bracelet, sir." She looked embarrassed.

"From a boyfriend?"

"No, sir. I wouldn't call him that."

"Well," I said, changing the subject. "We haven't had much chance to talk this set." I eased back, leaning against her desk still staring at the bracelet. "How are you holding up for the summer?"

"Fine, sir."

"Good, good. And your roommates? They fine too?"

"Uh, yes, sir."

"But—"

"But, what, sir?"

"You hesitated. I sensed a *but* coming. Thought you might have something to add."

"No, not really, sir."

"Come on, relax, O'Connor, this isn't a come-around. I'm not here to ask you rates. Speak up, please."

"Aye, aye, sir. Well, Amanda, uh, Miss White and I are doing fine. We're both a little concerned about Sara though."

I sensed this was coming. "How so?"

"She's having trouble, especially now that she's on crutches."

"She needs to get off them, and get off excuse squad," I said.

"She's demoralized, sir. And she's being humiliated."

"O'Connor," I said, in a fatherly tone. "That's what we do here, make it tough, challenge you, break you down. If you get a little humiliated or demoralized, that's part of the process. You're a smart cookie, you get that I'm sure."

"Yes, but Sara doesn't. And she's not getting any help from us, her classmates, the ones that should be helping. As you know, they call her names, to her face and much worse behind her back."

I cringed at her obvious truths. I'd observed the stuff to the face but not the intensity or frequency behind her back, what Maddy was suggesting. "Well, there's a shit-screen in every outfit," I offered. "She'll come around, maybe once she gets off crutches, she'll rally."

Maddy shook her head, "I don't think so, sir. There's a cruelty element that won't go away, crutches or no crutches."

"Cruelty?"

She hesitated, her guard up, feeling she might've gone too far.

"C'mon, O'Connor, permission to speak freely. Is Sedgley being overly harassed, by anyone in particular?"

"Yes, sir, I think she is."

"By whom?"

Maddy held tight, reluctant to finger any of her classmates.

"Okay, *how* is she being harassed?"

"It's the name-calling, sir."

"Everyone develops nicknames along the way. Sometimes it's a way for the group to show affection, that they like you."

"Sara Sludge? Or Miss Sludge, as Mr. Wise likes to address her? I wouldn't call that affection, more like third-grade bullying. Simple childish fear."

"Fear?"

"Sir, they see her messing up her rates, falling behind at PEP until blisters put her on the sidelines, on crutches. The crutches themselves, excuse squad, can't march, extreme introvert, only able to talk about things like religion when put in a social situation. She represents everything they fear, things anyone of them might become if it weren't for Sara holding down the fort for them. They, *we*, have put her in a box and are afraid to let her out."

"Is it really that bad? Has she completely alienated her classmates?"

"Yeah, it's that bad. She's hurting, for the wrong reasons, and I'm sick about it."

We grew silent. I scanned the room again noticing Sara's Christian influences, Bible verses under her blotter, a poster on the room's corkboard – half the poster, a pretty flower with a caption reading, *Wow, that's beautiful* – the other half, a black silhouette of the empty cross on Calvary reading, *I know, I made it.* Not a bad message but there was something subtly intimidating about it, something preachy. Yes, there were ingredients here to set her apart, and not in a good way. Sara had wandered into Hans Christian Anderson's tale, *The Ugly Duckling*, her egg having rolled into the wrong nest. But with this version, there'd be no hope of morphing into the beautiful swan. Instead, I sensed a tragic ending. I decided to switch gears, making a mental note to circle back with Sara later. "Hey, is that really you on stage playing the Fender Strat?" I gestured toward her blotter.

She blushed. "Yes. I was in a band briefly, in high school. We did mostly covers."

"Just covers?"

"Oh, we had some original stuff. Sort of a blend of surf music and punk rock."

"Sort of a Beach Boys meets the Sex Pistols?"

She laughed. "Yeah, but without all the testosterone."

I joined her laugh. "So, it was four of you? All girls?" I nodded at the picture. "You played and sang lead?"

Again the humility and cute, modest smile. "Yes, that was me."

"Out front like a regular Janis Joplin."

"I wouldn't go that far."

"Yeah, you're right. That didn't end so well." I gave a wink. "How about Helen Reddy, *I Am Woman*?"

"Gag."

We shared a chuckle finding commonality in our music taste and my jab at women's lib.

"So, what was the name of your group?"

"*The Willows*. We played at some dances and stuff, that's all."

"Impressive. Ever do any recording?"

"Oh, you know, a few demo tapes here and there." Maddy looked up and grinned. "Cut a record at a little place down south, Muscle Shoals. Ever hear of it?

"Muscle Shoals? As in *Sweet Home Alabama*? Are you kidding?"

She laughed easily like we were a couple flirting in a bar. "Of course, I'm kidding," she said, casually leaning in, brushing my forearm with her soft hand, her fingers sliding across my wrist, the charm bracelet making its sound.

I blanched. She froze. The touch was electric. Our eyes made contact as I stepped back. Maddy flashed a deceptive smile as if recognizing, only for a moment, the attraction between us, the power she briefly held. We'd forgotten our roles, who we were, where we were. Oh, there was electricity all right, and it came without warning, jolting us back to reality.

"Uh, you should probably get back to your watch station," I said.

"Aye, aye, sir." She moved for the door.

"Oh, one more thing."

Maddy turned, her eyes lifted in expectation. "Yes?"

"Get rid of that bracelet. You shouldn't be wearing it. It's against uniform regs."

"Aye, aye, sir." She quickly departed and disappeared down the long hallway.

Before the week was out, before I left for the Med, I had a talk with the plebes and with my classmates, but I never did talk to Sara herself. And I didn't call on Maddy again. I simply couldn't, for obvious reason.

# 14

## ACADEMIC YEAR

Thursday, September 9, 1976

RETURNING TO THE NAVAL ACADEMY after Labor Day, spotting the Chapel dome for the first time in the afterglow of extended leave and easy pace of summer cruise with its adventure and exotic liberty is, at best, a paradoxical, bittersweet experience. You are greeted with joy, reunited with your classmates all safely returned to the bosom of Mother B, swapping stories of high jinx and escapade. But you are also greeted with a staggering academic course load, long hours of study, exams, formations, marching, and a multitude of uniform and room inspections. Despite forging that stronger bond of friendship and basking in the camaraderie, paradox and bittersweet are ample words describing the abrupt seasonal transition to life back in Bancroft Hall.

God, we're back, I mused. It's like déjà vu all over again. I was sitting in my room, having unpacked my uniforms, organized my closest and lugged our huge stereo system in six boxes up three flights of stairs from storage, the one Neil and I jointly purchased our youngster year at the Mid Store. Stereos are a very important part of life to midshipmen, practically defining who you are by how big your speakers are and how many watts your amplifier can generate. Proof was at hand as I clearly could hear a fellow mid blasting his from an open window several decks above onto the Red Beach celebrating the Brigade's return. The sound level was cranked to at least 100 decibels, treating the entire sixth wing to Emerson Lake and Palmer's very apropos, *Karn Evil 9*, better known as *Welcome back my friends, to the show that never ends*. Well played, I thought. You'll probably get fried but at least you'll go down for a good cause. The lyrics were perfect.

There was much to do in the five days before classes, mundane stuff like finishing hauling gear from storage, purchasing textbooks, re-laundering uniforms, attending company meetings and a scheduled practice march-on for the Saturday home opener against Rutgers. I was taking a breather when Caleb, fresh from leave, pushed open our door scanning the room avoiding eye contact. "Oh," he said, stopping in his tracks. "I was looking for Neil."

Then he pivoted and made a quick exit. No hello, no how's it going, no how was cruise? It was obvious. He was still pissed and not talking to me. I'd fried him for DDO when I caught him using one of Sara's nicknames to her face specifically after ordering my entire staff to lay off. With that speech, and that Form 2, battle lines were drawn, I'd set in motion a schism that would likely divide the company in the coming months.

After Caleb, the company mate of the deck entered with a huge sack of mail. Bancroft Hall's post office had failed to forward any letters after my departure to the Med allowing it to pile up for a month. The mate, Roger Galvin, a third-class in our company, and plebe the last time I saw him, tossed two rubber-banded stacks on each side of our common desk. "Here's your lousy mail," he said, grinning. "Happy reading."

"Hey, Rog," I said, hoping I remembered his first name. I'd only known him as Mr. Galvin. "How's it going? Good summer?"

"Yeah, twelve weeks of heaven. Sucks being back here playing mailman though. They dumped four huge bags at Batt O. Had to haul them up here and spend the next two hours sorting it. Guess they don't believe in forwarding this shit anymore, huh?"

I could tell, he was enjoying having casual conversation with me after his year as a plebe. "Nah, let the car insurance and credit card payments lapse," I said, noticing two such bills in my stack.

"And get hit with all the late fees." He turned to leave. "Gotta keep moving. Join the Navy, deliver the mail."

"It's not just a job…" I added, smiling. "And enjoy youngster year. It's true what they say. It's all fruit."

"Thanks, good to know." He whirled around. "Hey, forgot to ask, how was detail? How were they?"

"How were who?" I said, knowing full well what he was talking about.

"You know, the girls. I hear we're down to two. Caleb's bragging he got one to quit. You guys make it extra tough on them?"

His comment stung. I'd just seen Sara's post on the company bulletin board this morning as did everyone else. "If you're referring to Miss Sedgley, let's just say she had some issues."

"I'll say she had issues. What an ugly broad. Good riddance to her. That other one, what's her name, O'Connor? Quite the babe, huh? Whatever made her want to come to this place? What a waste of talent."

Hearing Roger make his macho comments, I was starting to feel protective of our remaining two women as he continued to pry. "They'll be fine. My advice is to just be careful around them and leave it at that."

He gave me a sideways look. "Sure, Mitch. Whatever you say." He finally spun and left for good.

Again, I was bothered by this new third-class's brusque appraisal of two women he barely knew, probably hadn't even met yet. I would need to keep

231

an eye out for both Maddy and Amanda. No telling what attention they'd garner now that all four classes were back on the prowl, eyes and ears open, very much attuned to women living among us for the first time.

I casually rifled through my stack of mail in Roger's wake. Aimee hadn't been much of a letter writer during the last six months but there was a decent probability of at least several I'd missed due to the lapse in delivery over the past four weeks. I weeded out the junk, the bills and was left with three legitimate letters, two from my mother and one, just one, from Aimee. I breathed a sigh of relief not wanting to consider the alternative, that there might've been none. I saved Aimee's for last after reading and discarding everything else, sliding open the envelope addressed in her very distinctive cursive. Something told me to be careful. I wasn't sure why, or of what, but there was an intuitive unease settling in.

The letter, a simple two-pager, began: *"Dear Mitch, this is going to be a difficult letter to write but..."* I quickly dropped the page face down on my desk and felt my stomach sink. Not a great start. Why did I know this day would eventually arrive? Was it her lack of letters, her dodging of my invitations to come visit? I drew a deep breath and started again at the top.

*August 28, 1976*

*Dear Mitch —*

*This is going to be a difficult letter to write but I feel I owe you an explanation for all your unanswered letters, your Ring Dance invitation and other visit offers you've extended to me over the last nine months. I'm so sorry I've not been a good communicator and I've been unfair procrastinating writing this letter. You've been a wonderful friend over the last year, Mitch, and the few times we've been together have been priceless. I'm just sorry I haven't been able to find a way to visit Annapolis more often. It's a beautiful town and I'll always treasure the memories I have of us strolling the streets, the harbor, the romantic dinner and Christmas dance and your personal tour of the Academy itself.*

*So, where to begin...first off, I got a recent promotion at the radio station. I'm off the nightshift and doing the midday 10 – 2 show. They've also made me a sales manager in charge of finding more sponsorship participation for our evening programming. Basically, I sell advertising space to new clients. It's a lot of phone calling but it is more money – especially when I sell a new contract, yay. So, I've been busy, trying to balance my "new" life of radio show, selling and personal. I've started working out more, jogging 3 times a week like you – still a long way to go there. I did make it home to LA this summer. I needed to pick up the last of my things and say goodbye to Bill. The good news is, we're finally back on speaking terms. We were actually civil to each other and I stayed at the house this last visit. He's lonely, apparently broken it off with Penny and is looking again. I do feel sorry for him but there's so much history, so much bad blood between us. Who knows what our future holds — I do miss SoCal and it would be nice to have that link when or if I return.*

*I know it's obvious, I'm wandering and not getting to my point. This is hard, Mitch, and I'm sorry but here it is — we need to break up and end our belief that this relationship can work. The long-distance romance we both felt so strongly about last year seems like such a pipedream now. We're just too far apart to experience the joy we deserve. My new job at the station makes it hard to get away and I know you can't just drop everything on a moment's notice either. We really need more time together to make this work and you know me, not much of a letter writer, I guess. I've craved more time together, more than the thousand miles can give us, and I'm finding letter writing alone doesn't seem to help. I'll admit, it's my fault. I need contact, the day-to-day kind, just hanging out watching TV, walks, simple handholding and yes, of course, our intimate, wonderful sex. I have vivid memories of our lovemaking during the brief, but incredible visits and I will always cherish that. Of course, sex does not define a relationship but to me physical contact of all types is a very important part, a part that cannot be overcome by phone calls and letters and once-a-year visits.*

*I wish you good things, Mitch. I will always value our relationship and remember the love and kindness you gave me over the last year. I only hope you will remember us fondly and not hate me too much right now. Who knows, our paths may cross again someday. Fate is funny that way.*
*Love,*
*Aimee*

I set the letter down on my desk and closed my eyes. *Love, Aimee?* How could she use that phrase after all the preceded it? What kind of cruel, mixed message was that sending? If she was aiming at irony, she'd hit it. Love? As in, I love you so let's break up? Was she just trying to assuage her guilt by offering the word as a final token of civility? Or was she simply expressing platonic love, love you casually toss around with any number of friends in your life? My mind raced. Was there someone else? Was she needing a convenient exit? Would I ever see her again? There were a million things I wanted to say, questions I wanted answered. But sitting at my desk, isolated by a thousand miles and facing the daunting year ahead, I was filled with a firm resolve — I would not ask her a single question. I would not write back, I would not call, not now, not ever. My pride was in tatters and I needed to shelter my ego. The questions would stay within, left for me to draw my own conclusions. God, this sucked, the surprise, the timing, and yet I should've seen it coming like a freight train.

I sank deeper in thought recalling how we met in a bar on Seville Quarter in Pensacola during my second-class summer indoctrination training in

August of 1975. She had started her job as a local DJ and was living with her older brother, a second-class petty officer stationed at VT-4 working as a jet engine mechanic. She and her friends hung out a lot on the Quarter and had met many junior officers going through the training command. She told me I was her first midshipman. As we talked, she playfully referred to the JOs as a bunch of assholes interested in one thing, seemingly putting me on notice that I better not be interested in scoring tonight, mister. I hadn't thought that far ahead, maybe only getting to first base. Aimee was enchanting, tall, athletic, shoulder-length blond hair and dark, mysterious brown eyes. I couldn't take my eyes off her. Our training group, referred to as PROTRAMID 2B, had only one week before we had to fly to our next destination, Quantico, Virginia, to play Marine and I was eager to hang onto my newfound female companion and possibly enjoy some slow dancing later on. As the night progressed, Aimee and I, her girlfriends, the midshipmen contingent I was with, and pretty much everyone in the bar grew more intoxicated as the music swelled to an intensity making it impossible to talk. Aimee suggested we go outside to continue our chat. In no more than a minute on the patio, she deliberately leaned in and initiated a long kiss, our lips connecting, our tongues touching, our bodies pressing into one another in a way that could only be described as intense, primal, sexual. Mutual permission, consensus it seemed, was being given that said, yes, we'll be going beyond first base tonight. Aimee was a bit woozy as we walked back on the dance floor, the DJ calling for last dance. Our lips came together again while dancing to Bachman Turner Overdrive's, *Down to the Line*. With each wet kiss I was already imagining being deep inside her, moving in rhythm over her slick, energy-charged body. The dance floor itself was a melee, especially when Randy Bachman, playing his heavy metal guitar and belting out the lyrics, *Down to the line.*

Everyone was screaming out DOWN TO THE LINE on each refrain. There was a multitude of color lights flashing, dry-ice fog creeping around the stage, hands clapping in the air, people stomping. We were surrounded in a swirling madhouse of noise and sweat and sex. When the bright lights came back up and the barkeep announced closing time, things proceeded rapidly. Aimee took my hand and led me toward her Mustang parked out back. There was no chitchat, no playing it coy. We both knew what we wanted and spoke very little on the short drive back to her apartment, a sense of urgency pushing us up the stairs and through the front door. The motion itself was overpowering and unstoppable, like being sucked into the vortex of a tornado – no options, no decisions, just a path leading straight to the bedroom, straight to Aimee. When we'd finished, there was a swath of destruction, clothes, shoes, pillows, comforter, everything, strewn about the room but no guilt from our action, just a sense of calm, of understanding, like we'd known each other for years, that the connection was more metaphysical. Our conversation in bed afterward lasted hours, discussing god-knows-what. Everything. Nothing. I can't recall. Aimee sat up in bed in a black silk robe, knees to her chest, her hair pulled back in a ponytail looking absolutely adorable. I lay back on the pillow, my hands laced behind my head. I knew I would remember this moment the rest of my life. It was written in indelible ink. I would remember Aimee, I would cherish her and cherish the memory, always.

This was our tenuous beginning – of how we'd met and how I'd felt only minutes after making love to her. But it was also how I felt sitting in my room in Bancroft Hall more than a year later. This wasn't a mere sexual romp or a one-night stand. Okay, maybe it was – the spark perhaps – but after our little tête-à-tête that ran for two hours, we'd cemented a commitment to one another to begin a letter-writing campaign with promises of my returning on the first long weekend in the fall. We were in love, or so I thought. Warning signs abounded in the months after I flew down to Pensacola for the Veteran's Day long weekend using my free airline pass privileges. What a Charlie Foxtrot that was. I hopped a standby flight on Saturday via Atlanta into Pensacola that ran late, landing well past midnight, then caught the first flight back to Baltimore via Dallas early Monday morning. I was stressed all weekend and Aimee sensed it. Still, we had a marvelous Sunday to ourselves, spending most of it in her apartment getting reacquainted, her brother gone at sea on the USS *Lexington* supporting carrier quals. Aimee did make it up to Annapolis for the Christmas dance in December, but her letters trailed off soon thereafter. I told her I'd come down for Christmas leave but she said no, she'd be in California. I offered to drive down from the Bay Area since I'd be home too, but she again balked, offering some vague excuse. The big warning flag went up at Easter break. This time I had the full week off and couldn't wait to get back down to see her, especially after enduring the Dark Ages – that depressing period of perpetual cold and gray that descends on Annapolis between Christmas leave and spring break putting everyone in a funk. It was during a phone call in February I suggested we see each other. Well, you'd have thought I was the hitchhiker in the *Texas Chainsaw Massacre* threatening to come back to town and make house calls. She made excuses, hemmed and hawed, backtracked, nearly begged me not to come down saying, no, please, now is not good, some other time, please. Say what? I mean, what the f— Were we going out together or not? Since neither of us had told the other we wanted to break it off during the call, I considered it a sign to keep moving forward and reinitiated my letter writing after the break. But for every four of mine, Aimee would return maybe one. I could now see, looking back, with "Dear John" in hand, that she needed to deliver a knockout punch, that I was simply too dense to curtail my writing and let our relationship die a peaceful death. God, this was bad, the heartache, the sting of reality, everything. Why did she wait so long to end it? Why not back at

Christmas, or spring break, or during the summer? The year had dragged on, its path littered with telltale debris. Fall was bound to be a disaster.

Neil popped back into the room in his running gear, glistening with sweat, all grins. "Sure is great to be back, huh, roomie? Nothing like a nice head-clearing run along the seawall to reinvigorate your senses, give you a deeper appreciation for this marvelous place. Am I right or am I right?"

"Whatever."

Neil started peeling off his shirt and shoes and turned on the shower. "Hey, get some tunes on, for crying out loud," he said, gesturing at the stereo. "Got it all hooked up, right?"

Observing me parked on my side of the desk, idle and nearly catatonic, he pulled out one of his own LPs, placed the needle on the record and headed back to the shower undressing, singing as he went. But before Neil could enter the stall, our door swung open. This time Lonnie McCann strolled in, our company commander for the fall semester, clad in just PT gear. Lonnie appeared to have business on his mind but when he heard Neil's song emanating from the speakers, he stopped dead in his tracks and cringed, spying the offending Abba album cover on the desk. He gently wafted its fumes under his nose and made a face like a chef discovering a spoiled tray of beef. "This is bad, man, really bad. Lights out, I'm afraid." He faced Neil, standing naked before him. "Bang-A-Boomerang? Seriously? At least turn the volume down before they hear it in the hall. You're making us all look bad." Lonnie turned my way and gave a wink. "What's up next, the Partridge Family?"

Neil pretended to look hurt, all for show, of course. "Hey, don't even talk to me about music taste, Mister Chairman Emeritus of the Diana Ross fan club. Do you even own any other albums?"

"Just my Miss Ross," Lonnie replied, closing his eyes, feigning to hear her voice and entering a state of bliss. "One sweet artist, one sweet sound."

"Oh, brother." Neil rolled his eyes. "Feel free to jump in anytime, Mitch."

I remained silent, unable to participate in their light banter.

Lonnie opened his eyes and smiled. "See? He knows crap when he hears it."

Neil's hurt look returned. "Thanks a lot, roomie. Knew I could count on your support." He turned back Lonnie, "So, what's up, Lon? I know you didn't come all the way down here to debate the musical superiority of Motown versus Stockholm. To what do we owe the esteemed pleasure of our company commander's visit?"

Lonnie glanced at our closed door and lowered his voice, his countenance growing dark. "I wanted to give you guys a heads-up. Lieutenant Herrera saw Sedgley's picture and the dirty comment this morning when he came in." Lieutenant Mike Herrera was our company officer, a nuke-power submariner, a fair guy with a passion for avoiding confrontation and conflict at all cost. "He immediately yanked it from the board, not saying a word. Wanted to ignore it, I'm sure, but couldn't after realizing half the company had seen it. And shit like that travels like wildfire around the here. Hell, it's bound to hit Salty Sam's next column. Anyway, Herrera calls me in and basically goes ballistic."

"Ballistic?" Neil said. "We're talking about the same Herrera, right?"

"Yeah. Says he wants to, and I quote, find the culprit that penned that poison and have him castrated."

"Castrated?" Neil started laughing. "And I suppose he expects you to do it?"

"He wasn't clear on that point. Just wants 'em found before the Commandant hears about it. I don't think he was serious about the castrating part."

"What a relief." Neil turned my direction. "Hear that, Mitch? Castration is off the table, you're safe." Then, back to Lonnie, "This is really a no-brainer, Lon. It's pretty obvious it was Caleb Wise."

"Don't say that, man. Not unless you know." There was a pause. "*Do* you know?"

"Of course not," Neil said. "It was scribbled anonymously, done in the dead of night, same as Sedgley's picture. Hey, maybe it was the same person, that ever occur to you? Maybe Sedgley herself wrote it."

"Well, damn. Now there's a hot lead. Guess we'll never know for sure. She out-processed yesterday."

"I was kidding, Lon."

"Oh, really, Neil? I couldn't tell. I'm a little slow on the uptake today. Maybe next time give me a hint, okay?" Lonnie was smiling, playing along but he was stressed. This was his first crisis as company commander and he'd only been at it a day. "Look, this thing is volatile, man. There'll be some serious shit go down if we don't handle it right. I get the joking around but..."

I listened passively to Neil and Lonnie as they batted around the consequences of what would happen should Caleb, or anyone in the company, be implicated in defacing Sara's post. I couldn't have cared less. I wasn't interested, having been put out of commission by Aimee's bombshell. Besides, what was done was done. I was more concerned with the fate of our two women going forward, specifically Maddy. Everyone had their eyes on her since returning and the possibilities were nauseating. Lonnie was droning on about this and that, throwing in a bunch of handwringing and what-ifs. As he talked, I scanned the room aimlessly, becoming hypnotized by Lonnie's exposed, permanently swollen knee. A long zipper-like scar ran the length of his kneecap from the quadricep, over the repaired ligaments, terminating near the tibia – a wound that would've put Joe Willie Namath's

237

to shame. I tried to imagine the horrible pain he must've felt getting drilled in practice when his leg collapsed. It must've been excruciating. I felt sorry for him and glad I wasn't in his shoes – both then and now. Lonnie finally departed leaving me with Neil. Abba was still playing, but at a much softer volume.

"Okay, Mitch, talk to me," Neil challenged.

"Huh?"

"Don't give me huh. It's written all over your face. What the hell happened? Who died?"

Neil and I had shared our lives together over the last three years. There was very little he didn't know about me and vice versa. Still, I wasn't ready to talk and unsure I'd ever be able to discuss Aimee's letter with him. "Nobody died. I'm fine. Just trying to get used to being back, I guess."

"Oh, bullshit. But, hey, far be it from me to pry. When you're ready, I guess you'll tell me." With that, Neil slipped into the shower he'd started ten minutes ago and whisked the curtain shut.

Sunday, October 17, 1976

The last formal Tea Dance at the Naval Academy was held on a Sunday in October, at least in the traditional Tea Dance sense, and my role was to act as a chaperone. These compulsory dances existed solely for plebes and the reason for holding them was simple: plebes were not allowed to drag except on certain weekends during formal dances. The administration realized they'd created a Catch-22 with the plebe dating prohibition by denying them a chance to meet local women but encouraging them to attend the three or four formal dances given throughout the year. Good luck finding a date under those conditions. The solution? Hold a mandatory mixer early in the year on a Sunday afternoon, bus in local girls and pair them up with the plebes thus providing potential escorts to future formals. When I say, "pair them up" I mean in the literal sense – this is a forced date for the remainder of the afternoon. The Tea Dance format, referred to as Tea Fights among the mids, involves setting up a long curtain in the center of Dahlgren Hall's ice rink and dividing the women onto one side and the plebes on the other. Both lineup on their respective side, move forward until they meet at curtain's end and are paired by a first-class midshipman chaperone, setting up a true blind date for the afternoon's dance. The Tea Dance has existed for decades, having acquired a derogatory set of nicknames such Tea Fight, Pig Push, Hog Call, on and on. As I studied the Brigade Bulletin announcing the dance, there was no mention of just how it would function now that female plebes had been integrated into the Brigade. Would they line up with their civilian counterparts on the women's side or would eighty male civilians be bussed in and lined up with the thousand male plebes? I suspected the former. Where would they find eighty young men willing to come in and be subjected to this type of dating horror show? I set the bulletin down on my desk and realized with every new day we were in uncharted waters with the women, changing history, bucking a mountain of tradition.

One of the more notable changes was the Naval Academy now had female cheerleaders among its ranks. And I don't mean cheerleader women imported from local colleges as in years past. No, for the first time in history we had the domestic variety at the football season opener against Rutgers. A squad of six female plebes had been selected during the summer and integrated with six male upper-class cheerleaders. The girls had to learn quickly, polishing their skills and synchronization with the men right up to game time. They may have looked new, slightly out of place with their youthful looks and bobbed haircuts, but they showed a genuine exuberance and were completely capable of leading the Brigade in spirited cheers, turning cartwheels and doing handstands. The problem was the Brigade had neither the patience nor tolerance for this recent change to the lineup. They wanted their pretty coed cheerleaders back, the ones with long hair, overdone makeup, flirtatious looks and availability to date. At one point during the game, the mids started booing our girls while performing one of their routines. The entire squad turned around to look at the team on the field, thinking something bad just happened to Navy. You could see the frozen panic on the girl's faces when they discovered it wasn't Rutgers, or the refs, or something else gone horribly wrong. It was them. They were being booed simply for daring to suit up for the game and take the place of their civilian predecessors. In retrospect, it was sickening to witness this predatory behavior. Still, the girls soldiered on, determined not to be discouraged or run off. What other choice did they have? Then, to add insult to injury, during the second half, some of the plebes, under the direction of the upperclassmen, I'm sure, went over to the Rutgers' side of the field and "kidnapped" one of their cheerleaders, carrying her over to the Navy side and passing her up into the stands. She feigned embarrassment, of course, offering token resistance, playing along with the gag, even allowing some of the mids to cop a feel as they handed her up. It all seemed like great fun to the enthusiastic crowd but the subtle message to the new Navy cheerleaders was calculated and cold. *You don't belong, and you certainly don't have what it takes to replace the real women on the other side of the field*. It was a classic case of mob mentality causing half the stadium to act in a way they would never dream of as individuals, taking refuge under the protective clause, "they can't fry us all". Collectively the Brigade, we darlings of the nation, could behave like a pack of spoiled adolescents.

Despite the flak at the football game and public disavowing of women in our ranks, an interesting phenomenon was occurring. Since the Brigade had returned, friendships with the women were developing within the class of '80. These friendships, most platonic in nature, were based on recognizing a common interest, a common goal and respect for one another, much like any group thrust together in difficult circumstances might form. Initially, the men resented the women as they later admitted, because of perceived favoritism they would garner. Women resented the men because they generally felt unaccepted regardless of what accomplishments they might achieve. These were natural responses on both sides, especially given the pre-arrival bias that existed soon after Congress passed their law. The peer contact over the summer, and now academic year, was reducing the stereotype showing perhaps a glimmer of hope that things may work out after all.

I had the duty for the weekend when the Tea Dance rolled around, hence my job as one of its first-class chaperones. Two were needed from each company's duty section to staff the dance so I volunteered along with Posey Shelnutt, a classmate stuck on the duty with me. We took the short walk over to Dahlgren Hall together, wearing our service dress blue uniforms, each with a blue and gold U armband for Usher. I figured we'd likely end up working the line and be involved in the pairing exercise. This is going to be interesting, I thought, participating in the dance from a completely different perspective, playing God of sorts. History has shown some plebes meet their future wives at this dance.

"So, Pose, what do you think? You remember our first Tea Fight three years ago?"

We were walking along the terrace connecting Bancroft to Dahlgren. "Huh?"

I could tell, I'd broken his concentration on something completely unrelated to the moment. "You remember, back when we were plebes? You did go to the dance, didn't you?"

"Maybe," he said, staring off into space. "It's statistically probable."

The Pose was an enigma, drifty as a loon with a country innocence like something straight out of the Walton's. His eccentricities baffled us, but we liked him, our fondness growing over time. Posey came from Valdosta, Georgia, his slow-talking southern drawl, lanky build and funny name placing a huge target on his back during plebe summer. The firsties on plebe detail immediately pegged him as a hayseed with a relaxed brain and were continually on his case. But Posey persevered, surprising everyone, later becoming a top rower on the plebe crew team and standing first in the company at the end of plebe year academics. His class standing only improved youngster and second-class year and he was slated to graduate among the top five in our class, destined for nuclear power school on service selection night. Still, there was just something indescribably odd about the guy. He operated on a different wavelength never giving the impression he was smart as his lack of common sense and art for casual conversation masked any noticeable gifts of intelligence. He was the classic savant that hovered on the fringes of the Asperger's scale, unable to exchange pleasantries, understand sarcasm or laugh at simple jokes. He didn't date or own a car his first-class year but could solve complex fluid dynamics equations with an ease that would've confounded Bernoulli himself. His only real outside interests were church and old Louis L'Amour novels. He attended Chapel on Sunday, never missing a service, and never said a bad word about anyone. The Pose was an endearing, sensitive soul willing to offer the shirt off his back, helping us with our studies, quick to swap the duty with anyone in a pinch, never expecting payback, sharing care packages from home and loaning money without question. When Posey saw Sara's farewell post on the company bulletin board the morning it went up, witnesses said they saw tears streaming down his cheeks walking back to his room. And he'd never met her.

We entered Dahlgren Hall, the midshipmen's social center, through the side doors and breezed past the reception desk, down the wide staircase onto the main dance floor. The inside of Dahlgren Hall looked like a huge, open arcade with rows of lights lining its high arched ceiling. The vast ice-skating rink below doubled as a multipurpose area for dances, dinners and formal ceremonies. Dahlgren Hall also sported a small fast-food restaurant, the Drydock, that had recently been given permission to sell beer to the upper three classes. Today, the place was a madhouse. There were hundreds of girls of all shapes and sizes in semi-formal attire milling about on the bare ice rink floor on their half of the curtain with hundreds of sex-deprived male plebes on their half talking loudly, eager to take their chance at this form of roulette wheel dating after not talking to or touching a girl for at least four months. Posey and I walked up to a first-class that looked like he was in charge. He had four stripes on his sleeve along with his own blue and gold U armband. I didn't know him.

"We're here to usher," I said. "How can we help?"

He glanced at our armbands. "And you are—?"

"Mitch Baumann and Pose Shelnutt, 27th Company." I gestured at Posey. "Just say you don't need us, and we'll be on our way," I said with a hopeful grin.

"No, no," he said. "Derick James, 1st Batt Commander. We need you both." He gave us a quick look from top to bottom. "We'll use you," he said, pointing at Posey, "on the line downstairs. I'd like you, Mitch, up topside," he nodded at the mezzanine, "keeping an eye out for any funny business or any plebe trying to cut out early before the festivities begin."

I studied Derick's stern face. "You really think they'll try to ditch after taking the trouble to come over here in the first place?" I knew attendance was mandatory, but no muster had been taken. Most of the plebes I knew had been talking about this dance for weeks. And while they pretended to be grossed out by the thought of a blind date for the afternoon, they'd gone so long without any female companionship most seemed totally willing to accept this humiliating process in which to achieve it. The Tea Fight was practically a rite of passage, one every plebe class goes through and lives to tell – both the goodness and horror afterward. The plebes, at least the male plebes, were jazzed. I hadn't thought about the plebettes and what was going through their minds.

"Of course, they'll try to leave, they're here under duress. And they're scared shitless," Derick reminded us. "Anyway, we need to start this thing in five minutes. Mitch, go topside and try to keep order on the mezzanine. Once the pairing starts all those upperclassmen will start hooting and hollering, trying to offer coaching assistance to their plebes below. We need to make sure they keep quiet." He looked up in their direction. "They shouldn't even be here in the first place but there's no rule keeping them out." He gave a resigned shrug and turned back to us. "Pose? That your name, Pose?" Derick asked, not sure he'd heard correctly.

"Posey," said the Pose.

"Not much of an improvement," he muttered. "Okay, I need you to start herding the plebes into a line, then the girls, okay? We'll get this thing moving as soon as they're queued up."

"Seems to me we should just take down this here curtain and let 'em pick a mate for themselves," Posey said in his soft southern drawl. "Sure make things go easier."

Derick looked at Posey, then at me, a look saying, no, no, no, that will screw everything up. "Why you dumb hick, this dance represents decades of tradition. We're not here to change history or make things easier for the plebes."

"Who are you calling a dumb hick?" I said, stepping in on Posey's behalf. I didn't like this guy's attitude and felt protective of the Pose, and our company. "Why don't I come with you and let Posey do mezzanine patrol?" Posey was better at doing things on his own anyway, and again, for some reason, I didn't feel comfortable leaving him with Derick.

"No, he comes with me," Derick said. "And, sorry, I was only kidding about the dumb hick remark. You just keep order up in the peanut gallery and we'll handle things down here." He turned to leave.

I felt like snapping off a smart palms-up British salute and tossing in a sarcastic, *Yes, sir*, but kept my mouth shut. Derick was just doing his job, although he seemed to be enjoying it a little too much. I suspected he also enjoyed his little dig at Posey's heritage given his forward demeanor and aristocratic chin. I walked back up the stairs past the reception desk toward my assigned station. Dahlgren's mezzanine was a wide balcony extending the length of the hall on both sides with cushioned chairs and sofas providing an excellent view of the dance floor activity below. I knew all about the heckling and assistance the upperclassmen provided at these dances and observed the mob was in full force today. It was all part of the infamous Tea Fight experience for all participants steeped in tradition separating this dance from anything similar at our civilian college counterparts. I wasn't about to squelch or contain the exuberance let alone stop it, as Derick seemed to suggest was my mission.

I found a place to myself and leaned against the wrought iron railing as the assembly process began. Male and female gathered on each side of the curtain below and I spotted both dour and giddy faces as they snaked their way forward in the hook-up line. Derick stood at the far end of the curtain along with Posey and a third-class midshipman messenger of the watch. This is where boy meets girl, I thought, where the pairing occurs. Derick's third-class assistant made the pairing decision based solely on height-matching while Posey was assigned the task of making the formal introduction of the couple once they were united, each first whispering their names in the Pose's ear. I was having more fun watching Posey perform his ritual in the distant silence than the line activity itself, much like he was officiating a wedding ceremony – *I now pronounce you midshipman and future wife.* Still, after about fifty introductions, the Pose seemed uncomfortable and in need of relief. The upperclassmen on the mezzanine directly above the pairing station were already going wild, yelling, motioning, instructing certain individuals to move up or back in the line to get one of the good-looking girls. They'd continually offer either a thumbs-up or a cut sign to the plebes below. It was difficult to tell if their advice was designed to help the plebe or simply deceive him, let him think he was getting a hot babe right up until the last second before he was "bricked," the term for ending up with a loser.

I finally spotted some plebes from our company, Brownfield, Harrington and Poole, clustered close in line, cutting up, having fun, acting like they were God's gift to women as they bravely waited their turn. They looked like lambs being led to slaughter, oblivious of their fate, but eager to get on with the task. On the opposite side of the curtain, I spotted Amanda White, one of our plebes, standing with another female plebe from a different company. Both girls wore grim expressions among the hundreds of cheery civilian girls dressed in their stylish attire, streaming long hair and excessive makeup. Where was Maddy in all this? I hadn't seen her the entire afternoon.

As I watched Amanda make her way toward the front of the line, I felt a sudden, inexplicable urge to move closer to the pairing station. The yelling from the mob on the mezzanine had swelled in intensity, the upperclassmen screaming, *No, no, back, back!* I ran down the wide staircase leading to the floor, coming to a halt just behind the trio of Derick, his messenger and the Pose. The introductions continued as Amanda appeared from behind her side of the curtain. Her apparent date for the afternoon appeared amid much noise and jeering from the gallery above. Posey leaned in to catch the male plebe's name, much as he'd done for the last fifty couples.

"*Oh, SHIT!*" the male plebe declared before any introductions could be made, clearly unhappy with the paring. He looked up to the gallery and smirked, only to receive a barrage of catcalls and wild applause.

Amanda looked embarrassed like she just wanted to melt into the floor.

The male plebe, this arrogant prick, kept up his disappointment, yelling up to the gallery, "I can't believe it! I got bricked! I got stuck with one of the ploobs!"

I'd had it, with him and all his homies on the railing. I stepped in front of Derick and his messenger, getting right in the plebe's face. "All right, take it back," I said. "Say you're sorry to her."

He just froze and stared back at me.

"I said take it back, you son-of-a-bitch!" Restraint was lost. I'd forgotten our roles, our rank difference, protocols, everything. In the confusion that followed, I may have even lunged at him, I don't recall. Nonetheless, an unidentified classmate grabbed me from behind while another stepped between me and the plebe. Posey slid his arm around Amanda and quickly shunted her aside to a nearby bench. "So help me," I cried, "you take it back or I'll—"

A fight was about to break out. I was ready. I wanted to hit someone, the plebe, Derick, the messenger, anyone. I no longer cared. Pose came back whispering in my ear, calming me down and persuading the classmate to release me. I straightened my double-breasted jacket and glared back at them both.

"Who the hell do you think you are, asshole?" the classmate called. "Don Quixote?"

"Yeah I am. Fuck you." I recognized this guy, he'd been on the balcony only moments before, likely the plebe's squad leader or someone from his company. We were both eager to fight, drilling hate into each other, but our potential bout quickly lost steam as the mids surrounding us with much cooler heads prevailed. Finally, Pose steered me away to the bench where he'd deposited Amanda.

"Mitch, man, you were hotter than a two-dollar pistol back there. What happened?"

"I don't know, Pose. I guess it's the crudeness of the whole affair. It seems so demeaning, especially to the women." I looked at Amanda sitting next to me.

"That Derick fella calls it tradition. What are you going to do, take on the whole system?"

"Hey, haven't you heard? I'm Don Quixote."

Posey blinked twice, unsure of the reference, and returned to his station leaving us alone on the bench.

"Sir, do I need to get back in line?" Amanda said. "I mean it's—"

"Of course not. That'd be double jeopardy." I grinned. "The law's on your side."

"Thank you, sir."

"Don't even say that. I'm just sorry it happened. Those guys were way out of line back there."

Amanda offered a thin smile before looking down at her shoes.

"Hey, tell you what – I'll be your date for the rest of the afternoon, think we could get away with that?" I was kidding, of course, offering a kindness, nothing more. We both knew the regs.

"Sorry, sir. I can't play your Dulcinea. Not today."

I smiled at the witty comeback. "No problem, White."

"Besides, why does everyone think we always need rescuing in the first place? One side wants to harass us, the other side wants to rescue us. We're doing just fine. But thank you, though," she quickly added, afraid she'd stepped on my good intentions.

"You're welcome," I said. "And I'll try to remember that in the future." I went on to ask if she'd heard anything from Sara if they'd stayed in touch. She said only that Sara had made it back to Kansas and would likely enroll at KU in the spring. I let her know my feelings on the bungled handling of her final post by Lieutenant Herrera, our company officer. Herrera had been running his own scorched earth policy from day one. He was going to interrogate every individual in the company by sitting them down in his office, asking point-blank if they defaced Sara's post, and forcing a confession via the honor concept – that a midshipman will not lie, cheat or steal, and be subject to separation if found doing so. After some counseling on the matter, he was informed that using the honor concept to enforce an admin conduct violation was in direct conflict with the concept itself and considered unethical. Herrera ultimately backed off when he found there were other simultaneous, politically charged incidents around the Hall gathering notoriety, thus diluting ours. Amanda reminded me of the anonymous graffiti found scrawled in the woman's head in 34th Company around the same time as Sara's post. The threat was raw and just as hateful. *Hang It Up, Bitch!* it'd read. Surprisingly, no high-profile action had been taken when either epitaph had been discovered by the administration. The Academy was like that, wanting to project an aggressive, zero-tolerance image of sexual harassment but also adept at covering things up, doing proper damage control and handling things locally when able, when necessary. If the Commandant wasn't going active on these incidents, demanding answers, Herrera must've thought, why should he? By the time October rolled around, no culprit had surfaced, and Sara Sedgley was a distant memory.

The dance was about half over when I met Amanda back at her bench. She hadn't moved since making my final rounds as usher. I was eager to head back to the Hall after Derick informed me my duties were no longer required. I wasn't sure how to take that bit of news, hoping he wasn't going to fry me for my outburst earlier, which would've totally been his prerogative. "Hey, one last question," I said to Amanda as we stood up, preparing to walk back to Bancroft together. "Where was your roommate this afternoon? I never saw her."

I had clearly rattled her. "Uh, you mean Miss O'Connor, sir?"

"No, Miss White, I mean Indira Gandhi. Who do you think? Where is she?"

"I'm not sure, sir. I think you'll have to ask her."

I stopped walking. Amanda continued ahead hoping to dissuade further conversation. "You both knew this dance was mandatory, right?" I had to shout as she maintained her swift gait.

"Yes, sir," she called over her shoulder.

"Miss White, halt! Come back here when I'm speaking to you." I realized I'd gotten too familiar with her earlier. This was the result, the price paid for being chivalrous versus maintaining a proper relationship with a plebe. Again, a paradox, new ground for the Academy.

"Yes, sir?"

"I don't know where Miss O'Connor was this afternoon." I eyed her carefully. "But I suspect you do. I want to hear it from her though, directly from her. Tell her I want to see her after evening meal tonight."

"Aye, aye, sir."

"Okay, you're dismissed."

She hurried along the walkway ahead of me. I could have told her I wanted to see Maddy immediately but decided to create some tension, some suspense. Let them simmer, I thought. Still, I felt terrible. Today was not a good day for Mitch. Seeing all the pretty girls around Dahlgren Hall made me miss Aimee all the more. I'd felt as deprived as the plebes and unable to do anything about it. I'd also been thinking of my father earlier and realized the memory of his recent visit, wishing it'd been Aimee instead, conspired against me likely causing my quixotic outburst at the plebe and his asshole squad leader. I regretted getting too familiar with Amanda earlier too, giving the impression I was her friend. But most of all I was worried. I had a sickening sense I knew where Maddy was. I needed to confirm it first, then bring a halt to it if my hunch was correct.

Shortly after 7 P.M. I walked over to the girl's room, knocked once and pushed the door ajar. "This is Mr. Baumann. I'm coming in, are you decent?" I spoke loudly and plainly, announcing my presence.

"Yes, sir." It was Maddy. "You may enter."

I pushed the door fully open until it latched, the proper position when male and female were in the same room.

She sprang from her seat. "Midshipman Fourth Class O'Connor, sir, 8-0-4-4-5-1!"

Maddy stood at full attention behind her desk, still wearing her service dress blue uniform from evening meal. "Impressive, O'Connor, but drop the alpha code. This ain't plebe summer."

"Aye-aye, sir."

She looked stiff, formal, and very nervous. She'd been tipped off, which I'd intended. "Where's Miss White? She around?"

"No, sir. She just signed out for Nimitz Library."

"Fine. Sit down, please." She reseated herself on her side of the big double desk, I took Amanda's side, facing her. I intentionally chose to hold our meeting in the girl's room rather than make Maddy come to mine. I needed her to feel more comfortable, more willing to be forthright in the questions I needed to ask, which, I feared might wander into some gray areas. "Do you know what this is about?"

"No, sir."

"No? Didn't Miss White tell you I was looking for you?"

"Yes, sir, but she didn't say what it was about."

I was losing patience. "Cut the crap, O'Connor." I looked her directly in the eye. "Where were you this afternoon?"

"You mean the Tea Fight? Sir?"

I massaged my temples to show frustration, my elbows resting on the desk, hands covering my face. The moment called for some wicked sarcasm, but I held back. "Yes. O'Connor. The. Tea. Fight." I lowered my hands. "Where'd you go? Why'd you skip out?"

"Sir, I made the plebe muster for the dance in the company area, you know, before we headed over to Dahlgren Hall. But—"

"But you cut out once inside, right?" I completed her sentence. "In one door, out the other."

Silence.

I'd sniffed out the truth, virtually offering a confession for her. Maddy was puzzled, unsure how to reply or if she should reply at all.

"C'mon, O'Connor, confirm or deny what I just said." I wasn't going to let her off the hook. "You think people don't notice your presence or lack thereof? This shouldn't come as news, but you are very noticeable. You stand out, you're in a fishbowl here, with almost every guy in the place keeping tabs on you. You can't just leave and have it go unnoticed. Do you understand?"

"Yes, sir, I understand," she said softly, staring at her blotter. "I left Dahlgren before the dance started."

Okay, good, I thought. Admission. Proper handling would be to simply take this information and write her up for missing a scheduled evolution, twenty demerits, deposit the Form 2 with our company admin officer, investigation closed. But that wasn't why I'd come to her room. I was more interested in the gray area beyond. "Then what? I said. "You decided to take a walk? Get some fresh air, tour the Yard, perhaps?"

"Something like that. You know…" Her voice trailed off.

"No, I don't know. Something like what? Can you tell me where you, went?" I intentionally formed it as a question, not wanting her to construe it as an order. This question was the crux of my visit.

Maddy met my eyes, pleading silently for something, I wasn't sure. "Sir, I left the Yard, I did. So, go ahead, fry me. Pretty careless, I admit but I'd rather not explain the rest. I'm sure you know anyway." She reached for a tissue.

I closed my eyes, replaying our chance meeting in her plebe summer room back in July. I recalled the joking around, the easy laughter, the contact. Yes, I knew or imagined I knew, where she was this afternoon. I lowered my voice to almost a whisper. "Maddy, listen to me. If you're surreptitiously seeing an upperclassman, sneaking out the gate in his car or whatever, I urge you to stop, to stop now. As I said, people are watching. Your activity around here does not go unnoticed. If you're caught, you'll be looking at 150 big ones, 75 for unauthorized absence and 75 for fraternization. A couple of Class-A's as a plebe and you're gone. Neither of us wants that, right?"

"Uh, right, sir." It looked like she'd entered a trance, was no longer present in the room.

I stood. Maddy stood. "Okay, then," I said, restoring my voice to its normal level. "Do the right thing, O'Connor. Drop this guy, whoever he is." I turned and walked out.

It wasn't hard, but by checking around afterward, with Roger Galvin and a few other youngsters in our company, I pieced together a fairly obvious scenario. Maddy was seeing someone, a first-class in 28th Company, one of the second set squad leaders in the melded Oscar Company from the summer. I knew him – current 28th Company sub-commander, captain of the pistol team, wiry physique, gung-ho style, headed for Marine Corps infantry upon graduation, a squared-away mid – an overall stud. I suddenly hated him.

# 15

## GOOD INTENTIONS

Saturday, November 13, 1976

I SWUNG MY MG ROADSTER into one of the few open parking spaces alongside Farragut Field near the eighth wing, shut off the engine and sat alone in the darkness. The evening was frigid, and the car's interior cooled quickly from the brisk November wind off the Chesapeake. I'd just returned from Jack and Irene's, my sponsor's, after a light meal following Navy's final home football game of the season. We'd all been to the game and attended one of the big alumni tailgate parties afterward. I felt bad for cutting out early, making an excuse about an upcoming term paper but the truth was I was tired. And I didn't feel like going up to our company wardroom, watching more TV and seeing our drunk youngsters and second-class pour in from their liberty arguing about what channel to watch. As a first-class I had the entire weekend off and, like the rest of my classmates without the duty, should've been miles from here. My mind went back to Maddy and the meeting in her room nearly a month ago. I hadn't tracked her whereabouts closely but noticed she spent an inordinate about of time at Nimitz Library, even for a plebe struggling with nineteen semester hours. Tonight though, she could've been anywhere. I really hoped it wasn't with that guy in 28. I kept telling myself I was concerned for her future, not wanting it jeopardized by fraternizing and riding out the gate in upperclassmen's cars. That was the whole point of my counseling and warning in her room last month, right? But that was a lie. I was jealous, pure and simple. I felt a tug of competition at some primal level not wanting Maddy for myself but, more to the point, not wanting anyone else to have her. I wanted to think of myself as a mentor guiding a student, steering her clear of harmful obstacles. And if it meant encouraging or threatening her to dump this guy, so be it.

So, here I sat, in an unseasonably cold breeze off the bay under the shroud of darkness with nowhere to go on a Saturday night. I could see clusters of midshipmen, some with dates or recent pick-ups, coming and going from Dahlgren Hall in the distance. Another Saturday hop was in progress. Aimee drifted into my mind. I wondered what she was doing tonight in Pensacola a thousand miles away and tortured myself with images of her out having fun on a date of her own. Her letter was still very much in the forefront of my mind and I came dangerously close to doing a little drinking-and-dialing a few weekends ago from a noisy bar in Georgetown until Lonnie and a few other classmates grabbed my shoulder and steered me back to our table. I was pissed and told him to leave me alone — *let a man do what he has to do.* But I also ended up apologizing and thanking him profusely the next morning for preventing the call from ever going through. I was a mess, really.

It was time to get out of the car and brave the cold. The walk back to Bancroft would be short since I'd found a relatively close spot. I was contemplating this go-stay-go-stay when there was a rap on my passenger window. A petite figure in uniform was shaped in front of me but towering over the small MG. The figure bent down and met my eye, her face framed in the window. *Maddy?* I rolled down the passenger side. "O'Connor, what are you doing out here on a Saturday night? You scared the crap out of me."

"Sorry, sir, I just saw you pull up sitting there. I'm taking the long way back from the library, out for a walk."

"A walk? It's freezing outside." She was clutching a notebook. "What have you been studying there?"

"Oh, this? Just a little project I'm working on."

I was skeptical. "Which class?" All the plebes took a very standard load of courses.

"Not for a class. Just some extracurricular research."

Just then we noticed three mids in uniform and overcoats walking in the road, headed our direction. "As if you have time for extracurricular research," I spoke in a low voice as the mids passed. They minded their own business but got a good look at our little scene. A few more were off in the distance. I pushed the passenger door open. "Better get in and sit for a minute. I don't want anyone else getting the wrong impression."

She sat low in the bucket seat next to me and took a deep breath. The car was quiet for a moment filling up with her sweet fragrance in the confined space. I was at a loss given how quickly things had changed in front of me. "Who were you waiting for out here?"

"No one, sir."

"No one? I find that hard to believe."

"It's the truth." She sounded indignant. "I was out for a walk and needed away from the library. I rate this, you know. We've got liberty. I'm not breaking any regs."

"Please don't quote me the regs, O'Connor. I know better than you what you rate and don't rate. It just looks suspicious, that's all."

"Why?"

The two mids in the distance earlier were getting closer. From their silhouettes, I thought I recognized them. "Okay, enough of this," I said. I started the engine and quickly pulled onto the narrow two-lane road. "Hang on."

Maddy smiled. "Ooh. Where are we going?"

"Just away from here. It was getting like Grand Central Station back there."

We picked up speed passing Halsey Field House pointed toward Gate 1. Maddy grabbed my windbreaker she'd been sitting on, slid low in her seat, as low as the small car would allow, getting nearly horizontal and burying her face under the jacket. This was a wise move but not one I'd anticipated. I thought, how many times has she performed this little ritual? We sailed straight out Gate 1, past the guard shack and more midshipmen heading into town for liberty.

"Okay, all clear," I said, sarcastically, once in the harbor area and pointed across the Eastport bridge. "You can come out now."

Maddy punched my arm softly but remained crouched low in her seat. "So, where're you taking me?" she said, like things had just blossomed into a big adventure.

"Nowhere." I wasn't about to give her the impression I had a plan. But here we were, out of the Yard, moving with purpose for parts unknown. Cruising along, I was reminded of an earlier thought, admitting I didn't want to date Maddy, to have her for myself, but I didn't want anyone else to have her either. "So, is this the first time you've done this?" I asked. "Riding out the gate curled up like that?"

Maddy remained silent.

"Is it?"

"I'm not answering that. If that's what this drive is turning into, an interrogation like some jealous boyfriend, then—"

"Jealous boyfriend?" I started laughing. "This is about getting us out of harm's way just now, not—" I paused, unable to complete my sentence. A moment passed.

"Yes?" She grinned back. "Please, continue."

I remained quiet and drove on. We were free from the Yard and the vibe between us had changed, like we were reprising the roles in her room during plebe summer, both of us briefly shedding our rank difference and resuming our friendly chat. We entered a small park in Eastport at the far end of Spa Creek, the road terminating in a cul-de-sac with a boat ramp and lone streetlight facing a large expanse of dark water. I pulled over next to the light pole, shut off the engine and doused the headlights. Everything went dead silent. Maddy looked around, appearing nervous. "So, this is your plan? Take me to some remote park at night, kill me, dump the body?"

"Relax, O'Connor. I told you, I don't have a plan. You know what I did back there and why."

"Yes, I know what you did." Maddy smiled. She rested her hand on my

251

thigh and leaned across the tiny console. The feeble streetlight cast a soft shadow across her face revealing only a silhouette, a stunning facial profile. She brushed a lock of hair back from her cheek and leaned toward me. I moved closer, unable to stop, and pressed my lips to hers. Our ensuing kiss felt natural, a continuation, a release of tension that had existed since the summer meeting in her room. We kissed again, longer, with more passion, pressing into each other until I felt her stop, her body relax. I figured she was sending a warning, for us both to halt our reckless behavior before it got completely out of hand. I quickly sat upright, recentering myself in the bucket seat.

"Why'd you stop?" she said.

"I thought *you* were stopping."

"Well, I wasn't."

"But you made it seem— You sort of pulled back, didn't you?"

"I didn't."

"All right then, maybe it's a sign. Maybe we need to cool it."

"Mitch, I'm okay with things but if you're not, then maybe we should cool it."

I was taken aback hearing her use my first name for the first time. Things really had gotten out of control. I'd gone too far, and it all happened so quickly, in the blink of an eye. "I'm sorry. This was my fault. I didn't mean to take us out here, to mislead you. To hurt you."

"Hurt me?"

"Yes, I'm sorry."

"Grow up. I'm fine."

The car grew silent, both of us staring out the windshield as the water shimmered against the shoreline. The right thing to do was start the car and head back. I was saddened and embarrassed we'd misread each other. By the same token, I was relieved. My intention was never to bring Maddy out here in the first place, the whole thing an accidental encounter but I was struggling with how natural things had developed in its wake. I let out a spontaneous laugh, causing her to jump.

"What's so funny?" she said, eying me suspiciously.

"Oh, nothing. It's just that sometimes—" I turned to face her. "Why are you here, O'Connor? What made you decide to come to the Naval Academy?"

Her eyes grew large, inquiring if I'd lost my marbles. "What kind of question is that?" She thought about it for a second. "Why are *you* here?"

"I asked you first."

"Because of your father, right? He was a pilot in World War II. He's your hero and now you're honoring him? Is that it?"

"*What?*" Her casually turning the tables and tossing in my father threw me for a loop. "Where'd you hear—? How'd you know that?"

"He was with us in the Wardroom for evening meal back in the summer. The plebe regimental commander, Mr. McDavid, introduced him, remember?"

"Yes, I remember." After my father's performance at dinner that night, I'd hoped to forget the whole thing. It was still as fresh as yesterday, but I was stalling, playing it cagey. "Okay, so I came to this place to be a pilot too. Big deal. It's just that things change, it's complicated right now." I recalled my father's words to me in Memorial Hall, the drift in his speech, his reticence to stand up at dinner.

"How complicated can it be? You walk down to Mitscher Hall on service selection night, pick Naval Aviation and never look back. Done deal. That'll be me in three years, that's for sure."

"I'm glad you're so cocksure of yourself, O'Connor. Maybe you want to focus on getting through the rest of your plebe year first."

"What do you mean? I am focused. I've got a 3.2 QPR going into ten-week exams."

"What I mean is riding out the gate in upperclassmen's cars, crouching low in the passenger seat, wearing civilian clothes, dating, fraternizing. Your entire behavior – it's got to stop. What if you're caught? It'll be goodbye USNA, hello junior college."

Maddy started laughing. "Oh? And what about the upperclassman that invited me into *his* car, drove me out the gate to some backwater park and fraternized like hell just now?" She was smiling, but serious. "I suppose he has a *Get Out of Jail Free* card?"

"You know what I mean. Think of tonight as an isolated incident, a counseling session, perhaps." I was going out on a limb calling it a "counseling session" but kept rolling. "I'm talking about riding out the gate regularly, trapesing around town in civies, going beyond the seven-mile limit, drinking – all of it. I don't care who you're with, eventually you will get caught. How hard do you think it was for me to find a few people willing to talk, to get the lowdown on who you're dating? Remember what I said earlier? Think fishbowl, O'Connor."

"I don't know who your sources are, but this is only the second time I've ridden in an upperclassman's car. And dating? I'm not dating anyone. Yes, you noticed I disappeared at the Tea Fight. I drove up to Severna Park for the afternoon with a guy from 28th Company. *That* was your basic isolated incident, and it was stupid. He was interested in one thing and one thing only. And he didn't get it, I might add." Maddy paused to draw a breath. She no longer appeared angry but was still agitated. "Mitch, I think I see what you're trying to do. I do. And I think it's honorable, in a sort of perverse, misguided way. Some of your other classmates are not so honorable. They're either monstrously crude or overly sweet before they propose we steal away to an isolated part of Bancroft Hall for a quick blowjob."

Her candor shocked me. "I had no idea."

"Yeah, well, I'm getting pretty good at deflecting it." She managed a weak smile.

"Is it really that bad, around the Hall I mean?"

She didn't respond, which spoke volumes. Outside, a light snow began to fall. I watched the tiny flakes swirl in the arc of the streetlamp and considered starting the car to head back for real this time. Maddy needed to make taps in less than an hour.

"I came here because my father is my hero too," she blurted out rather randomly.

"Hang on. I never claimed my father was my hero. Those are your words. I'll concede, he provided some influence, a guiding presence, perhaps. Maybe, I don't know."

"Oh, that's right. It's complicated. For me, it was easy, there was no question."

"Really? Your father fly in the war too?"

"Hero doesn't necessarily mean flying in aerial combat."

"You're right, it doesn't. And again, I never claimed my father was my hero." Denying my father hero status and claiming he only provided some influence in my life was a lie. He was the primary reason I was here. I had sought my appointment to the Naval Academy solely to impress him, to regain his attention, his affection, but after his behavior during the recent visit, I felt I'd been subconsciously distancing myself from him and sabotaging his memory. His entire stature, his persona, was unraveling before my eyes.

"Well, you started it," she said. "You asked me earlier, why I came here. It was an easy decision. My father didn't fly airplanes. He's a retired Navy commander, an aviation intelligence officer, someone I always looked up to but was gone an awful lot."

"Welcome to the club," I said.

"Still, he was our glue, he bound us together, even when he was deployed – all of us, Mother, my older brothers, my sister, me. I always admired his strength and the love he showed my mother. I wanted to be that person. Now, with the help of Congress, Title IX, Women's Lib, whatever, I'll—"

"Your family was close? Your mom dealt with the separations okay?"

"She did. They loved each other. We'd draw tight when he'd leave and run with open arms when he'd return. When I was little, I thought everyone's father went on deployment. It was what fathers did. When I got older and discovered the opposite, it made me admire him even more."

Given my plight and personal experience, I didn't have the heart to continue, getting force-fed her version of the Brady Bunch. "So, you knew you were going to join the Navy your whole life?"

"No. I was headed to Notre Dame, Dad's alma mater, on a swimming scholarship, but when this opportunity came up, it was easy to pick. I got some additional encouragement from a family friend – a grad himself."

"Some big admiral, I suppose?"

"As a matter of fact, yes. Harlan Tennant. I mean Admiral Tennant, a three-star now. My dad served with him at the Pentagon in '73 before we retired in Annandale. Also served with him on the *USS Independence* back in the '60s. Ever hear of him?"

"No."

"Us kids called him Uncle Harley but that doesn't sound right now that I'm here. He's going places, I'm sure. Naval Aviator, slated to take over as Commander, Seventh Fleet next year. I even wrote my essay about him, used my dad and him as examples of why I wanted to attend the Academy."

"You wrote an essay about Uncle Harley?"

She laughed. "It was part of the nomination process, you know, to get your congressman to nominate you to a service academy."

"I never wrote an essay," I said, surprised to learn they might now be using this as an extra winnowing tool given the sharp rise in applications since the Vietnam War.

"Well, I had to. Wasn't too hard. Figured I'd earn some brownie points mentioning his name, that I knew him growing up. He told me he was in the Tonkin Gulf in '64 when the North Vietnamese first started shooting at us. Sort of bragged it, actually. I followed up with some more research to make it sound authentic."

"Impressive," I said, wishing I at least knew *of* him. "Sounds like a decent guy."

"He was, at one time. Seems kind of arrogant now that I'm grown up, a bit of an asshole, I'm afraid. But I guess all flyers are, right?" Maddy smiled and bumped me with her shoulder, a gesture that hinted at intimacy like we might get close again after our misstart.

I leaned toward her in anticipation of resuming where we'd left off if nothing more than to erase the awkward moment earlier.

Maddy stayed put. "Mitch, let's not," she said. "I know you're not that dense, that you recognized what I was offering earlier. You hesitated, for good reason, I'm sure. And I can respect that, I can. You've got other things on your mind."

I laughed. "If you only knew."

"Then let's head back. I need to make taps in half an hour anyway."

"Very well." I started the car, and we rode in silence during the short distance back to the Yard. When I stopped at the seawall and shut off the lights, I spoke one final time. "Maddy, I'm sorry. I like you too but there's too much at stake here. You need to stay focused. Hell, *I* need to stay focused. You shouldn't even think about dating – not until next year, right?"

Maddy stared ahead, her face a blank.

"You need to come to terms with why you're here – to get your BS, not your MRS."

Silence.

"Right?"

She pushed the car door open, gave a smirk and gathered her notebook. "Right," she said, then disappeared, cutting across Farragut Field into the night.

# 16

## ON WATCH

Saturday, November 20, 1976

THE LAST WEEKEND BEFORE the Army-Navy football game, with all the usual celebration and high jinx in full swing, found me stuck with the duty, my last until the semester ended. I was standing the Bow Wow watch in the battalion office when a call came in at 2250, ten minutes before taps. Cory Hunter, the midshipman in charge of battalion office, my assistant of sorts, picked up, spoke briefly then covered the receiver mouthpiece with his free hand.

"Mitch, it's the OD," he said, whispering loudly. "He's over at the base hospital, says he wants to speak to the Battalion Officer of the Watch."

I rolled my eyes. "Now what?" I picked up the phone. All I wanted was to end this watch in the next hour, peacefully, without incident. I took a deep breath. "This is the Fifth Battalion Officer of the Watch, Midshipman Baumann, may I help you, sir?"

"Midshipman Baumann?"

"Yes, sir."

"This is Lieutenant Commander Callahan. You the current Bow Wow for Fifth Batt?"

"Yes, sir." *Didn't I just say that?*

"Then I need you over here at the base hospital, ASAP. I'm holding four youngsters from your battalion that need to be escorted back to Bancroft Hall and written up, all four of them."

"Yes, sir, I'll be right over," I said. "Can you say what I'll be writing them up for?"

"I most certainly can. Drunk in public, disorderly conduct. Stupidity. I'll think up some more charges on your way over. One of them took a leap off the Eastport bridge, for crying out loud!"

I wasn't sure I'd heard him correctly. "You say one of them jumped off a bridge?"

"That's what I said. In full uniform. Just get over here and pick them up. I can't wait around all night."

257

"Aye, aye, sir."

I hung up the phone. Under normal circumstances, I would've been laughing my ass off. A drunk mid decides to jump off the Eastport bridge in full service dress blue uniform? Un-fucking believable. Instead, I stood up slowly, donned my cover, reattached my sword and spoke very calmly to my battalion office messenger, a plebe from our company. "Grab your pen. Grab your notepad. We're taking a ride over to the base hospital."

It took more than an hour to get the full picture of what had occurred. There were statements taken from all four youngsters, discussion with the harbor patrol boat officer that fished our jumper from the water and hospital release forms to sign. The attending physician stated that other than minor shock and hypothermia, which he'd treated, our mid would be fine. Riding back to Bancroft Hall in a skimpy hospital smock, wrapped in a wool blanket, our mid didn't look so fine. The consequences for his daring but foolish jump were slowly sinking in, that he was going to be fried, big time. When I got back to the battalion office, I was hoping to quickly make my logbook entry, sign the taps report, pipe-down the watch and get some shut-eye. Instead, I was greeted with our second snafu of the evening.

"Mitch," said Cory, "Another problem. We've got a UA on one of the company's taps reports. Someone from 27."

"Oh, of course, we do," I said, sarcastically. "We're on the eve of Army Week. Which one of our intrepid mids got shitfaced and couldn't find his way back to Bancroft, or is out on a recon moving the F-4 to the Supe's front yard again as we speak?"

"No one. It's one of our plebettes, Miss O'Connor. And she's still not present."

I looked up at the office clock on the wall – midnight-thirty. "She's not up in her room? Where is she?"

"They don't know. The duty section's checking around right now. Neil King just phoned down ten minutes ago. Still no O'Connor."

My stomach knotted. I was pissed and worried at the same time. This was exactly the type of behavior I told Maddy I wanted stopped. Yet something told me my hunch was wrong, that Maddy was not out riding around in another midshipman's car. She'd been truthful the other night, I was certain. "Okay, I'm going upstairs. I want to talk to Neil. Have you passed the taps report to Main Office?"

"Not yet. They just phoned asking why they don't have it. It was only a plebe messenger, so I told him to standby."

"Let me check things out first. If you don't hear in ten minutes, go ahead and pass the report with the UA on it."

"Roger."

I grabbed my cover, running up the single flight of stairs to our company area. *Maddy... Where the hell are you?* Something felt really wrong.

I met Neil back in our room. He was changing into his uniform in anticipation of being called to Main Office, but so far no one had sent for him. "So, how'd this go down? I asked. "Has anyone talked to White?"

"Of course, we have, Mitch. I just got back from her room."

"And?"

"Not much to tell. We did our room check at 2305. Miss White present, Miss O'Connor, not present. I asked White where she was, or if she knew where she might be. She says, 'No, sir, I don't have any information, sir.' That was it, end of story."

"Christ, Neil. That's the only question you asked? Think Columbo, man, ask the follow-up." I was shocked. "I'm going down to her room now. This is ridiculous."

"Mitch," Neil called out as I headed out our door, "She could be anywhere. Probably snuck out with some guy, their car broke down or something."

My stomach dropped. Was he right? Was Maddy—? No, I wouldn't allow myself to believe that scenario. I ran down to the girl's room and banged on the door twice. "I'm coming in. It's Mr. Baumann."

"You may enter, sir."

Amanda was sitting on her rack, the overhead lights out per regulation but the shower light was on, casting a dim glow about the room. "All right, where's Miss O'Connor?" I said, wasting no time, flipping on the overheads.

"Sir, as I told Mr. King, she should be back."

"That's not what I asked. I asked, where is she? Where'd she go tonight?" Think, Miss White, think. This is important."

"I don't know. I don't. Earlier in the week, she mentioned she might go see that new movie, *Carrie*, over in Eastport. But that'd be over by now."

"*You think?*" I looked at my watch: 12:50 A.M. "The last show ended two hours ago. Besides, she's not going to violate taps over a stupid movie. C'mon, Amanda," I intentionally used her first name and lowered my voice. "Where is she? Did she sneak out again with that guy in 28?"

"No, sir. I'm certain she didn't."

"How certain are you?" This probably didn't need asking, it just fell out.

"Sir, she doesn't like that guy. She never did." Amanda paused, shifting her position on the bed, speaking softly. "What she really—" A new thought occurred. "Wait, I just remembered. I think she said she was going to the movie with her sponsor. She might've gone to her sponsor's house first."

I jumped to my feet. "You're just remembering now? Why didn't you think of that an hour ago?"

Neil entered the room before she could answer. Despite his glum look, I asked, "Is she back? Did you guys find her?" I really wanted to hear some good news.

"No. That's why I came for you. I think we should call the OD, maybe

259

go down to Main O."

"Hang on," I said. I stuck my head out of the room and yelled to the CMOD in the hall at his podium. "Hey, Buell! Get down here. And bring your sign-out log with you."

Buell grabbed the big green book and chopped towards us. He looked flustered, unsure if he should greet us, stand at attention or sound off. After all, it was 1 A.M. He was thinking his watch should be over but recognized something important was going on, that he'd better pay attention. He popped open the log to today's date and held it out. "Sir, here are all the entries for—"

"Just give it to me," I said, yanking it from his hands. I quickly scanned for Maddy's name. "Bingo. It was right here all along. Neil, look." I pointed to an entry penned in Maddy's handwriting along with a copy of the special request chit excusing her from evening meal formation. The entry read:

| Name | Destination | Time Out | Time In |
|------|-------------|----------|---------|
| *Mid'n 4/c O'Connor* | *Sponsor's, Perry Circle* | *1700* | |

"Wow, Dick Fucking Tracy," he said. "Guess we can call Main O now."

"Not so fast." I turned to Amanda. "Miss White, who's Maddy's sponsor? What's their name?"

She thought for a moment, a look of disappointment forming on her face. "Sir, I can't remember. It's some CEC officer, works over in Halligan Hall, family lives just outside Gate 8 in one of those big apartment buildings. That's all I know, that's all Maddy ever mentioned."

"Okay." I looked up at Neil. "Shouldn't be too hard to find. We need to get their number, call them tonight."

"Shouldn't we just notify the OD, let Main Office handle it?"

"Who, Lieutenant Commander Callahan? I was with that numb nuts at the hospital tonight. He wouldn't dream of calling anyone at this late hour and disturbing their sleep over a simple UA. He'll just want to make sure she's written up by either you or me, that the Form 2 is on its way and that his ass is covered."

"You don't know that."

"You're right, I don't. Go ahead, notify Main Office, tell the OD. I don't care. I'm still going to find the sponsor and call his quarters as soon as I get the number. In fact, I may even take a walk over there."

"Mitch, what the hell's gotten into you? Are you crazy? You don't need to go banging on doors, not tonight. What's got you so—"

I interrupted. "Because, Neil, we need to go active on this thing, right now. The sooner we find her the better. I have a bad feeling about this, I really do." I glanced at Amanda. She looked frightened, which preyed on my own fears. It was probably my urgency, my tone, not Maddy's absence that was frightening her, but I wasn't sure. "Anything else you can tell us, Miss White? Anything at all?"

She closed her eyes and shook her head. She was scared.

Neil and I walked back with Buell to his watch station to use the phone, but it was already ringing when we got there. Buell picked up, gave his perfunctory greeting and immediately handed me the receiver. I hoped it was good news about Maddy. "Midshipman Baumann, may I help you, sir?"

"This is the MOOW. Am I speaking to the Battalion Officer of the Watch?"

"Yes, you are. This is Mitch Baumann."

"Mitch, where the hell's your taps report? The OD's going wild. Christ, it's 1 A.M. We should've had it an hour ago."

"Didn't he tell you I was with him at the hospital until a half-hour ago? I just got back to my company area. We're checking on a potential UA right now."

"Well, stop checking and come down to Main O. He wants to see you and someone from your duty section before he pipes-down the watch."

"Okay, fine," I said, brusquely. "I want to see him too. We're on our way down." I hung up, turning to Neil. "C'mon, roomie. Let's take a walk down to Main O."

"Mitch, before we go, you may want to tone down some of that attitude. Callahan has every right to ask us why he doesn't have that report."

"Yeah, he does. And I have every right to ask him to do something with the information I'm about to provide. Let's go."

We moved at a quick pace through the empty corridors of Bancroft Hall, Neil struggling to keep up – down the flight of stairs to zero-deck, along the nearly quarter-mile of passageways and multiple company areas before coming to a final flight of stairs leading up to the Rotunda and into Main Office. I was in a hurry – not to present my stupid taps report but to convey a sense of urgency to LCDR Callahan and his MOOW to call Maddy's sponsor, tonight.

Main Office was fully staffed, every watch stander's eye on me when we walked in. The MOOW met us at the door. "He's in here," he said, guiding us to a private office.

LCDR Callahan was standing behind his desk. He looked up when we walked in. "Sir, Midshipman Baumann. And this is Midshipman King, 27th Company duty section," I said, nodding at Neil. "Reporting as ordered, sir."

"Ah, Baumann. We meet again, and so soon."

"Yes, sir."

"What's going on over there in Fifth Batt tonight? Why're the natives so restless?"

"Army Week, sir. Something like that." *Why's he asking me this again?*

"We needed that taps report over an hour ago. What's the story?"

261

"Sir, as I told the MOOW, I just got back to the battalion office thirty minutes ago. I was informed about a UA. We were just doing a little investigating first."

"Unsat," he said, frowning. "Your MCBO should've passed the report, you should have written him up and then you could've done your investigating."

"Her."

"Who?"

"Her. The UA, sir. It's a female plebe. We've got the sign-out log and her special request chit. She went to her sponsors at 1700, never signed back in."

"Well, then, she's UA. Is she spending the night?"

"No, sir." Plebes weren't authorized to spend the night outside Bancroft Hall, even with a special request chit. *He should know that.* "I recommend we contact Miss O'Connor's sponsor, tonight, right now, to see what he knows, if he can help."

Callahan thought for a moment, the wheels turning in his head, weighing what a 1 A.M. call to the house might yield, if anything. "Who is the guy?" he said. "Do we have his number?"

I was hopeful. "We're checking now, sir. He's a CEC officer, lives just outside the back gate on Perry Circle."

Again, the thoughtful pose. Then, "Nope. There's nothing he's going to tell us that will make any difference tonight. I want you to write up this Miss O'Connor and if she's not back by tomorrow morning, I'll call the sponsor, and then the Commandant."

"But sir, I can easily find the guy's name and address. We really should call, ask what they did tonight, where they went, when Miss O'Connor departed. Or, if in fact, she did spend the night." Maybe Maddy had crashed at their place even though she didn't rate it. This would be a minor infraction compared to what she was facing otherwise.

"I appreciate your concern, Mr. Baumann, I really do but it doesn't matter. If she's spent the night, so be it. If not, we'll find out where she went in the morning. We're not calling the sponsor's quarters, not at this late hour."

"But sir, what if—"

"I said *no*. I'm not contacting anyone, not tonight." Callahan's eyes narrowed in on me. "And that goes for you too. No one, I repeat no one in your duty section, you or anybody, will attempt to contact the sponsor tonight. We'll deal with this thing in the morning if she's not back. Do I make myself clear?"

I hesitated before responding. Callahan raised an eyebrow. Neil glared at me and jumped in. "Yes, sir, very clear, sir."

"All right, then. Good night, gentlemen, you're both dismissed."

Neil and I turned to leave.

"And I want that girl written up. Tonight."

"Aye, aye, sir," I replied in a whisper, heading out the door. *Whatever.*

Neil and I returned to the sixth wing at the same brisk clip as our walk to Main O. I made a beeline to the battalion office. Neil followed me inside. "Did you find him?" I demanded of Cory Hunter, storming right up to his MCBO desk. "Our CEC officer on Perry Circle?"

"I most certainly did. Wasn't too hard, just a simple process of elimination." Cory pointed at two phone books, one for Bancroft Hall, one for the Naval Academy proper, and handed me a slip of paper.

"You're a genius, man. I owe you."

Cory basked in the compliment while Neil got in my face. "Mitch, have you lost your mind? Didn't you hear Callahan? He specifically ordered you, or anyone in the duty section, not to contact the sponsor tonight."

"I know. But he never said anything about company officers. I'm calling Lieutenant Herrera right now. I'll persuade him to make the call."

"Oh, brother. Mitch, I really don't think that's a wise move."

I ignored Neil, found the number to Herrera's quarters, picked up the phone and dialed.

"I'm leaving," Neil said. "I'm not going to be a party to this."

"And you don't have to be." I listened to the phone ring in my ear. "Sleep tight, roomie."


Sunday A.M., November 21, 1976

I was shocked when I hung up the telephone. Either I was losing my touch or Herrera wasn't fully enough awake to comprehend what I was telling him. In any case, he thanked me for the call, my concern, and said to sit tight until the cavalry arrived in the morning. *Until the cavalry arrived?* What the hell was that supposed to mean? We're talking about a missing plebe midshipman. A missing *female* plebe midshipman, for crying out loud. She wasn't out drinking, passed out on someone's couch or taking an unauthorized weekend outside the seven-mile limit. She wasn't out on a recon raid, hadn't scaled the wall. She was missing and she needed our help.

I went to bed at 0200, tossing and turning in my rack for the balance of the night. When 0700 finally came, I arose and dressed back into my uniform to resume my watch as the Bow Wow, one that wouldn't end until I was relieved at 1730 this afternoon. I had a very clear mission to complete before I left the watch, one that flashed in my head before I'd dozed off. I wouldn't wait for Callahan. I wouldn't wait for Herrera. I would take a walk out to Perry Circle, introduce myself to Maddy's sponsor and pay my respects on a pleasant Sunday morning visit.

It was bitter cold under blue sky when I set out on foot, a trek that led me through the center of the Yard, past the Superintendent's quarters, the Chapel, the parade field, over a causeway, out Gate 8 and up a hill to eight

263

neatly arranged three-story apartment buildings ringing a manicured lawn. I covered the mile-plus in my service dress blues, white gloves and sword as gusty winds swept crisp autumn leaves across my path. I eventually spotted the address Cory gave me, 8 Perry Circle, Quarters E, on the third building up the hill. I gave a shiver. Almost there, I thought. I confirmed Maddy's sponsor's names, *LT and Mrs. Robert Clausen, CEC, USN*, on the mailbox at the base of the steps. Other bits of scribble on Cory's slip of paper were their home phone number, Clausen's billet, his work address and phone number. I scanned the information one final time before stuffing the paper in my trouser pocket and walking up the narrow indoor stairs to their front door.

Thankfully, the family was home. Ringing the buzzer, I could hear noise leaking into the vestibule – a small child's footsteps, a muffled television, the aroma of breakfast cooking. A woman in a white robe opened the door with a big grin. Her expression quickly changed when she noticed me standing at the threshold, grave-faced, in full uniform.

"Oh." Obviously, I wasn't the neighbor she was expecting. "Yes? May I help you?"

"Good morning, ma'am. I'm Midshipman Mitch Baumann. I'm looking for Lieutenant Clausen. I need to speak with him if I may."

"Of course. Come in, Mitch, please. Sit down, I'll go get him." She warmed quickly. "I'm Jan, by the way." Her pleasant manner and grace suggested she'd greeted many midshipmen and other guests into her home. I eased into their living room, noticing a small girl of maybe three in pajamas parked in front of the TV. She turned around, made eye contact and giggled, then went back to her program.

Heavy footsteps reverberated on the hardwood floor; the man of the house approached. "Good morning. Bob Clausen," he said, projecting a hand. "What can I do for you?" He was dressed in sweatpants and a long-sleeved t-shirt, a moist towel draped around his neck suggesting he'd just returned from a run.

"Good morning, sir." I shook his hand. "Midshipman Mitch Baumann." I took a deep breath. "Sir, I'm from 27th Company and we're looking into a possible UA. Was a Midshipman O'Connor here last night? We show she was signed out to this address."

"Maddy O'Connor?" He was instantly concerned. "Yes, of course, she was here. Both she and Michelle Dobson, our other mid from 10th Company, they were both with us. We're their sponsors. You say they're missing?"

"I can't speak for Miss Dobson, sir. But, yes, Miss O'Connor didn't make taps last night and she's still not back in the Hall. I was hoping I'd find her here or you might know where she was."

"No. I have no idea. We went to an early movie over in Eastport, the four of us, then came back and made dinner. That was it."

"Do you remember what time they departed, sir?"

"Well, they left at different times." He shifted his stance. "And by the way, call me Bob." Bob placed a hand on his chin. "After dinner, Maddy said she needed to get back, but Michelle decided to stay and finish watching a TV program with us. I offered to drive her back to the Hall, but she insisted on walking, for us to stay and finish the program. I asked again, but she remained firm, said the air would do her good."

"What time was that, approximately?"

Bob thought about it. "Let's see, we finished dinner around eight-thirty. I'd say she left no later than 2100. I drove Michelle back right before taps, around 2245." He looked me directly in the eye. "Are you certain, she never made it back?"

"Yes, we're certain. I checked her room again before walking over here."

"My God, this is awful. What's being done? Have you notified the Officer of the Watch, her company officer?"

"Yes. I spoke to both of them last night."

"And?"

I thought for a moment before answering. On one hand, I wanted to report they'd done nothing, taken no action, told me not to worry and to stay out of it. On the other hand, I didn't want to further alarm Bob. I could see deep concern written all over his face, that he felt terrible for letting Maddy leave alone under the cover of darkness. I thought the same thing. *Why didn't you insist a third time, fool?* "And, the OD said he'd call the Commandant this morning if she wasn't back," I said. "I imagine that call's taking place right now. I told them about Miss O'Connor being here, so you may get a call too."

"Breakfast's ready," Bob's wife called from the kitchen. She came into the room, smiled at her husband, then me. "Mitch, please join us. Have you had anything to eat this morning, dear?"

I started to politely decline when Bob jumped in. "Maddy's missing, Jan. Mitch says she didn't make taps last night."

"What?" Her heart skipped a beat. "Missing? Oh, no, what on earth happened?"

"We're trying to figure that out now, ma'am." I didn't feel comfortable calling her Jan. "I'm really interested in what she might have said, where she was headed after she left your apartment."

Bob suggested we move into the adjacent dining area. Breakfast was served and he likely didn't want his young daughter picking up the serious nature of our conversation. "Mitch, please sit down," Jan urged. "I know you must be hungry. We've got plenty of eggs and toast."

I held up my hand. "No, ma'am, please, I really should be—"

"It's Jan," she reminded me. "And don't be silly. You can't go. We still need to talk."

"Jan. Yes, I'm sorry." I looked at the spread on the table – egg casserole, sliced fruit, bacon, toast, coffee, orange juice. It smelled heavenly. "Well, maybe just some eggs," I said. "Thank you." We seated ourselves around the table. "I really hoped I'd find Miss O'Connor here this morning, maybe she was sick or forgot to let us know or something," I said, as Jan poured my coffee. "Was there anything unusual she talked about or said? Where she might be headed afterward?"

"Not really," Bob offered. "She said she had a term paper due next week she still needed to finish. Both girls did. I figured that was what had her eager to get back."

"Did she mention anything about her family, her parents, where she lived?" This was a stretch, but I thought maybe something persuaded Maddy to go home to nearby Annandale, maybe a family emergency had occurred.

Jan spoke up. "We're supposed to meet them next week at the Army-Navy game. We're all going up to Philly and Maddy wanted to make sure she introduced us to her mom and dad. Said something about meeting a family friend as well, some admiral." She looked at Bob, "I can't remember his name."

"Tennant. Admiral Harlan Tennant," Bob said. "He's quite the wheel. Going to be taking over Seventh Fleet in February."

"Yeah, Uncle Harley," I said.

Bob and Jan laughed. "Uncle Harley?" Jan questioned, raising an eyebrow.

"That's what Miss O'Connor called him, as a kid."

They both stared, probably wondering how I'd acquired that personal tidbit. I finished my small portion of eggs and pushed the chair back. "Bob, Jan, thanks so much for breakfast but I really need to be getting back."

"Not yet, Mitch, please." She turned to her husband. "Bob, do you think we should tell him? This could be relevant now."

My heart stopped. "Tell me what?"

"Well, I guess we have to now," he said, revealing some disappointment, likely betraying Maddy over something she'd told them in confidence. "I don't know if this will help or tell us where she went but, yeah, Maddy told us about several harassment incidents involving a company officer."

"Lieutenant Herrera? Our company officer?" I was shocked.

"No, no. The Marine in 28th. Captain Manley. You know him?"

"Oh, yes, I know him." Manley was a very tough, no-nonsense Marine. He was known to have reservations about women at the Academy and was sometimes outspoken on the subject but still, harassment?

"Maddy spoke of several one-on-one "chance" encounters where he'd harangue her to quit, use derogatory female names, direct his firsties to conduct bogus room inspections, practically stalk her around the Hall. Said if she told anyone, he'd deny it."

Good God, I thought. A company officer? Before I could respond, Jan chimed in.

"She also told me one of the first-class in that company hit her," she said. "When they were in his car."

Both Bob and I stared incredulously. "Whoa, Jan, are you sure?" Bob asked.

"Of course, I am. Maddy told me last night when you'd stepped out. I wasn't planning on saying anything but, well, this is important now, isn't it?"

Bob continued to stare.

"Yes," I said, quickly. "Thank you, Jan. I think until she's found, everything is important." I stood. "Okay, I really need to be going this time. Again, thank you both for the breakfast." I reached for my cover, shook Jan's hand and moved for the door.

Bob stood up and walked with me. We stepped into the vestibule. "Mitch, I want you to keep me informed. Please let me know when you find her. In the meantime, if I can do anything to help, anything at all. I'm a little concerned over this one, I've got a bad feeling. This isn't like Maddy."

"I know. It isn't." I shook Bob's hand and headed directly back to Bancroft.

My mind raced as I walked. This was information overload. A company officer harassing a female plebe? It made no sense, but on some level, it did. Captain Preston Manley, USMC, was a hard-as-nails Marine infantry officer, the man with no neck as we called him, and had achieved hero status before arriving at USNA. He was assigned to the Marine Security Guard Battalion at the U.S. Embassy in Saigon during the final chaotic days of the Vietnam War in 1975 under Operation Frequent Wind. Many recall those iconic, end-of-the-war photographs of the UH-1 helicopter parked atop the embassy roof as a line of evacuees poured up the ladder, or Huey helicopters being pushed off the decks of carriers. What we knew was Manley was part of a small detachment of Marines holding back more than 10,000 desperate South Vietnamese during the evacuation and protecting the U.S. ambassador after the mob broke through the embassy gates. Manley and his team held firm, avoiding death numerous times before joining up with other men on the last chopper out. They landed aboard the USS *Okinawa* only hours before the Viet Cong hoisted their flag above the Presidential Palace in Saigon. He was the final Marine to step off the chopper and symbolically became the last U.S. servicemen out of Vietnam the day the war ended. Everyone at the Academy knew the story and easily recognized him around the Hall.

And what was up with this first-class, also from 28th, I thought, hitting Maddy, for crying out loud? I'd instantly known who Jan was talking about, the moment she'd let slip, "in his car." It was *Captain America*, my rival, captain of the pistol team, the firstie she'd ridden out the gate with last month during the tea dance. His name was Jon Sweet and he currently stood at the top of my shit list.  I needed to find him and have a little talk.

I entered the sixth wing and proceeded to 5ᵗʰ Batt Office to check in with my MCBO, see what had transpired in my absence, if anything.  "Herrera's up in his office," he informed me.  "He's looking for you."

Normally, Herrera wouldn't be at work on a Sunday, but things were popping, he'd been rudely awakened at one in the morning by the Bow Wow and given news, news he could no longer ignore.  The cavalry had arrived.  "Was he in civies or uniform?"

"Uniform."

Good, I thought.  "Okay, I'm headed up there now.  Anything from Main O this morning?  The OD?"

"Nope."

Not good, I thought.  "All right, be back in a few."

"Good luck, Mitch."

Herrera was at this desk, also in his service dress blues, when I entered his office.  "Good morning, sir," I said, strolling in and taking a seat before he even looked up.  All the first-class in 27 had a causal relationship with our company officer.  We'd been to his quarters many times for impromptu happy hours, gatherings known as "green lights".  We'd also gotten to know his wife and two young children, been to football tailgaters with them, drank beer, exchanged Christmas cards, etc.  Still, we maintained certain protocols, especially in Bancroft Hall, just a little less formally than the under-classes.  Herrera even encouraged the friendship.  He wanted to be liked by everyone.

"Morning, Mitch."  He looked up.  "I just got off the phone with Lieutenant Commander Jimmy Callahan.  He's the OD today, you know."

"Yes."

"I heard he ordered you not to call anyone last night."

"Just the sponsor," I said.

"Oh, but it was okay for you to call me at oh-dark-thirty, huh?  Wake *me* up instead of the sponsor?"

"Yes, sir."

"That's a fine line you're walking there, Mitch."  He looked out his window before eyeing me closer.  "Where were you this morning?"

"Over at the quarters of Lieutenant and Mrs. Robert Clausen," I said, confidently.  Better to appear confident than guilty.

"Where?"

"Miss O'Connor's sponsors."

He threw up his hands.  "I don't believe it.  Mitch, what the hell?" he said, lowering his voice to a conspiratorial whisper.  "You're really sticking your neck out on this one.  How'd you find them so fast?"

"What do you mean?"

"I mean they are still searching for their names over at Main O.  They don't have a clue.  Told them I'd find it for them.  Guess someone's beat me to the punch, done my job for me."

"Sir, it wasn't too hard. I asked Cory Hunter, my MCBO, to find them last night. He had the gouge in ten minutes." I let Cory's slip of paper drop to his desk. "So, I take it the sponsors haven't been contacted and the Commandant knows nothing?"

"No one's been notified. Christ, she's been gone less than twelve hours. We don't need to sound general quarters, not yet."

"I think we do," I said, under my breath.

"Maybe by evening meal formation tonight." Herrera switched gears. "So, what'd you find out at the Clausen's? Anything?"

"No, sir, not much. She left their place for Bancroft Hall after dinner at 2100. No contact after that. Don't you think someone should be calling Miss O'Connor's parents? Wouldn't they want to know about this? Hell, maybe she's at home. Can't we do something other than sit here with our thumbs up our, you know, while we wait for Main O to decide?"

"Look, I get the urgency you're feeling—"

*No, you don't.*

"But this has to be handled very carefully. We can't go notifying the Commandant on a weekend over a simple UA or alarming the parents about a potential missing child, especially when we know nothing, really nothing at all."

Oh sure, I thought, great plan. We're Sergeant Shultz, we know nothing. Then I thought about Jon Sweet, my last card to play. I needed to find this shitbird and talk to him tonight when he returned from his weekend leave. He had to have a role in this. "Sir, I guess I better get back down to Batt O, in case something develops."

"Yeah, go. Just finish out your watch and I'll let you know if I hear anything, and vice versa."

"Aye, aye, sir."

Sunday P.M., November 21, 1976

Sweet's company area was on 6-4, the top floor in the sixth wing. I trudged up the stairs and located the mate of the deck, inquiring the whereabouts of his room. He gave me the number and added, "It's in shaft alley, sir, last room on your left."

"Is he back from his weekend yet?"

"Yes, sir, I believe so. He should be in."

Shaft alley was a shipboard nickname applied to the narrow passageways in the sixth wing where the corridor dead-ended at a right angle to the main thoroughfare. It's where many of the upperclassmen preferred to live due to its privacy, where the company's collection of bad-asses and oddballs could be found taking refuge.

It was 2100. My watch ended earlier this afternoon with no news. Before heading home, Herrera told me he was going to meet with the on-coming OD and the Commandant to discuss the plan. As far as I knew, they'd neither contacted Maddy's sponsors nor her parents but I wasn't completely certain as I was no longer in the loop. It was unspoken that since my watch was over it'd be best if I just kept my inquisitive nose the hell out of it. I walked back to Sweet's room, admittedly, with a chip on my shoulder the size of a small truck.

I pushed open the door, double-checking the nameplate. Odd that the company commander and sub-commander didn't room together as most of the other companies did, I thought. I recalled a memory from our plebe year, the firsties in Oscar Company all calling him *Sweetie* that first summer, and he hated it with a passion, causing the nickname to stick longer than it should have. As far as I knew, no one called him Sweetie any longer, but I wasn't sure. After our plebe summer, we'd each gone to our new companies, me to 27, him to 28, and I'd rarely been up to 6-4 over the last three years.

I entered the room. "Jon, how are you?" I said. "Got a minute?"

He was alone, seated behind his desk in skivvies, his roommate apparently not back from his weekend. "Jonathan," he said.

"Huh?"

"I go by Jonathan."

This was a new twist, but, whatever. I hadn't seen him in a while. "Jonathan. Sorry. Got a moment to talk?"

"Depends. What about?"

Setting up defenses a little early, I thought. I glanced around the room. Marine Corps scarlet and gold posters hung everywhere.

*Marines, the Few, the Proud.*
*Marines, Swift, Silent, Deadly*
*Marines, Semper Fidelis*

Off to the side, a bumper sticker read, *I'm not Fonda Hanoi Jane* ☮ *American Traitor Bitch.*

"Going Corps after graduation?"

No response, just a cold stare.

"Look, I was the off-going Bow Wow this afternoon. We had a UA here in Fifth Batt last night. Midshipman Madison O'Connor." I studied his face for a reaction. "And she's still not back. I was hoping you might have a clue as to where she was."

"Now how the hell would I know that, Mitch?"

"Mitchell," I said, nodding back at him.

He raised an eyebrow. This would've been his cue to smile, to say *touché*, but he didn't. I'd unbalanced him. "Again, how the hell would I know that?"

"Oh, I don't know. Just checking around, thought I'd ask." My eyes wandered the room again eventually settling on an object hung near the windowsill.

Sweet's eyes slowly tracked with mine. He reached for the object, picking it up. "Ever see one of these?" he asked.

I shook my head.

"Military police Billy club. A Marine Corps second lieutenant gave it to me last summer when we were at Quantico. Pretty powerful little device, wouldn't you say?" He slapped his palm with it. "Take a look."

I didn't reach out, preferring he hold it. It was a heavily weighted black baton with a 90-degree stud handle, designed to either whack someone over the head or jab them sharply in the ribcage. It was a very intimidating, ugly weapon and seemed very much at home in the hands of this wiry little man.

Sweet sat back down and lit a Marlboro Red cigarette from a pack on his desk. "I don't know where you get off coming up here, asking me about Maddy," he said. "Like I'm supposed to know where she is."

"Well, do you?"

"No. Fuck, no. And I think it'd be wise for you to drop that attitude."

We studied each other, the air alive with tension.

"I know you've been seeing her," I said. "I know you drove out the gate with her on a Sunday last month."

"Well, now there's a revelation. Half the Brigade's probably been out the gate with her in the last month."

"Where'd you go?"

"Get out of here. Get the hell out of my room, right now."

"Where'd you go, Jonathan? Where'd you take her?" I couldn't stop myself. "Did you hit her when she was with you in your car? Did you hit her, big man?"

Sweet stood up. He glanced at his baton on the desk. "You care to tell me how you know that? Have you been going out with that little cunt too?"

I remained silent. We were face to face, just a breath apart.

"Tell me how you know that." He eyed the baton a second time. "Or maybe I just club it out of you."

"All right, *Sweetie*," I said, staring down at his sinewy five-foot-eight frame. "Just a reminder, I've got five inches on you and thirty pounds. I'm not Maddy. Make a move for that Billy club and I'll send you headfirst out that sixth floor window."

We glared in unflinching silence for several heartbeats, Sweet never making his move.

I turned to leave. When I reached the door, I was shaking. Sweet was built like a fireplug. I figured once he latched onto something, like a bulldog, he would never let go. Fortunately, he stayed put. I made my way down the stairs and back to our company area unscathed. The encounter hadn't gone quite as I'd hoped. Another classmate's wrath I must bear, I thought. Still, I'd gotten what I was after. Let him stew on that one.

Monday, November 22, 1976

Army Week events were in full swing with only five days until the big game, and still, no Maddy. It seemed surreal as these high-spirited events unfolded around me in the wake of Maddy's disappearance, like nothing unusual had occurred, like it was just business as usual. A bonfire was scheduled later in the evening in the center of Thompson Field, a pep rally in Tecumseh Court the following night complete with the Drum and Bugle Corps, cheerleaders, mascot Bill the Goat and thousands of screaming mids. A team sendoff in the Field House parking lot was set for Wednesday, Coach Welch and other dignitaries all to give inspiring, do-or-die speeches. Thanksgiving leave would start on Thursday, everyone scattering in all directions, reuniting at JFK Stadium in Philadelphia on Saturday morning for the march-on.

After my fourth-period class, I decided to pay another visit on Lieutenant Herrera before noon meal formation. I sensed his emanating vibe reminding me to keep my distance, to give him room to work, but I also knew he was a soft touch, someone I could press for information without becoming rattled or irritated. He was just too amiable to get in someone's face and say back off.

I walked into his office.

"Mitch," he said, looking up from behind his desk. "I know why you're here, and rest assured, we're doing all we can."

"Yes, sir. And may I ask what that is?"

"Well, for one, the NIS is now involved. They were notified last night and have a meeting with the Commandant later today, a meeting I've been asked to attend. NIS was the Naval Investigative Service. I was impressed. Calling them in was a bold move, a welcome move. The NIS was a government law enforcement agency that handled criminal investigations under the Navy's broad, global jurisdiction. I wasn't clear whether they were being called in to investigate Maddy for going UA or viewing Maddy's disappearance as a criminal act itself. I hoped it was the latter. "That's great, sir. But do you know, has anyone spoken to Lieutenant Clausen yet? Have Miss O'Connor's parents been notified?"

Herrera looked down at his desk as if some paperwork suddenly caught his attention. "Yes, the parents know. I'm not sure about the sponsor. In fact, I anticipate the parents being at our meeting this afternoon along with Commander Egan." Commander Egan was our battalion officer, in the chain of command between the Commandant and Herrera himself. Herrera looked up from his desk with a pained expression. "Mitch, you need to cool it, okay? This thing is hot and has the potential to explode, to turn into a real PR nightmare, and we have no knowledge, no concrete information to go on. Apparently, the parents have no knowledge either. They're sick with worry, as you can well imagine."

"Yes, sir, I can well imagine. And we certainly don't want any PR nightmares."

Herrera looked out his window, clearly reading my frustration and blunt tone. "I'm advising you, Mitch, leave this one alone. You did your duty as the Battalion Officer of the Watch. Let the investigation run its course and come to you, not the other way around. Don't go hunting everything down like it's your own goddamn personal mission. Do you understand?"

"Yes, sir, but—"

Herrera cut me off. "No buts," he said, lowering his voice. "Look, I get why you're so emotionally charged, why you're so determined to find her. You think I'm blind, that I don't hear things?" He folded his hands and rested them on his blotter. "So, let's just leave it at that and mind our own business on this one, shall we?"

I didn't respond, rising from my chair. How could he know about my drive with Maddy?

"You can go now."

Amanda was a mess when I sat with her in her room after evening meal. We agreed to skip the bonfire. I wanted to assure her everything possible was being done but I knew nothing more than when I'd left Herrera's office earlier today. After his meeting with the Commandant, and presumably Maddy's parents, he'd conveniently disappeared, never returning to his office. I asked Amanda if she'd ever met Maddy's parents, knew anything at all about them. She replied she'd briefly met them during Parent's Weekend. Also, she expected to see them again in Philadelphia at the game, but we agreed, it was highly unlikely they'd be in Philly this weekend. I thought about their family friend, Uncle Harley, also planning to attend. I wondered if he might help push the investigation along or if I could arrange a chance meeting. I reminded myself about Herrera's earlier advice. *Uh, Admiral, sir, I was wondering if you wouldn't mind helping me find Maddy O'Connor? I've been ordered to keep my big nose out of it but, well, if you could, sir, I think you could really lend some firepower...* Sure, that's exactly what I'd say. If he was any kind of family friend, he'd probably already made a few telephone calls on Maddy's behalf. At least I hoped so.

On Wednesday, the entire brigade was eager to depart for the long weekend commencing after the last class of the day. Neil and some other classmates were headed to his girlfriend's home in Potomac, Maryland for Thanksgiving and had invited me along. I declined, having already accepted an invitation from my sponsors, Jack and Irene, to dine with them. Walking back into the company area from my final class, Lonnie McCann corralled me and Neil into his room for an impromptu meeting.

"Hey, I hear some serious shit went down this weekend while I was gone," Lonnie said, directing us to some chairs. "So, Mitch, what do you know? What do you hear?" Both Neil and Lonnie leaned in, like I was about to recap all the baseball scores and highlights.

"What do *I* know?  You're the company commander, Lon.  What do *you* know?"

"Not much, Mitch.  Not much.  But I do know someone's been coming and going from Herrera's office like he has a revolving door.  And I know someone called Herrera's quarters at 2 A.M. on Sunday morning and later took a walk out to O'Connor's sponsors on Perry Circle.  Oh, and I know someone walked up to Sweetie's room Sunday night, of all places, and had a pleasant little chat."

"Yeah, Lon.  So, what's your point?"

"Hey, relax, Mitch.  You're among friends.  My point is, you're in a position to know more than those NIS jokers that are starting to nose around.  So, where do you think O'Connor ran off to?"

"I wouldn't know.  Herrera told me to back off, to stay out of it."  I was both surprised and disheartened by Lonnie's casual questioning like Maddy had taken off on a shopping trip and would show up in due time after she'd maxed out her credit cards.  He was purely after gossip.

"Yeah, but you've got to know something.  What'd the sponsor say?"

I launched into exactly what I knew, reluctantly at first.  I hadn't planned to go into detail, but it all fell out.  I was fighting this battle alone and felt anxious, unsupported and I needed an ally to hear my confession.  I told them I was frustrated by the sense of stalling, of everyone wanting to put on the brakes rather than strike while the iron was hot, while the information was still fresh in people's minds.  "It's like Herrera's participating in an unspoken coverup like he's hoarding information rather than sharing it.  Why wouldn't you use all resources?  I don't get what's driving him."

"Driving *them*," Neil corrected.

"Who?"

"The administration.  Them.  You want my theory?"

"No," I said, half-joking.

"This is new ground for everyone.  They don't have a clue how to react.  A male mid goes UA?  Oh, let's wait a few days.  He'll turn up.  Why he's probably flown the coop to Vegas or New Orleans, gonna get a little crazy before dropping his resignation letter.  Call in NIS, you say?  Don't be absurd.  A female mid goes UA?  Runs off to Vegas or New Orleans?  Not likely, but we don't know the habits of the female midshipman.  We've never met one before.  So, let's sit tight, circle the wagons until we know more, until we have all the answers."

"That's your theory, huh?"

"Yep."

"Pretty depressing."  I looked at Lonnie.  "They can't dodge a missing person like that.  Can they?"

"I don't know but they're doing it," Lonnie said.  "They certainly know she didn't run home to Mommy and Daddy.  They're both camped out in the 'dant's office, fearing the worst."

"I don't blame them," I said.

"I did hear something in our weekly batt staff meeting yesterday," Lonnie offered.

"Yeah?"

"It only confirms what Neil was spouting. NIS is involved but they aren't calling it anything right now. No foul play, no kidnapping. Not even labeling it a missing person yet, like she's playing hide and seek in Bancroft Hall. Anyway, the Annapolis Police got wind of it on Monday and are claiming jurisdiction since the sponsor's quarters are outside the gate. That was the last time she was seen, right?"

"Right. Sounds hopeful," I added. "The more the merrier."

"Yeah, but NIS will probably get them to back off. They'll claim it's Navy business and to stay the hell out."

"Figures." I wondered how the police got the tip in the first place. "And isn't it strange how they'll kick each other's ass over jurisdiction while the hot leads just melt into thin air?"

"And speaking of strange, you want to hear something else?" Neil asked.

"Here we go again," I said. "I'm betting it's not good."

"Maybe. Maybe not. On the eve of O'Connor's UA, sometime around 1800, the mate told me some commander came on deck, up to our company area."

"Who?" Lonnie and I said, in unison.

"Don't know. Mate says he was in civies. By the time he chopped up to him, the guy flashed his ID card, headed back down the stairs and was gone. Said all he saw was a picture and the bold letters CDR for his rank."

"He didn't ask for the guy's name, or get it off the ID card?" Lonnie said.

"Apparently not. Said he looked familiar though."

"Neil, for crying out loud. I was the Bow Wow that evening. Why didn't you have the mate report it down to Batt O?"

"Because it was probably nothing. The guy walked in, he walked out, then disappeared. No harm done. Geez, think about Homecoming. We get these geezers all the time, drunk alumni in civies flashing their ID cards, thinking they can just wander back to their old rooms." Unless you lived or worked in Bancroft Hall, you were not allowed to enter unescorted.

"Neil, you or the mate should've called me. This wasn't Homecoming weekend."

"Army Week, man." He shrugged his shoulders. "Same deal."

"Not really." I made a note to find the mate, follow up later. "Besides, if you thought it was nothing, why'd you bring it up?"

Another shrug.

"Mitch, what else happened on your watch?" Lonnie said. "Anything unusual?"

"You mean besides the youngster from 25 jumping off the Eastport bridge?"

Lonnie and Neil shared a chuckle. The story was making the rounds, already becoming the stuff of legend. "Yeah, besides that."

"Nothing really. We had some jackass call Batt O, claimed there was a recon in progress by a couple of our Whoop exchange cadets, said they were attempting to set all the yawls adrift in Santee Basin. When I got out there, nothing. Just another crank call to Batt O, send the Bow Wow on another wild goose chase."

I realized we were spinning our wheels with all this loose talk. More needed to be done, yet my hands were tied. I'd been warned. I could continue a personal investigation at my own peril, especially with the NIS, the Commandant and his staff involved, or I could set the entire matter aside, removing it from my head. Besides, I had my own problems – a term paper coming due, final exams to study for, grease to write. I'd have a nice Thanksgiving meal with Jack and Irene, attend the big game, complete all my work, then prepare for Christmas leave in the Bay Area, returning to the bosom of my wonderfully dysfunctional family.

# 17

## CHRISTMAS LEAVE

Friday, December 17, 1976

FLYING STANDBY AS A FAMILY MEMBER of an airline employee is always a dicey proposition, even when that employee is a senior captain with thirty years of service. The busy holiday season only compounds the risk. Nonetheless, I was lucky and ended up snagging the last available seat, a window in the coach cabin on a fully loaded DC-10 and was winging my way from Baltimore to San Francisco for the Christmas break. I stared at the landscape scrolling below, listening to Linda Ronstadt sing *Tracks of My Tears* on the cheap plastic headset. I thought of Maddy. There was no way I'd removed her or the investigation from my head. The longer it ran with no news, no findings, the more it loomed in my mind, intruding on my sanity. A few days before departing for the airport I had called on Bob and Jan Clausen, taking the walk to their quarters after evening meal. We compared notes, gaining nothing new from either side. I did learn it was Bob who tipped off the Annapolis Police after receiving no assurance from the OD late Sunday night that action was being taken. He and Jan were as sick with worry as Maddy's parents. We again agreed to stay close, to keep each other informed, but it was offered more as a courtesy than a real commitment. We weren't going to solve Maddy's disappearance on our own, especially since it'd been dragging on for more than three weeks. As much as it pained me to admit, Maddy was gone. She'd vanished into thin air and wasn't coming back.

I turned my thoughts to returning home, preparing for my own version of *The Fall of the House of Baumann*. I really had little idea of the mood or actual environment I'd be arriving in. My mother's letters always painted a rosy picture but came with subtle zingers buried in the text, like everything was grand only because she was holding it together with band-aids and baling wire. My main concern, of course, was my father. Since his summer visit, I'd lost hope that things would ever return to normal at home, that he'd regain control. I wasn't even sure he was living at home. My mother had spoken of longer and longer absences but not a complete departure from the scene. Still, if I correctly interpreted her ambiguous messaging, it sounded like she hadn't a clue where he was at any given time or when he'd be back. And Amber, what a wreck. My mother was less ambiguous on that topic, openly grieving over her sad saga. She'd go on and on about the ridiculous amounts of money required to keep her in private school and what a waste it was, yet report Amber was doing *so much better* since getting back from drug rehab at Lake Arrowhead, that she'd rejoined her school choir and was working with a tutor after class. Even with the tutor, she was facing many failed or incomplete courses thus forestalling a June graduation. I drew a deep breath sighing in joyless anticipation of the next two weeks as the big airplane made its touchdown at SFO.

After an awkward greeting at baggage claim and quick drive from the airport, I followed my mother, lugging my heavy suitcase up the walkway to our front door. Apparently, the automatic garage door had failed during the course of my father's latest absence, "And there just hasn't been a man around that can fix it for me," she lamented, parking her sporty Mercedes 450SL, a 50th birthday gift from my father, in the driveway and fumbling for her front door key.

"Yes, Mother, I'll take a look," I offered. God forbid she call a repairman and ease her heaping mound of burdens.

"And Christmas, well, I hope you're not too disappointed. There's just so much for me to deal with right now. As you can imagine."

"Yes, Mother."

I entered the house and was shocked. My mother's admission of a lack of holiday preparation was an understatement. Nothing had been done. In fact, the house was about as untidy as I'd ever seen it – dirty plates with food scraps on the coffee table, clothing strewn about the room, unopened mail piled on the dining room table, a general air of neglect to the entire home. It occurred to me this was a ploy, her way to guilt me with just how much of a struggle she'd endured over the last year, her entire world crashing in around her. *Now you can see for yourself,* her mess was saying.

"Guess we're not doing a Christmas tree this year, huh, Mother?"

She ignored the comment, strolling into the kitchen and helping herself to some red wine on the counter. "I hope they fed you on the plane. I just wasn't able to get to the grocery store today, what with all that's been going on."

"All that's been going on?" I said, staring at the stack of dirty dishes in the sink. "I'm not sure I follow."

"Don't start with me, Mitch. You've been gone an awfully long time and you're in no position to—"

"Gone a long time?" I said, cutting her off. "I've been at school, Mother. Now I'm home, home to spend Christmas with my terrific, loving family."

Again, she chose to ignore my remarks, adding more wine to her glass and directing me to follow her to the back of the house. She grabbed a stack of linens and entered my old bedroom. "Here, help me make up your bed," she said, ripping off the old sheets and tossing them in a corner.

"Where's Amber?" I asked, watching her move around the bed.

"Out."

"Out?"

"Yes, out with friends," my mother said, without looking up. "She comes, she goes. I don't ask a lot of questions."

"You should."

"I should what?"

"Ask a lot of questions."

She stopped her tucking and smoothing and looked at me. "Mitch, someday you'll understand. There are some battles I choose not to fight. Let's just leave it at that. Your sister's doing very well now that she's back and I'm not about to upset the balance. You'll appreciate this advice one day when you're a parent." Her tone seemed to imply I'd never appreciate this advice, the heavy burden she now bore. It was pointless for me to remain in the room, to try to converse with someone so hellbent on projecting such a perpetual state of misery, of wallowing in her victim status. I walked back into the kitchen, sat down at a barstool and helped myself to a glass of wine, surveying the backyard patio and pool in the quickly fading winter twilight. The house was dormant, a distant cry from the halcyon years of Christmases at the Baumann's. Missing were the festive lights in the yard, the glittering twelve-foot Christmas tree in the living room, trays of homemade fudge, neighbors dropping by for a splash of holiday cheer, us kids roaring around the cul-de-sac jazzed for Santa and all the presents he'd soon bring. I looked again at the silent backyard. It was as if someone had died, the house in mourning.

Dinner never came. *Yes, Mother, they fed me on the plane.* I was still hungry as it was now 9 P.M. I pulled a lukewarm turkey pot pie from the toaster oven and dragged a chair in front of the television. The Mormon Tabernacle Choir was performing *Handel's Messiah* softly in the background as I poured myself another glass of Mother's wine. She eventually reemerged from her bedroom in a green bathrobe, sitting down to join me, toting her own wineglass back into the room.

"My, we're certainly a pair, aren't we?" she said, intentionally inserting a vague, misery-loves-company camaraderie into the dour holiday mood.

"Just two peas in a pod, Mother."

"Mitch, I would appreciate it if you wouldn't use sarcasm. I'm doing the best I can, under the circumstances."

"What circumstances? I just got home. You need to tell me the circumstances."

"Well, I didn't think I'd have to spell it out for you but—"

*You will anyway.*

"Your sister. Oh, my, what a nightmare."

"You said she was doing fine."

"And your father, well, I hardly see him anymore."

"Where does he go, Mother?" I knew this was opening Pandora's box and was unsure if it was wise to head down this path, but after the horrible homecoming and two glasses of wine, I thought, what the hell. "And when was the last time you saw him?"

"1969."

"I'm serious."

"So am I. And I stand by my statement."

I knew she was referring to the change we'd all felt, the tectonic shift buried in the family past. I'd never pinned it to a specific year but 1969 seemed right. It coincided with the period my father started taking less interest in me and my activities. He'd stopped coming to my baseball games, supporting my Scout activities or showing any interest in Amber and her things. Still, this wasn't what I was after. "I mean, when was the last time he was home?"

"Two weeks, three weeks ago, a month maybe. I don't know. I told you in my letters, he comes and goes. They've got him on a new schedule, but he'll be back. He'll be back soon," she repeated, mostly to herself.

"Why's he doing this, Mother? What's he running from?" I'd finally gained the courage to ask. This was the heart of the matter.

"You really don't want to know," she said, with a lilt of superiority.

"What do you mean? Of course, I do."

She ignored my urgency. Our eyes locked. She flashed one of her all-knowing smiles and finished off her wine.

"Mother? For God's sake, just tell me."

"Oh, Mitch, darling," she said, continuing her melodrama. "I know you don't approve of me. You haven't in years."

Here it comes, I thought, the inevitable pity party. "Please don't change the subject. This isn't about you. I want to know where Dad goes. What's he do? When's he coming home? Do you or don't you know these things?"

Again, the intentional pause, the pursed lips. "He's seeing a psychiatrist, you know."

"Good, he should," I snapped.

"Some shrink in San Bruno."

"Did he tell you this?" I was hopeful they were still communicating, at least on an essential level.

"I received a call from a doctor's office last week, someone I'd never heard of. Of course, I played along like I knew who they were. They were wanting to reschedule a recent appointment he'd missed."

"How do you know it was a shrink's office?" What if he's just a regular doctor?"

She sighed. "Oh, son, please, give your doddering old mother some credit. I looked up his name in the Yellow Pages. Sometimes, I can think for myself, you know."

"Yes, Mother, your investigative prowess could rival Perry Mason." Despite her bombshell, I considered the information as progress. "At least he's seeking help. That's a good thing. Have you considered that?" But it wasn't a good thing, I thought, if he was ducking appointments.

"He'll lose his job if the airline finds out."

"What if the airline set it up?"

"Don't be absurd, Mitch. I know how things work. He'll be grounded if United discovers he's seeing a psychiatrist, or any kind of medical doctor, without their consent or knowledge. He could get fired and lose his pension."

"Really?"

"Really. And where would that leave me?"

Me. Of course, *me*. I needed to keep things on track. "Do we have a clue what might be wrong? Some kind of work issue? Depression, maybe?" I thought of his summer visit, our talk in Memorial Hall.

"Certainly not. He's never been depressed."

"Oh, so it's a simple case of not being able to find his way home after his trips? That's why he's setting up appointments with psychiatrists?" Did she not see what I saw last summer?

"I can't answer any of that. Stop asking me so many questions." She was clearly flustered, throwing up a defense for them both. "Maybe my perfect son has an answer."

"I have none, Mother. What's wrong with you? I'm only trying to understand what's been going on since I've been away."

"I told you, I don't know where he goes or what he does. Maybe you need to spend more time at home. Ask him yourself."

"Spend more time at home?" I was dumbfounded. "Mother, sometimes I think you've lost your marbles."

"See? That's what I'm talking about. You don't respect me. And you certainly don't appreciate me. If you'd only—"

"Enough, please." I'd had it. I stood up from my chair. "Is that all you think about? Me? Because it's all I ever hear. Me, me, me. Have you even once thought about him?"

"Have you?" she fired back. "Have you once thought of what goes on here while you're living your perfect little life back east with your future so bright?"

I thought about my so-called perfect life, of Aimee, of Maddy, of everything piling up here and at school. Sure, with my future so bright. "That's unfair, Mother. I'm doing what any parent should be proud of, if this was any normal kind of family."

She stood from the sofa, dribbling the last of the wine into her glass and gracefully swooping it from the coffee table. "I'm sorry we've all been such a *disappointment* to you," she said, tightening her robe, poised for her theatrical exit. "So, let's ask, who's thinking *me-me-me* now?"

Saturday, December 18, 1976

My mother and I are two different personalities, and we deal with residual anger in different ways. After our little showdown in the living room the previous night, I chose to retreat to a neutral corner, gain some perspective in the big, empty house and ignore her. Mother, on the other hand, had returned to full functionality, overcompensating as if nothing had occurred, no harsh words had been spoken, breezing into a room happy as a lark. This was how she greeted me the next day when she returned from Christmas shopping – a song on her lips, a spring in her step as I sat at the kitchen bar picking at a late lunch of leftovers. "Mitch, darling, I'm glad you're home. I have to bake some cookies for the ornament exchange party at the neighbor's later this evening and I need you to pick up Amber at school. Can you give her a lift for me? Pretty please?"

I looked at my watch. "School? It's 5 P.M, Mother. Besides, what's she doing at school on a Saturday? Isn't she on holiday break?"

"It's her choir. They're doing the dress rehearsal for the Christmas concert tomorrow. She should be done in an hour and will need a ride."

I'd heard nothing about any concert, when it was, or if we were attending. "Sure, Mother. Give me your keys. I'll go fetch her."

"Not now. In an hour."

"I'll go now. I could use the air." I snatched the keys from her hand and headed for the door. I needed a break from the house, the pounding silence, the memories, but mostly I needed space from my mother despite her conciliatory tone and sudden energy to reestablish the Christmas spirit. I was still mad, at her accusations last night, and general lapse in her duties at home. I didn't necessarily blame her for everything, but she was a convenient scapegoat making it easy to remain cool in the wake of her newfound happiness.

I found her new 450SL a joy to drive. It handled like a true sports car, not as well as my smaller MG, but had twice the power and a smoother feel to the road. And it still had that new-car smell. I wound through the residential streets of Mills Estates, twisting and turning at speeds faster than the posted 25 MPH, eventually arriving in the parking lot of the school. Mercy was a catholic all-girl high school situated on forty lush, wooded acres in the hills above Burlingame. The school itself didn't look like a school, at least at first blush. It more resembled a country club with its wide circular driveway, manicured lawn, tennis courts and stately administration building. This was a prep school for the Peninsula's elite, children from good families with money that were being given an amazing head start in life and able to pick from most any college they desired after graduation. In Amber's case, it also provided a rigid set of rules complete with school uniforms, a better teacher-student ratio than the public schools and more accountability. After her stint at Lake Arrowhead, I was buoyed by her reinvolvement in choir and working with a tutor, hopeful she was getting her life back on track and would soon select a college herself.

It was a short walk from the parking lot down the hill toward the chapel, which was integrated into the nun's novitiate, a larger building resembling a college dormitory. This was my first visit to the chapel, and I groped my way to the sanctuary following the soft echo of young voices singing. I gently cracked the door and peeked inside. Amber was one of about forty kids huddled closely on risers, focusing intently on their conductor. She was dressed marvelously, as all the girls, in a sleeveless black formal and a modest ring of pearls around her neck. The boys were dressed in black jacket, bow tie and white shirt. I barely recognized her, having only seen her on previous visits in ratty jeans and odd collection of t-shirts and baggy sweaters. The conductor had stopped the rehearsal and announced a quick five-minute break before resuming the final half-hour. Perfect timing, I thought. Maybe I could grab Amber and we could split early.

Amber immediately noticed me gawking and made her way down from the risers with the flow of kids. "What?" she said, approaching, feigning self-consciousness.

"I don't know. You look so grown up, so beautiful – all of you. That's all. Merry Christmas."

She eyed me carefully. "Now don't go getting sentimental on me, Baumann," she said. Despite our defensive posture, she hugged me dearly, leaning closer. "Thank you," she whispered in my ear. "Merry Christmas."

"You ready to go?" I said, knowing full well she had thirty minutes left but testing to see if she was willing to ditch early as she had with so many of her other classes.

"We still have one more song to practice. It's the finale. I really need to stay."

"No, that's okay. I'm glad you're committed. To finishing," I added. "That's great."

Amber gave a subtle smirk. She knew what I was referring to. "So, did Mom send you out here? To finally bring me back home?"

"What do you mean? Didn't she drive you to rehearsal?"

"Of course, not. I rode over here with my friend, Dez. Spent last night at her house too, just in case anyone was wondering. Or if anyone's been asking."

"Well, Mother's been busy today," I said. "Finally getting the house ready for Christmas."

Amber rolled her eyes. "Yeah, right."

I smiled, happy she was disappointed in Mother too. "What about Dad, Amber? Where is he? When's he coming home?"

"Didn't Mom explain? Give you her version?"

"Not really. She was rather vague on the topic like he comes and goes. Should be home eventually, just working from a different schedule."

"Different schedule? What a liar. He hasn't been home for two months, Mitch. Based on what he took, I'd say he's gone, for good."

My stomach sank, sensing the obvious truth. "So, he won't be home? For Christmas?"

"I wouldn't hold your breath."

"Have Mother and Dad split up? Was there some sort of fight?" I felt bad asking all these questions, but someone needed to fill me in, and I certainly wasn't getting an accurate picture from the lady of the house.

"He's gone, Mitch. There was no fight, that wasn't it. I called the airline, just to check on him, to see what city he might be in. They said he wasn't on the flight schedule, couldn't tell me anything other than he last flew in August. He's got to be living somewhere else now. North Beach with some belly dancer for all I know."

Again, my stomach sank. I didn't appreciate Amber's cynicism but nothing in my father's life was off the table. In the background the singing resumed, rehearsal had commenced. "And Mother knows none of this?"

"I don't have a clue what Mom knows. She lives in her own world. Look, I better get back to my spot."

Behind the doors, a group of soprano voices began singing softly in unison. They were soon joined by the altos and tenors in a breathtaking acapella harmony. My ears perked up. "My God, Amber, that song, it's beautiful. What is it?"

She pulled open the door as the choir spread into four parts. "It's a new rendition of Coventry Carol. Goes back to something like the 16th century."

"The voices. Where'd the men come from? I thought this was an all-girls school."

"Serra High. All-boys. Look, I gotta run." Amber quickly dashed back up the riser.

I sat down in a pew near the back to listen. It was a spine-tingling lullaby to the Christ child. Unaccompanied voices, forty strong, filled the chapel with a wonderful reverb, the purest ring I'd ever heard, pulsing, swelling, softening, intoning:

> *Lul-lee, lul-lay*
> *Thou little tiny child*
> *By, by, lul-lee, lul-lay*
> *Oh, sisters too, how may we do*
> *By, by, lul-lee, lul-lay*

There was just something so stirring about the acapella medium, an ethereal sound revealing God in song, providing a glimpse of heaven. The piece was the most beautiful choral music I'd heard and before long, tears were streaming down my cheeks. I was experiencing the burden of sadness yet a lifting of sadness, a wonderful paradox of emotional release manifesting with unstoppable, burning tears. I realized the entire choir could probably see me, especially Amber, and I turned away to wipe my cheeks, embarrassed at the loss of control of my emotions over something so simple as a bunch of high school kids singing a song. I stepped away from the pew and back into the narthex to await Amber's return. In reality, I felt better than I had in months, the flow of tears lightening a heavy load that had invaded my soul since September.

We talked easily on the drive home, catching up after not seeing each other for a year, overlooking our issues, our differences, sharing a concern about the growing tension at home – Dad's departure, Mother's denial. "What's it going to be like at Christmas?" I said, shifting the car into second. "Dad's absence? Are we supposed to just make believe he'll slide down the chimney on Christmas Eve and—"

"Hey, did you lose it back there in the chapel or what?"

I was surprised she was calling me it. Amber and I were experts at pressing each other's buttons, exploiting each other's weaknesses, but we'd been operating under a truce, or so I assumed. "Please don't change the subject."

"I thought it was sweet." She smiled at me across the console.

"I don't know what came over me. Stress or jetlag or something." I took a deep breath. "So, are we going to simply ignore the blank spot where Dad used to be?"

"Whatever. It's not like it's going to change anything."

"You think Mother believes he's coming back?"

"I don't know what she believes. She's crazy, you know."

"Sure seems that way. Probably just her way of coping."

"No, I'm serious. I think she's schizophrenic, batty as a loon."

I laughed, doubting Amber's diagnosis but not her passion.

"Go ahead, make fun," she said. "Unlike you, I'm stuck here. At least until I graduate. After that, I am so gone."

"College, I trust?"

It was Amber's turn to laugh. "Hardly. I think one parent's wet dream is enough for this family."

I was shocked by her sudden insult, momentarily unable to react. "Hey, wait a minute."

She immediately reached across the console and grabbed my free hand. "I'm sorry, Mitch. That was mean," she said. "Growing up in your shadow has been tough, especially with you gone and living with just *her*. It's Mom

I'm lashing out at. Forgive me."

I drove in silence, still absorbing her poison, the hurt she must've felt obliged to share.

"Mitch, I said I was sorry. C'mon. I envy you, that's all. You've got a life, a future ahead. And in a week, you'll be gone from all the madness, leaving me to deal with the crazy lady, alone."

"Your day will come. You won't be stuck here forever. And don't think for a minute that leaving home will solve all your problems," I said, thinking of my own. "Believe me, there are minefields out there just waiting. The trick is to see and avoid."

"Kinda tough when they're buried."

I pulled into the driveway and killed the engine. Amber closed her eyes, tilting her head back. "I can't," she said. "I just can't."

I rested a hand on her thigh and gave a brave smile. "Come on," I coaxed.

Her eyes popped open. "No, wait!" she said. "Let's take off. Turn the car around, drive us to the airport and let's hop a plane to Tahiti for Christmas using Dad's free passes. I'm serious. You and me, just disappear. What do you say?"

"I'd love to, but we can't. Our place is here," I said, in mock seriousness. But, oh, was I tempted. The shock value alone would be worth it.

She punched my arm. "You're no fun, you know that?"

We exited the car and walked up the steps, wondering which version of mother would greet us at the door. As much as Amber and I wanted to escape, we Baumann's were realists. We'd keep calm and carry on. Amber would perform her concert. I would return to Annapolis. We'd spend Christmas together, as one big happy family, minus one.

Monday, January 3, 1977

I was restless on the eve of my departure for Annapolis, eager to shed the drama on the home front and put Christmas behind me. Amber was right, I was in an envious state. I was leaving the madness but returning east would be no picnic either. I was sweating final exams and dreading whatever news there was on Maddy's ongoing investigation. I'd had no contact with Lieutenant Herrera, the NIS agents or any other Academy official, which I took as a bad sign, that the investigation had stalled and they'd neither found Maddy nor uncovered any new information during the holiday break.

I decided to take a walk, to clear my head and wander through the old neighborhood one last time, not knowing when I'd return. It was a breezy afternoon, the winter sun low on the horizon, a chill in the air. I left the cul-de-sac moving at a quick pace, glad I'd thrown on a light jacket. Making my way along the sidewalks I experienced a tug of sadness. California would always be my home, yet I was having doubts. There were wonderful memories from my youth bounding me to this part of the Peninsula. I would always be drawn to the creeping fog, the verdant hills, the smell of eucalyptus, the ocean, the scent of the tide. Yet these memories were becoming tainted creating an impulsive desire to disappear forever much as Amber had suggested with our escape to Tahiti. I slowed my walk and thought of Amber. She was at a tipping point in her life, a critical juncture in which she could either graduate and move on to college or continue her self-destructive behavior with her druggie pals. She just needed some stability at home. This was a horrible time for Dad to go AWOL, for Mother to become a basket case and for me to leave for my final semester. It would destroy any hope for a full recovery, ending her streak of lying, ditching school and casual drug use.

Deep in thought, I found myself one street over in front of the house where my childhood friend, Harold, had lived. Harold's family was from Germany, and, as I recalled, his mother and father were teenagers growing up in the thick of World War II near Hamburg, having later immigrated to the US in the 1950s. I surveyed the tidy front yard and well-maintained home wondering if they still lived here. A flashy 1977 Porsche Carrera was parked in the driveway with dealer plates. August, Harold's father, was part owner in a Porsche dealership and always drove the latest models off the lot. I was admiring the car when I heard my name being called from a distance. I turned and spotted a young woman in trendy workout attire, sweatband and blond ponytail jogging up to greet me. Her face was familiar, but I had difficulty believing this was the same person I knew in high school. "Krystal?" I said, taken aback as she made her approach.

"Hey, Mitch Baumann, I thought that was you." She embraced me in a warm hug. "How are you?"

"Well, certainly much better now." Her hug was a nice surprise.

She laughed, undoing her ponytail and swishing her bushy mane back to shoulder length. "So, how long's it been? Four years?"

"At least." Krystal was Harold's older sister by one year. We graduated from high school together after I was skipped ahead a grade in elementary school. I had such a crush on her in junior high, back when the girls matured ahead of the boys and my friends and I were still chasing lizards and shooting marbles. She was out of my league, but I tested the waters in ninth grade asking her to the homecoming dance thinking as Harold's friend I'd be a shoo-in. She turned me down, of course, preferring to pursue the older guys with their muscle cars and letter sweaters. We drifted as I became involved with baseball and other sports, Krystal caught up in her cliquish, popular-girl social strata. By the time we'd graduated, I'd become immune to her presence around the hallways, not saying more than two words our entire senior year.

"So, you're back at Annapolis now? Getting ready to graduate soon, huh?"

"Yep. In June."

"How about after graduation? They send you to a ship or something, right?"

"I'm planning on flight school down in Pensacola."

"Ooh, just like Dad," she said, sounding impressed. "Going to be a pilot, fly for the airlines someday?"

Her polite inquiry sounded less palatable to me than it would've a year ago. "Yeah, maybe. Who knows," I said, staring down. "So, what about you? What's Krystal's story these days?"

She shrugged. "I don't really have one. I graduated with my associate's from San Mateo a year ago. I may return to school, try nursing. Maybe write children's books on the side, become rich and famous, ha, ha."

"Hmm, nurse-slash-writer. Sounds like some long hours ahead." I sensed that neither were in her future. She was embarrassed and needed to fill the void with something positive. "What about Harold? What's he doing?"

"Working for his father. Wants to get into auto racing. Spends part of the year down in Ontario working in the pits or something, I'm not really sure. He's at the dealership today, otherwise you could stop in and say hello."

I observed Krystal as she spoke. She'd maintained her friendly charm, both sweet and candid, very much the girl-next-door persona I'd fallen for. She'd had many boyfriends later in high school, almost like she was collecting them on a whim. Now she seemed lonely, unmoored. We walked along in silence. It was my turn to say something. "So, Harold the racecar driver, huh?"

"No, more like Harold the dreamer." She gave an audible sigh. "Sometimes life seems, so, random, you know? You're gamboling along life's chosen path, then, *wham*, suddenly you're not."

"Uh-huh." We were no longer talking about Harold.

She stopped and faced me. "So, what about you, Mitch?" She flashed a quick smile. "You got a girlfriend? Someone waiting for you back east?"

Her sudden forwardness surprised me. I thought of Aimee and frowned. "I did. We were off and on. Then she jilted me, sent me a Dear-John letter."

"Oh, my."

"Yeah. *Wham.*"

"That's such a cowardly thing to do," Krystal said, like she knew Aimee and always suspected her of such behavior. She took my hand. "I'm really sorry to hear." Her tone suggested otherwise.

I thought of Aimee, jumbling she and the Maddy situation together, uncertain what I felt at any given moment. There was a time when I would've been flattered by Krystal's little inquisition, her prying interest in my relationship status. The door was open, both of us unattached. She was mildly coming on to me with her brief, sad history and renewed interest in my life. My, how things can change, I thought. It was only yesterday, that summer after ninth-grade hearing Bread's, *Make It with You* over and over, a sappy chick song ripe for teenage heartache, that I believed it was possible to fall in love simply by hearing a song on the radio. I was mad about Krystal that summer, even after she'd turned me down, dreaming one day for a second chance. My thoughts returned to Aimee. "Yeah, well, I'm over her," I said, realizing I was anything but.

"That's great. So how was your Christmas?"

"Not so great. My father left my mother, at least we think he did." I never intended to let this bit of news slip. Not until I heard it spring from my lips did I believe I'd said it. "I haven't seen him my entire visit. We really don't know where he is."

"Oh, Mitch, I'm so sorry. That's horrible. I hadn't heard." Her tone was sincere, unlike hearing my news about being dumped.

"Yeah, things are a mess." I was really socking it to her, giving her the complete lowdown on my woes, a one-two punch to a girl I hadn't seen or spoken to in nearly five years.

Krystal's mood seemed to sink. I'd given her more than she'd bargained for ending the tangent on our love lives. "When did they split up? My mother never mentioned anything."

Cornelia and my mother were friends, not super tight, but we both knew this was exactly the type of information my mother would unload on anyone in the neighborhood lest they hear from another source first, disallowing her proper spin. "I don't know if it's official yet or not. My mother seems to be in denial, like he's coming back. Amber seems to think otherwise."

"Oh, Mitch. I don't know what to say, other than I'm so sorry. I really liked your dad. And your mother too, of course."

"Thanks."

"I just saw him recently, you know. He was at our house the other day."

"Just saw who? My father?" I was shocked, unsure I'd heard correctly.

"Well, not that recent. Maybe during the summer, around June. I say recent only because he hadn't been to visit since we were kids."

This was bizarre. And she was correct about the visit. The last time my father visited the Hagl home was back in 1969. It was during the Apollo 11 moonwalk. They'd hosted a big neighborhood party for the occasion, and we'd all crowded around their big color TV set to watch Neil Armstrong and Buzz Aldrin take their first steps on the moon. I remembered that evening well. That was going to be me one day. "He just popped in? After more than seven years, for a visit?"

"Yeah, it seemed strange, not like a simple pop-in. Mother and Father knew he was coming. And I don't think it was a neighborly visit, more like he was after something, needed help or information maybe."

"What'd they discuss?"

"I don't know. They went off to a corner of the living room. I didn't think much of it at the time."

"Krystal," I said, my voice rising. "This is important. Will your mom and dad remember that discussion? Do you think I could talk to them about it?"

She seemed concerned I was pressing her with more urgency than seemed necessary. "Sure, come talk to them. But you can't right now, they're out for the evening. Come back tomorrow. I'm sure they'd be happy to—"

"I can't come back tomorrow," I interrupted. "I leave in the morning for Baltimore, to return to school."

"Well, I'm sure they'd love to see you. Call or catch us next time you're back."

"I may not be back," I said, with a touch of finality, glancing at my watch.

"Ooh, that sounds ominous."

"Not really. Look, I need to get moving, get packed for tomorrow." The sun had gone down, streetlights were flickering on.

"Sure, I understand." Krystal looked sad. The misdirection in our conversation had thrown her, made her uneasy. "Well, take care of yourself, Mitch. I'm sure things will work out."

"Will they?" I said, fretting like an old lady.

"Of course, they will." She reached out and we embraced in a second hug, longer than our first. As we relaxed our grip, she leaned forward and pecked my cheek catching the corner of my lips, more a quick brush than a real kiss. I was surprised but reacted in kind. This was a rare moment not to be squandered, like Halley's Comet coming back around, renewing a dormant schoolboy crush. I leaned in and we kissed in earnest – long, slow, with a hint of passion. There was an exchange of energy, a lifting of my spirits, my confidence restored. It felt good, refreshingly out of the blue and certainly nothing I could've predicted when I left the house in a stew only twenty minutes ago.

I smiled, still holding onto her hand. "Thanks, Krystal. That was a nice Christmas present."

"It was, Mitch. Happy New Year."

# 18

## THE DARK AGES

Friday, January 7, 1977

SPORTS ARE A MANDATORY PART of the curriculum at Navy. Either you participate at the collegiate level on a varsity or plebe team, or you go out for one of the many intermural sports offered throughout the academic calendar. I'd been back less than a week and was already in the swing of things finishing up an intermural company flag football game on a frigid overcast afternoon after six classes in a row – a 6N day for Navy. Lonnie played quarterback for our company team, having lost his opportunity to play on varsity due to the hatchet job the tackler did to his knee. He'd lost most of his mobility but was great in the pocket. And Posey was his favorite receiver. Rail thin, and six-foot-five, Posey would sprint downfield and extend his right arm straight up in the air as the target. Lonnie would stand rooted in the pocket just like Joe Willie himself and float a perfect pass hitting him directly on the palm of his outstretched hand. The Pose would tuck the ball to his chest and glide untouched into the end-zone – touchdown, 27th Company. We'd run several of these successful plays during the game and easily defeated our rival, 28th Company, 35 – 14. Lon, Pose and I walked together in a tight pack from the field after the game. We were the only first-class on the team and needed to discuss a little business as we walked. Lon, I could tell, was under a ton of pressure as our company commander, eager to shed his tenure in a few weeks with the beginning of the second set. The investigation had taken its toll – on him and Lieutenant Herrera since there'd been no real news since Maddy's disappearance in November. They were being squeezed to deliver some tidbit of information, shed some light and wrap this thing up and move on before it became a PR disaster for the Academy. Lonnie told us to expect a second wave of the investigation to begin soon.

"Hey, you want to hear a good one?" Lonnie said. We'd just stepped off the brown, frozen turf of the athletic field, crossing the road on our way to Bancroft Hall.

"I don't know. Do I?" I said, wary to engage in any wild speculation about

Maddy.

"They say they want to start the interviews next week. And get this, their list has shrunk from something like 4,000 to just ten."

"Ten what? Midshipmen?"

"Not all mids. Couple of company officers in the mix from what I hear."

I stopped in my tracks. "Just who's your source, Lon? You're telling me they've got ten suspects and they're all from the Academy?"

"I never said suspects. Just a list of ten high-interest persons they want to talk to."

"Haven't they even looked beyond the gates? Hell, she was last seen outside the Yard. Why aren't the Annapolis Police involved? Sounds like they're treating it like an inside job."

"They *are* treating it like an inside job," Lonnie said, his voice growing more troubled. "Herrera showed me the list. And you're officially on it, by the way."

"Good," I snapped. "I want to talk to those NIS idiots too. I want to ask them what they did over the Christmas break. Or more to the point, what they *didn't* do."

"I doubt you'll be the one asking the questions, Mitch. This is serious. You need to settle down. The investigation has finally come to you. That's what you've wanted, right?"

"Right."

"Then don't blow it, man. Work with them. Don't show that hostility you're showing me, or Herrera, or else—"

"I'm not hostile, Lon. If they want hostility, believe me, I can—"

Posey broke into the conversation, halting us both. "Do you think they'll want to ask me some questions?" Pose had been silent since the game had ended and now looked hopeful, as if he had something to report.

"Your name wasn't on the list Herrera showed me, Pose," Lonnie said. "Do you have some information? Something you'd like to share?" Lonnie spoke slowly as if talking to a child.

"I've got something in my room I think is important."

Lonnie and I exchanged looks. "What you got, Pose?" I said. "A computer printout with the perp's name at the bottom? Did you write a program that's figured this whole thing out?"

Posey ignored my jab at his nerd-dom. "I'd just as soon show you all back in my room."

"Sure thing, Pose," Lonnie said. "Let's go."

We were headed back to the company area anyway. The three of us hopped up the stairs and followed Posey down the corridor, mystified by what evidence he could possibly be hoarding. We gathered around his desk as he spun the dial on his lockbox and reached in. "I found this," he said. "Near State Route 450, just outside Gate 8."

Lonnie reached for it. "Whoa. What do we have here?" He was truly shocked, recognizing immediately, as I did, the significance, that this was valuable information if Posey did in fact find it where he'd said.

"It's a plebe shoulder board," Posey said, answering honestly, as if Lonnie were too dense to comprehend what he was looking at.

"Not only that," I added. "It's a *female* plebe shoulder board. Look at its size."

"No crap, guys." Lonnie said, rubbing his hand over his tight afro haircut. He looked up at Posey. "What the hell, Pose? Where'd you get this? Where'd it come from?"

"I found it like I said, near Route 450, Baltimore Road, outside Gate 8."

"When?"

"The morning after Miss O'Connor missed taps."

I zeroed in on him. "Posey, for Christ's sake, how'd you know to go out there? Looking for what?" I was beside myself that someone else had taken it upon themselves to do some investigating so soon after her disappearance. "Who put you on the trail?"

"Wasn't hard. I just looked in the company sign-out log Sunday morning before chapel and took a walk out the back gate towards Perry Circle."

"Did you talk to the sponsor too? Did you ring their bell?" I was incredulous. Clausen and his wife had said nothing of another visitor.

"No. The log only said Perry Circle, no address."

"When did you take your walk, big guy?" Lonnie asked.

"Around 0630, maybe 0700. Somewhere between there."

"And you found it just sitting in the road?" Lonnie held up the lone shoulder board.

"Actually, in the gutter near the road."

Lonnie and I exchanged looks again. "Pose, why didn't you come forward with this when you found it?" I said. "I mean, why'd you sit on it? This is huge."

"Yeah, Pose," Lonnie said. "This could be trouble. We need to turn it in, ASAP."

"Let him answer, Lon. Why'd you keep it to yourself?"

Posey hesitated, searching for a good answer.

"Pose?" Lonnie said.

"Lieutenant Herrera said we needed to let the investigation come to us," Posey snapped. "Not to meddle or cause any interference as the NIS performed their job. Of course, he said this after I found the shoulder board, but I figured it best to lay low, to turn it in when they interviewed me." Posey looked up. "You say I'm not on the list for an interview?"

"You are now, my man," Lonnie exclaimed. "You'll go straight to the head of the class after this little find. Geez, Pose, don't you know the difference between meddling and assisting? You shoulda turned this thing in as soon as you found it."

"Hey, cut the guy some slack, Lon," I said, coming to Posey's rescue. "You heard Herrera's speech at quarters before the Christmas break. He practically ordered us to do nothing but wait, to speak only if spoken to." But if I recalled correctly, it was my meddling that motivated him to make that speech in the first place, as if he were speaking to me personally.

Lonnie stood from his chair. "We've got to turn the board in now. Right now. I didn't see Herrera in his office when we walked by, I'm sure he's gone home for the day." Lonnie paused, looking at his watch. "Damn. I'd really rather gift wrap it to him, but this can't wait. Pose, let's you and I get out of our sweats and take a walk down to Main O. I'd rather get this into NIS hands sooner than later." Lonnie moved to the door then turned. "And start thinking up something smart to say when they ask why you held it for so long." He disappeared to shower and change.

"Mitch, you think I'm in trouble?" Posey said in Lonnie's wake. "I mean, it's the truth, the reason I kept it."

"Sure, Pose. No sweat. Just tell them the truth and you'll be fine."

"Well, I'm still a bit worried."

"Why? What's eating you?" I sensed more complication.

"I need to show you something else."

"Something else, Pose?"

"I found something else."

"What?"

Posey reached back into his lockbox. He slid out a long silver bracelet, one with small dangly orbs and embedded gemstones, maybe half a dozen encircling the bracelet itself. "This," he said, holding it to the light.

My eyes bugged out. *God no.* A sledgehammer had just been cleaved into my gut. Posey noticed. "Holy shit, Pose. Where'd you find this?"

"Same place."

"As the shoulder board? You sure?"

"Same place. About a foot apart, near the gutter." Posey looked frightened. "I'm in trouble, aren't I? It's hers, isn't it? Miss O'Connor's?"

"I don't know, Pose. Relax. What made you think it was hers? Did you ever see her wearing it?"

"No. They were just close together, so I thought to pick up both of them."

I studied Pose closely. "Why didn't you show this to Lonnie just now? There was a reason. You know it's hers, don't you?"

"No. I thought you might know. I mean, you and Miss O'Connor...you know..."

"No, I *don't* know, Pose." My tone was stiff. "It could be hers, just like the board could be hers. We don't know."

"Then we should just turn them both in, huh?"

A thought occurred. "Tell you what. Let me take a run out to Miss O'Connor's sponsor's house tonight after evening meal. I'll bring it with me, see if either Lieutenant Clausen or his wife recall her wearing it that night. I mean, you couldn't miss something like that on a person's wrist, right?"

"Then we turn it in?"

"Yes, Pose. Give me until tonight. Then we'll turn it in."

By the time I reached Bob and Jan Clausen's quarters, I was exhausted. My stress level had peaked since returning from Christmas leave. I'd left behind a mess at home, final exams were a week away and the whole Maddy affair was bubbling over in my mind threatening to wreck whatever sanity I had left. There'd been no news since her disappearance, and I'd been surprised nothing had appeared in the media. So far, the Academy damage control process was holding but the rumor mill was churning. Everyone seemed to blithely accept the fact she was gone, and it was becoming sport to tag onto the latest theory or hearsay offering completely unenlightened opinions, some of them absurd and downright cruel.

I'd shown up at Bob and Jan's unannounced with bracelet in hand hoping it was a different one than Maddy was wearing over the summer – the one I told her to take off. Fortunately, they were home just finishing supper themselves. Jan's eyes became as large as saucers when I showed it to her. Of course, she recognized it and remembered Maddy wearing it. When I explained where the bracelet was found, along with a single shoulder board from her overcoat, Jan's knees nearly gave out and Bob had to steady her. All three of us recognized the significance of the find. I'd almost hoped Jan wouldn't recognize it or deny it was Maddy's as it would mean the location of her disappearance was elsewhere, not at the intersection of Perry Circle and State Route 450, which blatantly suggested foul play. As I retraced her steps from Bob and Jan's quarters, located the curb where Pose had found the evidence, the picture became nauseatingly clear. She'd been abducted, at this exact point, no question. Perry Circle joins SR 450 after winding down the hill from the cluster of apartments. At the intersection is a small visitor parking lot on one side, a narrow walkway leading down the hill on the other. Maddy must've been walking down this path, in the dark, when she was greeted by someone parked in the lot, probably waiting for her. There was a struggle, the shoulder board popped open, the bracelet clasp gave way. Whoever it was probably didn't notice either item in the darkness. I gave a shudder. I may not have pieced it together perfectly but what I had, what I knew at this moment, was certainly more than the NIS knew. Pose and I should've just turned this piece of evidence over earlier this afternoon, same as he did the shoulder board. I was becoming more and more rattled by my acquisition of clues. The shoulder board alone, albeit a female plebe shoulder board, didn't suggest wrongdoing, simply a defective snap. But when coupled with a personal item such as the bracelet with a broken clasp, this suggested something else entirely. As a pair, they would substantiate the theory that there'd been a kidnapping.

Monday, January 31, 1977

I fell in love with Stevie Nicks of Fleetwood Mac on a gray afternoon in early '77. Their song, *Silver Springs* had just hit the airwaves, Stevie delivering an emotional refrain about the heartache and breakup of a failed relationship. The guitar's wistful moans and delicate echoes spilled from my speakers as the song began. The dreaded Dark Ages had finally descended on the Academy with all its might, creating a picture-perfect backdrop for me to lapse into a coma. Stevie's low voice added the necessary one-two punch to Lindsey's weeping guitar. I was sitting at my desk facing the gloom from the window, back from our brief semester break. I should've been ecstatic. It was the beginning of my final semester. Service selection, Hundredth Night, June Week, graduation, were all joyous events forming on the horizon. It would all be over in a matter of weeks. But, no, I was content to sit in my room by myself, wallow in self-pity and contemplate the haze gray overcast and freezing temperatures outside.

From my perch in Bancroft Hall, I watched cars silently crisscross the Eastport bridge above the icy harbor, imagining a brisk windchill coming off the bay. A pile of dead brown leaves swirled in the parking lot below. Legend has it John Phillips of the Mamas and Papas penned his song, *California Dreamin'* during his plebe year at the Academy on a similarly dreary afternoon in the Yard. While a touching notion, it was later proven he did no such thing, having never been to California until much later in life. Still, his colorful lyrics painted a lustful picture of her warm shores and sunny beaches, especially to a California boy stuck in Annapolis on a frozen day in January. His reference about being safe and warm in LA reminded me of Aimee. *Silver Springs* reminded me of Aimee. Stevie Nicks reminded me of Aimee. Lately, every friggin' sad song on the radio reminded me of Aimee and seemed custom-made. I needed to break the spell, dump this catatonic stupor ahead of its death grip and leave the room. I had Aimee's Dear-John letter, her last, spread out on the desk in front of me when Neil walked in, overnight bag in hand, freshly back from semester break. He read my face instantly.

"Oh, no. Here we go again. Say it ain't so. Please. Say you're not still obsessing over Maddy."

"I'm not still obsessing over Maddy," I said, robotically, staring straight ahead. "I'm fine."

"Yeah. And I'm Captain Fantastic and the Brown Dirt Cowboy."

I watched another pile of leaves swirl from the window. "What if they never find her, Neil? What if they never solve this thing?"

"Ah. So, you *are* still obsessing."

"I'm not obsessing. At least I wasn't until you brought it up." Neil looked down at my desk and noticed Aimee's old letter, the one we'd never discussed. "Is it wrong simply to want to know what's happened? What's being done?"

"They'll figure it out, Mitch. Just give 'em time. I hear they've already talked to Captain Manley and Sweetie up in 28th over the break."

I was intrigued by how Neil would know this. "And?"

"And they're still here. No arrests, if that's what you were hoping for."

I wasn't. But the idea of Sweetie being Mirandized and dragged off in chains held a certain appeal. "I guess I'll be next then. Lonnie said they were going to hit our company this week."

"Herrera will be next. Then you, me and everyone in the duty section that night. Pose too."

I thought about Posey and what else he might know or confess. The shoulder board and bracelet revelation still had me stunned. "Speaking of the Pose," I said. "He gave me something else before we went on semester break."

"Something else?"

I drew a deep breath and reached into my desk drawer. "This," I said, holding up the charm bracelet.

Neil took a long, close look without reaching for it. "And what is *this*?" he said.

"Pose found it next to the shoulder board."

"Pose found it? Oh, jeez, and I suppose it's hers, isn't it?" Neil's expression changed immediately. "Mitch, what the hell? I don't even want to ask why *you* have it."

"I wanted the sponsor to ID it, to see if they spotted Maddy wearing it that night."

"And?"

"It's hers, Neil."

"I don't believe it. You dumb bastard. What are you trying to do, get yourself arrested?"

"I went down to Main Office after hours to turn it in. Wanted to give it to the OD, but he was out and none of the mids on watch had a clue what to do, so I kept it. Told 'em I'd take care of it in the morning. I probably waited too long, huh?"

"You *think*? Just how long did you plan to sit on this bit of crucial evidence?"

"Oh, calm down. The NIS is moving at a snail's pace. I'll give it to them at my interview, tell 'em everything. It's no big deal."

"It certainly *is* a big deal. It's like saying, 'Oh, since you guys are so inept, I took it upon myself to track down this bit of evidence for you. And never mind I crapped all over it with my fingerprints and sat on it for three weeks, here it is now. I hope it helps.' Mitch, this does not look good, man. They're under intense pressure to name a suspect, find some hint of evidence. This'll be the perfect excuse to point the finger at you. Why'd you do this?"

"As I said, I had a hunch and acted on it. I'll give it to them. Don't worry about it."

Neil finally set down his bag and started unpacking. "Okay, I agree, things are moving much slower than they should. But you're playing with fire. You know that, right?"

"I know and I can't help it. I expected the NIS to walk in here with unlimited resources and grill everyone like Sergeant Joe Friday and have a collar within a week. Here we are more than a month in and there seems more effort at damage control than finding Maddy or the perp."

"Just turn in that bracelet, Mitch. Don't give them any excuses to make you their perp."

"I will. I will."

"Good." Neil breathed easier. "So, roomie, the final push, right? Turn on the big blue machine one last time, spit us out for good in June? I can't wait. I swear, the plebes in my squad better know the exact number of days, hours and minutes until graduation when I ask or I'll fry every last one of them." Neil noticed my glum look. "Oh, and Mitch, try to contain your exuberance. I can see you're just so damn happy to begin our final semester here at Canoe U. I know, it sucks, it's the Dark Ages." He stood behind me and massaged my shoulders. "But you've got to snap out of it, man. We're outta here in—" He glanced down at his desk calendar. "128 days and a wakeup!"

Neil was right, I needed something to snap me out of it. Things were going to get better, they had to. I thought this was as good a time as any to share what had been on my mind before he barged in the room. "So, Neil, you asked about Aimee at Christmas – how come you hadn't seen her, when was she coming back up for a visit."

"Hey, relax, man. I figured you guys were going through some difficulties. Long-distance stuff. Hell, Potomac seems like a trek for me at times. I can't imagine having a girlfriend a thousand miles away."

"I don't have a girlfriend a thousand miles away."

"Oh, she's moving closer, I trust?" He knew that wasn't the answer.

"We broke up in the fall. Remember, when you came into the room, took one look at me and asked who died?"

"Yeah."

"Well, she'd just sent me this." I handed Neil Aimee's two-page handwritten letter.

"A Dear-John?"

"Go ahead, read it. I should've told you a lot sooner."

Neil handled the pages very carefully, very respectfully. I'd never shared any of Aimee's letters with him, at least not let him read them, but this time it felt right, and he sensed the gravity. I needed a second opinion, advice, a friend, a cathartic moment, anything to help me purge the weight I'd carried since August. I carefully tracked Neil's expressions as he began to read, having memorized every word of Aimee's cautious and calculated prose. I knew exactly what he was reading when he was reading it. My eyes never left him. He smiled at her romantic description of Annapolis, her life at the radio station, shook his head at the suggestion we break up, raised an eyebrow at sex parts then, as if experiencing a eureka moment, he dropped the letter to the desk and said, "Man, that's no Dear-John letter. Not in my book."

"What do you mean? Of course, it is."

"Nah, you're way off. Just read it."

"I have. About a hundred times."

"Well read it a hundred and one times. Look at that last line, *Fate is funny that way.*"

"So?"

"*So?* Fate is funny that way? It's your move, man. She's practically counting on you to find her. Wake up, for God's sake."

Friday, February 4, 1977

It began with a legal-sized envelope protruding from my mailbox. About time, I thought, as I pulled it from the slot, opened it and scanned the enclosed memo's contents. The official communication was short and to the point:

*From:    Commandant of Midshipmen*
*To:      Midshipman First Class Mitchell J. Baumann, USN, 27th Company*
*Subj:    NIS Case File# A-76-0583DC*

1. *You are hereby directed to report to conference room #1 located adjacent to the Office of the Commandant, 4101, Bancroft Hall, on Monday, 7 February at 1100 for an interview regarding the subject investigation.*

2. *Subject investigation is being conducted under the jurisdiction of the Naval Investigative Service, Quantico, Virginia and the Washington, DC Field Office. You will give them your full cooperation and not discuss the interview's contents or proceedings with anyone.*

> *By direction,*
> *Byron Plum*
> *Captain, USN*
> *Deputy Commandant*

I would miss my fourth-period class and likely noon meal, but I wasn't concerned. I was eager to get started, answer their questions and tell them everything I knew after what felt like an eternity since that cold night in November. I planned to ask them some pointed questions too, like why the hell it's taken so long to get to these interviews. I considered bringing the bracelet as I prepared to head down to 4-1 but decided it might divert their attention as I walked in the room. Better to just tell them about it when the time was right and hand it over later.

I was calm, confident, almost cocky, striding into the Commandant's outer office. The receptionist guided me to an adjacent conference room. I was met by the two agents standing around its large table. The agent nearest me, tall and clean-cut, was dressed in a loose-fitting dark gray suit, coat unbuttoned. He greeted me, extending his right hand while balancing a Styrofoam cup of coffee in his left.

"'Morning. Special Agent Daryl Hanratty." He was smiling, but only slightly, as he flashed his badge.

"Good morning, sir. Midshipman Mitch Baumann."

"And this is Special Agent Scott Haney."

Haney extended his hand after flashing his badge without smiling or speaking. He was shorter, dressed in a similar ill-fitting suit. Haney eyed me as we took our seats, the two agents taking places on the opposite end of the table.

"Coffee?" Hanratty asked.

I declined, signaling I wanted to skip any preliminaries, that I was ready to begin and not waste any more time than necessary.

Hanratty began, pen in hand, notepad and coffee in front of him. Haney continued to stare. "Mitch, I assume you know why you're here, what this is about?"

"Yes, sir."

"This is an interview, nothing more. We're going to ask you some questions regarding our investigation into the matter of, well, into the recent disappearance of the fourth-class midshipman in question."

*Recent disappearance?*

"Do you understand?"

*And why not say her name?*

Hanratty looked up. "Mitch, do you understand?"

"Yes, sir."

"Okay, let's begin, starting from the top." He punched a small cassette recorder on the table and opened a manila folder, one which held my previously written statement. "When did you first meet Midshipman Madison O'Connor?"

*Boy, we really are starting from the top.* "Induction Day. July 6, 1976."

"And you were her…" He looked down at his pad. "Her—"

"I was her company commander," I said, filling in the blank. "For the first set of plebe summer. I met her at evening meal that night. She was seated at my table with her new classmates and squad leader."

"So, you were her company commander, directly in her chain of command?"

"Yes."

"How many between you and Midshipman O'Connor?"

"Two. Her squad leader, Caleb Wise, and platoon commander, Neil King."

"Hang on with the names, we'll get to them later. So, there were two first-class midshipmen between you and Miss O'Connor? During the first set?"

"Yes." *Where's he going with this?*

"As company commander, did you have any one-on-one time with Miss O'Connor, much time for personal interaction?"

"I spoke with her individually a few times but certainly not as much as Caleb. Excuse me, her squad leader."

"And during this individual time, what was discussed? Her performance, her progress during the summer?"

I thought back to our first one-on-one meeting in her room, when we were both on watch, the pictures under her blotter, her barging in and surprising me, catching me snooping. "Yes, more or less, stuff like that."

Haney raised an eyebrow.

I continued, uncertain of their knowledge. "We had our first meeting in her room a few weeks into the summer. I was inspecting it when she walked in. We went on to discuss her progress, how she felt, how she was coping."

"Anything else?" Haney interjected, speaking for the first time.

I met his gaze straight away. "Yes, there was something else. We discussed her roommate's performance, the difficulty she was having. Miss O'Connor was worried about her."

Hanratty looked down at his pad again. "Midshipman White? She was having difficulty?"

"No, not Miss White. Midshipman Sedgley. Sara Sedgley. She subsequently separated, quit at the end of plebe summer."

"Why'd she quit?" Haney said.

"As I said, she was having difficulties adjusting. Health issues, physical issues." *Does it matter? Aren't we here to discuss Midshipman O'Connor?*

"Mitch." Hanratty looked up, reading my mind. "I know this may not seem important, but it is. Everything we ask you is for a reason." His tone relaxed, became less formal. "Now Sara had issues, she quit. We know this. I want you to describe the dynamic that was going on in your company during the summer's first set, when you were in charge, when you were their company commander and Maddy and Sara and Amanda were all under your care."

*My care?* He surprised me by placing the onus on me and switching to their first names. In one sentence he'd implied Maddy was in my personal care, as was Sara and Amanda, and the "dynamic" was being called into question. "Agent Hanratty, when you say to describe the dynamic, do you mean the attitude at the Academy in general, or do you mean the dynamic between me and the three women?"

"Both. Were the women accepted initially, given preferential treatment? Or were they treated unfairly? Like perhaps, Miss Sedgley?"

"Now wait a minute. Who said Miss Sedgley was treated unfairly? She wasn't given preferential treatment, but she wasn't singled out for unfair treatment either. She had physical issues, she was on crutches half the summer, on excuse squad, but she was never picked on or grilled excessively. If anything, she was left alone more than the rest, when the company was marching or on the PEP field or playing sports."

"Was she harassed? For being a woman, for being perhaps something else?"

"No." My defenses were coming up.

Haney jumped in. "'Hey, Miss Sludge, what about you?'" he said, glancing at his notes. "'Is Brownfield hot?'" He met my eye. "And wasn't Brownfield, in fact, standing naked in front of the platoon wearing nothing but his jockstrap?"

I wanted to reply, no, he also had on his combination cover and a pair of shoes, but that probably didn't need mentioning. Haney's question was designed to unnerve me, to make me wonder just how much detail these guys had gathered in their little pads. "What's your point, Agent Haney?" He was beginning to get under my skin.

Hanratty spoke in his place. "Mitch, what was the attitude during the summer? Again, were the women accepted or was it your company's unspoken mission to run them off?"

"We weren't there to run anyone off. Of course not. I resent your implication."

"And yet there were derogatory nicknames being tossed in their face, bold sexual innuendo used in ranks, fraternization, rampant evidence of sexual harassment." Haney was looking up from his pad. "The list goes on, you know."

"We aren't accusing you," Hanratty jumped in.

*The hell you aren't.*

"We just want you to comment on the situation, the environment the women were immersed in. You're saying there was no harassment?"

"Well, okay, yes, there were two camps. One made it clear to all women that they did not belong. And yes, they were pretty vocal about it. The other, the majority, was supportive and fair." Just not as vocal, I thought.

"And which camp were you in, Mitch?" Haney asked.

"The latter. I hope."

"Mitch, tell us about Miss O'Connor," Hanratty said. "Was she a squared away mid?"

"Yes, she was. She was exceptional."

"Compared to whom? The other women?"

"Everyone."

"Everyone?" Hanratty conferred with his notes again. "Do you recall how she was ranked at the end of first set?"

I figured this might come up. "Somewhere in the middle, I think."

"Yet you say she was squared away, in fact, exceptional."

"So?"

"So, I'm trying to understand the disparity. Was she mediocre as her 17th out of 38 ranking suggests or was she exceptional?"

I'd had it with this line of questioning. These bozos were no closer to solving Maddy's disappearance than they were eight weeks ago, and this proved it. "Gee, I don't know, Agent Hanratty. What if I told you the entire 27th Platoon was exceptional? Or that the first sixteen were positively brilliant placing Maddy's seventeenth ranking as merely exceptional? Would that clear up the disparity for you?"

"Take it easy, Mitch." Hanratty looked at his watch. "We're only fifteen minutes into this thing and many more questions remain. These preliminaries are essential, so I suggest clear, direct responses so we can get through them. Along with a little more patience and a little less attitude," he added with a smile.

"Yes, sir."

"Okay, let's move on. Tell us about any other interactions you had with Miss O'Connor."

"You mean during the summer?"

"At any time, Mitch. But let's pick up after your chance meeting in her room several weeks in."

I truly had to think. There'd been no more private meetings during summer. But had I been in the girl's room any time during the first semester? Then I remembered. "It was after the Tea Fight, sometime in October."

"The what?"

"The Tea Dance, it's a hop for plebes, held on a Sunday. I met with her that evening, after the dance, in her room."

"Just the two of you?"

"Yes."

"Do you recall the purpose of the meeting?"

"Yes." I glanced at the water pitcher in the center of the table. "Do you mind if I have glass?"

Hanratty looked at Haney then nodded. Both men's eyes watched as I poured. After taking a sip, I resumed. "We discussed her reason for not attending the Tea Dance. I was an usher that day and noticed she was missing. I went to inquire why, to hear her excuse, in her own words."

"The dance was mandatory?"

"Yes." Another sip of water. "As it turned out she did indeed skip. She admitted it when I pressed her."

"Did you place her on report?" Hanratty said.

I squirmed in my seat, unprepared for this question. "No."

Haney was about to say something, but I talked over him. "I decided to give her a warning. There was no official muster for the dance, no chit to turn in, so I just wanted to let her know people were watching."

Haney stood up. "But the proper procedure would have been to place her on report, right?"

"No." I met this little prick's gaze. "Upper-class midshipmen are given discretion within the admin conduct system. I chose to give her a warning."

"Why?" Haney immediately fired back like a prosecutor going for the jugular. "Why would you do that?"

Hanratty held up a hand. "Hang on, hang on." Haney backed off and slowly lowered himself into his seat. "Mitch, did she tell you where she went in lieu of attending the dance?" Both sets of eyes were back on me. "What she did that afternoon?"

Since Lonnie had told me these guys had already talked to Sweetie and his company officer, Captain Manley, I figured they knew the score and were drilling in on possible inconsistencies in our stories, nothing more. "Yes, she told me," I said.

"And?"

"And, she admitted to riding out the gate in an upperclassman's car for the afternoon. They went for a drive somewhere and returned before evening meal formation. That's it." Picturing Sweet, I said, inaudibly, "You probably heard this already."

If either of the agents caught my latter statement, they ignored it. "And you most certainly wrote up Miss O'Connor for *these* offenses – fraternization and UA," Haney said, deciding to remain seated.

"I most certainly did not, Agent Haney. As I said, I used discretion, as is my right as a first-class midshipman." I knew what he was implying, that there was some sort of lover's triangle between Sweetie, Maddy and me and I was protecting her, giving her aid and privilege with hopes of winning her over.

"Mitch, were there any other one-on-ones after that? Any other meetings?" Hanratty asked, eager to keep moving forward.

Okay, here we go. "Yes, one more, I believe."

"When and where?"

"We talked at Nimitz Library, upstairs. This would've been in early November, a weeknight."

"And the purpose?"

I was getting tired of his implying every meeting was calculated, everything must have a purpose. "We bumped into each other. She was studying and we chatted briefly about the other night in her room. I wanted to caution her again, remind her about not riding out the gate in upperclassmen's cars. That it was risky and would jeopardize her status as a midshipman."

"How did she react?"

"She was respectful, we talked in hushed voices and she seemed to understand. It was a quick meeting, there were people watching. Then I left her to study. That was it."

"And that was the last time you talked to her, individually? That evening in early November?"

"I believe so."

"You're certain?"

"Yes."

"Okay, so tell us about the night she went missing, November 20th. You were on watch that night, correct?"

"Correct. I was the Bow Wow for Fifth Batt that evening." I went on to describe the Eastport bridge incident, how I was tied up at the hospital until after taps, coming back to Batt Office and discovering the UA, that Maddy was unaccounted for. I told them everything that followed in a very concise, orderly manner leaving nothing out. Every detail of that evening and the following morning was locked in my brain, as fresh as the day it occurred. We discussed my meeting with Bob and Jan Clausen, their reaction, their speculation about Maddy and our agreeing to stay in touch, to share any news we might hear or come across. "Have you even talked to the sponsors yet?" I said, trying to mask my frustration at having to relive that awful night and once again face the fact that Maddy was no closer to being found than the night she went missing.

"Yes, Mitch, we've talked with the Clausen's."

Haney jumped in. "And just a reminder here, you're not conducting this interview. We are, the NIS. We ask the questions, you answer. Not the other way around. Got it, Midshipman Baumann?"

"Got it, Agent Haney." If they'd talked to Bob and Jan, it had to have been on the phone. They admitted to me when I showed them the bracelet that they'd *not* been interviewed face to face, not yet. I stared back at Haney.

"All right, all right," Hanratty said, looking at his watch. "It's now noon. I suggest we all take a break, the air's getting a bit stuffy. Mitch, how about it? Take five?"

"I'd just as soon continue, sir. I don't need a break."

Hanratty and Haney stood up, Haney whispering something in his partner's ear. "Mitch," said Hanratty, "We need to step outside for a moment. Help yourself to some more water or coffee, it'll just be a second, okay?"

"Yes, sir, fine." I watched them leave. I wasn't sure if this was a stall tactic, to let me stew a bit, or if they legitimately needed to talk, to confer about my answers, my behavior. I thought about Neil's, Lonnie's and Herrera's caution about curbing my attitude and figured I was doing okay, holding my own. Sure, I'd rattled the agents, but they'd rattled me, especially this Haney fellow, intentionally rubbing my fur the wrong way. I began thinking of him as the bumbling Mr. Haney on Green Acres, the con man with the cheap suit and clip-on tie. I was smiling when they walked back into the conference room and took their seats.

"Mitch," Hanratty said, flipping his notepad back open. "Just a couple more questions on the night Miss O'Connor went missing. You say you went to the base hospital to escort some intoxicated midshipmen back to Bancroft Hall. What time did you leave the Hall for the hospital?"

"That would've been right before taps. Around 2250." *Why are we covering this again?*

"And what time did you arrive at the hospital? Did you get a ride?"

Okay, I'd omitted a small detail. Still. "The hospital duty van had to be called to come get us and was taking too long. I told my plebe messenger to wait for the van, that I was going to walk ahead. It's less than a mile. I arrived at the hospital about the same time as my messenger and the van."

"Why didn't your messenger walk with you? Why'd he take the van?"

"Because we'd already called it. And we were going to need it to get the four drunk mids back to the Hall. I don't see where this is going."

Hanratty ignored my last comment. "So, you said you were at the hospital for an hour and got back to the Hall around when?"

"Sometime after midnight. Say midnight-15, in the van, with my messenger and the four mids from 25."

"And you were informed of Miss O'Connor's UA at that time?"

"Yes."

"Was there anything else that caused you to leave the Hall before the call came from the OD about retrieving the mids from the hospital?"

We hadn't covered this. "Okay, yes. Around 2030, Batt Office, my MCBO actually, received an anonymous call about some of our Army exchange cadets untying the yawls in Santee Basin and setting them adrift."

Hanratty gave me an odd look.

"It was no big deal. It was Army Week. All kinds of shenanigans go on. In this case, the Army cadets were conducting a prank, what we call a recon."

"How long were you gone this time?"

I held up my hands, exasperated. "I'm sorry, Agent Hanratty, with all due respect, what does this all have to do with Maddy?" I was tired of saying *Miss O'Connor*, better to personalize it. "I mean, I'll grant you, some of this was outside the normal Bow Wow watch activity but, as I said, it was Army Week. What? You think Maddy was abducted as some sort of prank, a recon that

306

went awry?"

He ignored my plea. "Again, how long were you gone this time? Please don't make me ask a third time."

So, even Hanratty's patience was wearing thin. "Okay, probably an hour. I left Batt O at 2030 and got back around 2130, after inspecting Santee Basin."

"Did you go alone, or did you have your messenger this time?"

"No messenger. I went alone. And when I got out there, the yawls were fine. All snug, moored to their slips. Turns out the prank was on me. Again, not that uncommon for Army Week."

"So, you were gone from Batt O from 2030 to 2130 and then again from 2250 to 0015, a total of nearly two and a half hours."

"Yes, that's right." I really wanted to inject some more sarcasm into his latest statement but held my tongue. We were all getting punchy and I wanted to leave soon, still hoping to catch noon meal in the Wardroom. As I pondered pouring myself another glass of water, it hit me, the likely reason for Hanratty's need to hear an accurate accounting of my time. He was trying to establish a window for an alibi, to match my whereabouts with the approximate window of Maddy's disappearance, which would've been around 2100 according to Bob and Jan.

"And you didn't talk to Miss O'Connor or see her at any time that night, the night she went missing?"

"No. As I said, Agent Hanratty, the last time I talked with her was upstairs, in Nimitz Library."

Hanratty paused, his eyes locking on mine. "Mitch, let's stop playing games here, okay?"

"Playing games?"

"Yes. I'm going to ask you again. Did you see or talk to Miss O'Connor at any time after your exchange in the library?"

My stomach sank. I suddenly felt sick, knowing they'd somehow uncovered a significant omission to my story. But how? How'd they know about our drive? "Okay, yes," I muttered. "In my car."

Hanratty and Haney exchanged looks like they knew all along. "Whoa," Hanratty said, flipping through his pad and grabbing the folder on the table. "In your *car?*" he said, incredulously, feigning ignorance. "You said the last time you talked to her was in the library, around..." He consulted his notes. "Early November."

"Yes, I know what I said. I misspoke." I'm sure I looked guilty as hell. "Miss O'Connor and I last talked on Saturday night in my car, a week before she went missing. We took a short drive out in town. It was really a continuation of our talk in the library, one where I wanted to caution her on her non-reg behavior of riding out the gate in other mid's cars."

"And yet you chose to advise her of this non-regulation behavior while driving out the gate together in *your* car?" It was Hanratty's time for sarcasm.

"I know. I did it for the right reasons though. I realize, this looks bad."

"It does look bad, Mitch. Why this wasn't even mentioned in your written statement." He held up the folder. "How else have you misspoken today? What else is missing from your story?"

"Nothing else is missing." I shifted uncomfortably in my chair thinking of the charm bracelet in my desk drawer. "I've told you everything. I'm sure you can understand why I wasn't keen on admitting my drive out the gate with Maddy. Besides, I didn't think it was relevant." I went on to tell them about our stop in Truxton Park that night, our discussion for her to end the joyriding in cars and her admission to skipping the Tea Dance, that riding out the gate with another midshipman was an isolated incident. I never mentioned Jonathan Sweet, knowing they had talked to him already, wanting them to bring his name into the conversation, if necessary. I ended by telling them I'd dropped Maddy on Farragut Field before watching her slip away in the darkness. *That* was the last time I'd talked with her. End of story. I admitted I was sorry I didn't tell them straight away. When I looked at Hanratty and Haney, I could tell, neither of them were buying it.

Hanratty went back on the offensive. "Okay, Mitch, in light of what we now know, tell us about your relationship with Miss O'Connor. Was it more than just professional? Because she didn't get in your car that night simply to get lectured by an upperclassman, to face her wrongdoings and be counseled, right?"

"No, she didn't." I knew I'd royally screwed up. I'd lost credibility with my omission and now had to sit through any accusation they cared to level at me. "We had feelings for each other, yes, but we weren't "seeing" each other, we weren't secretly dating. It was more of a mutual, unspoken attraction, like keeping an eye on one another from afar. We understood there was no way we could act. And we didn't. She went out the gate with me once, we talked about a lot of things that night sitting in my car, but in the end, we both knew she needed to focus and finish her plebe year. In fact, I said as much when she departed, and she agreed. That was the last time we spoke, and that's the truth."

"When you say you talked about a lot of things, like what?"

"I don't recall everything. We talked about her family, where she was from, why she wanted to attend the Naval Academy, stuff like that."

"Anyone else she was seeing, an officer, another midshipman, perhaps? Did that come up?"

"Jonathan Sweet came up." There, I'd said his name. "Again, she maintained it was a one-time thing, during the Tea Dance. That was it. I'm sure you talked to him."

"Yes, we've spoken to him." Hanratty reached for the pitcher and poured himself some water. He offered to pour for me too, but I held up my hand, declining. "Tell us about Sweet. Do you two know each other?"

"Of course, we know each other. We were in the same company plebe summer, but we were never close, never really friends during these last three years."

Hanratty made some notes.

"C'mon, Agent Hanratty, I'm sure you know about our meeting in his room the day after Maddy went missing. And what happened, yes?"

"He said there were words, that you came up to his room and threatened him."

"Not before he threatened me." I was starting to get angry. Despite my earlier omission and associated guilt, I didn't like their implication, the sense that I was now being treated like a hostile witness, or worse, like their lead suspect. I needed to come clean about the charm bracelet before things got completely out of hand. "Look, gentlemen, I wanted to bring this up earlier, but the time never presented itself. I was given an item by my classmate, Posey Shelnutt, who found it the same time he found the plebe shoulder board, in the same location."

"You mean the shoulder board that was turned in three weeks ago?"

"Yes. Another item was found by Pose in the street next to it, at the same time."

"Another part of a uniform?" Hanratty and Haney both looked incredulous.

"No. A bracelet. I have it in my desk. I planned to bring it down."

I could see their wheels turning.

"In fact, I can go get it, now."

They eyed me carefully. "No, Mitch, no rush," Hanratty said. "No rush whatsoever. Why you've had it for three weeks now. What difference is a few more hours going to make? Or another day? Or another week for that matter? No, by all means, take your time. Deliver us this potentially valuable piece of evidence whenever it's convenient. Whenever it suits you."

They were truly scaring me. "I'm only trying to help," I said, meekly. "I'll go get it." I stood up.

Hanratty motioned for me to take my seat. "Mitch, let's stop for a moment, shall we?"

"Huh?"

"Yes, sit down, please. Let's pause and assess the situation, put the pieces together, see what we've got."

"Put the pieces together?"

"Yes, hypothetically speaking." He leaned back in his chair. "Here's a scenario: you're the kidnapper, you took her that night and murdered her."

"*Me?*"

"We're talking hypothetical, so bear with me. You now admit the two of you took a drive out to a park the Saturday before she went missing?"

"Yes."

"So, you asked Maddy out, under the pretense that it's a date. You've been keeping an eye on her from afar as you put it, you have a mutual admiration going, a crush perhaps, going back to the summer, back to your first encounter in her room. Maddy agrees to go along. She likes you. She trusts you. She's done this before, so why not? She sneaks out of the Hall, hops in your car, you find the park, appreciating its dark, remote location, its quiet ambiance. You shut off the engine and tell her we need to have a little talk. Maybe you don't like the fact that she's been seeing Jonathan Sweet, maybe you tell her to stop, for her own good, of course. She takes exception, tells you she'll see whoever she wants to see, that you're in no position to be jealous. The conversation doesn't proceed well. She tells you to take her back to the Hall, that this was a mistake. You're upset, you reluctantly drive her back but argue the whole time about her careless behavior. You hold out hope you can change her mind. When you pull into your parking spot back in the Yard, she tries to get out of the car, you grab her wrist, she pulls away and flees, disappears, as you put it, into the dark of the night. You're angry. You're also worried she'll tell, but really, who's she going to tell? She's broken about ten regulations herself, so you're safe."

"Agent Hanratty, please. You are way off base. That doesn't remotely resemble what happened that night." The truth was, except for the grabbing her wrist part, it eerily resembled what happened that night.

"Again, we're using our imagination here."

I shifted uncomfortably in my chair as Haney's eyes drilled in on me, observing every nuance.

Hanratty continued. "Which brings us to the night of her disappearance. You were on watch, but you still want to see her. You're still seething from last week. You notice she's signed out to her sponsor's, outside the Yard, clear out on Perry Circle, but she'll return sometime before taps. She'll have to. And, as luck would have it, she leaves early and decides to walk, the night air will do her good. You're on watch, you have rounds to make, you enjoy a sort of autonomous freedom, yet you're still on watch with certain constraints. And here's where we need to keep using our imagination." Hanratty paused to take a breath. "Mitch, remind me again, who found the missing plebe shoulder board? And this bracelet you now speak of?"

"Pose Shelnutt?"

"Ah, yes, Midshipman Posey Shelnutt. And where might he fit into all this? He's an odd duck, wouldn't you say?"

Bringing Posey into his "hypothetical" threw me for a loop. It also frightened me because I'd been wondering the same thing myself. Why the hell would Pose decide to wander out the gate early Sunday morning and "find" two of Maddy's missing articles, then hide them over Christmas break. "I'm not sure I follow the question, Agent Hanratty," I said, attempting to buy time. "We're all odd in some manner." I looked directly at Haney.

"Odd, indeed. But this guy, in fact, an idiot savant, a distorted view of reality, loner, extremely loyal, would do anything for a classmate, am I right?"

"I suppose. But still—"

"So, Posey waits patiently, as instructed, for Maddy to come down the walk from Perry Circle."

"*Posey?*"

"He's sitting in his car watching the steps the way a dog would watch for his master. He spies Maddy at precisely 2100, steps out of the car, tells her she shouldn't be out walking alone on a night like this. He offers her a ride back to the Hall and she easily accepts because, one, she knows him and, two, Posey is about as cute and harmless as a puppy dog. Instead, Posey decides to take a drive by the Santee Basin, coincidentally where our Fifth Battalion Officer of the Watch was dispatched. Maddy doesn't like what she sees when Posey pulls up and attempts to flee the car as soon as it stops along the sea wall. You grab her, you tell her to calm down, no one's going to hurt you. You just want to talk. She screams, says let go, drops something. You grab her arm harder and twist it. She hits you, you hit back, hard, maybe with a blunt object. She goes down. You didn't mean to hurt her, you had no choice. She screamed, she was making a scene. Besides, she was way out of line talking to you that way the other night. All you did was want to tell her she was wrong and needed to apologize. Now this – dead girl. You tell Posey to leave, get back to the Hall, you didn't see anything. Being the gullible child that he is, he does as instructed. He keeps quiet, he hides evidence. You toss the body in the trunk hoping no one sees you. You look around. The coast seems clear—"

It's at this point in Hanratty's narrative I had to laugh out loud. And my laughter was borne from relief that he'd completely missed the boat on the Pose. "Nice try. You had me going there for a moment. You really did."

"What?" Hanratty flashed a fake smile. "You don't like it? Am I not painting a clear enough picture for you?"

"Not painting an accurate picture is more like it. First, Pose doesn't own a car. I doubt he even owns a driver's license. Second, he would never intentionally hide evidence or cover-up being witness to a murder. He's abundantly open and truthful, practically to a fault. I'm sorry, Agent Hanratty, your narrative is flawed."

"Is it, Mitch? Is it that far off? What if we take Pose Shelnutt out of the loop? Is it still flawed?"

"Of course, it is."

"Oh, on the contrary. Without Posey, my narrative still has legs, in fact, it gets stronger. Can you account for your time, the full hour mind you, after you left the battalion office at 2030, walked to Santee Basin and returned at 2130?"

311

"Yes." I understood his point and had to think. An hour was a long time to simply walk out to the basin, make a two-minute inspection of the yawls and walk back. "I took the long way around," I said. "Through the Mid Store parking lot, around the first wing, Tecumseh Court and then into Dahlgren Hall. There was an informal hop that night, the place was packed. Part of Bow Wow's job is to patrol "Disco" Dahlgren and be on the lookout for drunken misconduct, mids out of uniform, wild behavior, that sort of thing. That filled the entire hour. I'm certain, yes."

"You talk to anyone along the way? Can anyone corroborate your journey?

"I'm sure they can. Someone must've seen me in Dahlgren. As I said, the place was packed."

"Can you name a specific person, someone you talked to, anywhere, that would remember seeing you?"

"I'm sure I can."

Hanratty made a point to open his notebook, flip to a blank page and position his pen, eager to write. "Go ahead, give me a name. I'm ready."

"I don't have one. But I'm sure many people saw me that night." I was starting to sweat. This was not going well. Hanratty was forcing me down a path, one I was certain he didn't truly believe himself. This was supposed to be his "hypothetical." "Look, I get it, you have a problem," I said. "A girl goes missing in the Yard at 2100, and because she was from my company and because I can't account for my exact presence at 2100, you pin the whole thing on me, mystery solved, case closed. You no longer have a problem. Is that the way this works?"

The agents exchanged looks. Hanratty rose, walked behind my chair and placed a friendly hand on my shoulder. "Ah, Mitch." He spoke in a fatherly tone. "That's not the way this works. I still have a problem."

"Yeah, what's that?" I felt extremely relieved, but perspiration had formed soaking the inside of my uniform.

"I don't have a body. And that's a big problem. In my little scenario, you would've either dumped the body in the bay that night or kept it in your trunk overnight and dumped it elsewhere. In any case, it would've washed up by now. Or, been dug up by animals in the shallow grave you would've hastily dug. We're still searching but that's my problem – no body after two months. Zip, zero, nada." Hanratty paused as if to consider the weight of his own statement. "We find a body, it's a whole new ballgame."

"Indeed."

He released his hand from my shoulder and faced me. "Mitch, you can go now. I think we're done here."

I was shocked but thrilled. *I can go now?* I felt I'd been through hours of intense interrogation, Hanratty just hitting his stride. Nonetheless, I stood, unsure if I should shake their hands. It didn't seem natural after being painted a murderer and kidnapper by these two men. "What about the bracelet? Should I, uh—"

Both Haney and Hanratty moved toward the conference room door, buttoned their jackets, smiled warmly, each shaking my hand. "Bring it by later today, just drop it with the secretary. We'll give her some instructions." Hanratty thrust a business card into my hand. "Thanks for your time today, Mitch. We'll be in touch."

I didn't just walk back to my room, I skipped. I wasn't sure what I felt but elation and relief were right up there. When I walked down to 4-1 earlier, I was confident, practically fearless. I was going to ask *them* the score, why *they* were dragging their feet, why *they* didn't have Maddy's disappearance solved. Near the end, I felt like slinking out of the conference room thankful for not being led out in chains. Their interrogation had scared the hell out of me. It was easy to see how innocent people confessed to crimes they didn't commit. These guys were pros at finding holes, inconsistencies and gray areas in the most innocent of suspects and their stories. I'd done nothing wrong, yet I felt guilty. Something was still gnawing at me though, something not quite right. How'd they know about my car ride with Maddy? I was certain she'd told no one. And shouldn't they have asked me more about the bracelet with the defective clasp and any conversation I'd had with Bob and Jan? That would've made me feel better, to show them I'd pinpointed Maddy's exact disappearance, time and place. Wouldn't they want this information, or had they already figured that part out? And all that callous talk about a body, as if it were just one more piece of evidence to be shoved in a bag. Until today, I'd been in denial, not admitting Maddy was dead, that she was only missing and would eventually turn up. Hanratty had filled my head with images of bloated corpses floating down the Severn River just waiting to be discovered by a jogger or fisherman, or baying hounds pawing wildly at a shallow grave beneath a tree in some remote park. These thoughts made my blood run cold. When I returned to the company area, it was mostly deserted. Everyone was down in the Wardroom eating lunch. I sat at my desk in the hushed silence, looked out the window and began to bawl. Maddy was gone, forever. If that wasn't clear before, it certainly was now. Hanratty and Haney *had* painted the perfect picture. They weren't hot on the trail of a runaway or a kidnapper demanding ransom, piecing together intricate clues as they went. They were chasing a dead body.

Tuesday, 8 February 1977

The Mate of the Deck stuck his head in my room, a third-class with the afternoon watch. I didn't have any classes after lunch and was trying to finish up a lab report for one of my engineering courses. "Mitch, Lieutenant Herrera wants to see you. He's up on 6-4 in Captain Manley's office."

"Right now?"

"Yeah. Said if you were in your room to come on up."

I sighed. I would need to put the rest of my class uniform back on, tie and all. "On my way. Manley's office upstairs, you say?"

"Yeah, and better put your spiffy back on too, him being a Marine and all."

I smiled. "They say what it was about?"

"Nah, he sounded pretty relaxed on the phone though, but that's just Herrera."

When I got up to 6-4 to Manley's office, the two company officers were seated around his desk appearing to have a pleasant chat, which I took as a good sign. Herrera looked up from his cushioned chair. "Mitch, thanks for coming up. You know Captain Manley, yes?"

"Yes, sir." Who *didn't* know him? The introduction, I suspected, was more for Manley's benefit. He extended a hand, not making eye contact. We shook briefly.

Manley was talking before I could get to my chair. "So, Mitch, how was your day in the breech yesterday?"

"You mean my NIS interview? I didn't think we were supposed to talk about it. At least that's what the memo from the Commandant stressed."

Herrera jumped in for Manley. "Mitch, we know you can't discuss the ongoing investigation, but we heard, uh, Captain Manley feels a crusade has been launched looking for, well, that their focus has not been—"

"That their focus has *certainly* not been on the ball," Manley said, completing the sentence. "What Mike's trying to say is they've turned their investigation into a search and destroy mission. Those two limp dicks who couldn't find their asses with both hands are onto something else. *This*." He waved a hand at some official-looking message on his desk.

"This?" I said. I had to chuckle at Manley's colorful description of Hanratty and Haney, but I didn't get the impression they were solely after harassment violations.

"Mitch," Manley said, making eye contact for the first time. "Did they, at any time, ask you about how the women were fairing since the summer. How they're being treated around the Hall?"

"Well," I thought back. "We touched on it, maybe briefly. Yes, as I now recall, one of their questions asked if I felt the women were accepted or was it our company's unspoken mission to run them off."

"See? I knew it," Manley said, pounding his fist on his desk. "This is exactly what I'm talking about."

I jumped from the sudden noise. "We didn't pursue it though. I felt they wanted to understand the environment, the attitude the women are dealing with, not necessarily put anyone on report."

"They ask you specifically about anyone?" Manley said. "Any female mid in particular?"

I thought about Sara and how Haney had pinned me down on the name-calling. "They did bring up Miss Sedgley, the derogatory nicknames, why she quit, stuff like that."

Manley shot Herrera a knowing look.

"What about O'Connor?"

"We talked a lot about Miss O'Connor, of course," I said. "They pursued some harassment stuff but—"

"Did they mention any other company officer's names, a battalion officer?"

"Not that I recall."

Manley gave Herrera another look. I studied each man carefully, wondering why I was here, where this questioning was going. Was it to corroborate Manley's suspicion that these two NIS bozos were here to investigate sexual harassment charges? Or were they simply giving it legitimacy along with Maddy's disappearance in an attempt to link the two? I was reminded of Bob and Jan's comments to me that Sunday morning at their quarters, about Manley possibly badgering Maddy about why she was here, about making disparaging female remarks to her face, about getting her to quit. This would fit the mold. Manley was a recruiting poster Marine brought to USNA as a company officer to promote Marine recruitment in the afterglow of his embassy triumph in Saigon. He was a natural leader and the mids flocked to him in droves, especially the ones wanting to go Marine Corps on service selection night. He wasn't a stickler for many of the "Mickey Mouse regs," as he put it, around the Hall unless it involved haircut and uniform standards. He carelessly slung his Marine profanity, drank beer with his firsties and enjoyed telling vulgar sea stories rich in the Corps vernacular. But more importantly, he achieved the results he was hired for, personally increasing Marine recruitment numbers among the class of '76 last year, exceeding the goal, and was on track to do the same this year. However, he was also unapologetically outspoken in his opposition regarding women at the Academy and had written a persuasive memo to anyone who cared to read it before the girls arrived in July. I think the administration initially tolerated Manley's attitude, appreciating his leadership gifts and combat experience, thinking he would round out the midshipmen's experience and eventually wise up and toe the party line.

"Mitch," Manley said, "I can see the wheels turning up there, so I'll just say it plainly to both of you. It's my humble opinion this entire fuckin' investigation has evolved into a witch hunt, a diversion, while they wait for a body to just magically appear. In the meantime, they cover their asses by taking action on all the outstanding harassment complaints that have been piling up. They are going door to door in Bancroft Hall intimidating every mid that ever spoke to O'Connor while they should be looking beyond these walls for a killer rather than what's it like to be some poor, picked-on woman

315

at USNA. There's been a murder, for Christ's sake." His eyes narrowed. He slowed his rant. "We met with the parents, Mike and me. Those NIS whiz kids tell you that?"

"No, sir."

"They're petrified."

"Who's petrified? The agents?"

He ignored the question. "They ask you about the family?"

"The O'Connor's, sir?"

"No, Mitch, the Pruitt's of Fucking Southampton. Pay attention." He flashed a quick half-smile to show he wasn't going for my jugular. "They ask you about her essay?"

I was now completely lost and afraid of appearing more confused. Was he talking about Maddy's application essay? The one she mentioned in my car that night? "No, sir. There was no discussion about any essay." I spoke confidently but was clearly at sea.

"What about Commander Fowler, over in First Batt? Or that other joker in 18th?"

"Uh, no, sir. No mention of Commander Fowler or—"

"You sure?"

"Yes, sir."

Manley stroked his chin. "Okay, fair enough." He stared at Herrera and me. "Still, these are leads, goddamn it. I don't get it. The clues are strewn before them like trash in an empty field. Why they're dragging their squid feet on this is beyond me." He paused, looking down at his desk again. "Ah, but who am I to question anything anymore? I'm history. Gone. Persona non-grata."

I had no idea what he was talking about, what any of this meant.

Manley continued. "I'm going to let you in on a little secret, Mitch. It'll all be public tomorrow anyway. I've received orders, fresh off the presses. I'm to leave good ol' USNA and 28th Company for good. Six months early in fact. And I'll tell you something else. I'm sorry, really sorry about that broad, O'Connor. She didn't deserve this. I just hope they can figure it all out, for her family's sake. They won't, of course, because either someone's pulling strings, or we've got the most piss-poor excuse for NIS agents ever put on the planet."

My head was spinning. Was Manley a suspect? Or was he a suspect at one time and now being shoved out as a token sacrifice for his vehement anti-woman stance? Could the Academy no longer cover for a squared-away Marine that was on the fast track to becoming a dinosaur in the age of women's lib? There was simply too much doubletalk coming at me too quickly.

Herrera looked disturbed. "Mitch, you're not to breathe a word until I announce the news at quarters tomorrow morning. I'll be taking over both companies under the direction of Commander Egan until a replacement is announced. Captain Manley has accepted orders back to Okinawa. That's all you need to know for now."

Herrera stood. It was like he was formulating the speech he'd give tomorrow morning, practicing hearing the words himself. I stood with him, taking my cue that the meeting was over. I wanted to say goodbye to Manley, wish him luck, something. He knew stuff, we still needed to talk. Instead, Herrera placed a guiding hand on my shoulder and steered me toward the door ahead of him, bidding Manley a good day for both of us.

When I returned to the company area, Neil met me at the stairs and directed me back to our room. "C'mon, Mitch. Got something you should know."

"What?"

"Just follow me to the room."

When we got there, Dan Buell, a plebe from our company was seated at Neil's desk. He started to stand but Neil motioned him back down. "Tell him, Buell, tell him what you found out."

"You mean from when I was on watch that night, sir?"

"Yes, yes. Start from the beginning where you told me about— Oh, the hell with it. I'll tell him." Neil looked at me. "Mitch, remember the night Maddy went missing? You were the Bow Wow? I was in the duty section? Buell here was the CMOD?"

I just stared back.

"Well, you were pretty steamed when you found out later we had an unidentified visitor come on deck and I never told you, right? Buell here, being the intrepid mate that night, never identified him except to say he was wearing civilian clothes and only saw CDR on his ID card when he flashed it. Never made a log entry."

"Yeah, so? Where's this headed, Neil?"

"Tell him, Buell."

"Well, Mr. King and I, sir, we went to some of the other company areas yesterday, checked some of their past CMOD logs. You know, from that night and—"

Neil jumped back in. "And, to make a long story short, ol' Detective Buell found two such logs with entries from November 20th – one from 1st Company and one from 23rd Company, both on zero-deck, both Mates of the Deck in fact recording the name and rank of our mystery guest as he passed through their area on his way up to us."

"Swell. And will our mystery guest please sign in," I said, sarcastically, not enjoying the drama. "Who was he, Neil?"

"Commander Richard Fowler, 1st Batt Officer," he said, proudly.

I stared at both Buell and Neil. "Yeah, okay. So, what's the link? What's it supposed to mean?"

Neil smiled, taking a sip from a Pepsi he'd just opened. "I don't have a clue, Mitch. But it's information. He took another sip and set it down. "You know, someone once told me, think Columbo, man, ask the follow-up. Ask yourself the follow-up. What was he doing in the Hall that Saturday night? In civilian clothes? Clear on the other side of the world?"

Neil had a piece of new information, true. He was excited, felt the call to action. I stood before him, thinking. Thinking. Thinking this was all meaningless, random shit. "I don't know, Neil. Ten thousand things must've happened that night. They can't all be connected."

"Yeah, but this deserves a second look. Doesn't it fit with any of the information the NIS boys might've shared or let slip yesterday?"

I was about to yell an emphatic *no* until I remembered what Manley had mentioned upstairs. "Hey, hang on, Neil. Hang on. This just might fit together with something. I'm not sure what though. Wait here for a bit, let me get back to you." I turned and ran back out the door.

# 19

## THE ADMIRAL

Friday, 29 April 1977

DURING THE FOUR YEARS at the Naval Academy, midshipmen are availed ample opportunity for indoctrination into the military etiquette and social strata of officer life. This includes dressy affairs such as the tea dances as a plebe, the formal hops as an upperclassman, dining outs and other less-formal occasions in the Yard such as attending a play or chapel or visiting your sponsor's. Attending the Superintendent's reception shortly before graduation is one of the final obligatory highlights on the social calendar.

The supe's reception was the reason Fifth Battalion's first-class were gathered at his grand mansion next to the Chapel on this spectacular spring afternoon. Neil and I and a few other company mates had made the short walk from the Hall and were now in the long receiving line to meet the dignitaries arrayed in the foyer like a military ball. Except this was not a military ball. It looked more like a who's who of the top brass on the Academy staff, including the academic dean and some three-star admiral I didn't recognize. All the senior officers, two of them flag rank, were lined up, wives next to them in semi-formal attire, facing the receiving line and being introduced to each midshipman as we passed. I was first introduced to the Superintendent, Rear Admiral Ervin Rodgers and his wife, Catherine. We knew her nickname was Cat but was always addressed as Mrs. Rodgers to anyone under the rank of full captain. She was a very gracious, petit woman playing the tireless hostess to the thousands of reception guests that trooped through her home each year. Rodgers himself was an impressive figure and minor celebrity within the service. He was the skipper of VA-173 based on the *USS Franklin D Roosevelt* in 1967 when he was shot down in his A-4, spending six years as a POW in the Hanoi Hilton. I was honored to finally meet him face to face and shake his hand. Next in line was the three-star I didn't know, and his wife. I did a doubletake when his aide introduced us. "Admiral Tennant, this is Midshipman Mitchell Baumann," he said, after reading from my nametag. I was momentarily dazed. *Uncle Harley!* I shook his hand firmly and offered a polite greeting. His wife seemed stiff, her hand

319

limp when I took it as if she were bored, just going through the motions.

After the receiving line, I gathered with a group of my classmates outside on the rear terrace, marveling at the guest list and the house itself. I'd never been inside the Superintendent's quarters nor viewed the Yard from such a vantage point. The four stories and 34 rooms along with a lush garden half the size of a football field were integrated skillfully into the Yard's tight design using every bit of scarce acreage that was allotted during construction in 1906. I stood overlooking the manicured lawn, the azaleas in fiery spring bloom and seeing Dahlgren Hall beyond the fence line at an unfamiliar angle that made me dizzy. In the foreground, down on the lawn were clusters of my classmates holding drinks, some from 28th Company. I spotted Jon Sweet, Dan Flores and a few others standing in a tight knot, laughing, as if sharing some inside joke. I felt a pang of remorse, reminded how the integration of women at the Academy had created a sharp divide among many of the mids this year, especially the first-class. Sweet and I were no longer on speaking terms after our confrontation in his room and Caleb Wise and I spoke only out of necessity. Many other friendships had suffered since the investigation. Battle lines were still drawn over the women and Maddy's disappearance, surprisingly, had not defused the situation. Her investigation had served only to create a deeper subtext of mistrust and unease among many of the mids in Fifth Batt, and Captain Manley's abrupt departure had fanned the flames. Now, after nearly five months since that night in November, there'd been no new developments, no newfound evidence, no arrests, no dead body, nothing. The NIS agents, Haney and Hanratty, hadn't been seen in weeks.

"You know, I get why Commander Egan's attending today but what's *he* doing here?" Neil said, nodding at the officer standing next to Admiral Tennant. He was referring to Commander Fowler, 1st Batt Officer. Egan was our battalion officer. Seeing him here made sense, but Fowler? None of his mids were in attendance. "He's the one those NIS clowns shoulda been asking some pointed questions."

I knew it bugged Neil that we never got a straight answer to Fowler's visit to our company area. "Guess he's a friend of the Admiral's," I said.

"Yeah, right."

"So, let's go say hello," I suggested. "To this Tennant fellow."

Neil jumped back. "Are you out of your mind? Why the hell would we do that? We just met them all in the receiving line."

"Yeah, but we're supposed to mingle, chat them up, be social. Isn't that why we're here?"

"Mitch, I'm not going over to shoot the breeze with some big admiral just for giggles. The guy has just taken over as Commander, Seventh Fleet. He reports to CINCPAC and the Joint Chiefs; he's met the President. What makes you think he's got anything to say to us? Or us to him, for that matter?"

"Oh, I don't know," I said, breaking with Neil and heading in Tennant's direction. "I think it'll be fun." *Uncle Harley, Uncle Harley,* kept flashing in my head like a neon sign.

I approached a group of about a dozen officers and mids ringing Tennant like worker bees surrounding their queen, all smiles, listening to him hold court. I stood on the outer fringes listening to what sounded like a colorful sea story, the Admiral waxing poetically about his role in the mining of Haiphong Harbor during the Vietnam War. I soon became captivated by Tennant, observing his soft-spoken manner, strong will, and command presence. He radiated a magnetic forcefield that I sensed could either attract or repel, holding the reins of power like a birthright. According to our program, he'd had nothing but success since graduation in 1949, gaining higher rank and responsibility and status as he climbed the ladder. I noticed his awards, six impressive rows of ribbons – the Legion of Merit with Combat V, Achievement Medal, Navy and Marine Corps Commendation Medal with Combat V, Air Medal with silver star among other decorations, topped with gold Naval Aviator wings. The guy was polished, no doubt, an accomplished leader and skilled politician, and, as Maddy reminded me, likely our next Chief of Naval Operations. I wondered how closely he knew the O'Connor family and just what his connection to the investigation might be. Hell, he'd have to be involved. I mean, a three-star admiral, a friend of the family, that family's daughter goes missing under a cloud of kidnapping and possible murder? He'd have to have a role in the ensuing investigation, turning the screws, keeping things alive with his significant weight and personal interest. After all, Maddy was his "niece," for crying out loud.

After the story ended and crowd thinned, I moved closer to Tennant feeling guided by an external force. Tennant was standing with Fowler and a lieutenant commander, presumably his aide, and now appeared in serious conversation. As I grew closer, his countenance quickly changed to a very welcoming, benign father figure as if eager to talk to any mid bold enough to make his approach. I reintroduced myself and added I was from 27th Company, hoping that rang a bell.

"Fine, son, that's great," he said, appearing to make no connection between Maddy and 27. "Was in 12th Company myself. Pleased to know you." He seemed distracted, his eyes scanning the room with a cool urgency tracking a person or competing event over my shoulder. "Jesus," he suddenly muttered. I was tempted to turn, half-expecting to see the Chapel dome imploding before my eyes but remained focused. "So, service selection occurred the other night," he continued, his eyes resettling on me. "Did I hear right?"

"Yes, sir." *If you call six weeks ago the other night.*

"Tell me, which branch are you headed for? And don't dare say nuclear power." His aide and Commander Fowler started cracking up as if on cue,

Tennant himself smiling.

"No, sir." I looked at Tennant's gold wings and proudly stated, "Naval Aviation, sir."

"Good, good. Glad to hear Rickover's demons didn't claim another soul for their silent service." More laughter by Fowler and the aide. "And your plans are to fly jets, get your hands on one of the new Tomcats, perhaps?"

"No, Admiral. I'm leaning towards the P-3 Orion, sir." I didn't dare add they'd be the best aircraft to make the transition to the airlines, multiengine and land-based.

"The P-3? Why hell, son, why would anyone do that?" Tennant looked at Fowler and smiled. "They're just a bunch of limited aviators – not truly part of the tailhook Navy." He placed a hand on my shoulder chuckling several times with his aide while Fowler just stood there, a stupid grin on his face. "Limited aviator," Tennant uttered over and over in a whisper, shaking his head like it was a bad word. "Remind me again, Mitch, which company are you in?"

"Twenty-seven, sir. Midshipman Madison O'Connor's company." There. I said her name. I hoped that finally made things clear.

His smile turned solemn, reflective. "Yes," he said, placing a hand on his chin. "Any news on that front?"

"I was hoping you'd tell me, sir. Miss O'Connor spoke often of you."

"She did, eh? Well, yes, I know the family. Very sad situation." He was either very sad or very uncomfortable, his face growing dark. "I've spoken with them, assuring them we're doing all we can."

"Yes, sir. And what is that, may I ask? The investigation seems to have turned cold. No news, no leads."

The looks on all three men's faces changed. I'd intended to put the NIS on report, throw them under the bus, but I'd gone too far. Still, I wouldn't get an opportunity like this again. I needed to keep pressing but Tennant's aide jumped to the rescue. "Midshipman Baumann, the Admiral just said—"

"I know. I know what he said, sir. I'm just surprised everything's stopped. There's been no further questioning, no activity. I think…" I looked right at Fowler. "I think they should expand the search before they shut it off entirely. Talk to some more people."

Tennant spoke up. "No one's shut anything off, not yet. And it would behoove you to leave it to the professionals. As I said, they're doing all they can."

"But—"

"Mitch, thank you for this chat." The aide placed his hand gently around my waist. "I think this concludes your time with the admiral. Come this way, please." He led me to a butler's pantry about twenty feet from Tennant and stepped back eying me, almost daring me to rejoin their circle. I instead turned and walked back onto the sunporch feeling numb.

*All they can, huh? You mean by assigning that crack NIS team of Stan and Ollie to the case? Letting the investigation run its course for months without a single lead or arrest? Turning it into a sexual harassment witch hunt instead of a murder investigation? Getting a decorated Marine officer fired, ruining his career? You're right, sir. You have done all you can, time to step aside.* I knew Tennant wasn't personally overseeing the investigation or supervising the NIS agency but figured he certainly could use his position of authority, his firepower, his personal connection to the family to apply pressure and make things move faster. Why did it seem like the opposite was occurring? Limited aviator. What an asshole.

Wednesday, 8 June 1977

June Week and graduation were a blur. Only Mother showed up and she arrived the day before, no Dad, no Amber. I was saddened to learn Amber had suffered a relapse and was running with her druggie crowd, coming home only sporadically to change clothes. This was inevitable given all that was going on at home, or *not* going on at home, that forced Amber's hand, allowing her to drift back to the dark side in the face of no suitable supervision by a set of functional adults. I'd foreseen as much at Christmas. I think Mother enjoyed springing the news then quickly followed up with, "And we're not going to talk about any of that. I'm here to see my son graduate."

The morning of June 8th was magnificent, a cloudless day under a bright blue sky. I'd asked Jack and Irene, my sponsors, to join us and they were eager and right on time. We gathered outside the Navy-Marine Corps Memorial Stadium's gate before the ceremony began. After some quick introductions I took my position on the field among my 900-plus classmates while Mother, Jack and Irene headed for their seats in the stands. Of course, Mother was dressed for the occasion in what I'm sure she deemed appropriate. Overdressed would've more aptly described it. She was wearing a black cocktail dress, pearls, stiletto heels and Gucci sunglasses, her hair done professionally into some sort of modern wave earlier this morning. She looked stunning for her age but out of place. Jack wore a pair of simple khaki slacks and Navy golf shirt, Irene in a pretty sundress and fashionable hat. They looked comfortable in their surroundings and happy to have been invited. I imagined them as my parents, desperately wishing they were, Mother simply the wealthy aunt asked to tag along as a courtesy by her sister, Irene.

The ceremony began on time, precisely at 10:30 with the national anthem and invocation followed by the introduction of the guest speaker, Vice President Walter Mondale. Mondale gave a disappointing, lackluster policy speech on nuclear weapon proliferation and our need to reestablish the SALT II discussions with the Soviets. Boring. Even the Superintendent looked catatonic as Mondale droned on from the podium. My mind wandered. I was still hung up on the investigation's gradual deterioration, almost like it was planned. I, like many of my classmates in the company had expected, had held out hope, that a resolution, a conclusion to the investigation would occur coinciding with graduation, that all things would be tidied up, a suspect named or Maddy found, something. Yet here we were, carrying on today like Maddy was just another bump in the road, something we felt for a few weeks back in the Dark Ages but had moved on. I was at loose ends over everything, a hollowness in my heart. I couldn't just move on. Here we were about to scatter for good and there'd been zero resolution, little hope of anything flickering back to life. What could I do? Just let it die?

After the speech, events moved quickly. It was time to receive our diplomas. I walked up on stage, was handed mine from the Vice President himself and shook his hand, posing briefly for a picture. Part of me felt like asking him pointblank, *What the hell's being done about Maddy?* But I didn't, of course. I simply turned and made my way down the ramp from where I'd come. The oath of office was administered next, the entire class being sworn in as newly commissioned ensigns or second lieutenants, then a congratulatory offering by the Superintendent. Finally, our class president took the podium, proposing three cheers for those we were about to leave behind. *Hip-hip-hooray-hip-hip-hooray-hip-hip-hooray!* The traditional hat toss followed, our old midshipman covers sent flying skyward. Jack, Irene and my mother met me on the grass field afterward for a quick round of family photos. Jack took several of my mother and Irene with me, each pinning an ensign shoulder board to my dress white uniform. I then insisted Mother take a shot of Jack and Irene flanking me, an arm around each, in what I imagined would be the real family photo, my dream parents.

Graduation was a relief, I admit, a closure to four long years. Still, I was just sad inside.

# 20

## PENSACOLA, FLORIDA

Thursday, 25 August 1977

I DIDN'T GO HOME TO CALIFORNIA after graduation. I couldn't. Instead, I chose to burn up my 30-day basket leave by driving up the east coast to Martha's Vineyard in my tiny MG. I couldn't afford to stay on the island, so I made a day trip out of it, riding the morning ferry out and spending the night back in Falmouth before a quick detour up the Cape. I was struck by the obvious contrast between the free and easy California surf culture and east coasters with their formality and self-imposed summer dress codes. It was everywhere – the conscious awareness of status, the attire, the posturing with their once-over glances. I swore after my Christmas visit, I wasn't going to return home, ever. Yet, after driving past miles and miles of gray ocean and unremarkable terrain melting into the meager surf, I was homesick. I decided to make the U-turn south, days ahead of my plan and continued at a snail's pace down I-95 making stops in New Haven and Manassas before arriving at my final destination on the Redneck Riviera.

To say Pensacola reminded me of Aimee was an understatement. I was captivated as soon as I entered the city limits, drawn to that exact nightspot where we met two summers ago, nearly two years to the day. I drove up to the bar, Phineas Phogg, sat out front in my car, engine idling, imagining hearing the music from that night, the deep bass from Bachman Turner Overdrive, the commotion on the dance floor, Aimee slipping her hand into mine and tugging me toward her red Mustang...

*Stop. Get a grip, Baumann.* I watched a couple exit the bar and jump into a waiting cab. I had no idea if she was still in town, but it didn't matter. *Aimee is gone. For good. Out of your life.* She'd made it clear in her letter she needed her space, a long-distance relationship simply out of the question borne of innocence and naivety.

When I checked into the BOQ at NAS Pensacola, I still had ten unused leave days I unknowingly surrendered when the duty officer stamped my orders. The hell with it, I thought. I had nowhere else to go until flight school started. Instead, I looked up some of my bachelor classmates that had

325

similar reporting dates and we got drunk, just totally shitfaced at many of the sleazy watering holes around Escambia county. I was rapidly embracing the life of debauchery and alcoholism in my first full month as an ensign. I drank more tequila shots than Sammy Hagar, played a lot of pool with my friends, looked for fights, drove home completely blotto at 4 A.M. and flopped on my BOQ mattress only to rinse and repeat the next day. It wasn't until I was driving home one night, listening to the radio at full blast, speeding back to base that I paused to consider the possibility I was living a dangerous life and that behaving recklessly just might have consequences, that this wave of destruction was an ebb and flow of all the anger and self-pity pent up inside when—

*Hello it's me…* the song continued with its melodic, introspective lyrics. I found myself singing along, enjoying its relevance and soaking up the mood, when all of a sudden lightning struck. "And that was Todd Rundgren from *Something Anything*. I'm Aimee Erikson and glad you're along with me tonight on the Coast 104—"

My God, it was her, Aimee, in a soft sexy, polished radio voice, one I hadn't heard. She hadn't left. She was still working the same job, likely living in the same apartment, going out with the same girlfriends, just waiting for me to swoop in and rescue her. I looked down at the radio dial as if expecting to see Aimee's face staring back. *Go find her. Take her back,* it said.

It took hearing her voice on the radio again, this time sober, to realize I'd given myself a tall order. Just go find her and take her back? Who was I kidding? There were two equal and opposite forces in play. First, I needed to resolve the conundrum Neil had placed in my head after reading her letter. *Fate is funny that way.* In Neil's version, Aimee was doing anything but letting fate take charge. She was moving the pieces around the board and I needed to wake up and play my part. Second, and this loomed large, if I found her, our "chance" rendezvous would put me in a highly vulnerable state and could end badly. I would risk never seeing her again, things not working out like some idyllic rom-com movie. It was the latter that petrified me – all or nothing, one of life's pivotal moments. *Fate is funny that way.* I was injecting free will, forcing an outcome.

Nonetheless, I was at the end of options on this bright, sunny morning in August. I'd come to terms with my self-destructive lifestyle. A change was needed, time to alter course and stop sitting paralyzed by doubt. Aimee finished work in the early afternoon. By following her regular radio show for a week, I learned she was still on the air from 10 – 2, the other night in the car, probably substituting for another DJ. My plan was to meet her at the Coast 104 radio building north of town when her shift ended. I wouldn't spy or stalk her. I'd simply pop into the lobby. *Hello, it's me.* Roll the dice, take my chances.

The air was oppressive when I stepped from my air-conditioned car,

Aimee's radio station a small annex next to what looked like an abandoned furniture warehouse. There were no other cars in the small lot out front. I entered the empty lobby and glanced around – no receptionist, no other visitors, nothing but a locked door with combination pad and telephone hanging on the opposite wall, the station's music spilling from an overhead speaker. I paced around the room before deciding to pick up the receiver. It rang instantly. "Hang on, I'll be right out," a lady's voice answered on the other end, then click. *Aimee?* I took a deep breath.

It wasn't Aimee. It was a cute Asian girl, no accent, barely twenty, introducing herself simply as Jasmine, no last name. "Can I help you?" she asked.

"Hi, Jasmine. I'm Mitch. I'm looking for Aimee." I spoke the words casually like we were all friends. When she raised an eyebrow, I continued, "Aimee Erikson. She works here, right? Her show just ended?"

Jasmine laughed. "I'm sorry, Mitch, you've missed her. I think she's off today."

"But I just heard her. On the drive over."

She laughed again. "Oh, no, it's just a tape today, same as we do nights."

"A tape?"

"Yeah, we've lost some DJs. We tape their shows, edit and replay them. Tapes are the only way to survive until we hire more staff. Fools a lot of people."

"Well, it fooled me," I said, sad I'd missed her yet experiencing an odd sense of relief at the same time. "Do you know when she'll be back?"

"She usually comes in Tuesdays and Thursdays to work her sales job, but I haven't seen her." Jasmine shifted uneasily. "You want me to tell her you stopped by, maybe leave a message?"

I considered writing a note but was losing hope, feeling like I'd gone far enough. Let her find me, I thought. "No. Thanks anyway. Don't bother passing a message. I'll catch her next time."

I bid a hasty goodbye, pushed open the lobby door and reentered the steamy afternoon heat. I had nowhere to go since making muster this morning, so I breezed past my car, deciding to take a late lunch at the Bennigans across the street in the strip mall. I needed to think. I mean, was I serious about seeing this girl or not? If so, then why didn't I press Jasmine for more information, tell her to relay a message? If not, then why was I here in the first place? I was seated in a big booth opposite the front door letting this schizophrenic exchange run in my head when a woman touched my shoulder from behind and instantly slid onto the cushioned bench across from me. At first, I thought it was the waitress.

It was not.

"Aimee! My God. Where'd you come from?"

She had a smile pasted on her face and seemed just as surprised to see me.

327

"Hi, Mitch." Upon closer inspection, it was more an embarrassed grin.

"I just came looking for you. I mean, they said you weren't in. How'd you find me?"

"We watched you cross the street," she said. "Both of us." Again, the embarrassed grin.

"Ah, so you *were* there." I suddenly felt better despite the deception. "Why didn't you come out? Why'd Jasmine lie?"

"She was just following security protocol," Aimee said, staring at the tabletop. She looked elegant, different than the last time I'd seen her more than a year ago. There was a calm, measured air about her. Her hair was cut shorter, to shoulder-length. Her pretty face hadn't changed but her outfit, a skirt and simple blouse with light make-up and necklace, gave her a mature, professional look. She slid from the booth and stood up. At first, I thought she was leaving. *And she just got here.* She stepped closer, near my side of the table. Her eyes beckoned, so I stood, unsure of myself. "Come here," she said, reaching out in an embrace with both arms, bringing me tight. I returned the hug, rejoicing in her touch, her body pressed against mine, breathing in her familiar scent. "It's been a long time, Mitch."

"It has." I was dizzy with joy when I sat back down across from her, both of us dabbing our eyes. Still, I proceeded cautiously, her "Dear-John" as fresh in my mind as if I'd just opened it. "And I'm at a loss though. What happened to us? Why the— Why the letter?"

"I don't know, Mitch. It's hard to explain. There were issues, I guess. Things, limitations. You were a thousand miles away. What was I to do?"

Her response puzzled me. It was as though I'd moved away after we'd met, I was the one that'd broken up with her, leaving her in the lurch. "Aimee, I wasn't always going to be a thousand miles away."

"I know. Let's just say a long-distance relationship wasn't working for me back then. I was having a tough time. I was mixed up." She laughed and covered her mouth. "Not that I'm perfect now, mind you, but I'm doing okay. You know?"

"I'm happy for you," was all I could manage. A lot of missing pieces needed filling in. Still, we had time. We were together. I would be patient.

"So, tell me. You've finally graduated, huh? Here to be a Navy pilot?"

I gave her the light version of my time at the Academy, telling her about finishing up my final year, eking out a 3.0 QPR, selecting flight school, very little of my family's woes of Amber and my parents, and certainly nothing about Maddy and the bungled, now stagnant investigation. I explained I was in the student pool, basically in limbo state after finishing six weeks of aviation indoc and, due to student backlog, awaiting primary flight instruction at Whiting Field. "What about you? I heard you on the radio the other night. Jasmine told me it was a tape, or was she lying about that too?"

"No, it was a tape. We're running the station with a skeleton crew, no way around it, I'm afraid. So, you finally heard me, huh?" Her face brightened. "How'd I sound? Did it surprise you?"

I wanted to say it shocked the hell out of me, sobered me right up, but I softened it a bit. "It brought me to you, Aimee. It's the reason I'm here." I let the significance sink in before continuing. "So, my turn. What's been going on in your life? Have you gotten married or something?" I wanted to head off any bad news before she could spring it.

"Good God, no. Of course, not. Is that what you thought?"

"I didn't know what to think. Your letter was a punch in the gut. It raised more questions than it answered."

"I know. And I'm sorry, Mitch. I may have jumped the gun on that." She went on a long narrative explaining about her stepfather finally remarrying, her brother leaving Pensacola, currently stationed in San Diego aboard the USS *Kitty Hawk*, other news, both good and bad, about the radio station, her new apartment, but no information whatsoever about her wild girlfriends, love life, or other men in her life. I didn't pry, sitting quietly listening to her tales of the last two years. It was presented as a hopeful picture, like the optimist Aimee was, but there was an emptiness in her tone, like something was missing, clearly not a man, but something else. Perhaps an underlying sadness that life wasn't bringing the joy she deserved, or expectations not being met. Or was she simply distracted? When she finished, she glanced at her watch, stood up and announced she had to make a quick phone call, that she'd be right back.

I nodded and stood, watching her thread her way to a bank of payphones in back. A quick phone call? To whom? This was maddening, frustrating, more pieces to fill in later.

Aimee returned to the table in no more than three minutes. "Mitch, I need to run. I'd love to stay and chat longer, but I can't." Her tone was final, non-negotiable.

I couldn't let her go. Something told me this might be it, her simple way to brush me off, for good. "Can you say where you're going? Can I come with you?"

"No, I'm sorry. Not right now. Maybe soon. Can I call you later?"

"Aimee. Don't do this. I haven't seen you in over a year. And I don't have a phone. Let me call you." I felt my stomach sink, I was losing her, emotions were rushing to the surface. "I—" I almost said it. *I love you. Does that mean anything? I love you.* I was that close.

Aimee sensed my predicament, my loss for words and jumped in. "Okay, okay." She took a deep breath. "I'm not sure about this but— Can you come over tomorrow? Are you free? Say 3ish, to my apartment?"

"Your apartment? What aren't you sure of?" *Too late for lunch, too early for dinner.* "As I said, I'm in the student pool. I make muster at eight then I'm free."

She jotted down an address on the back of a napkin. "Then come, Mitch. Just come." She reached out for a quick hug goodbye, leaned close to my ear and whispered, "I still love you, you know."

Then she slipped away and was gone.

I stood in the foyer of the Bennigans experiencing about every possible emotion a guy can when he's in love and perplexed by a mysterious woman. Watching her jog back across the street, her hair flowing in the breeze, I finally said it aloud. "I love you too, Aimee."

Friday, 26 August 1977

Driving out to Aimee's apartment I couldn't help but recall the poignant moments that linked our tenuous relationship that lasted exactly a year. Due to the impossible geography involved, I could count on one hand the times we'd seen each other face to face in that span. The reality was our romantic connection was sustained solely through a series of phone calls and letters ebbing and flowing on Aimee's whims. Sometimes I'd have difficulty recalling her face and I'd start to panic, craving her scent, her smile, her soft touch. I was in love and was forced to cope by staring at pictures under my blotter for hours or breathing in her perfumed letters kept in a box in my lower desk drawer. When her Dear-John finally arrived, I was stunned and swore I would not reinitiate contact. Yet here I was. Was the feeling mutual? Were we getting back together or was she just wanting to let me down easy, see an old friend one last time? I was fixated on what a "3ish" appointment meant – certainly not a date. It sounded more like an open house invitation. If I was to win her back, I would find out in the next hour.

I located the apartment building, a low-silhouette U-shaped brick structure situated on Pensacola Bay where Cervantes becomes Scenic Highway. My watch said precisely 3 o'clock when I stepped from the car. The parking lot was cluttered with Trans Ams and Z-28s with base stickers – flight students either at NAS Pensacola or Whiting Field. I wondered how many of these studs knew Aimee and were already hitting on her, the sexy DJ down the hall. The grounds and building itself were clean but tired, a common lawn area of mostly crabgrass, a barbeque grill stuck off to one side, an oscillating sprinkler trying its best to keep up in the afternoon heat. This was the perfect bachelor pad for a group of young ensigns, I thought. Split the $250-a-month rent, pocket the rest of your BAQ and spend it drinking and partying all over town. I stepped around a stack of empty beer bottles and ten-speed bike near the base of stairs leading to the second floor. Climbing to the upper story, I spotted Aimee's door and pressed the buzzer.

"Mitch," she said with a warm smile. "Right on time."

I sensed an expectation of a hug but after my earlier head games in the car, I was reticent, reacting more like this was a business meeting.

"Come in, sit down, please." I could tell, Aimee was on high alert, my coolness apparently bleeding through.

We took separate seats in the sparsely decorated living room, an awkward silence hanging in the air. Her apartment was tidy, some boxes stacked in corners like she was still moving in. "Nice place," I said, scanning from the couch.

"Yes, I found it shortly after my brother left for San Diego last month. It's a longer drive to work but it's clean. And affordable."

"And you've got a view of the bay." I nodded at the sliding glass door. "A small deck too."

"Yes."

"Better than the BOQ where I'm at, that's for sure." I glanced down the hall. "Two bedrooms?"

"Yes." She seemed to be stalling and shifted uncomfortably in her chair.

I wanted to ask why two bedrooms but held back. "So, Aimee, where were we yesterday when you had to run off? Everything okay?"

"I know. I was rather cryptic, wasn't I?"

"Sort of."

"Well, it's really no mystery." She made eye contact. "Mitch, I tried to find you. More than a month ago, I began a search. Do you believe me?"

"Yes." I was pleased, desperately wanting to believe her but held some doubt.

"I truly did. I knew you'd graduated so I used directory assistance to find your home number in California. Got your mother on the line, but she couldn't tell me much." Aimee tilted her head. "Don't you two communicate?"

"I didn't go home after graduation. And, no, we don't speak much."

"Oh." Long pause. "I'm sorry to hear. Well, anyway, our talk didn't last very long. She confirmed you'd be in Pensacola soon, if not already. And—"

"And, what?"

"She said she had no address or phone number for you. That she hadn't heard from you in ages."

I rolled my eyes. "That's such a lie. She came out for graduation. She knows how to reach me." I was getting angry. It would be just like Mother to not give out my address, implying her only son had abandoned her, claiming victim status to any caller on the line asking for help. "What else did she say? Anything?"

"That if I found you, to tell you everything's peachy in California, that she's getting along just fine, and not to worry about a thing."

I let out a quick laugh. "Yep, you talked to Mother all right. I'm the one that should be sorry, Aimee. She should have told you where I was."

"Well, it was a start. So, I drove down to the Naval Air Station, but didn't get very far. The Marine at the gate wouldn't let me in. Used a lot of ma'ams. No ma'am, sorry ma'am. Are you a dependent, ma'am? Then I can't give you any information, ma'am. Said I needed to call the training command or some such office."

I shook my head. "Not very helpful." But I was starting to feel a lot better about her intentions this afternoon, about things in general.

"Then fate intervened. I'd been thinking about you so much and suddenly there you were, out front, in the lobby."

"And this Jasmine chick says she hasn't seen you? That you weren't there. Why'd she have to do that?"

"As I said yesterday, it's part of the training. We get stalkers from time to time. Losers that want to meet their dream girl, the one on the radio, the one they've been fantasizing about. Stuff like that, you know?"

"Yeah. It's how *I* found you."

"Well, I'm glad you did. Loser." Aimee laughed, placing a hand on my thigh as reassurance it was a joke. I knew as much but nonetheless breathed easier. Our relationship was gradually righting itself, coming back to the previous levels of laughter and joy we'd experienced after our first night together. "So, anyway, Jasmine comes running back into the studio, to my desk and says, quick, come look, there was some cute guy here to see you. He's crossing the street now."

"Amazing."

Aimee slowly rose from her chair and joined me on the couch. She leaned in and we kissed for the first time in more than a year. It felt wonderful, natural, as if we'd not been apart for even a day, let alone the full year. We kissed longer with more passion. Then she relaxed and pulled back. "Mitch, I'd love nothing more than to continue this—"

I leaned in, kissing her a second time, holding her close. "In the bedroom, right?"

"Yes. I mean, no." She hesitated, biting her lower lip. "I mean, before we go any further, there's a reason I asked you out here, something I need to tell you."

"Oh? Sounds ominous."

Aimee glanced at her wristwatch and stood. "Come out on the deck with me for a moment." She slid the door open.

I stood with her. We stepped outside and leaned forward on the wooden railing surveying the bay. I felt queasy. Was the news I imagined in the car about to hit? The air was sticky, an oppressive blanket of humidity, the afternoon sunlight dancing on the water. A squadron of pelicans swooped by low and fast. A silence enveloped us, which I gathered was Aimee's intention, part of her plan.

She maintained her gaze toward the water. "Mitch, there was a reason I wrote you that letter last year, a single definitive reason."

"And?"

"My brother, Phil. He said I had to."

"Your Navy brother? Why that son-of-a—"

"Let me finish. He said it was for your own good, your protection."

"I don't follow."

"Let me ask you a question. While you're a midshipman at the Academy, you're not allowed to be married, right?"

"That's right. And you can never have been married," I added.

"Yes, that's what he said. He also said you can't have any dependents either, such as a child or stepchild."

"Yeah, I guess." I looked at her. "Aimee, where is this going?"

"You'd have been kicked out, right? If they found out?"

"Yes. But what does this have to do with anything? What are you getting at?"

Aimee slid the glass door open and reentered the apartment. Her buzzer had made a noise, someone was at the front door. I followed from a distance and observed the visitor, a woman about the same age as Aimee, standing at the threshold, holding a toddler, a small boy dressed in Flintstones pajamas and cute little slippers, maybe a year, year-and-a-half old. Aimee took him from the woman, kissed him dearly on the cheek, the boy smiled, then she whirled to face me. "Mitch, there's only one simple way to say this. This is Sean. He just turned one in May and he's our son."

# West of Annapolis

# Part III

# 21

## HAIL AND FAREWELL

June 1983

I TOOK A SEAT with Aimee among the sea of white-clothed folding chairs, two of about two hundred lined up in neat rows of ten. I gave a shiver even though I was wearing my full dress-white uniform. It was June, summertime in the Bay Area, yet the hangar was damp, residual nighttime moisture locked in until the massive hangar doors could be retracted in anticipation of the upcoming change-of-command ceremony scheduled to begin in fifteen minutes. The VP-25 hangar space was spotless and festive, two squadron P-3s parked as bookends at each edge of our gathering with colorful signal flags draped tip to tail. The flags also hung across the back of the raised stage which held chairs for the skipper, the XO, other senior officers and visiting dignitaries. A podium and microphone stood front and center.

The Navy's change-of-command ceremony is a tradition dating back to the era of wooden ships, a formal yet very efficient transfer of authority between an incumbent commanding officer and his relief. The ceremony's main purpose is to honor and strengthen the respect for authority and is conducted as an all-hands event during quarters. The crux of the ceremony culminates with the reading of official orders and boils down to two sentences. The outgoing officer turns and salutes his relief and says, "Sir, I am ready to be relieved." The relieving officer returns the salute and says, "Sir, I relieve you." That's it, done deal, authority transferred. Of course, there's the surrounding pomp and pageantry leading to the moment – the arrival honors, the National Anthem, an invocation, a keynote speaker. Then a few remarks from the outgoing commanding officer as he reflects on his tenure as skipper and imparts some final words of wisdom to his troops. Lastly, there's a benediction. The entire ceremony takes about an hour.

Today, per regulation and Naval Aviation custom, Commander Samuel Wilson (aka Yosemite Sam) will be relieved by Commander Richard Fowler as the skipper of VP-25 in the presence of the Commodore, the Wing Ten Commander, the incoming XO, a host of dignitaries and the entire complement of men and women of VP-25 itself, about 400 strong.

God have mercy, I thought, recalling Fowler's volatile tenure as squadron's executive officer. Thankfully, I wasn't in need of His mercy or deliverance from the dreaded CO Fowler. I'd detached from VP-25 yesterday per orders that had arrived two weeks prior, hence my presence in the gallery with Aimee rather than standing at attention in the ranks to either side of the stage. I glanced over and squeezed her hand. She smiled back. She was dressed for the occasion in a sapphire blue silk wraparound and looked amazing. We both felt good about the change the orders would bring in our lives. I studied my former squadron-mates standing at attention, their faces blank – not the grim expressions I'd expected, none showing concern for the tectonic shift about to take place in their lives.

Bright sunlight began streaming through the gaping hole at the end of the hangar as the doors retracted bathing the freshly arrived guests and dignitaries. The ceremony was about to start. I looked at Aimee again and was reminded of our discussion after returning from Annapolis, which seemed a lifetime ago but was only a matter of days. As expected, the visit had jarred loose a rush of memories and emotions, all of which needed explaining if Aimee and I were to arrive at a decision to return to the Academy and live as a family. First, there was the issue of Maddy, her disappearance and subsequent investigation, none of which I'd shared with Aimee during our marriage. I could never bring myself to face it, to adequately describe the emotional shock and dark stain indelibly planted on my soul. I'd meant to bring it up before we moved to Corpus Christi but kept stalling, erroneously concluding the memory would fade and become less significant as time passed. Pretty soon I'd dug myself a deep hole and gone beyond what seemed like a reasonable waiting period. Then there was the issue of forestalling my departure from active duty, either waiting to jump to the airlines or foregoing the option altogether. Aimee wanted to restart her career in radio. Sean would need to change schools. My mother would again become a basket case, her only son leaving for the east again. It all came to a head the evening I'd returned, Aimee and I sitting up well past midnight making the important decisions about our future, ones I'd been avoiding for more than a year.

The ceremony began, right on time at 1000. Al Quigley, my NAVCOM, and his wife Anne had joined us, sitting to Aimee's left in the gallery of seats. Al was still attached to VP-25 but off flight status, hobbling on crutches, attending weekly therapy sessions at Oak Knoll for his mangled, slowly healing right leg. He was not required to stand in ranks today and was questionable if he'd ever be part of an aircrew again. I reached across Aimee to shake Al's hand, giving Anne a nod and smile. They'd been through a ton in the last eight weeks – medical appointments, therapy sessions, specialist visits. I looked back at Al, connecting what we'd been through on deployment last year, our time together on the crew, our final flight in Adak and now, my last day in the squadron. We'd been tightly bound by recent events, as close as any two Navy comrades, and would no doubt remain friends for life.

The VP-25 officers had conducted a brief hail and farewell in the wardroom during a scheduled AOM earlier in the week welcoming the new XO replacing Fowler and two new ensigns that'd recently checked aboard. I was given the only farewell recognition. The skipper's farewell had been conducted at a squadron dining-in while I was on my Annapolis trip. I was sorry I'd missed it. My wardroom farewell was a somewhat humorous and touching affair, the whole thing pretty much unrehearsed and spontaneous. After three years and four months, I was given the chance to say goodbye as the longest member on VP-25's active roll, to provide a few good-natured parting shots at whomever I deemed appropriate. There wasn't a soul in the squadron present the day I'd checked aboard back in January 1980. I was called up in front of the room of approximately sixty junior and senior officers of VP-25 by Skipper Wilson. He smiled broadly, shook my hand and presented me with a squadron plaque, one that artistically blended a P-3 flying atop a submarine and our mascot, a ripped red fox with six-pack abs squeezing droplets of blood from the sub below. Our motto, *Semper Paratus*, Always Ready, was underneath on an engraved placard. I'd expected some token sarcasm by the skipper, maybe a jab at the restriction he'd put me on, but he offered none. He was in a fabulous mood and dredging up old wounds wasn't his style at an AOM where he was saying goodbye himself and to one of his more outspoken and "memorable" junior officers, as he put it. He ended with a brief, humorous recounting of our crew's final mission in Adak in SE-05, the fragile tactical success we'd achieved, the harrowing landing in the fog and just how much the repair of the wrecked P-3 had cost the Navy and our taxpayers. It was a funny story with no hard feelings, the accident board having freshly exonerated me of any wrongdoing or improper decision-making on station. Before I could give my little speech, our maintenance officer came forward and presented me with a picture, two photos mounted side by side in a single frame – the before and after of SE-05. The right was the beautiful after-shot of the repaired and repainted aircraft glistening in the sun, having been freshly returned to the VP-25 ramp after three months of TLC by the Naval Air Rework Facility in Alameda. The left was the before-shot – the damaged aircraft in same perspective with the punctured right wing, both engines torn up, the number four propeller missing entirely, the fuselage deeply gouged aft of the nav station window. Somehow, they'd managed to superimpose me in my flight suit standing in front of the carnage, a sheepish grin on my face with the caption reading, "Sorry, Dad, I wrecked the car." Everyone roared at the picture and the presentation from the MO. I figured it would one day make a nice conversation piece hanging in a future den.

After the laughter died it was time for me to speak. I was unsure of any words that might pop out, having prepared nothing. The moment called for something profound, sentimental and of course humorous. But it also needed to be quick. "Thanks, Skipper, MO," I said, clutching the picture. "I knew something was up when I went to check out of the squadron yesterday and the mess treasurer informed me my tab of $23.50 had suddenly ballooned to something like a million dollars." I turned back to the MO, still smiling. "I hope you'll take a personal check, sir." More laughter, most of it polite from the group. I turned to face them. "On a serious note, I think you always welcome this day, you relish it, to finally detach from sea duty and move on to the next chapter of your Navy life. But there's the sorrow of leaving behind friends and family that have sustained you through some pretty rough times. VP-25 has been my home, Aimee's and my Navy family for the last three years, and it's been a great experience I wouldn't trade for anything. Well," I said, gesturing at the picture. "Maybe I would've traded something to avoid *this* great experience." More polite laughter, a few shifting uncomfortably in their seats. I needed to end the platitudes and wrap up but something inside was urging me to remain standing, to press on.

"We all learned some of life's lessons very quickly that night in the throes of that emergency. Many of you, including the accident investigation board and folks at the Wing asked me the question what it felt like when that propeller blade tore into our skin over the Bering Sea in pitch darkness a mere two thousand feet above the sea." I now had everyone's attention, especially the nuggets. I couldn't have ended if I tried. Every eye in the wardroom was on me, every eye except Fowler, sitting in his chair next to the skipper looking bored. I continued. "My immediate answer, my honest answer to the board was to say nothing can prepare you for an emergency of that nature with so many things going wrong at once, certainly nothing our annual NATOPS check can cover." I paused, unsure of my ground but figured what the hell, this would be the last time I see many of these guys. I took a deep breath. "Sometimes Navy life seems like an endless series of challenges. You either accept the challenge and grow from it or like me, curse and resist it and suffer the consequences later, doing damage to all the things you hold dear – your career, your family, your marriage. I went up to Adak angry in the wake of my SDO restriction." I nodded at the skipper. "I was just counting the days until I could detach, peel out the back gate and watch those huge blimp hangars disappear in my rearview mirror.

"Then I got my wakeup call, literary, at two in the morning. As many of you know, my father passed away just a week before we went up to Adak, our crew's departure delayed so I could attend the funeral. After the accident, the board had drilled me hard on this point, asking me if I thought my father's recent death was a distraction, implying I might have been unfit to fly that night. I thought long and hard about that one. I thought about my father, his life, and the eulogy I'd delivered the day we buried him, a story I told about his imparting philosophy, words left to me without ever speaking them – to always do the right thing. I hadn't been living my life with those words in mind recently, but they were obviously running under the surface. He'd been through a life of his own, flying combat missions over Germany, a pilot himself, facing flak, enemy fighters, coming back from one mission so shot up, so wounded, his aircraft so disabled yet managing to make the landing, saving himself and crew and living to fight another day. If anything, his funeral, the memories he evoked, going to war, doing the right thing, acted in my favor that night as I prepared to bring our own flight back safely to Adak." I was starting to ramble, slowing my delivery, taking too much time, drifting to some elusive ending. "So, his recent passing was certainly not a distraction. I believe it saved us. That, of course, along with the many hours of training and repetition. They conspired to keep me in the seat to…" Words became elusive. "To return…" I was losing connection with the group. My eyes welled up.

The skipper came to my rescue. He leapt from his chair and stuck an arm around me. "Training and repetition, yes. But being able to return that ship and crew safely from a churning sea runs a hell of a lot deeper than memorizing a lot of NATOPS EPs." He eyed the group. "It's a testament to our culture of doing the right thing, to courage and character. That's what keeps any of us in that seat, gentlemen. These things are not given freely or learned overnight." He turned to me. "That's what kept you in that seat, Mitch. And that's what I expect – what the *Navy* expects – will keep any of you in that seat when things go wrong some night a thousand miles from home without a long, dry runway in front of you."

I was grateful and understood. His little speech, expressing what I couldn't, wasn't about my flight as my crew and I fought for our lives that night. Life is complex, he was saying. It's hard, and you never know when you'll be expected to take decisive, lifesaving actions. And goddamn it, you better have the strength, the character, and fortitude before you go hanging it out, putting yourself and others at risk. It was at this moment I would've walked through fire for Wilson, done anything for him – his Rough Rider storming San Juan Hill, his soldier on Omaha Beach, his wingman over Midway. I would've followed this man's lead into battle anywhere. VP-25 was going to sorely miss him.

The change-of-command ceremony concluded as my mind wandered back from the AOM, the memory and sensation of the skipper giving me a final hug in front of the entire wardroom amid applause. Aimee and I hung out on the crowded hangar floor after the departure of the dignitaries and entourage to say our final goodbyes to friends. Al and Anne were first, then Colby appeared, then Jamie and Horse and the rest of our crew. We'd already

341

said our goodbyes in separate social gatherings, long conversations, impromptu meetings and individual encounters around the squadron spaces earlier in the week. These last-minute handshakes and hugs seemed awkward and superfluous, words forming slowly laced with, "Safe travels," "Don't be a stranger," "If you ever get back to Moffett—"

Aimee and I needed to return to our quarters. The movers had departed with our household goods yesterday and we needed to prepare for our final inspection to clear base housing this afternoon before we could begin the long cross-country drive in the morning. I had one final official act in the duty office before we could depart the squadron. I needed a final stamp on my orders by the SDO and hoped to make it quick as I pushed the door open.

"Mitch," said Jake Burgess, rising behind his desk to shake my hand. "Thought you'd be by. How'd it go out there on the floor this morning?"

"Well, in case you haven't heard, you've got a new CO." I grinned. "Condolences, buddy."

"God, ain't that the truth. Never thought I'd say it but I'm going to miss the old man. The screaming, the cursing, his check rides from hell—"

"Yep, Yosemite at his finest." I dropped my orders to his desk. "Now if you could be so kind as to stamp and date these things making it official, I'll be on my way."

"Sure thing." He quickly signed them off. "Lucky bastard. And a company officer billet at the Academy to boot. How'd you manage to pull that off?"

"Long story. Sold my soul to the Navy, something like that."

"More like sold it to Wilson." Jake thought for a moment. "He's not such a bad guy, is he?"

"Treated me very fairly on this one."

"Didn't hurt you got an Air Medal out of it. Congratulations, by the way. You certainly deserved it."

"Thanks. Still waiting on NAVAIRPAC to endorse it, so we'll see."

"Aw, it'll come through. That was one hell of a flight, Mitch. I'm betting half the pilots in the squadron would've planted it in the ocean that night. They owe you more than a medal."

Just then Fowler pushed the door open behind me and entered the tight office space. He glared at Jake. "What the hell are all those parked cars doing in front of the VIP spots? They're blocking the Commodore's departure," he barked. "His driver and aide are going wild. What kind of SDO lets that happen? Get out there."

"On my way, sir." Jake threw on his cover and slipped out the door.

I turned around, orders in hand, face to face with Fowler himself. I'd hoped to avoid any contact in his new role as CO, wanting to depart quickly without a trace. But here we were. "Ah, Baumann, getting out of Dodge just in the nick of time, eh?" He was smiling but there was an underlying sneer. I'd seen this look dozens of times before.

I nodded back, not wanting to speak for fear of another confrontation as in Adak. His message, his facial features made it clear standing before me – there's a new sheriff in town, time for the outlaw JO to hit the trail. "Just signing out now, sir. Headed back east tomorrow." I took a second glance at Fowler. His expression seemed to relax. Maybe he wasn't sneering. Maybe he was hoping for some peace, some reconciliation on his special day, like, hey, no hard feelings. I suddenly felt bad, perhaps misreading him. Protocol and decency told me to offer some kind words. "And congratulations today – Skipper," I said, using the term for the first time and offering my hand. "It was a very nice ceremony. Best of luck with your new command, sir."

We shook hands as he eyed me again from top to bottom, both of us in our dress white uniforms. Fowler unclipped his sword and handed it to the assistant SDO, an enlisted kid from Jake's crew. "Let's take a walk, Baumann."

I followed him onto the hangar floor. The large crowd had mostly dispersed, many headed to the O-Club for the reception. Chairs were being folded, the stage cleared, stringers of flags being dropped. I hadn't planned on attending the reception. Aimee and I needed to hurry back to our house for the inspection. We continued deeper into the hangar passing two parked P-3s undergoing minor maintenance. Fowler finally spoke. "Pretty good orders, if you ask me. I presume you got what you wanted out of it, you and Alice?"

*Alice?* And yes, I got what I wanted out of it, I thought, no thanks to you. I was reminded of my conversation with my detailer, Hal Wilkinson, of how Fowler had tried to sabotage me by calling Hal's boss, bad-mouthing me in advance of my trip, recommending the Bureau take a pass on me. Despite his efforts, the Commandant gave the nod as did Hal and BUPERS. "It should be a nice two years, sir. For me and Aimee."

"You bet it will. Pretty laidback duty compared to the fleet." If he caught my name correction, he ignored it. "I was stationed there, you know."

"Yes, sir. Same time as me."

He flashed a look of surprise. He should've been able to intuit my graduation year, that I was a first-class at the start of his tour. He placed his hand on his chin like it was all coming back. "Guess we were shipmates in a prior life, huh?"

"Yes, sir." I was hoping he'd come to his point soon, why we were on this little walkabout in the first place.

We strolled side by side, keeping our eyes forward. "First thing you do when you get back there?"

"Yes, sir?"

"Is make sure you take the drive across the river to Captain Blake's on Mill Creek. Little waterside crab shack. Best in Maryland. And even better, the mids and tourists haven't discovered it. At least not while I was back there."

"Thanks, XO. I'll make sure we check it out." I caught myself. "Sorry. I mean, Skipper." The gaff was not intentional and certainly forgivable this close to his change of command. It was his chance to be a good guy, throw me a lifeline, say something like, hey, no worries, still getting used to it myself. But he didn't. Maybe he thought I was having a go at him for his Alice remark.

"Second thing you do?"

"Yes, sir?"

We stopped walking. He looked me in the eye. "Learn your job and learn it quick. Then learn your boss's job, his needs, and understand the competition around you. It'll be keen, nothing like the rocks around here."

"Good to know. Thank you, sir." This sounded like sage advice on the surface but seemed like a paranoid way to approach a new job, like everyone was angry, cut-throat, career-driven assholes like Fowler himself and to be careful and trust no one.

"They assign you a company yet?"

"Thirty-four, sir. I'll be their company officer when they return in August. Indoc'ing over the summer."

"Part of Sixth Batt, huh? Tucked into the far reaches of the eighth wing."

"Yes, sir. You were First Batt Officer if I recall, when you were there, right?"

"Right." Fowler gave me an odd look, like, how would I know this? *C'mon, I was there in '77, same as you.*

"Did we ever cross paths?"

"Briefly, sir. I was in 27th Company. We were at a Superintendent's reception a month before I graduated."

Again, he stroked his chin, struggling to recall.

I gave him a poke. "You were with Admiral Tennant. I'd asked him what was being done about the Midshipman O'Connor investigation." This was a blatant hint and I feared I may have gone too far given what I'd said to the admiral that afternoon. "I was concerned for her, sir."

Fowler's reaction was momentary shock when he heard Tennant's name. "Ah yes, Baumann. Now I do recall. You were acting like a real horse's ass and Tennant's aide had to remove you from the conversation." His shock had morphed to ire. "Yup, same old Baumann, challenging authority, even back then."

It was all coming back, to both of us. I wanted to ask him the question Neil posed to me before we graduated – just what were you doing up in our company area, in civilian clothes, the night Maddy went missing? Instead: "I was troubled with why the investigation had cooled, sir. Just wanted to express that to the admiral."

"It cooled because there were no leads. Nothing after six months. Waste of manpower to keep going. It was the perfect crime if you ask me."

*Perfect crime?* What a thing to say. I couldn't respond. I stood there slack-jawed. Fowler seemed to take pleasure in my reaction. "Well, so long, Baumann." He stuck out his hand. "My advice to you is keep your nose clean back there. Keep it glued to the grindstone, as they say. Capisce?" He was enjoying his little pep-talk. "You've joined the big-boy leagues, playing for keeps. No more hotdogging, ducking regs or schoolboy pranks like gluing bumper stickers to your boss's car if you catch my drift. That shit doesn't fly back there." He paused to give me a final once-over. "That's my advice, son, and it's the best you'll ever get." The fake smile returned. "You take care. Give my best to Alice."

That was it. I couldn't take it any longer. "It's *Aimee*, sir. My wife's name is Aimee, not Alice." I took a deep breath. "And I think they should reopen the investigation. There *were* leads, dozens of them. It was by no means the perfect crime."

"What's that supposed to mean?"

"It means the NIS should've interviewed a lot more people than just midshipmen, asked a lot more questions." I looked at Fowler for the last time and leaned in close. "I know you were there that night. You came up to our company area and ducked out when the CMOD tried to ID you, the night Miss O'Connor went missing. And they never approached you, never asked you a damn thing about it, did they?"

Fowler froze. His expression was priceless. I'd taken a chance, not knowing for sure if the NIS did or did not question his roaming the hall that night, but his stunned reaction confirmed everything. "Goodbye, sir. Good luck with your new command."

# 22

## EDEN

I WAS STILL RATTLED by my confrontation with Fowler when we started our drive eastward the following morning. I'd rocked him back on his heels which was not my intention, angering a very vindictive, mean-spirited commanding officer only hours after his taking the reins. I really wanted to forget the investigation that was now six years old, not reignite all the tension and unpleasantries I'd experienced in a place I'd sworn not to return, a place that was now my destiny.

We arrived in Annapolis on a Tuesday night amid one of Maryland's infamous thunderstorms after four days of steady driving in the Suburban, most of it along the I-80 corridor. We checked into the Howard Johnson's across the river and stood ready, on a gloriously sunny morning to tour and accept our new living quarters we'd been assigned on Pythian Road, inside the Yard. The movers would be allowed to unload our household goods any time after that. Despite being bleary-eyed and exhausted from the grind of the road, Aimee was eager to inspect what would be our home for the next two years. I was more concerned about what my own reaction would be as we made the right turn onto Boyer Road entering the Academy from its rear Gate 8. We were early for our appointment with the housing office, so I continued over the causeway to the center of the Yard feeling like a tourist driving my oversized family vehicle with wife and kids scanning for a place to park. I wanted to show Sean and Carlene the highlights, their first visit to the school, and Aimee's first since visiting me as a midshipman during the Christmas dance back in '75. I pulled into the empty lot in front of Dahlgren Hall. Aimee asked where everyone was as we strolled toward Tecumseh Court. I told her the Brigade had scattered for the summer and the new class of 1987 plebes hadn't yet arrived. I surveyed the vacant courtyard and Stribling Walk, a memory from an old catalog forming in my head – *T'ain't no mo' plebes, you say? The schedule (or so it seems) hardly ends before it begins all over again.* The place was a ghost town all right, graduation a faded memory, I-Day just around the corner. A few stray officers made their way up the steps to Bancroft Hall. I gave Sean and Carlene a handful of pennies and told them to throw them at Tecumseh, that it'd bring good luck.

"Throw them at what?" Sean said.

"That Indian statue up ahead."

The kids raced toward Tecumseh as Aimee slid her arm around my waist. "How you doing?" she said as we strolled. "You going to be all right?"

"Yeah, I'm fine." The truth was I felt odd like my head was spinning. I was standing in this very spot only a month ago with my detailer, Hal. Before that, it'd been six years before I'd felt these bricks under my feet. My sense of time was being warped. Were those *my* kids running rings around Tecumseh just now? I watched as Sean scattered his pennies, ricocheting them wildly off Tecumseh's broad chest. Carlene bent down to stack hers neatly at the statue's square base, picking up some of Sean's in the process. I looked toward Bancroft's huge columns and stone facade then spun the opposite direction staring down the tree-shrouded Stribling Walk toward Mahan Hall flanked by the Chapel to my left, Michelson and Chauvenet to my right. I felt dizzy. It was like the whole place was wrapped in an opaque layer of plastic, the buildings reflecting a blurry, underwater presence. "Whoa," I muttered to myself and stepped back.

Aimee quickly steadied me from behind. "Mitch?" What's happening? Are you okay?"

"I think so." I touched my forehead, feeling beads of sweat. "Guess I'm still a bit hungover from our long drive."

"Sure," she said, guiding me back to the passenger side of the car. "Get in, I'm driving."

We departed after Sean insisted on feeding one of the squirrels with some crackers in his pocket. Aimee herded the kids into their car seats, jumped behind the wheel and headed us back over the causeway to Pythian Road for our scheduled appointment with the housing rep.

Our building on Pythian, one for four lining the same side of the road, was identical to the one Bob and Jan Clausen had lived in, Maddy's sponsors back in '77, on Perry Circle outside Gate 8. Clinging to the railing as we climbed the interior steps of our new building, I swooned from the memory of Bob and Jan's building, experiencing similar glints of sunlight in the hallway and the sweet musty hallway smell, as fresh to my senses as the morning Maddy went missing. Aimee and I learned from the cheery housing rep that our apartment building, situated across from the base hospital and mirroring the ten units clustered around Perry Circle, was built in the mid-1930s as the need for Academy officer housing grew. The red brick exteriors and dormer windows resembled the colonial architecture of surrounding Annapolis with their slate roofs, common formal entrances, terrazzo floors and cast-iron stair railings. Since I was one of the more junior officers to rate this larger style quarters inside the Yard, we were given a unit on the top floor. The building itself housed six families, two per floor and, along with the formal entrance, there was a back staircase off each kitchen leading down to the basement garages, one per tenant. The same staircase also led to the fourth-floor attic with its dormer windows. Our housing rep explained the rooms up here, while stuffy in the summer, were used for maids in days of yore but now configured for additional storage, studios or guest rooms to host drags, midshipmen dates on the weekend. Aimee was nodding enthusiastically soaking all this in, charmed with the entire history and living experience, looking forward to meeting our neighbors and hosting drags of our own someday.

The truth was, we both loved the place and quickly settled in. The location was perfect aside from the late-night sirens from the nearby fire station and hospital, which would startle Carlene awake like clockwork. It was a small price to pay, given the huge upside of life in the Yard. Our unit had the same number of bedrooms as our duplex on Moffett but was twice the size. The military family lifestyle was extremely vibrant here with informal gatherings and barbeques every weekend, a super-strong support network, teenage babysitters for Sean and Carlene available like low-hanging fruit. This was a far cry from my days in Bancroft Hall, seeing the Yard anew as an officer on staff. We began thinking of our life on this side of College Creek (the waterway separating us from the main side) as the minor yard, affectionately referring to it as Ursa Minor. Yet it was only a short walk across the causeway or a footbridge to the Academy proper, quickly rejoining one with the horde of midshipmen in their numbers and might and their massive dorm with its own zip code. Life on our side was tranquil, especially on weekends – a world removed with its family swim center, crew team boathouse, empty baseball fields and lonely obstacle course. And, of course, there was the Academy cemetery with its adjoining base hospital, an irony lost on no one.

When my company officer job started in the fall, I was able to walk to work. It was a pleasant one-mile stroll in the morning from our apartment to my office on 8-3 in the eighth wing of Bancroft Hall, a sweaty journey but made beautiful after the summer humidity dried up, replaced with crisp autumn air and bayside breezes of early October. We began attending chapel services regularly on Sundays. I started working out during lunch, swimming laps in Lejeune Hall, the new midshipmen swim complex next door, meeting some other officers and faculty members. Aimee and I started having the first-class from my company over on occasion for "green lights," basically a glorified weeknight happy hour. They'd show up at our door in their casual civilian attire and leather jackets bearing a simple hostess or gag gift for Aimee, which she loved. We'd sit around, talk shop, have a beer or two and watch Monday Night Football, a few harmlessly flirting with Aimee in the kitchen, which she also loved.

One of the added responsibilities of a company officer I soon learned was being assigned several collateral duties, mostly to midshipmen activities around the Hall that needed some "adult" supervision. One of my added assignments was the designated officer representative for the 1984 Lucky Bag, the Academy yearbook. I had no experience in publishing or editing but fortunately had an officer assistant and extremely competent midshipmen staff that carried me, asking only that I keep them in operating cash, increasing their meager budget to pay the publishing company some rather large, unexpected fees. Aimee got involved too, but with a different midshipmen activity. It turned out the officer rep for the midshipmen-run FM radio station, WRNV, lived in our building. He was also a company officer and, like me with the yearbook crew, knew nothing about radio. He enlisted Aimee's help after I'd recommended her, Aimee herself delighted to get involved and work in radio again. The station had fallen on hard times after once thriving in popularity when I was a midshipman. Back in '77, Harry Chapin came to the Naval Academy giving a concert in the Halsey Field House and substituted the call letters in his song *W.O.L.D.* with WRNV. He sang out, "I am the morning DJ at W-R-N-V-V-V-V!" The crowd loved it and went wild, keeping the station on the map during those glory years. But like typical college radio station formats of its day, WRNV experimented with the emerging punk rock genre and added in too generous a mix too quickly propelling a near-fatal identity crisis. Sometime in 1980, listeners got fed up and changed the dial. The station had trouble keeping regular DJs, especially during exams, and began looping a series of taped shows, ad nauseum. The loops would sometimes run for days without anybody checking or listening. Aimee's intervention to the struggling station brought a resurgence in popularity and a sense of cool factor to tuning in again. She assisted the officer advisor, then started working directly with the mids, bringing an air of professionalism to the station. She taught the DJs little techniques, production shortcuts, humor, style and the proper way to arrange a playlist. Pretty soon some of the mids became established radio personalities around the Yard and in town. She'd keep the station tuned in constantly in our quarters, "just to keep tabs on things," she'd say. Truth was she adored her midshipmen DJs and thrived as their shows succeeded and brought in a larger, more diverse audience. She was happy to contribute to the station's success, fulfilling her need to be back in radio in the wake of her missed opportunity in San Jose.

As Aimee immersed herself at home and the station, I was invited by one of the Seamanship and Navigation instructors, a classmate of mine also stationed at the Academy, as a guest speaker in his Air Navigation class. Air Nav was a three-hour elective course for first-class midshipmen interested in Naval Aviation upon service selection. It basically served as a rudimentary ground school for mids entering the pilot and NFO pipelines after graduation, giving them a slight edge when they got to Pensacola. For my first appearance in their classroom in Luce Hall, I arrived finding the mids casually draped over their desks or leaning back in their chairs, all very nonchalant, like, oh, great, here's another aviator trying to scare the crap out of us about how tough it'll be in flight school.

I was disappointed to observe a few with longer, non-reg haircuts, and some with marginal uniform appearance. I started by giving my background, talking about P-3s and antisubmarine warfare. Many in the class, as I myself did, had an affinity for the P-3 with its land-based mission and easy hop to the airlines. Others fancied themselves as future fighter jocks, cocky and invincible, certain they would qualify for one of the few F-14 slots after completing primary. All listened to my talk respectfully, some interjected questions but it all seemed like polite boredom. Ten minutes in, a perceptive mid in the front row held up his hand after noticing the dark-blue and orange ribbon just below the wings on my uniform. He pointed, "Sir, isn't that an Air Medal?"

Soon the entire class was encouraging me to tell the story behind it. I was reluctant but went along, never expecting my guest appearance to turn into a *There I Was...* moment. But after tossing around terms like engine fire, catastrophic propeller failure, fuselage breech and rapid decompression, they were no longer yawning or bored. All sat upright and locked into the events as I unfolded them. As I finished with our successful landing back in Adak, the group let out a collective sigh of relief.

And since they'd coerced me into recreating the incident, making me relive a shorter version of the accident and residual trauma, I wasn't going to let them off the hook. I concluded with a single takeaway, something that needed saying now that I had their full attention. "I know, you're on top of your game right now," I began, pacing slowly in front of them. "Seniors, about to graduate, grab your sheepskin and scatter to the fleet. And I know the tendency is to seek the path of least resistance with all the Academy's nitpicky regulations and constant oversight, to coast when you can, and get all cynical when the stress bothers you, like cynicism is cool." I went on to remind them that in any dire situation staying cool, remaining confident, keeping your poise and sense of humor are essential tools. "Some of this attitude you've cultivated may be useful but please—" I implored them, "do not allow your cynicism to creep in and corrupt your idealism, what is still pure within you." I scanned to make eye contact. "You're leaps and bounds ahead of your contemporaries at other colleges, your value to the nation immense upon graduation. Carry that sense of commitment into the fleet, to your duty assignments. Don't become disabused by your idealism, gentlemen." I paused, making my way back to the podium. "Cherish it."

Standing there, I was struck by my sudden enlightenment on the subject wishing someone had reminded me of these things when I checked into VP-25 nearly four years ago. The mids stared back, silent, a few of them getting it, many not. I suspected they'd heard it all before. As I walked back to my office in Bancroft Hall, I thought, well, some things they'll just have to figure out themselves.

Aimee and I were busy with our new life, no question. Not that Moffett Field was slack, for either of us. In some ways we'd been busier at Moffett, but the pace was more disjointed and frenetic, more stressful with my irregular hours, the flight schedule and Mother's continual needs. A peace had settled in, a happy busyness from being on shore duty with its steady routine, its normal home life and yes, a mother 3,000 miles away. I quickly rediscovered and embraced the staff's wide access to the Academy's marvelous athletic facilities. USNA was like jock-o-rama. You could pick any sport and find a venue in the Yard, from handball to weightlifting, sailing to swimming. My irregular flight schedule and limited facilities at Moffett had made it difficult to establish any normal workout routine. I began swimming daily at lunch in a brand-new Olympic pool with very few lanes in use. Lejeune Hall was completed in 1981 after I'd graduated and was an enormous, state-of-the-art facility. I'd established a regular workout routine with a group of officers and professors during these lunch periods when I met Ryan McCrary, a Civil Engineer Corps lieutenant who lived in the building next door and worked in Halligan Hall. Ryan had been a swimmer on the varsity squad while at USNA. He was in the lane next to me and, after observing my slog back and forth lap after lap, decided I needed an intervention. He provided some pointers and we got to gabbing, picking out the common links in our Navy past. He'd been a surface warfare officer on a destroyer out of Mayport before making the jump to CEC. Ryan was quick-witted, outgoing and wore a perpetual smile. We found we enjoyed each other's company in and out of the water. Hearing him later describe his public works job in Halligan Hall, it wasn't lost on me he likely knew Bob Clausen, the CEC community being relatively small and close-knit. Bob and Jan were long gone, having rotated out sometime after I'd graduated but, like Maddy, I'd wondered about them ever since. I introduced Aimee to Ryan and we later met Ryan's wife, Sherry. They had kids, we had kids, all of us becoming fast friends instantly. We ended up doing all the touristy things together, seafood dinners around the harbor, bike rides in town, ice cream stops and day trips to the surrounding area.

Time moved quickly as we grew comfortable and happy in our surroundings. It was already November and preparation for Army Week was underway all around the Yard. I'd been thinking about Maddy more than usual for the obvious reasons as November 20th approached, the seventh anniversary of her disappearance. I wanted to downplay the significance of the date but the seasonal transition and spirited pace around the Hall made that impossible. After a slow walk home from the pool one day with Ryan, I decided to casually drop Bob's name to see if he knew him. Of course, he said. He went on to mention Bob was currently stationed at the nearby Navy Yard in DC working for NAVFAC, the Naval Facilities Engineering Command. He and Jan now lived in Silver Spring in the DC suburbs. This tidbit came from their annual Christmas card exchange.

After our talk, I was overcome by an odd emotion. I was angry at myself for pressing Ryan, for not welcoming the news I'd pursued in the first place. First, because Bob and Jan were nearby, I could drive to them in thirty minutes. Ryan's information was forcing me to act. Second, I knew Aimee wouldn't understand. There'd be more questions, another lengthy discussion and eventual disharmony around the house. I was setting in motion extraordinary steps to reignite the long-dormant investigation that Aimee knew I'd taken extraordinary steps to avoid. The whole Maddy affair would not leave my head. I needed relief, something to give me back a sense of closure but talking to Bob and Jan risked a slippery slope with no return. I took the drive out to Silver Spring on a Saturday morning, explaining to Aimee I had some nagging questions from that night in November that wouldn't go away. I needed to talk to Bob and Jan. I felt guilty wasting a perfectly good Saturday morning, offering Aimee a stupid grin and kissing her on the cheek saying I wouldn't be long. She rolled her eyes and said, "Just go. Do whatever it is you have to do."

From a Maddy perspective, the visit with Bob and Jan was a bust. It felt awkward from the beginning. We sat on their sunporch sipping coffee catching up on the last six years, delicately sidestepping the elephant in the room. Bob was now a lieutenant commander finishing up his current assignment at NAVFAC soon to relocate back to Port Hueneme on the West Coast where he'd started his career. Both he and Jan were eager to leave the DC rat race for the sunny shores of southern California. I gave them a brief rundown on my getting married, our two kids, our tour at Moffett and how I'd met Ryan. Once we were all caught up, Jan topped off our coffee and the talk turned to the inevitable. Neither of us was eager to initiate the discussion but I plunged ahead with my best recollection of my interview with the two NIS clowns, Haney and Hanratty. I told them how it appeared the NIS was more attuned to harassment violations than Maddy's disappearance and described the circumstances about Captain Manley, the Marine that'd been fired. I also told them about Commander Fowler's mysterious visit to our company area and coincidentally, my just finishing a tour with him as my XO. I hadn't spoken to Bob or Jan since I'd showed them Maddy's charm bracelet before my interview, and they listened intently to every detail. This was mostly new information for them. I could tell Bob was disturbed revisiting it, still possibly carrying the burden of letting Maddy depart solo from their quarters that night. He mentioned he and Jan met with Maddy's parents before moving from Annapolis to express their sorrow but with no meaningful exchange of information. He nearly broke down when describing Maddy's mother, the pained expression in her eyes, knowing Bob was the last to see her daughter alive. Jan quickly changed subjects and asked about the bracelet again – did it corroborate a hypothesis or contribute to the mounting pile of evidence? I explained I turned the bracelet over to some secretary after my interview and that was the last I'd heard. Jan remarked that seemed odd. I concurred. The conversation lapsed in awkward silence, their grandfather clock ticking softly down the hall adding a touch of finality to our morning. I stood to leave. We were at a dead end.

Returning to Annapolis along the Beltway, I felt more relieved than sad. Had there been any shred of hope, any new lead Bob or Jan might've not thought of earlier, I would've gladly kept going. I would've even stopped by the NIS regional office in DC. But there was nothing to act on. We'd covered it all, either back in the day or this morning on their sunporch. It was time to bury the memories, for good. I had every reason to be happy. I was enjoying my job, the daily challenges from my midshipmen, my occasional guest appearances in the Air Nav classes, my swimming with Ryan, the social life Aimee and I had carved out. In many ways, the Academy was our Eden, the Navy's little slice of paradise along the Severn.

Our building hosted a final home football game barbeque on the first Saturday in November in unseasonably warm weather. Over a hundred people showed up after the big game, wives, kids, girlfriends, significant others. Aimee and I hung out on the back lawn well after sunset, sipping wine from plastic cups, chatting with the neighbors until the cold forced us up to our apartment with about twenty diehards in tow. We stayed up late playing a free-for-all, scream-fest version of Trivial Pursuit after swilling way too much wine. Whoever yelled out the funniest answer, not necessarily the correct one, was awarded a piece of the pie from the group. I fell asleep that night at peace, thinking we'd hit the jackpot with these orders, that we'd truly been blessed. Aimee and I loved it here as we approached our six-month anniversary.

On Monday morning, I walked to work in the chill of the pre-winter dawn happy I'd remembered my gloves. Driving would soon become the warmer, preferred option. Still, the Yard was beautiful on this crisp fall morning as I crossed onto the main side of College Creek. When I arrived at my office on 8-3, the CMOD greeted me, informing me Lieutenant Colonel Walsh, our Marine battalion officer and my boss, needed to see me in his office. "As soon as he gets in," he said. I looked at my watch. 0715. Our staff meeting was scheduled at 0800. Whatever it was could not wait. I didn't waste time unlocking my office door, instead making a U-turn back down the stairwell, briefcase in hand, to LTC Walsh's office on 8-0. An uneasy shiver raced through my body upon entering his office, an intuitive sense all was not well. He didn't seem happy when he looked up.

"Good morning, Colonel," I said. "You wanted to see me?"

"Ah, yes, Mitch. Take a seat, please." He waved me to a chair. Still no smile.

I leaned to the edge of the cushioned chair, assuming a sitting form of attention.

Walsh made eye contact and spoke directly. "Mitch, I'm sorry to be the one to inform you of this but you're being court-martialed."

"What?"

"Yes, court-martialed." He let it sink in. "I'm not joking."

A numbness washed over me. I was paralyzed, instantly entering a state of shock. I opened my mouth to speak, and nothing came out. What had I done? It had to be serious, whatever it was. And yet, I couldn't imagine.

Walsh pushed a thick manila envelope across his desk. "This showed up in the Commandant's office late Friday."

I lifted the flap, slid out the top document and noticed the subject line on the cover letter. *The United States v. Mitchell John Baumann, Lieutenant, USN.* I quickly stuffed the letter back inside, horrified to see such language. I regained my voice. "I don't understand, sir. Why are you informing me of this? What have I done? What's this all about?"

"It's all in there," Walsh said, in a calm voice. "You need to read it."

My first thought was I'd been framed with Maddy's kidnapping and murder, that the NIS finally found someone to pin it on. But that was absurd. The investigation had been inactive for years. They weren't out to frame anyone. Then I thought I'd been improperly charged for popping positive on some drug test. I would've welcomed this as it would've been a huge error, something I could easily fight. I was no druggie. Then I looked up at Walsh. No, this was something else entirely. "Sir?"

"The package was addressed to the Office of the Commandant as your commanding officer. We discussed it over the weekend and agreed I'd be the one to inform you. It appears your old CO from VP-25 is charging you with violating a number of Navy regs in connection with that flight you took in Alaska."

"A court-martial? Why now? The accident board cleared me." It was true, the flight occurred back in March when Wilson was skipper and he'd done nothing but shower me with praise. Then I remembered the conversation in his office after I got back from Adak. *Fowler.* Fowler had threatened it. But could he court-martial me? He wasn't the CO then. I didn't understand.

"Apparently the accident board results have little bearing on the charges," Walsh said. "And they're well within the statute of limitations. I still need to read the entire package myself."

"So, what happens next?"

"You'll need to fly back to Moffett Field and meet with the Judge Advocate General. They'll formally charge you. You'll acknowledge the charges and then I suspect you'll need to find counsel." Walsh gave me a pained, fatherly look, like how could you let something like this happen? You came to us with the highest recommendation.

There was little else to say. I needed to tell Aimee. I needed to arrange transportation back to the Bay Area. God, this was awful. I felt I'd let everyone down, yet I felt I'd done nothing wrong. I needed to get a closer look at the charges. I stood to leave. All I could offer was, "I'm sorry, sir. I really am."

I'd scanned the charge sheet before leaving Walsh's office. Each seemed serious, closely tied to the events of Adak but utter bullshit at the same time. This was Fowler at his finest, flexing his command muscles and acting out of vengeance. He was sending a message to all his junior officers still onboard. *See?* This is what happens when a disrespectful, snot-nosed JO crosses me. Yet here I was, detached from VP-25, on the opposite coast, a preemptive strike arranged by Skipper Wilson for the very purpose of evading Fowler's crosshairs. What had gone wrong? I was still in a mild state of shock traversing the Yard back to our apartment. My whole world had gone upside down in the blink of an eye. I passed the Chapel, the Admin Building, the parade field with its autumn-flecked maples and backdrop of large brick homes filled with families, imagining how fortunate they were untouched by this personal tragedy which had fallen on me like an axe. How would I describe my shame to Aimee, my humiliation, the anger burning inside? I was headed back to Moffett to face an incomprehensible, life-altering event. I was being exiled from paradise like Cain in the Book of Genesis. My past had caught up with me, Eden no longer sustainable, Nod, my future. Was this the message God was sending me?

# 23

## THE LAND OF NOD

AFTER PASSING THROUGH Moffett Field's main gate, the road forms a Y encircling a vast lawn the size of two football fields, likely a parade field in the distant past. A row of mission-style administration buildings with red clay tile roofs dominates each side of the grassy expanse set in the shadow of the mighty Hangar One. This original part of the base dates to the 1930s airship era and the architecture is a pale nod to the famous Main Quad of nearby Stanford University a few miles north on El Camino Real with its own grand mission arches and vast spread of red clay tile. I'd always felt at home amongst the Spanish Colonial architecture that dominates much of California but today it was like a plague, an unwelcome sense I'd returned to purgatory.

The Judge Advocate General's office was situated near the center of the quad in a two-story building with a small parking lot. I parked my rental car out front and trooped up the dimly lit hallway to a second-floor suite of offices for my appointment with the senior JAG officer, a full Navy captain. After a brief wait, I was led into his inner office by the yeoman out front. We made quick introductions without any pleasantries. The captain turned to introduce a lieutenant commander, also a JAG officer, likely to act as his witness. The lieutenant commander, who bore a startling resemblance to Rod Serling, took a seat on a couch against the far wall. I sat in a chair directly in front of the captain. These preliminaries took less than a minute, both men making it clear with their expressions and mannerisms this was purely business. No refreshments were offered, no coffee, no water, nothing. The room was stuffy, a steam radiator clanking away under a window. I'd entered the Twilight Zone.

"Lieutenant Baumann," the captain began, staring at the file before him. A copy of the charge sheet prepared and signed by Commander Fowler was on top. "You are present today because you are being formally charged with the violation of four punitive articles of the Uniform Code of Military Justice. These charges have been referred to a proper convening authority and may result in a general court-martial. Do you understand?"

"Yes, sir."

"Okay, let me begin. You are charged with violating UCMJ Articles 92,

98, 108 and 111. The following are the associated specifications.

"First: In that Lieutenant Mitchell J. Baumann, U.S. Navy, did, on or about 15 March 1983 at or near Naval Air Station Adak, Alaska, knowingly commit an unauthorized release of classified information to an enlisted petty officer without proper security clearance, in violation of Naval Instruction OPNAVINST 5510 and Article 92.

"Second: In that Lieutenant Baumann did on or about 14 March 1983, consume alcohol within twelve hours of aircraft preflight time in violation of OPNAVINST 3710, Naval Air Training and Operating Procedures Standardization and Articles 92 and 111.

"Third: In that Lieutenant Baumann did, on or about 15 March 1983, allow unauthorized personnel, two female petty officers, on a naval aircraft while conducting a classified tactical mission in close proximity to the Soviet Union in violation of Navy regulation 0840 and –"

This is where I let things fade out and quit listening. I'd read the charges myself, in fact, had spent hours digesting them on the plane ride out. After reading the third, the captain went on to charge me with unauthorized shutdown of our number four engine while on station, a violation of a Wing 10 standing order and destruction of government property, basically a violation of Article 108. There were five charges in all, violating four articles under the UCMJ. Again, this was Fowler, and it was personal.

"Lieutenant Baumann, do you understand the charges and specifications as I've read them?"

"Yes, sir." I'd read them a hundred times already.

"Do you have any questions?"

"No, sir."

The captain looked up from the charge sheet and met my eye. "Do you understand you have the right to counsel and to have counsel present during questioning?"

"Yes, sir." I'd forgotten about the Article 31 rights, that they'd be part of the procedure.

"Do you understand you have the right to remain silent?"

"Yes, sir."

"And that any statements, oral or written, may be used against you?"

This was surreal and making me ill. I'd first heard these words on *Dragnet* when I was a boy. It was when Sergeant Joe Friday cuffed the bad guys and read them their Miranda rights. I was hearing the military's equivalent, their gravity just as intense. I felt light-headed like I might faint. I was no bad guy. These words couldn't apply to me.

"Lieutenant Baumann? Do you understand?"

I blinked back to reality. "Yes, sir."

"By signing the form, you are not admitting guilt, only that you are acknowledging the charges you've been read. You will need to find counsel.

I'd like to do the arraignment tomorrow, basically another meeting similar to this but with counsel present where you will make your plea." The captain looked up. "You *do* plan to have counsel represent you?"

"Yes, sir." I scribbled my name on their forms. I had no idea where I was supposed to find a lawyer in twenty-four hours.

"I suggest you go next door, meet with the DSO. They take drop-ins and can assign a government lawyer to represent you at no expense. Or, if you prefer, you may hire a civilian lawyer to represent you, but that will be at your expense, of course."

"Of course." I stood to leave. "Thank you, gentlemen. I trust we are finished?"

They both nodded.

I wanted out. It was clear these guys were not my friends or on my side.

I walked from the captain's office, across the hallway and down several doors to an open bay with three desks. Two were empty, a female lieutenant (jg) was sitting behind the third. I leaned in the doorway. "Excuse me, is this the DSO's office? They told me you take drop-in appointments?"

"No, I'm sorry, this is the Legal Services Office. The DSO is—" she looked up, "Mr. Baumann? I mean, Lieutenant Bau— Mitch?"

She looked familiar.

Before I could place her, she said, "It's me, Amanda White. Twenty-Seventh Company. One of your plebes? Remember?"

I felt embarrassed. Under normal circumstances, I'd have recognized her instantly. "Of course, I remember you." She stood and we shook hands. I stepped back realizing I was probably too dazed to ID my own sister. Amanda was not the 18-year-old kid I remembered but had matured into a pretty twenty-something. Her face was lean and tanned enhanced by a touch of makeup, her hair a bit longer, salon cut, not the shaggy mop I recalled from plebe summer.

"What brings you up here?" she said. "To the Defense Services Office, of all places?"

This was humiliating, having to explain my legal predicament to someone outside my family, especially to one of my plebes from first-class year. Nonetheless, I gave her a thumbnail of the whole mess, the flight in Adak, the vindictive Fowler, the charges just read to me. I tossed in I was married, two kids, currently stationed back at the Academy as a company officer.

This drew a surprise reaction. "The Academy? Wow. I'm not sure I could go back there. Not this soon."

I understood the underlying message to her question. She was bringing Maddy back into the conversation, interested in any residual influence she or the case still held over me. Was the vibe any more intense back in Annapolis proper?

"How's it working out?"

"Oh, you know, it's a plum assignment," I said. "We're enjoying it so far." I turned serious and lowered my voice. "Truth is, I'm reminded of her every day. It's hard not to. I find myself avoiding our old company area on 6-1. In fact, I try to stay out of the entire sixth wing whenever possible. When I was stationed here at Moffett, the memories faded. I'd swept the whole thing under the rug. But as I feared, all of it – Maddy, her disappearance, the investigation, came roaring back the moment I drove through the gate." I recalled my sensory overload the morning we toured our new quarters. I walked over to the window and looked onto the parking lot. "Have you heard anything new? Any update?"

"The investigation's still officially open."

"Yeah, I figured. Just no breakthroughs after six years?"

"No."

I'd hoped Amanda, in her JAG capacity, might've heard something, or been privy to some behind-the-scenes stuff. "So, what about you. How'd you end up getting into the JAG Corps?"

She went on to describe the process of applying during her first-class year, one of two from the class of '80 to be accepted. She'd received her JD degree from UC Berkeley, finished the Navy's J-School in January after passing the California state bar then assigned to the Regional Legal Services Office, Moffett Field branch, over the summer. She added the cost for this marvelous education was three more years of service obligation tacked on to her original five. "I'll be a lifer, for sure," she laughed, then switched subjects. "So, Mitch, you really need to find a competent defense lawyer regarding these charges. Someone good."

"What about you?" I smiled, offering a compliment, nothing more. "A lawyer fresh out of J-School, think she could handle it?"

Amanda didn't laugh. "I don't do that. Not yet. The RLSO provides legal advice and referrals to service members for things like financial guidance, notary, powers of attorney, stuff like that. You need the DSO." She nodded down the hall.

"So, just walk down there and take my chances with whoever's in?"

"No!" she said, urgently, then lowered her voice. "The JAG defender stationed here is a real idiot. I wouldn't go near him," she said, in nearly a whisper. "And you didn't hear that from me. The guy you need to see is in our San Diego office. He's exceptional. I highly recommend him."

"Clear down in San Diego? Who is he?"

Amanda paused to flip through her Rolodex.

I laughed. "Highly recommended, huh? You don't even know his name."

"I know him just fine. People call him the Monk. Hang on." She lifted out his card. "Leonard Monkowski, LT(JG), San Diego DSO. Did his law school in Florida. FSU, I believe. Phone number is on the card, although you may not need it."

"No?"

"He's going to be up here sometime tomorrow working another case. You should find him, set up some time."

"Hmm, a junior grade lieutenant, Half-ass U grad, goes by the Monk. Sounds like my kind of guy."

"Don't be fooled by his rank. And FSU's not a bad school. You were expecting Harvard Law, perhaps?"

"Why not? It's only my life we're talking about."

"Meet with him, Mitch. I think you'll be surprised."

"I'll try," I said, slipping the card in my pocket. "Your captain here wants to do the arraignment tomorrow."

"That's his problem. You've got rights. You get to call some of the shots now. They have to give you adequate time to find counsel, and that can take days, not twenty-four hours. Just tell his yeoman out front you can't do it tomorrow, that you're requesting more time. They'll set a new date."

"That easy?"

"That easy. Look, Mitch, these charges are serious. I don't know your XO, this Commander Fowler, but if he can make any of this stick then—"

"Then what?"

"Well. It could ruin your career, maybe worse. I really shouldn't speculate. I only advise you to find Monk, work with him, take the process seriously. Despite what ridiculous things you think of Fowler, he's submitted his charges and he's basically out of the loop. It's in the Government's hands and I'm certain they'll prosecute this aggressively."

I suspected as much. Still, there was so much out of my control, so much coming at me from different directions, my only recourse to take it one step at a time. I'd find this Monk fellow tomorrow and we'd chart the government's minefield together. Amanda's endorsement was good enough. I still needed to find a place to stay, get settled, call Aimee. I stood to leave. "Well, I'd better get going. Thanks for the referral. I assume we'll see each other again?"

"Sure, Mitch. I'll be glad to help. Whatever you need."

I grabbed my briefcase. "So, what happened after I left?"

"Huh?"

"You know, after I graduated? Was there any more talk, any activity at all on the case?"

"No. Nothing. After youngster cruise, I was shoved into 10th Company since I needed a roommate. Guess they figured it best to get me as far away from 27 as possible. I almost quit. Youngster year was a tough adjustment coming back after the summer, but I hung on. Did my remaining three years in 10, not a peep about Maddy."

"Nothing ever came out, no publicity, nothing in the papers?"

"Nope. We all learned the Academy was great at disseminating its zero-tolerance policy on sexual harassment, setting the bar way up there, and when there were violations, they came down hard, but they were also great about dealing with it behind closed doors, circling the wagons, experts at damage control. They treated the Maddy affair the same way." She lowered her voice back to a whisper. "I'm told some pressure was put on her parents, that they were told to keep quiet while the NIS ran down the hot leads, so as not to disturb the investigation by bringing a lot of publicity that might spook the perpetrators."

"And the parents bought that? They never talked to a reporter?"

"They must not have. I never saw anything in the papers, either before or after you graduated."

"Unbelievable." This confirmed my suspicion. "So, it really was about deflection, letting others take the fall for related transgressions while they flailed about on the real crime. Show everyone action was being taken, progress made, people fired."

Amanda's eyes lit up. "Hey. Speaking of people fired, remember Captain Manley, 28th Company officer?"

"Of course, I do."

"I bumped into him last month when I was down in San Diego. He's out of the Marine Corps, a civilian now—"

"Yeah, I figured he'd be out of the Corps. How'd you ever run across him?"

"Our services office down there liaises with civilian law firms from time to time, stuff like divorce or bankruptcy when a service member is involved. Manley works for a private security firm in Coronado, a partner or something. Anyway, he was doing some investigating for a client, a sailor involved in a messy divorce. He needed some paperwork, came into the office, we talked for a while. I told him I remembered him from the Academy. At first, he seemed aloof, like, big deal, until I told him I was Maddy's roommate. He grew serious and we chatted a bit more. Didn't say much about himself, just asked how I was doing, said he was sorry about Maddy, wished me luck. But I got the feeling he knew stuff, you know? Didn't seem interested in going down that path, like he had other things on his mind."

I was reminded of my meeting in his office with Lieutenant Herrera. "He does know stuff," I said. "He let some things slip the day before he was given the boot. At the time it all seemed random like he was bitter for being fired and giving the bird to everyone, but now I'm not sure." I tried to recall all that was said in that meeting with Herrera back in '77. "Do you have a card on him? Any contact information?"

"No. But I could easily get it. As I said, his firm is closely connected to the Navy. They do a lot of business with the sailor community."

"Yeah, I'll bet." I pictured a sleazy PI firm, investigators hired to trail sailors or their wives all over town suspected of cheating, that sort of thing.

"I can make a few calls." She placed a hand on her desk telephone. She knew what I was thinking.

"Nah, don't worry about it. As if I don't have enough on my plate."

"Sure, Mitch."

We stood and briefly shook hands. Amanda leaned in and whispered, "It'll be okay. I'll help if I can."

I forced a tiny smile. "Appreciate it."

There was much to do. I practically needed to make a list. First item was to get a postponement of the arraignment. Second was to track down this Leonard Monkowski, or the Monk, or whatever the hell he was called, and pin my hopes to him. I needed to call Amber, my mother, and Aimee, in that order. As I headed to my car my mind was a jumbled mess.

My problems were just beginning.

This is *Palo Alto*? I thought. Well, okay, East Palo Alto, but still… I cruised the street slowly, searching for house numbers of an address Amber had given me, part of me sad at what I was seeing, part of me resigned, knowing this was her reality, the price paid for a life of bad choices. I'd never been to this part of the Peninsula and was astonished at the disparity of neighborhoods and homes only blocks away on the "proper" side of 101. This side resembled a war zone. What began I'm sure as starter homes for returning World War II vets and their budding families had turned into a vast suburban slum. These mid-century cottages were now being rented, and trashed, by a variety of ungrateful, down-on-their-luck tenants as evidenced by the graffiti, the broken-down automobiles in people's yards and bars on their windows.

I spotted Amber's ancient VW Beetle, one she'd purchased to replace the original that'd rolled down the hill on Thanksgiving day. The house number matched the address she'd given me. Her yellow Bug parked out front confirmed I had made no mistake. Ugh, this was going to be tough. I opened the rickety gate and walked to the front door. My plan was to stay with Amber during my return to the land of Nod, hoping the stay would last no more than a week. The Moffett BOQ was full, the surrounding hotels too expensive and Mother's large home up in Millbrae too far. Besides, I wasn't ready to explain everything to Mother, not yet.

Amber greeted me in work attire, black slacks and polo shirt, a tiny smiley-faced *Goodwill* logo embroidered on one side, her name tag on the other. I'd last seen her about a month before we left for Annapolis and knew she'd moved out of Mother's, rented a place, purchased a car and acquired a female roommate. Before that, it was at our father's funeral only weeks after returning from her drug rehab stint in Colorado. We hugged on the steps, both of us sensing the irony of change brought about by my recent misfortune. My life was now in peril, Amber's transitioning to stability, a reversal of fates neither of us could've predicted.

The small living room was cluttered with many personal items spread amidst the modest furniture – stacks of unopened mail, magazines, a half-full laundry basket, a neatly folded quilt on the sofa. Things appeared to have been hastily tidied up for my visit. I smiled. This was Amber's well-intentioned effort to conceal my discomfort created by her chaos. "Oh, I brought this," I said, holding up a bottle of merlot. "Thought we could share it over dinner." I'd never been to Amber's house before or surprised her with wine. I sensed a sudden unease developing, of being thrust together and forced to act like grownups for the first time. "Monterey County," I added, looking at the label. "Thought it'd take the edge off before I get into my story later."

"You're kidding, right?"

"Oh." I took a step back. I'd surmised, perhaps incorrectly, that Amber planned to cook us dinner. "I'm sorry. Are we going out?"

"No, Mitch." She put her hands on her hips and glared. "I just spent thirteen weeks at Camp Columbine, remember? I can't drink. Not now, not ever."

"Oh, right." I'd forgotten, the Columbine Care Center. "I'm sorry," I said again, abandoning the bottle on a nearby end-table.

"I'm making us spaghetti. Nothing fancy, but it's quick, and all I've got. Do you have a suitcase or anything?"

"In the car." I pointed. "Look, Amber, I'm sorry. I forgot about—"

"Don't worry about it. It's my doing, my consequences, no one else's." She wanted off the topic. "Let's take a walk out back. I need a cigarette. I'll show you around."

"That'd be great." We stepped through a kitchen door onto a stoop facing the postage stamp backyard. The cottage was typical of others in the neighborhood – small rancher, two-bedroom, one-car garage, flat roof, narrow property line. The stucco exterior and wood trim were in sore need of paint, the backyard mostly compacted dirt and weeds except for a small clearing near the fence.

"This is my garden," Amber said, pointing proudly. "Well, *was* my garden. It was beautiful in the summer." She pointed at several tomato plants and four wilted, bare corn stalks. "The cherry tomatoes came in great, gave us dozens. The corn, not so great. I don't think I gave it enough water." She pointed at a kinked hose and plastic watering can. "Maybe next year I'll put in some squash. And I've always wanted to grow a pumpkin or two." We walked back inside the kitchen. My heart was melting. This was progress, a phenomenal turnaround, all while I wasn't looking. My jaded sister was trying to be normal, to embrace a life she'd spent many years railing against.

Amber put on a pot of water and started dicing mushrooms while I cleared the tiny two-seat table, removing breakfast dishes, scattered

363

newspaper and more unopened mail, mostly bills. I sat at the table and watched her cook. "So, how's Mother? You see her much?" I really craved a glass of that wine going to waste in the living room.

"Mother is mother," she said. "I see her on weekends when I'm not working. We talk on the phone. She seems more interested in Gwen, what makes her tick, than anything else around here."

"Gwen?"

"My roommate. Gwen. The bedroom you'll be sleeping in? Hello? I'm sure Mother's told you all about her."

"Oh, right." Gwen, as Amber had explained, was out of town for the week visiting family up in Portland. That was the only detail provided when she invited me to stay. I'd never met Gwen although I did learn from Mother, among other things, she was a lot older than Amber. "So, how's she adjusting to things, Mother, the newly bereaved widow?"

"Oh, she's fine. It's not like Dad was around much anyway."

"True." He'd left her five years prior, but Mother had always held an unspoken hope he'd return. She'd always bring him up in conversation as though he were on the golf course for the afternoon or in the next room watching a ballgame on TV.

"She's turned into quite the gossip, our mother," Amber continued, chopping lettuce for the salad.

"You don't say."

"Thinks the neighbors are spying on her. Complains about her health more, losing interest in the garden club, claims the housekeeping service is stealing from her, that sort of thing."

"Stealing? That's not good."

"Oh, Mitch, please. No one's stealing anything. It's just her way of getting attention."

I had to laugh. We were on the same wavelength, discussing the same person, a mother who'd spent a lifetime vying for attention through any means available. Amber went on about her job at Goodwill, how she enjoyed it and made her feel good to associate with and help the less fortunate rather than working in retail elsewhere. It was a start, she said, employment her rehab center had helped arrange. I studied her nimbly moving about the kitchen as though she'd been cooking for years. There was a spring in her step, a liveliness I hadn't detected earlier. Gone was the suspicious, skittish demeanor, the angry girl persona ready to flee at the drop of a hat after years of drug use and associated paranoia. She was finally putting her life together, finally able to support herself, gaining confidence from her new job, her car, *her garden*. Her face still bore a trace of wear, some early lines, but her complexion was good, eyes bright, otherwise the look of a youthful 24-year-old. Life hadn't treated her well but, as she said, these were her choices, her consequences. And she had accepted them and seemed at peace.

Dinner was simple but amazing. Amber said she'd finally perfected her sauce-making and had used fresh arugula dotted with home-grown cherry tomatoes on the salad. As we wrapped up and moved to the living room, I decided to get into my saga, one I'd hinted at but provided no details. We sat and I told her about the flight in Adak, about the trouble we'd encountered and the subsequent legal mess. Predictably, she reacted like Aimee, with huge doubt the Navy would ever court-martial anyone after pulling off such a daring feat.

"Well, they are," I said, then gave a brief rundown of the charges. I didn't go into who was doing the court-martialing or why, just that I was in a tough spot.

"You've got a lawyer, right? The Navy allows lawyers?"

"Yes, they allow lawyers. I'm supposed to meet with one tomorrow, goes by the name of the Monk." I smiled. "Comes highly recommended."

"The Monk, huh?" She wasn't amused. "Comes highly recommended for what? A foosball partner down at the frat house?"

"I'm told he's exceptional," I said, recalling Amanda's words.

"Well, I hope he is, Mitch, because this sounds serious." Her worried countenance eerily resembled our mother. "What can they do if, you know, if you're—"

"Found guilty? I don't know, probably discharge me. I need to talk to this guy tomorrow." I massaged my temples. "Let's not go into it anymore tonight." I really wanted a glass of that wine, or something stronger.

Amber reached across the table aware of my distress. "I'm sorry, Mitch," she said, taking my hand. "I really am. I wish there were more I could do."

"Thanks. I smiled and squeezed back. "You already have, so let's just drop it. What about you? What do you do when you're not working at Goodwill or tilling the soil or listening to Mother's woes?"

"I go to AA meetings. Twice a week, in the evening."

"AA, wow. And they're helping?"

"I live for them. I'd go every night if I could."

"Every night? Amber, there's more to life than AA meetings. You've made amazing progress. You seem to be in a good place now."

"A good place is when I'm most vulnerable to the drugs. I can't celebrate a good day anymore or pick myself up from a bad one. No margarita at happy hour, no glass of wine, nothing. That's when I really don't see the point of staying on the wagon. Life's highs and lows scare the hell out of me, and I struggle just to keep things at a dull, monotone hum."

I nodded yet couldn't imagine. My ignorance on Amber's addiction and emotional tug-of-war left me silent.

"So AA works. It keeps me on the straight and narrow. And the people are wonderful. There's a sense of honesty and love – things I've never felt from a group before. An instant acceptance," she added.

"What about rehab?  How was Colorado?"

"Colorado?  It was awful.  F– that place."

"F– that place?"  I grinned.  This was also an improvement.  Amber used to toss more fucks around than Richard Pryor.  "Was it tough?"  It was difficult to imagine a harsh bootcamp environment with the colorful brochures Mother had left lying around showing a posh mountain lodge and majestic snowcapped peaks.

"No drugs, no alcohol.  Nothing, for thirteen weeks.  They kept their promise on that.  But the stupid rules, the lockdowns, the horrible food, two to a room.  I don't know.  The final cost was obscene, the biggest waste of money ever.  I could've chained myself to my room at home for three months and done better."

"Is that where you met Gwen?"

"No.  I met her at the AA meetings, about three months ago.  She's great, by the way, a positive person, someone to look up to.  We got along so well, we agreed to rent this house, signed the lease a week later."

I looked closely at Amber.

"And no, Mitch, she's not a lesbian, if that's what you're thinking."

I laughed.  "Never crossed my mind."

"She took a real tumble.  Started on antidepressants after getting married and having a baby, mainly dealing with postpartum.  Began self-medicating after that with a range of drugs, valium, speed, opiates, bogus prescriptions, then arrest.  She lost her husband, custody of their child, a cute little eight-year-old girl.  Had a home in Marin, money, a pretty nice life."

"That's horrible."

"It's not uncommon.  People take falls.  AA's full of stories."

I thought about my own fall, still underway.

"And, Mitch, please don't say anything to Mother.  She's really curious about Gwen.  She's older, about ten years, and Mother keeps poking me with her usual BS.  What's wrong with that woman?  She looks like a hippie.  Why isn't Gwen dating?  Why isn't Gwen engaged?  Why isn't Gwen married?"

"Gwen, huh?"

"Exactly.  Those questions are obviously pointed at me."

"It's a generational thing," I said, smiling.

"It's a sick, manipulative Mother thing."

I wondered if Amber had a boyfriend, someone waiting in the wings.  "You think you'll be ready to start dating again?"

"Oh, I suppose.  But I'll let you in on a little secret," she said, lowering her voice.  "The drugs, they completely wipe out any sense of normalcy and screw with your priorities.  You're on a mission for one thing only.  Friends and personal relationships no longer matter.  Sex no longer matters."

I wanted to stick my fingers in my ears, sing *la-la-la-la.*

"All you think about is where the next hit is coming from.  Oh, sure, I had plenty of sex, straight, gay, three-way, but it's joyless, more like revenge, what feral druggies do when they're high."

*La-la-la-la.*

Amber noticed my disturbed look. "Sorry. That's just the AA talking. We're very open at the meetings. I guess I'm still adjusting, discovering what my new normal is," she said, drawing air quotations around "normal."

"Me too."

She paused, moving closer, observing my detached state, reading my mind. "Mitch, believe me, I know it's hard right now. But eventually things work out. Time heals. Aimee gave me a book at Thanksgiving, just before rehab. Do you remember?"

I remembered. "You read it?"

"Cover to cover. The first thing it said was, life is hard. As soon as you accept life is hard, it stops being hard. Something like that."

"Yes." I very much remembered the book, and my cavalier response to Aimee after she'd laid that bit of philosophy on me the night before Adak. I'd hit back, hard. Hearing it now from Amber made me want to cry. I'd been so angry, so full of arrogance and directed it at my family like a cruise missile. My, how life changes, I thought. "Don't let anyone tell you karma ain't for real," I said, my eyes wandering beyond Amber to a shelf on the wall. "Is that a picture of Mom and Dad?"

She turned around to look. "Yes. I've never kept pictures before. I thought I should have a few."

The photo showed them as a couple, taken at MacDill Field in Florida, 1944, just before Dad shipped overseas. "Mother has one too," I said. "In their den."

"It's the same one. She gave it to me on my last visit up."

I walked over to the shelf and picked up it. "God, Amber, they're so young. Look at Mother, barely eighteen years old for crying out loud." They both wore brave smiles. I studied my father closely wondering what his thoughts were at that moment, holding his new bride knowing he was headed to war, his world about to go inverted. "Were you afraid?" I whispered, holding the frame close.

"I'll bet he was," Amber said, placing her arm around me. "Were you?"

"When?"

"In Alaska. When your plane nearly crashed."

"That was different, there wasn't time. He knew," I said. "There was plenty of time to ponder his fate every time he went up."

"Well, he came back. And so did you. You didn't drown in the ocean. That would've been two airplane accidents in the family. Father and son, both dead in the water."

"Amber, *please.*" I'd never considered it that way, that I almost followed in his footsteps literally, both of us ending up in watery graves.

"Do you think he intentionally crashed his airplane, Mitch? That it was a suicide?"

"Suicide?" I was shocked. "What? No!"

"I do."

"Don't say that. You don't know."

"Not for sure. But I talked to him, on the phone up in Coeur d'Alene, a few months before his accident. I needed money for rehab."

"And?"

"He seemed fine. He was sweet, agreed, no problem. Told me he'd just renewed his private pilot's license. Wanted to start flying again, small planes."

"So? How's that make him suicidal?"

"It seemed odd. He wasn't exactly heartbroken when he left United. The way he talked to Mother, I figured he'd never touch another airplane."

And he hadn't, for five years. I could see Amber's point. But, still, her dark speculation came out of the blue, blindsiding me. I'd never allowed myself to consider suicide a possibility. "I figured his going back to flying was a good sign."

"Maybe, who knows."

"I guess I should contact this Ramona woman," I said, sighing at the inevitable. "I told her I would."

"His girlfriend? Yuk."

"Whatever she was." Like me, Amber was uncomfortable with the term. "We spoke at the funeral. Made it sound like she had information, things she wanted to share."

"Like what?"

"I don't know. She wanted me to come up to Idaho, show me something. At first, I suspected it was about money, but she quickly rebuked me on that point. I wasn't exactly coherent that day. Lots in my head."

"I remember."

"I wish I could." I wasn't keen putting more focus on this dark corner of my life. I wanted lighter conversation, away from funerals, death, rehab and court-martials. I switched us to something more amicable, recalling several humorous stories when we were kids. They seemed to lift our spirits, but after the laughter died, Amber grew quiet. I was sitting on the floor in front of the coffee table and watched her expression change from joy to sadness.

She looked up, brushing a tear from her face. "Mitch, I'm sorry. I wasn't a very good sister, was I?"

"Whoa, where's this coming from?" I said, at a loss. "You were fine." Her teen years had shaved lives off us all. Well, at least Mother and me. But this didn't bear repeating. Amber had paid dearly for her mistakes and was on the higher road to recovery and a promising life ahead. Why was she bringing this up now? "We all made mistakes back then," I said. "And I mean every one of us. Nobody's perfect, right?"

"No. I was awful. I treated you horribly."

"No, you didn't." I joined her on the sofa. "What are you talking about?"

She grinned. "Remember when I snuck up behind you at our pool? It was winter and you were skimming leaves. The water was freezing, and I pushed you in, clothes and all."

I laughed. I remembered. "Yeah, you were like four. I was beside myself with rage and wanted to shove you in too, but Mom stopped me. Typical brother-sister stuff. It's hilarious now."

"I know but—"

"Amber, don't beat yourself up. We were kids, we were happy. It was a better time," I added, implying things did indeed change later.

"I used to sneak up and poke you in the ribs too. You'd always scream bloody murder then chase after me." She laughed easily. "You used to hate that."

"I know. I was ticklish. Still am."

The smile faded. "Mitch, I don't know how to say this, but I wish I could erase so much of my life, mostly what came after high school. And so much more. I really want to change."

"I know you do."

"Sometimes I hate myself. I really do."

"No, you don't." I was puzzled by this sudden negative outburst but recognized its significance. I pulled her close for a hug. "Amber, you're awesome and you're beautiful," I whispered in her ear. "And you're doing great." I gently eased back, holding onto her. "Just don't poke me in the ribs right now, okay?"

Tears were streaming down her cheeks. She smiled and sniffed. "Okay."

It was getting late. I stood, needing to retrieve my bag from the car and get ready for bed. "You know, I really should go up there," I said, thinking back to Idaho. "I should. For both of us."

"Up where?" Amber said, reaching for a Kleenex.

"To see this Ramona woman. I could call her, drive up, when I have time."

"When on earth will you have time?"

"I don't know." I reached for the front door. "Maybe I'll get kicked out of the Navy this week. Then I'll have plenty of time."

# 24

## THE MONK

"SO, TELL ME ABOUT THIS FOWLER DUDE," the Monk said. "Why's he got a bee up his ass?"

I rolled my eyes at his mixing of metaphors and referring to a full Navy commander as "this Fowler dude." I wasn't sure what to make of this guy, smart or just empathetic as he drilled in on what he sensed, I'm sure, was the root of my problem. No harm continuing the interview, I thought. "Well, as I said, he's vindictive. It's in his genes. Doesn't seem to like subordinates. The more junior, the more the need to push them around, intimidate them, abuse his authority."

"Sounds like my kind of CO."

"He's not."

"Mitch, I was kidding, a little sarcasm. Lighten up, please."

"Lighten up?"

"Yes. If this thing goes to trial, there'll be plenty of time for seriousness. I'm only trying to gain a sense of the politics, the personalities right now. You and Fowler, the rest of the VP-25 wardroom, there's a history of clashes, I presume? When he abuses his authority?"

"Yeah, something like that."

"You pulled pranks. Had nicknames for him. Used them behind his back?"

"Hold on. Where's this coming from?" My defenses reacted immediately, feeling I was already on trial, not being interviewed by a prospective lawyer. "Don't you want to hear my side of the charges?"

"I've read the charges. I've read the entire file. Again, I'm trying to gain a sense, intuit some things before we—"

I interrupted. "Look, Monk, are you going to take the case or what?"

"—go into the arraignment, make your plea."

"Oh, so now you're not sure how I'm going to plead?"

"Mitch, calm down. You're getting ahead of things. I'm getting some preliminaries out of the way before deciding our best course of action."

"So, you're taking the case?"

"We still need to talk."

"It seems more like an interrogation. You're supposed to be on my side."

"Better to get this stuff out now. Tell me more about Fowler, when you first had words."

"Like a conversation?"

"Yes."

"Well, we first spoke in 1977 back when—"

"1977? I thought you said he joined the squadron in '82."

"He did. I knew him at the Academy, briefly, back when I was a midshipman."

Monk took a deep breath and picked up his pen. "Okay, let's start with 1977."

I began the narrative starting with the Superintendent's reception and recounted all I could about that date. I continued chronologically, expressing my feelings, my relationship, the squadron JO's relationships, my run-ins, primarily during his tenure as XO of VP-25. I left nothing out, eventually arriving at the Maddy investigation and my comments to Fowler the day I'd checked out of the squadron. None of this was in the file he'd read.

Monk sat quietly, nodding, encouraging, asking a few questions but mainly writing on his yellow legal pad.

I'd met Monk only hours earlier in Amanda's office. If I'd held an image of the tall, handsome, strong-shouldered defender of life's victims and underdogs then I was sorely mistaken. Monk was short, wore his hair uncombed and carried a bit of a limp. His wire-frame glasses were thick, and his face bore scars from what must've been a raging case of teenage acne. This was the nerdy kid in high school everyone picked on or beat up in the showers after gym class. Monk was up from San Diego wrapping up a plea bargain for some sailor involved in a UA and drunk and disorderly. He seemed bright and capable but carried his intelligence a bit too face-forward for my liking. Amanda had warned me of this, of his curt, dismissive attitude like he was way out in front of anyone he met, knowing everything before they did. She emphasized to not let this lack of people skills influence me, that this was the guy I wanted defending me.

Before Amanda introduced us, we'd met in her office at 0800 this morning, waiting for Monk, sipping coffee. She informed me of her activities after our chance meeting the day before.

"So, I talked to Preston Manley yesterday, on the phone."

"You found him, that quickly?"

"I found a card on his firm. Anyway, he said he'd be glad to talk to you, not sure he could help though, having been six years and all."

"Doesn't sound too eager."

"No, he was interested. You know how he talks, monotone, not much emotion." She looked up. "We can call him now if you'd like."

371

I thought back to our meeting in his Bancroft Hall office. There was no monotone that day. He'd bled out most of his emotion on me. "Nah, I'll do it later. Sounds like he's busy."

"C'mon, Mitch. Monk won't be available for another two hours. Just do it, while you've got a chance."

She knew I was stalling. I had no intention of reviving the investigation, poking around its lifeless edges when I drove onto base yesterday. My visit with Bob and Jan finally convinced me it was time to let Maddy go, for good. Then, wham, next thing I'm face to face with roommate Amanda and, in less than twenty-four hours, she's arranged a conference call with Manley to pick over the loose remains. I just didn't have the heart, or the energy to continue. As if I didn't have enough worries.

"I'm dialing," she said, picking up the phone.

"Oh, for heaven's sake, Amanda." It was too late to pry the receiver from her hand and slam it back on the cradle.

"It's ringing." She smiled and winked at me. Then: "Good morning, Pres?"

*Pres?*

"Sure. He's right here." She handed me the phone.

"Uh, good morning, sir," I said, making a face at Amanda.

Our subsequent conversation started slowly, like he was doing Amanda a favor, nothing more. After all, his firm needed to remain in good standing with the Navy and if it meant doing a little PR, a little schmoozing to keep relations in order, then so be it. However, it soon became obvious Manley was no schmoozer. He was gruff, asking me for details, things I didn't know or care to admit when we'd last met. I told him about the charm bracelet and the visit by Fowler to our company area the night Maddy went missing. The latter piece of information sparked his interest. A second visit? he'd said. I wasn't sure what he'd meant by a second. We didn't talk much after that. He bid a quick goodbye after assurance he'd be in touch. "Let me get back to you on this," he'd said. That was it. He hung up, end of call.

"That was quick," Amanda said, after stepping back into the office with fresh coffee, one in each hand.

"I think he got what he needed."

"What *he* needed? What about you?"

"I'm not sure. Apparently, Fowler had been to 6-1 more than once. That's the piece that jolted him."

"Didn't he share anything with you?"

"Not really."

"Nothing about Maddy's essay?"

"Essay? No, nothing about an essay." Then it hit me. Amanda wasn't the first person to bring up Maddy's admission essay, the one Maddy had told me she'd written that night in my car. Manley was the first. In his office, that day six years ago. "What's the deal with this essay?"

"I don't know. Something Maddy's parents told Manley when they'd met. Before he departed the Academy for good."

"Amanda, please," I said, holding up a hand. "This whole thing is making my head hurt. Mysterious visits, old essays, conversations with the parents. I need to swallow about ten Excedrin right now." It was information overload – zero to sixty in three seconds – too much for my distracted state of mind. Someone needed to get their hands on that essay. That was clearly the next step. "Look, keep a line open with Manley, in case he calls back, but I really shouldn't get any closer to this, not now, for a lot of reasons."

She could see I was agitated. "Sure, Mitch."

"And so that's Fowler, in a nutshell." I smiled at Monk. I felt I'd painted an accurate picture of a tyrant, a bully, a spiteful son-of-a-bitch with an axe to grind and ludicrous charges fit for the dumpster. "Any other questions?"

"Just one, Mitch."

"Shoot."

"Do you think painting Fowler as this loathsome asshole, a bully as you put it, is a prudent defense?"

"He *is* a bully. The court will see that."

Monk looked at his notes. "Or perhaps they'll just see a bitchy, whiny JO."

"Hey, you asked about him. Is it not prudent to torpedo Fowler on the witness stand?"

"If this thing goes to court-martial, I'd never *put* Fowler on the witness stand."

"Oh, so I'm going to take a plea, admit guilt? No trial. Is that where we're headed? If so, then I want to talk to another lawyer."

Monk picked up my file and waved it between us. "Unauthorized release of top-secret classified information? Drinking on duty, violating your twelve-hour rule? All the rest that's in here?" He dropped the manila folder back to the table. "The Government wouldn't care if Fowler was a card-carrying communist. Their witnesses corroborate these charges? Then it's lights out for Mitch, no room for a deal if we go to trial. You suffer the full consequences for something that appears very black and white."

I figured in a full court-martial, worst-case scenario, I was facing discharge, and that was only a remote possibility. Until now. I swallowed hard. "Okay, Monk. What am I looking at, worst case? What's the max the Navy can do to me?"

Monk placed a friendly hand on my shoulder, a gesture of pity. "Let's not discuss that now."

"C'mon, you've made your point. I'm scared shitless. Why not?"

"Because every case has its gray areas. Best not to discuss the extreme, not yet."

"You just said this one's black and white."

"I was being a lawyer. It's got some gray in it for sure, probably more than most. We just don't want it to go to a full court-martial."

"So, we make a deal? Is that it?"

"Maybe a different strategy." Monk paused, took the opportunity to pour himself some water. "Do you remember your Law 101 from the Academy?"

"I took a leadership and law course if that's what you mean."

"Did they teach you about Article 32?"

"I don't know. Probably. What's your point, Monk?"

"Let's presume you're innocent, of all charges."

"The law presumes innocence, that much I know. Right?"

"Let me rephrase. Let's presume this goes to a court-martial and you're found not guilty of all charges."

"Amen."

"Hang on. Now let's say it goes the other way, that you're found guilty."

"I'd rather go back to door number one."

"You're sentenced, discharged, less than honorable, maybe worse."

I gulped.

"Kicked out of the Navy, career ruined, future aspirations as a commercial airline pilot ruined, professional career anywhere in the private sector ruined, game over."

"Stop. We weren't going to discuss extreme. Why are you doing this?"

"Okay, so let's return to not guilty. What then?"

"I go back to the Academy, resume my job as a company officer and put all this behind me?" As soon as I finished my sentence, I knew that wasn't the right answer. I was being led to an alternate, much less appealing scenario.

"You're an officer with a promising career. The court-martial becomes a permanent part of your service record, guilty or not guilty."

"Okay, so you're saying even if I'm found not guilty and allowed to continue my naval service, my career is over. I'll be passed over for any more fast-track assignments or promotion?"

"Basically, yeah. Even a not guilty looks bad, that you even went to court-martial in the first place."

"So, I'm screwed either way," I said. "That goddamn Fowler. This was his plan all along." I eyed Monk, not expecting his reaction. "Why are you smiling?"

"Let's go back to Article 32. You know what a grand jury is, right?"

I nodded. "It's the civilian counterpart to an Article 32. An investigation to see if the charges hold water?"

"Indeed. So, there's been an Article 32 investigation by some line officer. His name's in the packet here." Monk pointed to my file. "It's similar to a grand jury, justification and decision to send it to a court-martial. The difference is we get to challenge the charges, just like in a trial. We can call witnesses, cross-examine their witnesses. It's called an Article 32 hearing."

"And potentially get the charges thrown out before it ever goes to a court-martial?"

Monk nodded.

"And that will prevent anything from ever making it to my record?"

"Bingo."

"So how do we do that?"

"I don't have a clue."

"What?"

"I'm kidding. It won't be easy, but it's our best shot. I may have to call Fowler after all."

"Sounds risky."

"It is. It means we plead not guilty to all the charges at the arraignment tomorrow."

I liked his term, *we*. "So, you're taking the case?"

"If you'll have me."

"Of course, I'll have you. Let's do this thing." I looked at Monk. His jaw was clenched, his features hardened into a mask of controlled rage. "What's gotten into you?"

"Oh, just putting on my game face. I fucking hate bullies."

The drive up to Mother's didn't take long. Traffic on the Bayshore Freeway was light and moved briskly on this Saturday morning. I made my way north from Amber's bungalow in Palo Alto in a heavy funk as cars zipped around me, the events of the previous week so surreal and elusive in nature, yet so tangible and catastrophic in potential outcome. I was not looking forward to meeting my mother, neither expecting to see her so soon after our summer departure for Annapolis nor having to explain my current predicament. Still, I couldn't ignore her upon my unexpected return to the Bay Area. Nor could I forgo paying a visit to our old homestead at the end of Latera Way. For reasons of simple comfort and refuge, I was relishing the weekend break, a chance to escape back to the familiar sights and sounds of the old neighborhood, breathe in the scents of my youth in the nooks and crannies of Chez Baumann. God, how I longed to be that kid in the cul-de-sac again, I thought as I pulled up to the house, carefree and spinning my bike in lazy figure-8s. I fiddled with the front door, finally pushing it open. I vowed I'd find peace, somehow.

"Hello? Mother? Anyone home?"

"Out here," came a faint cry from the backyard. Mother stepped through the family room's sliding glass door, ensuring it latched behind her. She was dressed in a well-worn utility apron, gloves and straw hat, a silver gardening trowel in her hand. "You caught me," she said with an embarrassed look, wiping her free hand on the apron. "Just putting in the last of my bulbs and emptying out the fuchsia boxes for the winter." She gave a quick laugh. "Look at me, I'm a mess." She actually looked good, a happy countenance and glow of exercise about her. Gardening had always been her tonic, a perpetual source of companionship and renewal.

"You look great, Mother." I gave her a quick kiss on the cheek and a hug, both of us holding on a bit longer than usual.

"Oh, Mitch, daring, you do surprise your mother. Let me look at you." She pulled back. "Why the return so soon? Is Annapolis taking a fall break? And why not Aimee and the kids?" She sensed trouble, diving right to the point. There was no such thing as a fall break.

"Well, we can talk about all that." I sat down on a barstool. "That's partly why I'm here."

"Would you like some coffee?" she said.

"No, thanks."

"Can I make you breakfast? Toast, anything?"

"No, nothing. Thanks."

"Well, I don't know why you didn't drive up yesterday when you got in." She looked hurt. "You're certainly welcome to stay with me, you know."

"I'm staying with Amber, Mother. It's closer to base. And easier to get around."

"Base? Why on earth? I thought you were done with Moffett Field."

"Just some unfinished business. That's why I'm back." The fresh coffee dripping in the pot across the counter got my attention. I wasn't prepared to spill my troubles just yet. "I believe I'll have some coffee after all." I stood, but before I could make a move, Mother had a mug in front of me and was already pouring.

"So," she said, softly, in a conspirator's whisper, "Tell me all about Gwen. What do you make of her?"

"Mother, I haven't had a chance to make anything of her. Gwen's gone for the week, up in Portland, I think, visiting family."

"Oh." She looked disappointed. "I didn't know she had a family. She just sort of popped into Amber's life one day. Family up in Portland, you say?"

Her art for boldface prying veiled as casual conversation was too easy to spot. "Mother, Amber's doing great," I said, getting back on topic. "She's working, she's paying her bills, she's got a garden—"

"She's going to AA," Mother threw in, hoping for surprise.

I halted and looked up. "Yes, she is. And it's keeping her clean and sober, on a path to righteousness. What's wrong with that?"

"Oh, nothing. Nothing, of course, dear. I worry about her, that's all. And that will never change. For as long as you're alive, Mitch, you and Aimee will worry about Sean and little Carlene, even when they're in their fifties and you're in the rest home, you'll still worry about them."

"I'm sure we will, Mother." I leaned over to her barstool and kissed her cheek which she seemed to appreciate, blushing with an approving smile.

"You've always been my Rock of Gibraltar, son," she beamed. "Amber's been my – well, you know, my Amber."

"She's changing, in a good way." I drew a deep breath, knowing the next part wouldn't be easy. "I've had some changes too, Mother. And not in a good way. Your rock is slipping from its foundation, I'm afraid." I looked her in the eye. "I need to tell you why I'm back."

"Oh?"

She was frightened so I began by first providing her more detail, more background about my flight in Adak, painting myself as the unshakable hero of the story in the face of unimaginable odds. I would never brag so brazenly to anyone else, but this was my mother, someone who'd never hear my words and deeds as bragging. Then I entered a soft, sorrowful tone, telling her about the charges against me, the vindictive XO and upcoming court-martial, the reason I had to return.

As expected, she stared in disbelief during my entire monologue, then stirred to life. "Oh, Mitch, all those legal terms. Court-martial. Arraignment. Article 32. It sounds so technical, so serious. What could possibly have persuaded them to do this? What'll happen to you?"

I shrugged. "I'm just taking it one day at a time. As I said, I've got a lawyer. The arraignment's on Tuesday. The hearing will likely start on Wednesday."

"I don't understand. What's the difference between the hearing and the court-martial? They sound like the same thing."

"I'm not sure I understand it that well, myself. The Monk, my lawyer, says the hearing may result in the charges getting thrown out, so it won't have to go to a court-martial."

"And that's good, right?"

"It is. If everything gets tossed before the court-martial, nothing is entered in my service record. Be like nothing ever happened."

"Whew. Well, that's what will happen then."

I smiled. "You've decided, huh?"

"That's right. I've decided."

I was pleased she was calm and supportive, even sympathetic. My biggest fear of her reaction to the news was instant meltdown, an over-the-top, drama-queen performance thinking that's what I wanted to hear. In doing so, she'd also divert the problem (and attention) to her and the burden she would have to bear. Thankfully, there was none of that. I wanted to compliment her restraint but was afraid it'd be construed as inciteful and ruin our fragile peace. Best just to take the gift and move on. "So, Mother, the backyard looks great," I said, surveying the pool and meticulous lawn from my barstool. "You're doing a marvelous job with the old homestead."

"I'm thinking of selling the old homestead," she replied instantly.

"Selling?" This came as a shock and visibly shook me. "Why would you do that? This is home. For all of us. You can't."

"It's getting too much for me to bear, Mitch." There was guilt in her tone. She knew what this home meant to me. "Something's always going wrong."

"But my whole childhood is contained here, these walls, this cul-de-sac. It's *my* Rock of Gibraltar. You can't just sell it."

"And I'm the one who has to deal with it. Alone."

"Okay, Mother, I get it. We won't be in Annapolis forever, you know." We may be back sooner than later, I thought. Moving in with you in fact, if things continue the direction they're headed. "I can help out while I'm home if you'd like. I thought you loved it here."

"Your father loved it here, dear. He picked the lot, built the house. This was his choice."

This was news. I'd just assumed they mutually agreed to settle in the suburbs, raise a family and grow old together. "So, he planted the garden, hung the fuchsia boxes, trimmed the roses, decorated the patio? All that?"

She smiled, not taking the bait. "If it'd been up to me, dear, we'd have stayed in the city. I loved San Francisco, our flat in the Marina District, city life, the formalities, the privacy." She became wistful. "Your father wanted you kids to grow up on the Peninsula, in a big house with trees to climb, a lawn with piles of leaves and a pool out back. That was his dream."

"But you made the house a home, Mother," I said. "Not him." I sharpened my tone, implying fault with my father for his absentee role, especially in the later years. "Dad was never around."

"He was."

"No, I'm sorry. He was not."

She sighed. "Mitch, when does this end? Wasn't the funeral enough? How much more mileage do you intend to squeeze out of this? When do you end the blame?"

"What do you mean, end the blame? How much longer are you going to stick up for him? Get a clue. He left us. For a new life." A voice told me to stop at the risk of sounding like her. "How can you continue to play the role of martyr and elevate him to sainthood? It's delusional, and certainly not honest. Aren't you even the least bit bitter?"

"I'm not bitter. I loved him. Even when things seemed lost, when he was lost. Someday you'll understand."

I was afraid of this. She was leading me to a place I couldn't bear right now. "I'll never understand," I said, dismissively.

"Why? Because he wasn't perfect? Because he didn't live up to your expectations?"

"Mother, stop. I can't do this now."

"Mitch, I know what you're thinking. You were neglected. You were shortchanged. You didn't get the fatherly attention you deserved. You feel you're still owed."

"Mother—"

"Just listen. When we got married, things were different. He was a different man entirely. You tell yourself things will never change but they do. The war changed him, it changed our generation. But when he got home, he adjusted. He had to. Everyone did. He got on with United, began his career, you kids were born healthy and happy, and we moved to the suburbs. The perfect life, right?"

"You would think." I wasn't going to stop her.

"But life isn't perfect. It never is. I became lonely."

"Mother, please."

"I became depressed. I had my own problems. You kids were small. You had so many needs. And your father was gone, a lot. We made friends, we tried to socialize with Aunt Carol and your cousins, but he and Uncle Hank would fight every time we got together, maintaining a feud that lasted twenty years. It became impossible to visit them. Your father drank more, stressed about his job more. Flying began to eat him up." She sighed. "If only you'd known him before, when he was different."

"Oh, please." I rolled my eyes. "Spare me the if-only-I'd-known-him-when-he-was-different speech. As if I had a choice!"

She didn't respond. Her eyes were shut, her lips tightened.

"Mother, I'm sorry."

No response.

I eased off. "Was there anything unusual that happened when he was overseas? He never spoke about that."

"Sure, things happened. Lots of things." She slowly opened her eyes. "I don't know any of the details. I didn't pester him, and he didn't volunteer. We just picked up the pieces and resumed our lives."

I sensed she knew stuff about the missions but wasn't ready to talk. "Tell me about Uncle Hank. Why weren't they close?"

"Oh, that man." She rolled her eyes. "He was an ass. I could barely speak to him at the funeral."

"That's the reason for Dad's problems? Uncle Hank?"

"It's complicated, Mitch. That's the only way I know how to describe it. But, oh, Hank could brag. Your father never bragged. He tended to compartmentalize. When the drinking started, Hank would turn to his time in the Army in Europe, where he'd tell brave stories about fighting the enemy from foxholes in freezing snow or tank battles lasting for days. He'd tell your father he should've been fighting on the ground and experienced real combat, not looking down from the air, returning from his missions to the booze-filled officer's club, hot food and a comfortable bed."

"He said that?"

"Jealousy was at the center, or a childhood grudge, something I never understood. Hank's time in the service was about the only significant thing he ever did, and he'd cling to it like a worn-out blanket. After he got out of the Army, he was always into some crazy get-rich scheme – shady land deals, franchise opportunities, pyramid schemes. He'd urge your father to invest, saying he'd found the deal of a lifetime, then call him a fool when he didn't. We tried to help them. Hank lost a lot of money over the years, and in the end, he lost his wife and two wonderful children."

"So, it was over money? Dad gave him money and invested. That's what did it?"

"Certainly not. He never gave Hank a dime for his schemes. Your father was cautious and sensible. And honest. Traits I'm sure that made an impression on you, Mitch, whether you're aware of it or not. No, something else got to your father. Things piled up." She paused to think. "And then they fell apart. It was that party, around the time we went to the moon, I believe."

"The moon?"

That night in bed I kept turning over the information Mother had given me peeling back layer after layer but bringing me no closer to understanding the man himself. I had bizarre dreams intertwining my court-martial, Uncle Hank, my cousins, Aimee and the kids, all who seemed to arrive on stage simultaneously in some sort of swirling madness where I was lost in a maze, inquiring frantically about directions to a courtroom amidst a series of walls and endless doors. I pleaded for help from my family and was met with a cool indifference like a petulant, crying child after being dropped at nursery school.

I awoke late on a gray Sunday morning in my childhood bedroom shaking off the haze of the dream and my displaced surroundings. I was left with an ambiguous sense of urgency pushing me to action but without a clue as to the dream's significance. I dressed quickly and informed my mother I was headed out. No breakfast, no coffee, nothing. I needed to pay a visit on the Hagl's and get to the bottom of things once and for all. After my father's funeral, Cornelia had invited me to come by, a courtesy, I figured, nothing more. It must've been daughter Krystal's comment at Christmas back in '77 that made things click, giving me the needed push to get out of bed. I took the short walk to their impeccably maintained ranch house one block over. I was conflicted, dubious as to what I'd gain from this unexpected pop-in. On one hand, there might be nothing for them to tell. They'd simply welcome me in and ask how I'd been over the last six years – how's life, what's new – mere neighborly courtesies. On the other hand, they might offer some disturbing revelation, something sensitive or shocking about my father I wouldn't be able to process. I stood on their porch debating the two alternatives trying to shut off the pounding instinct in my brain to turn and run like hell.

I pushed the doorbell and was instantly ushered into the Hagl's home, embraced as warmly as a returning son. Cornelia and August had been seated around the kitchen dinette overlooking their backyard with the pergolas and orchard trees. They invited me to sit and, without asking, Cornelia poured coffee and had a plate of scrambled eggs waiting in the wings.

"This is great," I said. "But you didn't have to. It's almost as if you were expecting me."

"We were, dear," Cornelia said, in her soft German accent.

"Huh?"

"Cynthia jingled us. She was afraid you might catch us by surprise. She's always been very thoughtful that way."

"Yes, she has," I reluctantly agreed. Inside I was pissed. Mother and I would need to talk later. "Still, it's not like I expected breakfast or anything. I only wanted to follow up with your invitation after the funeral. You know, just a brief visit to say hello," I quickly added.

"Of course, dear."

August smiled but remained quiet. I was unprepared how to begin the conversation, unsure of why I'd come in the first place. "So..." I stirred some cream into my coffee looking out at their peaceful backyard. "Mother mentioned something about the first moon landing, some big party. Is that about the time you met my parents?"

Cornelia wasted no time jumping in. "Yes, indeed, the moon. It was July." She turned to her husband, "1969, ja?"

August nodded. "We held a large block party for the moonwalk," he said, taking over, his accent a bit thicker than his wife's. "It was a celebration of grand German achievement."

*German* achievement? I waited for a smile, an indication maybe he was kidding or being ironic or perhaps self-deprecating. No smile. He was dead serious.

"Of American bravery and German technology," he added.

Oh, sure, I thought, now I get it. Wernher von Braun. The guy we got after the war who'd invented the Nazi V-2 rockets, then came over and designed the Saturn rockets for us. August's burst of nationalism threw me. It was as if he believed the Americans were monkeys, albeit brave monkeys, strapped aboard rockets that German technology built, hurling us to the moon and back. I wasn't sure if he talked this way to everyone or had special reason to point it at me. Taking credit for the Apollo program was an egregious stretch of his imagination. "I remember the block party," I said, deflecting his commentary. "Us kids playing outside while the adults socialized, waiting for the actual moonwalk later in the evening. We came in later and huddled around the TV. It seemed the whole neighborhood was there that night. My mother and father too. It was the first time you'd met them you say?"

Cornelia answered. "The first time we met your father, John."

"He didn't stay long," August added.

I imagine not. Not if you pulled that German technology shit on him too.

"He left right after the astronauts emerged, which I thought was unusual."

I stared at my coffee. That sounded about right, something unusual must've occurred that night. I retained the faint stain from his abrupt departure as did my mother.

"John excused himself, dear," Cornelia said. "To find the bathroom, I think. I pointed him down the hall and went back into the kitchen. Next thing I know, he's back in the kitchen looking as if he'd seen a ghost. It was just the two of us. He thanked me and said he needed to leave. And just like that, he was gone. He slipped out through the laundry room unnoticed among the many guests."

"Very unusual," August repeated.

Cornelia's description was disturbing but painted a picture of what was plausible, what could've easily been my father's behavior back then. Still, I was shaken and confused hearing it from a source outside our nucleus. I had no idea what would've spooked him and was afraid to ask. This was private stuff and my curiosity had suddenly hit a brick wall unwilling to probe further – not this morning with two people I barely remembered. I swallowed the last of my coffee and stood. "Well, this has been interesting," I said. "Thank you for breakfast and spending time to catch up. It's been wonderful to see you both, but I really should be going."

August seemed accepting of my departure, of the brief visit's purpose, and stood with me. Cornelia remained seated, "Please, Mitchell. You do not go, not yet. Tell us about your wonderful family, what you're doing now that you've moved back east. We've hardly seen you since you and Harold were boys." She'd picked up the vibe and eased me back to my chair, halting my rude exit.

"I'm sorry, Mrs. Hagl." I reseated myself and offered a summary of our time since the move, of receiving orders back to Annapolis, our quarters, my new job and how Sean was in second grade, Carlene starting pre-school. "We're enjoying life very much," I said, skipping the court-martial part. "It's a beautiful place and a nice change from the rat race I endured here at Moffett Field."

They nodded. A silence developed as they considered the mundane news.

"They grow up so quickly, you know," Cornelia said. "The children."

"Yes, they do," I agreed.

Another pause. The room remained quiet. I looked away, my eyes again settling on the placid backyard.

"It was the war, my dear." Cornelia broke my attention from two hummingbirds taking a drink from their feeder. "We need to talk about the war. Of course, you know this, ja?"

"I do?"

"That is why you're here," she said, making it sound like it was preordained. "John came back to visit us, years after the moon. We hadn't seen him since 1969 but he wanted to ask us about some things."

Things suddenly clicked. Krystal had told me about the visit when I saw her that Christmas, that my father had simply shown up. Okay, I thought, this is why I came.

She turned to August. "It was later, around the bicentennial celebration?"

"Yes, 1976," he said. "June."

"June, yes." Cornelia turned to me. "John first asked if we knew his family was from Germany. From Hamburg. I told him, of course. Baumann. How could that not be German? We knew Baumann's. And you from Hamburg of all places, I said. How nice. What a coincidence."

"Go on, please," I said, fearing what may come next.

"Well, we didn't know he was in those big planes that flew over us."

"We called them the four-motors," August chimed in. "They filled the sky back then."

"The B-17s, yes," I said. "He was a pilot."

"We know that now," Cornelia said. "However, then, well, we gave him quite a story, didn't we, dear?"

"He wanted to know. That's why he came. So, we told him."

"What it was like on the ground, you mean?" I asked. "During the raids?"

"He wanted to know the details," Cornelia said. "So, we tell you too?"

I drew a deep breath. "Sure."

August began. "Before the war, we lived west of Hamburg, near Pinneberger on the Elbe. I was nine years old when the war began. There was little change in our routine back in 1939. Rationing hadn't started. We had a large house, an automobile and a maid. My father worked as an engineer at the shipyards in Harburg. Times were favorable for Germany again, good fortune for my older brother and me. I had new clothes, a bicycle, schoolmates, everything a child could want."

His narrative was plain, but he sounded wistful. I expected him to toss in a nice compliment to Hitler and pay homage to the Nazi party. He didn't.

"Then the radio announced there was war in Poland. To end Russian aggression, we were forced to enter Poland and move east to take Warsaw. People initially cheered in the streets then quickly went back to their business. Sidewalk cafés were bustling, regular theater performances continued, we strolled outside in the evenings. The enemy airplanes didn't come until later. 1940. Nighttime bombers from the west."

"The British," I said.

"Yes. We'd hear them fly over, just a few airplanes at a time, then we'd hear their bombs hit. Distant explosions that did very little damage, none in our area. It was mostly a small disruption, certainly nothing my father ever worried about."

"Didn't you run to shelters when they came?"

Cornelia's took over. "After a while, we learned to go, yes. I grew up different than August. I was also nine, but we lived in Hammerbrook, large rows of apartment buildings near the city center. After Poland, we were given instructions. They taught us how to fight fires and convert our basements into shelters. Pretty soon, larger public shelters were constructed. The hospitals were reinforced, and huge searchlights started appearing in parks and on street corners. For some reason, the searchlights with their big lenses scared me. The nighttime bombings continued in 1941 and '42 but all were nuisance raids. One night, a single bomb hit an apartment building a block over from us and started a fire that was quickly put out. We were led to believe we were successfully turning back the British, demoralizing them, that the bombings would end, and the war would soon be over."

August: "The turning point was 1943. Things got worse, not better. The British started daylight bombing with their Mosquitoes. The nighttime bombing continued but with more airplanes, more success. The nuisance raids were over."

Cornelia: "Then came July," she said, gravely. "Seven nights of continual bombing with thousands of aircraft. We went down to the shelter on the second night after seeing the pathfinder airplanes drop their flares, bright red and green lights falling just blocks from us. The sirens went off and we went down. Daily trips to the shelters were becoming commonplace, but we were still scared. The night before, a huge section of the city was set afire and was still burning. The next night was the worst. For nearly an hour the blasts struck above us, cracking timbers and starting more fires. We had small handpumps to bring in air, but soon only smoke came through and we stopped pumping. Air was being sucked away from the shelter. It became hot and hard to breathe. Someone went to the door, to open it but it was jammed. Things suddenly grew dark."

Cornelia hesitated, shutting her eyes, obviously reliving the horror. August took her hand.

"I must've fainted because when I awoke someone had carried me to the street. It was nighttime but the sky was bright as day. The city around us was burning, everywhere. I was carried to Alster, the big lake in the center of the city. Everyone that could walk or run was taking refuge near the big lake. We watched the city burn from fire all around us. The next morning, we were taken out. My sisters and I were evacuated, put on a train with many other children and sent to live in the countryside. I spent the rest of the war moving town to town, church to church, until reuniting with our mother in the town of Koblenz, many miles to the south. It was on May 20th, 1945 – my fifteenth birthday."

August: "Our family stayed. My father had an important job at the shipyard and my brother, 17, was taken into the Wehrmacht in 1941. Rationing started that year, we let our maid go and made our house more secure. I stayed home with my mother listening to the war reports on the radio. The news was all glorious, of course. Herr Goebbels was claiming victory on every front. We stopped worrying about my brother, last heard from near Stalingrad, hoping he'd be home soon, and everything would return to normal. This was late 1942. We never heard from him again. He'd been killed, obviously. The official notice came months later. It was after the British raids on Hamburg center in 1943 that the big American four-motors came, bold formations filling the sky in broad daylight. Their bombs stayed away from the city in the early raids, mostly hitting the docks, the oil refineries or the factories."

I knew this was not my father but remained quiet. He hadn't shipped out to England yet, his Hamburg mission destined for December 31, 1944. I knew the date solely from his list of missions still hanging in its frame on the den wall of our home.

August continued. "But the Americans started with their carpet bombing as the war progressed. My father was killed in late 1944 traveling home from work at Blohm and Voss, a nearby submarine yard, after the Harburg factory was destroyed. There was little discrimination between civilian and industrial targets near the end. Dust and smoke hung in the air continually from early '45 until the end of the war. Food became scarce, available only on the black market. There was a famine as the city became cut off by the advancing armies. The Russians were closing in from the east, the British from the west. Near the end, we weren't sure if the city would be defended or not. We feared the Russians might take us and heard horror stories of their rampant raping and looting. Then we heard the British were coming from the west and rejoiced. First a single tank arrived, then two more. The invasion came peacefully, thank God. There was no shooting. For us, at this point, the war was over."

I took another deep breath. Cornelia was shaking and took my hand holding it firmly in hers. Their dreadful war odyssey sounded horrid, and I fought the urge for tears. Their tales were heart-wrenching and unimaginable. But there was an aftermath.

August: "Occupation followed. The army kept the peace, curfews were put in place and there was little incident. But half the city was in ruins, a million people either displaced or dead. There were no communication links to the outside world, and famine was very much alive. Harburg was also a mess, sunken ships, blocked harbors, collapsed bridges, no train service. We began searching for relatives. Messages were left on community center billboards but without food or shelter, Mother and I decided to move south with many other refugees."

Miss Klara, I thought. August's mother. I was reminded of her story at Thanksgiving.

"We kept moving, all the way to Koblenz. It was a long journey, some by train, some by truck but the last part mostly on foot. At least there was food and water. Life was more resilient as we moved farther south. We initially shared a basement, a former air-raid shelter, with another family. There were so many refugees fleeing from the east because of the Russians. Schools didn't resume for another year. That's when I met Cornelia. We were sixteen. We married at eighteen and finally got to the United States in 1950 after turning twenty."

I provided a faint smile, warmed by their happy ending but disturbed, unable to speak.

Cornelia: "Thank God for the American president, Harry Truman. August and I finally made it out after he signed the Displaced Persons Act." She grinned at August. "And with a little help from our Lutheran Church. Germany was struggling to house its refugees. They couldn't possibly rebuild fast enough. The US and Canada opened their borders. We learned a bit of English, were given the chance to immigrate and we took it."

"And thirty years later, we are here," August said, grinning back at his wife. "Things didn't turn out so bad?" He tenderly kissed her cheek and she spoke some words in German. They had been blessed after all the tragedy in their early lives and took solace having reconciled the irony of being bombed by the same people that now genuinely welcomed them as family.

I really felt the need to head home. Despite their happy ending with America opening her loving arms, I didn't feel closure or in possession of some profound revelation about my father. While certainly making repeated bombing runs over numerous German cities could take its toll, especially when given the unpleasant opportunity to meet some of its citizenry below, was this enough to haunt him, I thought, to wreck his career, ruin his family life? What horrors had he seen? "Did Dad hear any of your stories?" I asked.

"We tell him exactly as we tell you," Cornelia said. "He listened quietly, offered a polite apology for the war and any suffering the bombings may have caused. He also said he was sorry for August's father and older brother. He was distraught, a mess really, but looking for something else."

"So, he didn't break down? This wasn't what he came for? No open confession to blatant war crimes? No connection to some distant cousin he obliterated. What then?"

Cornelia looked at August before speaking. "The night of the moon party, when he left like he'd seen a ghost. That's what he was after when he returned several years later."

"You mean something here, in this house?"

"Yes."

"*What?* What possibly would've haunted him nearly twenty-five years after the war and then send him here if it wasn't to apologize or look for some long-lost Baumann?"

Cornelia turned to August. "A doll," they said, in unison.

Mother was sitting on the sofa in the living room pretending to be busy with her knitting, anticipating my arrival when I came through the door. I stormed into the room. "We need to talk," I said, unzipping my windbreaker.

"What, Mitch? What did you find?"

"You mean you don't know?"

"Don't be absurd," she said, dropping her work. "I have no idea what you're talking about."

"Of course, you do. You tipped off August and Cornelia. You told them I was coming over." I looked at her. "Why?"

She said nothing.

"Mother, how much do you know? I get the feeling it's a lot more than you're letting on." I was angry, pacing about the room. "What happened to Dad over there? He didn't just fly his missions, drop a few bombs, and come home to a ticker-tape parade. What are you not telling me?"

"I'm afraid I don't know as much as you think."

"Well, tell me what you *do* know."

"Not much."

"Mother."

"Some things were better left unspoken after he returned. I ignored a lot. We'd been married only a week, neither of us knowing if he was coming back. Then suddenly his missions were over and he was home. He'd made it. And yes, he was different – quieter, soft-spoken, less demonstrative. His reclusive behavior left a chill between us. I wasn't about to question what he'd been through. It was none of my business. We had a life to build. We needed a home, he needed a job, and we had no idea where to begin."

"He didn't just jump to the airlines right after the service?"

"I worked that first year, in a department store. He stayed in the reserves, visited some war buddies and became sort of a nomad as he half-heartedly looked for work. He even considered selling insurance and moving us to Chicago of all places. Instead, we moved to California after he interviewed with United at the urging of a reservist friend. He had no intention of becoming an airline pilot."

"He was unemployed, for more than a year?"

"Yes. And I'll tell you this one thing about his war experience because it's all I know. Something did happen on one of his missions near the end, around 29 or 30. It was to Hamburg. There was trouble, flak or something.

The plane lost a couple of engines and sank lower and lower as they approached the North Sea. They ended up ditching and spending the night in a raft before being picked up by Air Sea Rescue the next morning. That's how he got his Air Medal and Purple Heart."

I just stared in disbelief. I'd never heard any of this.

"And that's all I know. That's all he ever told me."

"So, he crashed his airplane in the North Sea, was rescued the next morning, and that's all he ever said?" I wasn't angry at either of them for this undisclosed fact in his service. I too never pressed my father, letting his wall of impressive pictures and medals in the den tell the story. But why would he not feel comfortable talking about it, something as eventful and heroic like that? I pondered her words, allowing a silence to build before changing subjects. "Mother, what do you know about a Muschi doll?"

"A what?"

"It's an old German doll. He was captivated by one he saw in Krystal's bedroom during their moon landing party back in '69. That's the reason he paid a visit seven years later. Obviously, he'd been carrying the image the entire time and it got the better of him. Something drove him back to take a look, ask them some questions."

"I don't know anything about a doll." She was emphatic.

"Are you sure? He's gone, Mother. There's no reason to hide anything now."

"I'm telling you, I know nothing about some old doll."

I studied her face. She sat in cold silence, angry, perhaps, but wasn't lying. But, oh, her curiosity was on high alert. Her expression seemed to demand I tell everything August and Cornelia said, especially now that I'd brought this mystery doll into the picture. I recounted everything they told me about their war experience, which wasn't much she didn't already know. Then I got to the doll. "He went back to their house, sometime in the summer, 1976." I looked at her. "You knew about that visit, right?"

"Maybe. I don't know."

"Well, he asks very nicely to see this old doll he noticed on a visit a few years back. Does Krystal still have it? he asks. May I see it, please? They tell him yes and go fetch it." I paused. "Does any of this sound familiar, Mother?"

"No!"

"All right, all right." I held up my hands. "I believe you."

"Just tell me the rest," she said, her eyes shut, bracing for the worst.

"Not much more to tell. He holds the doll. He strokes the doll. He gets emotional, cries a bit, asks where the doll came from. Cornelia tells him it was hers, given to her as a girl, one of the few possessions that survived the bombings she kept throughout the war. When Krystal was born, Cornelia gave it to her, placed it on a shelf in her bedroom where it remained. Dad found it in 1969 and became obsessed with it, I guess."

Mother's eyes shot open. "Obsessed?"

"Well, no. Obsessed is my word. But they said he was very taken by it. That his curiosity of the doll was the main reason for the visit, not so much to hear their account of the war in Hamburg."

"And they didn't discuss his connection to the doll, why he was smitten?"

"He didn't volunteer any additional information and they didn't feel it proper to ask. He simply thanked them and went on his way. End of story."

"End of story?" Like me, she had hoped for more. "It all seems very strange."

"Very strange, indeed, Mother. I don't know what to make of it."

I left the homestead early Sunday evening and drove back to Amber's in Palo Alto. The visit had allowed a deeper insight into my father's ordeal and the aerial bombings, but it was like peeling an onion. I was nearing the center yet achieving nothing close to full understanding. What possible link would a German doll have to a bomber pilot that never set foot on German soil? I'd turned it over and over walking back from the Hagl's, concluding some questions may never be answered. I needed to refocus on the present. The upcoming week was going to be brutal. My arraignment was scheduled for Tuesday, the Article 32 hearing set for Wednesday, the court-martial sometime after that. There was much preparation and strategy to discuss with Monk. I needed to put my father and his World War II saga aside. I'd hit a dead end.

# 25

## INTO THE BEAST

THE HEARING ROOM WAS SMALL, dominated by an oak conference table with seating for ten. Extra chairs lined the walls leaving minimal floor space in which to maneuver. Three large windows with blinds drawn allowed bright rays of morning sunlight to stream in providing relief from an otherwise very claustrophobic, cluttered feel to the space. Up front, an American flag and Navy flag stood limp on their poles looking out of place, like they'd been dragged in at the last minute for the hearing. My arraignment was yesterday in this very room and lasted ten minutes. With Monk at my side, I pled not guilty to all the charges as planned.

Today would begin my Article 32 hearing. I glanced at the wall clock. 0730. We were thirty minutes early. Monk's plan was to arrive ahead of everyone else and set the tone, to send an early message that we were out front and prepared to end this charade today. At least that's what he told me last night when we ended our strategy session at midnight. For twenty minutes this morning we'd been alone staring at the wallpaper. "Relax," he assured me. "This is where it gets fun."

"Fun for you, maybe."

At 0750 a lieutenant walked in carrying a stack of files bound by a thick rubber band and set them on the conference table along with his coffee. He was a pilot like me and had a VP-46 nametag above his right breast pocket on his khaki uniform.

"Ah, the Investigating Officer," Monk said, standing to shake his hand. "Len Monkowski." Monk turned and gestured at me, "And this is Mitch Baumann," he said smiling genially like we were all friends gathering for happy hour.

"Les Donahue," he said, returning the greeting. "And I know this guy." He looked at me and smiled. "Who doesn't?" He shook my hand. "Good to finally meet you, Mitch."

I was stunned, unsure how to react. Did he know me simply from spending weeks pouring over the charges and my career and now felt like we were close friends? I'd never seen him before.

"Mitch," Monk began. "Les here was the one designated by the Wing to

390

conduct the investigation into the charges. He's here to present his findings under oath and will sit here." Monk pointed to a spot at the table. "He's a line officer like you, from one of the other squadrons on base."

"Have we met?" I asked Les.

"Not before today."

Monk seemed to be enjoying taking early charge of the hearing, describing to us line officer rookies how things work in the world of the Judge Advocate General. Next entered a lieutenant commander JAG officer along with an enlisted petty officer, both carrying briefcases. Introductions were made, much more formal than with Donahue. Monk turned aside, explaining this was the prosecutor for the Government and the court recorder, a Navy yeoman. Finally, a full Navy commander entered the room, another JAG officer. I followed Monk's lead, standing up, as did everyone in the room.

"Good morning, gentlemen. I'm Commander Richard Ray. I'll be the Hearing Officer for today's proceeding." He appeared older than his rank suggested and very distinguished, resembling a handsome Clark Gable with glasses. Ray gestured at the lieutenant commander. "This is Rory Pritchard, acting prosecutor for the Government. And to his left," he squinted to look at the nametag, "Lieutenant Donahue, the Investigating Officer. Do I have that right?"

"Yes, sir."

"And lastly, our recorder." He nodded at the yeoman in the corner chair then looked at Monk. "Are there any questions before we begin?"

"No, sir."

Commander Ray nodded at the Investigating Officer. After some preliminaries regarding Article 32 procedures, he said, "Lieutenant Donahue, you will begin with the opening statement of the charges then move to your findings." He turned to the Monk. "Lieutenant Monkowski, the Government will provide substantiation of each charge via either written statements, teleconference call or personal appearance from their witnesses. Defense counsel will have the opportunity to challenge each charge, each witness statement and/or their actual testimony here today. You will also be given the chance to call your own witnesses as needed. Both Government and Defense will be allowed a summation before the court renders a decision on each charge's merit to proceed to court-martial." Back to Donahue, "Okay, Lieutenant Donahue, you may proceed."

Donahue looked down at his file and the papers spread before him. He read verbatim from a prepared opening statement, giving his name, his role as investigating officer and his own brief background as a pilot and line officer assigned to VP-46. My thoughts suddenly ran cold. My little pep-talk with Monk in the conference room prior to everyone's arrival had convinced me all charges would be dismissed before noon, that this was in fact a charade. Yet here we were, listening to the Hearing Officer, this full commander, explain the formal procedures in careful legalese and measured tone before turning it over to Les Donahue with his thick file and staid demeanor. I was now convinced I was doomed. The hearing would last days, not hours. The Government certainly wouldn't drop all charges after taking the trouble to develop them, especially that thick file on the table, I thought. Some would stick, they'd have to. It was court-martial here I come. My stomach sank, my bowels ready to give way. I looked at Monk. He was staring out the window mindlessly doodling on a yellow legal pad, black Sharpie in hand, as Donahue droned on. "On the first charge of consumption of alcohol within twelve hours before preflight, I'd like to begin by reading the statement of witness number one, a Mr. Julius Bang, retired chief petty officer and bartender on duty the night of," Donahue looked down at his papers, "14 March 1983, at the Husky Club on Naval Air Station, Adak, Alaska." The statement, in effect, read, I, Julius Bang, hereby observed a group of junior officers enter the Husky Club just before 2000 hours (which, from the tone of his words suggested he didn't much care for seeing junior officers enter his seedy but beloved bar). These officers ordered many pitchers of beer and margaritas between 2000 and midnight, he went on to say, and all were in a rowdy, highly intoxicated state when they departed after midnight. His final sentence claimed he served us our last pitcher before midnight but was certain our departure was well *after* midnight. The statement was full of half-truths, supposition and overconfidence in his power of observation, written with a professional flair that suggested he'd been coached. Donahue concluded the reading, dropping the paper statement to the desk, and looked up. The room was silent.

I turned to Monk, still doodling, and whispered, "Is it our turn to speak? Don't you want to cross-examine?"

No response.

"Object?"

Monk smiled and shook his head.

"C'mon. Something."

"Not yet," he said, showing no interest in what he'd just heard from Donahue. He wrote on his legal pad, *Patience*.

Donahue continued. "Our second witness is Lieutenant Aubrey Moskowitz, a nurse stationed at the NAS Adak hospital from May 1982 until present. She was present in the Husky Club the night of March 14." He read Aubrey's statement, which contained a lot of words and little substance. At the end, she seemed to corroborate Bartender Bang's story that liquor was flowing freely when she arrived at our table before midnight and still flowing when she departed after midnight. This was bullshit and I turned to Monk imploring him to stop the reading and jump in.

"Hang on," he whispered.

At this point, a yeoman entered and whispered to the Hearing Officer.

"Gentlemen, I'm told we've got our witness," Commander Ray said, "Lieutenant Moskowitz, on the line."

With this, the yeoman leaned toward the center of the table, pressed a button on the conference room speakerphone and fiddled with the volume. "Go ahead, ma'am, can you hear us?"

"Yes," said a scratchy female voice on the other end. "I can now."

Commander Ray spoke again. "Lieutenant Moskowitz joins us via teleconference from Adak, Alaska." He spoke into the phone's tiny speaker box in the center of the table. "Lieutenant, can you hear us clearly?"

"Yes, sir."

"Okay, very good. As you were prepped, your statement concerning the night of 14 March has just been read by Lieutenant Donahue, the Investigating Officer. The defense counsel is present. He is going to ask you some questions. Do you understand?"

"Yes, sir."

Ray nodded at Monk. "Okay, Counsel, you may proceed."

"Lieutenant Moskowitz," Monk said, diving right in. "Forgive me, but I'm still a little vague after hearing your statement regarding your relationship to this group of officers. Just how did you come to know the defendant, Lieutenant Mitch Baumann, on the night of 14 March?"

Brief pause on the line. "I didn't say I knew him. I said I observed a group of them, Baumann included, drinking in the Husky Club well after midnight."

"And you hadn't met the defendant before that night?"

"No. I never met any of them," she replied, rather haughtily.

"But you sat with them, at their table?"

Another brief pause. "Yes."

"Who was present at the table when you arrived? Can you identify any of them?"

"I don't remember names."

"Can you describe them? How many?"

"Look, it was a long time ago. Maybe four or five of them. Two women, three guys, something like that."

"And Lieutenant Baumann was present? You're certain of that?"

"Yes."

"Can you describe Mr. Baumann?"

"Object." It was Rory Pritchard, the prosecutor, speaking for the first time. "There's no point in Ms. Moskowitz trying to describe the defendant over the telephone."

Commander Ray spoke. "Objection noted but unnecessary." He turned to Monk. "Mr. Monkowski, this is a hearing, not a court-martial. Witness can positively identify the defendant when this goes to trial and she's present in the courtroom."

"Thank you, Commander."

I poured some water and took a gulp. Great, I thought, everyone seems to agree I'm going to trial.

"Okay," Monk continued, "You say you don't recall names or faces. How can you positively say it was Lieutenant Baumann who was drinking after midnight?"

"They all were drinking."

"All were drinking, fine. What brought you to their table that night? What made you decide to join them?"

Initially there was no response, just a soft, long-distance hum. Every eye was glued to the speaker box.

"Ms. Moskowitz, are you there?"

"Yes."

"Okay, good. You agreed to sit down. Why?"

"I don't know. I was passing by, someone said, 'Hey, honey, grab a seat.' So, I obeyed. I slid into a chair and sat." She made the act sound distasteful, like sliding into a dentist's chair to have work done.

"And," Monk paused. "What time was this, approximately?"

"I already told you. Before midnight, maybe 11, something like that."

"And there was liquor all around the table, as you put it?"

"All around."

"Then you departed. What time was that, approximately?"

"After midnight. Maybe a quarter-after."

"Did you leave alone?"

More long-distance hum.

"Ms. Moskowitz? Did you leave alone?"

"I might've walked out the door with someone from the table. I don't recall."

"And this was a quarter-after, around 0015, you say?"

"Yes."

"And was it with Mr. Baumann?"

"No."

"Who then?"

"Look, I don't know what this has to do with anything. As I said in my statement, I observed these officers drinking at their table before midnight and I observed them drinking *after* midnight. Isn't that the question, the reason I'm here? They broke their twelve-hour rule, what more do you want from me?"

Monk pulled a file from his briefcase and removed a single piece of paper. "I'm going to read from a statement – one like yours that's also been entered into the record. This particular statement comes from a Lieutenant (jg) Wayne Horseman." He let the name sink in then repeated it. "Wayne Horseman. Does that name ring a bell?"

Exasperated, "Yes, but—"

"And I quote from Mr. Horseman: *I met Aubrey standing at the bar around 2300. We made idle conversation. I kidded her I was John Fogerty playing a USO tour in Adak and invited her to join our "band" at the table. She sat with us until Jamie Morgan, our TACCO, announced we had a preflight at noon the next day. This was precisely 2340 because I looked at my watch when Jamie said we needed to wrap up the party. I suggested to Aubrey that we head to her place. We left the Husky Club together no later than 2345.*"

I loved the fact that Horse used her first name in his narrative, implying an intimacy between them I knew Monk enjoyed reading aloud while probably causing Nurse Aubrey to cringe from embarrassment on the other end of the line.

"I would like to point out to the court," Monk said, "that due to the couple's departure time, it would've been impossible for either Mr. Horseman or Ms. Moskowitz to know if the defendant continued to consume alcohol past his midnight prohibition once informed of his noon preflight the next day. And therefore, it is also impossible for Ms. Moskowitz to accurately testify to this fact."

"Object," Rory Pritchard cried again. "Defense counsel is attempting to establish the fact it's common knowledge the couple left at 2345 because their witness says they left at 2345. That Ms. Moskowitz's version is unreliable and therefore must be fabricated."

"Commander Ray," Monk said. "I'd like to continue, if I may."

Pritchard kept going. "This is nothing more than an attempt to discredit a witness simply because she departed with one of the men at the table that night. She is a senior lieutenant, a licensed Navy nurse skilled in observing human behavior, and her testimony is relevant. The defense counsel has intentionally set up this conflict with the male officer to embarrass Ms. Moskowitz."

"The defense counsel has set up this conflict because someone isn't telling the truth," Monk retorted. He turned to Ray and spoke calmly. "Commander, I have something that should help resolve the conflict. If I may, sir?"

"Continue, counselor."

"Thank you. These are statements from two additional witnesses present at the table the night of 14 March I'd like to read." Monk held up two curled sheets of thermal fax paper. "The first is from OS2 Kerry Sullivan, the second from OS3 Robin MacHold, again, both stationed at NAS Adak and present the night of—"

Pritchard cut in, "Hold on. I've never heard or read these statements. They were never introduced as evidence into this proceeding."

"I'm introducing them now," Monk said. "We received these statements via fax over the weekend from Petty Officers Sullivan and MacHold. These women were part of the group in question that night." Monk spoke directly to the Hearing Officer. "Commander Ray, I'd like to introduce these two signed statements, drafted and sent by Ms. Sullivan and Ms. MacHold via fax, with originals in transit, and ask they be accepted as evidence into this Article 32 hearing."

I knew Monk had worked hard over the weekend to track down and gain additional statements from Kerry and Robin regarding our night in the Husky Club. Kerry had transferred from Adak and was now stationed in Rota, Spain. Robin was still with the NAVFAC in Adak and both were scheduled to testify for the prosecution later by conference call, if necessary, regarding their unlawful presence on our ill-fated flight. They'd been positioned as Pritchard's star witnesses. Monk's ability to contact them, urging them to submit statements on my behalf on short notice was a major coup.

"Commander Ray? May I proceed, sir?"

Ray thought for a moment and provided his ruling. "All eyewitness statements are considered relevant and will be included in any Article 32 investigation. Evidence of this nature must be heard and weighed before the decision is made to send to a general court-martial. Yes, despite their late appearance, I will allow the statements into the record as part of this hearing. Counsel, you may proceed."

"Thank you, sir." Monk began reading Kerry's statement. *"Robin and I were introduced to LT Baumann and his crew in the Husky Club at approximately 2100 on a Monday night by LTJG Horseman…"* Her account was raw, unedited, and Monk struggled with her loopy handwriting and blurry fax image but recited it confidently as though Kerry were in the room reading it herself. Her description tended to ramble and read more like a diary entry than an objective witness report, but you could tell, she was doing her best to come to my rescue on short notice. *"Then that nurse came, LT Moskowitz. Mr. Horsman, who everyone was calling Horse, brought her from the bar. It was obvious she'd been drinking. We all had, but she was tipsier than the rest. Before long, she and Mr. Horseman were making out at their end of the table. We ignored them and our talk turned professional, about the upcoming Delta ops – all unclassified, of course. Mr. Baumann was the clear leader of the group, asking a lot of questions. He then conferred with Mr. Morgan, his TACCO, after a talk with a lieutenant commander that entered the bar much later. It was 2340 when Mr. Morgan informed the others of the noon preflight the next day. Mr. Horseman and the nurse promptly left the club at 2345. We finished our beers at 2350 and departed at 0010. There was no drinking by anyone, Mr. Baumann included, after midnight. We left the club and went our separate ways. I hereby swear this statement to be true and correct to the best of my knowledge. Respectfully, OS2 Kerry Sullivan, USN."*

I breathed a sigh of relief. She'd mentioned nothing of our decision, our *drunken* decision, to invite the girls to go fly with us the next day. Of course, the Government was going to press both she and Robin later as witnesses on this exact point. They would also stress they were both unlawfully present on an operational mission chasing a real-world Soviet target within fifty miles of Mother Russia. I thought it decent of her not mentioning those details in her statement.

Robin's statement was very similar but without the clear resentment toward Nurse Aubrey. Her times matched Kerry's perfectly and exonerated me and the crew of any drinking past our midnight curfew. I knew Monk provided guidance as they carefully prepared their master timelines and list of names and events so both would be consistent and fulfill a minimum standard of information. But their style, their words, were uniquely their own and one-hundred percent accurate.

Monk quit reading and looked at the speaker box. "Ms. Moskowitz, are you still with us?" He twiddled the volume knob. "Ms. Moskowitz?" He looked at Ray, "Did she hang up or what?"

Commander Ray looked at the box. "Apparently."

"No matter. I'm finished." This time Monk looked at Rory Pritchard. "Back to you, Mr. Prosecutor."

Commander Ray looked at his watch and interrupted Pritchard before he could speak. "It's 1145. Let's take this opportunity to recess for lunch. We can reconvene at 1300. Are there any questions or further comments?"

There were none.

"Very well, gentlemen, hearing adjourned."

We walked back to Monk's makeshift office, a small cubicle in a windowless corner of the DSO bay. He dialed the phone and ordered some deli sandwiches from the Exchange for him and I, plus the stenographer. Once the sandwiches arrived, Monk eagerly dove in wolfing down a ham and cheese on rye like he hadn't eaten in a month. I left mine in the wrapper, not hungry, wanting to discuss the morning's testimony. "Great job, back there," I said. "Do you think it made an impression?"

"Absolutely. We can bury the drinking charge," Monk said, with a mouthful of food. "One down, four to go."

"You sure? I mean—"

"Mitch, those girls love you. You saved their lives, best witnesses in the whole world for the defense."

"But it's the truth. None of us touched a drop after midnight, including Kerry and Robin."

"I know, man," Monk said, gulping his diet Shasta. "All I'm saying is we own those two, they'll do anything for you. And we'll need that spirit later for the other charges."

Monk was referring to their alleged unauthorized presence on the tactical mission. He kept calling it "alleged" presence like he was going to make them disappear from the manifest. That was impossible and I said so, not nearly as optimistic as Monk, yet buoyed by his confidence. "So, what's next, who do we have after lunch?"

Monk frowned. "Jamie Morgan. He'll be present in the room for his testimony."

"That's good," I said. "Jamie's a friend. He'll back me up."

"Yeah, except he's been called by the Government. I'm not sure what ol' Rory has up his sleeve – for having him sit in person, I mean. From Morgan's written statement, he could easily become a witness for the prosecution."

"Jamie's always been a straight-shooter."

Monk took another swig of soda. "Exactly."

We sat in silence for a moment when Amanda burst around the corner. Wide-eyed, she saw me sitting with Monk and said, "Oh my God, *there* you are. I've been looking for you since your hearing broke."

"Been here the whole time," I said, calmly unwrapping my sandwich.

"Well, you need to come with me." She looked at Monk. "Can I borrow him? We need to talk," she added, "in private."

Monk smiled at her choice of words, unsure of her intentions. "Sure, take him," he winked. "He's all yours."

She grabbed my hand and yanked me from the chair.

"Just have him back by 1300," he yelled.

Amanda quickly led me to the bay where her workspace was located. "Sit down," she said. "You're not going to believe this."

"Believe what?"

"Just sit down. You need to hear this sitting down."

"Okay, okay. What's going on?" I wasn't sure if this was some spicey female drama or she truly had something earthshattering to tell me. In the wake of the hearing, I wasn't prepared to absorb a whole lot of new stuff.

"I just spoke to Pres Manley, on the phone."

"Wonderful. And?"

"Oh, Mitch, you're not going to believe this. He's made a connection." Amanda sat down across from me and lifted her notepad from the desk. "He's headed to Atlanta. Right now. Today." She was about to burst.

"Okay, tell me," I said, not feeling her enthusiasm. "What's so special in Atlanta?"

"The federal prison."

"Federal prison?" She now had my full attention. "In connection with Maddy's case?"

She nodded.

"Holy crap."

"That's what *I* said, holy crap. He's going to meet an inmate there." She opened her pad and flipped through some pages. "Manley has a buddy from Quantico, now with the FBI. He called last week. They've been communicating ever since."

"Wait. Who called who? This FBI guy called Manley?"

"No, the other way around. After we talked to Manley last week something must've clicked, so he made some calls." Amanda looked at her notes again. "Chad Peters, that's his name. He's a special agent with the FBI, Main Justice. They're going down to Atlanta together, likely to coincide with—"

"What's main justice?"

"Huh?" Amanda stopped and looked up, obviously frustrated. "Main Justice. FBI headquarters, Washington, DC. Don't interrupt. Do you want to hear the rest?"

I took a deep breath. "I don't know, do I?" Obviously, this was not the reaction she'd hoped for.

"Mitch, this is important. It's good news. I thought you'd be pleased. Isn't this what we wanted?"

I gazed out the window. "Sure. I guess." I was less enthusiastic. The timing on this thing sucked. I was in the middle of a fight of my own and here she was, dragging me back into the past, something I'd put on the shelf years ago. Fat chance of leaving it there now. "It's just that I'm a bit distracted right now." I gestured back toward the hearing conference room. "Can't you see that?"

She was unmoved. "What I see is I'll be going this alone." After my tepid response, her energy bubble had burst. She stood from the chair. "You should probably get back. I can handle it from here with Pres."

"Amanda, sit down. I'm sorry." Despite my legal mess, she'd aroused my curiosity. Had ol' Pres Manley cracked the case? After one call? "Let's start over," I said. "Tell me, please, who is Manley going to see at Club Fed tomorrow?"

She reseated herself and pulled her notepad close. "I already told you, he's meeting with this FBI agent buddy of his, Chad." She looked at her notes. "The agent wants to interview an inmate, someone they put away a few years ago that Manley thinks had a connection to..." Amanda bit her lip.

"Go on, please. A connection to what? To Maddy's disappearance?"

"Her murder, Mitch. She's dead. They know this now."

Her words stung. I'd buried Maddy in my mind years ago, making the same horrible assumption but never expecting to hear it so bluntly played back to me. "Okay, so what's next?"

"Let me finish my notes." She flipped a page. "This guy they put away, back in '81, apparently, was part of a duo working for a private eye firm that went to the dark side. Two thugs from a firm based in Ellicott City, Maryland, started moonlighting, performing covert dirty work for any client willing to hire them and pay their exorbitant fees. It started out very low-profile and quickly crossed legal and ethical lines. Tricks like planting fake evidence on a cheating spouse in a divorce case or breaking into a home to rifle through a plaintiff's financial records. It later grew into some blackmail gigs for some high-vis corporate executives or kidnap and ransom for rich family clients. I think that's how they eventually got caught. There was a pile of money to be made and they got greedy and careless."

I was starting to form a picture but unclear how Amanda and Pres knew to contact this FBI agent friend and ask about these bozos in the first place. "How'd they find them and what's the link between their activity and Maddy? Why fly down to Atlanta so soon?"

"Manley thinks the guy in prison wants to make some sort of deal. He's filed dozens of motions and appeals that are going nowhere. He's getting impatient, wants to short-circuit the system and implicate his partner. Maybe. He's not sure."

"But why now? What changed things?"

"It was the call Manley made to the FBI agent. He was the agent on the case that put the pair away in '81. During the investigation, they found a possible link to the crime in Annapolis in 1976. After the FBI talked to the NIS, they deemed the information as noteworthy but nonrelated, convinced by the NIS it was a dead end. It didn't matter, the FBI had plenty of evidence to put the pair away on multiple other crimes."

"But this was a murder, for crying out loud, not blackmail or breaking and entering."

"Exactly. And Manley's call with information to his friend Chad Peters confirmed his suspicion that the trail was not a dead end, that there was in fact a link. He now seems eager to follow up."

"So, Peters and Manley are just going to go down there, walk into the cell and ask this goon, 'Hey, did you and your partner by chance commit an abduction and murder in Annapolis back in 1976 among all your other crimes? We were just wondering...'"

"Yeah, something like that. As I said, the guy appears to want to make a deal. Maybe admit guilt, make a new plea. His lawyer will be present when they meet."

"Lawyer, huh?"

"These are really bad guys, Mitch." The other one's doing hard time in Pennsylvania. The pair weren't exactly on speaking terms after their arrests. Manley wouldn't or couldn't tell me the rest. He was acting mostly on a hunch and needed to meet with his agent buddy. Still, he knows more than he was letting on. But I trust him."

"When will we know more?"

"He promised to call me in a few days if the trip pans out. He did want to impress on us both that one thing is clear now about Maddy's case."

"What's that?"

"I'm only quoting."

"*What?*"

"That it was a professional hit."

I walked back into Monk's cube and dropped to my chair. My head was spinning, barely able to comprehend the information just handed to me. Monk picked up immediately. "What the hell happened to you?" he said, pushing my partially eaten sandwich at me. "Better finish up. We need to be back in the conference room in ten minutes. I want to be early."

"I'm not hungry."

"Oh, really. What a surprise." He studied me closely. "Mitch, what happened back there? What'd Amanda tell you just now?"

"I'd rather not get into it," I said, avoiding eye contact. "Do we really have to go back to the hearing? I'm no longer up for this. Can't you file a, you know, a motion to postpone, get a continuance or something?"

"Why?"

"I just told you, I can't go back in there. I'm no good to you right now. Just get them to postpone it for a day. Can you do that?"

"No. And I can't file a continuance. We're already underway. Besides, we've got Jamie Morgan coming to testify, in person, and there's a conference room full of people. Can't you tell me what's going on?"

"It's about that missing person I told you about from college. It's got nothing to do with the hearing. That's all I can say."

"All right, tell you what. I'll suggest to Commander Ray after Jamie's testimony we shut it down for the day. Would that help?"

"I don't know, I guess."

"Mitch, we gotta keep moving. We just had a victory before lunch. The Government will back off the drinking charge, they'll have to. So we stay on the attack. Better to get Jamie's statement fleshed out here than at trial."

I admired Monk's hard-charging optimism. It was helping to clear my head after the Maddy intrusion. "Why is Jamie's statement suddenly so important that he has to come in? Don't they believe him?"

"That's what has me concerned. There's no need to drag Jamie into the conference room. We're just going to have to roll with whatever Pritchard has planned and recover on the fly. I may have to take your suggestion and request we adjourn until tomorrow anyway, depending on how it goes."

"C'mon, Monk. We've read his written statement. It's fine. You said so yourself. Jamie's a friend and truthful to a fault. They're not going to find any holes."

"Maybe. Maybe not."

"Oh, so now the statement's not fine?"

"Look, it's neither damaging nor exonerating. It doesn't get you off, but it doesn't help their case either. That's the thing. Pritchard can't squeeze more out of the statement just by reading it aloud. Still, bringing Jamie in is risky. And Pritchard doesn't take risks. He's had to have deposed him, must've made some kind of deal, or some kind of threat..."

I listened as Monk's voice trailed off. During our prep, he was always spinning out scenarios and having raging debates in his head, letting his formidable ego do battle with reality as he plotted our strategy. Sometimes he would riff for hours. "Well, we're going to be face to face in a few minutes," I said, finally cutting in. "You better be ready with something."

Monk stood. "We're just going to sit tight. For the next two hours, it'll be the Rory Pritchard show."

The entire hearing team was assembled back in the conference room when we entered. We were a few minutes early and the last to arrive. Monk and I threaded our way to our seats, Monk nodding at Commander Ray. As Hearing Officer, Ray opened things back up. "The hearing will now come back to order," he spoke before turning to Monk. "Lieutenant Monkowski, is the defense ready to proceed?"

"Yes, sir."

He looked at Rory Pritchard. "Commander Pritchard?"

"Yes, sir."

Ray turned to Donahue. "Lieutenant Donahue, is your witness ready?"

"He is, sir." Donahue rose from his chair and opened the conference room door and in popped Jamie. If he was sitting outside as Monk and I breezed by, I'd completely missed him. Jamie took a seat at the far end of the conference table from Ray in the chair reserved for witnesses. I made eye contact. Jamie tried to smile but his demeanor was stern, serious. It was the first time I'd seen him since the squadron change of command in June.

Donahue spoke. "I interviewed Lieutenant Morgan on 10 July and again on 1 September in connection with the events in Adak, Alaska on 14 and 15 March 1983 and his role in these events. I have also received a written statement from Lieutenant Morgan, which has been entered into the record, which I will now read aloud." Donahue read Jamie's written statement nonstop. It was two pages of clinical description beginning with our gathering in the Husky Club, the preflight briefing at the ASWOC the next morning and our subsequent flight into the evening hours. Both Monk and I had read Jamie's statement a dozen times and there were no surprises. Jamie's experience as VP-25's legal officer allowed the statement to sound official and cut through the typical verbose, awkward prose of many first-time witnesses. The narrative was encouraging, making the progression of events sound trivial, as if nothing had gone wrong, no regulations bent or broken. The two women were clearly present on the flight, but he noted no discrepancies or surprise. Like permission had been given in advance by the mission commander, Lieutenant Baumann, and that was good enough. Regarding the top-secret sub position information, Jamie noted he suspected Hodges was briefed beforehand (again by Lieutenant Baumann) but had identified the sub position himself on the acoustic sensor gear during the mission. There were no incriminations, no mention of warnings or confrontations, no disagreements throughout our mission, only the two facts that (1) yes, women were present on the mission and (2) Hodges appeared to have knowledge of the *USS Phoenix* before it showed up on his grams. No mention was made regarding the number four engine shutdown.

Donahue barely finished reading the statement when Pritchard jumped in. "Lieutenant Morgan, you were the TACCO on Crew 4 in Adak during the period of 14 and 15 March, is that correct?"

"Yes."

"Tell us about the preflight on March 15. When did you learn of the women's intention to accompany your crew on the mission? And were you surprised?"

"Well." Jamie preceded slowly in measured tone. "I met them in the briefing room at the ASWOC before Lieutenant Baumann arrived. They were dressed in flight suits and asked about the preflight briefing and where they should wait until takeoff time."

"Were you upset to learn they'd be flying with you?"

Jamie didn't immediately respond.

"Lieutenant Morgan?"

"I was neither surprised nor upset. I hadn't been informed of any additional passengers on the manifest and was unsure where the request might've come from. I don't typically ask a lot of questions before a mission."

I had to hide my smile. Jamie always asked a lot of questions before a mission. He was interested in every aspect and curious by nature.

"Did you in fact learn from OS2 Sullivan, one of the women, that they were invited by Lieutenant Baumann in the Husky Club. In the bar that night?" Pritchard placed special emphasis on the words, *In the bar that night*, implying all sorts of impropriety with the invitation.

"She said someone suggested the idea."

"But Mr. Baumann endorsed it?"

"Yes."

"In the bar that night?"

*Oh brother.*

"Yes."

"Did you think it unusual, even improper, that such an invitation was given to two women? That it might be against the regs?"

"Yes."

"And you informed Mr. Baumann of your concerns?"

Jamie hesitated. "Yes."

Monk jumped in. "Object. Witness was not present *in the bar that night* when the invitation was given." Monk was clearly mocking Pritchard. "He would have no way to confirm if Mr. Baumann did or did not endorse it, *in the bar that night.*"

"Sustained. Government will cease this form of leading the witness. Court is well aware of when and where the invitation was given."

I was glad when Monk finally put a halt to all this yes-yes-yes bullshit, his late objection notwithstanding. But I was becoming very disturbed by Jamie's easy compliance and Pritchard's brazen method of steering him beyond the original statement.

Pritchard resumed his charge. "Lieutenant Morgan, just a few more questions. Did Mr. Baumann ignore you in the, uh…" Pritchard shot Ray a deferential glance. "In the Husky Club, when you informed him your crew had been put on the flight schedule for a noon preflight the next day and they'd need to quit drinking?"

"He didn't ignore me, he said—"

"He said, and I quote, 'Hey, I haven't seen any flight schedule with our names on it.' Isn't that what he told you?"

"Yes."

"And then you said, 'C'mon, Mitch, I just informed you.'?"

"Yes." Jamie's countenance was that of a zombie.

"Seems to me he was clearly attempting to abrogate his upcoming twelve-hour prohibition on alcohol."

"Object." Monk jumped in sensing his earlier victory with the girls slipping away. "It's already been established no drinking occurred by any member of the crew after midnight."

"Has it?" Pritchard raised an eyebrow. "Let me switch gears," he said, turning to Jamie and looking at some notes. "Lieutenant Morgan, regarding the release of top-secret information to Petty Officer Hodges that night, did you inform Mr. Baumann you were troubled, that you said, and I quote, 'I wish you hadn't said anything to him about this. It could make things difficult later on?'"

"Yes. I said that."

I wondered where the hell Pritchard was getting his information. No one overheard our conversation in the aircraft that night. And it certainly wasn't in Jamie's written statement.

Monk frowned but kept quiet.

Pritchard kept up the offensive. "And regarding the unauthorized shutdown of the number four engine, didn't you warn Mr. Baumann about the standing order by saying, 'I'm just quoting from the Wing 10 Op Order, providing you guidance, that's all. Obviously, it's your decision.'?"

"Yes, I said that."

Monk cleared his throat. "Commander Ray, I'd like to—"

Pritchard kept charging like Monk and Ray weren't in the room. "And when you said, 'It's your decision,' you were referring to Mr. Baumann's loitering of the number four engine against Wing 10 policy, am I correct?"

"Yes."

Pritchard turned to Ray. "Commander Ray, I'd like to ensure the account of the damage to SE-05, the P-3C flown the night of 15 March, be entered into the record to substantiate the charge of destruction of government property." He held up a thick folder stuffed with technical descriptions of the damage, dozens of maintenance action forms and a raw account of the repair and cost estimate from the subsequent prop malfunction. The obvious message was I'd caused this simply by violating the Wing 10 loiter directive, regardless of what the accident investigation board said earlier.

We were being gutted on all fronts, no question. This frank, sobering testimony by Jamie was something neither Monk nor I anticipated. Apparently his written statement, prima facie, wasn't good enough for ol' Pritchard. It didn't paint a damning picture, so he decided to put Jamie on the stand to frame the charges in a more serious manner, more in line with what he needed to get them to a court-martial. I was absolutely confounded at how easy Jamie was rolling over and how confident Pritchard seemed by quoting our conversations from the mission, almost like he had a wire on one of us. Monk had confirmed Jamie wasn't under subpoena today, that they typically don't use this tool in an Article 32. What had Pritchard promised Jamie that obliged him to spill the beans on these private conversations? Or worse, what did he threaten him with?

Then a thought occurred to me, a horrible one, and I audibly gasped.

For a moment, everyone's eyes in the room turned to me.

Pritchard shot me an odd look. "No further questions, Commander," he said, nodding to Monk. "Your witness."

I expected Monk to come unglued, to stand up and make a fuss about how we never got to depose Jamie ourselves, how his written statement didn't include *any* of this new testimony, how none of this was given to us during discovery. He didn't. He sat calmly and did something equally shocking. "I have no questions for the witness, Commander Ray. I'd like to request we adjourn and pick up with Mr. Morgan tomorrow." He offered no explanations, no excuses, nothing. I looked at my watch. It was only 1400.

"Very well," Ray said, looking at the wall clock. "We'll conclude the hearing for today. My calendar is full tomorrow, so we'll resume on Monday at 0900. Are there any questions? Government? Counsel?"

There were none.

"Okay, thank you, all. Hearing adjourned."

Everyone stood to leave. I glared at Monk. Jamie bolted for the door. He was the first to leave the room.

I stormed back to Monk's cube and plopped in my old chair saying nothing. Monk came running up from behind stopping at the entryway out of breath. "Now, Mitch, take it easy. I had to call a recess. This was going to end —"

"Why the hell didn't you challenge Jamie before suggesting we quit for the day? It looks bad letting Pritchard's victory hang in the air over the weekend. Doesn't it? Can Pritchard do that? You know, bring Jamie in without allowing us to depose him? Shouldn't that stuff have been in his original statement and already entered into the record?"

"This is an Article 32. Pritchard was only fleshing out Jamie's statement. Not everything gets put into a statement. You should really be asking where'd all those private conversations come from? I thought you said Jamie was your friend."

"He is."

"No one else would've been privy to all that stuff. Jamie just threw you under the bus."

"I know. It's baffling."

Monk squeezed between my chair and sat down at his desk. "C'mon, we're okay. Best this stuff come out today. It's over, Pritchard's shot his wad. He addressed all five charges, so we'll just pick up the pieces on Monday. What'd I'll tell you before we walked in there?"

"You told me a lot of stuff. What?"

"That this was going to be the Rory Pritchard show this afternoon, right? That'd we'd have to sit and take it. We've still got cards to play."

"I need to talk to Jamie."

"Oh, no you don't. He's gone to the dark side. We've got work to do and you look like shit. Take the rest of the afternoon off and we'll meet at my Q room tomorrow morning."

"Monk, I don't know what work we've got left." I stood to leave, still reeling from Jamie's testimony. "All those quotes Pritchard rattled off?"

"Yeah?"

"Every word of it was true."

# 26

## REGROUPING

ON THE WAY OUT THE MOFFETT GATE, I stopped to grab an early dinner at Two Guys, a little Italian bistro Aimee and I fell in love with while stationed here. The place was always lively and the food excellent. This afternoon the atmosphere felt sterile and unfriendly like I was alone in a foreign country. I drove back to Amber's exhausted and despondent over the day's events replaying every aspect of Jamie's testimony in my mind. It was only five in the afternoon and Amber wouldn't be back from work until seven. I realized as a gracious guest, I should help get dinner started but was carrying a load of pasta and bread in my stomach and more food sounded awful. I realized what I should do is call Aimee.

After a lot of sulking, I dropped into a beanbag chair in Amber's living room and picked up the phone. My mind toyed with the idea of hopping back in my rental car and just driving, driving in any direction away from my troubles and the land of Nod. I saw no value whatsoever in putting Jamie back on the stand on Monday. To what purpose? Was Monk going to pull some alternate version of reality from thin air and twist Jamie into believing it? I invited the girls. They were present on the flight. I passed top-secret information to Hodges. I shut down the engine. The engine came apart. Those were the simple facts. I would go to court-martial, get sentenced, be tossed from the Navy, and work at K-Mart the rest of my life. I shut my eyes and massaged my temples listening to the phone ring in my ear, realizing it was almost 9 P.M. in Annapolis.

"Hello?"

"Aimee. Hi."

"Mitch, I was hoping it was you. How'd it go today?" She sounded optimistic, hopeful for some good news. "Are they going to throw out the charges?"

I wasn't ready to unload, desiring some domestic chitchat first. "How's it going there? How are the kids?"

"The kids are fine. I miss you, and I'm worried. Tell me what happened at the hearing today."

"First tell me something about Sean and Carlene."

"Well, let's see." Her tone was gentle but eager to return to the news. "Sean decided he was going to run the obstacle course on Hospital Point today with one of his buds. Fell off the high bars, got a few cuts and bruises."

"Is he all right?"

"Oh, he's fine. I put a band-aid on him, good as new. Says he's going to try again tomorrow."

I had to smile. I would've done the same thing at seven. "Carlene?"

"Well, Carlene got a pet goldfish yesterday. Took her out in town, she was so excited. She picked out a big fantail."

"She pick out a name yet?"

"Mister Bubbles."

"Of course."

"I think she overfed him last night. Mister Bubbles didn't look so great this morning, but I think he'll live."

"That's good."

I wanted more, but Aimee remained quiet. We'd covered the preliminaries and she was ready to move on. I didn't blame her. I always wanted the bad news first.

"So, the hearing opened today, right on time and we wrapped up a bit early. Round one, I guess. This thing may go a few more days. I'm not sure."

"But it went well? And this Monk fellow, he's as good as you hoped?"

"Monk's fine. Look, Aims, if truth be told, it really didn't go so well today. Monk asked for an early recess, to regroup, I think."

"Regroup? What happened, what went wrong?"

I wanted to tell her *Jamie went wrong*, that he threw us all for a loop, but held back knowing Aimee would struggle to find it credible. She adored Jamie. "Just a little surprise in the testimony, that's all. Nothing we can't fix by Monday."

"Hmm."

"Yeah. So anyway, not to change subjects…" I definitely wanted to change subjects. "But after this thing is over, I may want to drive up to Idaho, you know, for a quick visit."

"Idaho?" She paused, her wheels turning. "But you'll be coming home first, right?"

"Well, I'm on the West Coast now. I just thought—"

"Mitch, I'm well aware of what's up in Idaho but why the urgency? What's changed?"

"Amber and I were talking the other night. She put a new spin on Dad's accident and—"

"And this Ramona woman's just going to spell it all out for you? Is that it?"

"I don't know, Aims. Maybe. There's still a lot of questions. I told her

I'd come up sometime and, well, now might be the best time. I don't know."

Silence.

"You there?"

"Yes. Do you really have to do this now?" There was frustration in her voice. "You can't just walk away from your job. Are you planning to take leave after the court-martial or something?"

"I may not need to take leave after the court-martial."

"My God, what are you saying?"

"Nothing. Nothing at all. I just may have some time after."

"After what? After you get kicked out of the Navy?"

My turn for silence.

"Mitch?"

"Things didn't go well today, Aimee. That's all I'm saying. And yeah, who knows how it'll end if I go to court-martial. I may have time for a lot of things. Maybe even grad school, huh?"

"Grad school."

"Yes. Or any number of options."

"What went wrong today? Did one of your squadron buddies testify against you or something?"

She was perceptive as usual, always willing to dive into the tough issues. No sense in holding back. "Yes. Jamie came in and gave testimony today. His prepared statement was very predictable, very supportive." I took a deep breath. "But under oath, he confirmed a lot of damning conversations he and I had during the flight. Private conversations."

"This is Jamie we're talking about?"

"Exactly. It was like he was being coerced or had been threatened with something. It was in his eyes like something wasn't right. There's no way he'd have told the prosecution all those behind-the-scenes conversations, and yet they had the information and made him corroborate it on the stand."

"That's not Jamie."

"I know. And I was suddenly struck by a revelation this afternoon sitting in my chair listening to him and the prosecutor go on." I recalled my involuntary gasp and felt the same sensation now. "Remember, a few years ago, when you first met Jamie, you mentioned something to me?"

"Yes."

"You know what I'm talking about, right?"

"Yes." She knew exactly.

"Well, I'm thinking that was the threat he was working under today. That Rory Pritchard, the prosecutor, was told certain things about Jamie, things you intuited as soon as you met him."

"Are you referring to the conversation we had after Jamie came to dinner back in '81?"

"Maybe."

"Now Mitch, how could Jamie being gay be used against you?"

"Whoa, hang on." She'd said it, the word I could barely bring myself to admit. I spoke slowly. "Are you still convinced he's gay?"

"Of course, I am. Lisa and I both saw it. It's pretty easy for a woman to spot, easier than men. And if they're threatening that dear man to use it against him. How could they?"

"Because, Aims, if it's true, then he's history. The military has no tolerance for openly gay men. And I'm certain he doesn't want to lose his career, so he's cooperating."

"He's *not* openly gay. Are you sure they'd get rid of him?"

"If the wrong people find out, or force him to admit it, then yes, I'm sure. Out of the closet on your own, or if someone outs you, either way, you face mandatory separation." I wanted off the gay topic. The whole thing made me ill, that the Navy could separate someone so dedicated and true, so cut out for Navy life. "Look, I'll call you tomorrow. Monk and I are going to review some things, we'll be okay. It could all be over on Monday."

"Have you told Monk your theory? Will you talk to Jamie, later I mean?"

"Monk says I shouldn't talk to Jamie. And no, I've said nothing to him about Jamie's uh, issue."

"Mitch, I'm so sorry. I want to be there with you. You certainly don't deserve this mess. You really need to stand up and fight back with all you've got. Everyone knows it's Fowler. Are you sure Monk's the right lawyer for you? Is he helping at all?"

"Yes, Monk's fine. I trust him." I looked at my watch. "Hey, I really need to get going. Amber will be home soon, and I don't want her barging in on the call and have to reexplain everything." I needed to end but sensed Aimee wasn't ready. "Is everything else all right at home?" I continued. "Everyone in the building taking care of you?"

"Everyone's been great. Ryan's been asking about you, misses you at the pool. I've been talking to him and Sherry every day. All the other neighbors too."

"Great. "Well, I guess we should—"

"Oh, I almost forgot. There is something else. I got a call from a Bob Clausen, the guy you drove out to see a few weeks ago? He was that girl's sponsor, right?"

*That girl.* "You mean Maddy. Yes, Bob and Jan were her sponsor." I was going into shock. "What'd he say? What's the news?"

"That he's got a copy of her essay. Got it from her parents and said you should call him."

"Wow, fantastic. I will." *God, this thing will never end.* "I'll call him as soon as I can, maybe tomorrow. Did he say anything else?"

"No, Mitch. He didn't say much. And he didn't seem to think it was fantastic. What essay is he talking about anyway?"

"Maddy's application essay. There must be something in it, some new clue. I'll talk to him tomorrow and let you know. You say you didn't talk long?"

"No. He sounded sad, not like he'd found any long-lost clue you mention. We ended it pretty quickly after that."

"Just let me call him." As if I don't have enough to worry about, I thought. "And I promise, I'll call tomorrow with any news on the hearing." I needed off. "Okay, love you, bye."

"Oh. I guess we're done then. Okay, love you. *Bye*," she said, sharply.

Instantly I felt awful. "Aimee?"

"Mitch?"

"I'm sorry. I just—"

She interrupted and sighed. "Mitch, I know it's hard right now. You've got a lot going on. And I want to be there for you. I do. Just promise me you'll take care of yourself. Get some rest and find some peace. Promise?"

"Promise."

"All right, then, call me tomorrow. I do love you."

"I know, Aims. I love you too."

I knew I'd rushed things trying to end the call with the abrupt love-you-bye routine. Aimee's tone had been supportive throughout, but she seemed preoccupied and stressed near the end. And who could blame her? I'd given her some heavy stuff to process, adding to her own heap of worries about our near-term future. Was I getting kicked out of the Navy? Was I driving to Idaho? Was I plunging head-first into a dormant investigation about a girl Aimee had no desire to hear about? These were things that would drive any spouse crazy, isolated at home, feeling out of control, helpless, frustrated, afraid. I knew because these were my emotions too.

We returned to the conference room on Monday morning at 0900 picking up where we'd left off Thursday. Jamie was not invited back as our strategy had taken a major turn during the weekend. Monk and I had spent most of Friday and Saturday preparing for the big showdown as Monk kept calling it, one where he was determined to put Jamie back on the stand and "put his nuts in a vise" getting to the source of his testimony once and for all. I'd left him alone on Sunday so I could take care of some personal business. Monk was still at it Sunday night because he'd called me at Amber's around 10:30 P.M. "Change in plans," he'd said. He would not use Jamie after all. Said he'd lined up testimony from two new sources.

I sat uneasily in my chair understanding very little of the purpose of the two witnesses Monk intended to call. Commander Ray resumed the hearing by turning to Monk. "Defense counsel, please call your first witness." The door swung open and in walked a senior chief petty officer in fresh khakis, one Monk had found at the last minute from the Wing 10 staff across the field who'd agreed to come in on short notice. After a bit of haggling with Pritchard over this late addition, the senior chief was sworn in.

"State your full name, rank and current billet, please," Ray said.

"Donald R. Mullen, Aviation Warfare Systems Operator Senior Chief, Patrol Wing 10 Assistant Training Officer, sir."

"Do you swear to tell the truth, the whole truth and nothing but the truth, so help you, God?"

"I do."

"You may proceed, Mr. Monkowski."

"Thank you, Commander." Monk dove right in. "Senior Chief Mullen, how long have you been in the Navy?"

I smiled. *All me bloomin' life, sir...*

"Twenty-one years and two months."

"And of that time, how long have you been designated as aircrew?"

"A little over twenty years."

"And of that time, how long serving as P-3 aircrew?"

"Fourteen years. The other six in P-2 Neptunes," he quickly added.

Pritchard gave Monk a hard look, implying how much of his resume do we have to sit through? I expected a fiery objection, but he remained silent. He had no idea where this was going.

"Senior Chief, can you explain your role as Wing 10 Training Officer?"

"Assistant."

"Yes, I'm sorry, Assistant. Please explain what the job of Assistant Training Officer entails."

"Well, I assist the Training Officer," he smiled. "And I oversee the training curriculum of all the AWs, ATs and AOs in the seven squadrons attached to Wing 10."

"Quite a large responsibility, yes?"

The senior chief shrugged. "I suppose. Yes, sir."

"And, let the record show," Monk turned to the stenographer, "you've been selected by the FY-1984 E-9 Selection Board for advancement to Master Chief, is that correct?"

A humble, "Yes, sir."

Pritchard couldn't keep quiet any longer. "Is there a point to all this?" he said, throwing up his arms and glaring at Monk. "We all know that—"

Monk cut him off. "Senior Chief, what level of security clearance do you currently hold?"

Pritchard went silent and looked at the witness.

"Secret. SBI."

"Not top-secret?"

"No, sir. My previous jobs and current job as ATO do not require top-secret."

Monk switched gears. "Senior, how many special crew hours do you have in P-3s as an AW sensor operator?"

"Approximately 2,500."

"And in that time, did you ever see or track a US nuclear sub on your AQA-7 acoustic sensor gear?"

He laughed. "All the time, sir."

I wondered where Monk had obtained his technical knowledge to drill down this deep asking about SBIs, special crew hours and AQA-7s. Certainly not from me.

"Hang on," Monk said. "You tracked US nuclear submarines all the time? Wouldn't that require a TS clearance?"

"No, sir."

"Please explain."

"Well, there are really two types of missions where you might see or work with a US boat. The first type is training – where crews go down to SoCal and track a nuke that's putting out augmented frequencies in the water for easier detection. The AWs are briefed on those augmented freqs and set up their gear accordingly. Again, this is done for training purposes and is not classified as top-secret."

"But, in the course of tracking, do you ever see the real frequencies? The un-augmented frequencies?"

Mullen shifted uneasily in his chair but continued. "Sometimes. You have to really look hard and know what you're looking for, but yes, you can see a US nuke on the equipment."

"Okay. Tell us about the second type of mission."

"Well, it would be a special operational mission, not training. There are rare cases where a VP crew is tasked with guiding a US attack sub into position behind a Soviet boat, to put it in trail for various operational reasons."

"Various reasons?"

"To take it out, if necessary. To kill it. But in peacetime, it's usually to gain acoustic intelligence or observe their tactics.

"Ah. So, let me ask, as an AW sensor operator, when you fly one of these missions, are you briefed ahead of time? Are you made aware your flight will be guiding a US sub in trail of a Soviet?"

"No, sir, not officially."

"Not officially. But you're implying you are made aware at some point, that unofficially, you might see a US sub on your grams during the mission?"

"Yes."

"Who makes you aware?"

I looked around the conference room. You could have heard a pin drop. Everyone's eyes were glued to Senior Chief Mullen staring in rapt attention, hanging on his every word.

Again, the uneasy shift. "Well, any number of officers with the TS clearance, sir. Usually in the ASWOC after the formal briefing – the DBO, the TACCO, the mission commander may mention something."

"Okay, hang on again. Let me get this straight. The DBO, the TACCO, the MC." Monk used his fingers to tick them off one by one. "Are you saying they all are violating security regulations by telling you about a possible US sub during the mission?"

"No, sir."

"Again?"

"No, sir, they're not violating security regulations. There's a protocol, a difference, depending on the phase of the mission and what eventually occurs."

"Continue."

"While it's true that US submarine positions are classified top-secret when operational there's a subtle difference between knowing it and the data itself that gets recorded, such as position, course, speed, depth, acoustic intelligence, et cetera."

"And what is that difference?"

"Knowledge of the sub's positional information, while top-secret, is considered *perishable*. The difference is recorded data is considered top-secret *non*-perishable and handled as such. There are specific guidelines in the Wing 10 Op Order that I helped to write on how to handle perishable and non-perishable classified information. I called out the specific paragraph in my written statement to the court."

"So what happens to the recorded data? Data that you see and record on your own AQA-7 gear?"

"If an operational US sub has been detected, the debriefing officer will classify the artifacts obtained on the mission as top-secret – computer tapes, audio recordings, sonograms, navigation logs, miscellaneous notes. It's during debrief the mission gets its official upgrade to top-secret designation and the artifacts are treated and stored as such."

"Okay, thank you, Senior Chief. Just a few more questions. When you were aircrew, were you ever informed about a US sub potentially being part of your operational mission, you know, in advance of going flying?"

"Many times, sir."

"How can that be? Isn't that a violation?"

"No. It's considered perishable as defined by the op order. MCs and their sensor operators discuss it all the time before a mission. It would be considered negligent not to."

Monk let his final sentence hang in the air before closing in for the kill. "Okay, one last question. In your expert opinion as a senior chief AW with over twenty-one years in the Navy, serving as current ATO for Wing 10 and author of the Wing 10 Op Order, would Lieutenant Baumann have violated UCMJ Article 92 and OPNAVINST 5510 by informing his Sensor 1 operator about the USS *Phoenix* and her mission before going flying that night?"

Every eye was still pinned on Mullen.

"No, sir. He would not have."

"Okay, thank you again, Senior Chief. We have your written statement on file." Monk held up two sheets of handwritten chicken scratch and handed them to Ray. "Unless the Government has any questions for the witness, this completes my examination."

"None," Pritchard mumbled, staring at his legal pad.

Ray lifted an eyebrow. "Okay, then. Witness is excused."

Perfect, I thought. Brilliant. I wasn't aware of the fine-line distinction between perishable and non-perishable until today and doubted Fowler or the JAG did either. Where'd Monk find this guy? I wanted to reach over, pull him close and kiss his rugged, pockmarked cheek.

Monk was on a roll and didn't even blink when Commander Ray asked if he wanted a break before his next witness. "No sir, I'd like to proceed by calling Captain Roland McKinney, Patrol Wings Pacific Operations Officer."

And just like that, in walked a senior naval officer in service dress blues, four gold stripes on his sleeve, carrying his cover in his right hand. This was amazing, Monk being able to round up these two witnesses on short notice. He was flying by the seat of his pants and Pritchard knew it.

McKinney took his seat in the witness chair at the end of the table. Pritchard was on his feet before Ray could swear him in. "Commander Ray, if I may, sir, please." His tone was urgent, desperate sounding. "This is the *second* person in the chair this morning that we've had no advance notice of appearance. I object to this parading of undisclosed last-minute witnesses by the defense and request the captain be dismissed until the Government can understand his role in connection with this hearing, have him deposed and his appearance subsequently entered into the record."

Monk rose from his chair across the table, both lawyers now on their feet. I suspected Monk didn't want to allow Pritchard any edge when addressing Commander Ray. "I can explain his role right now, sir. Captain McKinney is the WINGSPAC operations officer and has been asked today to appear as a material witness. He has no specific knowledge of the events in Adak nor the charges facing the defendant. He has not produced any written statement to the court in advance and is here purely to address Naval Regulation 0840 and 0841. He is an authority on," Monk paused to look down at his notes, "OPNAVINST 3710 Naval Air Training and Operating Procedures Standardization, and Patrol Wings Pacific operational policy. I ask that he be allowed to testify today specifically to refute the charge of unauthorized personnel on naval aircraft."

Ray turned to Pritchard and spoke in an exasperated tone. "Mr. Pritchard, we've covered this already. This is the Article 32, not the general court-martial. I will allow any relevant testimony to be gathered here today and entered into the record as it is necessary to weigh the merit of the charges and guide the court's decision before sending the case to trial. Understood?"

"Yes, sir."

He and Monk took their respective seats as Commander Ray swore in the captain. When he finished, he said, "You may proceed, Counsel," nodding at Monk.

"Thank you, Commander." Turning to McKinney, "Captain McKinney, sir, I'd like to thank you this morning for agreeing to make an appearance on such short notice."

"That's fine," he replied softly.

I studied the captain in the chair. He was tall, at least six-three, with a large neck and athletic physique, possibly with college football or lacrosse in his background. He looked familiar but I was certain I'd never met him. His uniform was sharp and freshly pressed, common for a senior officer on the Commodore's staff, his naval aviator wings and five rows of ribbons, impressive.

"Captain," Monk began, "Is it correct, as WINGSPAC operations officer, your duties include overseeing the general administrative and operational actions of the P-3 patrol squadrons based both here at Moffett Field and in Barber's Point, Hawaii?"

"Yes, that's correct."

"Is it also correct that your office routinely creates policy and makes decisions on who may fly as passengers on those aircraft?"

"No, it isn't."

Monk blinked. "Excuse me? You don't make the determination on who flies on your aircraft?"

"We do not, generally speaking. Naval regulations and NATOPS, specifically 3710.7, provide very clear guidelines."

Monk's surprise disappeared. Either this was lawyerly theatrics, or he was truly caught off guard by the captain's abrupt *no*. Captain McKinney was crisp and business-like in his answers, possibly pushing back at Monk's early attempts to steer him too quickly and inaccurately to a desired outcome.

"I see. Thank you, sir. Can you please provide us with some examples of where your office might provide specific guidelines regarding who can fly, and not fly, on P-3 aircraft under administrative control of Commander Patrol Wings Pacific?"

"Yes, we require more detail for situations where Navy regs and NATOPS cannot provide. The P-3 is a large aircraft and, as you know, was once a Lockheed civilian airliner known as the Electra. The ASW-configured P-3s can carry up to 23 crew and passengers and unique situations can arise with classification of these passengers."

"So, for example, a P-3 may carry passengers on a…" Monk again conferred with his notes, "A reposition flight, a pre-deployment or VIP flight, transport from point A to B, et cetera?"

"Correct."

"Are there other types of flights where passengers may be carried?

"Yes. Training missions, demonstrations, flights for members of the media and other officials."

"You mean civilians? Civilians can fly in naval aircraft?"

"Yes. Under the authority and guidelines of 3710."

"So, in the case of active-duty military, specifically the passengers present on Lieutenant Baumann's flight the night of March 14th, they would fit the definition of authorized passengers per 3710, yes?"

"They would."

Pritchard, who'd been following this exchange like a tennis match was convinced he was losing another witness and spoke up. "I'd like to jump in with a question, if I may, Commander." He looked at Pritchard.

"You may."

It had been explained by Commander Ray earlier in the hearing that since this was not a court-martial, the formal rules of examination and cross-examination did not necessarily apply, that if the defense or prosecution needed clarification on a point or had a question they needn't wait until the other side rested, provided they poised their question by first deferring to Ray.

"Thank you, Commander." Pritchard turned. "Captain, with respect to this passenger status you speak of, are these same passengers allowed to fly on naval aircraft within thirty miles of the Soviet Union?"

Okay, here we go, I thought.

"Yes. With the proper training."

"And what training would that be, sir?"

"Standard aircrew training. A syllabus that includes parachute, ejection seat, SERE, DWEST, things like that," said the captain, ticking them off one by one.

"Okay, so, let me understand. Any passenger flying in close proximity to Soviet airspace on naval aircraft, in this case, within thirty miles in the PARPRO system, would first have to have completed SERE, DWEST, all the necessary things you speak of, in advance, correct?"

"No."

"No?" Now it was Pritchard's turn to look surprised.

"First, these are aircrew requirements I've listed, not for passengers. Second, there are special cases where passengers *are* allowed in the PARPRO system on an operational flight."

"Special cases though, right?"

"Yes. There's been precedence established over the years where naval engineers, civilian scientists and government contractors have gone on high-priority P-3 missions to help gather special intelligence on Soviet submarines, all in close proximity to the Russian landmass. Training requirements for these types of passengers are typically waived by the Wing, someone at my level."

"Can you provide some examples of these special missions, Captain? Reasons why they need a waiver?"

"Beartrap, DMP, icepack ops. These all require special measuring apparatuses, equipment run by engineers or scientists."

Pritchard paused, stroking his chin. Things were percolating in his head. "Yes, I understand. And this waiver, it is important because aircrews that go through the training, specifically SERE School, are trained as such because there is a risk of capture if the airplane goes down so close to the Soviet Union while on an operational intelligence-gathering mission? Is that correct, sir?"

SERE stood for Survival, Evasion, Resistance and Escape. It was a mandatory one-week training course given to aircrew in the remote high desert outside San Diego and was modeled after POW experiences gained in Vietnam. The students were set loose in the desert, told to survive and evade, ultimately being captured by the "enemy" then taken to a prison camp, beaten, tortured, waterboarded and shoved in tiny boxes to test their resolve. It was the student's duty, once in the camp, to resist and, if possible, attempt escape. The entire purpose of the training was to emphasize the US military's Code of Conduct, apply it in a practical environment and learn one's breakpoint and limit of endurance.

"Yes, there is that possibility," replied the captain. "What's your point?"

"My point is, sir, that when you sign a waiver, the Navy is taking a huge risk letting civilians without this training fly so close to "enemy territory." They are not SERE trained, they haven't taken DWEST. This is certainly not something you would sign simply for a couple of enlisted OSs stationed at the NAVFAC wanting to go joyriding, especially *female* OSs with no engineering or scientific credentials to speak of?"

"I don't sign the waivers," McKinney deadpanned. "They are delegated to the local operational commander to make the decision and, under my authority, approve or deny permission of any passenger, or passengers in this case, on any operational flight."

"So, in the case of a flight out of NAS Adak, Alaska, who would have been the proper delegated authority to approve passengers on an operational P-3 flight?"

"The CO of the squadron. Or, in the case of Adak, his OINC."

"Ah, so in this case, it would have been Commander Fowler, OINC at the time of the flight?"

"If he was the OINC up there, then yes. He could've okayed it."

"And since we know Commander Fowler approved no such participation of the two NAVFAC women on this flight and proper authorization was not achieved, then Lieutenant Baumann was certainly operating well outside the boundary of his own authority as PPC by allowing them on board." Pritchard didn't phrase his last statement as a question to lead the captain. This was his summation, his coup de grace. He was finished. He'd made his point and looked at Monk with a satisfied smirk.

Captain McKinney remained silent.

Monk stood up. "All right, hang on," he said. "Defense completely rejects the Government's phrase, *joyriding*. Both Petty Officer's MacHold and Sullivan did not go flying that night for the purposes of *joyriding*." Monk exploited Pritchard's reckless use of the term like a pro. "They went as experts in their field to assist against a very high priority target as designated by CINCPAC Fleet – a Soviet Delta IV nuclear ballistic missile submarine. They'd been tracking this target for weeks in advance on their sensor gear at the Naval Facility in Adak and were completely qualified to offer their expertise to the aircrew on station that night. In fact, from the accounts of the mission, their presence aided in detection of the Delta, did it not?" Monk turned to Captain McKinney. "Sir, let me ask you a hypothetical. If you were the OINC in Adak on the eve of this very critical mission, would you have authorized the two NAVFAC operations specialists as passengers on the flight?"

I cringed. Monk was taking a huge risk with this question. I was no lawyer but certainly understood the cardinal rule that you never ask a question, especially in court, to which you did not already know the answer. In this case, I knew Monk had no chance to prep McKinney. Both he and Pritchard had been pushing the envelope this morning, taking their chances probing this last-minute witness.

Captain McKinney didn't answer immediately. He maintained a thoughtful pose and was about to speak.

Pritchard jumped in. "Object. Captain McKinney's answer, regardless of his position and authority, is immaterial. He was not the OINC that night and therefore his answer, regardless of what he might say, should have no bearing on the conduct of the defendant acting outside his authority by inviting the two women along. That's really the issue here."

Monk looked at Ray. "Is the Government finished? Can the witness please be allowed to answer the question?"

"Witness will answer the question," Ray said, shooting Pritchard a scolding look.

"Captain McKinney, sir?"

All eyes went to McKinney.

Again, the thoughtful pose adding a touch of finality. "Yes, I would have allowed the two operations specialists on the flight. Again, a precedence has been established—"

"No further questions, Commander," Monk said.

"Government?"

"No questions, sir. I stand firmly on my last statement."

"Witness is excused." Ray turned to Monk after Captain McKinney stepped away from the table and exited the conference room. "Okay, who's next, Counselor?" he asked, implying what other surprises do you have in-store today?

"That was my last witness, Commander."

Ray turned back to Pritchard. "Mr. Pritchard, do you intend to call any more witnesses today?"

"None, sir. However, I'd like to point out to the court that despite the captain's final answer, Commander Fowler, the current commanding officer of VP-25, was the OINC in Adak during the flight in question and permission *was not given* for these women by Commander Fowler to fly with Mr. Baumann's crew."

Monk's turn. "And I'd like to point out the current operations officer from Patrol Wings Pacific just now testified that he would have authorized them."

"But Commander Fowler did not," Pritchard responded.

"Has Commander Fowler testified to this fact?" Monk asked. "Do we have a written statement from him?"

I was getting nervous. We all knew Fowler had given no statements and was not a witness for the hearing. He had submitted the charges to the Judge Advocate General and had been expected to step back and let the proceeding run its course. In fact, Monk himself said he'd never call Fowler as a witness.

Pritchard waited for a moment. "Commander Fowler did not authorize those women."

"Commander Ray," said Monk, "I'd like to request a private conference with you and the investigation officer, Mr. Donahue. May we step into your office for a moment?"

Ray nodded. I had no idea what Monk was up to. He had gone completely off-script by bringing Fowler, and now this side conference, into the mix. The threesome stepped outside leaving Pritchard, the stenographer and I to stare at each other in awkward silence. They were gone for approximately five minutes.

When they were reseated, Ray spoke. "The hearing will now adjourn for the day. Due to the Thanksgiving holiday, we will resume on Monday, 28 November at 0900 in this conference room. At that time, Commander Richard Fowler will be called as the final witness for the Defense. Hearing dismissed."

Everyone filed out of the room.

I maintained a poker face until the door was shut then turned to Monk. "What the hell? You said we'd never—"

Monk expected my reaction and cut me off. "Mitch, I know what we discussed. We are so close to getting the charges dropped, we really are. Time to put Fowler in the chair and end this nonsense."

"But he didn't authorize the women. I never asked his permission."

"Yes. And at the end of the day, it will be a minor footnote on this case. It's trivial. Not important right now. You gotta trust me on this one. We'll meet at my place tomorrow and then I'm headed back to San Diego for the long weekend."

"Minor footnote, huh?" I was stunned.

Monk meticulously placed his files, array of pens and yellow legal pad back in his briefcase, closed the lid and headed for the door. He turned and smiled. "Hey, by the way, what are you doing for Thanksgiving?"

I didn't respond. If he was inviting me along to San Diego it was assumed because he offered nothing more before closing the door behind him. I remained seated alone in the empty space with the same thought – just what *was* I doing for Thanksgiving? I desperately needed to talk, but not to Monk. That could wait until tomorrow. I needed someone else.

Castro Street in Old Mountain View – I was standing in a crosswalk searching for a tiny Mexican restaurant hidden somewhere across the busy street. This would not have been my first choice, I thought, but I would've agreed to any venue. There was no way Monk was going to prevent this meeting. Jamie was amenable to meet after working hours and had suggested, "Someplace quiet and off base." I was happy he'd proposed dinner as our phone call wrapped up. I couldn't accept breaking contact as Monk had demanded. During the entire ordeal with Jamie, even after his testimony, I never felt our friendship was hanging in the balance. I knew long before he'd submitted his written statement or came into our conference room to be sworn in he'd remain true, never lying or stretching the truth to conform to peer pressure or honor a friendship. It was always *just the facts ma'am* with Jamie. So, when his testimony went south on Monk, I just rolled with it. What bothered me was the look in his eyes. Jamie appeared to have been coerced into following Pritchard down a predisposed path, one that wasn't asking him to lie, just reveal more than a close friend would volunteer to a hostile prosecutor. I mean, how did Pritchard and Donahue get those verbatim snippets of our private conversations? Certainly not from the Jamie I knew.

I finally located the restaurant. It was wedged between a bank and a dry-cleaner on the old-town mall, an easy miss until I caught the whiff of fresh tortillas and roasting maize. This was going to be a difficult meeting, I thought, taking a seat alone in the small dining room. Waiting, my mind began to disassociate, fretting about my time away from Annapolis. I missed Aimee and the kids and felt guilty being apart from my job as company officer, one I'd started only five months ago. I'd need to call Lt Col Walsh, update him on the hearing's woeful progress and make excuses about the wheels of justice turning slowly. It had been four days since the hearing began and would be another full week before it would resume, every member scattering for the long holiday weekend. Monk himself was heading home to San Diego. I had no clue into the Monk's private life other than he was unmarried and living with some coed liberal arts major attending San Diego State. I debated flying back to Annapolis for Thanksgiving but nixed it as being impractical given the time constraints and cost. This seemed sad and outrageous, separated from my wife and kids on our first major holiday in Annapolis considering this was supposed to be shore duty. I pondered the alternative, spending Thanksgiving at Mother's with Amber and her roommate, Gwen. Not a bad alternative but certainly not my first choice. I recalled last year's event where Amber confessed to a second rehab during turkey dinner, her car rolling down the hill into the neighbor's house during dessert, my flying all night before, getting into an argument with Aimee then getting yelled at by Skipper Wilson in my father's den – back when my father was alive and well living in serene, picturesque Coeur d'Alene, Idaho. My God, had it really been a year? It seemed like ten.

I spotted Jamie entering the front door and raised my hand. He smiled and nodded, making a beeline for the booth. He was dressed in casual civilian attire, same as me – chinos, polo shirt and docksiders, the same civilian clothing available to servicemen on the cheap at Navy Exchanges around the world. We shook hands, maintaining our grip an extra second, truly glad to see each other. I was relieved but unwilling to dive straightaway into the weighty issues we'd come to discuss. Instead, I asked Jamie about news from the squadron.

"Oh, you know, the final push to get readiness up before we leave for Kadena," he replied.

"Ugh, another six-month deployment. Time flies. When do you leave?"

"You mean, when do *they* leave? Skipper's plane departs on 6 January. Guess when I detach?"

"5 January?"

"Yep."

"Perfect. Your orders came. Congratulations. Where're you headed?"

"Got my first choice, an ROTC unit at Rennselaer in upstate New York."

"RPI, back to your alma mater, right?"

"Yeah. Will try to finish an MBA in my spare time, ha."

"If anyone can do it, Jame, it's you. Again, congrats."

"Thanks," he said.

Our waitress arrived with two Dos Equis's and we drank in silence.

"So catch me up, Mitch," Jamie said, eager to fill the void. "How's life treating you back at the Academy? How's Aimee?"

"We love the place. Certainly a different perspective than being a mid there. Going to be a sad day when our two years are up. Not sure what's in store after that."

"Airlines, right?"

"Not a hundred percent. I'm considering my options. May decide to stay in. What do you think about that?"

Jamie's mouth dropped. "No way. Mitch Baumann, a lifer? What's Aimee going to say?"

"Oh, she'll be fine with it, either way. I think she's adapting pretty well to Navy life."

"She's a fantastic lady, Mitch. Tell her I said hello, I miss her."

"I will, thanks." We both sensed the obvious discomfort talking about my personal life and plans knowing damn well that any career, as a naval officer, future airline pilot or bagboy at Safeway, hung in the balance based on decisions yet to be made at the hearing and subsequent court-martial. I wanted to give the impression Monk and I had things under control, we were weathering the storm and the whole mess would be dismissed as early as next week. But I was struggling. "You know, this thing makes me feel like my life has narrowed to a path leading to an incredibly wobbly footbridge without railings," I said. "And I need to get across. But I'm blind, Monk is my guide, and a drop to either side is fatal."

"Mitch, I feel horrible about—"

"No, no, don't even go there." I held up my hands. "You did nothing wrong. You told the truth. This is my doing."

"It's Fowler's doing," he said. "He started camping out on my desk as soon as you detached."

"Because you're the squadron legal officer?"

"Yeah. He knew Wilson wouldn't stand for him bringing charges against you. He had to wait, and he did. Exactly one day after the change of command."

"I figured as much. Still, it's not your fault. What I'd really like to know is…" I hesitated. This was my challenge to Jamie. It was the crux of our dinner meeting. "How did Pritchard get those conversations? Our exact words? That drove Monk crazy. We never planned for that part."

"Les Donahue, the investigation officer, got a listen to the ICS tapes from our mission. Some of it was on the recordings."

"Whoa. Why wasn't that given to us at discovery? It should have been, right?"

"Right. I told Pritchard that. He claimed the tapes were top-secret, which they were, so he tried to bury it, was careful not to reference his source. Monk has a case. If he wants to take the discovery violation to Commander Ray, I'm sure he'd entertain it."

I was outraged and buoyed at the same time. Here was a ray of daylight our case needed, it was good news, but something still bothered me. "Jamie, still, some of our conversations were not on that ICS tape. Pritchard quoted me in the Husky Club and ASWOC like he was sitting at our table. What's up with that?"

"You're right," he said, sorrowfully. He looked down and lowered his voice. "He got that from me."

This was the part where I was supposed to get indignant. *And why the hell did he get it from you?* But I'd already talked to Aimee, already made my supposition about Jamie's motivation and had no intention of confronting him directly on it. "And you felt called to offer it?"

Jamie didn't respond, leaving me with the sense he didn't want to discuss it further, that we were finished – our conversation, our dinner, our friendship. I had nothing more to add.

After a long silence, Jamie spoke. "Mitch, you speak of a narrowing of your life down to that wobbly footbridge, Monk as your guide?"

I looked up from my beer. "Yeah."

"That's an apt analogy. That was me too, I was at that same bridge last week. I felt awful afterward. I needed redemption after that horrible testimony, so I had a long talk with Monk Sunday morning."

"Yesterday?"

He nodded. "I know both Captain McKinney and Senior Chief Mullen from my work with the Wing. I informed Monk and encouraged him to use them as material witnesses. Walked him through some of the technical stuff, some regs too, drew him a map of sorts. Monk's a pretty quick study."

"Yeah, he is."

"I really wanted him to dump all over Rory Pritchard. What a scumbag lawyer."

"I was wondering where Monk suddenly became an expert," I laughed. "You should have heard him reel off some of our technical jargon. That certainly didn't come from me."

"Yeah, Monk had very little time to prep them Sunday night."

"Prep must've gone well. They did great." I was starting to feel better, warming back to Jamie and his stab at redemption. "So, Monk calls me late Sunday night, says, 'I really wanted to rip Jamie a new one on the stand tomorrow, but we've got a change of plans. Two surprise witnesses. Tell you about them tomorrow.' Click. Pritchard was so pissed he couldn't see straight." I laughed again, almost uncontrollably, encouraging Jamie to join in.

"I trust it went well," he said pensively, a direct contrast to my newfound mirth.

"It did, it did." I wanted to assure him all was good.

Another silence. Jamie was slow to warm, his mood still dark. We sipped our beers quietly. "I want to stay in the Navy, Mitch. You know, make it my career."

"Yeah. I kind of figured that. Admiral."

"Got some great orders out of VP-25. Rennselaer. Looking at possibly a DESRON staff on the East Coast after that."

"Sounds like all the right tickets to punch." I wondered where this was going. "Jamie, I need to be frank, and tell me if I'm out of line, but…" I swallowed hard. "Were you threatened by anyone, Fowler, Pritchard, anyone, to give that testimony? I was just wondering because—"

"Both."

"Huh? Really?"

"Fowler went to bat for me with my detailer, got a verbal from BUPERS, exactly the orders I wanted. Then Pritchard comes along, says the orders may be in jeopardy, certain other factors might be in play.

"That sounds like a veiled threat."

"Just clever wording. He wasn't exposing himself. Wanted to make it sound like he'd heard things, passing on advice. Like he was watching out for me."

"But the underlying message was clear."

"When Fowler said he'd heard there was a potential snag at the Bureau about the time I was told to draft my statement concerning our mission and everything that followed, yeah, the message was pretty clear."

"Jamie, man, you had some legal training. Isn't that, like, witness tampering or something? Aren't they breaking the law?"

"They weren't going to touch my orders, Mitch. That would've been boldface extorsion. No, it's something else."

My stomach knotted. This was the delicate issue I'd come to confirm. "I spoke with Aimee," I said. "Last Thursday after your testimony—"

Jamie's sighed. "Well, I'm betting she'll never want to speak to me again."

"No, you're wrong. She adores you. You're as good a friend to her as me. And we talked about, you know, that something else you just mentioned."

"So, you figured it out? She told you?"

"Aimee spotted it shortly after she'd met you."

"Oh." Pause. "She did, huh? That long ago?" Jamie laughed for the first time since sitting down. "Well, women can sense things. She's pretty sharp. As I said, she's a wonderful lady, Mitch. Make sure you hang onto her."

I gave him an odd look.

"Seriously."

"I will," I said, feeling defensive for no reason like he was seeing into my marriage.

"She's been a true friend. Yeah, we've even talked on the phone a few times, mostly when I was having my doubts, my issues."

"You talked? To Aimee?" I was flabbergasted. "When?"

"It's okay. Just a few times. About stuff, you know, relationships. She knows about my friend in VP-46, shared some things about, well, you guys too. Just talk. You know…"

Just like two girlfriends, I thought, just like Aimee and Lisa. Our conversation was going deeper than I'd anticipated or was comfortable with. So, she knew more than she let on the other night. In any case, I had my confirmation from Jamie himself on why things went south at the hearing. Time to move on. "Aren't you concerned?" I said. "That you're still vulnerable of being exposed by Pritchard after your good deed on Sunday?"

"Yeah, I figure he'll smell a rat after he connects the dots to McKinney and Mullen. He'll probably out me and there'll go my career."

"He can't do that. We'll figure something out." I was thinking of Monk.

"I doubt it, Mitch. My friend in -46, there's already been talk. Either the investigation officer, Donahue, or someone else told Pritchard. People just *love* to talk. But whatever happens, happens. I don't care. I'm grateful I was able to come back and help after they tried to sink you. I just hope it ends well and the bogus charges are dropped."

"So do I," I said, wanting to believe it as much as Jamie. "By the way, Monk's putting Fowler on the stand next Monday. Did he tell you that?"

Jamie gasped. "No way. Are you kidding?"

"I'm not. I'm meeting with him tomorrow to understand where this wild notion came from in the first place. The accident board never dinged Fowler for the questionable PMCF, just the maintenance crew for ignoring some of the gearbox mods. I'm guessing he wants to grill him on the engine thing."

"That's not it, Mitch."

"No?"

"I gave Monk more ammunition on Sunday than just McKinney and Mullen."

"Fowler?"

"Yeah. But he wasn't supposed to put him on the friggin' stand. What's he thinking?"

"What'd you tell him?"

"Ho-boy," Jamie sighed. "Let me explain. What I'm going to tell you stays between you, me and Monk."

426

# 27

## TWO BAD GUYS

I TRUDGED UP THE STEPS to the second floor of the JAG building. Practically my second home, I thought, as I approached Amanda's office. The lights were out throughout the building except her LSO bay, everyone scattered for the Friday after Thanksgiving. Amanda was a model of concentration as I knocked on her cubicle's doorframe stirring her attention. "Morning, Mandy, thanks for coming in. I know this is your day off."

"Morning, Mitch." She smiled and wrinkled her nose at the nickname. "Yours too, I imagine."

"Yeah, well, I've had more than my share of time off," I said, thinking of my neglected job back at the Academy. "So, what've we got?"

"Sit down, please." She motioned to the only other chair in her cube. "We have some time before the call." She glanced at her watch. "Coffee?"

"All coffee'd up, thanks." I was eager to hear the news she'd so urgently discovered a few days ago and prepare for our conference call with Pres Manley in thirty minutes.

"Well, I need a cup. Just going to pop down the hall to the machine. Back in a sec, okay?"

"Roger." As she bounded from the cube, I marveled that this was the same wide-eyed plebe I'd met in the wardroom back in '76. She appeared very much in control of her life, very confident where she was headed. I thought she'd be a much better role model for Amber than this Gwen, her current roommate. I'd met Gwen yesterday at Mother's during Thanksgiving and she seemed dear yet older and a mass of insecurities. By my reckoning, it was a case of the blind leading the blind. But she and Amber were in it together, piecing back their lives, and that was the whole point. Who was I to judge?

Amanda strolled in, fresh cup of coffee in her hand. "Let's take a walk down to the conference room, get set up for the call."

I stood. "Ready when you are."

We walked down a darkened passageway to a familiar door. Ugh, the hearing room, I thought. I held it open for both of us and flipped on the overhead lights. Why'd she have to bring me back here? Amanda explained this was the only speakerphone on the floor and we needed a room to ourselves. It'd be especially private with the entire building nearly empty. I sat down in my old chair, Amanda taking a seat across the table where Pritchard sat. She dragged the speaker device and its tangle of wires in front of us. "We've still got a few minutes before Pres said to call. Maybe we should go over some preliminaries first. I'm not sure how much he'll be able to tell us. But it sounds like they're close."

"Close to what?" I wasn't in an optimistic mood.

"Close to…" She gave me a frustrated look. "Solving this thing, what else?"

I was tempted to blurt out some sarcasm. *Wow, you mean he's found Maddy? Where's she been all these years?* Instead: "He got the essay, right?"

"Yes. And thank you. I'm glad someone's stayed in touch with the O'Connor's. I feel guilty for letting them slip away over the years."

"Well, don't look at me. This was all Bob Clausen. And I'm not sure he or Jan stay in touch regularly either. It was probably my visit to their house in Silver Spring in October that reenergized Bob to make the call." After Aimee told me Bob had received a copy of Maddy's application essay from her parents, I made sure he faxed a copy to both Amanda and me and kept the original for himself. After reading the essay numerous times we were still puzzled as to what we were looking for, so Amanda went ahead and sent a copy to Pres Manley.

"Mitch, I know you can't talk about your hearing but how's Monk working out? You guys hit it off well?" She added a quick laugh, implying no one really hit it off well with Monk.

"He's fine," I replied. "So far, so good."

"I know he's got his share of quirks and can come across as an arrogant jerk, but I like him. His heart's in the right place."

"He's a killer," I said, smiling. "And I don't see the arrogance that much since the hearing's started."

"Hmm. That's odd."

"What?"

"Well, he's obviously not feeling in control. When he knows his stuff, which is 99% of the time, he's an arrogant jerk. When you don't see it that means he's got a confidence problem."

"Oh, great. Thanks for that."

"I'm joking. He's got a whole range of personalities in case you haven't noticed."

"Tell me about it. Sometimes he's up, sometimes he's down. He pings off the walls, he goes into trances and mutters to himself. I think he's schizophrenic, or ADD, or something."

"Just the something," she said, opening her spiral notebook. "Well, I'm glad he's working out for you."

"And I'm glad you warned me about that stuff before I met him. Otherwise, you'd have been my lawyer."

"And you'd have been on a fast train to Leavenworth by now."

I froze. Her stab at self-deprecating humor was sweet but a full court-martial and incarceration were still very real options in my mind.

Amanda noticed my reaction. "Sorry. That was in bad taste."

"No problem… It was funny, actually. Hey, before we get started, different subject."

"Sure."

"You looking for a roommate by any chance?"

Her eyes grew large. "What kind of question is that? Are you needing a new place to stay?"

I laughed and held up my hands realizing how absurd that sounded. "Not for me. My sister. I was just wondering."

"Oh." She thought for a moment. "I'm sorry, has she had another—"

I sensed her reticence immediately. "No, no, nothing like that. She still has a roommate." *Why'd I bring this up?* "It's just, well, you'd be…" I laughed again to dispel the notion I was serious. "I think you'd be a good influence, that's all. I'm sorry, let's forget it. We've got bigger fish to fry."

"Well, I guess I could talk to her."

"No, that's all right." I'd clearly rattled her. "We don't need to be tackling this right now. Let's just move on, please."

"I'm flattered you'd ask." She took a quick breath, shaking off the diversion. "Okay, then. Let's recap where we are before I dial." She looked down at her page. "First, Pres Manley and this Agent Peters buddy of his from the FBI traveled to the prison in Atlanta more than a week ago. They met with a convict, I just found his name, a Lyle Humphries. He's completed a year of a five-year sentence and yes, Pres confirmed the whole point of the meeting was to hear about a possible deal in exchange for some new information he's willing to offer, likely on his partner."

"The meeting already happened though, correct?"

"Yes. I'm hoping it's part of the reason for the call today. I got the feeling they still have some holes and want either you or I to clarify some things, not sure."

"Again, tell me the link to this guy and Maddy's – disappearance. How'd they put it together?"

"It's two guys, one in Atlanta, the other in Pennsylvania. They were suspected by Peters of being involved with Maddy's disappearance during the investigation in '77 but it was dismissed after consultation with the NIS. The FBI had enough evidence from their other crimes to put these guys away, so they backed off and let the NIS run solo with Maddy. And we know how that turned out. So, that's why Pres felt drawn back in – after you told him whatever it was on the phone a few weeks ago."

"I didn't tell him much." I thought back – the charm bracelet, the second visit to the Clausen's, Fowler coming on deck the night of Maddy's disappearance. I wasn't sure which piece of information, if any, had tripped him.

"Okay, I'm dialing," Amanda said. She punched the speakerphone. A loud dial tone filled the room followed by a series of digital beeps, each one slowly entered on the keypad. I noticed the Washington, DC area code.

Loud ringing. Amanda twiddled with the volume knob.

"Pres Manley here," came the reply over the box. He spoke fast, making his three words blend as one.

"Pres, good morning, it's Amanda. And I've got Mitch Baumann sitting here with me."

"Standby. Let me go on speaker."

Some mild jostling. We glanced at each other. "Speaker?" I whispered. We'd expected Pres to be solo, at least for this initial call.

After a beat. "Okay, much better. And I've got Special Agent Chad Peters, FBI, with me. We're actually using his office here in DC."

Amanda was about to speak but Pres continued.

"And, full disclosure, we have two other guests in the room with us this morning."

Another pause, Pres dragging the phone and mumbling to someone on his end. I turned my attention from the box to Amanda and mouthed, *Who?*

She shrugged and shook her head.

"I'd like to introduce Bill and Rebecca O'Connor, Maddy O'Connor's parents. They're sitting in today at their own request." Some more mumbling. "And at the behest of Agent Chad Peters."

I quickly punched the mute button on our speaker box. "Holy shit! Did he say Maddy's parents are in the room?"

"Sounds like it."

"What the hell?"

"This is a surprise to me too."

Another man's voice was speaking.

"Better get off mute," Amanda said.

I punched the button again.

"Pres, we're still here," she said. "Did you say Mr. and Mrs. O'Connor are there with you?"

"Mitch, Amanda," a second male voice said. "This is Chad Peters. Is it all right to call you by your first names? I think that'd be fine with everyone here." A pause. "Yes, Bill and Becky O'Connor are with us this morning. I anticipate this to be an informal meeting."

Before we had a chance to respond, Peters continued.

"Allow me to explain. I know you probably weren't expecting a full house today, but a lot has happened in the last two weeks and there's been some new activity I'll share. I won't be able to tell you everything. In fact, I need you, Mitch, to provide some information, fill in a few holes first. And just a heads-up, I'll be recording this entire conversation. Do you have any issue with that?"

How were we to respond? Yes? No? I opened my mouth to speak.

"Mitch, Amanda? Bill O'Connor here. As Chad explained, I'm sure this is a surprise to you both, to have Becky and me on the call, but I think he's got some good news on the recent progress. We're all here to respond to some urgent questions that should tie things together. And Amanda, it's great to hear your voice again, sweetie. It's been a long time. Mitch, I'm pleased to finally meet you and grateful for your continued concern for Maddy and effort you've shown to bring the case back to life. I can't tell you what it means to Becky and me."

There was a pause as Bill seemed to wait for a response. My mind raced. What could I possibly say to this couple that had lost their daughter over seven years ago to a brutal murder? *Oh, yes, Mr. and Mrs. O'Connor, pleased to meet you. I knew Maddy well, a sweet girl, a wonderful person. Did I mention I was in love with her once, a long time ago? I'm so sorry for your loss.* No way, I just couldn't. Instead: "Thank you, sir. We're here to help."

"Mitch, Chad Peters again."

"Yes, sir?"

"Just to start with, a few questions on Maddy's essay. First, nice work prompting Bob Clausen to get back in touch. His call to the O'Connor's enabled us to find a second copy of her essay, one we didn't know existed until Becky, her mom, found it in Maddy's personal possessions – boxes that were moved to their attic for storage when she left for the Academy."

"What happened to the first copy, the original?"

"Mysteriously disappeared. That's all I can tell you right now. As you know Maddy submitted it to her congressman along with a letter requesting a nomination back in 1975. All part of the application process, you know."

"Yes."

"After she was nominated, her congressman's office forwarded every applicant's paperwork to the Naval Academy Admissions Office in Leahy Hall. Didn't keep any copies for their own records. Standard practice I'm told. Back in 1977, the NIS seized Maddy's admission documents including things like her pre-candidate questionnaire, high school transcripts, SAT scores, medical exam results, recommendation letters, stuff like that, a whole folder full. Turns out the lone document they were searching for was apparently missing, conspicuously absent among a file with virtually everything else intact. This missing essay did raise questions but wasn't considered crucial since no one knew what it contained and therefore held no relevance to the case. And no other copy was known to exist." Peters changed direction. "Mitch, you knew of this essay before Maddy went missing? She told you about it, yes?"

I thought back to the one time she'd mentioned it – in my car during our rendezvous and escape to the park that night exactly one week before she went missing. "Yes, she told me she'd written an essay as part of the admission requirements." I swallowed hard, hoping I wouldn't have to admit to the location or circumstances with Maddy's parents hanging on every word. What was happening? Was I being investigated? Were charges being pointed back at me after I'd rushed in to help?

"So, you knew of the essay, and you've had a chance to read it. Mitch, I presume you read a copy of the essay before forwarding it to Pres and I?"

"Yeah, I read it." My defenses were coming up. "So did Amanda."

"No, no, that's okay. I hoped you did. That's what I want to talk about. Tell us," he said, shifting direction. "What were your impressions?"

"My impressions? On what?"

"Anything. Anything in particular."

I felt I was being led to some distant answer Peters needed to hear. He was fishing for something. "Well, Maddy seemed to be writing about the two people she admired, that influenced her the most when it came to defining role models in her life, you know, as she considered her future – her father and this Admiral Tennant fellow, a friend of the family, right?" I was hoping Father Bill would jump in and back up my assumption about Tennant. Peters' motive had me worried.

"Mitch, when Maddy told you about the essay she'd written, did she make any side comments about Admiral Tennant? Anything at all – about her relationship, how long she'd known him, her impression of him, as a child, as a midshipman?"

I was hoping he'd leave this alone. I was being forced back to our joyride in the car that night. "Well, yes, she did mention he was on the move, going places. Might even be the Chief of Naval Operations someday."

"Anything else?"

Yes, I thought, there was something else. Our conversation was coming back slowly – Maddy admitting to using him to earn "brownie points" with the selection board by claiming a close relationship with a well-known admiral. And her mentioning doing some deep research on him, learning his role in the Tonkin Gulf incident, for what I assumed was to create a more authentic essay. And lastly, her calling him a bit of an asshole when I led with the comment that he sounded like a decent guy. "She said she researched his career a bit, you know, to make her voice sound more knowledgeable when she wrote about his duty stations, combat action, awards and decorations, stuff like that."

"Did she mention discovering anything in particular? Any abnormalities or discrepancies?"

"No." I thought back. "No mention of anything like that."

There was a long pause on their other end. "Mitch, Amanda, pardon us. We're going to go on mute for a sec. Be right back."

"Okay." I pushed our own mute button and turned to Amanda. "What the hell's going on? What do you make of this? His questions?"

She shook her head.

"I'll be honest," I said. "I'm a little concerned."

"Me too. I'm guessing they found more stuff in Maddy's boxes besides that essay."

"Really? Like what?"

"Not sure. Maybe Maddy had a—"

Just then, "Mitch, Amanda. Chad Peters, we're back. Sorry for the interruption."

I came off mute. "That's okay, we're here." *God, what's next?*

"Mitch, this is Bill O'Connor again. I know some of these questions may seem a bit strange. I've spoken with Chad and Pres here so allow me to share some background on Admiral Tennant. We met back in '67 aboard the Indy – the *USS Independence*. He was the skipper of VF-41 and I was one of the wing's AIOs. We did two cruises to the Med in '67 and '68 and I got to know him, and eventually his wife, Marilyn, very well. In fact, he took me under his wing and helped get me some orders I needed to get back to the States when Becky was sick. They were both great, and we began seeing them socially when we were stationed here in DC. When it came time for Maddy to write her essay for the Academy she wanted to write it solely about me but I suggested she include Harley so, yes, as you learned, she did do some research filling in her knowledge on his career. It was these research notes, along with a notebook she'd been keeping on him, even at the Academy, that Becky found when we went looking for her copy of the essay."

There was a pause at their end, some more mumbling. Amanda and I maintained a stare at the speaker.

Bill resumed. "That's really it. Harley and Marilyn became close friends along with our children, their children. His career was really taking off and he ran in some larger circles but yes, I would have considered them friends of the family in that period of our lives."

This all seemed very interesting, but I wasn't getting it. What was the point?

"One last bit of info," Bill added. "Back in '68, aboard the Indy—"

"Yes?"

"Harley Tennant, Commander Tennant at the time, made friends with another officer during the second cruise. He was an aviator, part of ship's company, the catapult officer, I believe. His name was Lieutenant Commander Richard Fowler. You know him, yes?"

"All right, hang on," Peters jumped in. "Thanks, Bill, let's not get ahead of ourselves."

I about slipped off my chair after hearing Fowler's name mentioned. It wasn't so much that the three men were stationed together on the Indy. The Navy can be a relatively small community. Officers with similar warfare specialties and career paths often intersect over the years. The thing that jolted me was the fact Bill considered this relevant, that it meant something to him, to the case.

"Mitch, just a few more questions about your conversation with Maddy," continued Peters.

*Geez, this guy is a pit bull.*

"The night you last saw her, in your car—"

*Oh yes, my car, you just had to bring that up.* "Hang on, Agent Peters. I'm happy to cooperate, but you seem to know everything already."

"Yes, we do, Mitch. We have the transcripts from your NIS interview back in '77. We share things like that, you know. And I will say, that car ride in town had you pegged as their prime suspect for about a week there."

"What?"

"Relax, please. That's not what this is about. We've obtained some new information, thanks to you, Amanda and Pres and I just need you to corroborate a few things."

I took a deep breath. "Okay."

"This is important, and I need you to think back to that night in your car in '76. Think hard. When Maddy told you about Tennant, that she did some research on him, did she at any time say she'd uncovered anything new?"

"No." I thought we'd covered this.

"Anything about a notebook she was keeping?"

"About a what? I'm not following." I clearly wasn't.

"The research, on Tennant. Did she admit to finding, how shall I say, any new information since arriving at the Academy?"

"Again, Agent Peters, she said very little about her essay that night, and nothing about any ongoing research. It was a very brief part of our overall conversation."

"Okay, fair enough. Let me ask, when you dropped her off at the athletic field…" He paused, possibly to consult his notes.

I was about to bust having to sit through this interrogation with Maddy's parents likely sitting on the edge of their chairs imagining all kinds of inappropriate behavior in the car that night. Prime suspect, my ass. "Hold on, please, Agent Peters, Pres, Mr. and Mrs. O'Connor," I said. "Let me ask a question. You mentioned a significant breakthrough in the case, some new information coming to light, thanks to Amanda, Pres and I. Can you please share what you've uncovered? What happened two weeks ago in Atlanta? I assume this is what brought the case back to life, not some essay on an admiral seven years ago." I winked at Amanda hoping she'd agree. No harm in asking, I thought. I needed Peters and Manley to come clean, give us more insight and make us feel part of the team.

"That's a fair question, Mitch. We'll need to take another break. I'm going to go on mute again. Give us five minutes." With that, the line went silent.

Here we go again, I thought. In the interim, Amanda and I stared at each other, we speculated, we got more coffee. I used the restroom. Amanda returned some calls. The break lasted more like ten minutes but when Peters was back, he was speaking in a softer, whisper-like voice. "All right, Mitch. We just said goodbye to the O'Connor's. They've departed my office. It's just Pres and me."

"Okay."

"I can tell you he and I traveled to the federal prison in Atlanta on 16 November. We met with one of the inmates."

"Right." I waited, hoping there was more, that he didn't clear the room just to tell us this one thing I already knew. "Keep going, please. This is why the FBI is now involved, yes?" I knew it was, remembering Amanda speculating she thought this convict, this Lyle Humphries in Atlanta, was wanting to make a deal in exchange for information. "What'd this creep in Atlanta tell you?"

"Okay, I'm going to make this short, basically the same thing I told Bill and Becky this morning. I owe you that much. I'm not at liberty to discuss everything but our man in Atlanta, Mr. Humphries, became suddenly willing to offer new testimony on the case, basically rat out his old partner doing time in Pennsylvania as a trade for early parole, and a few other things I can't get into."

"So these guys were, how do I put it, professionals? Hit men or something?"

"No, nothing like that. They worked for a PI firm near Baltimore, and a sleazy one at that. They were small-time hoods, at least until that night in November."

"Who hired them? Who did they work for?"

"I'm sorry, that's all I can tell you other than, well, to aid his cause he's given us a lead on where we can dig up a body."

"A *WHAT?*" Amanda and I both gasped. Did we just hear correctly? "My God. Have you found her yet?"

"I said, *a body*. Until we find something, it's a random tip from a desperate hood. Could be any number of things but we've got several agents on it as we speak. I'm going out to the site today. It's all brand new, unfolding as we go. And it's as much as I can reveal."

That was it, he would go no further. I was shocked he told us that much, and from the way it sounded Peters himself likely exposed more than planned by bringing the body into it. We ended the call with Pres telling us he'd stay in touch via Amanda and let her know if there was news or if anything changed. He added to standby, that they expected news very soon.

"Why can't they tell us who hired them?" I said, after Amanda had coiled up the speakerphone wires and shoved the box aside. "I mean they pretty much told us everything else. And what was all this stuff Peters kept asking me about inconsistencies in Maddy's research? Like she'd uncovered some new details on the Kennedy assassination.

"Pres asked me the same questions a few days ago. Wanted to know if Maddy ever confided things her research was uncovering. I told him no, that I wasn't even aware she was doing any research beyond her normal studies." She met my gaze. "They're on the trail of someone, Mitch. This convict, Humphries, has named the client they were working for. It's just a matter of running down some leads, and that's the part Peters can't reveal. I'm sure we'll hear from Pres in the next few days."

"What else did Pres say, when you talked to him a few days ago? Anything more than Peters just told us?"

"Just a couple of things. Said Humphries claims he wasn't at the scene, was working in Baltimore the same night tracking some Sun reporter that was going to interview Maddy."

"A reporter?"

"Apparently they never planned to kidnap her. Just stalk her, intimidate her, maybe talk her out of this essay. Then that night Maddy comes down the steps outside Perry Circle, sees the van and this big guy gets out. He's alone. He may have demanded something. There are words, there's a struggle, she screams, and he takes her down trying to keep her quiet. It was all a mistake, a big accident, or so he claims. Wasn't supposed to happen that way, according to Humphries, based on what his partner told him."

"So that's really the whole thing? This guy wants out of prison for admitting his partner did it, it was an accident, and oh, by the way, he wasn't even there?"

"More or less. Pres says the FBI will run down his alibi, where he was that night. They have the missing shoulder board and charm bracelet. Dusted them for prints again but came up empty. Got some good ones on you though, and Posey Shelnutt."

"Good ones on me, huh?" I hoped her last sentence was sarcasm. I started to speak, feeling guilty for Posey and me seven years after the fact. "But we—"

"I wouldn't worry about it, Mitch. They know how the evidence was obtained. Water under the bridge, Peters told Pres. So, anyway, they told Humphries and his lawyer no dice on any deal until they could corroborate his story or talk to his partner. Until then, you're just a lying snitch, Pres said. That's when he must've told them about a body."

I pushed back my chair. There were still too many unanswered questions, too many loose ends. "Why were these guys stalking Maddy? What was their motive? Obviously they were hired, but by who?"

"It'll come out."

"It better," I said. "After coming this far." Amanda was growing pensive, and I turned away to the window. "God, I can't believe this thing could actually be put to bed, after all these years."

"I know."

"The entire grisly mess."

Amanda let out a quick sob and caught herself.

I whirled around. Tears were starting to flow. "Are you okay?" I moved back to the table and sat next to her. "They're getting really close," I said. "This sounds like good news."

She sniffled and brought a Kleenex to her nose. "I know. It's just that, well, Peters says they're going to find the body. Imagine, finding Maddy after all these years. They might've already found her for all we know." She dabbed an eye. "I wasn't prepared to hear that. I told myself as the years passed, it was never going to happen, they'd never find Maddy or her killer. Now that we're close, I guess it's hitting me hard, harder than I expected, that's all."

I nodded. I was getting emotional too, trying to imagine the bittersweet sensation of solving Maddy's disappearance but also having to face the raw truth of what happened, a blow-by-blow description of the facts, of what went wrong that night, and why. I thought of the parents, Bill and Becky. How much had Peters shared with them? All of it? Do they know about the search for their daughter's remains, underway as we speak? God, what a prolonged nightmare it must've been for them, especially the mother who kept quiet during the entire meeting. After a few minutes of sitting in silence, I stood to leave the conference room. "You want to head back to the office?" I said. "Maybe grab some lunch?"

"No, you go ahead. Hit the lights on your way out though. I think I'll sit here a few more minutes."

"I can stay. You sure you're all right?"

"I'll be fine." Amanda maintained her blank stare at the wall. "Mitch, I think we know who hired those two men," she said in a flat voice.

"I can't even imagine if it's true. Things seem very surreal right now." I reached for the doorknob. "I'm going out for a drive, maybe over to Santa Cruz. If anything comes up, you've got my sister's number, right?"

"I do."

"Hang in there, counselor, we'll know something soon." I forced a smile and closed the door leaving her alone. We were both wrecks. We knew Maddy would be found in the next few days, a killer named. And it wouldn't be either of those two goons in prison.

# 28

## FOWLER ON THE STAND

I WAS STUCK IN MORNING COMMUTE on the 101-freeway heading south to base. A steady rain was falling from the first storm of the season, the roads were slick, traffic backing up in a sea of red taillights. The car wipers were beating, the radio droning softly in the background. My future was still pathetically murky with no resolution, no sense of control and no single piece falling neatly into place. It had been exactly three weeks since I sat in Lt Col Walsh's office and received word of my court-martial. My exile to the land of Nod, now at nineteen days and counting.

I fiddled with the radio dial trying for a new station. I needed to control something, even if it was simply to rid my world of the annoying song. I wondered just how much more of this extended absence Walsh and the Academy would tolerate. I'd been sent out to Moffett under two weeks of TDY orders with an agreement to phone back daily. Walsh sounded fatherly and understanding during our initial calls, but I sensed frustration in his tone after telling him I needed an additional two weeks serving to compound the guilt I felt over my lengthening predicament. And then there was Aimee. She seemed to be coping well with the help of the neighbors but was obviously worried and running out of patience.

We were to resume today with our climactic power move – Monk putting Fowler on the stand. I was still vague on the entire strategy as Monk swore from the beginning nothing good could come from making Fowler testify. What had convinced him otherwise? Jamie? To me, Jamie's inside knowledge, while helpful, was mostly hearsay, a wobbly compass designed to point Monk at a potential cache of information with no guarantee of reward. For the last three weeks, Monk and I had prepared diligently, running down any lead, any new witness, but to me it all felt like an exercise in futility as the hearing dragged on. Was Jamie's intel really going to be the big game changer and split things open for us?

My mind continued in a detached, fretful stream of consciousness as I entered the hearing conference room. I barely remembered driving through the main gate, parking my car and walking up the steps of the JAG building. But here I was, seated, Monk next to me, the hearing board present and everyone ready to resume. Suddenly, Fowler walked in. He smiled at Rory Pritchard and Commander Ray and took his seat. Poof. My reality was shifted back to the present.

Fowler was quickly sworn in. Monk stood and cleared his throat. "Commander Fowler," he began, his tone measured and full of derision. He held up a single sheet of paper handed to him only moments ago. "Your witness statement, I presume? From the events in Adak?"

"Yes."

"Given to the defense counsel just minutes ago." Monk eyeballed Rory Pritchard, then Commander Ray, implying Government obstruction by intentionally sitting on this item of discovery. "Never mind the witness was summoned nearly a week ago. That we are only receiving his statement this morning."

Pritchard stared back. *And your point?*

Monk refocused on the statement, his eyes scanning it rapidly as if speedreading. "I see, Commander Fowler, that you were the executive officer of VP-25 during the events in Adak?"

"Yes."

"And currently the commanding officer?"

Fowler didn't respond. Monk was buying time, merely probing Fowler's current state of mind. "Commander Fowler?"

"Yes, I am currently the CO of VP-25, just like the statement says."

"Thank you, sir. And where were you stationed before receiving orders to VP-25?" This, I doubted, was in Fowler's short statement.

"I was in Washington, DC, assigned to—" Fowler stopped and turned to Commander Ray. "Before I continue, I don't see how this question has any relevance to the proceeding."

"I'm sorry, sir," Monk interrupted, "It wasn't in your statement, and I wasn't given much time to prepare for your appearance this morning." Monk knew the answer, and he'd had plenty of time to prepare. He was already setting the trap.

Fowler eyed Ray, his look saying, *Do I really need to answer this kid's question?*

"Please answer the question, Commander," Ray responded.

Fowler's eyes narrowed. "I was assigned to the staff of the Deputy CNO for Information, Plans and Strategy." He flashed a superior grin at Monk. "At the Pentagon." *There you go, smartass.*

"Impressive," Monk said, clearly not impressed. "When was this? Approximately?"

"1979 to 1982. Approximately."

Monk peered at his notebook for a moment. "And before that, from 1976 to 1979, you were stationed at the Naval Academy as a battalion officer on the Commandant's staff, correct?"

Fowler was aghast. Not so much from the fact he was a battalion officer in that period, but that Monk already knew both facts and was simply jerking him around. "Correct—" He started to add something, but Monk cut him off.

"And you were the OINC, the Officer-in-Charge, of the VP-25 Adak detachment from 15 March to 20 May, were you not?"

Fowler gave Monk a hard look, not answering.

"Commander, this is relevant. You were the OINC in Adak during the period I just mentioned and during the defendant's flight in question?"

Again, a delayed response. "Yes, correct again, genius. I was the OINC."

Monk ignored the sarcasm. "Commander, please describe what an OINC does, the nature of his duties."

"Just like the title suggests. He's in charge of the squadron detachment, the skipper's representative on the scene. His duties are much like any CO, the job I now hold in VP-25. Like any position of high authority, the OINC is responsible for the safe and effective operation of the squadron's assets, its airplanes, its aircrews. He oversees everything and reports to the operational commander as well as the commanding officer of the squadron. Very high authority, very important position in a forward theater."

"Thank you, sir. However, as I understand, isn't the OINC job traditionally reserved for someone more junior than a squadron executive officer? A department head perhaps, someone being groomed for command?" Monk was suppressing his delight. This was part of his trap, painting Fowler as an XO in need of remedial training, his question designed to rile Fowler and bring Pritchard to his feet.

Pritchard took the bait, jumping right in. "Commander Ray, I'd like to call a halt to this line of questioning regarding Commander Fowler's duty stations and billets. It's irrelevant and borders on harassment. He has been brought in to testify, at the defense counsel's behest I might add, regarding events the defendant now stands accused, not to review his career with a fine-tooth comb. And I might suggest that—"

"I believe in light of Captain McKinney's testimony last week," Monk interrupted, "Information regarding Commander Fowler's duty stations, specific duties as OINC, and his actions are especially relevant."

"I'd like to finish, please," Pritchard said. "And I believe you cannot belittle a senior officer's role as OINC just because he may have been considered over-qualified by customary standards."

"Now hold on there," Fowler said, looking at Pritchard. "Who said an OINC has to be a department head? Who said a squadron XO is considered over-qualified?"

"No. I'm sorry, sir." Pritchard was back-peddling. "I didn't mean to imply… You were certainly qualified, maybe a bit senior, that's all. Ah, let me switch gears." He paused and took a deep breath. Pritchard was being forced into defending Fowler, rushing in too soon. But nonetheless, he looked committed. He continued. "Sir, how long have you known the defendant, Lieutenant Baumann?"

"Too long. Ha, ha." Fowler looked around the room thinking his dim retort might earn him support and a few laughs. We all sat and stared. Fowler looked like an ass. His lack of self-awareness and timing was embarrassing. In any other circumstance, I'd have felt sorry for him.

Pritchard offered an obligatory smile, forced again to show some level of support for this key witness on which everything now hinged. "Yes, sir," he said, breaking the awkward silence. "In fact, you were first introduced to Mr. Baumann when you joined VP-25 as executive officer in," Pritchard looked down at his copy of Fowler's statement, "May of 1982, correct?"

Fowler straightened in his chair, giving Pritchard a more sober response. "Yes. That is correct."

Pritchard's face relaxed. He seemed concerned about Fowler's volatile temperament but keen on extracting a few facts before letting Monk continue to have his way. "And under what circumstances were you introduced to Mr. Baumann, after you'd joined the squadron?"

"Well, I'd have to say that..." Fowler appeared in serious thought, stroking his chin. "Hmm. It would have to be the bumper sticker incident."

"Excuse me?"

"Yes, that's right. He vandalized my car in the parking lot shortly after my taking over as XO by gluing a bunch of, how shall I say, inappropriate stickers to the rear bumper."

My eyes bugged out. I was about to speak. Monk kicked my shin under the table and wrote on his legal pad, *QUIET. All good.*

Fowler continued. "Now I can enjoy a laugh as much as the next guy but those stickers, those slogans were downright disgraceful, and anti-American. Plus, it took some special solvent to remove them entirely."

You could see Fowler still seething at the memory, angry as the day it happened since no culprit had been named, no punishment meted out. His erroneous assumption had been to finger me. Pritchard seemed eager to move on but didn't react quickly enough to provide the necessary change in direction.

"And this wasn't the only time in my acquaintance with this officer..." Fowler looked around the room, disdain in his voice having to associate me with the term, *officer.* "With Mr. Baumann, that I observed this juvenile behavior and complete disregard for authority."

"Go on, please," Pritchard said, his voice flat, unsure this was a wise move.

"Yes," Fowler said, giving Pritchard a stare. *Isn't that why I'm here?* "Well, I can't list everything, and certainly not in any particular order, but I recall an incident where he intentionally skipped a crew debriefing at the ASWOC after a mission."

"And this was part of his duty? To attend the debrief?"

"You bet it was. He was the mission commander on that flight for crying out loud. Felt it was beneath him. Or his time too valuable to be bothered."

I expected Monk to object. This was purely inflammatory and speculative. Fowler could not have known what was in my head when I skipped the debrief. Monk remained silent when I eyed him. He double tapped his legal pad, emphasizing his previous instruction.

Fowler went on. "Missed their crew qual, as I recall. Affected overall squadron readiness."

"A pattern was developing with this type of behavior, yes?" Pritchard said, now encouraging Fowler. He must've thought skipping the debrief was significant and worth exploiting.

"The pattern was developed long before I ever arrived," Fowler responded, happy to keep going. "Mr. Baumann violated rules and regulations at will during my tenure as XO. There were the pilot training flights to Klamath after the commodore prohibited them, his routinely skipping the birdbath after overwater flights, multiple crew rest violations, the bumper stickers, of course, and his general encouraging of other junior officers to ridicule me."

*Oh, brother, what a crock.*

Fowler reached for a sip of water and resumed. "Probably the most egregious behavior was his public criticizing of my pilot skills. He and some other junior officers made an elephant poster and hung it in the squadron wardroom implying my approaches and landings were not up to snuff. EAs, or Elephant Asses was the term he used, I believe."

*That poster wasn't about you, dipshit*, I nearly screamed.

Pritchard must've sensed the lack of credibility Fowler was creating as a witness with his paranoid accusations and stepped back in. "Commander, let's return for a moment to your period as OINC back in Adak on 15 March."

"Of course," Fowler said, lowering his voice. His quick acquiescence signaled agreement he'd broadly digressed from their general talking points and was grateful for the rescue. He wasn't that dense.

"Regarding the two female petty officers from the NAVFAC flying with Mr. Baumann's crew on their tactical flight." Pritchard paused to look at his notes. "Testimony has been given that authorization for them to fly is delegated by WINGSPAC to the commanding officer, or in this case, the OINC, his representative in Adak."

Fowler beamed. This line of questioning had obviously been rehearsed. "Yes, that is correct, sir."

"Were you aware these two women, these two petty officers…" Again, Pritchard referred to his notes. "Petty Officers Robin MacHold and Kerry Sullivan, were on the flight after it departed Adak at 1600 on 15 March?"

"I was not, sir."

"When did you learn of their presence on the flight?"

"After the flight landed the next morning. I was gathering artifacts that I knew would be needed for the accident investigation. Copies of the flight schedule, aircrew flight logs, maintenance records, the manifest. That's when I caught it."

"Petty Officers MacHold and Sullivan were listed on the flight's manifest?"

"Yes."

"So, for this specific event..." Pritchard looked down again. "AK 44-83 on 15 March, an operational mission against a Soviet submarine within thirty nautical miles of the Russian coastline, the Kamchatka Peninsula, did you, at any time, give your permission to Mr. Baumann, or anyone on his crew, to add these two female petty officers to the manifest?"

"I did not."

"Did Mr. Baumann, or anyone on his crew, seek your permission in advance, during preflight or in the ASWOC before or after the briefing? Or at any time?"

"He did not, sir."

"Thank you, Commander. Now, just a few questions regarding the engine shutdown on station." Pritchard was eager to keep up the cadence, the rhythm he and Fowler had now developed. Monk remained silent, doodling small cartoon characters on his legal pad. "Is it true, sir, that there are separate regulations regarding the loitering of the P-3's number four engine on-station depending on which theater of operation the aircraft is in?"

"Yes, there are."

"Please describe the primary difference in these regulations."

"Well, they are governed by the particular operation order. For P-3s operating in the Seventh Fleet AOR under CTG 72, a P-3 is permitted to loiter the number four engine when operating on-station at or above 2,000 feet MSL. When operating under Third Fleet AOR and Patrol Wing Ten however, loitering of the number four engine is not permitted."

"According to the accident investigation findings, did Mr. Baumann, as PPC, loiter the number four engine while on-station?"

"Yes, he did."

"Thank you, Commander," Pritchard concluded. This appeared to be his planned ending.

"And I might add, this was a serious breach of regulation as it endangered the crew, the mission and ended up causing a great deal of costly damage to the aircraft."

"Thank you, Commander."

"Mr. Baumann has a long history of undermining responsibility. His illegal shutdown of that engine was the culmination of his contempt for the

Navy and highlights his rebellious nature, most of which I've already covered."

"Yes, sir, thank you again."

Fowler was on a roll. He'd been eager to rip into me, airing his grievances and painting a picture of a reckless junior officer seemingly fixated on causing trouble, despite Pritchard's attempt to wave him off, to quit while they were ahead. "I'm certain his judgment was clouded by his late return from the Husky Club the previous night," he complained. "Why, we haven't even discussed his violating the twelve-hour rule on alcohol consumption and ignoring crew rest requirements."

Monk smiled and kept doodling. Fowler had no knowledge of the previous testimony on the drinking charges and how the Government's star witness, nurse Aubrey, had stumbled and was mertilized by Monk during his cross.

"The guy is a hotdog and a danger – a danger to himself and others, and to the proper order and discipline within the squadron."

Everyone remained silent when Fowler quit talking. He'd anticipated Pritchard would pick up the volley and keep things alive like two eager children whacking a pinata. Pritchard said nothing.

"Of course, this obviously boils down to a case of raging immaturity," Fowler said, filling in the void. He'd departed from their script and was unable to stop hitting on the personal issues, the lies and misconceptions he felt very passionate about since twisting them into his own version of the truth. "Most junior officers come around during their first tour," he said. "But Mr. Baumann, well…" He looked at Pritchard. "You know the story with these types, they're practically sociopathic. They enter a pattern of self-destructive behavior, breaking rules, hurting themselves and others around them in the interest of appearing cool." Fowler smiled, pleased with his summation and amateur diagnosis. "I'm certain the court will agree and come to the right decision regarding these charges." He folded his hands ready to depart the room. "That's all."

"Thank you, Commander." Pritchard nodded to Monk and Commander Ray, hoping to get Fowler out of the chair. "No further questions, sir."

Fowler slid his hat from the table and stood.

"Uh, no sir," spoke Monk. "We're not quite finished. Just a few more questions if I may."

Fowler sat back down but was clearly not happy. "I thought you already had your shot," he muttered, hoping for support from Pritchard or Ray.

Monk ignored the jab. "Commander Fowler, when Mr. Pritchard asked how long you knew Lieutenant Baumann you said, and I quote, 'Too long.'"

Fowler looked irate hearing his botched joke played back to him.

"You later agreed it was in May 1982, when you joined VP-25 as the executive officer. Is that period, correct? The first time you'd met Lieutenant

Baumann?"

He shifted uneasily in his chair.

"Commander?"

"Yes. Sometime that year."

Monk looked down at some notes. "Isn't it true, sir, that you in fact met Lieutenant Baumann when you were stationed at the Naval Academy in 1977? When he was a midshipman?"

"How would I remember that? There were thousands of midshipmen. How am I supposed to recall meeting each one?

"Weren't you present at a Superintendent's reception in April of that year with an Admiral Tennant when you were introduced to Lieutenant Baumann?"

Fowler smiled, suddenly amused by the question. "Yes, in fact, now I do recall. Mr. Baumann was disrespectful to the admiral and his aide had to intervene. I'm glad you asked this question because it further underscores the history of this officer's—"

"Commander Fowler, what is your relationship with Admiral Harlan Tennant? Do you have a personal connection? Are you acquaintances, or perhaps friends outside the Navy?"

Fowler's eyeballs about popped out.

Pritchard bristled. "Object," he protested. "These questions have no bearing whatsoever on Mr. Baumann's actions, either at, or after a reception that took place over six years ago."

"Sustained." Ray looked at the court reporter. "Strike the questions." He turned to Monk. "Mr. Monkowski, unless you can establish a precedence or the need to question any relationship between these two senior officers, I suggest you move on with your examination."

"Thank you, sir." Monk smiled at Fowler maintaining eye contact.

I had to marvel at Monk's smooth, unflinching ability to toy with Fowler while under Commander Ray's authoritative eye. His leading questions aimed at our first meeting, the superintendent's reception and Fowler's relationship with Tennant were merely designed to rattle him, jar loose some half-truths and undermine his credibility before moving to the more crucial section of his crafted plan.

"I'd like to return again to your previous testimony, Commander," Monk said. "When Mr. Pritchard asked if Lieutenant Baumann sought your permission to add the two petty officers to the manifest, you said, 'He did not, sir.' Is that correct?"

"That is correct." Despite being on firm ground, Fowler looked wary.

"Mr. Pritchard also asked if any crew member perhaps sought your permission to add them?"

Fowler banged the table. His pasty complexion reddened. "Haven't we covered this already?" He looked at both Pritchard and Ray, then back to

Monk. "No one asked my permission, not that night, not the next night, not ever, to let those two girls go fly with Mr. Baumann!"

Monk eyed Fowler closely. "No one, sir?"

Fowler hesitated for a moment. "No one."

"You're certain?" Monk held up his notepad. "Because I'd like you to recall a conversation on the afternoon of 15 March you had in the ASWOC to discuss permissions for Mr. Baumann's flight. Any recollection of that, sir?"

"I had no such conversation where I would've given my permission," Fowler said with startling authority.

This guy is such a liar, I thought.

"Do you not recall a conversation with Lieutenant Commander William Olivares, the ASWOC Operations Officer, around 1500 that day? Didn't he inform you of the two petty officer's intention to fly with Mr. Baumann's crew and ask your permission on behalf of Mr. Baumann?"

Thank God for Jamie and our dinner meeting, I thought. He'd withheld this piece of information during his appearance earlier in the week fearing for his own future. This little gem and a whole laundry list of things on Fowler he'd gained as Legal Officer came out Sunday night during his interview with Monk.

"Commander Fowler? Please answer the question, sir."

"I don't recall," he said, angrily. "He and I spoke, yes, many times but I'm afraid someone's misinformed you about Olivares asking for permission, let alone my giving it."

"Do you know where Lieutenant Commander Olivares is right now, sir?"

"I'd have no way of knowing."

"He's currently assigned to VP-1 in Barbers Point, Hawaii." Monk pointed to the speakerphone. "I can have him on the line in twenty minutes to testify if that would help clear up who might be misinformed."

"That won't be necessary."

"Oh? So, he did ask for permission, on behalf of Mr. Baumann?"

"Look, there was a lot going on in those two days. We were all very busy with the high tempo of operations and getting very little sleep. And it was a long time ago. I repeat, I had many conversations with Olivares in that period, but I don't recall him ever asking permission to let two women fly on one of my airplanes."

"Did he ever ask you for permission, for anyone to go fly?"

"I don't recall—"

"All right," Monk said, cutting him off. "Then I suggest we call a recess to aid in the commander's recall, and so that I may arrange the necessary teleconference with Mr. Olivares. I will call him as a witness as soon as he can be brought on the line."

"Hold on," Pritchard said.

Ray, keen to get Fowler out of the chair to clear his head, overruled Pritchard. "Hearing will recess for thirty minutes to allow the conference call to be arranged. We will resume with Commander Fowler's testimony at 1100 followed by Lieutenant Commander Olivares, pending his availability, later this afternoon."

Everyone stood, the room was cleared. I tailed Monk back to his office wondering when he'd spoken to Olivares or if he'd received a written statement from him. Things were finally progressing at a breakneck pace, Monk seeming to have all the pieces in place to knock down Fowler and the last two charges.

"So, you've talked to Olivares?" I said, once we were seated. "He'll be standing by the phone awaiting instructions, ready to testify?"

"Not quite."

"What?"

"Calm down. VP-1 is on deployment to Cubi Point in the Philippines. He's been a bit harder to track down than I thought. They said his crew was in Diego Garcia."

"Great. That's exactly halfway around the world. And you're going to have him on the phone, no prep, no advance statement, in what?" I looked at my watch, "Like thirty minutes?"

"We're playing chess here. I shouldn't have to explain this to you. Fowler can't dodge my questions any longer. You heard Ray. And he's not going to perjure himself. Stick with me on this, his goose is cooked."

"Oh, so no phone call?"

"No," he said, with an abrupt arrogance, cutting me off. "Don't be dense."

"Well, at least we're sure Olivares asked permission, right?" I knew nothing of this fact until last week.

"Jamie was a wealth of information. We're going to see that more come out in the hearing after the break."

"So, you're planning to use it all. Everything?" I was nervous. Jamie had told us some shocking tales of Fowler and his actions in the wake of submitting his court-martial charges. And I was confident they weren't lies coming from Jamie, but using this raw, unverified intelligence in court could prove risky.

I was surprised when I looked over Monk's shoulder and saw Amanda striding by our cubicle at a quick pace, her head bobbing above the low walls. In her wake were three men I'd never seen before dressed in civilian coats and ties along with someone I thought I did recognize. Pres Manley? They whizzed by so quickly and disappeared into the LSO bay where Amanda worked, I didn't have time to spring from my seat to get a clear ID or ask Amanda who they were. The activity was unusual, their skulking movement through the office spaces arousing suspicion. Something was up.

After our twenty minutes had passed, Monk and I made our way back to the conference room and the hearing resumed. "Mr. Monkowski," Commander Ray said after we were all assembled and seated. "I trust you've made contact with your witness, Commander Olivares, and that he'll be available to testify?"

"Still working on it, sir. We should be fine for this afternoon though."

Ray nodded.

God, Monk had us out on a ledge. He'd just lied to Ray as no calls had been placed to VP-1 either in the Philippines or Diego Garcia during our short break. Fowler was back in his chair looking less agitated than before but still not the model of calm and composure Pritchard had hoped.

*Right where I want him*, Monk's ego was saying.

"Commander Fowler," Monk began with the same trace of derision as his morning opening. "Just a few more questions if I may." He grinned. "Hopefully we'll make this as painless as possible. Would you agree, sir, that your charges against the defendant are rooted in a personal grudge and therefore baseless?"

This was an outrageous way for Monk to resume his examination. Even Ray looked shocked. Pritchard was out of his chair in a second ready to object.

Ray held up his hand anticipating Pritchard's usual rant. "Mr. Monkowski, I would advise you stick to the line of questioning you were pursuing before the break unless you are finished with the witness. In that case, we'll move on to Lieutenant Commander Olivares as soon as we can establish contact."

I gulped. Ray was already calling Monk's bluff.

"Sir, I am not finished with the witness. Given Commander Fowler's earlier testimony, I contend at the root of these ridiculous charges against my client lies a personal grudge."

Monk, just let him step down, I thought. He's already embarrassed himself.

"A personal grudge. One so long-running and so deeply held by Commander Fowler that it motivated him to initiate weak, untenable charges with the mere hope a court-martial entered into Lieutenant Baumann's record, whether found guilty or not, would bring his promising naval career to a halt and ruin his chances to obtain professional employment in the civilian sector."

"Every one of these charges has merit," Pritchard said, lifting up his thick file from the table. "Each one can stand alone. And they all merit being sent to a full court-martial."

Ray spoke in a firmer tone than usual. "Mr. Monkowski, I'll ask again, is the witness excused? Are you ready to move on?"

"No, Commander. I need to continue my questioning to substantiate my earlier point, that this grudge lies at the heart of the charges and therefore, the charges themselves are unfounded and deserve to be dismissed – all of them. May I continue, sir?"

Ray nodded but was on high alert, remaining vigilant to Monk's intentions of pulling off this delicate balancing act. I was concerned, as Ray, that Monk would aggressively attack Fowler rather than his frivolous charges and go well beyond proper decorum and respect entitled a senior officer. Ray would then have to intervene protecting Fowler and reprimanding Monk. Game over, Mitch goes to court-martial.

Monk resumed under the watchful eye of Ray and Pritchard. "Commander Fowler, you are the accusing officer in this court-martial, are you not? You submitted five specific charges to the Judge Advocate General recommending court-martial and are the sole signatory on the charge sheet. Is that correct, sir?"

"That's right."

"And is this the first time you've submitted charges recommending court-martial against the defendant, sir?" Monk nodded at me.

"It is."

"You never initiated proceedings against Lieutenant Baumann at perhaps another time that would've led to a court-martial during your tenure executive officer?"

Fowler understood where this was headed. "If you're referring to the bumper sticker incident, I believe I've already covered that."

"Not in its entirety, sir. If I may..." Monk conferred with his notes. "Once you discovered these inflammatory stickers on your car, how did you determine it was the work Lieutenant Baumann?"

"I never said—"

"You said, and I quote, 'He vandalized my car in the parking lot shortly after taking over as XO by gluing a bunch of stickers on it,' unquote. Sir, I ask again, how did you determine this was the work of Lieutenant Baumann?"

Fowler looked like a trapped fox. "I had a gut feel—"

"A gut feel? Yet at the time you were willing to attempt to court-martial Lieutenant Baumann over it, regardless of proof, following your gut feel." Monk looked at his notes. "Did you initiate paperwork for a special court-martial against him after the bumper sticker incident?"

"Well, I—"

Monk abruptly changed tack. "Sir, did you call a Captain Raymond at BUPERS back in May of this year in an attempt to overturn Lieutenant Baumann's orders to the Naval Academy?"

Fowler gave me a hard stare upon hearing the question. "Well, I might've talked to someone at the Bureau back then. We discussed a lot of things—"

"Did you not specifically recommend the Bureau take a pass on him?"

"All right, I see what's going on." Fowler sat up in his chair. "Yes, I most certainly did recommend a pass."

449

"Why, sir?"

He immediately launched into the litany of reasons he'd given Pritchard earlier – vengeful, immature, disrespectful, hotdog—

"Yes, I see, sir. All those things," Monk said, sounding agreeable. "How did you feel about Lieutenant Baumann's airmanship skills? Was he a good pilot?"

"He was dangerous."

"Dangerous?" Monk raised an eyebrow. "Yet his squadron ground job was the Pilot Training Officer, he was a NATOPS qualified instructor pilot and one of only three junior officers in the squadron certified by the Wing as a P-3C mission commander. Let me ask a question. Would a commanding officer bestow all those designations and responsibility to a pilot that is considered dangerous?"

"I wasn't the commanding officer who *bestowed* those designations."

"Fair enough, sir. Was Lieutenant Baumann considered a good pilot around the squadron?"

"He was average, I would say. He seemed to have the respect of his peers and members of his crew." This was a huge concession.

"Especially after the Adak flight?"

"Perhaps, yes." Another concession.

"Then you weren't surprised to learn that Commander Wilson, the CO at the time, recommended Lieutenant Baumann for an Air Medal after that flight? That it was deserved?"

"I wasn't surprised, no."

"Did you feel it was deserved, sir?"

"I felt... Well, it wasn't my position to say if it was deserved or not deserved. I—"

"You didn't make your position known, to anyone?"

"I did not."

Monk stood from his chair. "You didn't voice your concern to NAVAIRPAC in San Diego? Did you not call a..." Monk quickly referred to his notes. "A Commander O'Meara, an acquaintance of yours, in an attempt to undermine the citation and subsequent award of the medal? In direct disobedience of Commander Wilson?"

"That call was not about—"

"Sir, when you flew your post-maintenance check flight on SE-05 in Adak, did you log the flight time as one hour on the post-flight paperwork?"

Fowler looked taken aback by the quick change in direction. "Yes, I did."

"When in fact the actual flight time was recorded as ten minutes in the Squadron Duty Officer's log, then somehow got *adjusted* to one hour?"

Fowler finally went ballistic. His eyes narrowed, boring in on Monk, then Ray. "That's an outrageous lie," he shouted, his face now bright red. "Look, I don't know what testimony has been given—"

"It's all right here," Monk said, smiling, holding up his notepad and the SDO logbook.

Pritchard jumped to Fowler's rescue reciting his long list of harassment claims to the court. "...and I'd like to request that Commander Fowler be dismissed," he said. "That the hearing be concluded, and the court rapidly move to a decision sending all charges to a full court-martial."

Ray appeared frustrated by Monk's wild west show and the entire unorthodox exchange but was prepared to rule on the objection.

"I'll offer my summation now, sir," Monk said, calming things by speaking softly in direct contrast to the chaos he'd just created. "Regarding the five punitive charges and violation of the UCMJ articles, we've had more than enough evidence introduced and testimony given to refute each one and obviate the need of a court-martial for my client. One, Lieutenant Baumann never violated his 24-hour alcohol prohibition, we now know this. Two, he had secured permission for the two women to fly that night via Lieutenant Commander Olivares, and Captain McKinney endorsed it. Three, from Senior Chief Mullen, we learned that Lieutenant Baumann was well within his boundary to inform his sensor operator about a possible encounter with the USS Phoenix and that there was precedence of this sharing of information among many aircrews. And lastly, we've established that an aircraft operating out of NAS Adak falls under both the authority of Third Fleet or Seventh Fleet AOR and thus can be subject to one or both operation orders. Since the mission was supporting a Seventh Fleet asset, the USS Phoenix, operating far west of Adak in the Seventh Fleet AOR, Lieutenant Baumann did not violate the Wing 10 directive by loitering his number four engine. The accident investigation board also found no fault with that decision."

Monk was on fire but his last argument about the engine hadn't been tested and was on shaky ground.

Nonetheless, he continued. "And the subsequent damage to the aircraft and destruction of government property charge, well, we need to look no further than the accident investigation board's findings with the faulty propeller governor and rushed maintenance procedures with the engine change, not my client. He wears an Air Medal today for his actions that night." Monk paused and calmly took a sip of water. "Again, gentlemen, things should have never come this far. Why, this entire proceeding seems to be the result of a personal vendetta, the charges a manifestation of misguided hatred brought on by a vindictive executive officer against an exemplary pilot. And why? For exhibiting outspoken leadership skills amongst his crew and his peers, thus creating an inexplicable friction with Fowler himself? And what was at the root of this friction? Disgust? Envy? Revenge exacerbated by Skipper Wilson's public praise of Lieutenant Baumann? Especially given the testy relationship between the XO and CO themselves?"

I looked at Fowler. He was seething, a lock of white hair hanging over his reddened forehead. I suspected he wasn't supposed to hear this preamble to Monk's summation and should have been dismissed long ago.

Pritchard stood. Here came another fiery objection –

"Mr. Monkowski," Ray jumped in. "I caution you on your tone and speculative nature defining this senior officer's behavior and motivation. You will cease or risk contempt charges and severe reprimand from the court."

"Yes, sir," Monk said, softening his tone. "I'll just reiterate that I respectfully ask the court to drop all charges against my client and cease plans for a full court-martial proceeding. There's no merit to any of the charges as has been proven during the course of this hearing." Monk took another sip of water. "That's really it, Commander. Thank you. I'm finished. Defense rests."

Ray spoke, "Uh, Mr. Prichard? Does the Government have a summary, any closing remarks?"

Instead, Fowler spoke up. "Yeah, I've got some closing remarks."

"Commander Fowler," Ray said quickly, eager to get Fowler out of the chair. He should have cleared him from the room long before the summation process started. "You're dismissed, sir. Thank you for your testimony today."

Fowler ignored Ray's dismissal eyeing me with daggers. "How dare you question why these charges were brought. As if anyone in this room doesn't know the answer. Revenge? Envy?" He maintained his lock on me as if I'd spoken the words and not Monk. "Try willful, dangerous, disrespectful, and law-breaking." Fowler turned toward Ray. "In all my twenty years of naval service I have never encountered a more despicable officer, one so in need of correction and punishment for such bold acts of wrongdoing. Just look at him, sitting there all smug, like he's too good for all of us, like he's got the whole system beat and can challenge any of us at will."

Ray broke in, "All right, Commander Fowler, that'll be enough. Thank you. You're dismissed."

Fowler continued as though Ray hadn't spoken. "If this court has any balls," Fowler eyed Ray, "it will not only send this *gentleman* to court-martial, it will strip him of his wings, his commission and send him packing with a dishonorable discharge into a very cold, unsympathetic civilian world. Mr. Baumann should never fly again, period. He's unfit. Unfit for duty that is, except for maybe cleaning the urinals at Dodger Stadium after nickel beer night."

Ray abruptly stood from his chair. "Mr. Fowler," he cried. "I said you are *dismissed*, sir." Ray moved forward, closer to Fowler as though he was personally going to extract him from the conference room. Fowler stood and grabbed his hat in one grand gesture. The two men faced each other, eye to eye.

Fowler backed off, reaching for the door and turning to me. "You're finished, Baumann. I don't care what it takes or how long. People like you are garbage and should be flushed from the system."

I stood. Monk stood with me, extending an arm across my chest. "No, sir, you're the one that's finished," I said, taking a chance based on what I saw earlier during the break. "It's liars and cowards like you who should be flushed from the system. I'd check my six from now on. You never know who's watching."

There was an eerie silence after Fowler slammed the door. Commander Ray looked troubled. He had no gavel but was filled with resolve to resume control. He firmly shut his thick copy of *Manual for Courts-Martial,* slowly looked up letting a calm build in the wake of Fowler's departure. He removed his glasses and spoke, "Court is adjourned, and members dismissed. The hearing is hereby concluded."

Ray had barely finished his sentence when Monk scurried around the large table leaving his briefcase and papers spread out in disarray. He grabbed my arm. "Hurry up, let's go. Follow me."

I hesitated. "What's the rush?" For better or worse, the hearing was over. "Where're you taking me?"

"Come on, just follow me," he said, practically shoving me out the door.

We rapidly descended the stairway toward the building's main exit. Amanda appeared magically from a side hallway and joined us. A small crowd of official-looking men had gathered in the main parking lot. Fowler proceeded directly toward his Corvette oblivious of their intentions. We stopped, observing from a short distance.

"Commander Richard Fowler?" said an imposing figure in a dark suit, holding up a badge.

Fowler's mouth dropped open seeming to sense trouble but looked lost, almost like a child. He simply nodded.

"I'm Agent Peters. And this is Agent Fitzpatrick. We're with the FBI. You are under arrest, sir. Please come with us." Agent Fitzpatrick gestured at a dark sedan, the rear passenger door already open. Preston Manley and a third agent stood close by.

"Arrest? For what?" he cried. "For *what?*"

"Kidnap and conspiracy to commit murder," said Peters, guiding Fowler to the car.

"Murder?" he said, his voice gaining strength. "Have you men lost your minds?"

"Place your hands on the roof of the car, sir."

Fowler complied but seemed to be hyperventilating. "This is outrageous, a terrible mistake!"

Agent Fitzpatrick quickly conducted a pat-down search then instructed

Fowler to place one hand at a time behind his back before handcuffing him and guiding his head into the automobile. I could hear them beginning the Miranda rights as they shut the car door and sped off, Fowler breaking into tears.

I couldn't believe my eyes, dumbfounded by the entire two-minute scene as it'd unfurled before me – shadowy figures moving silently and efficiently in the foreground speaking in muffled tones. I wasn't sure which emotion to feel or if any remained after coming off weeks of hearing. Monk draped an arm around my shoulder. "C'mon," he said, "Let's go back inside."

# 29

## THE VERDICT

WE WERE HUDDLED IN AMANDA'S OFFICE a minute later. Pres Manley spoke first. "Well, that's one traitorous son-of-a-bitch down, one to go," he said, proud of his work and the collar just now by the FBI. Monk and I were standing with Manley, Amanda sitting behind her desk. We all needed to unwind after the tense but amazingly quick arrest of Richard Fowler in the parking lot. I was still trying to digest the entire event and in need of conversation.

"Traitorous?" I said.

Manley ignored the question. "That Fowler, what a goddamn amateur."

"Well, that amateur dodged arrest for seven years," I said, immediately regretting my words. I knew Manley had skin in the game and I didn't want him thinking it was a dig at him. "I mean—"

"He didn't dodge shit. He was just lucky the FBI backed off the NIS investigation when they did. Otherwise, those two dirtbags would've rolled over in a second if they'd been questioned about it."

"And there were markers all over the place, all those trips he made to 6-1." Amanda said. "I think Fowler got lucky too."

"He even told me it was the perfect crime," I said, recalling our conversation in the hangar the day I checked out of the squadron.

"He said that? What an arrogant prick." Manley looked at his watch. "I'll tell you what, I'd hate to be his wife right now. I suspect the FBI is ringing her doorbell, informing her about the perfect crime and the arrest of her perfect husband."

"So, it was Fowler that hired those two goons?" I said, stating the obvious but wanting Manley to keep talking. He seemed in a jovial mood and I wanted to coax more information out of him.

"He was working a favor."

"Huh?"

"They trailed O'Connor for two months, starting in October, fed information directly back to Fowler, her whereabouts, her encounters, who she was seeing."

"That makes no sense," I said. "A private eye firm? To trail Maddy? For what? Fraternization violations?"

"They even followed you out to Truxton Park that night, Mitch. Who knows what might've happened if one of those shit-for-brains stumbled out of the bushes and made his presence known."

I sank in my chair considering our drive to that remote waterfront park and Manley's ominous statement. "So that's how those two NIS agents knew about our rendezvous when they questioned me," I said. "You're telling me Fowler tipped them off? Trying to tie me to the murder?"

"Yeah, more or less. He pulled a lot of strings."

"Pres, this is insane. He did all this because he wanted to nail Maddy for dating other midshipmen?"

Manley held up his hands. "No, no, no. There was a hell of a lot more at stake than who O'Connor was *seeing*."

I felt compelled to come to Maddy's rescue. "She wasn't *seeing* anyone."

Manley raised an eyebrow.

"She told me so, and I believed her," I shot back.

"That's true, Pres," Amanda jumped in. "Mitch was the only one she snuck out with. Except for Jonathan Sweet, and that was a mistake. He was after something else, I'm afraid."

"I know about Sweet," remarked Manley. "I'm pretty certain now that was Fowler too." He paused, reached for his briefcase and grabbed a folder. He slid out a piece of paper. "You can forget about Sweet, the fraternization and the sexual harassment. It was really all about this," Manley said, smacking a piece of paper and handing it to me.

I glanced down. "Maddy's essay. So what? We've all read it."

"Yes, we have." He snatched it back. "The essay. It's all about this lousy essay. If she'd never written it, none of this would've ever happened." He let it slip from his hand and float to the desk.

I was still puzzled.

"Okay, so I'm sure after reading the thing, you've figured out it's not about the lousy essay."

"Pres, you just told us it *is* about the essay."

"I lied. And yet, the essay became the hottest property since Boardwalk to Fowler and those two numb nuts he hired. He even broke into Leahy Hall to steal the original. O'Connor wrote the damn thing but didn't realize what she had until after arriving at the Academy." Manley let the weight of that sink in before continuing. "The real work was in her research kept in a notebook after arriving at the Academy."

"Pres, excuse me. I may be slow coming up to speed but you're talking in circles. Why did Fowler think the essay was so important? Was it the essay or the research?"

Monk spoke for the first time. "Mitch, Fowler was protecting someone. I mean, look no further than the essay's subject." He turned to Manley. "You said earlier Fowler was working a favor. It was for Tennant, right?"

"Correct, counselor. Admiral Francis Harlan Tennant, Deputy CNO for Information, Plans, and Strategy – Fowler's mentor. Got him command of a VP squadron for that favor. Seems O'Connor had a pretty boring admission essay, just a rolling list of duty stations and medals until she got a last-minute tidbit from the man himself bragging about a little action he allegedly took part in the Tonkin Gulf back when the whole Vietnam war got started. So, she included it."

"Allegedly took part?" Monk said. "This is the Tonkin Gulf Incident we're talking about? How we went to war?"

"Right again. So, what else do we know about the events of August 1964?"

I jumped in. "It was around August 2nd, right? Three North Vietnamese torpedo boats attacked the destroyer *Maddox* in international waters and were later repelled by F-8 Crusaders from the aircraft carrier *Ticonderoga*. The torpedo boats were either damaged or sunk. Nothing alleged about it."

"Great, Baumann. You took History 101. What happened next, on the eve of August 4th?"

"The North attacked again?"

"Did they, now?"

"Of course, they did." Amanda chimed in. "This time the *Turner Joy* and the *Maddox* got hit."

"And three days later," Monk said, "Congress passed the Gulf of Tonkin Resolution giving Johnson all the authority he needed to conduct full-scale war against North Vietnam."

"That's right," I followed up, turning to Manley. "So, big deal. Tennant was there, in one of the fighters. And Maddy reported it in her essay."

"Do you know who else was there, in one of the other fighters?"

"They didn't teach us that in History 101." I smiled at Manley.

"Try then-Commander James Stockdale, CO of VF-51."

"The senior POW at Hanoi Hilton Stockdale? Now Admiral Stockdale?"

"Same one." Manley's eyes darted around the cubicle. "Also, the same one that led the retaliatory raid on August 5 at the Vinh oil and gas storage depot." He then stuck his head over the wall to scan the bay and lowered his voice. "Look, what I'm going to tell you is pretty hush-hush but since the arrest of our intrepid Commander Fowler today, it's going to break really quickly. O'Connor actually spoke twice with Stockdale after entering the Academy and—"

"I was just going to say," I interrupted. "Maddy met Stockdale, we all did, when he came to our company area in Bancroft Hall back in the fall of '76. He'd just received the Medal of Honor earlier in the year and was present for a brief ceremony to dedicate his old room in the Hall as one of the Medal of Honor rooms."

"I remember too, Mitch," Amanda said. "Maddy was more comfortable than the rest of us to approach and speak to senior officers. She mentioned to Stockdale she was a Navy junior and her family knew Tennant. Just wanted to establish the fact that she knew him, and they flew together off the *Ticonderoga*. Her way of being friendly, I thought."

"As I recall," I said, "There was no meaningful exchange of information at the ceremony. Their conversation lasted less than a minute. Maddy took some friendly heat from her classmates later, schmoozing with some famous admiral, but that was it. Nothing more came of it."

"Oh, yes, it did," Manley said. "Plenty more. She went back to see Stockdale a second time, chasing him down after his Forrestal Lecture to the Brigade later that night. This time he told her some things, not much, but that's when she began her notebook."

"You mean the notebook the FBI, Agent Peters, told us about in our telecon last week?" Amanda said. "The one they found in the O'Connor's attic along with her essay?"

"That's the one. No one knew it existed until last month."

"Wait," I suddenly blurted out, "I did," shocked by my own realization. All eyes were on me.

Amanda tilted her head. "What?"

"She had a notebook with her, when we took our ride out in town. When I asked what class she was working on, she told me it wasn't for a class, just some extra-curricular research. I was doubtful, but that had to have been the same notebook, right?"

"The timeline fits," Manley said.

"So, Pres, tell us why this is all so hush-hush as you put it. What did Maddy discover in her research, what did she know?"

Manley's eyes narrowed. "This stays between us in this cube until it hits the news wire."

"News wire?"

Manley began. "Both Stockdale and Tennant flew on the *Turner Joy*, *Maddox* skirmish on August 4th. Tennant was supposed to fly as Stockdale's wingman but was late taking off due to a mechanical. Well, as you may remember, the *Maddox*, perhaps a bit gun-shy from her skirmish from two days prior, reported more attacks from approaching torpedo boats. Boats were approaching from everywhere they claimed. Stockdale arrives on station, flies over the ships, searches for anything to attack but sees nothing. He reports to *Maddox* he sees nothing. He flies back to the ship and reports nothing. Enter Tennant. He arrives on station late, after Stockdale departs and is caught up in the radio chatter and falsely believes he sees torpedo boats making runs on the ships. Claims he crisscrossed over the top of them, firing his guns, driving them to retreat."

"And this was untrue?"

"Never fired a shot. Tennant arrives back on ship, gets debriefed by the squadron AIO and together they cook up a story, one that makes Tennant a hero, and one that conveys a shocking message to Washington that Johnson and McNamara desperately need to hear. That there was a second attack thus providing Johnson all the horsepower he needed to enter the war and stop the North's aggression once and for all."

"How the hell did they pull that off – Tennant and the AIO, that is?"

"The report was sent up the chain along with many others and kept quiet. The AIO had early support from the *Maddox* skipper himself, before he recanted, about seeing boats. This guy stuck his neck out and Tennant rode along, desperate to further his career and outshine his own skipper, Stockdale. Anyway, Washington ran with the Tennant version, ordered the retaliatory attack, passed the Gulf of Tonkin Resolution and the rest, as they say, is history."

"What happened to the AIO? Wasn't there a subsequent investigation?"

"He and Tennant stuck to their story. Lied under oath. Of course, this all comes out after Stockdale was shot down and taken prisoner. The AIO, I'm told, later died of cancer sometime in early '69."

"Leaving Tennant as the only one holding the false narrative."

"Yep. And he lived in the clear as long as Stockdale was a guest at the Hanoi Hilton. When Stockdale and the other POWs were released in '73, Tennant must've been wary, but nothing was ever reported. Folks in Washington were eager to put the whole Vietnam mess behind us. My guess is Stockdale knew his role in leading that retaliatory raid based on false intel and feared he may divulge it during the many torture sessions he endured. Came home and kept quiet until he met Maddy. Gave her a small tidbit to run with after hearing Tennant's claim."

This was a lot to swallow, I thought. A lot to take in. "So, Fowler is told by Tennant to keep an eye on Maddy, that she could potentially blow the coverup? Tennant knew this?"

"Of course, he knew. He bragged in a weak moment to O'Connor for her essay never dreaming it would start things rolling. Then there were multiple tipoffs as Maddy began her quest. Her request for documents under the Freedom of Information Act, her trips to Nimitz library, books she checked out, oh, and the Baltimore Sun reporter. This finally got Fowler to act and put those two guys onto her."

"A reporter?" Monk said.

"I remember," I said, turning to Amanda. "You mentioned that Humphries fellow was stalking a Sun reporter the night Maddy went missing, right?"

Manley responded. "Another fuck-up by this crack team of hoods. The reporter was a friend of Bill O'Connor's, a classmate, I think. All he wanted to do was interview daughter Maddy about her plebe year at the Academy.

Wanted to do it at the Army-Navy game in Philly. So, Fowler somehow gets wind of the interview fearing O'Connor is going to spill the beans about Tennant and—" Manley paused and shook his head. "I think if there was going to be a murder that night, it was the reporter. I'd say he literally dodged a bullet. O'Connor was a mistake."

"But there was no link? This reporter didn't know anything about Vietnam, the Tonkin Gulf, Tennant's lies?"

"Hell no. As I said, these bozos were way in over their head, but the money must've been good, and they were following orders. Ol' Fowler kept rolling the dice."

I took a deep breath trying to assimilate the rapid-fire information. The final pieces were fitting into place like a complex jigsaw puzzle and I was certain more details would emerge. "So, what happens to Tennant? He's now at the center of the murder, the coverup, everything, right?"

"He should rot in hell for what did. Think about it. He lied to pump himself up but Johnson and McNamara, the real culprits, used those lies to escalate the war into oblivion. It was the secret that could never come out. For twelve years Tennant held the lid on things until his "niece" came along and created this shitstorm. I lost a lot of friends in those jungles. Almost bought it myself in Saigon on the last day of the war. Why, if I ever see that son-of-a-bitch face to face, I'll probably choke him slowly with my bare hands."

"They'll probably arrest him before you'll get your chance, I'm afraid," Monk said.

"Tennant is next? He's the next domino to fall?"

"I'd hate to be in his shoes right now," said Manley. "He's going to get wind of Fowler's arrest in the next day or two and go batshit. Our esteemed admiral will have no place to hide."

We sat silent for a moment to contemplate how that scenario might go down, what it might mean to history, to the nation.

Manley reached for his briefcase and placed the essay back inside the folder. "I need to shove off, folks. This thing's bound to grow legs and be with us for a long time. And remember, keep quiet until it hits the press."

"Hopefully sooner than later," I said. I took a deep breath and closed my eyes. "God damn him, God damn Harley Tennant."

"Oh, rest assured, He will all right," said Manley.

"It's ironic, isn't it?" Monk said, a touch of finality in his voice.

"What's that?"

"That Tennant started the whole war for Johnson. He was present when those first shots were allegedly fired in '64. The first man in a shooting war who didn't fire a shot." Monk let that sink in. "Then Pres here is present when the last shots were fired in '75. The last man out. Bookends to history. Poetry, man."

Manley wasn't amused, likely having arrived at Monk's conclusion long ago. "Yeah, and between those bookends, 2.7 million Americans were sent over and 60,000 never returned. Either killed or MIA. And for what?" He shook his head slowly before closing his briefcase and heading for the door. "Nice working with all of you," he said. "If you're ever down in San Diego, look me up, we'll have a beer." We quickly shook hands and bid him farewell. "Didn't say I'd buy though." He winked and was gone.

I followed Monk back to his makeshift office in the next bay, jumpy and eager to head for the door myself. The hearing was over, albeit sans verdict but I needed to call Aimee. Manley's astonishing tale had forced me to relive many of the painful memories leading up to Maddy's disappearance and horrifying demise. Then having to digest that huge data dump about Tennant and Vietnam. I needed to clear my head and call my wife.

Monk plopped down at his desk and offered me a chair. "Sit," he said.

"No, I have to get going. Need to make some calls."

"Yeah, I figured." A yellow slip of paper on his desk caught his eye. "Hey, look at this," he said. "Ray must've just called." He read the phone message and thrust it at me. "Says he'll have a decision and recommendation to the convening board by 0900 tomorrow."

I scanned the note before wadding it into a ball and tossing it to the wastebasket. "Great. On to the court-martial," I said, feeling the irony after all we'd been through today. "Couldn't ask for a more poetic ending to promising naval career, huh?"

"Mitch," he said, winking at me. "You're home free. Go home, make your calls, give Aimee the good news."

I'd grown accustomed to Monk's brash, ego-driven optimism early in our relationship. There was no mountain he couldn't climb. But as the hearing dragged on, its finality looming, I found it difficult to partake in his backslapping machismo. "See you at nine," I said. Under the circumstances, it was the best I could offer.

I swung into the JAG building parking lot and leapt from my rental car. My watch said 0845. I flew up the stairs eager to confront whatever fate awaited me as I was never one to delay or avoid bad news with hopes it would just disappear. Despite Monk's sanguine nature and positive spin, all hope was drowned out last night as I contemplated how bleak my world would become if found guilty at some future court-martial. Fear was guiding me up the darkened stairwell to find Monk on this sunless morning, not hope.

I stuck my head in his cube. Empty. His desk light was on, his briefcase on the table, but no Monk. I jogged over to Amanda's area arriving at her desk out of breath. "Morning, Mandy. Is Monk around?"

"Oh, Mitch. Sit down, please." Her eyes were conveying a form of sympathy I'd not seen before like she knew something was up. "Monk's here

461

somewhere. I saw him earlier."

"I'll find him," I said.

"No, no, have a seat. I think I know where he is."

I slid into the chair forcing myself to relax.

Amanda was back within a minute. "He's on his way. Said to give him five."

"Hey, no big deal. It's only my life we're talking about. Shoulda told him to take ten." I was experiencing a sudden loss of urgency now that I was in the building. I studied Amanda's face. Something was amiss. "So, what gives with you? It's the hearing, isn't it? You and Monk know something."

"No, I'm still a mess from yesterday," she said, ignoring my latter comment and sitting down next to me. "Aren't you?"

"Which part?" I smiled. "Pres's rewrite of the Vietnam War as we know it, the FBI's arrest of Fowler for murder, or my impending court-martial?"

"All of it. I don't know how you're able to function."

"Practice."

"I'm still processing the arrest and what it means. I hardly slept last night."

"You're referring to the tip about Maddy?" I couldn't bring myself to say, "the body."

She nodded.

"Yeah, guess they needed that last tangible piece of evidence before they arrested Fowler. They found her, didn't they?"

She bit her lip and nodded again.

"At least it's closure. Did they say where?"

"Truxton Park," Amanda spoke softly. "Exactly where Humphries told them to look."

"*Truxton Park?* Tell me you're kidding. I mean...you know what that means?"

"Probably part of Fowler's plan – a bit of insurance to link you if they found her sooner than later. At least that's what occurred to me last night. Who knows?"

"My God."

"I know – it's sick. I hope they lock him up forever." She changed subjects. "Say, I spoke to the O'Connor's. They're going to hold a memorial service."

"They never had one?"

"I think they always held out hope she would come home. Just walk through the door some evening and surprise them. We all did."

"I know." I watched Amanda closely. She wasn't in tears but acting very somber, very reflective. "Are you going to attend the service?"

"I'd like to," she said. "Not sure I can get back though. It's going to be in Annandale, right before Christmas."

"Great," I responded, thinking I could probably attend being in nearby Annapolis. But did I really want to attend? Could I bear to attend? I couldn't answer those questions, at least not at the moment. "So, what do you and Monk know about Ray's decision?"

She abruptly stood. "Let me get us some coffee first."

I moved to block her exit. "Amanda, do you know? Did Monk say anything? Am I going to court-martial or not? Tell me the truth."

"Oh, so you want the truth this time." She smiled for the first time this morning. "Okay, let's see. Yes, yes and—"

Instantly Monk popped into the office, interrupting Amanda, as if on cue. He was carrying a large manila yard-mail envelope stuffed with a thick document in one hand and a shiny red apple in the other. "Hey, there you are," he said, his jaw-dropping open, surprised I hadn't skipped town and flown off to Venezuela. He didn't look happy.

"All right, Monk. Let's have it. What's the news?"

"Mitch, you need to sit down," he said gravely. "I need to explain a few things before—"

"Goddamn it. Just tell me. Am I going to court-martial or not?"

Monk looked at Amanda then at me. "Here, read it yourself." He handed me the envelope with its weighty contents.

"There must be a hundred pages here." I fiddled with the string on the flap. "What am I supposed to be looking for?"

"It's right there. On top... Oh, just give it to me." Monk grabbed the document back in frustration. "You're so helpless, Baumann. How's about I just read it for you?"

"Maybe you should." His glib attitude shocked me. I couldn't tell if he was joking or ready to lower the boom.

"Let's see..." Monk held up a cover sheet that appeared to be an official memorandum. He read: "Memorandum for Captain Austin Newell, Judge Advocate General, San Diego Naval District, Moffett Field Branch. From: Commander Richard Ray, JAG Corps, USN, Hearing Officer. Subject: Article 32 Hearing for Lieutenant Mitchell John Baumann, USN.

"On 28 November 1983, pursuant to blah, blah, blah, blah, blah – after testimony given in the court of – more legal blah, blah, blah." Monk dropped the first sheet then several more to the floor and kept reading. "Okay, here's the upshot, our actum finalem:

"The court hereby recommends to the convening authority on the charge of unauthorized release of classified information, in that (1) Lieutenant Baumann did not violate Article 92 of the Uniform Code of Military Justice and that a court-martial is not warranted and that the associated specification be dismissed.

"(2) In that Lieutenant Baumann did not violate Article 111 of UCMJ— Oh, the hell with it." Monk dropped the packet to the desk. "Bottom line, you're a free man, Baumann. Ray's recommending no court-martial and that all five charges be dropped." He looked up and flashed a huge grin, a patch of oily hair hanging over his forehead, his pock-marked face never more apparent. "Nothing in your record. Nothing to your commanding officer. Never even happened." He took a bite of his Red Delicious as if to say, how 'bout them apples?

Silence followed. It took a moment to adjust to what Monk had just said. *Free man. Charges dropped. Nothing in record.* I lifted the packet from the desk and held it in my trembling hands. Words were not forming.

"I think he's in shock," Monk said through a mouthful of apple, winking at Amanda.

Amanda broke the spell leaning toward me and embracing me in a big hug. "Congratulations, Mitch," she whispered. "I knew things would work out. You did it."

I returned her hug then stepped back. "No, I didn't do it, I'm afraid. *He* did it," I said, jabbing Monk in the arm. "So, nothing? No court-martial, nothing in my record?"

"Not a thing."

"When can I leave?"

"Anytime."

"Man, I owe you, Monk. I owe you a ton." Shear relief was now washing over me. It was finally sinking in.

"All in a day's work," he said, still grinning like an idiot, feigning humility.

I reached out and grabbed him, pulling him close practically in tears.

"Hey, hey, take it easy, big guy," he said, backing up, smoothing his uniform and laughing. "Save the mushy stuff for your wife."

# 30

## HITCHING A RIDE

IT WAS AROUND 11 A.M. when I left Amanda's office and departed the building for good. Good riddance, I thought. I wanted so badly to put Moffett Field in my rearview mirror, blow past the guard at the main gate as a final symbolic gesture of my newfound freedom. Saying goodbye to Monk and Amanda was a difficult and bittersweet moment. I loved them dearly yet leaving them behind felt good, a complexity of sadness and relief. My life could move on.

Amanda and I spoke of Maddy one final time. We'd pondered the downside of attending her memorial service grappling with the sense it would act as the opposite of closure after seven years, more likely to rip the band-aid off the wound rather than heal it. I envisioned large, blown-up photos of Maddy scattered around the chapel on easels, innocent and joyous shots much as I'd seen under her blotter plebe year. Then meeting her parents and all the sad faces. I just couldn't bear it. Amanda must've felt similar emotions, of course, neither of us admitting or expressing them. We simply hugged, said goodbye, and made hollow promises to attend the service, to see each other there, knowing we probably wouldn't.

Afterward, I made some celebratory phone calls, first to Aimee and then Lt Col Walsh to let them know the good news, that I'd be returning to Annapolis in a few days. The next two calls were more difficult, pushing me outside my comfort zone, but necessary. I arranged for a quick road trip in pursuit of the final pieces of missing information about my father. The first stop on the "Quest for Truth" tour would be a short drive across the San Mateo Bridge to the Hayward Air Terminal to meet Jeff Bailey at his hangar office.

Jeff was my father's last copilot before he retired, the one who encouraged me to give him a call when we'd met graveside at the funeral in March. Jeff was currently flying Learjets for a charter outfit he and a fellow Air Force buddy from Vietnam started shortly after leaving United in 1978. Jeff told me they had a fleet of two new Lear 35s and an old Aero Commander they got on the cheap. I found one of Lears glistening on the tarmac, plugs and covers removed, ready for flight as I pulled into the hangar parking lot. Jeff appeared from a side door of the tall building and made a purposeful stride toward my car. He was wearing a flight officer's white shirt with gold captain epaulets and aviator shades. I was thankful as I probably wouldn't have recognized him given our previous meeting circumstances.

"Looks like you're going flying," I said, shaking his hand.

"I am, I am," he replied, pumping my hand a little too hard. "Thanks for coming." He seemed rushed.

"We can do this some other time, you know."

Another jet was taxiing nearby, and I didn't catch his entire reply. Jeff held the door open to the hangar and guided me inside. "There, out of the elements. Much warmer."

"And quieter," I said. "Again, if you have to go fly, I can come back."

"No, no." Jeff held up his hands. "We've got plenty of time. Besides, I won't be back until Friday, so it's now or never." We walked down a short passageway to his first-floor office that overlooked the ramp. "Here, sit down, please," he said. "We've got an hour, then I need to get over to base ops to file my flight plan. Wheels up in…" He glanced at his watch. "Ninety minutes."

"Where're you headed?"

"Spokane. A reposition to pick up two VIP passengers then fly them down to Burbank."

"Sounds like fun."

"It's all right, I guess," he said, smiling. "It's a job."

I could tell, though, he was enjoying it. His easy-going demeanor and friendly responses gave him the aura of a contented man. "But better than the airlines?"

"Oh, I liked United well enough."

"Why'd you leave?"

"Well, there's an answer to that too," he said. "How much time you got?"

"I have all the time in the world. You're the one on the short fuse." I felt the need to change subjects and let Jeff unfold the story of my father on his terms. My eyes settled on a dozen or so military aircraft photos adorning his office wall. "Those are F-105s." I pointed. "You flew the Thunderchief in Vietnam?"

"Good eye. Flew the -105G Wild Weasel version based out of Takhli Air Base, Thailand. Two tours, a hundred missions. Got shot down once and was rescued. As they say, a hundred takeoffs and ninety-nine landings, not bad, all things considered." His grin revealed an honest attempt at humility masking what must've been a gargantuan ego back in the day.

"Pretty impressive," I said, marveling at Jeff's accomplishments, which was an understatement. The Wild Weasel mission in Vietnam was flak and surface-to-air missile suppression allowing the more vulnerable fighter-bombers to come in behind them and drop their loads on the target under a reduced ground threat. In his -105, Jeff would've purposely come in high to bait the SAM sites into firing, revealing their ground radar, then a wingman would come in low and blast the site to smithereens. Jeff, however, would've been left with the daunting task of dodging the SAM now headed in his direction. My understanding was the Wild Weasel squadrons in Vietnam took heavy losses throughout the war, many pilots shot down either becoming POWs or KIAs.

"Your father's service was impressive," he said, initiating the conversation he knew I was delaying with the small talk. "He blazed a trail with all those early daylight bombing raids, no fighter protection, concentrated flak towers lining the Elbe, hanging everything out in those low and slow B-17s. I can't imagine flying combat in one of those."

"He talked about his flying in the war, did he?"

"Not much. As I said, he was the quiet type. Kept a lot of stuff bottled up, I suspect."

"No kidding."

Jeff let my sarcasm slide and lowered his voice. "Mitch, I can't speak to everything you don't understand about your father. Small talk eluded him. He wasn't very free with his thoughts or emotions."

"No argument there."

"Okay, so I'm stating the obvious. But I know you came looking for answers, something deeper you're counting on me to deliver." Jeff took a breath. "I can only offer insight by telling you the story of that night in August of '77, his final flight with United. That's why I gave you my card and that's why I suspect you're here today."

"It is," I said, feeling my palms start to sweat. "Go on, please."

Jeff sat behind his desk nervously spinning a coin in small circles. "I joined United in '71 coming off six years in the Air Force. Started out in DC-9s, was about to make captain in '75 but switched to the newer DC-10. The -10 was the future, a true push-button airplane like nothing any pilot had ever flown. And the frocking pay after you made captain was amazing. So, I joined your dad's crew as a newbie with 35 hours in the -10. He had something like 10,000 hours and had already amassed a thousand in the -10 alone. We were a good match, and he was a good instructor. He motivated you with his calm demeanor and instinctive knowledge of flying. Nothing could rattle him, and nothing escaped him. After all those combat hours in Flying Forts then DC-6s and -7s where every flight was an adventure, where throwing a prop or losing an engine was routine, it was safe to say he'd seen it all. This was the guy you wanted in the left seat if you were a passenger. I was a cocky fighter jock willing to take risks. I still had a lot to learn about airline piloting, and he taught me, mostly by his example."

Jeff hesitated, feeling good about his lead-in, his tribute to my father, but seemed reluctant to continue. He was on the verge of revealing the damaging side of the tale, of how my father behaved that night, and it disturbed him to divulge bad news to a son that seemed to idolize him. "Jeff, please go on," I said. "My father's gone. I appreciate the kind words, but I need to hear this. It's okay."

"Right." Another breath and a nod. "Unto the breach. Your father was quieter than usual that afternoon as we ran through the pre-start checklist and pushback. Normally I could get him talking about last night's Giants game or the 49ers chances in the fall or how it felt to play a round at Pebble Beach."

I smiled but offered nothing. Like many, he knew Dad on that superficial level – his willingness to allow chitchat on the small stuff. Yet it pained me when we'd met at the funeral to discover Jeff had no clue my father had a son or daughter back home.

"Our flight that day was scheduled to depart San Francisco around 3 P.M. and arrive in Boston just after 11 at night. Everything was routine during takeoff and climb out. I noticed John declined dinner when the stewardess popped her head in and there was lighter than usual conversation in the cockpit. Normally I could count on Bob Smythe, our regular flight engineer, to engage in even the most mundane topics but since your father was quiet, we took our cue from him. I wasn't concerned. It was a beautiful summer evening to fly. Winds were light, visibility fantastic over most of the country and the view spectacular. I always find it enjoyable to watch the landscape scroll by when things get slow in the cockpit. After sunset, the entire eastern seaboard was lit up shimmering beneath the starry night sky. They'd even predicted Northern Lights at altitude.

"After what seemed like hours of silence other than the incessant low-level chatter on the radios, your father made a comment to no one in particular, almost like he was talking to himself. 'We need to watch number four,' he said.

"A nighttime thunderstorm was brewing off our right wing and you could see flashes of cloud-to-cloud lightning below our altitude. Detroit was off our nose at 2 o'clock. Cleveland and Buffalo directly ahead. Isolated storms on summer nights over the Midwest are very common and I was fiddling with the weather radar for a clearer picture when I heard your father say, 'There it goes, number four is acting up again.'

"I was concerned and reacted immediately. The DC-10, as you know, only has three engines and number three is on the right wing. There is no number four. Still, I scanned all the engine instruments. Everything was nominal and within range. I questioned your father. 'Captain, do you mean number three? Is there something wrong with three?'

"This was when he got confused and looked at me crossly. 'No, it's number four. Don't you feel that vibration? Just keep an eye on it. We may have to feather it after we come off the bombing run.'

"'Bombing run?' I whispered, turning to Bob at his flight engineer station behind me. I was afraid to offer any follow-up. We were still at cruise, just under two hours out of Boston talking to Toronto Center. I decided to ask your father if he'd like to take a break, get out of the seat and stretch a bit before we started our descent. This was when he came undone.

"'A break? Don't be foolish. We're two minutes from the IP. Look below, see all the fires?'

"I looked out the windscreen. Just the beautiful lights of Detroit on the right, Flint and Saginaw up on the far left. 'Those are city lights, Captain.'

"'Those are fires. Hamburg's on fire. That's our target.' He pointed at Detroit. 'We've got to drop over there. How'd we get so far off course?'

"At this point he disengages the autopilot filling the cockpit with the menacing aural disconnect horn. He puts the airplane in a sharp right bank and says, 'Pilot to Navigator, what's our heading to the IP? I need the new heading to the IP.' He pushes the nose down in a 1000-foot-per-minute descent aiming us right at Detroit. At first, I didn't react. I couldn't. The captain was in charge and had taken control of his ship. Never mind he'd departed the airway and our assigned altitude.

"Toronto Center was on the radio in two seconds. '*United 15 Heavy, Toronto, I show you drifting right of course, descending through flight level 350. Are you requesting a weather deviation or needing assistance?*'

"I heard the call but ignored it instead waiting for your father's next move, asking myself what the hell I should do. 'Captain Baumann,' I said, forcefully. 'John? Sir? Do you hear? ATC wants to know our intentions. What do I tell them? What are our intentions? Why are you turning us?'

"He said, 'There! There!' and pointed. 'We've been spoofed. The Krauts lit those fires intentionally. The target's over there.' He pushed the throttles all the way forward until the engine over-temp lights flashed on. The master caution illuminated with a series of aural chimes and the overspeed alert started clacking.

"This was when Bob Smythe, our FE, climbed from his seat reaching between us to retard the throttles and help me with your father. As we got him unstrapped and tried lifting him from the seat, he started to fight, waving his arms and grabbing at my face. In the meantime, Toronto Center was squawking over the radio telling us to state our intentions while vectoring other traffic away from us in a steady stream of mad instructions. '*Eastern 720, make an immediate right turn to 180, descend and maintain flight level 320. Allegany 1120, expedite a descent to flight level 330, traffic will cross your one o'clock less than a mile, a DC-10 a thousand feet high.*' He was on a tear like a cattle auctioneer, issuing a steady stream of instructions to all the aircraft packed in the lanes around us. He needed to clear the airspace from this rogue radar blip on his scope. '*And Toronto,*' replied the Allegany pilot. '*We've got the traffic. Looks like he'll pass directly over the top.*' There was a pause on the radio then,

*'Jee-sus that was close!'*

"We eventually sprung John from his seat but not before Bob placed him in a chokehold. It took both of us to force him into the left jump seat and get him belted in. I climbed into the empty pilot's seat and reengaged the autopilot. It was at this point one of the stewardesses started banging on the cockpit door after unsuccessfully trying to raise us on the cabin interphone. After our first deviation, I'm sure she was wondering about the sanity of her flight crew. We let her in, explained the situation and she was able to get John to eventually take a sedative, which helped. She was calm and professional and spoke very tenderly to him.

"Things began to settle down, but we were still headed in the wrong direction. Bob climbed into my empty right seat while I informed Toronto we'd had a minor medical problem in the cockpit. They got us turned around, back on course, asking if we were declaring an emergency and wanted vectors to the nearest suitable airport. We were only an hour out of Boston, maybe a bit more, so I told 'em no, we'd continue to our destination, that everything was under control."

I closed my eyes trying to fight the images Jeff described, of my father's hallucinations, his erratic behavior in the cockpit and the skirmish with his two crewmen wrestling him from the seat. And just how close they might've come to a midair collision.

"Seventy minutes later, we landed without further incident which was not the best decision. In fact, it was later confirmed landing at Boston was the wrong decision." As Jeff finished, he had the same pained expression as before, like he'd betrayed someone – my father, me, himself, the man on the moon, anyone – and felt awful.

I reassured him all was well, that I sought this information out. "Why was Boston the wrong decision? Wouldn't that have been in the airline's best interest?"

"When the NTSB investigated along with United, they concurred the correct decision would've been to land sooner, either in Detroit or Cleveland. The passengers already knew something was up with the erratic maneuvering. I basically lied to them and said we had a minor autopilot malfunction and things were under control for an on-time arrival into Boston. We continued and landed without further incident. The passengers bought the explanation and were happy not to divert. And they never knew how close we came to that Allegany."

"Yeah, ignorance is bliss," I said. "I think you made a good decision."

"Apparently the NTSB thought otherwise."

"Is that the reason you left United?"

"Nah. I was contemplating it anyway. But after the preliminary incident report hit the street with a copy in my record, I figured it best to skedaddle. Best decision I could've made. Owning and operating a charter service flying the rich and famous around the country in these hotrods is much more fun."

"Sounds like it," I said, looking at the snazzy Lear parked on the ramp. This was a part of aviation I'd never considered. I hardly knew it existed and that there was money in it. The schedule would be more unpredictable but the destinations much more varied and exciting, as Jeff explained, with flights to all the·jet-setter hangouts – Vail, Aspen, Sun Valley.

"So, you said you're out here on Navy business?" Jeff asked.

I gave him the short version of my saga briefly explaining the legal entanglement from my flight in Adak, the flight itself and emphasizing everything was now behind me. "Just a little explanation to the lawyers and I was free," I said, making the entire mess sound like the Navy's fault and I only needed to make an appearance to set things right. "Well, it was a bit more complicated than that but it's all good. Headed home to Annapolis soon."

"Into BWI?"

"I have one more visit before I hop back east."

"Ah, the homestead." Jeff knew we'd lived in Millbrae.

"Nope. Coeur d'Alene. I'm driving up from here. Today."

"Drive? To Idaho? Mitch, are you out of your mind? That's like a thousand miles."

"It'll help clear my head, prepare for my meeting."

"Meeting? Who the hell are you meeting, some—" Jeff paused. "Oh, I get it. That's where your father had his accident. Who's up there? A friend, some distant relative?"

"I'm really not sure what she is. That's partly why I'm going."

I could see Jeff processing the information. *She.* He obviously didn't know about Ramona. "Mitch, don't drive up there all night by yourself in a rental car. Hell, the drop-off charges alone will kill you. Let me fly you up."

"Fly? You said you were headed to Spokane."

"Have you even looked at a map, Magellan?" Jeff was smiling. "Spokane is like thirty miles from CDA. I can have you up there in two hours. You can cab over to the lake."

"What about your passengers? You want me rubbing elbows with the rich and famous?"

"It's a reposition to Spokane. Just me and Tom, the copilot. C'mon, Mitch. I'm not taking no on this. You're coming. Dump your rental at the FBO, grab your bag. Wheels up in thirty minutes."

I considered his offer. Ramona wasn't expecting me until late tomorrow. Still, listening to Jeff's reaction, twenty-four hours of solo driving did sound insane. "Okay," I said. "I'm in."

"Good deal. Maybe we'll get you in the right seat for a spell too."

The Lear was every bit the hotrod airplane Jeff described. It was tiny and shaped like a bullet with fins. I couldn't stand up in the cabin and had to

471

squeeze through the clamshell door to enter. Still, it had a miniature lav, big leather seats, decent-sized windows and a bar up front stocked with real booze. After taking off from Hayward, we reached our cruising altitude of 41,000 feet in a matter of minutes. The aircraft's sizzling performance specs were an understatement. I'd never been this high and the rim of the atmosphere was the deepest shade of blue I'd ever seen. The P-3's cruising altitude was 27,000 feet and could make 330 knots on a good day. I knew from Jeff's bragging, we were moving at 500 knots, barely 60 under the speed of sound, and would make Spokane in an hour and fifty minutes.

The Cascade mountain range, which we'd just entered, was spectacular from my vantage point. We were over Mount Shasta on a northerly heading, and I was admiring the snow-capped peaks and crystal-clear lakes. My thoughts turned back to Jeff's story and how it fit together with other pieces I'd learned about my father since his small plane accident. It was difficult to picture him having what amounted to a raging fit at the controls of his DC-10 followed by a complete mental breakdown with the stewardess sedating him. But at the same time, it was information, valuable information, a painful pill to swallow yet therapeutic evidence at a deeper level. And it made sense, finally – this culmination of odd behavior, long absences, lengthy silences, his estrangement from my mother. It was a beginning, a candle amid much darkness. Still, I was nervous as I neared Ramona. The candle could either illuminate a treasure trove or touch off a keg of dynamite.

As I stared at the ground below, the spell was broken by a gentle touch of my arm. It was Tom, the copilot, asking if I wanted to go up front and fly. I hopped up welcoming the timely intrusion and made my way forward. "Climb in," Jeff said, gesturing at the empty seat.

I surveyed the tiny cockpit imaging what contortions would be necessary to insert myself safely into the right seat. "How?"

Jeff laughed. "As they say, you don't fly the Learjet, you wear it. Right foot over the pedestal first, then your left."

I gingerly hoisted my big shoe over the throttle quadrant, right first, then left, careful not to disturb or bump anything. "Good God, this thing's more cramped than my MG," I said, once seated and strapped in. "I'm already claustrophobic."

"Yeah, you get used to it." Jeff disengaged the autopilot and said, "Okay, she's your airplane."

"Whoa, okay." I quickly placed both hands on the yoke. I hadn't touched an airplane in six months since my final flight, a pilot trainer, in VP-25. Jeff had the airplane trimmed up nicely and it held the current altitude and heading until I made small movements on the yoke and column. The small craft responded instantly feeling very much like my MG while maneuvering within our assigned airway. There was a sense I could snap roll it just like the Blue Angels and be back on course in a second. Jeff let me remain in the seat and continue flying as we started our descent into the Spokane area. Flying the correct descent path, altitude rate and heading was challenging at first. I over-corrected on everything giving poor Tom in the back a very bumpy ride during our descent. Once we'd leveled out at 4,000 feet, I thanked Jeff and climbed out of the seat allowing Tom back in for landing. Flying the high-performance airplane with its powerful jet engines was a blast, nothing like the paralyzingly slow P-3, but I wasn't smitten. Flying wasn't in my blood like it was Jeff's. I guessed I was more like my father. Flying was a job. Granted, a much better job than a lot of others but at the end of the day, a job. What I found missing more than flying was the vibrant Navy life I'd left behind in Annapolis. I missed Aimee, I missed my kids, and craved to get back to the life I'd started. But first I needed to visit with Ramona and put my Quest for Truth tour behind me for good.

After a smooth touchdown at Spokane's international airport, we taxied up to the FBO which was basically a gas station for airplanes with a luxurious lounge inside for VIP passengers. I extracted myself from Jeff's flying carnival ride and said my goodbyes. "Thanks for the ride, Jeff. And thanks for the stick time, I'll make sure to log it, ha."

We shook hands. Jeff pulled me in for a quick man-hug then stepped back. "Take care of yourself, Baumann. You're a good man. And so was your father. I hope you find what you're looking for up here." He reached in his pocket and fished out a business card.

"I already have one."

"Take another," he said. "If you're ever looking for life after the Navy – well, you know where to find me."

"Appreciate it, Jeff." I felt like adding thanks but no thanks, but that would've been rude. I turned to go inside as he and Tom chocked the airplane and called for the fuel truck in preparation for their leg down to Burbank.

The lobby of the FBO was quiet, only a couple of people milling about. There was a counter with a receptionist, a well-appointed waiting area with comfortable furniture, a coffee bar and two projection TVs playing different news channels, their volumes muted. I was pondering where I might find the desk for rental cars when one of the big TV screens caught my eye. The TV was tuned to the headline news channel of Cable News Network. The anchor was mouthing words I couldn't hear with half the screen displaying a still photo of a naval officer. I instantly recognized the photo and made a beeline to the TV raising the volume to an audible level. The anchor continued, "...*Admiral Harlen Tennant, Deputy Chief of Naval Operations had recently been nominated to take over as CNO in January and was undergoing a difficult confirmation hearing on Capitol Hill yesterday after some highly classified information on the Vietnam War surfaced during testimony. His apparent suicide at his quarters in the Old Naval Observatory in Washington, DC comes as a shock to the military and the nation. The motive remains unclear as to why he drew a small arms pistol and fatally shot himself this morning at 10 A.M. Eastern Time. What we do know is he was being investigated for a possible link in the kidnap and murder of a female midshipman from the U.S. Naval Academy in 1976. Whether the hearing testimony and murder investigation are linked remains to be established. A suicide note has not been found. We will provide more details as they emerge from the shocking death of the Navy's top-ranking admiral, Francis Harlen Tennant. Stay tuned to CNN Headline News for the most up-to-date coverage."* Below the official photograph flashed his full name, his rank and span of life: *1927 – 1983*, before fading to the sports coverage.

Oh, Uncle Harley, I thought, reminding myself of a Dickens quote. Poor, wretched Uncle Harley.

# 31

## REGARDING YOUR FATHER

THE DRIVE ALONG THE I-90 CORRIDOR from Spokane to Coeur
d'Alene was not very spectacular – brown, rolling scenery giving way to low
hilltops and scrubby pines. It wasn't until I emerged on the other side of
Coeur d'Alene proper at the eastern fringe of the lake did the vistas become
stunningly beautiful. This was where the address on Ramona's contact card
led me, off the interstate, down a steep county road to a cluster of cabins
surrounded by towering ponderosa pines all within a stone's throw of the
deep-blue lake.

I thumbed the edge of her card, one she had thrust into my pocket after
the funeral, pondering the pretentious initials after her name – RN, MA LPC.
Why the hell not state your credentials in plain English? I thought. I'll admit,
I wasn't in the best state of mind for this rendezvous. What had felt like a
wise, selfless plan a few days ago had morphed into one of fear and
confrontation the closer I got to ground zero.

I pulled into a gravel driveway with the number matching her card on the
mailbox. Ramona greeted me on the stoop of her craftsman-style cottage
dressed in a flowery bohemian muumuu holding a mug of dark tea. I tried
to suppress a smile. She was making it too easy for me to maintain an image
of this aging hippie I'd imagined hiding under the nurse's scrubs at the
funeral.

"Mitch," she said softly, beckoning me closer. "It's so nice of you to
come."

I wasn't sure if the moment called for a hug, a kiss on the cheek or what.
I settled for a gentle handshake. "Yeah, here I am," I said, slightly self-
conscious for not being more effusive. "Sorry for showing up so early. I
planned to drive but flew into Spokane on a private jet at the last minute on,
well, a buddy's charter service."

"Ah, Jeff Bailey, I presume."

I was taken aback. "You *know* Jeff?"

"I know *of* him. Your father's copilot." She turned to face me. "Mitch,
I know a lot of things, okay? That's why you're here."

"It is?"

"And you don't want to make that drive, trust me," she said, whirling around toward the front door. "Come on in, let me get you something to drink."

I eyed her mug. "Tea?"

"Unless you want something stronger." She pointed at several rows of planter boxes near the porch. "I grow the lavender and jasmine myself. Crush them into a nice mix."

"Of course, you do," I said, responding with more judgment than intended. "No thanks. Not much of a tea drinker, I guess."

"Well, it's either that or water," she snapped.

"Ramona, forgive me, that didn't come out right." I'd crossed a line. "It's been a long day – a long two weeks, actually." I felt squeezed now that I was in her presence, on her turf. My subconscious reaction was to assume a defensive posture against the potential train wreck headed my direction.

"Don't worry about it," she said with a dismissive wave of the hand. "Let's go out on the deck and catch the sunset." She leaned in closer. "And I may have some wine in the fridge, if that would be better."

"Fantastic." I laughed. "In fact, make it a double."

She led me through a screen door to a wooden deck that was as big as the cottage itself and carried out a wineglass filled to the rim. She also refilled her tea. "So, tell me, how'd you finally find time to come up and pay a visit?" We both sat down around the table. "You seemed so distant and busy with your life when we met, going here, going there," she said, sipping her tea with an air of judgment herself.

We both were on high alert, my protectiveness as evident as Ramona's clinical demeanor. Nonetheless, I felt we needed to cut the chitchat if we were going to bear our souls and have some meaningful conversation. "So, is this where you and my father lived? In this house, together as a couple?"

She smiled at the blunt question. "So, is this where you turn the tables, put *me* on the defensive?"

"Oh, I'm the one that's defensive?"

"Please, Mitch, don't pretend. Of course, you're defensive. I understand your feelings, they're natural."

"You understand? Like some kind of shrink?" I thought of her card. "Is that what you are?"

"I'm an ER nurse at Kootenai hospital."

"But you talk like you're a counselor. Isn't that what the MA LPC is?"

She laughed. "Very good. You can read a business card. Yes, I have a master's in counseling from Chico State but since coming to Coeur d'Alene I work as an RN at the hospital. I got my RN long before my MA."

"Sounds like you spent a lot of time in school."

"I guess you could say I was on the twenty-year plan. I drifted a lot in between."

"Drifted?" I said, skeptically envisioning a hippie, flowerchild lifestyle.

"Yeah, Mitch, I drifted. After all, it *was* the sixties," she said, sharply. "There was all this dope-smoking and protesting and flag burning business to attend to first."

"Is sarcasm part of the MA curriculum at Chico?"

"Is judging others part of yours?"

I smiled at the comeback. "Okay, peace. I just thought that, as you pointed out, coming of age in the sixties would've led to some of those lifestyle choices, yeah."

"Put it this way, I was present. I did some things, saw some things, but I got my life together. I grew up." Her eyes darted from my head to toe, examining me for clues. "Eventually we all do."

Her last part was obviously aimed at me. The sun was getting low, the temperature sinking fast. Slivers of the cobalt blue lake shimmered between the tall pines. "Is that another cabin?" I said, pointing to the nearby woods. "It's so close to your deck."

Ramona took a sip of tea. "It's where your father stayed. It's part of the property – what I call a casita."

"He stayed there? Not in the house?"

"I think the previous owner built it as a workshop. My plan was to start a counseling service, use it as my office—"

"But then you met my father."

"We met long before deciding to settle here."

I shivered, looking at the lake again. "It's getting cold out."

"Mitch, there's a story behind how we met, and I'm prepared to tell. We've actually got a lot of ground to cover tonight, and I can see you're already getting nervous."

"I'm getting cold."

"And nervous." She smiled playfully.

"Ramona, it's November. We're on a deck and the sun is going down. I'm freezing. Can we please go inside?"

As we made our way back to the living room sofa, I reminded myself to unwind, to let down my guard a little. She was seeing through most of it anyway and it made no sense to hide or dance around issues I'd sought out by coming in the first place. I swallowed the last of my wine. Ramona filled my glass a second time before lighting a fire in the fireplace. "So, you were headed to Alaska when we met at the funeral," she said, plopping down across from me. "What'd you learn up there?"

"Learn?" I stared out the picture window. The sun had set, and I guessed I'd be spending the night, perhaps in the casita. But there'd been no offer. "I wasn't supposed to learn anything. I was serving my country."

"Very admirable, Mitch. So, what did you learn?"

"Why do you keep asking that? I learned Alaska is not a nice place in the winter. I learned how to fly a broken airplane back to the airport and land in some pretty nasty fog."

"What else?"

"What do you mean what else? I learned the Navy is an imperfect bureaucracy. That it lets flawed individuals into positions of power." I was thinking of Fowler.

"Like any large organization with people?"

I smiled. "Yeah, I suppose."

"So you had an accident? With your airplane?"

"We threw a prop out over the ocean, lost a couple of engines but made it home safely. Obviously."

"What happened after you landed? Did the Navy help you deal with any post-flight trauma?"

"They court-martialed me."

Ramona started laughing. "I'm sorry, forgive me," she said, covering her smile with a hand. "You have a way with words. Is that what you're referring to by describing the Navy as an imperfect bureaucracy? Because you were court-martialed?"

"I wasn't actually court-martialed. I had this lawyer—"

"I can't imagine what they'd charge you with after saving an airplane and its crew."

"Oh, they found nearly half a dozen things."

"But why?"

"I don't know. It's complicated."

"You must have some idea."

"It really came down to one odious individual with a personal vendetta. The one who charged me."

"The one the Navy let into the position of power?"

"That's right."

"What would've been his motive in the first place after pulling off a feat like that? To try to court-martial you?"

"His motive? He was a horrible person, a liar, a bully, a criminal in fact." I resented her question, implying I may have brought on the troubles myself. "You're asking why this guy singled me out, why I was chosen as someone worth targeting. Is that it?"

"Mitch you're a smart, perceptive individual. Certainly smart enough to avoid the crosshairs of a vindictive bully with power."

"So you're suggesting I intentionally goaded him, the court-martial charges are my fault?"

"I'm suggesting something must've motivated you. That perhaps you're hardwired to react a certain way, poking at authority, or a bully. Or maybe a large organization, lashing out at many things—"

"Why are we discussing this?"

"—even your family."

"Oh, my family now?" I'd heard so much of this argument before, from friends, from Aimee. She was hitting on a familiar theme, but I couldn't bring myself to simply nod and agree. "Look, Ramona, this is about my father. I didn't come up all the way up here for one of your personal therapy sessions."

"I think you did," she said softly.

I remained quiet. She was probably right.

"So, tell me about your wife, Aimee. How's she dealing with all of this?"

"All of what?"

"Everything. Your family, life in the Navy, your father, the court-martial—"

"Do we really need to go into this?"

"Yes. In just a few words."

"All right, that's easy. She's been nothing but supportive throughout. I love her, unconditionally. She's my soulmate, a wonderful mother to our children, a very gifted, multi-talented person. What more is there to tell?" I was happy to confess my love for Aimee but suspicious of Ramona's intentions. "Next question."

"How about your mother?"

"*Really?*"

"Again, just a few words."

"She's much too complex for just a few words. Okay. She's been a wreck since my father left, always needing help. She draws you into every one of her problems making them yours. She's quirky and tends to the melodramatic, but I love her. Of course, I do."

"Amber?"

"Same. Complexity of a different ilk, but I love her like a sister." I leaned forward. "Can we move on, please?"

"My point is everyone deals with the stress of domestic crisis differently. Your father became distant, neglectful of his family's needs. To cope, your mother drank more, became flighty, realized she could no longer rely on him, so she started leaning on you or anyone who'd pay attention. Your sister dropped out altogether choosing a self-destructive path of drugs and alcohol. You became an over-achiever, believing awards and better grades at school would restabilize your family life." She allowed me a moment, observing how I was taking her rapid-fire diagnosis. "Which brings us to our main character."

I groaned.

"So, tell me about your father."

I remained silent.

"Mitch…"

"I'd rather not."

Ramona stared.

I finished off my wine.

"Okay, then, I guess we're done." She slapped her thighs and stood. "Time for bed. Come, help me make up the guest room."

"C'mon, Ramona. You know what I mean." She was playing a transparent version of poker forcing my bluff. I'd come to her seeking answers about my father's mysterious behavior, to gain clues from his darkened past. I certainly didn't come to get psychoanalyzed.

"Just start with something, anything," she said gently. "Share your feelings about him. It's okay."

Here was my cue, permission to speak the unspeakable, things I'd never uttered out of respect, even to Aimee, things my entire life I'd not dared scream out and kept inside for reasons of shame or embarrassment. "Okay. I'm resentful, I'm saddened, I'm disgusted with him," I said. "He missed my childhood. He missed being the father he could've been. He missed Boy Scouts, father-son campouts, Little League, high school baseball games, my graduation from Annapolis, my wedding for crying out loud. He should have been there. He could have been there – for all of us. And he wasn't. Instead, he just turned his back on the whole family and disappeared to live with some woman in the mountains. Shame on him. There. You happy?"

"What about anger?"

"Isn't that implied in everything I just said?"

"Then say it. Say you're angry."

"I'm not supposed to get angry. That's the source of all my problems, according to you."

"I never said that."

"So, it's okay to be angry? To lash out?"

"Depends on who you're lashing out at. You're being intentionally obtuse." She stood to stir the logs in the fire. "Mitch, you know where I'm headed. This is about you and your father. And I'm guessing for years you've directed this misguided anger at your family, the Navy, anyone who was in your line of fire except your father."

"He was never around," I shouted.

"He was."

"But he's gone now, isn't he?"

"He was around long enough. Why didn't you talk to him? Later, as an adult?"

I thought of my aborted attempt before Adak. "Oh, as if—"

"Why not?" she demanded. "You knew where to find him."

"I don't know." I was still rattled. "You tell me, counselor."

"Because you idolized him. You couldn't risk bursting the bubble that held your dreams of following in his footsteps, even if it meant creating a distorted view of reality or denial altogether. And after you'd so methodically tried to impress him, to pattern your life after him, you discovered he seemed indifferent, sad, that maybe he was trying to protect you."

"Protect me? Protect me from what?"

"From bad choices." She met my eye. "From maybe having to go to war."

I thought back to our talk in Memorial Hall at the Academy my senior year.

"In any case, it only served to anger and confuse you as you grew older."

I let Ramona's words fade, hearing my father's again. *You know, I never really expected you to do this. You had other options, Berkeley, Stanford...* I stood, moving off the sofa to kneel at the hearth. *To fight so someday you wouldn't have to.* I stared into the fire and played with the poker. Was this my creation? Had I not considered his point of view? Had I poked at everything and everybody, stoking the flames, resentful from a lack of understanding? Was that easier to do rather than confronting my father? "Still," I said. "I'd think a war hero father would be flattered, overcome with joy by his son's desire to follow in his footsteps." I was on the verge of tears. "Wouldn't *he?*"

"Of course, he would."

"Then, what the hell? Why'd he tell me I had other options – Berkeley, Stanford?"

"Why do you think?"

"Don't give me that! He could've made his point differently. Couldn't he?"

"Well, this is where it gets complicated, Mitch. We spent many hours together. There are things you still need to hear, things he never told you about his war experience that, how shall I say, changed him in ways we were working with right up until – his accident."

*Complicated. Many hours together.* Was this her hint at a relationship that was more than platonic? Or that his accident was... I pushed a tear away and returned to the sofa, sinking in and clutching a pillow tightly to my chest. I was going to hear this whether I liked it or not.

"We met at an art show in Mendocino," she began. "In early 1981."

Around the time he disappeared from his condo in San Bruno, I thought.

"John was living in a dilapidated cabin south of Fort Bragg near the coast."

"My mother said he was living in Mendocino proper." I'd pictured a small house with a tidy yard.

"He was trying his hand at painting. Seascapes, I believe."

"What?" This blew my mind. "Did you ever see any of his work?"

"No."

"Then I presume he had little success. The only painting he ever did at home were kitchens and bathrooms. Maybe a fence or two. He must've really snapped to think he could paint landscapes."

"Seascapes."

"Whatever."

"It's not that uncommon with PTSD. The mind seeks escape to something peaceful, something solitary."

"Whoa, hang on. *PTSD?* He didn't suffer from PTSD. He came home from the war and was as normal as could be for many years afterward. How would you know about PTSD? You can't make that diagnosis thirty-five years after the war."

"Mitch, I've spent every year since 1975 working with Post Traumatic Stress Disorder patients. Let me assure you, I most definitely can make that diagnosis."

"Where'd you work, at some VA hospital handing out food to the homeless? Helping some scarred Vietnam vets reenter society?"

"Don't you dare. This conversation ends right here if you're going to make fun of our veterans or don't care to learn about PTSD."

"Okay, okay, I'm sorry." I held up my hands. "I had no intention of making fun of our veterans. I'm sorry."

"Thank you."

"Very admirable coming to their aid considering your generation."

"Thank you. After all, we were all about peace and love.

I wanted to add, *and dope,* but that too would've ended our conversation right here.

"I grew up in Orange County, Southern California, graduated high school in '62 and got accepted to San Jose State. That was a big deal since I was from a lower-middle-class Italian family in the wholesale fruit business. Needless to say, I deeply disappointed them in 1965 when I dropped out to follow some friends up to San Francisco."

"To Haight Ashbury, no doubt."

"No doubt, smart aleck. The commune lifestyle was rampant. And yes, I protested the war, did some drugs, burned my bra, even took the bus to Washington to march in '67. Most of those years were a blur. I don't remember much. What I do remember is an unforgivable incident I was involved in around 1969 that changed me forever.

"It happened at the Golden Gate National Cemetery, same one your father is buried. A group of us got word there would be a big military funeral for a soldier killed in Chu Lai and we all thought what a perfect time and place to hold a peace rally. So about fifty of us show up with signs, banners and megaphones and start heckling the mourners. Well, we thought it was a military funeral and everyone would be in uniform. Only a few were, mainly the honor guard. The rest were family members – mother, father, sister, brother and the like. Nonetheless, we all start chanting, calling them things like baby killers, yelling welcome home, pig, the only good pig is a dead pig, may you burn in hell, stuff like that."

"Peace rally, huh?"

"Yeah, I know. But keep in mind this was right after Calley and the My Lai massacre. When it came out in the press, we were reenergized to protest our war-criminal government."

"Christ Ramona, that was a funeral for a family who'd just lost their son you were protesting, not our war-criminal government."

She nodded her head. "It wasn't my finest hour."

"So, what happened next?"

"I got arrested is what happened next. But not before seeing the family closeup, the father in his shabby suit herding his poor family in a tighter circle with this horrible, strained look of confusion on his face. It wasn't anger. It was just this deep, pained state of confusion and sorrow. He looked like a simple blue-collar sort, probably spoke broken English much like my immigrant father. His eyes were locked on mine, silently communicating, why are you here, why would you do such a thing?

"We were arrested minutes later after a cemetery security guard called the cops. They hauled us off to a jail in South San Francisco and had to free us the next day."

"Why?"

"Some anti-Vietnam pro bono lawyer friend came in screaming about false arrest and first amendment rights, so they were forced to expunge our records and let us go. A huge victory for the draft dodgers and peace freaks, huh?"

"No."

"You're right. At least for this peace freak. I never forgave myself for the lack of accountability as a human being to my fellow man that day. What kind of person does that? But the passion didn't die overnight. I finally become completely disgusted with the commune lifestyle and its squalor in 1970. Went back home and worked in the family business before reentering college at USF in '72 earning my bachelor's RN in '75. I worked at a clinic in Santa Rosa and ran across a lot of Vietnam vets. They were filling the ERs, being turned away from many VA hospitals and had no place to go. Many had minor physical ailments, some were homeless, but they all carried similar traits of mental affliction and anguish. The father in the cheap suit kept coming to me in my dreams every time I treated one of these men. It was a call to action, saying do something. Help these people."

"But still, I don't get the parallel of these PTSD Vietnam vets with my father, who came home and was a productive citizen."

"There's been a generational study concerning PTSD. Until recently, medical science, and hence society, hasn't documented or recognized the delayed effects of war on returning soldiers. During World War I, any ill effects from the stress of combat was called shellshock. In World War II and Korea, they labeled it battle fatigue. As if getting a soldier away from the shelling or the battle would cure the problem and it would magically disappear. And there was a fair amount of this treatment, of getting servicemen temporarily out of the battle zone, especially during World War II. They'd give them a furlough or send them to a rest home for a few weeks. Then, if they were deemed physically fit, it was back to the fighting."

"I remember my mother mentioning he went to a country estate outside London with his crew for ten days of rest. I believe the term was R & R."

"That's right, he did. And that's exactly what it was for. I've got some information that will likely clarify things and put a timeline to it, things your father kept bottled up for a long time."

"Things he told you, here in this house?" I said, still clutching my couch pillow.

"We had our initial sessions after I encouraged him to leave that cabin in the woods and move down to Santa Rosa to be closer to the clinic. He did, of course, and I was immediately drawn to his case. He was my first World War II patient."

"Drawn to his case?" I said, skeptically.

"Okay, I know what you're thinking, Mitch. So, let's clear the air on that right now. Your father started off purely as a patient. As I said, I was drawn to his case and he was slow to open up. After we'd made our first breakthrough was when a friendship developed. He still needed a lot of work and became eager to talk. I couldn't continue to see him at the clinic, so our lives came down to one of those forks in the road."

"To stop seeing him or quit? An ethics thing."

"Right. I'd been a nomad most of my life, so I made a suggestion."

"To pull up stakes and move up to Coeur d'Alene?"

"I'd been here once in the mid-sixties. It was perfect for us both, serene and isolated. I was ready to make a change anyway, to start my own practice."

"And he just agreed?"

"He went along, yes."

I was dumbfounded with each step in my father's odyssey, that he was being so easily led by this newfound woman and acting so out of character. "And he lived in the casita out back?" I pointed in the general direction.

"Yes. And I started working as an RN at Kootenai. We needed the money and I had yet to land any counseling patients."

"He didn't contribute?"

"Most everything he had, his pension, your parent's savings and investments, they all went to your mother. And I encouraged him to do that."

I sighed. I was exhausted and stared at the ceiling. None of this was helping.

"We need to continue, Mitch," she said, noting my unwillingness. "There's more."

"Of course, there is," I said taking a deep breath.

"So—"

"Wait," I interrupted. "Before you continue, was it… Do you think it was his intention to…" I couldn't finish the sentence.

"His intention to what?"

I waved my hand. "Forget it. Just tell me the rest."

"I'll answer anything."

"No, please. Just finish."

"Okay, I'll try to make it brief." Ramona gave a weary smile and slid open a table drawer producing a notepad. "These are highlights from his file I jotted down. I can cover most from memory, but this will help."

I dribbled the last of Ramona's wine into my glass and leaned back. "Shoot."

She glanced at the pad. "Your father's airplane ditched in the North Sea returning from a mission, his thirtieth in fact. Did you know that?"

"Not until recently. Apparently, he didn't feel it significant enough to tell me when he was alive."

"Well, it certainly *was* significant. The mission was to Hamburg and it's the reason we're here tonight. I'll come back to that in a minute. First, I want to talk about your father's overseas tour before Hamburg." She looked at her pad. "It's September 1944 and he's on a 48-hour pass to London and meets a local citizen during a night air raid. They are caught outside the shelter and decide to watch from a distance. After the raid, they strike up a conversation and the man invites your father to come home to his flat to meet his family. He's very impressed that your father is a B-17 pilot and wants to show his gratitude. At the flat, he meets the man's wife and his two young children, a boy and a girl. The girl is approximately eight years old." Ramona paused to look up. "Does any of this sound familiar?"

"None of it."

"That's what he told me. Anyway, he befriends the family and returns to their London flat for dinner around December. It's almost Christmas and he brings them some gifts – he uses his rations to buy up chocolate bars for the kids, coffee and sugar for the mother and a special gift for the little girl."

"Oh, God." I let out a gasp. "I know where this is going." I felt like I'd just been punched in the gut and sat up. "The special gift is a doll, right? A German Muschi doll?"

"I thought you knew none of this."

"I just found out. Friends of the family."

She glanced at her pad again. "Ah, the Hagl's."

"Yes. I connected some of the dots on this trip home. They couldn't tell me any more than that. Keep going."

"After Christmas he's scheduled to fly his thirtieth mission to Hamburg on December 31, 1944 as what would be part of the biggest single raid by the Eighth Air Force flown to date. As you can imagine he has some trepidation

485

about bombing a city where his ancestors had immigrated to the US only two generations prior. The bigger problem he said was Hamburg proper had been bombed for many months and there were no real military targets left to destroy either there or in nearby Harburg, the industrial center. This was purely going to be an exercise in carpet bombing."

"He was troubled by that, wasn't he?"

"Yes, he was. They encountered German fighters after making landfall which took out some of their formation until the P-51s arrived and jumped into the fight. The flight to the target became less hazardous until the flak started, the heaviest he'd seen. His aircraft took a hit and exploded during the bombing run quickly losing altitude and breaking formation. The explosion knocked out two engines and they were now a sitting duck for any German fighter that cared to attack. To remain in the air, they jettisoned everything they could, deciding to stick with the crippled airplane rather than bailout over Germany. It would be a low and slow flightpath home but on two engines, one barely pulling, it was really an unavoidable descent into the sea. Your father learned they'd lost four crewmen, but their bombs had made it to the target. As they left the continent, he realized they'd never make it across the North Sea, so they contacted Air Sea Rescue and prepared to ditch. The plane went down, bouncing hard several times before settling. The aircraft quickly sank before all the rafts could be deployed and two more men were lost. At sunset, only four remained, two in each raft, but the rafts got separated sometime after dark. The winter sea was bitter cold, your father's raft had a slow leak from battle damage and began to take on water. Fortunately, there was a handpump and the two men took turns pumping all night to remain afloat and out of the freezing sea. The next morning Air Sea showed up and plucked the two nearly lifeless men from their raft. They found the second raft, both occupants dead – victims of exposure. Your father and his flight engineer were the only two survivors and the only reason they didn't die was the vigorous hand pumping – it was enough to keep them from freezing to death."

I couldn't help but recognize the eerie parallels to my Adak flight. If we'd have ditched into the Bering Sea that night, our crew would've likely suffered a similar fate. "I never knew any of that, the story behind his Air Medal and Purple Heart. I'm certain that experience would've been devastating, especially to the pilot in charge."

"That's only half of it," Ramona said, putting down her notepad. "When he was released from the hospital, he had an instinctive, urgent need to pay a visit on his adopted family in London. He felt strongly about seeing them before completing his five missions and shipping home. Before Hamburg, he was going to wait but something was driving him. When he made it to the London flat neighborhood, he could see it'd been bombed. Apparently, a V-2 rocket had struck the building next door and leveled the entire block the day before. Of course, he panicked. He ran through the rubble, digging frantically where the flat had stood looking for any trace of the family. He asked neighbors, bystanders, the police, the fire brigade, anyone who might've seen them. They were never found. The nightmares and hallucinations soon began. He would return to the flat in his dreams digging for the googly-eyed baby doll with the bonnet and rosy cheeks amidst the rubble. It became an obsession. An image of the frightened little girl hearing the rocket motors, clutching her doll in fear as the rocket hit would haunt him the rest of his life."

"But his obsession faded over time, right?"

"It didn't fade, Mitch. It's all part of delayed-onset PTSD. He put the doll in a deep hiding place along with memories of the family, of Hamburg, the freezing night in the raft, his missing crew and the guilt from the countless carpet bombings, some, his own relatives. The years of unresolved trauma were triggered by the visit to your neighbors and finding an exact replica of the doll. The Muschi doll was just the tip of the iceberg. He was dealing with multiple issues in the aftermath of his DC-10 flight, forced retirement, hallucinations that wouldn't end, the shame of abandoning his family – no single one strong enough to topple him but when combined, well, you get the picture."

I remained silent.

Ramona stood and quietly tended the fire.

I leaned forward on the sofa content in the stillness, feeling the warmth from the coals, hearing the gentle pop from the logs. It was getting late, we needed to wrap up. "You spoke of progress when we met at the funeral," I said. "After his experiences came out during your sessions, was he showing improvement? Were there any changes or breakthroughs after a year?"

"I would be a horrible counselor if I told you there was no progress during our time together. The sessions on the deck, long walks in the woods, trips into Spokane and Seattle, why we—"

"You make it sound so romantic."

"It was therapy, Mitch, and he had made remarkable progress. He started teaching ground school at the local flying club. He renewed his CFI license and started teaching students to fly, to get their private pilot's license. These were all positive steps. But he also suffered from insomnia, tremendous bouts of depression and we struggled with his medication. It was when he was returning from Missoula at twilight, after his medivac flight when, well, you know the rest. His plane disappeared below the radar and crashed in the lake." She studied me closely, waiting for a reaction.

"Medivac? He was flying a medical patient? I thought you said he was flying one of his students that day."

"He was. More came out after I returned from the funeral, part of the investigation."

"What else?"

She hesitated.

"Ramona, what else came out?"

"You're spending the night, you know," she said from her place on the hearth. "Did I mention that earlier?"

"Hang on. You know, don't you?" I was certain. "You know what I was about to ask earlier?"

"Mitch, come with me for a moment." She stood and led me down the hall to a spare bedroom.

I had no choice but to follow, my senses on alert.

She flipped on a light and tossed me some fresh sheets. "Here, help me make up the bed. You can sleep here tonight."

"Ramona," I said, breathing easier, "you sure have a flair for the dramatic. I thought you were going to drag me down here and show me the infamous Muschi doll. That he'd found it or something."

She turned to a dresser drawer and pulled out a large shoebox.

"Oh, God. He *did* find it."

"Afraid not." She handed me the box. "I want you to read what's inside before turning off the light tonight. It should answer all your questions."

"So, this is why you wanted me to come up here, after the funeral?" I lifted the lid and peeked inside. "Wow, I would've sworn it was the doll."

"We found more than a doll tonight, Mitch. I hope you've found some peace." She smiled. "Read what's inside. We'll talk in the morning."

"No, I'm afraid we're done," I said, aiding her with the sheets. "I'll read what's inside but I'm on the 0600 flight to San Francisco tomorrow morning connecting to Baltimore. I'm going home." I let the words sink in, enjoying their sound. "I'm finally going home."

"Well, then. I guess this is goodbye. You'll be in the air long before I'm awake." Ramona came over to my side of the bed and hugged me dearly. "Mitch, you're a remarkable soul. This time together has been precious. You've been through a lot this past year and you're still dealing with issues. Please, for your sake, keep my card and call me when you get home, or anytime. We'll talk. Or talk to someone, but you should keep this up, keep seeking help. Keep seeking the truth."

"I will," I said, ending our long hug. "This has been helpful tonight. Intense, but helpful. You were a wonderful comfort to my father, I'm sure." I stepped back. "One last thing though."

Ramona waited. "Anything."

"What I'd like to know…" I momentarily froze, opening my mouth, attempting words. "What I need to know is…"

I pressed the button on my airline seat, leaned back and shut my eyes allowing the cabin white noise to lull me into a deeper state of calm. I *had* been through a lot this past year and still had issues. And I learned more about PTSD than I cared to in this lifetime, but my arduous journey had been worth the cost. There were things I would never know, things Ramona could never explain and things I could never express, but that was okay. Sometimes matters of the heart are best left unspoken. Truth is found by not getting tangled up in simple words.

Pondering time and circumstances, I concluded I was the same age as my father when he ditched his airplane into the bitterly cold North Sea at sundown. When I was a boy, he seemed larger than life, but he changed before our eyes. Flying the endless string of combat missions, the night in the raft, losing his crew members, befriending a London family, losing them, trying to piece together the complexity of war, man's inhumanity to man as he put it, and doing it up close and personal in real-time. Post-traumatic stress? Yeah, you bet. Growing up, we lived with the changes in my father. His PTSD spread among us like a virus, its volatility awakened by the random discovery of a cloth doll leading to his complete breakdown while piloting his airliner, to skipped appointments with doctors, the shame of early retirement, missed parental duties, separation from a wife of nearly forty years, depression, reclusiveness, drifting, and finally, his calamitous ending in his Beech Baron on the lake.

I feared I'd put Ramona in a tough spot last night with my awkwardly phrased question inquiring about the possibility of a suicide. Her gift to me in the form of that shoebox was possibly the best way to explain things, something I could save and frame later. I'd stayed up well past midnight reading and rereading her saved newspaper accounts of my father's final flight from separate editions in the *Coeur d'Alene Press*, complete with history and pictures from his World War II and United days. The initial article came out the day after the accident simply reporting the crash of a small twin-engine airplane on Lake Hayden along with the name of the pilot, John Baumann, age sixty-three. The article reported he was flying solo and was found dead at the controls by rescuers, the cause of the accident to be determined. The follow-ups came out in the Sunday edition more than a week later and contained some very flattering reporting – two full pages worth beginning inside page 2. The headline read:

*Pilot Killed on Lake Hayden After Performing Life-Saving Medivac Flight to Boise*

The in-depth article began with the facts from the previous report but went on in glorious detail about a World War II B-17 hero and retired United Airlines DC-10 captain, John Baumann, making his final flight in Coeur d'Alene after a life-saving medivac – flying a six-month-old baby girl from the Flathead Indian Reservation to St Luke's Children's Hospital in Boise – one with a congenital heart defect needing a life-saving operation that couldn't be performed at the local hospital in Missoula. He'd landed at the Missoula airport that day preparing to fly a student when the scheduled helicopter for the medivac suffered a mechanical problem. The crew were in a pinch and asked if he could fly the infant girl and attendant nurse the 250 miles to Boise? Of course, he'd said, "Let's go." He took the student pilot in the right seat with the nurse and baby in the back. It was during the return flight from Missoula after dropping the student he faced stronger than anticipated headwinds back to Coeur d'Alene and was light on fuel. The Baron ran out of gas ten miles from the airport at low altitude and could not glide the remaining distance to the runway. "Instead, Captain Baumann decided to ditch in the open water of Lake Hayden so as not to endanger any of the local population. Radio reports from the tower confirmed the decision. His plane skipped across the lake several times before flipping over and sinking rapidly in the shallow water."

This was no suicide, obviously. Ramona had read my mind by handing me the newspaper accounts. She'd added that before his final flight they'd agreed to drive back to the Bay Area, that Dad was doing well enough and wanted to return home. She was to accompany him. It would be a difficult, bittersweet homecoming, one where she'd meet my mother and would offer to help with the transition. Instead, Ramona said wistfully, she ended up making the drive solo – to his funeral.

I closed my eyes and thought, *What if...* What if he had enough gas to make the airport? What if he ended up returning to Mother and his family? What if he never stumbled onto Krystal's Muschi doll? How differently would things have turned out? *What if...* I could torture myself the rest of my life with such questions. Instead, I needed to focus on the real outcome, the final outcome – the fact he simply ran out of gas and was now resting in peace with the Lord and his B-17 crewmates he'd lost on that flight so many sleepless nights ago. That was the important thing. Time would heal. Life would move on. I was going home. I was going home to Aimee and I would find my own peace.

# EPILOGUE

## ONE YEAR LATER

We threaded our way through the grass along the crisp rows of countless white marble headstones. There were eight of us today, our first collective family visit to the Golden Gate National Cemetery to pay our respects, my first since last Thanksgiving. What a difference a year makes, I thought, reminding myself of the excruciating, protracted ordeal 1983 brought to the House of Baumann. The weather was breezy and cool under a bright blue sky allowing the upright headstones to pop in the sunlight.

"I'm afraid we're lost, Son," cried my mother, negotiating the uneven terrain in her high heels, balancing a vase of flowers in one hand, her purse in the other.

"Over here, Mother." I pointed. "Here it is."

Our group came to a halt in front of my father's grave, first Mother, as she gently placed the vase containing a thick cluster of blue irises, her favorite flower, at the base of the stone. Aimee along with Sean and Carlene followed, falling into place next to their grandmother. Were those really my kids? I thought, observing them walking solo apart from Aimee. They were growing up so fast. Next was Amber and her new beau, Jim Tate, a USNA Class of '80 grad from one of the squadrons at Moffett, introduced by classmate Amanda. He was a nice kid, a good influence. Mother had whispered they were practically engaged. Bringing up the rear was Ramona, trying to act respectful by not intruding too closely. As she passed, I put my arm around her waist. "Thanks for coming," I said as we made our way to the headstone.

There wasn't the shock of sadness seeing my father's headstone for the first time as there was during last year's visit. Today my heart experienced a stirring of love and a leap of pride. The stone was engraved in standard Veterans Affairs script:

John K. Baumann
1st Lieutenant
U. S. Army Air Corps
World War II
Dec 26, 1919 – Mar 5, 1983
Air Medal   Purple Heart

I'd prepared a reading. It was not my intention to read aloud the note I'd written to my father the night before, rather just place an envelope on the grave. But while composing the short missive, the urge to give the reading to my family felt apropos in the wake of my prior performance. I recalled my father's actual funeral where I'd prepared virtually nothing and ended up giving a somewhat rambling eulogy then being escorted away before I could finish. Today I would finish what I'd started. As I unfolded the letter, Jim Tate leaned in and touched my arm. "Holy smoke," he whispered. "Your father's in great company. You see that?" he pointed. "That's Chester Nimitz over there."

"Hmm, yeah," I nodded and began to read. "Dear Father..." I looked up and smiled, suddenly aware of the religious overtones and formality for this intimate group. "Okay, let's start over." My eyes settled back to the paper. "Dear Dad..." No more deviations, I told myself. "When we last spoke at your funeral, I failed you and have waited too long to say I am sorry. I let you down. I let our family down. I let myself down. You deserved better and your legacy deserved better." I shifted to a preamble for everyone to hear again, things I was able to deliver coherently at the funeral covering Pearl Harbor, my father's call to duty, his desire to fly, getting married to Mother a month before shipping out, the thirty-five missions, Purple Heart, Air Medal and a long career with United. Then I came to the point, the reason I'd asked everyone here today.

"When we last talked at your funeral, I said you'd left me with a lifetime of questions. That one day we'd sort it all out. Well, here we are. When I made that claim almost two years ago, it was phrased in anger, demanding answers, like I was owed, the victim of some horrible childhood trauma. Little did I know the answers would come – that they would reveal themselves in the shape of a future nightmare called 1983. I was placed in a crucible and given a series of life-altering challenges, challenges I didn't ask for, but ones I deserved. Call it payback, call it karma, but those were the seeds I'd sown.

"This is awkward to say but perhaps easier now that you're gone. And forgive me. You weren't the perfect father. I wasn't the best son. I was angry, especially when you were gone. I felt I deserved more from you – things other boys were getting at home that I was missing. I was embarrassed, I was sad, I was confused. And later in life, I carried my pent-up anger like a burdensome cross.

"I didn't know how complicated it was to be a father. When your children are young, it's easy to connect. They adore you unconditionally. I understand that now as I prepare for my own children to grow into their teen years. I admit I threw up barriers as a teenager when it was easy to blame you for every angry impulse that entered my head. I see clearly how my anger has intruded on being a better father, a better husband, and my anger has certainly led me down a more difficult path I never would've chosen. Yes, I got into fights in high school, got ejected from ballgames my senior year, got restricted to base by my CO and was nearly court-martialed because of my anger.

"It's time to set aside the anger and grow up. I know I told you, Mother, or anyone that would listen I would follow in your footsteps – serve in the military and one day become an airline pilot. I worshipped you, Dad. I still do. Your strong work ethic and imparted philosophy of doing the right thing always made such a deep impression, traits I never thought I possessed or grasped in their entirety until this year. And now I realize it doesn't matter the vocation or life's chosen path – just that you do it with honor and passion.

"I'm on that path today and have made the decision today, in fact, that I will remain in the Navy. Duty still calls. I have accepted verbal orders to my next assignment, a staff position on a cruiser-destroyer group homeported in San Diego. Yes, I'm finally going to sea after all my landlubber years in the Navy, which now looks to be the full twenty. I anticipate there'll be joy and hardship in the path I've chosen – a ship tour, a second flying tour and maybe one day, command of a squadron. I've got a beautiful, supportive wife and family behind me and I know we'll make it.

"It's now up to us, Dad, the ones still here, to carry on the great task of life before us. You left us too soon yet your legacy, and the legacy of those that surround us will shine as our guiding light." I paused and looked up. "I'd like to recite a brief quote that I memorized in high school but never understood its true impact until now. It's from Lincoln, a piece of his Gettysburg address:

*It is for us the living, rather, to be dedicated here to the unfinished work which they who fought here have thus far so nobly advanced. From these honored dead we take increased devotion to the cause for which they gave their last full measure of devotion. That we here highly resolve that these dead shall not have died in vain.*

"You certainly have not died in vain. Your memory, your inspiration, your service, your guiding light will serve this family for many generations. Airline pilot after retirement?" I smiled. "Maybe. We'll see. I love you, Dad. Rest in peace."

I lifted my eyes from the letter and surveyed my family. We were a somber group in need of some levity in the wake of all this healing. I stuffed the letter back inside the envelope and rested it against the headstone. Amber was making an impish face trying to disguise what looked like tears. "Now don't go getting soft on me, Baumann," I said, leaning in and giving her a light hug. "Nice outfit by the way," I whispered. "Much better than the goth maxi and derby hat you wore at the funeral."

She grinned back. "And I see you finally ditched those gay Murjani jeans from two years ago."

"Now, you two. Don't start," Aimee cautioned, but was smiling too.

493

I slung my arm around her and took Carlene by the hand as we began to fan out toward the cars. "Hey, Amber," I said, over my shoulder. "When are you two lovebirds going to tie the knot? Mother says you're practically engaged."

Amber surprised me by taking the bait, sprinting up behind and poking me hard in the ribs, just like when we were kids. I let out a yell and chased after her. We left the others behind, running ahead in the grass and laughing like children amidst the hallowed gravestones under the bright blue sky.

# ABOUT THE AUTHOR

Ed Borger is a 1980 graduate of the U.S. Naval Academy and former P-3 Naval Flight Officer serving on active duty from 1980 to 1986. He is currently is employed by Honeywell Aerospace and lives with his wife in Charlottesville, Virginia.

Made in the USA
Monee, IL
12 July 2023

39061514R00293